BIGGLES'
SECRET ADVENTURES

BIGGLES'
SECRET ADVENTURES

Captain W. E. Johns

SevenOaks

This edition published in 2010 by

SEVENOAKS
An imprint of the
Carlton Publishing Group,
20 Mortimer Street,
London W1T 3JW

Biggles' Second Case First published in 1948
Biggles Breaks the Silence First published in 1949
Biggles Gets His Men First published in 1950
Biggles Follows On First published in 1952

A catalogue record for this book is available from the British Library

ISBN 978 1 86200 784 0
Illustrations by Studio Stead

Typeset by e-type, Liverpool
Printed in Thailand

Contents

Introduction

This third fantastic four-book omnibus of aviation adventures featuring Squadron Leader James Bigglesworth, better known as Biggles, takes our hero and his intrepid team beyond the devastation of the Second World War but never far from the shadows of deadly danger, dark deeds and dastardly intrigue.

In Biggles, W.E. Johns created the quintessential British hero – a thoroughly decent chap who can always be relied upon to save the day in an impeccably well-mannered way. Biggles and his crew were beloved by boys aged 7 to 77 for their rip-roaring adventures across the globe; the enduring appeal of Biggles' adventures over the last 80 years standing testament to the quality of the fast-moving, action-packed nature of the stories and the immense popularity of the characters. Whether they were fighting Germans in the First or Second World War, thwarting master criminals, or going in undercover to prevent the cold war turning hot, Biggles and his team of Algy, Ginger and Bertie, were what every boy wanted to be – courageous in battle but fair and merciful; able to think on the hop and handle tricky situations; masters of technology and expert innovators; and they always returned home safely.

Most importantly perhaps is the level of believability ingrained in each adventure. Johns was a combat pilot in the Royal Flying Corps during the last months of the First World War and later served with the Royal Air Force until his retirement in 1927. As such, the descriptions of technical detail and the capabilities of the aircraft are faultless. Whether it be the Tarpon torpedo bomber, the converted Wellington, or the Sea Ranger flying boat featured in this collection, Johns puts the reader in the pilot's seat of these fantastic 'machines', as they are known in the books.

It is inevitable that the Biggles books have attracted criticism in more recent years for presenting views which are now seen as rather outdated and sometimes politically incorrect. It must be remembered, however, that W.E. Johns wrote the first Biggles adventures nearly 80 years ago. While some of the views expressed and attitudes displayed are certainly 'of their time', this does not detract from the enjoyment that Johns, a master storyteller, provides for his audience. The four stories in this collection are admirable examples of Johns' imagination and skill.

In *Biggles' Second Case* Biggles, Algy, Ginger and Bertie hunt down a rogue German submarine, *U-517*, captained by the ruthless Von Schonbeck, carrying a cargo of gold stolen from Allied ships during the Second World War. On their way to recovering the gold they have to depth charge a submarine and escape a firing squad.

Biggles Breaks the Silence takes Biggles, his team and his friends the Grimes to the Antarctic to stop treasure from the lost wreck of the *Starry Crown* falling into the hands of villainous thugs. Before claiming their reward for salvaging the treasure, our heroes have to fight off an axe-wielding madman, rescue Ginger from the clutches of the brutal Lavinsky, and fight a gun battle in freezing Antarctic temperatures.

Biggles Gets His Men when the team investigates the disappearance of some top-secret scientists. The 'three vees' lead Biggles' adventurers to the outer reaches of the known world – the lawless and ungovernable border region of China, Mongolia and Siberia.

Here they mount a daring rescue mission that sees them having to spring Biggles from captivity and fight an old enemy before bringing the scientists safely home.

In *Biggles Follows On,* Biggles and Ginger venture behind the iron curtain on the trail of British Army deserters and bump into Biggles' arch enemy von Stalhein. The story takes them from London, to Prague, to Berlin and finally to China where they enlist the help of old friends Gimlet King and Wung Ling to drop behind enemy lines, rescue their man and foil von Stalhein and the red menace once more.

Fasten your seatbelts – you're in for a bumpy ride with Biggles & Co!

BIGGLES'
SECOND CASE

CHAPTER I

Aftermath of War

Constable 'Ginger' Hebblethwaite, of the Scotland Yard Air Squad, regarded the other three members of his division with moody disfavour. They were Sergeant Bigglesworth, D.S.O., D.F.C., and Constables Algy Lacey and Lord Bertie Lissie, all of whom had left the Royal Air Force to form the nucleus of a flying unit attached to the Criminal Investigation Department. It should be stated that Lord Lissie had for so long refrained from using his title that he had almost forgotten that he was a peer of the realm.

'What I say is this,' remarked Ginger, with gloomy emphasis, 'if Raymond can't find something better for us to do than sit here working out schemes to provide policemen with wings, schemes that are always turned down by the Treasury on account of expense, it's time we asked for our discharges and went off on our own.'

'Where?' asked Biggles.

'Anywhere,' returned Ginger vaguely, waving a hand in the direction of the window, presumably to indicate the blue sky.

'Doing what?' inquired Biggles.

Ginger hesitated. 'Anything,' he retorted, still more vaguely. 'I want action,' he went on, warming to his subject. 'I wasn't cut out for the Chairborne Division. In six months we've had one case.' A note of bitterness crept into his voice. 'What's wrong with our crooks? Have they lost their nerve or something? The miserable truth is, they're not so snappy at getting into the atmosphere as Raymond expected they would be.'

Biggles frowned. 'I don't know that I approve of the familiar way you refer to the Assistant Commissioner of Police, and an Air Commodore at that, by his bare surname, as if he were a sort of lackey. There's something in what you say, I'll admit, but *he* can't help it if the best crooks continue to travel on wheels, or on the soles of their feet.'

'While they do that we shall just sit here and wear out the seats of our pants to no purpose,' growled Ginger.

'All right. Our appointment was only temporary so there is nothing to prevent us from asking for our discharge tickets when we feel we've had enough of doing nothing. I don't like it any more than you do. As a matter of fact, I spoke to the Air Commodore about it only yesterday. He said he'd try to find us a good line in crooks if we'd hang on a bit longer.'

Ginger shrugged. 'Okay. Tell him to get busy. This messing about an office waiting for an enterprising crook to take flight isn't my idea of a gay life.'

Biggles took a cigarette from his case, tapped it on the back of his hand and looked at Algy and Bertie in turn. 'How do you fellows feel about it?'

'Frankly, I'm getting a trifle browned-off,' admitted Algy. 'This is a nice little office, as offices go, but rooms always did give me a sort of shut-up feeling. I need air; and I like to be able to move without bumping into something.'

'Same here, old boy – absolutely,' declared Bertie. 'The fug of the central heating in this bally mausoleum is slowly choking me to death – if you see what I mean? Give me the jolly old wide open spaces every time – yes, by Jove!'

The door opened and Air Commodore Raymond stepped into the room. 'Did I hear someone talking about wide open spaces?' he inquired.

'You did, sir,' answered Biggles. 'I'm afraid there's mutiny brewing here. Apparently Scotland Yard isn't big enough to house these skylarks.' He indicated the others with a jab of his thumb. 'They were just remarking that if they don't soon stretch their wings their feathers will start to drop off.'

The Air Commodore smiled. 'In that case I shall have to do something about it,' he announced. 'As a matter of fact, I came here to discuss this very thing. Talking of spaces, I have in mind a space so wide that no one – as far as I know – has ever got to the other side of it. As for fresh air – why, they can have a million square miles of it all to themselves.'

Bertie opened his eyes so wide that his monocle fell out. But he caught it deftly. 'Really? By Jove! That's marvellous, sir – absolutely marvellous.'

'Come down to my office and I'll show you what I mean,' invited the Air Commodore.

They all followed the Air Commodore to his private office where they were requested to be seated. Only the Air Commodore remained standing, and he took up a position – in the manner of a schoolmaster – in front of a large-scale Admiralty chart that had been fastened to the wall.

'Now, gentlemen,' he resumed. 'We have before us a case that should provide you not only with those things for which you are pining, but provide them in quantities sufficient to satisfy even *your* extravagant requirements. The problem is not precisely the one for which you were originally enlisted into the air branch of the C.I.D., because, for one thing, the men against whom you will be opposed are outside the jurisdiction of the Yard. The matter is largely political, as opposed to criminal. Your opponents have as yet committed no actual crime in, or against this country, although there is every expectation that they will unless we take steps to prevent it. Further, they are not airmen. They do not – as far as we know – possess an aircraft. They may never fly. Nevertheless, the case is one in which we on our side might with great advantage employ aircraft. Indeed, the time at our disposal is so limited that no other vehicle would be of the slightest use. Make yourselves comfortable while I run over the summary of evidence. It will take a little while.'

There was a pause while chairs were drawn closer to the chart.

'The story opened during the latter part of the war,' continued the Air Commodore. 'The U-boat had been beaten in the Atlantic and our lines of communication with the Empire were running pretty well; nevertheless, a number of ships disappeared, in rather mysterious circumstances. They vanished. There were no survivors. Until recently there was not the slightest indication of what happened to them. Curiously enough, all these ships were lost in the same area; that is to say, within a few hundred miles of each other. The area concerned was the South Indian Ocean. The ships were on the Grand Circle route between West Australia and the Cape of Good Hope. Now it happened that these ships were important – or four of them were. They carried a considerable quantity of bullion, gold which had been mined in Australia and was on its way to Great Britain. When I tell you that the value of this gold was in the order of five million pounds sterling you will perceive that we are dealing with what the Prime Minister might call a sum of money of the first order. Naturally, the Bank of England and the Admiralty supposed this money to be at the bottom of the sea, beyond hope of recovery, but evidence has just reached us which suggests that they may be wrong; and the manner in which this evidence was brought to light was, to say the least of it, dramatic.' The Air Commodore paused while he picked up a long ruler that lay on his desk.

'A week ago to-day, a man, a German, reported himself at British Headquarters in Germany, and asked for an interview with the Commander-in-Chief, the reason given being that he had important information to impart. There was a delay. While the visitor stood in the vestibule, waiting, another man entered. This man, too, we presume, was a German. Without the slightest warning of what he intended, he drew a revolver from his pocket and fired three bullets at point-blank range into the body of the man who stood there waiting. Having done that he bolted, shooting down a civilian who tried to intercept him. The assassin, I am sorry to say, got clear away, but unfortunately for him, and fortunately for us, as it turned out, the victim of the attack was not dead. He died later, but before he died he made an astonishing statement. Admittedly, it was supported by no proof, but considered in connection with what we know to be fact there is sound reason for thinking that the man told the truth. A dying man has no reason to lie, anyway. And now, here, briefly, is the statement of the man who was shot – as it was hoped, to seal his lips for ever.' The Air Commodore picked up several sheets of foolscap paper pinned together at the corners.

'The name of the murdered man is common enough in Germany. It was Muller. During the war he had been a sailor in the German Navy, serving for three years in U-boats. His final appointment was in the U-517, under the command of Captain Ulrich von Schonbeck. The Admiralty know all about von Schonbeck. He was a typical specimen of a hard-boiled Prussian Nazi – efficient, ruthless, and a fanatical admirer of Hitler. According to Muller, von Schonbeck was specially chosen for an assignment of unusual importance. It was this. In their pre-war preparations for a world war the Germans had established over the Seven Seas a number of secret U-boat bases. At the moment we are concerned only with one of them. It was on an unknown island in the South Indian Ocean. I'll come back to this *unknown* aspect of the island in a minute. Von Schonbeck's job was to get to this base and from it attack our ships that were operating between West Australia and South Africa. Actually, he was to do more than attack these ships. He was to seize the gold they were carrying, gold that would enable the Nazi leaders to buy badly needed commodities from neutral countries. It must be conceded that von Schonbeck did his job well. He got away with five million pounds' worth. With that we have no quarrel. It was all part of the grim business of war. But it seems that in order to cover his traces he not only sent every ship which he intercepted to the bottom; he murdered in cold blood every man, woman and child aboard them. You must understand that some of these ships were steamers carrying passengers. If Muller is to be believed – and as I have said, there is no reason to suppose he lied – von Schonbeck's usual method was this. He would stop a ship and order the crew and the passengers into the boats – having stated his intention of sinking the ship. He would then take the gold and sink the ship. This done, he would turn the U-boat's machine-guns on the helpless life-boats – with what result it is easy to imagine.'

'Swine,' muttered Biggles.

The Air Commodore ignored the interruption. 'In this foul work Muller admitted that he had taken a hand, acting under orders which he dare not disobey. It now becomes easy to understand why these ships disappeared leaving no trace behind them. Very well. It was too far, and too risky, for von Schonbeck to come home after each sinking, so the gold was stored at his island base, pending instructions from Germany.

'That was the position when the war ended. Von Schonbeck was still in the South Indian Ocean with the loot of his many raids safely tucked away. He had no intention of handing the gold back to us. With the Navy on the watch for him he dare not even risk trying to get it home. So he did what so many pirates have done. He buried it, and with an empty U-boat made his way back to Germany to find out what was happening. He didn't hurry. He prowled home in easy stages. In fact, he was so long getting home that the U-517 was posted as missing, presumed lost. Another reason for the delay was this. Von Schonbeck, instead of proceeding to the nearest port, as he should have done, made his way to one of the small German islands in the Baltic. Leaving the submarine hidden, with the crew still on board, he went to Berlin to reveal the existence of the gold to the surviving leaders of the Nazy party. At least, that's what he told the crew, and it may have been true. Apparently he failed to make contact with his Nazi friends, and finding himself with five million pounds' worth of gold which nobody knew anything about, he conceived the bright idea of keeping it for himself – or so we may presume. As a proposition it must have looked not only attractive, but simple. Into this plot, on his return to the U-boat, he took his first lieutenant, a brutal fellow named Thom. They still had the U-boat, remember, and the idea now was that they should return to the island, collect the gold, refit and re-fuel from the secret stores and then go on to a creek in the Magellan Straits. From here the gold could be transported by easy stages up South America to a small town in Chile, where there was still a large German colony. Von Schonbeck, Thom, and the crew, could then live in luxury for the rest of their days.

'That was the plan as it was put to the crew. The crew had to be told, of course, as they would be needed to man the U-boat. We now come to the first snag in this pretty scheme. Not all the men wanted to go. The murdered man, Muller, now comes into the picture. According to his dying statement, five men, of whom he was one, had had enough of the sea. Three were married and were anxious to get home to their families. Apart from that it seems that these men did not altogether trust von Schonbeck and Thom. Having seen something of their unscrupulous methods it seemed to these men that von Schonbeck, rather than share the loot, would be just as likely to bump them off when he had no more use for them. But the point is this. Von Schonbeck, having told the crew what he intended, now found himself in a quandary. If he allowed these five men to go it seemed not unlikely that they, or one of them, would sooner or later spill the beans – perhaps sell the information to us. But it did not come to that. Von Schonbeck took jolly good care it didn't. The suspicions of the five men who refused to go were well founded. Von Schonbeck and Thom, aided by the rest of the crew, shot them in cold blood and threw their bodies into the sea. Now, had all these men been dead we should have known nothing of this; but for once von Schonbeck's brutal efficiency let him down. Muller, although wounded, was still alive, but unconscious. The cold water revived him, and with the help of the tide he was able to reach the nearby shore. But he must have been seen, or else some peasants who befriended him unwittingly betrayed him. About that we don't know. Muller didn't know. All we know is, Thom was soon on his track. Unfortunately Muller was unaware of it. He made his way to Berlin, and burning for revenge after the foul attempt to murder him, as soon as he was able he went to our people with the object of betraying the plot. You can guess the rest. Thom, still on his track, caught up with him while he was waiting for an interview at General Headquarters. Thom shot Muller, got away, and no doubt made straight back for the U-boat. Muller, this time mortally wounded, only lived long enough to tell us the story I have just told to you. By this time no doubt the U-517 is on its way to get the gold.'

CHAPTER II

Biggles Asks Some Questions

'If I may interrupt, I'd like to be a little more clear on that point,' put in Biggles. 'Are you sure the U-boat has headed back for the Indian Ocean?'

'Not absolutely sure,' admitted the Air Commodore. 'Muller gave us the name of the island in the Baltic where the submarine had hidden herself, and we weren't long getting to it; but by the time we were on the spot she had gone. Of course, there is just a chance that von Schonbeck is still lying low somewhere in the Baltic, but if the vessel has gone, and it certainly has gone, it seems far more likely that it is on its way to its South Indian base. I can think of no reason why von Schonbeck should delay putting his plan into operation – can you?'

'No,' admitted Biggles. 'If the U-517 has got clear of the North Sea, then von Schonbeck looks like getting away with it.'

'If our judgment of the situation is correct the U-517 has been on its way for a fortnight,' said the Air Commodore. 'Muller was unconscious for some days; we had to wait for him to come round to learn what it was all about. Von Schonbeck had plenty of time to slip away. But there is one thing he does not know. He doesn't know that we are wise to his scheme. He doesn't know that Muller talked. He thinks Muller was shot dead by Thom – that he died instantly.'

'How can you say what von Schonbeck thinks?' asked Biggles quickly.

A ghost of a smile softened the Air Commodore's austere features. 'Our Intelligence people are good at dealing with situations of this sort,' he said dryly. 'They issued a story of the shooting for the Press. It was not exactly true, in that it asserted that the man murdered at British Headquarters had died without opening his lips. His name, and that of his assailant, were unknown. The motive of the crime was, therefore, a mystery. That was the story we put out in the newspapers. Thom would certainly see a newspaper because a criminal always makes a point of reading the Press notices of his crime, in the hope of learning how much the police know, or what they think. Thom would show the paper to von Schonbeck, and we can imagine the two scoundrels patting each other on the back at their astute handling of the situation. No word of the truth has been allowed to leak out, so von Schonbeck and his crew of cut-throats must believe that they are now safe from pursuit. That is about the only trump card that we hold.'

'The Navy has been looking for the U-517, I presume?' queried Biggles.

'Of course. So have Coastal Command and the Fleet Air Arm; but von Schonbeck must be an expert at dodging anti-submarine patrols or he would not have lived as long as he has. He's a wily bird. We haven't seen a sign of him.'

Biggles frowned. 'But we ought to be able to catch him.'

The Air Commodore shook his head dubiously. 'I should like to think so. But we are up against a big snag. We don't know the name of the island for which the U-boat is making – the island where the gold is hidden.'

Biggles looked surprised. 'But surely Muller told you the name of the island?'

'He did not, for the simple reason he didn't know the name of it himself. It was always referred to by von Schonbeck as The Island. That's what I meant when I described it a moment ago as an unknown island. In fact, incredible though it may seem, the island may not have a name. It may not be shown on Admiralty charts.'

Biggles' eyes opened wide in astonishment. 'Is that possible?'

'Easily. Perhaps we had better have a word or two about islands. In your study of Admiralty charts you must have noticed, scattered about the oceans, tiny specks against which occur the letters, E.D.?'

'I always understood they meant, Existence Doubtful.'

'Quite right,' confirmed the Air Commodore. 'These are mostly islands which have been reported as having been sighted by ship's captains, but could not afterwards be found by Admiralty survey ships or other craft. Unfortunately for us, the South Indian Ocean is particularly rich in such islands. I have been over at the Admiralty making inquiries about some of them.' The Air Commodore picked up some slips of paper that lay on his desk.

'For example, there is Swain Island,' he resumed. 'It was first reported by Captain Swain in 1800. He did not land. Several ships have seen the island since, and yet, absurd though it must seem in these days of swift transport, we still don't know where it is. In 1830 a Captain Gardner fixed the position of Swain Island, yet when two of our survey ships went out it was not to be found. In 1841 Captain Dougherty passed the island at three hundred yards and kept it in sight all day. He has described it in some detail. Later it was seen by a Captain Keates. It was seen in 1885, 1886 and 1890. In 1893 a Captain White sailed round it and reported it to be eight miles long and eighty feet high. No one has seen it since. Every attempt to find it has failed. In recent years Captain Scott, the famous Antarctic explorer, sailed over the spot and reported soundings of three miles! As late as 1932 the Admiralty erased the island from its charts; but it is hard to believe that all those captains could have been wrong. Yet where is the island? We don't know. Nobody knows – except possibly von Schonbeck, if it happens to be his secret base. Unfortunately Swain Island is not an isolated case. There are several islands that seem to be playing this glori-fied game of hide-and-seek, so you see how complicated becomes our quest for this slippery Nazi and his U-boat? Take the Auroras. Here we have a group of islands playing the same game. They were first reported in 1762. And the Royal Company Islands which, having been on our charts for years, were removed by the Admiralty in 1904 because no one could find them. But let's not waste time on islands that may or may not exist. The story of one is the story of all the others. Let's consider South Indian Ocean islands that *do* exist. They alone are enough to give us a headache, for there are plenty of them scattered over a few million square miles of ocean. They are all uninhabited. Some have not been visited for thirty or forty years. In fact, there are very few people alive who have seen them, let alone landed. Any one of them might be von Schonbeck's island.' The Air Commodore indicated a spot with his long pointer.

'First, there are the Crozets,' he went on. 'It's quite a big group. The largest is Possession Island. Then we have St Paul Island, Prince Edward Island, Macdonald Island and the Heard Islands. Here we have Penguin Island, a sheer rock rising a thousand feet out of the sea which has never been landed on. Here we have Flog Island, Inaccessible Island, Earl Island.' The Air Commodore moved his pointer. 'Over here we have the Apostle group, two large islands and ten smaller ones. I must tell you that some of these islands are the peaks of extinct volcanoes – and not so very long extinct, either. They hold boiling springs. If you stir the ground it smokes, reeking of sulphur. On the other hand, some of the islands are of considerable size. Kerguelen Island, for instance, is forty-five miles long by eight miles wide.'

'And do you mean to say, sir, that no one lives on an island of that size?' Ginger asked.

'I do. The chief trouble is, there is no communication with anywhere. Kerguelen is two thousand one hundred miles from the nearest inhabited land. Who's going to live in a place like that? One might as well live on the moon. Fancy having toothache, and the nearest dentist over two thousand miles away! Then again, these islands are not the voluptuous desert islands of romantic fiction. They are bleak, cold, inhospitable, treeless. None has been fully explored. There are quicksands to contend with – glaciers, torrents, roaring waterfalls. Deep fiords cut into them as they do into the coast of Norway. On ninety-nine days out of a hundred the wind comes screaming across thousands of miles of ocean to vent its fury on its first obstruction.'

'Then nothing lives on these beastly islands – what?' murmured Bertie.

'Oh yes. There is quite a lot of wild life – sea-birds, seals, penguins. There are rabbits, wild hogs and wildcats, descendants of domestic animals left behind at some time or other by passing ships. It must be possible to live on at least some of these islands, though, for in 1821 the survivors of a ship named *The Princess of Wales* were on the Crozets for two years before being picked up. As far as the Admiralty is aware the last visit to the Crozets was in 1901. This is what Admiralty Sailing Directions have to say about Kerguelen: "Notwithstanding its natural defects and desolate character it is not without value. It has safe and commodious harbours and an abundance of fresh water. Kerguelen has never been explored, the boggy nature of the interior making this extremely difficult. The western coast is under the constant bombardment of gales and high seas.'" The Air Commodore tossed the paper he held on to his desk. 'Well, there it is. Von Schonbeck is undoubtedly making for one of these islands, on which he has hidden a treasure worth five million pounds; but from what I have said you will have gathered a rough idea of what sort of job you will have to find him.'

Biggles smiled wanly. 'I was wondering when you were coming to that.'

The Air Commodore laughed. 'You didn't suppose that I was giving you a lecture on islands merely to pass the time, did you?'

Biggles shook his head. 'No, sir. But why pick on us? I mean, how does the Yard come into the affair? I should have thought the matter was one for the services – the Navy or the Air Force – to handle.'

'In a way it is,' admitted the Air Commodore. 'But the thing is one of those complicated affairs that occur from time to time. Strictly speaking, the rounding up of the U-517, of all U-boats, is the Navy's business. From the criminal angle, the shooting of Muller and the civilian who tried to stop Thom, the matter is one for the German police. Situated as they are there is little they can do, so they have asked for our co-operation. Then there is the question of the gold. It was heavily insured, and the companies concerned came to us, the proper civil authority, to protect their interests. We automatically watch the political side. As a result of this, to prevent overlapping, the Government has put the investigation into the hands of the Yard, with power to call on the fighting services should they be required. We have in fact invited the Navy and the Air Force to co-operate by calling on them for assistance. So far they have failed to achieve any result. Now, I'm afraid, ships are out of it. If von Schonbeck has slipped through the cordon which the Admiralty threw from the English Channel to the Shetlands, and it begins to look as though he has, he must be well on his way. What course he will take on reaching the Atlantic we don't know, and it would be futile to guess. What we do know is that his objective is in the South Indian Ocean. But, as you will see from the map, that particular ocean covers a large portion of the earth's surface. To search millions of square miles of open water by surface-craft, for one solitary U-boat, would take years. Our only hope of covering such a vast area is by employing aircraft, and that is where you come in. As it is, von Schonbeck may reach his objective and scoop the pool before we can get there.'

'But how are aircraft going to operate in the locality of these islands, with the nearest base more than two thousand miles away?' demanded Biggles.

'There will be a base nearer than that,' declared the Air Commodore. 'We are going to establish one.'

'Where?'

'Kerguelen Island. Five million pounds are at stake and that's a lot of money. The British supply-sloop, *Tern*, is already on its way to Kerguelen from the Falkland Islands, carrying food, stores, oil, petrol, and other things you will be likely to require.'

'And we, presumably, shall take up residence on Kerguelen, and from there proceed to engage ourselves in a task compared with which the finding of a needle in a haystack becomes a simple matter?'

'That, exactly, is the idea,' agreed the Air Commodore.

'You'll pardon me for saying that it doesn't set me on fire with enthusiasm.'

'It should be interesting.'

'What should be interesting – the sea? Millions of miles of nothing but water? Water in large quantities always looks alike to me. There's a limit to the time I can look at it without getting bored.'

The Air Commodore smiled. 'When can you be ready to start?'

Biggles shrugged. 'Tomorrow, I suppose. That is, we can start ambling towards the Southern Hemisphere. I take it that we can make our own arrangements for getting to Kerguelen?'

'Of course.'

'When will the *Tern* be there?'

'She'll be there before you.'

'And having found the U-517, what do we do about it – always bearing in mind that if von Schonbeck spots a British aircraft prowling around he'll know why it is there … and not forgetting that his ship carries the latest thing in anti-aircraft guns?'

'You'll report its position by radio and endeavour to keep it in sight.'

'Why not sink the blighter and have done with it – if you see what I mean?' suggested Bertie.

The Air Commodore looked pained. 'By the time you find the U-517 it will probably have the gold on board. Five million pounds at the bottom of the Indian Ocean is no earthly use to anyone.'

'Of course – absolutely. Silly ass I am – what?' murmured Bertie apologetically.

'How many men comprise the crew of the U-517?' asked Biggles.

'Twenty-five, including the captain – all selected seamen.'

'Rather more than we could handle if we caught up with them somewhere.'

'Definitely. This crew fought the British Navy for three years – and got away with it. They must be tough. We'll get them if we can, but the gold must be our first consideration. Any more questions?'

Biggles thought for a moment. 'I don't think so, sir. If anything occurs to me I'll let you know. Meanwhile, I'd better start making arrangements.'

'Good. The Navy is still on the job. If we get any signals I'll pass the information on to you. You get yourselves to Kerguelen for a start. The *Tern* will be there. The skipper has orders to reconnoitre for the best landing-area. He is letting us know the precise position. You'll have to use a marine aircraft, of course – presumably a flying-boat.'

'I don't feel inclined to try putting a land machine down in a bog,' murmured Biggles.

'Quite. With a flying-boat, from Kerguelen you'll be able to cover a pretty wide area. There's really no need for me to warn you, I know, but for Heaven's sake be careful with your navigation. Sitting here, Kerguelen may sound a big mark to fly on; but there's an awful lot of water where you're going, and if you miss the island there'll be nothing between you and the South Pole.'

'I'll watch it,' promised Biggles, rising. 'Come on chaps – we'd better look out our winter woollies.'

CHAPTER III

Von Schonbeck Strikes First

'There is always a peculiar fascination in watching a ship put to sea, but on this occasion it means more than usual – a lot more.' Biggles spoke. With the others standing beside him he was watching the *Tern*, a speck in a world of restless water, standing away to the western horizon, with the wind, blowing half a gale, tearing the smoke from her funnel and beating it down into a back-wash of flying spray.

A fortnight had elapsed since the conversation with Air Commodore Raymond at the Yard, a busy fortnight in which they had transported themselves from the centre of civilisation to the fringe of the known world. In that time there had been no word of von Schonbeck or the U-517. Not that this surprised Biggles. As he remarked, with the oceans of the world from which to choose, the cleverest U-boat commander in the Nazi service would not find it hard to disappear.

For the rest, the preliminary preparations had gone, to use a well worn expression, according to plan. The captain of the *Tern*, a cheerful young lieutenant who had been invalided from the Fleet Air Arm, had done his job well, both in his selection of a site for the base and its establishment. At the end of a long, almost land-locked creek, protected on the windward side by a range of gaunt hills, had been erected two iron-roofed Nissen huts of service pattern. One was the mess, living- and sleeping-quarters. Packing-cases served for chairs and table. The most conspicuous article of furniture was a small but powerful radio instrument. The other hut housed the stores – tinned foods, spare parts, emergency repair kits and a few cases of small-arms ammunition. A short distance from these buildings was the 'dump,' consisting of three circular erections of hand-picked stone, covered with tarpaulins, securely anchored against the wind. These contained petrol in the regulation four-gallon cans, oil, and a dozen depth-charges, aircraft type. A spring-fed burn, gushing noisily close at hand, provided unlimited water.

With the departure of the *Tern* the radio was the only link with the outside world, a world that now seemed as far removed as the moon. There would be no transmitting though, Biggles decided, except in case of emergency, for the obvious reason that signals might be picked up by the enemy, who was also equipped with wireless; but there was no reason why they should not listen to messages from home. Von Schonbeck, of course, would be able to hear these; but he would not know to whom they were directed, for the Yard call signal, for the Kerguelen base, consisted only of the cypher X L. Conversely, the party on the island would be able to pick up any messages sent out by von Schonbeck, although as far as they were aware there was no reason why the Nazi should use his wireless.

The last 'leg' of the outward flight had been made in one hop from South Africa. Two aircraft were in commission, both of the same type to prevent duplication of spare parts. They were twin-engined, flying-boat, amphibious monoplanes of the *Tarpon* class, war machines that had been specially designed for long-distance marine convoy work, and which were still on the secret list when the war ended. In the design of this aircraft, high speed, which is not essential for convoy work, had been sacrificed for robust construction and endurance-range, the two qualifications, declared Biggles, most to be desired for the task on hand. For reasons of weight limitation, armament had been arranged more for defence than attack: two fixed machine-guns mounted one on either side of the hull firing forward, and a similar mobile weapon covering the tail. The attack weapon of the *Tarpon*, against hostile marine craft, was the depth-charge, and the hull was equipped to carry two such charges of five hundred pounds each. In other respects, with the exception of some small arms, rifles and automatics which Biggles had added, the war-load was normal for a naval aircraft during the closing months of the war.

Biggles had flown out in one, with Ginger as second pilot. Algy and Bertie had flown the other. Biggles had resolved that in the ordinary way only one machine would be in the air at a time, the other remaining in reserve. He had no intention, he asserted, of marooning himself on a place like Kerguelen, without a means of getting off it. True, the Air Commodore knew where they were, and could always send out a ship or a relief aircraft; but it might be some time before the relief vessel arrived, and should a casualty occur the delay might mean the difference between life and death. Moreover, the only way help could be called was by radio, and should von Schonbeck pick up the S O S he might decide to come along and investigate – a contingency which, in view of the number of men at the German's command, Biggles preferred to avoid. Hence the two *Tarpon* aircraft.

The *Tern* had remained with them for two days. Then, after a final cheery meal on board, the robust little vessel had set off on the return passage to its station. Those who were to remain watched it forging its way, sometimes half hidden by spray, across a desolation of water.

Ginger looked about him. The scene, both land and sea, was

as melancholy a spectacle as could be imagined. It was a world without colour. The land, what could be seen of it, was mostly sheer rock: grim, black, basaltic cliffs. The sea was black; not the clear blue-black of ink, but a greenish black, except where the wind caught it and whipped the surface to slaty-grey. The sky was like a dome of lead. A curtain of cloud, unbroken by a single rift, stretched from horizon to horizon. There was a feeling of rain in the air. Far to the south, an iceberg, draped in tenuous mist, was drifting sluggishly across the face of the water. A few gulls wheeled, screaming defiance at the intruders.

Ginger walked a little way to the crest of a hill that commanded a view inland. It was just the same. Not a tree broke the barren skyline. Not a roof. Nothing but rock and harsh, wiry grass pressed flat by the everlasting wind. The dominating impression conveyed by the picture was utter loneliness; not the friendly loneliness of a quiet spot in rural Britain, with telegraph poles on the horizon and the distant hum of traffic in the air, but a vast hostile loneliness that was like a cold hand on the heart, reminding a man what a puny thing he is compared with Nature untamed.

Ginger walked back – rather quickly – to the others. The *Tern* was hull down.

'Let's go inside and have another look at the map,' suggested Biggles.

They went in. Biggles unfolded his map on a packing-case and studied it for a little while without speaking. He had ringed the base in red ink. From it, radiating like the spokes of a wheel, were pencil lines to other islands. Beside each line was marked the distance and the compass course.

'I suppose the first place to explore is Kerguelen,' said Biggles, glancing up. 'From the air it shouldn't take long. If von Schonbeck's secret depot is somewhere here on the island we ought to see it.

I can't believe that a number of men can use any place for three years without leaving traces visible from above, no matter how careful they may be. But there is one big snag against aerial reconnaissance. I own that I did not realise it until we got here and saw the sort of place we were in. If von Schonbeck is in fact established on Kerguelen, he'll see us – or our aircraft – before we see him.'

'What of it, old boy?' asked Bertie.

'Only this,' said Biggles slowly. 'Not being a fool, von Schonbeck will realise instantly why an aircraft is in this part of the world. He'll know that it doesn't take many men to maintain a machine. He may decide to play the same game as ourselves. That is, he may come gunning for us. He has twenty-five men. There are four of us. I don't object to numerical odds, within reason, but if the hare suddenly became the hunter we might find ourselves in a mess. We should have to bolt – and consider ourselves lucky if we got away. That would be a pretty state of affairs to report to Raymond, wouldn't it?'

'But we could call Raymond on the radio and tell him where von Schonbeck has his hide-out … if I make myself clear?' suggested Bertie. 'Raymond could send out a whole bally fleet of destroyers.'

'Yes, he could,' admitted Biggles, with bitter sarcasm. 'And by the time they got here von Schonbeck would be a thousand miles away with the gold under his conning tower.'

'By Jove! Yes. Never looked at it like that – silly ass I am,' muttered Bertie.

'If we can't fly to make our reconnaissance, what's the answer?' asked Algy.

'We shall have to fly, of course,' returned Biggles. 'But before we take off I think we ought to do a bit of footwork, to make sure that the Nazis are not sitting on our doorstep. When we have made certain that they are not within striking distance, at any rate, we can start flying.'

'But if we spot the submarine depot it comes to the same thing,' asserted Ginger. 'How are four of us going to attack twenty-five?'

'We couldn't,' admitted Biggles. 'Our play would be to sink the sub, if it was in shallow water, or put it out of action. That would keep the Nazis here, as safe as if they were in prison, until the Navy could collect them.'

'This is all assuming that the Nazis are at their base,' put in Algy. 'What happens if we spot the U-517 at sea? We shall have no means of knowing whether or not it has the gold on board. If we sink the sub, bang goes the gold, and the whole object of the expedition will sink with it. If we don't sink the sub it will simply submerge when it sees us and get away. Then we have to start looking all over again.'

'I've considered all these snags,' averred Biggles. 'Frankly, I can't see how we can make a definite plan. The only thing we can do is wait until we do spot the submarine, and then act for the best as the conditions suggest. We're just as likely to spot the sub at sea as in some anchorage. No doubt it will travel on the surface for normal operations – I mean, until it hears us or sees us. Anyway, whether we like it or not, von Schonbeck will have to spend a certain amount of time on the surface to charge his batteries. During the war that was usually done at night. We may do some night flying – high-altitude work – while there is a moon. The best thing of all would be to find the submarine base while the U-boat is absent, perhaps before it gets here, and destroy the fuel supply. Von Schonbeck must be relying on finding oil at his secret base. Without it he would be helpless. He couldn't get anywhere. He'd just have to stay where he was, and that would suit us very nicely. The big question is, has von Schonbeck reached his base yet? We don't know and we've no means of finding out until we spot the sub, in which case its course should tell us something. Admiralty experts know pretty well the speed of the U-517 class of submarine, and they assured me before I left London that it couldn't get here to Kerguelen, if this was its objective, before the twenty-fourth. This is the twenty-first. If they are right we still have three days. They may be wrong. Von Schonbeck may have a card up his sleeve. Again, the sub may not be heading for Kerguelen. The gold may be on some island nearer to the mainland.'

'It all sounds pretty vague to me,' sighed Bertie.

'It is vague,' admitted Biggles. 'We shall just have to do the best we can with the data available. We're here, anyway, and that's a start. We've no time to lose. Once von Schonbeck gets to his hide-out it won't take him long to load up his gold and turn his nose towards South America. We must nab him before he starts on that tack or we shall need more than luck to catch him. If—'

Biggles broke off, tense, in a listening attitude, as from far away there came three unmistakable gunshot reports – a single shot closely followed by two more. He looked at the others, sprang to his feet and made for the door. Before he could reach it, the hut vibrated with the long dull roar of a distant heavy explosion.

Another moment and Biggles was outside the hut, gazing in the direction in which the *Tern* had last been seen. Twilight was darkening a world already gloomy, so at first nothing could be seen except the vast expanse of empty sea; but after a little while it became possible to discern a smudge of smoke being blown along the horizon by the wind. Without a word Biggles ran to the nearest aircraft, cast off and jumped aboard. The others followed. Biggles was busy for a moment in the cockpit. The engines came to life, to roar – as it seemed – defiance to wind and wave. The machine moved, swinging round in a swirl of foam to face the open sea. In two minutes it was in the air, heading for the smoke which was now dispersing.

'What was it, do you think?' asked Ginger, who was sitting next to Biggles.

'I don't know,' answered Biggles in a hard voice, 'but I've got an idea. I hope I'm wrong … but I'm afraid …'

He zoomed to a thousand feet and then put the aircraft back on even keel. What he was thinking Ginger did not know – but he could guess. For his eyes, too, were on the smoke. There was nothing else. Whatever had been under it, to cause it, had gone. From their elevated position the *Tern* should be in view. But it was not. There was nothing beside the smoke – nothing except the grey, heaving ocean.

Reaching his objective Biggles banked slightly, continuing the bank into a circle, looking down through a side window with eyes that were never still. 'Look for a conning tower or a periscope,' he snapped. 'If you see anything start to break surface, yell.'

Ginger did not answer. He, too, was staring down. There was little to see – a spreading patch of oil, some debris and a raft on which two men were lying prone. They did not move. He moistened his lips, which had gone dry.

Said Biggles: 'I'm going down. Keep watching.' He subjected the area to a final searching scrutiny and then landed near the raft, taxiing on until one wing was over it. 'Take over,' he ordered curtly, and climbing out ran along the wing until he could drop on the raft.

Out of the corners of his eyes Ginger saw him take one look and clamber back. 'All right,' he said. 'I'll have her.' He dropped into his seat and took off, climbing steeply to resume his scrutiny of the ocean.

'How about those fellows? Are we going to leave them there?' asked Ginger.

'There's nothing we can do for them – they're dead,' returned Biggles shortly. 'I daren't hang about. We might get what they got.'

Algy came forward. 'What was it – the *Tern*?'

They did not move.

'Yes. With a hole blown in her side by a torpedo, she must have gone down like a broken bottle.'

'How do you know it was a torpedo?'

'It couldn't have been anything else. She didn't blow herself up and gunfire wouldn't have sent her down in five minutes. Two men got away on that raft. I remember them well – two nice lads, they were. Now they're dead. Riddled with bullets. There can't be many swine in the world who'd do a thing like that. Von Schonbeck is one of them. This is his hunting-ground. He's back at his old game.'

'Does that mean he knows we're here?' asked Algy.

'Not necessarily. At least, it's unlikely that he knew when he fired the torpedo, although he probably knows now.'

'Then why should he do a thing like that?'

'The *Tern* was a British ship. Spite would be ample motive for a Nazi of von Schonbeck's type.'

'What do you think happened?' asked Ginger.

'The skipper of the *Tern* knew all about the U-517,' answered Biggles. 'In fact, he told me that he'd been ordered to keep an eye open for her. I'd say the ship spotted the submarine, running on the surface, and fired a shot across her bows to halt her. Von Schonbeck answered with a torpedo. The *Tern* would see it coming and have time to fire two more shots before it hit her. One torpedo was enough. After that von Schonbeck followed his usual procedure of destroying evidence by machine-gunning the survivors.'

'To do that he must have stayed on the surface.'

'Of course. He dived when he heard us coming.'

'You think he heard us?'

'Bound to. Had we not come along he'd probably still be on the surface, gloating.'

'So he knows we're here?'

'He knows there's an aircraft in the vicinity. He may not know why, but from what we know of the man he must have a pretty good idea.' Biggles raised his eyes from the water. 'Well, it's no use looking for him now; he'll stay submerged until he's well out of the area.'

Biggles flew back to the base and landed. No one spoke while they were tying up. Ginger was depressed, appalled, by the tragic end of the *Tern* and its cheerful company. Grim-faced, Biggles strode on to the hut. He waited until the others were inside, with the door shut, before he spoke.

'This makes a difference,' he said, dropping on to one of the packing-cases that served as chairs. 'We've got to go back to war conditions. The first thing is a black-out … and when I say black-out I mean a real black-out. Von Schonbeck will have guessed by now that we are after him. At any rate, he must know that an aircraft is here; but he doesn't know where it is based, and I don't want him to know. No lights after dark, or he soon will know. The U-517 carries guns – heavy guns, too. If von Schonbeck located us he might well attack us. He could sit a mile away and shell us to blazes. But let's have supper and turn in. Tomorrow we'll give Kerguelen the once-over.'

'Von Schonbeck has a big advantage,' observed Ginger moodily. 'He can hear us when we're on the move, but we can't hear him.'

'Nevertheless he has a handicap that doesn't affect us,' asserted Biggles.

'What is it?'

'Oil. Oil is to a submarine what his scent is to a fox. He can't move without it. The latest submarines are fitted with every conceivable device to prevent oil from escaping – special valves on the propeller shaft, and so on – but she still can't move without leaving a trace. It's impossible to keep the deck clear of oil. The guns need oil to keep them working smoothly. When a submarine dives some of that oil comes off, and in a smooth sea it only needs a few drops of oil to leave a stain, perhaps a trail. A sub that has been at sea for a long time, due to general wear and tear and perhaps a leaky plate or two, leaves a trail that can be seen for miles. The trouble during the war was, thousands of ships were on the move, all leaving trails. Damaged tankers were spilling hundreds of tons of oil. Planes were crashing in the sea, all spilling oil. But there's nothing here to spill oil – *except the craft we're looking for*. Okay. Fix a blanket over that window somebody and I'll light a candle.'

CHAPTER IV

Biggles Looks Round

After a fairly comfortable night, a night that passed without incident except that Ginger was more than once awakened by the howling of wildcats, break of dawn found Biggles outside the hut surveying the sea for signs of the U-517, and the sky for indications of probable weather conditions. The others joined him.

The prospect was not one to arouse enthusiasm. In the wan light of early dawn, land and sea looked even more depressing and bleak than on the previous evening. Ginger made a remark to this effect, whereupon Biggles replied, dryly, that as according to Admiralty Sailing Directions these conditions persisted for three hundred days of the year, the sooner they accustomed themselves to them the better. 'I was hoping to catch sight of the U-boat,' he added, 'but no doubt von Schonbeck is too wily a bird to surface near his latest sinking, knowing that an aircraft is in the offing. Still, we know he's arrived, and that's something. Moreover, he can't be far away. I don't mind telling you that the sinking of the *Tern* has made me sick and savage. It makes our account with this cold-blooded Nazi a personal one. Really, we ought to report the sinking to headquarters, but I don't feel inclined to risk giving our position away by using the radio. It will have to wait. Let's have breakfast and get busy.'

The meal over, Biggles picked up his binoculars. 'Before we start flying operations, as I suggested yesterday, I think we ought to have a look round from the nearest high ground to make sure that the U-517 isn't skulking in some hole within earshot. Algy, I shall have to ask you to stick around here and keep an ear to the radio in case any signals come through. I aim to be back by lunch-time, so see what you can turn out in the grub line.'

Biggles, Ginger and Bertie, set off, heading for a towering rock massif that rose up behind the camp at no great distance. During the climb, from time to time Biggles paused to scan the sea and the coastline through his binoculars, but each time he returned the glasses to their case without comment. The summit was reached in just over an hour, and from there a long and careful reconnaissance was made of the view it commanded.

For some time nobody spoke, probably because there was no specific object to call for remark; but Ginger, as he surveyed the scene, was appalled by the fearful character of the place. It was worse, far worse, than anything he had imagined. To left and right ran a rugged coastline, sheer rock in most places rising straight out of the sea, sometimes to a height of not much less than a thousand feet. Into these cliffs, untold ages of corrosion had cut narrow inlets of depths varying from a hundred yards to a mile or more. Within these confines the water lay black and still. Here and there a mass of cliff had fallen, leaving numerous small islets to provide a perch for gulls, penguins and seals – the only living creatures in sight. Not a tree, nor even a bush of any size, could be seen. The only growth was a stiff wiry grass that bent under the breeze. This did not grow in broad patches, in the manner of turf; it occurred only in low-lying areas and sprang up in the form of great tussocks.

Said Biggles, pointing to some that lay below them: 'I should be sorry to have to walk through that stuff. I'd wager it's peat bog between those tussocks. It looks like moss, and so it is, but if you stepped on it you'd probably go straight through up to the neck. I've seen that sort of stuff before, in northern Canada.'

Inland, the terrain rose in a succession of steps and screes to a considerable height before falling into what appeared to be a vast central basin, too distant for details to be observed.

'I say, old boy, what a place, you know, and all that,' remarked Bertie.

'As you say, it's a place,' agreed Biggles. 'Place is the word. The Nazi Higher Command knew what it was doing when it selected this God-forsaken area for a secret base. Not much risk of interference. Von Schonbeck has this advantage, and we should do well to remember it: having been cruising in these waters for three years he probably knows every hole and corner. We know nothing about it, and the chart shows very little, so if it comes to a matter of hide-and-seek he's likely to win the game. Take a look.' He passed the glasses to Bertie, who, after a while, handed them on to Ginger. Through them the stark inhospitality of the island could be fully appreciated.

'Before we go back we'll cut across to that shoulder of rock on the right,' decided Biggles. 'It blots out a lot of the sea that lies behind it. We may as well have a look at all there is to see while we're at it.'

'It all seems a pretty hopeless business to me, old lad, if you don't mind my saying so,' observed Bertie, as they descended. 'Instead of tearing up and down and round and round these bally rocks why not shoot across to the Magellan Straits and wait for the blighter to show up – nab him as he goes through – if you see what I mean?'

'It happens that the territory on either side of the Straits is not British, and there's no airfield, anyway,' answered Biggles.

'We could sit on the sea.'

'The sea would be more likely to sit on us,' asserted Biggles. 'From what I have heard of the Magellan Straits even the biggest ships reckon to take a pounding going through, in which case it makes no appeal to me as a parking-place for an aircraft.'

'Absolutely, old boy – absolutely,' agreed Bertie.

On the way to the new objective the party had to pass near the inner end of an inlet of some size. Here the rocks had tumbled down in a wild chaos of boulders to end in a short, rough shingle beach. Biggles stopped, looking at something. Putting up his glasses he looked again. Presently, without a word, he changed direction towards the object that had claimed his attention. Reaching it he said quietly: 'We needn't wonder what happened here.'

'Poor wretches,' breathed Bertie. 'Tough luck – what?'

Ginger did not speak. There was really nothing to say. What lay before them told its own story, and the story was one of shipwreck and disaster. A few rotting timbers that had once been a ship's lifeboat lay just above the high-water mark. Strewn about were some empty biscuit tins and a water keg. More poignant than these was an oar that stood up with its lower part held in a cairn of stones; it had fallen askew, but from the blade still hung the tatters of what had once been a man's shirt. Nearby, under the lee of a rough windbreak of stones, lay five skeletons.

'God! What a place to be cast away,' breathed Biggles, in a voice low and vibrant with sympathy. 'What a hope they had. I wonder who they were? They managed to reach land, and this was the land they reached. A lot of good it did them.'

'Some of von Schonbeck's victims, who managed to get away,' suggested Ginger.

'Quite likely.' Biggles shrugged. 'Well, staring at these poor bones won't bring them back to life; we'll leave them here to their loneliness. They should help us to remember what happens to castaways on Kerguelen.' Striding on he led the way to the top of the rock that had been their goal. As he breasted the final rise he uttered an exclamation that brought the others quickly to his side. By that time the glasses were at his eyes, focused.

Following the direction Ginger made out a vessel about five miles away. 'A ship, by jingo!' he exclaimed.

'She looks like a whaler,' said Biggles, without lowering the glasses. 'It's unlikely that any other sort of ship would have business here.' He continued his scrutiny.

In fact, he watched the ship for so long, with a deepening expression of surprise on his face, that Ginger was constrained to ask: '*Is it a whaler?*'

'It is,' answered Biggles. 'Heading south-east.' He lowered the glasses a trifle.

'Now what can you see?' asked Ginger impatiently.

'I can see what looks to me suspiciously like a trail of oil. It starts out there in the general direction of the ship and runs back towards the southern tip of this island. That means she must have been here – or else she passed pretty close.'

'But the oil—'

'There's nothing remarkable about that,' broke in Biggles. 'A whaler, I imagine, would always leave an oil trail. Modern whalers render the blubber down on board, and I reckon a ship doing that would fairly drip oil, particularly if she had been through heavy weather. All the same …' Biggles shifted the glasses slightly and continued to stare. 'She certainly is losing some oil,' he went on. At last he lowered the glasses. 'I'd like to have a closer look at that ship,' he said slowly. 'After we've been home I think I'll fly out and give her the once-over. There's nothing else to be seen from here, so we may as well start back.'

As they approached the huts Algy could be seen standing outside, waiting.

'What's the news?' called Biggles.

'The air has been fairly buzzing with signals,' answered Algy.

'For us?'

'No – they're in code.'

'The deuce they are.' Biggles increased his pace until he came up with Algy. 'Were these two-way signals?'

'Yes.'

'H'm! That's interesting. We know the submarine is about. Von Schonbeck might use code. But who would he be talking to? What was the strength of these signals?'

'They sounded pretty close, to me.'

'Did you keep a record?'

Algy held out a sheet of paper.

Biggles glanced at it and shook his head. 'No use amateurs like us trying to decode that,' he muttered. 'Scotland Yard could do it, no doubt. They've specialists trained for the job. But to get this to the Yard and wait for a reply would be too slow to be any use.'

'Send the thing by radio,' suggested Bertie, polishing his eyeglass.

'And tell the people who sent out the signals that we've picked them up? Not on your life. If there are transmitters in the region you may be sure they'll have operators always on duty. Von Schonbeck will know where we are, soon enough. I'm keeping off the air until it's absolutely vital that we use it.'

'You think von Schonbeck was behind these signals?' suggested Algy.

'I don't think there's much doubt about it,' returned Biggles promptly. 'There's no need for anyone to use code now. Admittedly the Admiralty might use code, but it's unlikely that there are any warships within a thousand miles of us. The question is, who was von Schonbeck talking to? I wonder ...' Biggles paused. 'From the top of the hill we spotted a whaler standing away to the south-east. As soon as I have gulped a spot of lunch I'm going to have a closer look at her.'

'But I say, old boy, there's no need for a whaler to use code,' protested Bertie.

'Not when her business is catching whales,' answered Biggles vaguely.

'Have you any reason to suppose that this one isn't catching whales?' queried Ginger shrewdly.

'I don't know,' answered Biggles thoughtfully. 'A whaler would be a very useful parent ship for a submarine – for refuelling, and so on. I had a good look at that ship this morning.'

'So I noticed,' put in Ginger.

'She was too far off for me to make out the flag she was flying, but there was something about her behaviour that struck me as odd.'

'What was it?'

Biggles took out a cigarette and tapped it on the back of his hand. 'It was this. A few miles to the east of that ship there was a school of whales. The look-out must have seen them. The business of a whaler is to kill whales, so one would have thought that the ship would have turned towards them. As far as I could make out it took not the slightest notice of them.'

'Perhaps it already had a full load?' suggested Algy.

'In that case why was it heading south-east, when it should have set a course for Europe or North America?'

'I see what you mean,' said Algy softly.

'We know the U-517 is in the vicinity – within, say, a couple of hundred miles at the very outside,' resumed Biggles. 'That being the case you may wonder why I haven't started a systematic combing of the ocean, looking for her. The answer is I want von Schonbeck to reassure himself that all is well. After he sank the *Tern* and heard us coming — if in fact he did hear us — he would dive, and stay submerged. It would be some hours before he surfaced. He would feel pretty safe last night, but with the coming of daylight he would certainly be on the alert. By giving him a rest we may catch him napping. In view of what we have seen today there seems a chance that the whaler is a German ship working with him. It may have a rendezvous with him. Let's have a look at the map to get an idea of where the whaler is making for. Speaking from memory there's nothing in that direction but water.'

Sitting on a packing-case Biggles opened the chart and looked at it. 'We needn't waste time on this,' he went on. 'If the whaler holds on the course it was making when we last saw her it will touch nothing till it comes to the polar ice-pack. The nearest land is here, this island to the east, although there's a doubt about that.' He pointed to a remote speck that carried the name Corbie Island (E.D.). 'Corbie Island, even if it exists, is two hundred miles away to the east of the whaler's last known position. It's a long way from here, but we'll have a look at it sometime. Meanwhile, let's eat. After lunch I'll take Ginger with me and have a look at these whale-hunters. You, Algy, and Bertie, will stand by for radio signals, and be prepared to fly the spare machine if it is needed.'

The meal did not take long, for Biggles, when busy, occupied no more time with food than was necessary to support life. As soon as it was over he donned his flying-kit and strode down to the mooring. Ginger followed.

In a few minutes the aircraft was in the air, climbing towards the leaden cloudbank that still covered the sky.

CHAPTER V

The Whaler

At two thousand feet, just below the ceiling, Biggles levelled out and turned to the south-east. To Ginger he said: 'Keep your eyes mobile. The U-boat may be about. Watch the creeks and inlets for oil tracks. The wind seems to be freshening again, so I'm afraid we shan't see much.'

Looking down Ginger regarded the surface of the globe, or as much as he could see of it, with morbid curiosity. Most of the island was now in view. The only part hidden was the southern tip where haze restricted visibility. As far as the land was concerned the spectacle offered nothing new; it was merely an extended version of what had been seen from ground level – an expanse of colourless wilderness, bleak and desolate in the extreme, with drab green areas marking the low-lying portions. These, he assumed, were the bogs referred to in the Admiralty description. The coastline was as irregular as the outside of an unfinished jig-saw puzzle. The sea offered even less to the eye. On every side it rolled away to pitiless distances, unbroken by any object except far to the south, where a line of icebergs and floes marked the outer defences of the polar regions. Of the submarine there was no sign, nor was the whaler in sight. The oil trail that Biggles had observed was still there, a sinuous grey mark across the surface of the ocean, narrow at the head and widening towards the tail where it swung round in a mighty curve towards the southern tip of the island.

'I fancy the wind has veered,' remarked Biggles. 'That trail is not as clear as it was. If a sea gets up it will soon be wiped out altogether; but it's still clear enough to give us the general direction taken by the whaler. Hello! There are the whales, just breaking surface. The whaler doesn't appear to have interfered with them.'

Ginger gazed with curiosity at the sea-monsters, looking from the air rather like a line of torpedoes floating on the surface of the water. 'What are you going to do first?' he asked. 'Are you going to follow the oil trail to the ship or to the island?'

'For a start I'm going to have a close look at the ship,' answered Biggles. 'Then we'll come back and check up on where the oil starts from.'

'You said you'd expect a whaler to leak oil,' reminded Ginger.

'Yes, I know,' returned Biggles. 'But to leave a trail like that I reckon a ship would have to be losing more oil than seems reasonable. If it goes on, by the time she gets to port her tanks will be dry. Of course, it's always on the boards that she has been lying in the lee of the island refining blubber, in which case she would get pretty dirty. I'd like to spot the U-boat. She'll travel on the surface while she thinks she's safe.'

'With a snappy look-out on the watch for danger,' put in Ginger.

'No doubt.'

Ginger said no more. Biggles flew on, and soon afterwards his questing eyes picked up the whaler, hull down, over the starboard bow. 'There she is,' he said. 'Check up on her course.'

'I make it a point or two east of south-east,' declared Ginger a few minutes later.

'That's about it,' agreed Biggles. 'I wonder where she's making for – if she isn't hunting whales? Her present course won't take her to Corbie Island – at least, not if the island is anywhere near the position shown on the map. Of course, the island may not exist. The letters E.D. give us fair warning of that, so we can't blame the Admiralty if it isn't there.'

'This looking for an island that may not exist is an unsatisfactory business,' opined Ginger. 'I should have thought that by this time the Admiralty would have pinned down every square yard of dry ground between the Poles.'

'They'll do it now no doubt, now that we have aircraft with a range of thousands of miles,' answered Biggles. 'It would have been a long and tedious business to do it with surface-craft. There wasn't much point in it to justify the expense. No one wanted these islands, anyway. Air transportation has now given remote islands a new value, as refuelling stations for trans-ocean runs.' As he finished speaking Biggles cut the throttle and began to glide towards the whaler, now in full view some three or four miles distant. 'Hello! Did you notice that?' he asked sharply.

'She's changed course – if that's what you mean,' replied Ginger. 'You can tell that by the wake. She's heading pretty nearly due east now.'

'Quite right. She's only just spotted us. I wonder why she changed course? And come to think of it, that vessel must have been travelling flat out to cover as much water as she has since we last saw her. What was the reason for that?'

'Maybe she's a modern ship.'

'She must be, to travel at that rate.'

The aircraft dropped lower, rapidly overhauling the object of the conversation. Men could be seen on the deck, looking up. One waved. A flag fluttered to the peak.

'She's Norwegian!' cried Ginger.

Men could be seen looking up. One waved.

'Say she's flying the Norwegian flag,' corrected Biggles. 'It isn't quite the same thing. A dishonest ship can fly any flag. Still, I believe Norway has the biggest whaling fleet afloat, so there would be nothing remarkable if she was Norwegian. Pity we can't make out her name, but we shan't be able to see it from the air.' He made a circle round the ship, which held on her course.

'Let's try being friendly,' suggested Biggles. He opened a side panel and waved.

The men on the deck of the ship, seven or eight of them, waved back.

'Can we speak to them?' asked Ginger.

'No,' answered Biggles. 'If we ask them who they are and what they are doing they might tell us anything, and we should have no means of checking up on it. If she is a consort of the U-boat we should merely reveal that we were suspicious of her without gaining anything.'

'Then there's nothing else we can do,' said Ginger.

'Nothing. We may as well go back. No use wasting petrol. We shan't learn anything more here.' Biggles turned away and started back over his course, keeping parallel with the oil trail. 'I still say that ship is losing more oil than she should,' he murmured pensively.

He did not speak again until Kerguelen was almost under their keel. Then he said: 'There's the end of the oil trail, plain enough. The ship must have been lying in that cove.' He pointed. 'I think we'll go down and have a look round.'

Dropping lower, the aircraft passed over a narrow neck of water, not more than a hundred feet wide, with precipitous sides, and found herself over an almost circular cove of some size. As a harbour it was perfect, as perfect as anything an architect could design, yet from the sea its existence would not have been suspected.

'Spare my days!' exclaimed Biggles. 'Look at the oil! That whaler must have burst a tank to make all that mess. I don't like the look of it. Keep your eyes skinned for anybody or anything moving. This is just the sort of place von Schonbeck would choose for a hide-out.' He put the machine in a turn and held it so until they had made three complete circuits at a height of less than a hundred feet. 'Of course, this may be a bona-fide whaling depot,' he went on. 'It's a depot of some sort, there's no doubt of that, and the place has been used recently. That's a camp down there.'

'I don't see any camp,' said Ginger.

'Look again,' invited Biggles. 'Look beyond that strip of shingle beach at the inner extremity of the cove. Those lumps are too square and regular to be natural rock formations.'

'Ah,' breathed Ginger. 'I get you.'

'We'll go in,' decided Biggles. 'If you see a movement, yell. I've got a feeling we're on the track of something.'

For a moment or two Ginger could see no movement of any sort, and he said so; then he cried out tersely: 'Steady! What's that between the rocks? There's something moving. It's a—'

He was cut off by a blinding flash followed a split second later by an explosion so violent that the blast, striking the under-surfaces of the aircraft, caused it to yaw wildly.

Biggles slammed on full throttle and zoomed. 'What the deuce!'

Ginger looked about him in no small alarm, fully expecting to see the smoke of a shell-burst, for he thought, naturally, that they had been shot at. But the sky was clear. The only smoke was a grey cloud that drifted across the cove from the point where the explosion had occurred. He continued to watch. Biggles continued to fly round, taking evading action.

'What in thunder was it?' he questioned, wonderingly.

'I don't know,' replied Ginger, in an astonished voice. 'I was just going to say that the thing I saw moving was a pig.'

'A *pig*! Ah. It must have been one of the wild hogs. So what? Hogs don't handle guns.'

'It may not have been a gun,' suggested Ginger.

'I think you've got something there,' returned Biggles in a curious voice. 'Let's try again.' He throttled back and put the machine in a new glide towards the anchorage. Nothing happened. The only sound was the gentle sighing of wind over the planes. On the ground nothing moved. The machine went on down, Biggles flying with one hand on the stick and the other on the throttle ready for instant action. Still nothing happened, and presently the machine landed, to run to a standstill near the beach, a position from which signs of human occupation ashore were at once evident. The keel of the aircraft grated gently on the shingle, where several gulls with oil-smeared wings tried in vain to take flight. Some lay dead.

'This place has a suspicious smell about it,' said Biggles quietly. 'But the smell I can smell isn't whales. It's machine oil.' For a minute or two longer he sat still, eyes active, hand on the throttle ready for a quick move; but nothing happened, and presently, satis-fied, he relaxed. 'Let's go ashore,' he suggested.

Ginger went forward, dropped the anchor and stepped down into two feet of oil-coated water. Biggles joined him, and together they walked slowly up the beach towards three small rock buildings that Biggles had observed from the air. Ginger was quickening his pace when Biggles laid a restraining hand on his arm. 'Just a minute,' he said in a tense voice. 'Take a look at that.' He pointed.

Ginger stared with startled eyes at the object towards which Biggles had directed a finger. At first he could not make out what it was, although it had a sinister look about it. It appeared to be a red stain, surrounded by red splashes. Some loose, soft-looking fragments lay on it. 'My gosh!' he exclaimed in a horrified voice. 'It's blood.'

'It couldn't be anything else,' said Biggles.

'What do you make of it?'

'I don't make anything of it – except that somebody, or something, has just met with a nasty accident. That blood's fresh.' Biggles spoke, but he did not move. The muscles of his face were tense. His eyes were never still for a moment; they went from point to point, always returning to the gruesome stain.

Ginger's eyes, too, were taking in every detail of the scene. It was now obvious that the place was, or had been until recently, a camp. The main features were the three huts, or cabins. There were other, smaller, erections. All were built of the rock of which the island was composed so that they blended into the background and could not have been seen from a distance. Faint tracks led from hut to hut, and to the beach. There were a few other objects, none conspicuous in itself but together giving the impression of human occupation – a heap of driftwood, an empty can, a scrap of paper, a piece of orange peel. There was one very curious object. On a flat boulder, about thirty yards from where they stood, rested a biscuit tin. The label it bore was new, untarnished by weather. Biggles looked at it for some time. Then he moved, slowly, step by step, towards the ugly stain and the fragments that lay on it. Stooping, he touched a piece.

Ginger was nearly sick when he realised suddenly what it was. His lips curled as he muttered: 'Flesh.'

Biggles laughed – a short nervous laugh. 'Call it meat,' he corrected. 'You said you saw a pig – a wild hog?'

'Yes.'

'This was it. Something tore it to pieces – small pieces; and I've got a pretty good idea what it was.'

'It could only have been a bomb.'

'Something of the sort. The poor beast took fright at our arrival, and was running away— Stop! Where do you think you're going?' Biggles' voice was crisp.

Ginger had moved forward. 'I was going to see what was in that biscuit tin,' he explained.

'It might be better to find out without touching it,' suggested Biggles grimly. 'Lie down.'

'Lie—?'

'Don't argue. Lie flat.'

Ginger, his face a picture of astonishment, obeyed. Biggles also lay down. He drew his pistol and took careful aim at the tin.

Ginger waited.

'Hold your hat,' said Biggles curtly. His pistol spat. The tin moved a few inches, that was all. He fired again. This time the crack of the weapon was followed by a vicious tearing explosion and the shrill whine of flying splinters. Grey smoke drifted. Debris pattered down. Silence returned.

Staring, Ginger saw that the tin, and most of the rock on which it had rested, had disappeared. His voice, when he spoke, was thin and dry with shock. 'What the dickens was that?'

'Booby trap,' answered Biggles quietly. 'That wretched hog saved *our* bacon,' he added with grim humour. 'Nazis have been here. We shall have to watch where we are putting our feet. And I'll tell you something else. Nazis don't set booby traps for penguins or wild hogs. Von Schonbeck knows we're here.'

CHAPTER VI

Tragedy Ashore

Ginger, looking thoroughly shaken, rose slowly to his feet, glancing around with no small apprehension. 'I don't like this place,' he decided. 'Let's get out of here.'

'I don't like it either, but we shall have to look at it,' answered Biggles.

'You think this was von Schonbeck's camp?'

'Yes – either his main base or an emergency depot.'

'Why not wait for him to come back?'

'Unless I have missed my guess he isn't coming back. Had he been coming back he would have left a guard over the place; and he would hardly have set booby traps. No, this was von Schonbeck's dump; when he went he went for good.'

'With the gold?'

'I don't think so,' said Biggles thoughtfully. 'I look at it like this. Whether this was von Schonbeck's base or not he was pretty certain to have a refuelling station on Kerguelen, which, after all, is the biggest island in the South Indian Ocean. He probably arrived about the same time as the *Tern*, or soon afterwards. Naturally, he would wonder what she was doing here, and watch her. He may have guessed the truth. Anyway, I'm pretty certain he saw us arrive, or heard us take off when he sank the *Tern*. For whom, except us, would he have set booby traps? He realised that he couldn't very well use Kerguelen at the same time as an aircraft without being spotted, so he cleared out, and knowing that sooner or later we should spot this camp, made arrangements for our reception. The booby trap is a Nazi speciality. Had that hog not come nosing around we might have stepped right into the trap, too.'

'But how does the whaler fit into the picture? Her trail brought us here.'

Biggles considered the question. 'I don't know – yet. We may find out presently.'

'If this was one of von Schonbeck's refuelling stations, and he's pushed off, it means that he had to abandon his oil. Yet he'll need plenty to get him to the Magellan Straits.'

'We'll see about that,' declared Biggles. 'Judging by the mess I'd say von Schonbeck has taken most of his oil with him. We'll soon see if that's true by having a look round, but, by thunder, we've got to be careful how we do it.'

'You're telling me,' muttered Ginger.

'Stay where you are for a minute.'

Biggles made a long and intensive survey of the camp before he moved, and then gave it as his opinion that provided they had only booby traps to deal with they were reasonably safe, now that they were alive to the danger. With his pistol he fired off two more rather obvious traps. One was a large flat stone, in the manner of a door-step, at the entrance of the nearest hut; the other, inside the building, was a case of chocolate so arranged that anyone lifting the lid would be blown to pieces. Biggles took no risks, choosing his path carefully without touching anything that could be avoided. Several times he fired at suspected traps that turned out to be harmless. Very little had been left behind. As he remarked to Ginger, if von Schonbeck knew that he was being sought by the British authorities, as it was now evident that he did, it was unlikely that he would leave any clue to his whereabouts. A careful inspection revealed only a few cases of sundry stores, some emergency tools and boxes of ammunition.

The big discovery was a concrete oil-tank that had been sunk into the rock about fifty yards from the camp. It was nearly empty. Biggles pointed to a dark, even line that ran completely round the wall, about four feet above the present level of oil. 'That tells a story,' he remarked. 'For a long time the oil must have stood at the upper level, where it made a mark. That, I fancy, was the period when the submarine returned to Germany after the war ended. Within the last day or two the oil was reduced to its present level. What happened was, von Schonbeck came back and refuelled. There's one thing wrong with that argument, though. No submarine could have the capacity for the amount of oil that has just been taken from this tank – not in one loading.'

'Perhaps it made two trips. I mean, it could have shifted some of the oil and come back for more.'

Biggles shook his head. 'No, that won't do. Had two loads been taken there would have been a delay between the two loadings, in which case the oil would have made a second mark – a slight mark perhaps – where it rested in the interval. When the oil was pumped from this tank it was taken at one go.'

'Von Schonbeck may have chucked the oil away to prevent us from using it?' suggested Ginger. 'Goodness knows there's plenty of oil on the water.'

'I can't accept that,' replied Biggles. 'A gallon of oil, on water, will cover an area of miles. It only forms a very thin film. We're talking about tons of oil. Where has it gone? There is only one reasonable answer to that. If von Schonbeck did not make two or three trips, and I don't think he did – I doubt if he'd have the time, anyway – someone must have helped him. In other words, another vessel besides the submarine has been here. There aren't many ships in these waters. In fact, there's only one that could have done it – our friendly Norwegian whaler. This is all confirmation of our suspicion that the whaler isn't what she pretends to be. I'm almost certain now that the whaler is acting as consort to the submarine.'

'But would a Norwegian ship do that?'

'Not willingly – we needn't doubt that. But don't forget that von Schonbeck is a Nazi. We know something of his methods. The whaler might have been pressed into his service. Just how we don't know, but in due course we shall find out. In the meantime I shall work on the assumption that the whaler is acting with the submarine, carrying reserve oil.'

'It may have been doing that all along,' said Ginger. 'When Germany grabbed Norway she grabbed her ships.'

'That may be so, but I have a feeling that this is something new,' averred Biggles. 'Had the whaler been working with von Schonbeck during the war, Muller, the chap who was shot in Berlin, would have mentioned it in his statement. There's no doubt that a tanker would be invaluable to von Schonbeck, taking into consideration his proposed long run to Chile. Well, now he's got one.'

'What are we going to do about it?' inquired Ginger. 'If what you say is right, it would hit von Schonbeck a crack if we sank the whaler; but I imagine it wouldn't do to sink a ship on the high seas flying the Norwegian flag.'

'True enough,' asserted Biggles. 'It's a bit hard to know what to do, and that's a fact. It's no use our following the whaler because we couldn't do that without being seen or heard. The whaler would warn the submarine by radio that we were about. The two ships would certainly not make contact. In fact, it's more likely that the whaler would push off and lay a false scent to take us off the trail. But I think this is going rather far, considering all the evidence we have is circumstantial. We have no actual proof that the whaler is in the racket, although the fact that she is at this moment heading for nowhere in particular is in itself suspicious. Still, suspicion isn't proof.'

'You think that the whaler has a rendezvous with the submarine?'

'That, of course, is the obvious answer. The signals Algy picked up were probably messages between the whaler and the submarine. The sub could hide from us by submerging, but the whaler must stay on the surface, and from the fact that we turned up this morning to have a look at her she must know we are suspicious. At the same time, von Schonbeck is no doubt astute enough to know that we wouldn't risk a row with Norway by interfering with a ship flying the Norwegian flag. If, subsequently, we could prove that the vessel had been pressed into von Schonbeck's service it would be a different matter, but even then Norway would probably take a dim view of it if we sank one of her ships without consulting her. To report the situation to Raymond, who would then have to deal with the matter through diplomatic channels, would be hopeless. It would take weeks.'

'You're making it all sound very difficult,' argued Ginger. 'What *can* we do?'

'Before doing anything else we shall have to go home for some more fuel,' asserted Biggles. 'Then we might have another look at the whaler to check its course. There's just a possibility that we might strike the whaler and the submarine together – although I suppose that's hoping for too much. An alternative would be to locate this place Corbie Island and see what goes on there – if anything.'

'We could always track the whaler by following the oil trail,' suggested Ginger.

Biggles glanced at the sky. 'I'm not so sure of that. The wind is freshening and a heavy sea would soon wash out the trail.' He thought for a moment, tapping a cigarette on the back of his hand. 'There is one encouraging point arising out of all this. I don't think von Schonbeck has got the gold yet. The whaler is heading roughly south-east, so if our deductions are correct the sub has gone in that direction since sinking the *Tern*. If von Schonbeck had the gold on board surely he would be on a course north-west for Chile, going at full speed to get clear of this area as quickly as possible. We'll have a final look round and make for home.'

Without speaking again Biggles made another examination of the camp without discovering anything of interest. Finally he climbed to the top of a low cliff that backed the shingle beach to see what lay beyond it. Ginger followed, and looking round saw on all sides the dismal desolation to which he was becoming accustomed. The shore line beyond the cove was now visible. It was dead, empty, except at one place where a flock of sea-birds were wheeling and swooping with a good deal of noise. Biggles raised his binoculars and studied the spot. He did not speak.

'See anything?' asked Ginger.

'I'm not sure,' answered Biggles slowly. 'But there must be something there or the gulls wouldn't behave like that. Maybe they're squabbling over a dead sea-creature – a whale, perhaps. I can just make out something tumbling in the surf, but I can't see what it is. Let's go and have a look. It isn't far.' He put his glasses back in their case and set off towards the clamour.

The walk took about ten minutes. Most of the gulls retired to a distance when the men approached; others hung about, circling, uttering the mournful cries of their kind. A short and rather dangerous descent took Biggles and Ginger to the shore, and after a final clamber over the rocks they reached their objective. They stopped. Neither spoke.

Near the rocks, rising and falling in the restless surf, were the bodies of two men, a short distance apart. Not without difficulty Biggles got one ashore, and a glance at the face was enough to tell Ginger that the man had not been dead for long – a few days at most. The body, as was to be expected, was that of an ordinary seaman, a tall, fair-haired, well-built fellow in the early twenties, clad in the usual blue jersey and trousers. There was nothing to indicate who he was. But the second body was more fruitful of information. This time it was an older man, grey and grizzled, his clean-shaven face tanned by wind and sun. He wore a jacket, and faded rings of gold braid on the sleeves revealed that he had been an officer. But what held Ginger's gaze was a small round hole, blue at the edges, over the right eye.

'This fellow wasn't drowned – he was shot,' said Biggles in a hard voice, as he felt in the inner pocket of the jacket. He brought out a number of letters. The ink of the addresses had run from immersion in the sea, but the words were still legible. In each case the name and address was the same. Biggles read it aloud. 'Sven Honritzen, Maritime Hotel, Oslo.' He glanced up and met Ginger's eyes. 'Norwegian,' he said laconically. 'The thing begins to hook together. This poor chap must have been one of the original officers of the whaler. I say original because I doubt very much if the officers now on board are Norwegians. The other fellow was a rating on the same ship. So the whaler *was* Norwegian. Von Schonbeck has been at his dirty work again. It doesn't need much imagination to read the story. The whaler was here on legitimate business. Unfortunately for the skipper von Schonbeck saw it and decided the ship would be useful to him as a mobile base. He may have given the crew the chance to work for him, or he may not. Either way it would have come to the same thing in the end. We know how von Schonbeck disposes of evidence. These men were murdered in cold blood. There may have been others. Von Schonbeck has taken over the ship, with a crew of his own on board, no doubt. Of course, there may still be some of the original hands on board, working under pressure. A Nazi would think nothing of shooting anybody who refused to work for him.' Biggles stared moodily at the bodies, the corners of his mouth turned down in hard lines. 'My God! The score against this inhuman devil is mounting,' he burst out suddenly, as if his passion had burst through his natural restraint. 'We'll get him. We'll get him if we have to follow him to the Arctic and back again to the Antarctic! I'm always cautious about judging other men, but this cold-blooded brute isn't fit to live.' He recovered his composure with an effort, and went on slowly. 'Well, I suppose it's no use sitting here looking at these poor fellows. There's one last thing we can do for them. Give me a hand.'

The bodies were carried above the high-water mark. A grave in the rocks was out of the question, but plenty of loose rock was available, and at the end of half an hour a tall cairn marked the last resting-place of two sailors who had gone down to the sea in a ship, never to return.

Biggles unstrapped his flying-cap and requested Ginger to do the same. Then, with the salt wind ruffling his hair, and the gulls mewing a melancholy requiem, he said *The Lord's Prayer*.

'Amen,' said Ginger at the conclusion, and replaced his cap.

'All right,' said Biggles quietly. 'Let's go.' He set off at a fast pace up the cliff.

'Take it easy – what's the hurry?' complained Ginger.

'I'm anxious to have a word with von Schonbeck,' answered Biggles curtly.

Ginger glanced at his face and said no more. He had learned when not to talk.

CHAPTER VII

Ditched

Biggles hardly spoke on the way to the base, where the others were found waiting with some anxiety. They had no news, however, beyond a report of more signals so strong on the air that the transmitter was obviously at no great distance; but as these, as before, were in code, they conveyed no information beyond the fact that they had been sent.

Over lunch, for the benefit of Algy and Bertie, Biggles narrated the events of the morning. 'The most important thing about these developments is this,' he concluded. 'I'm pretty certain von Schonbeck hasn't picked up the gold yet or both he and the whaler would close down on radio signals and hit the breeze at top speed for South America. They'll get clear of this area as soon as they can, you may be sure; and that being so I feel inclined to prang the U-boat on sight – if we can find her. We could look for the gold afterwards. I'm not concerned overmuch with the whaler. It's von Schonbeck I'm after. The first thing to find is the U-boat.'

'Even if we located her I fancy we should have a job to catch her on the surface,' opined Algy. 'Von Schonbeck must know all there is to know about dodging aircraft.'

'I quite agree,' returned Biggles. 'But that submarine can't stay at sea indefinitely. She's bound to make a landfall somewhere, even if it's only to pick up the bullion. Our best chance is to catch her at moorings, and I'm going to have a shot at doing that this afternoon.'

'Where?'

'Corbie Island. In view of what we've seen that seems to offer the best chance. Even if the U-boat isn't actually there we might learn something.'

'Such as?'

'If the place has been used at all. If von Schonbeck is in the habit of using the island there are certain to be traces of his visits. If the gold is there he is bound to go there eventually, in which case he might find us waiting for him.'

'You've picked on Corbie Island on account of the course taken by the whaler, I suppose?' put in Bertie, polishing his eyeglass.

'Yes.'

'But the whaler wasn't actually heading for Corbie Island,' reminded Ginger.

'I wouldn't be too sure of that,' argued Biggles. 'Don't forget there is some doubt – a big doubt, in fact – as to the position of the island. You can bet your sweet life that if anyone knows just where it is it will be von Schonbeck. From a high altitude we ought to be able to spot it, even if it means quartering several hundred miles of water. I'm going to look for it, anyway. I'll take Ginger along – and a couple of depth-charges, in case they're needed.'

Bertie looked disappointed. 'I say, old boy, isn't it time we had a cut in?'

'Perhaps it is,' agreed Biggles. 'But for the moment I'd sooner play safe. In these waters you never know what you're going to run into, and I should feel a lot happier knowing that we had a machine in reserve. You and Algy stand by for a signal. If we need help I'll call you out. You'll get a turn presently.'

'As you say, old warrior,' sighed Bertie. 'You know best.'

Biggles finished his coffee and got up. 'Okay. Let's refuel and get off.'

Twenty minutes later, with Ginger at his side and two depth-charges on board, Biggles took off, and climbing steeply for height, headed for the estimated position of Corbie Island. Looking down, Ginger observed from the 'white horses' that now flecked the sea that the wind had freshened to half a gale. For a short distance from the southern tip of the island a flat area marked the oil trail but, as Biggles had predicted, it was fading quickly in the more turbulent water.

For an hour Biggles flew on, his eyes for ever roving the forbidding waste of water. Icebergs came into sight far away on the starboard bow, and soon afterwards, the whaler.

'Take a look at her,' invited Biggles. 'She's back on her old course – that is, the course she was on when we first spotted her, before our arrival caused her to change it.'

'Are you going over to her?' asked Ginger.

'No,' decided Biggles. 'She wouldn't tell us anything if we did. We shall do better by keeping clear. The horizon is getting too hazy for my liking. Maybe it's only local; cold air in the region of the icebergs might cause that. If the wind veers to the north, bringing in warm air, it will probably get worse. We may have a look at the ship on the way back, but first of all I want to locate Corbie Island and plot its exact position.'

An hour later the aircraft was over the spot where Corbie Island should have been, according to the chart. It was not there. No land of any sort, not even a lonely rock, broke the endless procession of waves. Biggles re-checked his calculations and found them correct.

'Well, that's that,' he remarked. 'We can't blame the Admiralty.

They gave us fair warning with the letters E.D. This is where we begin looking.'

'In which direction are you going to start?' inquired Ginger.

'The direction that the whaler was taking before she altered course,' returned Biggles. 'When she turned she was heading for the South Pole. Her skipper must take us for complete fools if he thinks we are to be kidded that he has business *there*. I'm more convinced than ever that the ship is making her way to Corbie Island. There's no other landfall she can make. And if the whaler is heading for Corbie Island she is being guided by von Schonbeck, or his men, not by the Admiralty chart.'

Biggles swung away on his new course. For twenty minutes he did not speak. Then a grunt of satisfaction left his lips. 'There it is,' he muttered. 'That's the island. So it *does* exist. It's only about eighty miles from the estimated position, and that isn't such a big margin of error considering the expanse of water involved. If we achieve nothing else we shall at least be able to correct the Admiralty chart,' he concluded dryly.

The aircraft flew on towards the island, now revealed as a strip of land some ten miles long by two or three miles wide, as rugged, barren and windswept as Kerguelen. Biggles made no attempt to conceal from possible watchers his intention of surveying the island, knowing such a course to be futile; for even if he took cover in the cloud layer overhead the engines would be heard – must already have been heard – by anyone on the island. So he throttled back and began a long glide towards his objective, with the result that by the time it was reached the aircraft was down to a thousand feet.

'By gosh! There's the sub!' cried Ginger suddenly. 'She's there! We've got her!'

Biggles said nothing. The need did not arise, for he could see clearly the object that had provoked Ginger's exclamations. It was the submarine – or a submarine; and there could only be one underwater-craft at such a place. It was lying hard against a natural rock-quay, well sheltered from the weather in a snug little cove with an entrance wide enough to permit the passage of a fair-sized vessel.

Ginger kept his eyes on the mark. 'I don't see anyone moving,' he observed.

'If the sub is there you can bet the crew isn't far away,' returned Biggles grimly.

'What are you going to do?'

'I'm going to give von Schonbeck something that should keep him on that lump of rock until the Admiralty can send a destroyer along to pick him up,' answered Biggles. As he spoke his left hand moved towards the bomb release. With the other he straightened the aircraft until it was gliding on a direct course for the U-boat.

'Look out!' shouted Ginger suddenly, in a voice shrill with alarm, as nearly a score of men dashed out from places in which they had evidently been hiding.

Biggles did not answer. He flicked the throttle wide open and held on his course. The engines roared and the machine gathered speed.

An instant later the flak came up. And it came in such quantity and with such accuracy that Ginger was startled and amazed.

'Those fellows have had plenty of practice,' said Biggles through his teeth. His expression did not change nor did his eyes leave the mark.

Ginger held his breath. The aircraft still had a quarter of a mile to go and it was rocking through a hail of tracer shells and machine-gun bullets. It was hit, not once but several times. Ginger could hear metal ripping through wood and fabric. It seemed like

'By gosh! There's the sub!' cried Ginger suddenly.
'She's there! We've got her!'

suicide to go on, but he knew it was no use saying anything; knew that nothing would cause Biggles to abandon his attack while he still had a wing to keep the machine airborne. He felt the machine bounce slightly as the depth-charges left their racks, and was shifting his position to watch their downward track when an explosion nearly turned the machine on its back. It plunged wildly as it recovered, but even so he thought they were down. Then, with fabric streaming from the port wing, Biggles was taking evading action, and taking it desperately.

'Did I get her?' he snapped, the object of the attack still paramount in his mind.

Ginger looked down but could see nothing clearly for smoke. He noted, however, that the smoke came from the position where the submarine had been. 'I don't know,' he told Biggles. 'If you didn't hit her it was a pretty close miss.'

Still pursued by fire the aircraft was down to a hundred feet, racing over the sea with the island slipping away astern.

'There's nothing more we can do here. I'm going flat out for home,' declared Biggles tersely.

'I shan't burst into tears over that,' answered Ginger. 'One run through that stuff was enough.'

Biggles swung round on the homeward course. 'You'd better have a look at things,' he ordered. 'I'm afraid we were hit pretty hard.'

'I can smell petrol,' replied Ginger.

Proceeding with his inspection he saw that the aircraft had suffered considerably. There were several holes in the hull. Splinters of wood and broken glass lay about. Both wings were lacerated. A whole section had been torn out of the port wing where it had received the direct hit that had turned the machine over. These things did not worry him unduly, for the modern military aircraft is built to withstand punishment. The main thing was, the engines were still running, and while they continued to do so the machine would probably remain airborne. What did worry him though was the smell of petrol. Petrol was in fact slopping about the floor. Making his way to the main tank, two clouds of suffocating spray told their own story. He went back to Biggles.

'We've got it in the main tank,' he reported. 'Two holes – bad ones.'

'Can you plug them?'

'I doubt it, but I'll try.'

'Don't overdo it. If you feel the fumes are getting you down come back to me. We'll land and do the job afloat.'

'You'll never get down on that sea – it's running a gale,' declared Ginger. 'The hull is holed, anyway.'

'Do what you can.'

Ginger retired to the tank, and with the equipment provided for the purpose succeeded in plugging one of the holes. The second one was beyond him, but he did the best he could with it. When he had finished the inside pressure was still forcing petrol through the leak. Gasping for breath, for the fumes in the cabin were suffocating, he staggered back to Biggles and reported the situation.

Biggles glanced at the petrol gauge on the instrument panel. 'We shan't get home,' he answered calmly. 'Call Algy on the radio and ask him to come out to meet us. Tell him to stand by to pick us up when we hit the drink.'

'Do you think we shall last as long as that – I mean, till he gets here?' asked Ginger anxiously.

'Frankly, no,' returned Biggles evenly. He altered course slightly.

'What are you doing?' queried Ginger.

'Making for those icebergs. There should be slack water under the lee of them. We shall stand a better chance there than on the open sea. Tell Algy what we're doing. Give him the position of the island, too. Tell him the sub is there, and my orders are that he carries on if he fails to find us in twelve hours.'

'Von Schonbeck will pick up the signal,' warned Ginger.

'We can't prevent it,' said Biggles. 'Get busy. We haven't much time.'

'Okay.'

Ginger went off to the radio compartment. One glance was enough. The instrument was a shell-shattered wreck, damaged beyond all hope of repair. He went back to Biggles, relieved that the aircraft was still running fairly smoothly. 'No use,' he reported tersely. 'The transmitter looks like a cat's breakfast.'

Biggles' jaws clamped a little tighter. 'I doubt if it would have helped us much even if it had been in order.'

'How – why?' asked Ginger sharply, not liking the expression on Biggles' face.

'Take a look outside.'

Ginger looked out through a smashed side window, and understood. Grey mist was closing in all round. There was no horizon.

'The wind's swinging round to the north,' said Biggles quietly. 'I was afraid of it. It's been inclined that way all day. The fog's getting worse, and it's getting worse fast. We should just have time to reach the 'bergs.'

'That'll be a lot of use if we're blanketed in murk,' said Ginger bitterly. 'Algy won't be able to find us even if he comes looking when we don't turn up.'

'Sitting on a 'berg won't be as bad as rocking on the open water trying to keep the sea out,' asserted Biggles. 'There's the ice, straight ahead. We should just about reach it.'

Biggles' prophecy was not far out. By the time the outlying 'bergs were reached the engines were choking as the fuel petered out; and the mist had thickened to a white clammy fog. There was fairly smooth water in the lee of a big 'berg, and towards this Biggles turned the aircraft. It did not take long to go down, for the machine had been forced to under a hundred feet to keep the sea in sight.

'I'm going down on that slack water,' announced Biggles. 'We'll see how she goes when we get her down. If she fills with water faster than we can bale it out, or plug the holes, I shall try to run ashore on that floe at the tail of the big 'berg. I've enough petrol in the gravity tank to do that.'

'Get as close as you can,' implored Ginger. 'That water looks cold.'

'I daren't land too close for fear of tearing our keel open on submerged ice,' answered Biggles. 'I'll do the best I can, but I'm afraid we're going to get our feet wet.'

He landed about a hundred yards from the big 'berg. It was an anxious moment, but nothing happened except that the water started pouring through the holes instantly, as was to be expected.

'We're filling,' warned Ginger, who was watching. 'She'll be awash in five minutes if you stop.'

Biggles did not answer. He switched over to gravity, and under this new brief lease of life the engines carried the aircraft on and up a shelving bank of ice. There was a nasty crunching sound as the keel grated. In a few yards the friction brought the aircraft to a halt; and there it remained, half ashore, the tail trailing in the water, rocking gently in the swell.

Ginger crawled out on to the ice and tried to haul the machine higher, but in this he was unsuccessful.

Biggles joined him. 'We have at least got our feet on something solid,' he observed optimistically. 'I think the machine will ride all right where she is unless a big sea washes her off, or' – he turned his eyes to where the high end of the 'berg towered above them – 'or unless that pile falls down on us.'

'Is it likely to?' asked Ginger, consternation in his voice.

'Quite likely. Lumps of ice break off a 'berg as she melts. A blink of sunshine melting one side can cause a 'berg to overbalance and turn turtle.'

'Then I hope the sun stays where it is,' said Ginger fervently. 'Don't tell me any more horrors.' He stared at the white pall that now hemmed them in. 'Curse the fog,' he muttered.

'Unfortunately cursing it won't shift it,' returned Biggles evenly. 'There is this about it. The thing cuts two ways. If Algy can't find us, neither will the whaler. Of course, there's a snag, and it's a nasty one – or it will be if the fog persists. We're drifting, and even when Algy realises that we must be ditched he will have no means of checking our drift. Consequently, if the fog lasts for any length of time we shall be miles off a straight course to the island. He won't know where to look for us. I hope we don't drift too far north.'

'Why north, particularly?'

'Because north is the direction of the temperate zone. The farther north we drift the faster will the ice melt. But let's have a look at the machine to see if there is anything we can do. It'll be something if we can put her in a condition to keep afloat – in case the ice starts melting under our feet.'

Ginger stared into the fog, blowing on his hands, for the air was bitterly cold. The breeze seemed to be dying. The only sound in the frozen world in which they stood was the crash and crunch of ice as distant 'bergs collided. He shivered.

'Come on,' said Biggles shortly. 'Let's get busy.'

CHAPTER VIII

Algy Takes a Hand

As the afternoon gave place slowly to a long dreary twilight, for the twentieth time – or it may have been the thirtieth – Algy left the hut, made an anxious reconnaissance of the sky and returned to Bertie, who was sitting by the radio.

Bertie raised his eyebrows.

'Not a sign,' informed Algy.

'Really?' Bertie looked puzzled. 'But I say, old boy, what on earth can they be doing?'

Algy shrugged. 'Ask me something easier. But I can tell you this. There's a change in the weather. It's getting colder. I'll tell you something else. If Biggles isn't back in half an hour we shall know he won't be coming back. He'll be out of petrol. That is, if he's been in the air all this time. Of course, there's a chance that he may have landed somewhere – Corbie Island, or maybe on Kerguelen.'

'What I don't understand is, why he hasn't made a signal – being as how he's so late – if you see what I mean?' murmured Bertie. 'He must know how anxious we are, and all that. This bally instrument is dead. Not a squeak.'

'So you said before,' answered Algy. 'That's what I don't like about it. Everything seems to have gone off the air. That may be coincidence, or it may not.'

'You think maybe there's something cooking?'

'Maybe. No use guessing. We can only wait.'

'How about going off in the spare machine to see if we can spot anything?'

'Not yet,' decided Algy. 'You know what a stickler Biggles is for orders. He said stay here. If he came back in a hurry and found we'd beetled off on our own account he'd have a few short sharp words to say about it. We'll give him a bit longer.' Algy looked at his watch. 'If he isn't back in say, half an hour, we'll go and have a dekko. I can't help thinking that if he was in trouble, ditched, for example, he'd get in touch with us. In fact, one would think that would be the first thing he'd do. We'll give him a bit longer.' Algy sat on a packing-case and stared at the floor.

Half an hour passed. The radio remained dead. The only sound that came from outside was the distant lap of water and the melancholy cries of sea fowl. Algy dropped his cigarette, put his heel on it and got up. 'Okay,' he announced. 'Something's wrong. Let's go and have a look round.'

Picking up his flying-cap he walked to the door, opened it, but instead of passing on he pulled up short on the threshold with an exclamation of dismay.

'What's wrong old boy?' asked Bertie quickly.

'Fog,' answered Algy. 'Fog, of all things. We're grounded.'

Bertie walked to the door and stared at a blanket of grey mist that was slowly blotting out the scene. He did not speak.

'That settles any argument,' said Algy wearily, 'Biggles must have seen this coming. If he could have got home he'd have come home. He's down, somewhere – and there's nothing we can do about it.'

'We can keep an ear open for him – put out flares and that sort of thing, if he should turn up,' suggested Bertie.

'We can listen, but I don't think we shall hear much,' retorted Algy dubiously.

His pessimism was justified. As darkness deepened the fog closed in, enfolding everything in its clammy embrace.

'We may as well go inside and make ourselves comfortable as stand out here in this perishing "pea soup,"' said Algy at last.

They went in and closed the door. Bertie lighted a lamp and for a while they discussed the situation that had arisen. But at the finish, as Algy remarked, there was still nothing they could do about it. 'While this fog lasts we're tied to the carpet,' he averred.

'If it lifts at daylight we'll have a look round. Meanwhile, we may as well get some sleep.'

Dawn, to his unspeakable relief, found the fog lifting, or dispersing. 'By thunder! It's cold,' he exclaimed. 'There must be ice about. Let's grab some coffee and get away.'

Ten minutes later the reserve machine was in the air with Algy at the controls, heading in the general direction of Corbie Island, the last known objective of the missing aircraft; and the flight that followed was similar to that made by Biggles the previous day. Visibility was still far from good; indeed, after going some distance, right across their course a heavy bank of fog still clung to the sea.

'Better go over that stuff,' advised Bertie.

'No,' argued Algy. 'I'm staying low, where I can see the drink. Biggles may be on the water and I'm not going to risk passing him.' Taking the machine down to a hundred feet he put the nose of the aircraft into the fog, and a minute later received such a shock as he had seldom experienced. His eyes were on the water, just discernable through the mist. Something – he knew not what, unless it was a highly developed instinct for danger – made him look up and glance ahead. A white mass of what at first he took to be opaque mist towered above him. For a second the curious irregularity of its outline puzzled him; then, suddenly, he realised that what he saw was not mist, but solid ice. Snatching in his breath from sheer shock he dragged the control column hard over into his thigh, and as the aircraft swung back over its course, zoomed high. A gasp of relief left his lips as the machine merged into clear air.

'Here, I say, old boy, what are you playing at?' protested Bertie, who had been staring down at the water and so had not seen the 'berg.

'That fog has too many solid patches in it for my liking,' muttered Algy grimly, moistening his lips. 'We nearly rammed a thousand tons of ice. I ought to be kicked from here to Halifax for not having the sense to realise what was causing that murk. I'll take your advice and go over the top.'

'Absolutely – I should jolly well think so,' murmured Bertie. 'No joke ramming a beastly iceberg.'

The aircraft roared on.

Clearing the fog-belt Algy saw an open sea ahead. He scanned it quickly and anxiously, but of the missing aircraft there was no sign. 'I'm going right on to Corbie Island,' he told Bertie.

'Suits me, old lad,' replied Bertie.

They were nearly an hour finding it, for, like Biggles, they quickly ascertained that it was not at the position shown on the chart. Circling, and climbing at the same time, it was Bertie who saw the remote speck of land creep up over the horizon.

'Yes, that must be it,' agreed Algy, when Bertie called attention to it. 'We'll go and give it the once-over. If Biggles isn't there then I shan't know where to look, and that's a fact.'

A reconnaissance of the island revealed nothing – that is, no mark of occupation.

'There's a jolly little cove down there, suit a submarine very nicely I should think,' remarked Bertie as they circled.

'I see it,' returned Algy. 'I don't see anything in it though. In fact,

I don't see anything here to detain us. We might as well get back.' He turned the nose of the machine on the homeward track.

The only thing that happened during the first part of the return trip was that the weather definitely improved. Indeed, a streak of pale turquoise-blue sky appeared behind a rift in a cloudbank. In view of this Algy was not surprised to note that the fog-belt had dispersed, leaving the drifting floes and 'bergs in plain view. Not that these meant anything to him. There was no reason why they should. As masses of ice they were merely things to be avoided – or so he thought until a shout from Bertie brought his eyes round, questioningly.

'Look! Over there!' cried Bertie, shaken for once from his inconsequential manner.

Following the direction indicated Algy saw what appeared to be an extensive black scar on a floe that formed the tail of an iceberg of considerable size. For a little while, as he flew nearer, losing height, he reserved his opinion; but when, with a sinking sensation in the stomach, he observed the charred and blackened remains of an aircraft, he knew the worst. Or he thought he did.

'That's them,' he said in a voice that he did not recognise as his own. 'They must have done what I nearly did – tried charging through the fog and hit the 'berg. They were burnt out. We'll go down.'

Bertie did not answer.

Algy went down to make a safe landing as near to the wreck as he dare, afterwards taxiing on to the edge of the floe. Having made the aircraft fast they went on together.

There was no doubt in Algy's mind as to what they would find. With the wreck he was not concerned. His eyes probed it, looking for two bodies, for experience told him that those in the machine could not have escaped. But he could see nothing that looked remotely like a body; and when at length he stood right against the burnt-out wreck, and could still see no bodies, he uttered an exclamation of amazement in which there was a suspicion of rising hope.

'They're not here,' he said in an incredulous voice.

'But I say, that's odd – deuced odd,' declared Bertie, polishing his monocle furiously.

'I don't get it,' asserted Algy, looking around. 'Hello! What's this?' he went on sharply, and moved swiftly towards a stain on the ice some twenty paces from the wreck. It was red. There was one small splash with a few odd drops round it.

'I say, old boy, that's blood,' said Bertie, stooping. 'One of them must have been hurt.'

'That's obvious,' returned Algy. 'All the same there's something queer about this. If one of them was hurt badly enough to make a mark like this surely there ought to be a trail of blood leading from the machine to this point.'

'One of them might have been pitched out when the machine struck the ice,' suggested Bertie.

'It's just possible, but in that case I should have thought the mark in the ice would have been more definite,' returned Algy. He examined the ice critically. 'Yet I don't know,' he went on pensively. 'There are faint signs, marks, that a body could have made, lying here. But where are they now? With the machine burnt out they had no means of getting off this 'berg.' He turned bewildered eyes to survey the seascape. Nothing moved anywhere, only icebergs, icebergs with dark blue water between them. A feeble sun glinted on the tips of the big 'bergs. 'I don't know how it was possible, but the indications are that the injury that produced the blood was caused after the machine landed,' concluded Algy.

'Here, I say, what about this for an idea?' went on Bertie. He pointed to a tall pinnacle of ice that rose above the floe on which they stood. 'Now then. If a plane collided with the top of that 'berg it would be bashed about no end. Lumps of ice would be knocked off and fall to the bottom. I don't see any broken ice. And by Jove! I'll tell you something else. If a plane collided with solid ice the longerons would be buckled like corkscrews – wouldn't they?'

'Yes,' conceded Algy.

Bertie pointed to the remains of the machine. 'The longerons are as straight as crankshafts,' he declared.

'True enough,' agreed Algy. 'What you mean to say is, the machine didn't crash?'

'Absolutely.'

'But if it didn't crash why should they land here?'

Bertie shook his head. 'Ah! Sorry, old boy, but I don't know the answer to that one.'

'Okay. Then let's say that for some reason unknown Biggles landed here voluntarily,' resumed Algy impatiently. 'So what? Neither Biggles nor Ginger would be likely to set fire to the machine.'

'No, they would not,' agreed Bertie.

'Then who did?'

'You tell me,' pleaded Bertie. 'I'm no bally detective.'

Suddenly Algy took a pace forward and for a moment stood staring at something that projected from the blackened engine cowling; then he wrenched it out and held it up for Bertie's inspection. 'Look at that!' he exclaimed in an understanding voice. 'That isn't part of an aircraft. That's a piece of shell casing. Flak, by thunder! That's the answer. Now we're getting somewhere. Biggles found the submarine. He bombed it and got shot up. Remember the two depth-charges he carried? They're not here. Why not? Because he used them. Fool that I am for not spotting that immediately. The machine was hit, forced down and landed here. That's it. That's what happened.'

'And what happened next?' queried Bertie.

'The machine took fire on landing and was burnt out. One of them must have been wounded but didn't start to bleed until he was clear of the machine.'

Bertie nodded slowly. 'All right. One was wounded. He lay on the ice, bleeding. The other stood by. Then I suppose they both jumped into the sea?'

'Don't be a fool,' snapped Algy.

'Then what happened to them?'

Algy walked back to the bloodstain, stared at it for a little while, and then started casting around in increasing circles. He stopped suddenly and let out a yell. 'Here we are!' he cried. 'This is the way they went.'

Bertie joined him and saw at his feet odd spots of blood forming an irregular trail. Following it, he quickened his pace when he saw a small object lying on the ice some distance ahead. Reaching it, he picked it up. It appeared to be a small piece of bloodstained rag.

'That's Biggles' handkerchief,' said Algy in a dull voice.

They continued to follow the trail, with the drops of blood occurring farther and farther apart. It ended where the ice ended at the sea.

Automatically Algy raised his eyes and followed the trail out to sea as if it continued there. He started and clutched Bertie's arm. 'My God! Look there!' he cried in a strangled voice.

Bertie looked. A quarter of a mile away two polar bears were swimming strongly towards another 'berg.

For a little while time stood still. Without speaking, Algy and Bertie watched the bears reach their objective, clamber on the ice and then turn to stare at them. One uttered a hoarse growl. Its breath showed white, like smoke.

'I don't think it's much use looking for bodies – here,' said Algy.

'Nor I,' returned Bertie.

They turned away.

CHAPTER IX

What Happened on the Ice

Algy's summing up of what had occurred on the iceberg was correct to a point.

Following their discussion on the situation Biggles had made a systematic inspection of the machine in the hope that it might be made serviceable as a surface-craft, if not as an aircraft. 'What I should really like to know is, did I hit that submarine?' he remarked as he worked.

'If you didn't actually hit it you were pretty close,' Ginger assured him.

'I don't know much about submarines, but I imagine that any sort of serious damage would keep the U-boat where she is for some time,' went on Biggles. 'Quite aside from that she wouldn't dare to put her nose into any civilised port where there was a properly equipped workshop.'

Proceeding with the examination, it was eventually decided that while at a proper service station the machine might be made airworthy, situated as they were nothing they could do would achieve that object, even if fuel was available.

'I'm afraid there's nothing else we can do except wait,' announced Biggles. 'Algy should find us when the weather clears. The thing I'm most afraid of is, if he goes to Corbie Island looking for us he may get what we got. With both machines grounded the outlook would begin to look dim.'

'Very dim,' muttered Ginger. He started as from no great distance came a splintering crash. 'What the deuce was that?' he demanded.

'Two 'bergs colliding, I imagine,' returned Biggles. 'Or else—' He broke off and looked hard at the ice on which they were standing.

'Or else what?' inquired Ginger anxiously.

'Or else it was a big 'berg breaking up,' said Biggles quietly. 'This ice is damp. It's giving. We must be drifting north.'

'And the fog is lifting,' asserted Ginger. 'Look – there's another 'berg. And there's—' He broke off, staring.

There was no need to say more. The fog was, in fact, lifting, so that other 'bergs could be seen. But it was not ice that had so suddenly frozen Ginger's tongue. It was the whaler. Fog-bound like themselves the ship lay hove-to less than a mile away.

'Quick,' snapped Biggles. 'Get out of sight.'

They moved swiftly, but even so they were too late. A shout from the whaler came eerily over the dark water.

'They've seen us,' said Biggles.

'They've seen us all right,' declared Ginger bitterly. 'They're lowering a boat. What are we going to do about it?'

Biggles shrugged. 'There's nothing we can do about it. We can't fight a whole ship's company and it would be silly to try. Funny thing, I clean forgot the whaler. I suppose there's nothing remarkable about her turning up here. They'll have seen the aircraft so they'll know who we are. Well, it will be interesting to see just who is running the ship.'

'A lot of good that'll do us, if they follow their usual practice of bumping off anyone who gets in their way.'

'Ah well, we shall see,' murmured Biggles.

The whaler's life-boat forged on towards the 'berg under the impetus of six oars. Two men sat in the stern. Both wore navy blue reefer jackets over grey sweaters. On their heads were peaked caps bearing weather-faded gold badges. One, an elderly, heavily built man, with a broad flattish face in which were deeply set small calculating eyes, held the tiller. His companion was a different type. He was tall. His face was thin and colourless, and set in such hard lines that it might have been carved out of grey granite. His eyes, pale blue, were on the castaways.

Biggles walked slowly to the edge of the ice and waited. 'They're Nazis all right,' he said in a low voice to Ginger, who stood with him watching the oncoming boat. 'Just look at those faces, and those square heads. I've never been able to decide whether Nazis are born with something in their mentality that gives them faces like that, or whether it is something they acquire.'

'What does it matter, anyway?' growled Ginger. 'They look as though they had never laughed in their lives.'

'They probably haven't,' murmured Biggles.

The side of the boat grated gently against the ice. The rowers shipped their oars. Two jumped ashore and held the boat while the two officers in the stern got out. Both carried automatics. The heavily-built man, from his manner obviously the senior, eyed Biggles with a sort of grim satisfaction.

'So!' he exclaimed.

'So what?' inquired Biggles. 'Why the armament?'

The Nazi did not answer. His eyes lifted and surveyed the aircraft. 'So!' he said again.

'It is them,' said his companion, speaking in German.

The other walked on slowly towards the aircraft. The two sailors who had come ashore picked up rifles that had been lying in the boat and motioned to the castaways that they were to follow. Presently all six came to a halt a short distance from the machine.

'Anyone would think they'd never seen a plane before,' breathed Ginger.

'It isn't that; it's merely that they have a pretty good idea that they've seen this one before,' returned Biggles.

Without haste the burly man turned and addressed Biggles in fair English. His voice was harsh and his manner domineering. 'What you do here?' he demanded.

'We were waiting to be picked up,' answered Biggles. 'We had a forced landing.'

'What brought you to these waters?'

'My own business.'

'Ah! And what was that?'

'Suppose I ask some questions?' retorted Biggles. 'What ship is that out there? Who are you? And what are German naval officers doing on a ship of the Norwegian Mercantile Marine?'

'My name is Thom, Leutnant Thom,' was the answer. 'That may mean something to you?' The German eyed Biggles quizzically as if to note the effect of his words. 'The Norwegian ship you speak of has been taken over by the German Navy.'

'You've heard, of course, that the war is over?' queried Biggles evenly.

'That is where you are wrong,' was the curt reply. 'For some of us the war will never be over. Heil Hitler!'

'That war-cry is out of date, even in Germany,' said Biggles.

The German walked over until he stood within a yard of Biggles, facing him. 'What were you here looking for?' he asked.

'I've found what I was looking for,' returned Biggles softly.

Without warning, without the slightest hint of what he intended, the German's left arm flew out like a piston rod straight into Biggles' stomach. The blow was followed by another, from the right fist. It took Biggles in the face with a vicious smack and stretched him on his back on the ice. He lay still. Blood flowed from his nose across his face to make a little pool on the ice.

'You swine,' rasped Ginger. He made a dash at the German, but one of the sailors caught him by the arm and swung him round.

Thom laughed unpleasantly. His manner was easy and confident. He spoke to one of his men, jerking his head towards the aircraft.

Ginger went to Biggles, took his handkerchief from his pocket and wiped the blood from his face. He was still doing this when he was jerked roughly to his feet by the collar. Looking round he saw that the aircraft was in flames. Thom laughed again. The party began to move towards the boat, which was still waiting at the edge of the ice. Biggles, still unconscious, was dragged along by the jacket, and at the end bundled into the bottom of the boat. Ginger was pushed in.

The fog closed in again as the boat was rowed towards its parent ship, and Ginger reflected bitterly on the evil luck that had caused it to lift at such an untimely moment. The boat was guided to its objective by frequent hails. The prisoners were taken aboard and locked in a reasonably decent cabin. Soon afterwards the timbers vibrated as the engines were started, and at the same time Biggles opened his eyes.

He looked at Ginger and said: 'Where are we – on the whaler?'

Ginger nodded. 'That swine Thom hit you as dirty a blow as ever I saw.'

Biggles sat up, feeling his face tenderly. 'He's a Nazi,' he said simply. 'You must expect Nazis to do that sort of thing, just as you'd expect a mad dog to bite.'

'Are you all right?' asked Ginger anxiously.

'No bones broken, anyway,' answered Biggles, standing up and testing his limbs. 'Don't worry. We haven't finished yet. With any luck at all I'll hand back to Mr Thom what he gave me – with interest. What's happening?'

'Nothing, except that the ship is under way, moving dead slow on account of the fog, I suppose.'

'Bound for Corbie Island, no doubt. We should soon know whether or not I hit the U-boat.'

'Von Schonbeck isn't going to greet you with open arms if he guesses it was you who dropped those depth-charges.'

'From what we know of von Schonbeck he wouldn't greet anyone with open arms, not even his dying mother,' returned Biggles, moistening his bruised lips. Borrowing Ginger's handkerchief he dipped it in a can of water and bathed his face.

'Thom evidently guessed what we were after,' offered Ginger.

'Bound to. What else would we be doing here but looking for him? I should say these pirates have got the situation pretty well weighed up. One thing they may not guess is that we have a spare machine.'

'Algy will wonder what has happened to us.'

'He may find out. Let us hope so. He's our trump card. Better not talk about him, though, in case anyone comes eavesdropping.'

'Sure you're not hurt?'

Biggles smiled faintly. 'Those two punches shook me up a bit,' he admitted. 'They'd have shaken anyone. I wasn't ready. I shall be all right presently – a couple of black eyes and a bit stiff in the tummy, maybe.' He sat down on one of the two bunks. 'We might as well make ourselves comfortable until we get to where we're going.'

'You think Thom is going to make contact with von Schonbeck?'

'I'm pretty sure of it. He wouldn't have bothered about taking us with him unless he was due to meet a superior officer. He'd have left us on that ice-floe, stiff – or heaved us into the water. Did you see anything as we came aboard?'

'Some sailors.'

'Did any of them look like Norwegians?'

Ginger shook his head. 'Couldn't say. They didn't speak. Just stood watching.'

'We shall soon know,' murmured Biggles, stretching himself on the bunk.

'They took our guns,' said Ginger.

'They wouldn't be likely to overlook a simple precaution like that,' returned Biggles dryly. 'Not that guns would be much use to us now. Brains are the only things that'll get us out of this jam. There's this about it. We're not rushed for time. We're a long way from Corbie Island, if that's our destination. At the rate we shall travel through this ice region we shan't arrive much before dawn. That'll give us time to think things over.'

It was, in fact, in the grey light of dawn that the whaler arrived at a landfall which, watching through a porthole, Biggles recognised as Corbie Island. As he expected, the ship turned into the cove where the submarine had been moored. With what interest he watched to see if the U-boat was still there can be imagined. For a little while, as the whaler was coaxed in, travelling dead slow, he had reason to hope that he had sent the U-boat to the bottom with his depth-charges, for he could not see it – at least, at its original mooring. Then, to his intense disappointment, he made out the long, grey shape hard against the rocks farther in the cove. It was movement and sounds of human activity that revealed the submarine's new berth, for the vessel had been so cleverly camouflaged that it was almost impossible to distinguish it from the rocks to which it was made fast. He noticed that rocks had even been strewn along the iron deck in such a way that it would be practically impossible to spot the submarine from the air, even from a low-flying aircraft. Indeed, as the whaler drew near he observed that it was against air observation in particular that the U-boat had been camouflaged. And presently he noticed something else. The submarine was not on even keel. Her knife-like bows were too far out of the water. This, he thought, could hardly be accidental. It was more likely, he decided, that the vessel had been damaged and was now being repaired – a supposition that was supported by activity around her. All this information he passed back to Ginger as the whaler glided on to an anchorage some sixty or seventy yards from the U-boat. He saw Thom go ashore, to be met by a man in naval uniform who now emerged from a small rock-built structure. It was still too dark to distinguish features or badges of rank, and in any case the newcomer had his coat collar turned up against the biting wind; but he had no doubt as to who it was.

'Von Schonbeck is here,' he told Ginger. 'The next few minutes should be quite exciting.'

He watched Thom and his captain while they stood for a short time in earnest conversation. Then Thom returned to the whaler.

'This, I fancy, is it,' Biggles told Ginger.

His suspicions were confirmed when a minute later footsteps sounded in the gangway outside the cabin. The door was thrown open. Thom stood there, with two sailors armed with rifles.

'This way,' he ordered.

The party made its way to the deck where a number of sailors stood by to watch the little procession. Biggles noticed that they stood in two groups, and he thought he could guess the reason. One party were Germans, originally members of the U-boat's crew, for they were all dressed alike in the usual heavy trousers and sweaters worn by the crews of underwater-craft. Those comprising the other group, a smaller group, from their nondescript garments were ordinary sailors, probably Norwegians, the surviving members of the whaling-ship's company. Their expressions were different from those of the Germans. On their faces could be perceived such emotions as sympathy, commiseration and encouragement. However, neither Germans nor Norwegians spoke as the party descended the ladder that had been lowered and entered a small boat which was rowed quickly to the shore.

The man whom the prisoners had every reason to suppose was von Schonbeck stood waiting. He was younger than Biggles had imagined. Much younger, in fact. He might have been twenty-five years of age, not more; and as far as actual features were concerned no fault could be found. But here again, in the truculent bearing, the cold, humourless face and the hard, merciless mouth, Biggles recognised the typical Hitler fanatic. As he had on more than one occasion remarked to Ginger, they all appeared to have been cast in the same mould – as in fact, in a way, they were.

The party assembled, von Schonbeck lost no time in coming to the point. Considering Biggles with frosty hostility he said, in good English: 'You know who I am?'

Biggles answered: 'I think so. You're von Schonbeck, aren't you?'

'Captain von Schonbeck is my name,' was the brittle rejoinder. 'Of the German Navy.'

'There is no German Navy,' reminded Biggles quietly.

'I am an officer of the German Navy,' rasped von Schonbeck.

'There is no such thing,' returned Biggles coolly. 'You may be on the high seas under arms, but that only makes you a common pirate.'

Von Schonbeck drew a deep breath and changed the subject. He jerked a thumb towards the U-boat. 'Are you the man who did this?' he inquired, with anger hardening his voice.

'Did what?'

'Damaged my submarine.'

'I tried to sink it, if that's what you mean,' returned Biggles calmly. 'It's some comfort to me to know that I damaged it. I was afraid I'd missed it altogether I must be out of practice. Is the damage serious?'

Von Schonbeck's cold blue eyes remained on Biggles' face. Into them crept a suspicion of curiosity, as if the prisoner's nonchalant manner puzzled him. 'I was afraid at first that it was,' he said slowly. 'However, my chief engineer assures me that we shall not be delayed more than twenty-four hours.'

'I'll try to do better next time,' promised Biggles.

'There will be no next time,' answered von Schonbeck grimly. 'When I have finished with you, you will be shot.'

Biggles raised his eyebrows. 'Finished with me?'

'No doubt you are wondering why you were brought here?'

'No.' A ghost of a smile crossed Biggles' face. 'I hadn't even given it a thought.'

Von Schonbeck stared hard for a little while. 'There is a confidence in your manner that excites my curiosity,' he admitted.

'It would be still more excited if you knew what I know,' replied Biggles.

'Indeed! Then let us proceed to find out what that is. You will be well advised to answer my questions truthfully. Who sent you out on this errand?'

'What errand?' inquired Biggles blandly.

'Your errand was to find me, was it not?' snapped von Schonbeck, who seemed to be on the way to losing his temper.

'As a matter of fact it was,' admitted Biggles.

'Who sent you?'

'The British Government.'

'Ah! How did the British Government learn that I was coming here?'

'There will be no next time,' said von Schonbeck.

'You'd be surprised if you knew how much they do know about you.'

Von Schonbeck's mouth set in even harder lines. The corners came down. 'Very interesting,' he grated. 'How did your Government get this information?'

'That, I'm afraid, I shall have to leave you to find out from some other source.'

'Be careful not to drive me too far.'

'From what I know of you, von Schonbeck, you need no driving to do anything – and as that includes murder you can't go much further,' said Biggles evenly.

The Nazi stared. For a few seconds he seemed to be at a loss for words. Then, with an obvious effort, he recovered his composure. 'So you don't feel inclined to talk, eh?'

Biggles shook his head. 'Not at the moment, and when I do I like to choose my company. But isn't it rather cold standing here? We've had no breakfast, you know.'

At this juncture Thom broke into a spate of words, as if he could no longer contain his fury; but von Schonbeck silenced him with a gesture. Not for a moment did he take his eyes from Biggles' face. 'You are what you English would call a cool customer,' he remarked. 'But that won't help you now,' he added. 'What other ships, if any, are looking for me?'

'I can well understand how anxious you must be to know that, but you can't seriously expect me to tell you,' rejoined Biggles.

'It would make things easier for you if you changed your mind,' suggested the Nazi.

'I doubt it,' murmured Biggles sceptically.

Again von Schonbeck hesitated. 'I'll give you a little while to think it over. I realise, of course, that you must find your present position vexatious.'

Biggles shrugged. 'Please yourself. For the moment my time is yours. But if you must keep us hanging about I'd appreciate some coffee.'

'I'll see that you get some,' promised von Schonbeck. Turning to Thom he went on, in German: 'Take them back to the ship. I'll talk to them again later.'

The prisoners were returned to their cabin where, soon afterwards, sure enough, the coffee arrived – coffee, biscuits and a small tin of butter. The man who brought these refreshments departed, locking the door behind him.

'Von Schonbeck isn't such a bad sort after all,' remarked Ginger, pouring the coffee.

'Pah! Don't let yourself be taken in by this boloney,' muttered Biggles. 'Make no mistake, von Schonbeck hates the sight of us. No doubt he always did hate anything British, but now we've beaten Germany he must hate us with a hate you and I could scarcely understand. He'll shoot us when it suits him. The only reason we aren't stiff now is because we possess information he must be desperately anxious to have. He wants to know how much we know, and what steps the British Government have taken to round him up. Upon that information his life depends, and he jolly well knows it. He's put us here while he thinks of a trick to wheedle the information out of us – either that or he hopes we'll lose our nerve and squeal. I'm not complaining. That suits me fine, because it gives us more time to find a way out of this jam.'

'And it gives Algy a little more time—'

'*Ssh!*' Biggles raised a warning hand, glancing at the door. 'I wouldn't talk about that now,' he said softly. 'They may be listening. We'll confine this conversation to things that don't matter. If you have anything to say that does matter, whisper it.'

'How long is this going on do you think?' asked Ginger.

'Not long. Until tonight perhaps – or tomorrow morning. Remember what von Schonbeck said about the damage. His engineer said it would delay the sub for twenty-four hours. I take that to mean if she hadn't been damaged she'd be away by now. It also means that as soon as the sub is ready to travel she'll go. That's when the showdown, as far as we are concerned, will come. Meanwhile, let's keep an eye open through that porthole to see what happens ashore. We may learn something.'

CHAPTER X

Algy Carries On

Meanwhile Algy and Bertie were having an adventure of their own.

After sighting the bears, from which they drew natural but quite wrong conclusions, they did not stay long on the iceberg. There was inevitably a brief debate as to what course they should pursue, for Bertie could see no point in returning to Corbie Island after having drawn blank there earlier in the day. But Algy was not so convinced by this line of argument, pointing out that if Biggles had been shelled by the submarine he must have been pretty close to it, in which case von Schonbeck would take every possible precaution to hide his ship from air observation. This, at Corbie Island, would not be difficult, he averred. He was therefore in favour of making another, a closer inspection of the island, and the water surrounding it.

In the end a compromise was reached. In any case it would be necessary to return to Kerguelen for more petrol before going to Corbie Island. So it was decided that they should make a reconnaissance of all the icebergs in the region, for which they had sufficient fuel, on the off-chance of finding Biggles and Ginger; failing in this they would return to Kerguelen for petrol and then, conditions permitting, make another trip to Corbie Island. This settled, the aircraft was taken into the air and the survey of the ice-floes begun.

It was a dismal business, for while not admitting it neither entertained any real hope of finding anything of interest. Visibility was far from good, but it might have been worse, although even in bright sunshine the scene would not have induced high spirits. On all sides lay a restless ocean of dark, cold-looking water, dotted by 'bergs, floes and fragments of ice of all shapes and sizes. The picture was one of utter desolation. Apart from an occasional seal there was no sign of life.

For half an hour Algy maintained his patrol, flying in wide circles, examining each piece of ice methodically but without result. Arriving at the extremity of the ice he turned towards Kerguelen with the disconsolate remark: 'No use.'

'Better have a look at that odd 'berg, old boy – the big fellow over there,' suggested Bertie, pointing to a solitary mass of ice that floated a little apart from the main field.

'Okay,' agreed Algy, without enthusiasm; and he was bringing the machine round in a shallow turn when he saw something that caused him – to use his own expression – to stiffen on the stick. From behind a rugged pyramid of ice piled up in the middle of the 'berg had appeared a figure, the figure of a man.

'There's one of them!' shouted Bertie.

As Algy flew, now with the nose of the aircraft well down, a second figure appeared and joined the first. Another followed, and another and another, until by the time the 'berg was reached five men stood staring upward. With one accord they waved.

'Good Lord!' ejaculated Bertie. 'What do you make of that?'

'I don't know,' answered Algy slowly. 'They may be some of von Schonbeck's men,' he added cautiously.

'Go nearer,' suggested Bertie. 'They can't hurt us.

Algy went lower. 'I don't see any ship,' he muttered. 'There's something mighty queer about this. Who on earth are they, and how did they get there?'

'Let's ask them – what?' suggested Bertie cheerfully.

Algy flew lower over the little group, tilting a wing so that he could get a clear view. Upon this the men waved more vigorously, making beckoning signs that could only mean they were anxious for the machine to land.

'I'm going to risk it,' decided Algy, and after making another turn put the machine down on the water to finish its run not far from the ice. The five men came scrambling towards it.

Algy opened the cockpit cover and stood up. 'Who are you?' he shouted.

'Sailors,' was the answer, spoken in English with a pronounced foreign accent. 'Norwegian sailors.'

'Good Lor'! They must be part of the crew of the whaler,' declared Bertie.

'I think you're right,' answered Algy. 'All the same, keep your gun handy in case it's a trap.' He taxied on, slowly, until he was almost within touching distance of the ice. 'Who speaks English?' he inquired.

A tall young fellow with blue eyes and long flaxen hair held up a hand. 'I speak,' he announced.

'Who are you and what are you doing here?' demanded Algy.

'I am Axel Prinz. We are sailors from Norwegian whaling ship,' was the answer. 'Our ship is taken by submarine pirates. She goes away and we are left on ice.'

In view of what he knew Algy found this explanation so feasible that he hesitated no longer. He threw a line ashore. As soon as it was caught and held, followed by Bertie he stepped on to the ice.

It did not take the Norwegian who spoke English very long to tell his story. In effect, it amounted to this. With rifles and binoculars he and his four companions had gone off in a small boat to hunt for seals on the floes. This was three days ago. While they were some distance from their ship they had seen an astonishing sight. A submarine had appeared. It had fired a shot at the whaler, forcing the ship to heave-to. The whaler had then been boarded by men from the submarine. There was shooting. Bodies, or what from a distance looked like bodies, had been thrown overboard. Then the submarine and the whaler had sailed away together. That was all. The five men, unable to do anything, had been left behind, and they had, in fact, abandoned all hope of being picked up when they heard the drone of the aircraft. What the submarine was doing – indeed, what the whole affair was about – they had not the remotest idea.

Algy, sympathising with their plight, told them as much as he thought necessary. While not divulging its purpose in those waters he explained that the submarine was a Nazi raider. He also told of the discovery of the two dead Norwegians on Kerguelen Island, information which was received by the sailors with sorrow and anger.

'But the war is over!' cried a grizzled old man, who evidently could speak some English.

'There are still Nazis who do not think so,' answered Algy.

'Pah! These Nazis!' The old man spat his contempt.

'I say, you know, what are we going to do with these chaps?' Bertie asked Algy.

'Obviously, we can't leave them here,' replied Algy. 'The only thing we can do is take them to Kerguelen. They'll be all right there until a ship comes to take them off.'

'Where's your boat?' Algy asked Axel, looking round for it.

'It was crushed in ice during the fog, or we should have tried to reach Kerguelen,' was the answer.

'Have you seen anything more of the submarine or the whaler since they went off?' asked Algy, on the off-chance that they had. 'I ask because we've lost some members of our party, too,' he added.

To his surprise Axel had a lot more to say about this than he expected. In fact the conclusion of the young Norwegian's story threw a new light on the entire situation. He asserted that on the previous evening the whaler was observed coming back. They thought, naturally, that it was coming to pick them up. Then a fog had blotted out the scene. Soon afterwards an aeroplane was heard in the distance. The engines stopped and they thought it had landed. Later the fog lifted for a little while, and through the binoculars they saw the whaler again. It was a long way off. They watched it lower a boat, which went to a nearby iceberg. They could not see what happened on the 'berg, but presently a great cloud of smoke went up as if a big fire had been lit. The boat was returning to the whaler when the fog came down again and they saw no more.

To this enlightening recital Algy and Bertie listened with mixed emotions of relief and consternation. 'Things are not as bad as we thought, but they're bad enough,' said Algy to Bertie. 'The whole thing is plain enough now. Biggles went to Corbie. The machine was hit by gunfire and came down near the ice. The Nazis on the whaler spotted it. They picked up Biggles and Ginger, set fire to the machine and went off.'

'That doesn't explain the blood,' Bertie pointed out.

'There must have been fighting, and I can well understand that,' said Algy.

'The question is, where has the whaler taken them?'

'To meet von Schonbeck, I should say,' answered Algy. 'That means Corbie Island, unless they have a rendezvous on the open sea, which doesn't strike me as very likely.'

Bertie looked worried. 'But I say, old boy, what are we going to do about it?'

'That will need thinking about,' returned Algy. 'It looks as if my hunch about Corbie Island is right. That's where we shall finish up, I fancy, sooner or later. But the first thing is to get these chaps to Kerguelen. They must be in need of a hot meal.'

'It's going to be a bit of a squash, if we try to pack them in for one hop,' opined Bertie dubiously.

'We can manage it,' declared Algy. 'We haven't far to go. Let's get them aboard. There's no point in hanging about here any longer. We'll keep an eye open for the whaler as we go. We shall need more petrol in the tank before we start anything.'

The Norwegians were squeezed into the machine. Squeezed is the only word. But the machine had plenty of reserve power, and once in the air made no difficulty of its extra load.

On the run to Kerguelen, Algy devoted his attention to the problem that now confronted him. He knew that strictly speaking Biggles would wish him to proceed with the original quest, regardless of personal considerations. This, eventually, he was prepared to do, but for the moment he had no intention of ignoring Biggles' predicament. That, in his heart, came first. The gold could wait. If Biggles and the gold could be collected together, and this he thought was just within the bounds of possibility, so well and good. The first place to explore, he decided, was Corbie Island, but it was now clear that if the whaler or the submarine was there, a direct landing and a frontal attack was out of the question. Still, there were other ways, and by the time he had put the machine down at its Kerguelen base he had well turned them over in his mind.

In the hut he put the matter before Bertie and his new allies, whom he felt were now personally concerned in the affair in that they had comrades to avenge and a ship to recover. He talked while the Norwegians consumed a satisfying meal, prepared by one of their party who happened to be the whaler's cook. Algy announced his intention of visiting Corbie Island. It would be rash, if not futile, he asserted, to attempt this in daylight; but it might be done at night. The island was several miles long so it should be possible to affect a landing without being seen or heard. There would be a long walk to the cove which he suspected was the anchorage used by the submarine, but that couldn't be avoided.

Axel now made a statement which made it clear that the Norwegians were likely to be more helpful than Algy had supposed. In the first place they knew Corbie Island quite well, having landed there several times on previous voyages for fresh water and the wild cabbages that grew there. And they still had the guns which they had taken with them on their sealing expedition. So it seemed that they would be useful both as guides and as fighting allies. Not only were they willing to take part in an expedition, but they were burning to go, to redress their wrongs. This suited Algy very well and he expressed his satisfaction.

'All right,' he concluded. 'You fellows have a rest and a clean up while I'm getting the machine ready. We'll start at sundown, weather permitting.'

CHAPTER XI

Cut and Thrust

Biggles and Ginger, from their cabin prison in the whaler, had seen plenty to occupy their minds and provide them with subjects for conversation. A great noise of hammering and banging came from the submarine, and a party of men could be seen working in a cradle slung over the stern. Others worked from a small boat, evidently part of the U-boat's equipment.

'It looks as if I got a near miss close to her rudder, which may have affected her steering gear,' said Biggles thoughtfully.

The next thing that happened was the warping of the whaler flush against a low cliff, where she was quickly and cleverly camouflaged with netting of a nature and colour which called from Biggles a remark that it must have been specially designed for the locality.

'The Germans always were thorough in little things,' he observed, with grudging admiration. 'This is a really clever job. Von Schonbeck is taking no chances. We're well covered against air reconnaissance – and so, I see, is the submarine. It would take a wizard to see anything here except rock and water.'

'Maybe it's a good thing for us,' said Ginger. 'We should look silly if Algy came over, spotted the whaler or the submarine, and handed out a couple of depth-charges.'

'Algy may come, but unless von Schonbeck is fool enough to reveal his position by opening fire, I doubt he will see us,' returned Biggles.

'You don't think von Schonbeck will open fire?' queried Ginger.

'Not unless he has reason to suppose that he has been spotted. There isn't much point in hiding a target and then giving the position away by taking offensive action. If von Schonbeck is half as clever as he is reputed to be he won't make that blunder.'

Confirmation of this was soon provided. The drone of aero engines announced the approach of an aircraft, which those in the cabin knew could only be their reserve machine.

'Here comes Algy,' said Biggles quietly. 'We shall soon see how it goes.'

On the submarine, in response to a whistle, all movement ceased after the workers had dived for cover. The aircraft came on. All remained still. Gulls drifted languidly over the scene. The aircraft circled, and at length disappeared from the vision of the watchers. Its receding drone told them that it was retiring.

'They didn't spot us,' said Biggles. 'If they had they would have hung around for a bit, even if they didn't take action.'

The work on the submarine was resumed. The day wore on. Later, a parade of men was held on a level area of rock. Both von Schonbeck and Thom were present. Some of the men were issued with picks and shovels. Biggles counted fifteen men in all. 'I wonder what all this is about?' he questioned, as the party, after turning with military precision, marched off and was soon lost to sight.

More time passed. Work on the submarine was continued. The prisoners were served with a plain meal. Biggles continued to watch through the porthole. Suddenly he gave a low whistle. 'Take a look at this,' he invited.

Ginger, who was reclining on a bunk, joined him, and saw four men staggering along carrying an oblong wooden box obviously of considerable weight. It was deposited on a rock near the submarine's conning tower.

'What the deuce is it?' queried Ginger.

'I'll give you two guesses – and you ought to be right each time,' answered Biggles. 'The picks and shovels should have told us what was afoot.'

'I still don't get it,' muttered Ginger.

'Have you forgotten what brought von Schonbeck here – and us, too, if it comes to that?'

Enlightenment dawned in Ginger's eyes. He drew a deep breath. 'The gold!' he burst out.

'That's a bullion box those fellows are carrying,' Biggles told him.

'They're digging it out and getting ready to load up.'

'That's what it looks like,' agreed Biggles.

'And we're stuck here and can't do anything about it.'

'Not a thing,' agreed Biggles again. 'Here comes another lot.'

A second party of four men came into sight carrying a box similar to the first. The original four were on their way back. As the two parties passed some joke was evidently exchanged, for there was laughing.

'They seem to be happy,' growled Ginger.

'So would anyone be with five million pounds to spend,' said Biggles, smiling.

'You seem to be taking all this pretty lightly,' remarked Ginger, looking hard at Biggles.

Biggles shrugged. 'Moaning won't get us anywhere will it? The sub still has a long way to go.'

The work ashore proceeded without hitch, both on the submarine and with the transportation of the gold. The stack of boxes near the U-boat grew steadily in size. Eventually, von Schonbeck and Thom reappeared.

'I should say that's the lot,' said Biggles.

Towards evening there was a further burst of activity. The cradle over the submarine's stern was drawn up and the camouflage removed. After everything had been made shipshape von Schonbeck and Thom went aboard.

'Now what?' asked Ginger. 'Don't tell me they're going to move off?'

'The gold is still ashore. They wouldn't be likely to go without it,' answered Biggles dryly.

Soon afterwards the meaning of this latest manoeuvre was made clear. The U-boat's engines were started and the vessel moved out to open water. One or two turns were made, after which she returned to her mooring.

'They've tested her,' said Biggles. 'Apparently she's all right.'

'Which means she'll push off.'

'Not necessarily. They've got to load and stow that gold, and that will take some time. By the time they've done that it will be dark. Of course, von Schonbeck may decide to go right away, but on the other hand he may prefer to wait for daylight before taking his ship through that narrow channel to the open sea. He's got the whaler to dispose of, anyway. I don't suppose he'll leave it here.'

Nightfall put an end to further observation. When darkness closed in the gold was still lying on the rock, which, as Biggles remarked, tended to confirm his opinion that von Schonbeck intended to wait for morning before taking his ship out to the open sea. And the fact that only a sailor came to the cabin, bringing more food for the prisoners, supported this view.

'Yes, it looks as though they're going to spend another night here,' asserted Biggles. 'That suits us as well as anything. It gives us a bit more time, anyway.'

'A bit more time for what?'

'Oh – anything,' said Biggles nonchalantly.

'You think Algy might come back?'

Biggles considered the question. 'He might. We've no real reason for supposing that he will, though. And even if he does it's hard to see what he can do.'

'That's cheerful,' muttered Ginger.

'Unfortunately, my lad, it's the truth – and it's always as well to face up to facts. Dawn tomorrow will be zero hour – as far as we're concerned, anyway.'

After that they fell silent. There was nothing they could do except lie on their bunks. After a while, Biggles' steady breathing told Ginger that he was asleep.

At some time he, too, must have fallen asleep, although just when that happened he could not remember; but he was awakened by heavy footsteps outside the door, and the turning of the handle.

Biggles, who was already up, threw him a glance. 'This, I should say, is it,' he said quietly.

The door was opened and Thom, an expression of malevolent satisfaction on his face, stood on the threshold. He beckoned to Biggles with a peremptory finger. 'Come,' he ordered.

Ginger, thinking naturally that he was included in this invitation, moved towards the door; but with a harsh 'I did not say you,' Thom thrust him back with unnecessary violence.

Anger tightened Ginger's lips and set his nostrils quivering; but Biggles caught his eye and shook his head so slightly that the movement was almost imperceptible. 'Put your hackles down,' he said softly. 'It won't help matters. So long – in case.'

With that Biggles was bundled out of the cabin. The door was slammed and locked, leaving Ginger alone inside. He strode to the porthole, through which the bleak grey light of dawn was filtering.

Biggles realised that he was being taken ashore, to von Schonbeck, for the interview which had been promised; and the reception that awaited him as he stepped ashore near the U-boat left him in no doubt as to the finality of its nature. The gold boxes, he noted, were no longer there. In their place stood a file of six sailors who eyed the prisoner with hostile curiosity. Each man carried a rifle and wore a cartridge belt. At a short distance von Schonbeck was waiting, legs apart, service cap at a jaunty angle, a cigar between his teeth, hands thrust deep into the pockets of his short blue coat. Biggles smiled cynically, realising that he had been marched past what was obviously a firing party for no other purpose than intimidation.

'We are about to move off,' greeted von Schonbeck affably. 'Have you considered my proposition?'

'There was nothing to consider,' returned Biggles briefly.

The Nazi's expression did not change. He tapped the ash from his cigar. 'I am trying to give you a chance for your life,' he announced.

Biggles raised his eyebrows. 'I should never have guessed it.'

'I mean what I say.'

Biggles shook his head sadly. 'Even if I could accept the word of a Nazi – and the events of the war have shown what a flimsy thing that is – I would tell you nothing,' he said quietly. 'Go ahead. Do what you like. The only thing I have to say to you, von Schonbeck, is this. You still have a long way to go.'

'It may be that your young friend could be more easily persuaded,' said von Schonbeck thoughtfully.

'Try, if you like, but I think you'd be wasting your time,' opined Biggles.

'Ah well.' Von Schonbeck sighed – or pretended to sigh. 'You British always did have a reputation for being pig-headed. You'll see where that will get you at the end.'

'Your own methods during the war can hardly be described as overwhelmingly successful,' returned Biggles, a suspicion of a sneer creeping into his voice.

The thrust went home. The German scowled. 'This is not a good moment to remind me of that,' he rasped. 'When this affair is over there will be one damned Britisher the less, anyhow.' Von Schonbeck paused, and with an effort checked his rising temper. 'But to argue about things that are past at a time like this is folly,' he went on. 'Now then, as one officer and gentleman to another—'

Biggles looked incredulous. 'As *what*? An officer and gentleman? God save us. Von Schonbeck, you're just a cheap, cold-blooded murderer, high on the list of war criminals. Very soon every newspaper in the world will carry the story of your crimes, your butchery of helpless women and unarmed seamen. You may shoot me, and since a hyena can't change its coat I'm sure that was always your intention; but, believe me, I'd sooner go out here and now than live another twenty years with a reputation like yours. They'll put your photo in the papers, and every decent seaman between the Arctic and the Antarctic will spit when he looks at it. That should leave you in no doubt as to what I think of you.'

Thom took a swift pace forward and struck Biggles across the face with his open hand.

Von Schonbeck, whose face had flamed scarlet, laughed harshly. 'What you think of me is of no importance,' he grated. 'It is what I am going to do to you that will count.'

'Go ahead,' invited Biggles.

Von Schonbeck barked an order. Two men seized Biggles by the arms and jostled him forward a little way until he stood with his back against a face of rock. Another order and the firing party lined up in front of him. Another order and they came to attention.

'Would you like a bandage over your eyes?' sneered von Schonbeck.

'No,' answered Biggles evenly. 'There's nothing a Nazi can give me that I can't take.'

Von Schonbeck raised his hand.

'Take aim,' Thom ordered his men.

The rifles of the firing party came to their shoulders.

The crash of an explosion shattered the silence.

Biggles stumbled and fell flat.

CHAPTER XII

Ginger Starts Something

Now while Biggles was taking what he had good reason to suppose would be his last view of the earth from the inhospitable rock of the island, Ginger, still secure in the whaler, was nearer than ever before to panic. Watching through the porthole he saw Biggles taken ashore, saw von Schonbeck standing there, saw the firing squad and guessed its purpose. Yet there was nothing he could do. Absolutely nothing. He tried to do something, of course. In sheer despair he wrenched at the door handle, kicked the door and tore at the metal frame of the porthole, although he knew that these efforts were silly and futile. His only comfort – a poor crumb of comfort indeed – was the thought: 'I shall be next.'

At this juncture, while he was still staring ashen-faced through the porthole, a sudden noise behind him brought him round with a nervous start, in such a state of agitation was he. He saw that the door had been opened. A face, a leathery, weather-beaten face, alert with apprehension and anxiety, was peering into the cabin. The eyes met Ginger's. After a furtive glance along the corridor behind him the man made a swift beckoning movement with his hand.

Ginger felt intuitively that this man was a friend. Indeed, his attitude and manner almost proved it. So the question he asked was really automatic. 'Who are you?' he demanded.

'I friend,' was the terse reply. 'Come. Come quick. We go.'

'Go where?'

The man made a gesture of urgency. 'Hide. Germans shoot.'

The man's English was limited, but the words he did use were pregnant with significance. In any case Ginger was in no state to be particular. He was prepared to go anywhere, do anything, if only to get out of the cabin. 'Are you a Norwegian?' he queried, although here again he was pretty sure of his ground.

'Yes, me Norwegian,' was the quick rejoinder. The man laid a finger on his lips. 'Come. Not any noise,' he warned.

Still without knowing exactly what the man intended beyond the obvious fact that he proposed deserting the ship, Ginger followed his new acquaintance into the corridor, along which they passed swiftly to a flight of steps which, as it soon turned out, gave access to the deck near the bows. From this point Ginger made a lightning survey of the ship for possible danger. There were several sailors in sight. All were lining the rail overlooking the shore where a drama was being enacted, their attention riveted on it, as was natural. Ginger's guide, impatient at the brief delay, plucked him by the sleeve, and lifting aside the camouflage netting indicated that they should climb the low cliff against which the ship was moored. But in this simple manner of escape – for it was evident that the Norwegian did not look beyond that – Ginger was not prepared to participate. In point of fact escape was the last thing in his mind. The thought dominant in his brain was how to help Biggles. His eyes were on the shore and he could see clearly enough what was about to happen. The question was, how to stop it, and this was not so clear. The Norwegian was still hanging on the cliff, waiting, so Ginger ran to him and asked him if he had a pistol. Just what he would have done with this weapon had it been available is a matter for conjecture. It seems likely that he would have launched, from long range, a single-handed attack on the firing party, and lost his life for his pains. However, this did not occur for the simple reason that the Norwegian had no pistol. Indeed, he had no weapon of any sort, as he explained by eloquent gestures. Ginger, by this time in a fever of consternation, turned away, and in doing so collided with a weapon the like of which he had never seen before although his common sense told him what it was. It was the heavy harpoon gun, mounted in the bows, by which the whaler slew the great sea beasts for which it was designed. The massive point of a steel harpoon, with hinged barbs, a fearful-looking instrument, projected from the muzzle.

Ginger caught his breath as he realised the possibilities. He had an insane desire to laugh. 'Is this loaded?' he demanded of his companion, who by signs was still imploring him to escape while the opportunity offered.

The man shook his head.

'Where are the shells?' demanded Ginger. 'Quick!'

The man pointed at a stoutly-built wooden box, almost the size of a chest, clamped to the deck near the gun.

Ginger threw open the lid and saw rows of enormous cartridges. 'How do you load this thing?' he asked in a hoarse whisper.

The man joined him. 'Are you mad?' he asked with some agitation.

'Yes,' answered Ginger frankly. 'How do I load it?'

The man started to explain, but Ginger, unable to follow his instructions, broke in impatiently. 'Load it.'

The Norwegian, with a deftness obviously the result of long experience, slipped a cartridge into the breech and closed it. 'She is ready,' he said simply. 'She fire when you pull trigger.'

With a sort of delirious joy Ginger grabbed the weapon, swung the muzzle round – for it moved on well-oiled bearings – and took rough aim at the party on the shore. To his horror he saw that the

Ginger grabbed the weapon, swung the muzzle round.

sailors had raised their rifles. His finger coiled round the trigger. With a vicious jerk he pulled it, and then stepped back to watch the result.

There was a violent explosion, much louder than he expected. The harpoon, glinting as it caught the light, flashed a graceful curve through the grey atmosphere. Behind it, sagging slightly, trailed the line to which it was attached. Until this moment Ginger knew nothing of the line. Not that it made any difference.

The harpoon missed the target at which it was aimed by a fairly wide margin, although that is no matter for wonder. It hit the conning tower of the submarine with a metallic clang, glanced off, and spinning wildly whirled on towards the group assembled behind it. Ginger saw Biggles fall flat and for a ghastly moment thought that the harpoon had hit him. Thom spun a good dozen yards and went down, screaming. The rope, coiling like a snake in convulsions, threw the firing party into confusion. In actual fact Ginger was not at all sure of what had happened. One thing, however, was certain. He had interrupted the proceedings. Satisfied with his efforts so far he turned to reload the weapon, but the Norwegian clutched him by the arm and shouted to him to run. This, really, was sound advice, but Ginger was in no mood to listen to advice, good or bad.

From then on the affair was chaotic. Shots were fired. By whom, who at, and from where, Ginger had no idea. There was shouting. The old Norwegian was yelling in his own language. The sailors who had been lining the rail had turned, and they, too, shouted as they ran towards the gun, some in German and some in what Ginger supposed to be Norwegian. What is commonly called a free fight started. The old Norwegian picked up an iron spike that lay near the gun and threw it. It struck the leading German in the face and knocked him down. Ginger closed with the second. He went down under his man, who was a good deal heavier, and was getting the worst of it when the body pressing on him went limp. Pulling himself clear he saw a Norwegian swinging a wooden mallet in a sort of frenzy. Everywhere men were fighting, wrestling, some standing, some falling. It was evident that now the revolt had started, now that the Norwegians had turned on their captors, they were wiping out old scores and doing it with gusto.

Ginger took no further part in this particular affair. The mêlée was too confused, and although for the moment the Norwegians appeared to be more than holding their own, in his heart he felt sure that in the long run they would lose, because they were outnumbered. He was thinking, of course, of the Nazi crew on the U-boat, who, he was certain, would soon be aboard to quell the rising. And thinking on these lines he could find time to be sorry for the disaster which, he supposed, he had brought upon the unarmed whalers. He was anxious, desperately anxious, to learn what had happened to Biggles, and in the hope of ascertaining this he made his way to the rail which commanded a view of the scene ashore. There, an unexpected sight met his gaze. As far as he had been aware there had been no Norwegians on the island; so if there was any fighting at all, he assumed that it would be Biggles against the rest. But this was not so. Another battle, a battle in which firearms were being used, was being waged ashore. Perhaps 'battle' is not the right word. It appeared that a small party of men, Biggles amongst them, was making a fighting withdrawal towards the interior of the island. From here, too, shots were being fired. Ginger could not understand it at all. Not that he tried very hard. His chief concern was that Biggles was still on his feet, and seemed to have found some unexpected allies. Where these had come from he could not imagine. It was all very puzzling.

A new factor now appeared on the scene – or rather, over the scene. In a vague sort of way Ginger connected it with the happenings ashore without being able to reach anything definite in the way of understanding. It was the aircraft. It appeared suddenly over the crest of a hill some distance away. Ginger shouted from sheer excitement. A whistle shrilled on the shore, and the Germans who had been pursuing Biggles and his unknown friends began running back to the U-boat. Biggles and his party now turned back and pursued the Germans, who, in response to von Schonbeck's frantic shouting, converged on the U-boat and dived into the conning tower.

The aircraft came on. It still had some distance to travel, however, to the scene of hostilities; and when it did reach them it circled as if the pilot was undecided as to what course to take. This Ginger could well understand. A newcomer to the scene, he realised, would find it hard to sort out the combatants. The result of this hesitation was that by the time the machine reached the cove the submarine was under way, nosing towards the passage to the open sea. From the behaviour of the aircraft Ginger thought that the pilot – Algy or Bertie, he knew not which – had only just spotted the U-boat; but when the pilot did see it he came straight on. A depth-charge came sailing down. Ginger ducked, for the missile seemed to be coming uncomfortably close to the whaler. There was a thundering explosion. Ginger jumped up and saw that the depth-charge, obviously aimed at the U-boat, had missed its mark. It had fallen some distance astern. A quick-firing gun on the deck of the submarine started pouring up flak, forcing the aircraft to take evading action. Nevertheless, dashing in it sent a second depth-charge hurtling down. Again Ginger ducked, for this one, dropped in haste, looked like coming nearer. Again an explosion thundered, flinging columns of water sky-high. Again Ginger popped up, in time to observe that the shot was another miss. He groaned with disappointment. Then he remembered that the gold was on board the U-boat, a fact of which the pilot of the aircraft must be unaware, and he was glad, in a way, that the submarine looked like getting clear. He had no idea of the depth of the water in the cove, but should it be very deep, and it might well be, there was a good chance that the gold would have been lost for ever.

The U-boat, after rocking dangerously in the tremendous swell set up by the explosion, moved on towards the entrance. The whaler rocked too, so that Ginger was hard put to keep his feet. Spitting flak the U-boat held on, followed by the aircraft, still taking evading action, the only sensible thing to do in the circumstances, as Ginger realised. The machine took no further offensive action because there was nothing more it could do. It carried no more depth-charges, nor, for that matter, any other weapon powerful enough to impede the progress of the submarine. The *Tarpon*'s machine-guns were no use against a steel hull, so the submarine ran on through the channel to the open sea where, after the gunners had retired, it submerged and was lost to view. Not forgetting the gold, Ginger was conscious of a sense of frustration and disappointment.

Still somewhat dazed by the speed of events, and aware that the pandemonium behind him had subsided, he turned to see what had happened. A litter of bodies on the whaler's deck revealed at a glance the fury of the struggle that had been waged. It was equally clear that the whalers had won, for all those still on their feet were Norwegians. The old man with the leathery face – now bloodstained but twisted in a grin of triumph – was there.

Now that the affair on the whaler was over Ginger had no time to spare for it. He was more anxious to make contact with Biggles. So with a shout of congratulations and thanks to the Norwegians he went back to the rail, nearly being hit by a bullet as he did so. Realising that those ashore must be unaware of what had happened on the ship, and that they would naturally suppose it to be in enemy hands, he jumped up and waved his arms, at the same time shouting to call attention to his presence. Out of the corner of his eye he saw the aircraft coming in to land from the direction of the sea; but his attention was really on the shore, where a little knot of men stood together, one of them bending over something that lay on the ground. Biggles was amongst them. He looked across the water at Ginger and waved. He spoke to the men around him, with a result that two of them got into the little boat that had taken him ashore and rowed out to the ship.

Five minutes later Ginger was on the island talking to Biggles. The object on the ground turned out to be Thom. He was not a pretty sight, for the harpoon had gone clean through him.

Ginger shuddered. 'Did I do that?' he asked aghast.

'It was a good shot whoever did it,' declared Biggles. 'Did you fire the gun?'

'I did,' admitted Ginger.

'With more practice you'll be able to go in for whaling when you get too old to fly,' said Biggles. Then he became serious. 'You were just about in time, although at first I thought the harpoon was going to get me. I saw it coming and went flat. But let's get the situation straightened out. What's happened on the ship?'

'The Norwegians took a hand and cleaned up the Nazis,' explained Ginger. 'Where the deuce did these other fellows come from?' He pointed at three more men coming towards the scene. One of them was Algy. 'That means Bertie must have been flying the aircraft,' he concluded.

'Evidently,' replied Biggles. 'I'm still not clear as to what has happened, except that an attack on the Nazi camp was launched just about the time you fired the gun. But here comes Bertie. No doubt he'll tell us all about it.'

The aircraft had taxied up to the rock and Bertie had jumped ashore. He reached the party at the same time as Algy, who was plastered with mud and breathing heavily.

Bertie started when his eyes fell on the mangled remains of Thom. Adjusting his monocle he regarded the spectacle with disgust. 'Here, I say, you know, who made that beastly mess?' he inquired weakly.

'Never mind that,' answered Biggles. 'We're waiting to hear your end of the story.'

'Ask Algy,' pleaded Bertie. 'I'm still all of a dither. Did you see that bally submarine shooting at me? No joke, I can tell you.'

'You needn't tell me,' said Biggles curtly. 'I've had some. Go ahead, Algy.'

Algy explained how he and Bertie had picked up the Norwegians marooned on the ice, had landed at the far end of the island during the hours of darkness, and were getting into position to attack the Nazi camp when the firing of the gun had upset their plan. However, they had pressed on the attack, after which Biggles knew as much about it as they did.

'Well, it seems to have worked out all right,' said Biggles at the finish.

'You're not forgetting that von Schonbeck has got away?' Ginger pointed out bitterly.

'And I'm not forgetting that we've got away, either,' returned Biggles. 'An hour ago I wouldn't have given an empty petrol can for our chance. Von Schonbeck has gone and he's got the gold with him, but he's not home yet; with any luck we'll catch up with him before he gets there. Those cookies of yours, Bertie, were pretty close, and if they haven't loosened some plates I shall be surprised. The best thing we can do is get back to base and talk the thing over. Before we do that, though, we'd better see what we have on our hands here.'

'How about chasing the sub?' suggested Ginger.

Biggles shook his head. 'Not a hope. Von Schonbeck will stay under water for as long as he dare, knowing there's a hostile aircraft about. Not that it would make any difference if we did spot him. We've nothing to hit with.'

'If the U-boat is likely to leave a trail why not follow it?' suggested Ginger.

'What's the use of following a trail if you can't hurt the thing making it?' returned Biggles. 'Even if we had more depth-charges, and improved on Bertie's bombing, Raymond wouldn't thank us for sending the gold to Davy Jones. That isn't the idea. And there's no sense in burning petrol for nothing; if we happened to run into a gale it would take us all our time to get home, anyway.'

'We could look and see if the U-boat is leaving a trail,' pressed Ginger.

'Take a look at the weather,' invited Biggles. He pointed.

Glancing up, Ginger saw black squall clouds racing low across the sky. A rising wind was tearing the surface off the water. 'Okay,' he said in a resigned voice.

A check disclosed that of the original Norwegian crew twelve were still alive, including those who had been picked up on the ice-floe. One had been killed during the fight on the whaler, and three others wounded, although not seriously. One of the shore party had a slight gunshot wound. Of the Nazis, apart from Thom, three had been killed and four wounded. It turned out that the captain of the whaler had been murdered by the Nazis when the ship had been seized, but the first mate was still alive and asserted that he was able to take the ship to port.

'What are we going to do with the prisoners?' asked Algy.

'We certainly can't clutter ourselves up with them,' answered Biggles. 'There seems to be quite a dump here, with food and medical stores, so I think the best thing is to leave them here to look after themselves for the time being. We'll notify Raymond at the first opportunity; no doubt he'll send a ship out to take them off.'

One other point of interest came to light. The whaler, as Biggles suspected, had taken on board most of the reserve oil from the secret base at Kerguelen, the Norwegians explaining that it had been von Schonbeck's intention to use the whaler as a mobile base, and perhaps as a blind to hide his activities. For this purpose he had, as was known, put a Nazi crew on board from his own ship.

'Which means that his own crew must be shrinking,' observed Biggles.

After a short debate the matter was left thus: the Norwegians were to take their vessel to Biggles' base at Kerguelen, from where, after refitting as far as possible and restoring their wounded, they could make their way to their home port of Oslo, to report their version of the affair to their owners and the Norwegian Government. This would leave the airmen free to pursue the U-boat in the remaining aircraft. In the first place, however, they would have to return to base to refuel. They would take up the hunt from there.

'Do you think you will catch these swines?' Axel asked Biggles.

'I think we have a fair chance,' was the reply. 'If our depth-charges have strained some of the U-boat's plates, and that seems likely, she will leave an oil trail that we should have no difficulty in picking up. Once we find the trail we'll play cat and mouse with her until we catch her on the surface.'

'The one snag is,' he told the others later, when they were on board the machine, 'now von Schonbeck has the gold we mustn't sink him if it can be avoided. Of course, now he knows that we're after him he may change his plans. He may give South America a miss and decide on some other hide-out. He has a lot of places to choose from. However, we'll talk about that later.'

He took the machine off and headed for Kerguelen.

CHAPTER XIII

Von Schonbeck Tries Again

Leaving the Norwegians to follow in the whaler in their own time Biggles set his course for base. There was a delay as the aircraft passed over the area where the U-boat had disappeared, some time being employed in searching for indications of her track; but crested waves were now chasing each other in endless procession across the ocean, and with spindrift flying above them reconnaissance was hopeless and yielded nothing.

'I'm afraid it would need a lot of oil to show on a sea like that,' observed Biggles critically. 'If this weather persists for any length of time we're going to have a tiresome job picking up the trail. We may never find it. In fact, everything may now depend on the weather. It raises another possibility. If the sub is damaged, and if the sea gets worse, she may not be able to ride it out, in which case she'll go to the bottom taking the gold with her and no one will ever know for certain what did happen. That would be a most unsatisfactory end to the story.'

The machine went on to make a somewhat hazardous landing at the Kerguelen base. The water inside the cove was calm enough, but the air above it was tormented by treacherous gusts, due to the rugged nature of the terrain. In these the aircraft bucked and rocked before sliding down to rest in the sheltered anchorage. The machine was soon made fast, and under Biggles' orders it was refuelled forthwith in case it should be needed in a hurry. The party then retired to the hut for a quick bath and a badly needed meal. While they were eating, from time to time Biggles threw anxious glances at the window and the howling gale that now raged outside.

'It looks like working up for a real snorter,' he remarked. 'It's no earthly use going out in that. We might as well make up our minds to it and settle down to take it easy.'

He was right. The storm persisted, with squalls of hail, sleet and snow. It raged all that night, all the next day and all the following night. With visibility zero the airmen could do nothing. They were grounded. Biggles spent most of the daylight hours staring out of the window, smoking an endless chain of cigarettes, seldom speaking except to refer to the situation. The others, knowing what the enforced inaction was doing to his nerves, fell quiet. Of course, they too felt the strain – or rather, the slackening of the strain and the inevitable reaction.

'What I'd like to know is this,' remarked Biggles once, flicking the ash from his cigarette. 'How much oil had von Schonbeck got aboard when he pushed off? He went in a deuce of a hurry, don't forget. Most of his reserve fuel was in the whaler. He'd need full tanks to make the Magellan Straits – that is, if he's sticking to his original plan. We were on the whaler when she made Corbie Island, and after that we were always on it or near it. I can't recall seeing or hearing anything like refuelling operations. On the other hand, of course the submarine may have been lying there with full tanks. It's an important point. After running through a sea like this the state of her tanks will play a vital part in the game, because they'll control her endurance range. But there, it's no use guessing. I wonder how the whaler's getting on? Undermanned as she is the crew must be having a pretty thin time out there in that perishing murk, with ice about.'

'I can't help thinking we ought to radio Raymond and tell him the position,' put in Algy, moodily.

'And I can't see that it would do any good,' returned Biggles curtly. 'He's too far away to help us, considering the time factor. If it comes to that we should be no better off if we had a dozen planes here. They'd all be grounded. If von Schonbeck picked up our signal – and you can bet your sweet life he's listening for signals – it might do a lot of harm. It would tell him that we're still on the job and perhaps give him an idea of where we're working from – if he doesn't know already. Radio silence will keep him guessing. It's better that way.'

On the morning of the third day the storm blew itself out. The wind dropped to an occasional gust and the sea began to subside. Biggles, his irritation gone, became the very spirit of activity.

'I'm getting off right away, taking Ginger with me,' he announced crisply. 'I don't know when we shall be back. We may be some time. If von Schonbeck has managed to ride out the storm he should be a long way off by now; but he won't be outside our range, I think, because he wouldn't risk running at full speed through a heavy sea. Still, he's an old hand at this game and we shall have to be prepared for tricks – tricks like laying false trails by means of oil barrels with holes punched in them to allow the oil to seep out.' Biggles spoke to Algy. 'When we come back, if we've found nothing you can carry on. If necessary we'll fly complete circles at increasing distances until we do strike the trail.'

'There may not be any trail. The storm may have washed it out,' suggested Algy.

'Maybe. But the sea is down now and if the sub is still travelling she'll be leaving signs which we ought to see as we cut across them. There is this in our favour. There aren't likely to be any other craft about to mislead us.'

'And suppose you find the trail – what then?' inquired Algy.

'I shall follow it,' answered Biggles. 'If the sub is running under water, which is unlikely, or if she dives when she sees us, I shall call up Raymond, pin-point the position, and ask him to throw a cordon of anti-submarine craft round the whole area. The sub won't be able to sit on the bottom in these waters; they're too deep; and if the engines are running sound detectors should pick them up. Sooner or later the sub will have to surface if only to charge her batteries; and even if von Schonbeck realises that he is being dogged he'll have to carry on because he wouldn't dare to risk running out of fuel. It's a long way to the Magellan Straits. If his tanks dried up he'd be finished. He'd be a mere hulk, a floating tin can with no means of getting anywhere and at the mercy of the first storm that blew along. Diving wouldn't save him. A few near misses with depth-charges would either send him to the bottom or bring him to the surface. But the first thing is to find the submarine. By the way, you fellows keep an eye open for the whaler. It's time she was here. Come on, Ginger.'

Biggles strode down to the machine, which was soon in the air, flying under the usual leaden sky over a sea that still heaved in the aftermath of the recent storm. But the wind had died away and the waves were fast going down.

'In a couple of hours, if there's no more wind, she'll be flat calm,' said Biggles confidently, as he climbed for height. 'I'm setting a course to fly a big arc right across the region between Corbie Island and the Magellan Straits,' he announced. 'Keep your eyes open and tell me if you see anything – anything at all.'

'Okay,' acknowledged Ginger, and the search began.

For more than two hours the *Tarpon* roared on an outward course across a sullen waste of water. Nothing was seen. Absolutely nothing. Not even an iceberg or a solitary whale. Ginger, aware that they were hundreds of miles from home, or, for that matter, from the nearest land, regarded the featureless expanse below with rising apprehension. He could not help remembering that the best aero engines sometimes fail, that they were over the loneliest place on the globe, and, moreover, at about the limit of the range. From his manner Biggles might have been unaware of this. Consequently Ginger drew a deep breath of relief when the nose of the machine began to swing round.

'Queer,' said Biggles. 'Dashed queer. I would have wagered twelve months' pay that the submarine was losing oil. If there was oil we should see it.' This was obviously true, for the sea now lay as tranquil as a pond.

'He may have changed his mind and gone another way,' suggested Ginger.

'Then he must have another oil dump somewhere or he'd never make a landfall,' declared Biggles. 'He's a long way to go, even to South America. I'll try farther out.'

For about twenty minutes Biggles flew on, and then turned for home on an even greater circle than the outward journey. Ginger said nothing but he was far from happy. Biggles was taking chances, which was not like him. They were cutting the petrol supply fine, even in still air. A head wind now would be worse than a calamity. It would be fatal, inevitably fatal. However, his fears proved groundless, and the aircraft reached its base with only failure to report.

'Refuel and take over,' Biggles told Algy wearily. 'Try a different track.' He started as if a thought had occurred to him. A puzzled frown creased his forehead. 'By the way, where's the whaler?'

Algy shrugged. 'She hasn't come.'

Biggles' frown deepened. 'Hasn't come? What the deuce can she be doing?'

'The bally storm may have delayed her,' suggested Bertie.

'Of course it would,' acknowledged Biggles. 'But a whaler is built for salt water and she'd see it through. Storm or no storm she should have been here before this. Good Lord!' His eyes opened wide. He pursed his lips. 'I wonder...?'

'Wonder what?' prompted Algy.

'That ship is loaded with oil and von Schonbeck knows it. I wonder if he's had the nerve to turn back and ... It's the sort of thing he might do. I ought to be kicked for not considering the possibility.'

'I wouldn't worry,' said Algy. 'There's probably a simple explanation for the delay. It's far more likely that the whaler slipped under the lee of Kerguelen while the storm was on instead of battering her way against it.'

'It might be,' agreed Biggles. 'I'll tell you what, Algy. Fill up with petrol, and for a start fly back towards Corbie Island to see if you can spot the whaler coming. That'll settle any argument. Take Bertie with you for a breath of fresh air. This hut stinks like the fo'c'sle of a Dutch onion boat.'

'Here, I say, old boy, I was only making Irish stew,' protested Bertie. 'Jolly good stew, too. Try some?'

'We'll take a chance,' agreed Biggles, smiling.

Algy went off, taking Bertie with him, and soon afterwards the roar of engines announced their departure.

As Algy swung round the northern tip of the island on a course for Corbie, he flew as a man flies on a simple routine operation. He was quite sure that he would see the whaler ploughing along bound for the aircraft base; and the last thing he expected was anything in the nature of excitement. And at first events fell out much as he expected. In five minutes he spotted the whaler slogging along the lee of Kerguelen, northward bound.

'There she is,' he told Bertie casually. 'I was right. She's been sheltering from the storm. I'll go down and give them a wave; then we'll beetle back and let Biggles know it's okay.'

In accordance with this simple programme Algy cut his engines and, altering course slightly, began a long glide towards the ship. But as he drew near his easy attitude changed. He stiffened, bending forward to peer through the windscreen. Bertie did the same.

'Am I seeing things or is there something queer about that ship?' muttered Algy.

Bertie screwed his monocle in his eye and looked again. 'If you ask me, old boy, I'd say she's been dragged through hell backwards. Must have been the bally storm that knocked her about – what?'

'Not on your life,' snapped Algy. 'The wave wasn't created yet that could tear that hole in her side. She's been shelled, and hit – and hit hard. By thunder! Biggles was right. Von Schonbeck has been at her again. I'm going down.'

'Here, take it easy, old boy,' murmured Bertie uncomfortably. 'She may have the beastly Nazis on board, and all that.'

'No!' shouted Algy, as they swept low over the whaler. 'That's Axel standing on the wheelhouse. He's waving. He wouldn't be allowed to do that if there were Nazis on board. I'm going to risk it.'

He swung round, dropped a wing and side-slipped down, to land and come to rest about a cable's length from the whaler. Axel appeared at the rail, beckoning, so he taxied on until by scrambling along a wing he was able to grab a rope which Axel threw to him. In a minute he was aboard. 'What's happened?' he asked breathlessly.

He asked the question automatically, for he knew what the answer would be. At any rate, he had a pretty good idea of it. The condition of the ship, as he saw it from close range, told its own story. On reaching the deck a swift glance around confirmed everything, if confirmation were needed. The superstructure was a wreck. Standing gear was a shell-torn tangle. Splinters lay everywhere. There were bloodstains. Old Leatherface sat at the foot of the mainmast, cheeks grey under their tan. Some members of the crew were trying to clear up the mess. Pumps were working. All this Algy took in at a glance before turning horrified questioning eyes to Axel.

'The submarine shelled us – but we still have the ship,' announced Axel, smiling ruefully.

'But what happened?' persisted Algy.

'When the storm was bad, being short-handed we decided to run into the cove at the southern end of the island for the night,' said Axel simply. 'The submarine was there. We did not know it. It was dark, very dark. But in the morning there she was, getting oil from the tank on shore. There was much oil on the water. It may be the oil from the tank, or perhaps what your captain said was right, and the submarine is damaged. I do not know. But when we are seen the Nazis run to their guns and fire. We slip our cable and back out, but we are hit many times. It was bad.'

'When was this?' asked Algy quickly.

'This morning.'

'And where is the submarine now?'

'When last I see her she is in the cove.'

Algy's manner became brittle. 'Can you handle the ship?'

'Yes. We are making water, but hands are at the pumps and I think we shall be well.'

'Good. Bring her along. I must let my chief know about this.'

'Yes.'

'See you later.'

Algy scrambled back along the wing to drop into the cockpit. 'The submarine has been at Kerguelen all along,' he told Bertie tersely.

'She's lying in the cove at the southern tip of the island, presumably the one where Biggles found the dump. The whaler tried to get in and was shelled. Axel says she was still there when he left. I'm getting back.'

The engines roared, and the aircraft, after cutting a creamy scar across the black water, rose into the air. Five minutes later it was down again, at its base. Algy jumped ashore and raced for the hut. As he neared it the door was thrown open and Biggles appeared, his face asking a question, as if he had seen Algy's haste.

'What is it?' he demanded sharply.

In a few words Algy reported the position.

'Stiffen the crows!' exclaimed Biggles furiously. 'And I didn't guess it. No matter. We should get him now. He can't have got far.'

'He'll dive when he sees us,' warned Algy.

'If he's out of the cove he will.'

'What then?'

'I'll bring him up with depth-charges.'

'You'll be more likely to sink him – and he's got the gold aboard.'

'Okay, then I'll sink him,' rasped Biggles. 'But I'm not letting him get away. He may still be in the cove, taking in oil or repairing his ship. If he is, we've got him. We'll shut him in.'

'How?'

'By blasting the entrance of the cove. It's very narrow. Or better still, we'll bottle him in by using the whaler as a block ship. We'll sink her across the entrance.'

'The owners won't be pleased if you sink their ship.'

'What's a whaler when five million pounds are at stake?' rapped out Biggles. 'I'll tell you what I'm going to do. Taking depth-charges I'm going to the cove, dropping you at the whaler on the way. Tell Axel to turn his ship round, and under all the steam he can raise make back for the cove. He's to get her crossways across the entrance and open his seacocks. If the sub tries to get out he must ram her. We shall already be there, holding her in. If von Schonbeck tries to get out I'll lay a couple of depth-charges across his bows. The great thing now is speed.'

'What do I do when the ship sinks under me?' asked Algy coldly.

'Swim,' answered Biggles shortly. 'But if you have any sense you'll have a boat ready to take the ship's company ashore. You should be able to hold the Nazis if they come for you. We'll do our best to help you. But the first thing is to get the sub bottled up. It's no use planning beyond that. Afterwards we'll see how things go.'

'And if the sub is already at sea?'

'I'll plaster her. If you see that happen tell Axel to bring the whaler here.'

'Okay,' agreed Algy.

'Let's get cracking,' said Biggles.

CHAPTER XIV

The Pace Quickens

With full tanks, two depth-charges, and the entire party on board, Biggles took off and raced low towards the last known position of the whaler. It was still there, so he landed, and after a few words with Axel, outlining the plan and telling him what he wanted him to do, leaving Algy on board he took off again and headed for the submarine's hiding-place. Fifteen minutes later it came into view, with oil spreading out in a broad fan-shaped stain from the narrow entrance, and from then on the action was swift and fierce.

It was at once evident that the aircraft had arrived just in time – in time, that is, to prevent the U-boat from gaining the open sea, where no doubt it would have submerged and perhaps disappeared for all time. The submarine, with von Schonbeck and several members of the crew on deck, was moving towards the channel at a speed which suggested that he had heard the aircraft coming and was now trying to extricate himself from a position that might well prove desperate. He had in fact almost reached the channel by the time the aircraft was over the scene.

The reception the *Tarpon* received was much as Biggles expected. No amount of camouflage could help the U-boat now. It could only fight. The crew jumped to their action stations and flak came streaming up. Biggles was ready for it. He promptly took evading action, and diving low dropped his first depth-charge in the channel, partly in the hope of blocking it by a landslide or to cause the U-boat to swerve. Not knowing the depth of the water in the cove, which might turn out to be too deep for salvage operations, he did not attempt to get a direct hit, which he might well have scored. In one respect he was successful. A great spout of water leapt high into the air. As it subsided it piled itself into a mighty wave which struck the U-boat a glancing blow across the bows before half burying her under foam which swept across her deck and carried overboard at least two members of a gun crew.

The effect of this was to throw the U-boat off its course so that for a little while it was in some risk of colliding head-on with the cliff. To save his ship von Schonbeck was forced to continue the turning movement. He made a half-circle, narrowly missing some rocks, so that by the time the manoeuvre was complete the U-boat was stern first to the entrance – a state of affairs which suited Biggles very well, for a start, anyway. All this time flak was coming up, and it continued to come up, so that conditions in the aircraft were far from comfortable. Indeed, as far as Ginger was concerned it looked like being the final showdown. Either the aircraft or the submarine, in service slang, was about to 'have it.' But as it turned out the end was not yet, although it was getting close.

Biggles, feeling that he now had the whiphand, sheered off a little to see what von Schonbeck would do. He was too old a hand to take more chances than were demanded. The Nazi did not keep him waiting. With its propellers creaming the water the U-boat turned again towards the entrance, as if determined at all costs to escape from the trap in which it now found itself. Biggles was equally determined that it should not get out. He waited a little while, turning constantly to spoil the aim of the gunners, and then went down in another steep dive. Von Schonbeck must have known what he intended, but there was nothing he could do about it. He had no room to manoeuvre, for any sort of turn would involve him in a collision with the cliffs guarding the entrance.

Biggles let go his second depth-charge, and this time it looked as if it would hit the U-boat. It nearly did. It burst so close that it half lifted the submarine out of the water, and at the same time threw her on her beam ends with such violence that before she could recover her steel hull had scraped against a projecting shoulder of rock with sufficient force to make her reel again. It was obvious to those in the air that she must have been damaged, and the action her commander took practically confirmed it. The U-boat began to travel hard astern towards the landing beach by the depot.

This Biggles only saw in a fleeting glance, for his attention was now fully occupied with the plane. A shell, one of the last to be fired, had burst under the tail unit, inflicting such damage as to cause it to become almost unmanageable. Indeed, for a minute or two, those on board thought they were quite out of control. Biggles managed to make some sort of recovery, but realising that it was not possible to remain airborne without risk of a serious crash he looked about for a place to get down. He might, of course, have landed on the water, but he felt it was almost certain that his keel had been damaged by shell splinters. Moreover, it would mean landing in the cove, in which case he would become a sitting target for the submarine's guns. That, obviously, was out of the question. The only flat area round the actual cove was the beach for which the U-boat was making. That, for equally obvious reasons, was no use. As far as the rest of the island within gliding distance was concerned there was only one reasonable area; this was what appeared to be a slightly undulating expanse of moss that topped the cliff near the entrance and fell back towards the main terrain of the island. It was on this that Biggles decided to put the aircraft down, so lowering his wheels he put the plan into execution. The aircraft bumped, bounced, bounced again, and then, dragging in the moss and squelching water under its wheels, it ran on to a groggy landing, to finish one wing down due to the wheel on that side sinking deep into the moss. A stream of machine-gun bullets whistling past the tip of the exposed wing made it abundantly clear that the airmen were not yet out of danger, although fortunately a long, low fold in the ground near the rim of the cliff protected the lower part of the aircraft, including most of the hull.

'Outside everybody,' snapped Biggles. 'Keep your heads down.'

Those in the machine jumped clear and dived for cover. A few more bullets came whizzing over, then an uneasy silence fell. With brackish peat water oozing through the moss under his weight, Biggles crawled to the top of the rising ground, and peeping over saw the U-boat, apparently beached, near the depot. Not a soul was in sight, so after watching for a little while he dropped back to the others.

'We've given von Schonbeck something to think about, anyway,' he announced, with satisfaction in his voice. 'All the same, we're not sitting very pretty ourselves. In fact, we seem to have arrived at a state of stalemate. The sub is damaged, no doubt of that, but how badly we don't know. Unfortunately we're on the carpet ourselves so there's nothing more we can do. What I mean is, if von Schonbeck decides that his damage isn't serious, and tries to rush the entrance, we've no means of stopping him. Our big chance is, right now, to block the entrance with the whaler and seal the submarine in before von Schonbeck can get moving again. The whaler isn't due yet, but she must be getting close. The next two hours ought to settle things one way or another.'

'In the meantime, old boy, what do we do?' demanded Bertie.

'First of all we'll have a look at the machine to see how bad the damage is,' answered Biggles. 'If we can't get her off again we're going to have an awful long walk home. If you like, Bertie, you can take a rifle and try sniping anybody you see moving about the sub, but they're either inside or else they've taken cover in one of the huts. Keep watch, but don't get sniped yourself.'

'Not me – no bally fear,' declared Bertie, going off to fetch the rifle.

Biggles and Ginger examined the machine. The damage was serious but not vital. Elevator controls had been cut and there were some nasty holes through the tailplanes, fin and rudder; but there was nothing that could not be repaired, temporarily, given time. Biggles decided to start work right away.

From time to time Bertie, from his selected position, passed back information. 'I think the blighters are inside their beastly sardine can,' he called. 'I can hear 'em banging about. Straightening things out, and so on. There's a lot of oil round her.'

'I should say von Schonbeck is doing some quick patching up with a view to getting out before we hit him again,' said Biggles. 'He must have seen us go down. He may think he has plenty of time. Our trump card, the whaler, will shake him when it turns up and sinks itself in the entrance of his bolthole. Keep an eye open for the ship, Bertie, and let me know when she turns up.'

Biggles and Ginger carried on with their work. Time wore on without any new development. A feeble sun, blinking mistily through the clouds, climbed over its zenith and began to sink towards the west.

'The tide's coming in. I believe it's floated the sub off the beach,' called Bertie.

A quarter of an hour later he spoke again. 'She's started her engines. She's moving.'

Biggles frowned. 'I shall be sick if she manages to slip out after all,' he muttered to Ginger.

'Is there nothing we can do stop her?'

'Not a thing,' returned Biggles. 'If the whaler doesn't turn up we're helpless – anyway, until we can get back to base for more depth-charges.'

'Here they come!' shouted Bertie. His rifle cracked, and cracked again.

The bang of a gun and the scream of a shell made Ginger jump.

'What goes on?' called Biggles.

'It's the whaler!' yelled Bertie. 'She's nosing into the entrance – didn't see her before – bally cliff was in the way. Jolly good show.'

Biggles and Ginger dropped what they were doing and, crouching low, ran to the top of the rise. Biggles took one look and snapped: 'Get another rifle, Ginger.'

A three-sided battle, if battle it can be called, now developed. The U-boat directed its fire against the whaler, whose purpose by this time must have been apparent. A machine-gunner, from behind a steel shield, directed his fire along the top of the cliff to protect the submarine's gun crews at whom Biggles and Bertie were sniping. This state of affairs, however, did not last long, one reason being that the whaler was now in the channel, and it was evident that should a collision occur between the whaler and the U-boat, the latter would get the worst of the deal. The submarine stopped, and then began to back towards the beach she had just left. Its guns continued firing and the whaler came in for a good deal of punishment.

'They've done their stuff,' said Biggles suddenly. 'Axel has opened his seacocks. The whaler's settling down. Von Schonbeck must realise it. He knows it's all up. At least, he knows he'll never get out of that cove without a lot of high explosive to shift our block-ship. I can see Algy. They're lowering a boat – about time, too. Not seeing the machine Algy will wonder what has happened to us. We'd better let him know where we are so that he can join us.' Dropping back and crouching low to keep out of sight of those on the U-boat, Biggles ran along the top of the cliff to a point immediately above the whaler. Then, by shouting, he made contact.

It was half an hour before the crew of the whaler joined those on the cliff, for as they were unable to scale the cliff with two wounded men the boat had to be taken to a beach outside the entrance and a landing effected there. However, at the end, the two parties were united on the cliff near the aircraft.

Algy arrived smiling. 'We've put the cork in the bottle,' he announced. 'Von Schonbeck is inside for keeps.'

'He's inside for some time, anyway,' agreed Biggles. 'But I wouldn't bet too much on keeping him there indefinitely. He's a cunning devil.' Briefly he explained how the aircraft came to be grounded.

'What's the next move, then?' asked Algy.

'I haven't decided yet,' answered Biggles. He glanced at the sky. 'It's getting dark. We look like being here for the night. Von Schonbeck may not be content to leave us here though, covering the submarine, and the entrance to the channel, as we do; so we'd better get into some sort of position for defence.' Biggles broke off and thought for a moment. 'I think the time has come to let Raymond know how things stand,' he continued. 'With the U-boat immobilised, von Schonbeck could do nothing even if he picked up the signal. Yes, I think that's the best thing. I shall have to remain here to see what happens. The machine should fly all right now, although it wouldn't do to chuck it about. I'll tell you what, Algy. Take Bertie and the wounded Norwegians with you and push along to the base. Make radio contact with Raymond. Tell him the story and how we're fixed. Ask him for instructions, or, alternatively, ask him to do something about it. Daylight should last just about long enough to see you home. In the morning you'd better come back here to let me know what Raymond says. Meanwhile, the rest of us will stay here and keep an eye on things. Von Schonbeck may try something. A Nazi of his type isn't finished until he's dead.'

'Okay,' agreed Algy. 'You're sure the machine's all right?'

'She'll fly, and your engines are okay, but you may find her a bit groggy on rudder control.'

Algy nodded, and moved quickly to carry out his instructions, for the light was fast fading. The wounded Norwegians were lifted into the machine. Bertie followed.

'Don't let that blighter do us out of the gold,' he adjured Biggles. 'I've always wanted a nice big piece of gold to play with.'

'I'll watch it,' promised Biggles smiling.

With no small anxiety those who were to stay watched the machine take off and disappear into the northern sky. No flak came up. In the vicinity of the submarine all remained quiet. The only sounds were the murmur of the eternal waves fretting along the shore, and the plaintive cries of the gulls.

'Tomorrow, I think, should see the showdown,' opined Biggles.

CHAPTER XV

The Clock That Ticked Again

Dawn broke dull and drear, with a suspicion of frost and a threat of snow in the air. It found the little party on the cliff chattering with cold, and, with the exception of Biggles, who appeared oblivious to weather conditions, with small enthusiasm for the work ahead. Even Axel, who was on watch, glowered into the thin grey mist that enveloped them, reducing visibility to a hundred yards so that the submarine could not be seen, although its position could, with fair accuracy, be judged. No sound came from the U-boat. In fact, it was a long time since any sound had been heard, apart from the lap of water against rock.

Ginger spoke. His face was pale and nipped from the penetrating cold. 'I wish this infernal mist would lift,' he muttered. 'Algy will never risk flying in this stuff.'

'The trouble is, at this time of the year it may go on for days,' answered Biggles. 'We've got to be prepared for that. On the other hand it may blow away. It only needs a slant of wind to shift it, and wind is a common commodity in these parts.'

'What the dickens are we going to do?' asked Ginger. 'If we go on sitting here I'm liable to die of starvation – if I don't freeze to death first.'

'I've no intention of staying here,' returned Biggles. 'That silence across the cove isn't natural. Von Schonbeck should be doing something. Dash it, he *must* be doing something. But what? I'm going to find out.'

Ginger's eyebrows went up. 'You mean, you're going to have a crack at him?'

'Not necessarily,' answered Biggles. 'But if this fog doesn't clear in an hour I'm going to make a reconnaissance of the beach to find out what is going on there.'

'Alone?'

Biggles considered the question. 'No,' he decided. 'In this sort of weather I'm all against breaking up my force while it can be kept intact. There are nine of us all told, and with pistols and rifles we're pretty well armed. Just how many men von Schonbeck has available we don't know, but he hasn't as many as he had. We've whittled them down a bit. Assuming that he started with twenty he can't have more than ten or a dozen left. Of course, they're better equipped than we are because they've got machine-guns, but even so I think we ought to be able to put up a fair show if it comes to a scrap.'

After that they fell silent again. It grew a little lighter, but the mist still clung like a clammy veil to the knoll on which the party squatted. Biggles looked at his watch and got up.

'Okay,' he said. 'I'm not waiting any longer. Let's move along and see what goes on. We'll form up in line, keeping in sight of each other, and move slowly down the hill to approach the beach from the rear. If there's trouble we can retreat back here. I don't think von Schonbeck will risk trying to dislodge us because he would be bound to have casualties, and if he loses any more of his crew he won't have enough to man his ship. All right, let's move along. No talking. We shall be able to move quietly over this moss. With luck we ought to be able to get pretty close to the submarine without being seen. If we can pick off a few of them so well and good, but I don't want any firing until I give the word. Is that clear, Axel?'

Axel answered that he understood perfectly, and repeated the orders in his own language to those of his countrymen who knew no English. The party, keeping in line and with weapons at the ready, then moved off, descending a long incline which ended at the same level as the beach and perhaps a quarter of a mile from it, with a fold of rising ground between the two areas. Ginger moved next in line to Biggles. The uncanny silence persisted. With deep moss underfoot the advancing party might have been a line of slate-coloured ghosts.

The first objective, the dip at the foot of the incline, was reached without incident. Still no sound came from the submarine, and to Ginger the eerie silence took on the unreal character of a dream. In the dip Biggles halted the line by a signal, and by a sweep of his arm swung it round directly towards the beach. The march was resumed. Still no sound came from the submarine.

The near end of the beach came into view and the advance became more cautious. At the point where the moss gave way to shingle Biggles halted and peered ahead, eyes trying to probe the mist. He could just vaguely make out the shape of the U-boat, but it was still indistinct and there was no movement of any sort. He went on again, his body tense, pistol gripped in his right hand, halting for a moment after each step. Still nothing happened. Gradually things began to take shape – the hull of the submarine with the conning tower rising from it, a line of debris along the high-water mark and the squat stone houses beyond.

Biggles beckoned Ginger nearer. 'Pass word along the line to beware of booby traps,' he said softly. 'There may be an ambush. If firing starts remember that we retire on the knoll.'

Ginger nodded and went off on his errand, leaving Biggles staring at the submarine.

By single paces Biggles advanced again, eyes switching from one object to another, nerves braced from the strain of expecting every step to end the uncanny silence.

Still nothing happened. A black-headed gull swung on rigid pinions over the steel hull and with a mournful cry soared into the mist whence it had appeared. Biggles went on until he stood near the water's edge less than twenty paces from the U-boat. Dirty, oil and weather-stained, it had the appearance of an abandoned hulk. The conning tower was open. He stood there motionless, surveying the scene, for perhaps five minutes. Then he signalled to the party to rally on him. One by one they came, in silence.

Said Biggles to Ginger, who was the first to arrive: 'If this is a trap it ought to have been sprung by now. I don't get it. There's something unnatural about this set-up. What the devil is von Schonbeck doing? He can't have just shut himself up in his ship.'

'Maybe they're in one of the huts,' suggested Ginger.

'Even so, you'd think they'd put out a guard, and a guard would have seen us by now – unless he's asleep; and I can't imagine anyone under von Schonbeck's command going to sleep on duty. However, we'll soon settle it. Stand fast while I have a look round.'

Standing on the beach Ginger watched Biggles advance warily to the nearest hut, look inside, and pass on to the next. It seemed to be asking for trouble. Every second he expected to hear a shot and see Biggles fall, and cold as he was, perspiration broke out on his forehead from the strain of waiting. He drew a deep breath when Biggles came back and joined the party.

'They've pulled out,' he said shortly. 'It's the only possible answer. That's something I did not expect … unless…?' Biggles walked on a little way and then, stopping suddenly, pointed to a line of torn and buckled plates in the submarine's side. 'That must be the answer,' he said. 'That must have happened when she collided with the rock. Von Schonbeck daren't take his ship to sea in that state, and I doubt, even if he had unlimited time at his disposal, whether he could make good the damage. Yes, that's it. Bottled in by the whaler and with his ship out of action he must have decided that nothing was to be gained by staying here. He's taken to the country. Watch your step. Don't forget what happened the last time we were on this beach.'

'What are you going to do?' queried Ginger.

'We might as well have a look inside the ship as we're so close,' answered Biggles.

'But von Schonbeck wouldn't leave the gold behind,' asserted Ginger.

'No. If they've gone I imagine they'll have taken it with them, or buried it somewhere,' returned Biggles. 'But we'll have a look round inside all the same.'

Motioning the others to wait, taking Ginger with him, Biggles waded out to the U-boat, climbed on board the deck and made his way to the conning tower. At a distance of half a dozen paces he halted and called sharply. 'Von Schonbeck!'

There was no answer.

Biggles called again. 'I'm waiting for you,' he added.

Still no answer.

Biggles shrugged. 'I don't think he's here,' he said in a low voice. 'We'll soon make sure.' He went on to the conning tower, mounted it and looked down. For perhaps half a minute he waited. Then he climbed in and disappeared from sight.

Ginger hurried after him, and looking down saw Biggles standing pistol in hand at the foot of the steps near the periscope control. He went down and, joining his chief, looked about him with curiosity, conscious of a queer sensation now that he was actually standing in the ship they had come so far to find. All around were the intricate instruments and equipment of the U-boat. He noticed a conspicuous clock. It had stopped at one minute to twelve. An unnatural hush possessed the ship, unnatural because with so much mechanism about he felt that some of it should be working. But nothing moved. The silence was the dead utter silence of the tomb.

It was perhaps on this account that a sound, when it came, was all the more noticeable. Without speaking Biggles moved forward a few paces, quietly, to get a clearer view of the gangway leading aft. It was as he did this that the sound came. The clock had begun to tick. Biggles' eyes flashed to it, so did Ginger's. Biggles looked at the steel floor on which they stood. Ginger's eyes followed, wonderingly, surprised and not a little alarmed at the sudden stiffening in Biggles' attitude. He saw, lying across the floor, a thin strand of copper wire, a strand so fine that had it not been for the light catching its untarnished surface it would not have been noticeable. It was broken, and lay curled back upon itself like a spring.

Biggles spoke. He said one word. He uttered it in a voice so clipped that Ginger obeyed it on the instant. The word was; 'Bolt!'

Even as Ginger shot up the conning-tower steps he had a shrewd idea of what was happening, or what was about to happen. Reaching the deck he did not stop, but ran along to the nearest point of the beach, jumped ashore, and went on running. He could hear Biggles close behind him. 'Bolt!' he shouted to Axel, who, with his rifle half raised, was looking at him in astonishment.

'Run for your lives!' shouted Biggles, as he took a flying leap on to the shingle.

The entire party raced along the beach.

It had covered about a hundred yards when from behind there came such an explosion as Ginger had never heard. An instant later

Biggles, pistol in hand, stood at the foot of the steps.

what felt like a solid wall of air struck him in the back and threw him forward on his face. Half dazed by the shock he started to pick himself up, aware that there were others in positions similar to himself. A movement behind made him turn still further. He was just in time to see the submarine settling back into the water. The centre part was still raised high, but it had broken across the middle. Above it towered a mighty column of smoke. From the beach near the entrance of the cove sped a terrifying tidal wave. It struck the cliffs that guarded the entrance flinging spray nearly to the top, and then rebounded.

'Look out!' shouted Biggles, and scrambling to his feet made for the rising ground behind the camp.

The wave, with the relentless force of an express train, came after them. It all but had them. The curling crest crashed forward and down some thirty yards behind them so that the spreading rush of water licked their heels. Then it was all over. The wave receded. The water in the cove boiled for a little while, then fell quiet. Hard against the beach lay the U-boat, its hull distorted, its back broken.

Biggles sat and looked at it for a minute without speaking. Then he laughed quietly. 'What a beauty,' he murmured.

'What's a beauty?' demanded Ginger.

'That booby trap,' answered Biggles. 'I never saw a better one.'

'We nearly didn't see that one,' growled Ginger.

'You're right. It was pretty close,' admitted Biggles. 'Had we been talking we shouldn't have heard the clock start ticking, and had the clock not started ticking I shouldn't have spotted that wire.' He smiled. 'If we hadn't spotted the wire we should have made the fastest take-off ever. I should think the bomb, or whatever it was, exploded in the U-boat's remaining store of torpedoes and shells. Von Schonbeck must have heard the bang. From where he is he can probably see the smoke. Only an intruder in the submarine could have set off the bomb, so by this time he is no doubt having a chuckle at our expense and patting himself on the back for his ingenuity. He's justified, mind you. He might have got the lot of us at one go. He's going to have a horrid disappointment though when we turn up again.'

'Algy and Bertie must have heard that bang, too,' remarked Ginger. 'They'll be worried.'

Biggles glanced at the sky. 'The murk's lifting,' he observed. 'A clear sky will bring Algy along hotfoot to see what goes on. Hark!'

Faintly on the still air came the drone of an aircraft.

Ginger cocked an ear and listened. 'Okay – that's the *Tarpon*,' he announced. 'Algy has only to make a dud landing now and we *are* in the soup.'

'Let's go back to the cliff and show ourselves,' suggested Biggles.

CHAPTER XVI

Biggles Offers Terms

The party hastened back to the top of the hill. By the time they had reached it the mist had been lifted by a watery sun and the aircraft was circling preparatory to coming in. To Ginger's unspeakable relief it made a safe landing, whereupon the party moved forward to meet Algy and Bertie who now descended.

Algy's first words were: 'What the deuce was that bang?'

Biggles told him, jerking a thumb in the direction of the shattered U-boat. 'Did you make contact with Raymond? That's the important thing at the moment,' he asked.

'Yes, we got through without any trouble,' returned Algy. 'It took some time but I gave him the complete gen.'

'What did he say to that?' inquired Biggles.

'He said okay, stand by.'

Biggles frowned. 'Stand by for what?'

Algy shrugged. 'He didn't say.'

'Well, I call that pretty good. How long does he expect us to stand here?'

'I imagine he'd have to do some thinking before he made a plan of operation.'

Biggles nodded. 'Maybe he thought it unwise to announce his plans over the air in case the wrong people picked up the signal.

All the same, I wish I knew what he intended doing. Von Schonbeck is on the move; he's got the bullion with him so it won't do to leave him too long to his own devices.'

'But he can't get off the island, old boy – if you see what I mean?' put in Bertie.

'I'm not so sure of that,' answered Biggles, looking round. 'That fellow will be a menace until he's dead and buried.'

'But even if he got away he couldn't take the gold with him,' said Algy.

With his hands thrust deep in his pockets and his head bent, Biggles paced up and down. 'Let's try to get the thing in line,' he said curtly. 'Von Schonbeck knew that he was in a trap – there was no escape out of the cove, anyway. The only course for him, when you come to think about it, was to retire to the interior of the island taking the gold with him. What next? Well, five million in gold is something. A man with five million pounds' worth of metal is in a position to bargain.'

'For what, old lad? I don't get it,' murmured Bertie, polishing his eyeglass.

'His life, for one thing. Suppose he buries that gold. Who is going to find it on an island this size? That you can't dig up an entire island is proved by the fact that there is still a twelve-million-pound treasure on Cocos Island, although scores of people have tried to find it – and Cocos is nothing like the size of Kerguelen. Very well. Let us say we go after von Schonbeck and catch him. Or suppose the Government landed troops here and rounded him up. He just smiles blandly and says okay. Hang me if you like, but if you do bang goes your gold. He may say, let me go and I'll tell you where the gold is. So what? The gold doesn't mean much to us. For one thing it isn't ours, anyway. But the people who actually own the gold might be willing to bargain. What is one man's life to a fortune? But it may not come to that. The point is, von Schonbeck, by pulling out, is still at large with the gold. He's gaining time if nothing else. If he could get away, get clear of the island, he might return later for the gold.'

'How could he get away?' asked Algy. 'If we leave him here he's likely to be marooned for the rest of his life.'

'Don't you believe it,' said Biggles scornfully. 'To start with I've got an idea that he's got a boat with him. They were using a collapsible boat to repair the damage round the stern of the U-boat at Corbie Island. That boat was housed just aft of the conning tower – but it wasn't on the sub when we boarded her just now. Von Schonbeck may have that boat with him. The scoundrel is a seaman – we must grant him that. With decent weather he might push off and make a landfall at some other island. Long trips have more than once been made in an open boat. Of course, he wouldn't be so crazy as to attempt to take the gold; but if he got away he'd find it easy enough to come back later on, in a ship of some size, and collect the bullion. Amongst the German settlements in South America he'd find plenty of ships' captains willing to take a chance on that.'

'This is all supposing that he has a small boat,' put in Axel, who had followed Biggles' argument with profound interest.

'All right, let's suppose he hasn't a boat,' replied Biggles. 'That doesn't mean we can just stand bye waiting for Raymond to do something. If once von Schonbeck gets into the mountains of the interior it would need an army to get him out. To bring here the number of men that would be required for the search, together with stores and equipment, would cost nearly as much in cash as the gold is worth. What would be the alternative? To leave him here, marooned? To leave that bunch of Nazis on the loose would be like leaving a pack of wolves. Don't forget that once in a while ships call here – whalers, sealers, and so on. Von Schonbeck and his bunch would grab the first one to come in, scupper the crew and get away with it. One factor which we must never forget is this; von Schonbeck knows that his neck is practically in a noose if he is caught, and desperate men take chances.'

'So what's the answer?' asked Ginger helplessly.

'There can be only one,' returned Biggles. 'We've got to go after von Schonbeck. We've got to locate him, watch him, and if possible keep him on the move, so that he gets no chance to bury the gold. I needn't point out the snag in that. We've got to find him and catch up with him before darkness falls. Give von Schonbeck one night in these hills and if I know the man he'll appear tomorrow without the gold. He can't have got a great way yet. Hearing the explosion he may take his time, supposing that we've been blown sky-high as he intended, and as we jolly nearly were.'

'And having spotted him what do we do about it?' asked Ginger, a trifle sarcastically. 'Our rifles and pistols will make a poor showing against the machine-guns which we know they've got – at least, I imagine they won't have left them behind.'

'I'll grant you that,' agreed Biggles. 'All I can say is, we'll deal with that situation when the time comes. Man for man we must be pretty evenly matched.'

'The first thing is to find the blighters – find 'em, that's the thing,' declared Bertie.

'Bertie,' said Biggles evenly, 'you've said it. Let's get mobile.'

'We can't all get in the plane,' Axel pointed out.

'There's no need – yet. I'll take my three friends with me. You'll stay here with your party, Axel, and keep guard over the remains of the submarine. Should by any remote chance reinforcements arrive from my chief, Air Commodore Raymond, you can tell them where we are and what we are doing.'

Leaving the Norwegians on the cliff the others climbed into the aircraft. Biggles took off and headed for the interior of the island.

'See what I mean about looking for a few men in that mess,' he remarked to Ginger, indicating the gaunt rugged mountains which piled up behind rolling foothills that came down nearly to the sea. 'Finding a needle in a haystack would be easy compared with digging out a handful of men from that mass of rock. But von Schonbeck can't have reached the mountains yet.'

'This is not going to be a very nice place for a forced landing,' murmured Ginger, regarding the terrain below and in front of them with misgivings, and remembering the patched-up condition of their aircraft.

Biggles smiled faintly. 'We've flown over worse country.'

'Maybe, but I don't think you ever heard me say that I enjoyed it,' replied Ginger.

The unexplored interior of the island now presented a panorama as forbidding as could be imagined. Near at hand, the first impression was of a bleak, lonely expanse of rolling moorland, dotted everywhere with dark grey stone, either loose boulders or outcrops of the bedrock. The low areas were occupied by sheets of black, evil-looking water of unknown depth. Beyond this foreground, as the terrain rose it broke into tier after tier of rock ridges terminating in a tremendous massif of peaks, with glaciers streaking the ravines and depressions. What lay in the valleys between the mountain ranges was a matter for conjecture, for all that could be seen from the air was sombre shadows through which water, spilling off the rock slopes in numerous falls and cascades, forced a tortuous course. In one place smoke rose in a tenuous cloud, betraying the volcanic nature of the island. Looking at this harsh picture Ginger found it easy to understand why the island had never been properly explored, much less surveyed.

Biggles pointed to a pass that cut through the nearest range; it looked as though it had been smashed open by a giant axe. 'If von Schonbeck wants to get into the mountains that's the way he'll go,' he asserted. 'There's no other way that I can see. We'll try that one first, anyway.'

The *Tarpon*, flying at a thousand feet, roared on, and five minutes later Biggles' surmise matured into fact. 'There they are,' he said briefly.

Peering down the others saw a line of men, mostly in pairs, moving like sluggish ants towards the pass. They were as yet perhaps two miles from it, having covered some ten to twelve miles since leaving the sea.

'The dirty dogs haven't made a lot of ground,' observed Bertie.

'That ground is probably a lot rougher than it looks,' answered Biggles. 'Moreover, they wouldn't be able to take a straight line. They'd have to go round the lakes, and those outcrops of rock. Apart from that, look at the loads they're carrying.'

'The bullion boxes,' breathed Ginger.

'That's why they're marching in pairs,' said Biggles. 'For two men one of those boxes must be a heavy load; but von Schonbeck isn't going to leave it behind – no fear. There he is, marching ahead. He's looking up at us – you can see his face.'

'They haven't got the boat with them,' observed Algy.

'They may have parked it somewhere near the sea. As it is, they're carrying about as much as they can manage.

Ginger could see the men. 'Fourteen,' he counted aloud. 'One way and another we seem to have accounted for a few since we started.'

'How about accounting for a few more?' suggested Algy. 'Our fixed guns need warming up – we haven't used them yet.'

Biggles did not answer immediately. He went into a wide flat

turn, watching the men below struggling on, obviously with difficulty, towards the hills.

'We can't go on flying round them indefinitely. Next thing we
shall be out of petrol,' prompted Ginger.

'I'm going to give them a chance,' decided Biggles.

'Nobody in his right mind gives a mad tiger a chance,' growled
Ginger. 'Nazis don't appreciate chances; they've proved that often
enough. A chance will only give von Schonbeck an opportunity to
trick you.'

'I don't think he'll do that,' returned Biggles softly. 'I can't help
feeling that some of those men may be ready to pack up. They must
know the game is finished. I hate killing a rat in a trap. A beast
can't help being what it is. Pass me that message bag – or, better
still, take over for a minute. Don't go too close to them.'

Ginger glanced at Algy, smiling wanly. Bertie's eyes met theirs
in turn. Each knew he was thinking the same thing. This was
Biggles all over. Having got his man on the spot he had to give
him a chance. That was his code, just as von Schonbeck's code was
the Nazi code. It seemed silly – yet was it? wondered Ginger. A lot
of people around the world respected this strange British idiosyn-
crasy.

They watched Biggles write his message, and sign it. He read it
over to them: 'Pack up. Leave the gold where it is. Start marching
back and you will be treated as prisoners of war. Suggest you let
your men decide for themselves. Continuance towards the mountains will signify your refusal of these terms, in which case we shall
take action to stop you.'

Flying on over the fugitives he dropped it overboard. It fluttered
down. Watching, those in the *Tarpon* saw it strike the ground about
a hundred yards from the men, who halted while one of them ran
out, picked it up and handed it to von Schonbeck. Dropping their

loads the Germans mustered round their leader in a little group, a position in which they remained for some minutes, during which time the aircraft continued to circle.

'What goes on?' muttered Ginger suspiciously.

'They're probably talking it over,' returned Biggles, banking slightly to keep a clear view below. 'Hello!'

The ejaculation was prompted by a sudden movement. The group broke up in a manner which could only mean disagreement. Five men broke away from the main body and started running. Guns flashed. Puffs of smoke spurted. Three of the runners fell. One turned and fired back at the main body, scoring a hit. The two surviving runners went on to take cover behind an outcrop of rock.

'Some of them have had enough, anyway, and I don't wonder at that, when they see what's ahead of them,' murmured Biggles. 'Amazing, isn't it, how these Nazis so often finish up by shooting each other. God save us from such a hellish creed. Well, it looks as if von Schonbeck has decided to go on. He has lost six more of his men. That leaves eight. Yes, there they go. They're having to abandon some of the gold, but they're hanging on to as much as they can carry. Gold. Gold and blood. The old, old story. Funny how the two things go together. Well, if that's how von Schonbeck wants it, that's how he can have it. Hold your hats – we may get something back.'

Biggles swung the *Tarpon* round and put his nose down in a steep dive.

A line of tracer bullets rose gracefully to meet it.

Short jabbing flames spurted from the muzzles of the *Tarpon*'s twin guns. Two lines of bullets flashed down.

CHAPTER XVII

Clean-Up On Kerguelen

The result of the *Tarpon*'s dive was to send the U-boat crew running for cover, of which plenty was available in the form of loose rock. Two men fell, although one of them, apparently only with a slight wound, continued to crawl on to what he evidently considered a safe place.

'That leaves six,' muttered Biggles, as he zoomed up after the attack. On the ground, all that could now be seen were the gold boxes, lying where they had been abandoned.

'Now what?' inquired Algy. 'You can't get 'em while they stay as they are. They can afford to stay there, but we can't hang around. As soon as it's dark they'll push along into the hills.'

'Every word you say is true,' agreed Biggles. 'That's why we can't allow that to happen. I'm going down.'

Ginger looked startled. 'You mean – land?'

'There's nothing else we can do,' averred Biggles. 'It will start to get dark in an hour or two. We shan't have time to go home for more petrol. We'll settle this business right here and now. I'm not going to risk losing touch with von Schonbeck at this stage of the proceedings.'

'It'll be four of us against six, old boy,' Bertie pointed out.

'Oh no it won't,' returned Biggles evenly. 'As soon as we're on the carpet Algy can take off again and fetch Axel and his Norwegians. I'm sure they'll be glad to be in at the death.'

'By Jove! I say, that's an idea,' declared Bertie.

'Thank you,' acknowledged Biggles. 'The point is, where do we get down? I'd like it to be ahead of them if possible, or at any rate on their flank, so that we can keep them where they are. I hate walking, and if it comes to a race up those slopes we may lose.'

Casting about, Biggles descended on an area of what appeared to be smooth moss, between a quarter and a half a mile from the fugitives. Here, curiously enough – or it struck Ginger as curious at the time – there were no rocks; just a broad flat patch of thick sphagnum moss of many hues – green, yellow, orange, red. It was on this, after a cautious survey of the surface for obstructions, that Biggles landed. And as his wheels touched, and the full weight of the aircraft settled down on them, he knew that something was wrong. The machine rocked in a most extraordinary way, as if it were rolling on soft eccentric wheels. The others noticed it and looked through the side windows to see what caused the phenomenon.

Ginger cried: 'What the dickens!'

Then, suddenly, he knew. The aircraft was rocking, bouncing up and down with a slow sickening movement. All around, in the proximity of the aircraft, the earth seemed to be rocking, too. At first he thought that their landing had been coincidental with an earthquake – a not unnatural assumption, for that was the general impression created, and the island was, after all, volcanic. The moss was literally quaking – but not the distant view. The hills were steady enough. The quake was curiously local. It was when he realised this that the first suspicion of the truth struck him, and when the truth did dawn on him his mouth went so dry with shock that he could hardly swallow.

The aircraft, still bouncing slightly, finished its forward run.

'Sit still everybody,' said Biggles, in a quiet but tense voice. 'We're on a bog.'

No one moved. No one spoke while the aircraft came gently to rest. The rocking movement ceased. The moss assumed its original firm appearance.

'Take it easy,' cautioned Biggles. 'Things may not be as bad as they seem.'

'I should jolly well hope not,' muttered Bertie, who had turned slightly pale, 'I once saw a chappie in a bog. He—'

'Tell us about it some other time,' interrupted Algy, through his teeth.

'Shut up a minute,' put in Biggles curtly. 'This is no time for fooling. You'd better get the hang of what's happened. We're on the worst sort of bog. What we have landed on is really a thick layer of scum, over water or soft mud, on which moss has grown. The scum is only floating. That's why it rocked when we touched down. The scum sagged under our weight. If our wheels break through the crust we can say goodbye to the aircraft. I should say the risk of that is pretty big at the moment because our weight is all concentrated on one spot. We must alter that. The only way we can do it is by getting out. Algy will stay. As soon as the others are out he'll take off – or try to.'

'What's wrong with taking off right away?' asked Ginger anxiously.

'I daren't risk trying to get off with this load on board. The lighter the machine the better chance she'll have.'

'Here, I say, old lad. You're not suggesting that Algy leaves us standing on this bally crust, or whatever it is?' said Bertie in a horrified voice.

'If we step out we're liable to go straight through,' asserted Ginger.

'Just a minute, don't get so excited,' snapped Biggles. 'Nothing much has happened yet, and nothing may happen. I'll get out first to test the ground.'

'Don't be a fool,' protested Algy.

'Don't worry. I'll take a rifle in each hand. If my legs go through the rifles will catch on the moss and support me. If that happens you'll have to haul me back and we'll try something else. The idea isn't original. In bog countries people walk about with a plank for the same purpose that I, not having a plank, am using the rifles. If the crust supports me – okay. The others will follow. Keep a fair distance apart. We'll make for the rising ground in front of us, where the rocks start. That's the end of the bog.'

'What about me?' demanded Algy, with some concern.

'You'll be all right,' declared Biggles confidently. 'Even if your wheels break through the wings will support the hull. Your job is to get off and fetch the Norwegians – but you'll have to find another place to land when you come back. I'll get out now. Sit still, the rest of you.'

The others watched while Biggles opened the escape hatch. Then, taking a rifle in each hand, and holding them as far away from his body as possible, he stepped out. His feet sank into the moss; black water oozed up round them, and the immediate area sagged a little under his weight; that was all.

'Okay!' he called. 'I think it's all right.' He thrust one of the rifles back into the cabin, and holding the other at right angles from his body he started walking slowly towards the nearest rocks, about a hundred paces distant. Slight as the movement was, it was sufficient to set the whole bog rocking again. Tense with suspense those in the aircraft continued to watch, watched while Biggles, maintaining an even pace, not even hurrying when he was near the rocks, made the passage.

Pent-up breath escaped from those in the aircraft when Biggles jumped to show that he was on firm ground. He sat on the nearest rock and waved.

'My godfathers!' exclaimed Bertie. 'What a bally nightmare. I'll go next.' Adjusting his monocle and taking a rifle he walked slowly to the rock where Biggles was waiting, smoking a cigarette.

Ginger followed. A few yards from the firm ground his impatience overcame caution and he made a rush for safety. Instantly his feet went through the scum and he found himself standing waist deep in coal-black mud. The others hauled him in.

'You dirty fellow,' said Bertie, wrinkling his nose. 'By gad! How the stuff stinks.'

'I thought I was going to be sick,' explained Ginger. 'That bouncing feeling got me in the stomach.' He wiped his forehead.

Biggles faced the aircraft and waved to Algy to take off. 'Von Schonbeck must have heard the machine land,' he told the others. 'If he sees it take off again maybe he'll think we're all away.'

There was no talking while Algy took off. For fifty yards the machine rocked as though it was riding an ocean swell; then Biggles drew a deep breath. 'It's all right,' he murmured. 'He'll make it. He's practically airborne.'

A few seconds later daylight appeared under the *Tarpon*'s wheels. Algy climbed a little way, and then, turning, headed back for the cove.

'We're well out of that,' observed Biggles. 'Let's see what von Schonbeck is doing.' Walking fast he struck off on a course which, he explained, he hoped would cut across the Nazis path before they could reach the comparative safety of the hills.

After five minutes' sharp walking, from the top of a rise the Nazi party came into view, less than a quarter of a mile away, still making for the pass. Progress was slow, for four of the men were staggering under a heavy weight.

'He's had to abandon most of the gold, but he's hanging on to as much as he can move,' observed Biggles. 'He can't bear to let it go. The gold bug must have bitten him badly, as it's bitten others. Well, he'll see where it will get him. Come on.'

The party now moved forward at the double, still taking a line that would cut off von Schonbeck from the hills. And this, curiously enough, was achieved before they were seen – or, at any rate, before von Schonbeck, perceiving his danger, took steps to prevent it. A shot rang out and a bullet zipped through the scrub near Biggles' feet. He dropped flat, motioning the others to do the same. 'This will do,' he said.

The Nazis had by this time taken cover, so that they could not be seen, but their position was revealed by some loud talking. In particular, von Schonbeck's voice could be heard, pitched high.

'I fancy he's having a job to hold his men together,' remarked Biggles.

A moment later three men broke cover and ran as if to take up fresh positions outflanking the attackers. Biggles fired. The man at whom he aimed stumbled and pitched forward on his face. Bertie and Ginger fired together, apparently at the same man. He fell. The survivor of this futile counter-attack, bending low and swerving, ran back. Biggles fired and missed.

'They won't try that again,' he observed. 'Two down … that leaves four. Apparently von Schonbeck intends to fight it to a finish. Well, that suits me.'

There was now a period of calm. Biggles worked his way forward a little, as did the others, to close the distance; but the Nazis were behind cover and could not be seen. Four bullion boxes had been stacked together, and Biggles suspected that the Nazis were behind them. Refusing to risk casualties by a frontal attack he began to creep towards a new position from which the boxes could be enfiladed; but by the time he had reached it twilight had dimmed the scene, and all that could be seen distinctly was the silhouette of the mountains against the sky. The rest of the world lay in shadow, vague, menacing, lonely. Somewhere in the distance a bird wailed. A salt wind, bitterly cold, sighed across the dismal moorland.

Presently, on this breeze, came a drone, a drone that grew swiftly stronger.

'Here comes Algy,' said Ginger.

'Goodness knows where he'll get down,' answered Biggles, looking worried. 'This is a tricky place at any time, but in the light I'm afraid it's asking for it. But there's nothing else for it.'

The aircraft came on, and presently it could be seen, flying low. The bog, apparently, was Algy's landmark, for he flew straight to it, and then came on to sweep low over the scene of operations. Whether or not Algy saw the opposing parties on the ground, was not, at this juncture, apparent. It turned out subsequently that he did not. Biggles dare not risk standing up for this would have meant exposing himself to the enemy's fire. However, Algy went on, and after circling once or twice went down. His engines cut out and the aircraft merged into the colourless background.

The others listened, trusting to their ears to tell them what their eyes could not. Every sound of an aircraft landing was of course familiar to them. They heard the hum of the wind over the lifting surfaces. Then came a sharp, vicious thud.

'He's hit a rock,' said Biggles in a hard voice.

Came another moment of silence; then a harsh, splintering crash.

'I was afraid he'd got it,' said Biggles evenly. 'Listen. We shall soon know how bad it is.'

Voices could now be heard, perhaps a quarter of a mile away – perhaps a mile. It was hard to judge distance. Biggles moved to a higher point and strained his eyes in the hope of making out the shape of the *Tarpon*, but in vain. The background was too broken up by rock. There was more talking; then a voice called an order sharply.

'That was Algy's voice,' declared Ginger.

'I don't think the crash could have been very serious,' said Biggles. 'They were too low – just gliding in; somehow we've got to make contact. We must let them know where we are or they may open up on us.'

'How can we make contact?' asked Ginger. 'The Nazis are between us. If we try to by-pass them it will be pitch dark before we get in touch with Algy.'

'There's only one way,' replied Biggles. 'We'll start the ball rolling. You and Bertie open up a brisk fire on those gold boxes while I move forward. Then I'll open up and cover you while you join me. Let's go. I'm getting cold.'

In accordance with this plan of attack Ginger and Bertie started firing at the gold boxes, the outlines of which could still be seen. Biggles dashed forward. There was answering fire from the boxes, but he ran fifty yards before he dropped, and bringing his rifle into action brought a quick fire to bear on the enemy's position. Bertie and Ginger appeared beside him. By this time weapons were flashing at several points.

'I think Algy has got the hang of it,' declared Biggles. 'He's got his fellows advancing, too.' Cupping his hands round his mouth he shouted: 'Algy! Can you hear me?'

An answering shout came across the solitude.

'Keep moving forward!' shouted Biggles. 'Close in on the boxes. They're straight ahead of you.'

For perhaps five minutes a minor battle raged, apparently without casualties on either side. Biggles and his party continued to advance in short rushes. Algy and his Norwegians did the same. Then, when they were within a hundred yards of their objective, the end came quickly.

A man sprang up from behind the gold boxes, and with his hands held high ran towards Biggles shouting 'Kamarad!' He did not get far. Another figure rose up behind him. A pistol flashed, and the would-be prisoner sprawled headlong.

'Nazis usually end by shooting each other,' said Biggles.

'Look out!' exclaimed Ginger sharply.

The man who had fired the last shot, instead of dropping back to cover had dashed forward. Bending low he continued to run. His figure and his peaked cap revealed his identity. It was von Schonbeck. He did not run towards either of the attacking parties, but went out towards the flank between them, as if concerned only with escape. Biggles sprang up and ran too, firing an occasional shot as he ran.

'Be careful!' yelled Ginger. 'That's the direction of the bog.'

Biggles knew it. He also had good reason to suppose that the Nazi did not know what he was heading for. He shouted to him to stop, not once but several times. Von Schonbeck's only answer was to turn and fire a shot from his pistol before going on.

Biggles followed. He was perhaps fifty yards behind von Schonbeck when the German reached the bog. He shouted a warning, dire, imperative, but the German ran on, with the ground under his feet beginning to rock with a long, ominous swell.

Biggles raced to the edge of the bog and then stopped. He shouted a final warning. Whether the German heard it or not, or whether, having heard it, decided to ignore it, will never be known. But he must have realised his danger, for instead of running in a straight line he began to swerve, as if seeking firmer ground. Once he turned and, poised unsteadily, fired another shot. Biggles returned it. Both missed. Von Schonbeck went on, running hard, dodging as he ran, presumably to escape the shots he thought might follow him.

In the end it was this method of retreat that destroyed him – or so it seemed to Biggles, who stood watching. Biggles was just beginning to get anxious, fearing that his man would reach the other side after all, when the Nazi, in making a swerve, stumbled and fell. There was a horrid sort of *plop*, something between a thud and a splash. Von Schonbeck did not rise. Where he had fallen appeared a black stain. It quivered for a little while, then settled down. The Nazi did not reappear. Silence settled on the scene.

Biggles pocketed his pistol and was tapping a cigarette on the back of his hand when Bertie and Ginger joined him.

Ginger stared out over the morass. 'Where is he?' he asked breathlessly.

'He's had it,' answered Biggles laconically, dropping into service slang. He pointed to the ominous stain. 'That's where he went through. Maybe it was the best way. It saves us the trouble of taking him home and saves the country the expense of a trial.'

Algy, Axel and the Norwegians came up to report that there were two dead Germans lying behind the gold boxes.

'Then that seems to be the lot,' observed Biggles. 'There's no longer any need for hurry. It's all over.'

CHAPTER XVIII

The End of the Trail

Algy jerked an apologetic thumb in the direction of the crashed *Tarpon*. 'Sorry I made a mucker of it,' he said moodily. 'I was in a hurry to get down. There was a place where I thought I could get in between some rocks, but I was wrong. I hit a lump at the end of my run and she tipped up on her nose. No one was hurt.'

'I wouldn't worry too much about that,' replied Biggles. 'It means that we shall have to walk home, and we had that in front of us, anyway – unless we were prepared to risk a night take-off and landing. It's— Hello! What the…!' He swung round as from near at hand suddenly burst the roar of a high-powered aircraft.

'A Nimrod!' cried Ginger in astonishment. 'What the deuce!'

'A Nimrod usually means there's an aircraft carrier in the offing,' said Biggles.

'Here, I say, by Jove! There's another!' exclaimed Bertie, dropping his monocle and catching it deftly in his left hand.

'It looks as if Raymond has decided to take a hand,' surmised Biggles.

'Trust reinforcements to roll up when the show's all over,' said Ginger, a trifle bitterly.

'I wouldn't say that,' reproved Biggles. 'Raymond wasn't long getting on the job, you must admit, when we told him we needed help.

Apart from that I'm relieved to know that we shan't be marooned on Kerguelen. I, for one, have seen enough of it.'

'Absolutely, old boy, absolutely,' murmured Bertie. 'Beastly place.'

'That Nimrod pilot has spotted us, but he has too much sense to try putting his kite down in this wilderness,' remarked Biggles, watching the nearest machine which, after circling overhead, made off in the direction of the cove. 'We'd better start walking,' he added.

'What about the bally gold?' inquired Bertie.

'Unless you feel like carrying it, it can remain where it is for the time being,' returned Biggles. 'There's nothing on the island likely to touch it. Let's get cracking.' He struck off at a steady pace in the direction of the cove.

It was a cold, hungry, weary party which, sometime before midnight, plodded back to the starting-point, although it must be admitted that the last few miles were shortened by the appearance of bright lights in the vicinity of the cove. While some distance from the beach, the superstructure of a tall ship, anchored just outside the entrance, became visible.

'It's a carrier all right,' declared Ginger. 'There she is.'

'Looks like the *Vega*,' said Biggles. 'She must have been lying somewhere handy to get here in such a short time.'

A figure moved forward out of the shadows. 'Quite right, Bigglesworth,' confirmed a voice – Air Commodore Raymond's voice. 'You didn't suppose I was abandoning you in these God-forsaken seas, did you?'

'I didn't even think about it,' replied Biggles. 'I was too busy looking for what I came here to find.'

'And you've found it, I see,' observed the Air Commodore, inclining his head towards the shattered U-boat.

'Yes, we found it,' agreed Biggles.

'Where's von Schonbeck?'

'He's somewhere between the top and bottom of a bog of unknown depth about twelve miles inland,' informed Biggles. 'I doubt if it's worth looking for him. Some of his men are lying about though, so you'd better send out a working party in the morning to tidy the place up.'

'And the gold?' There was more than a trace of anxiety in the Air Commodore's voice as he asked the question.

'That's kicking about, too,' announced Biggles. 'It's all yours.'

Raymond smiled. 'So you don't want it, eh?'

Biggles shook his head. 'All I want is a bath and a bed.'

The Air Commodore laughed softly. 'No doubt that can be arranged. Come aboard,' he invited, and walked towards a motor boat, manned by naval ratings, that waited near at hand. 'You'll be able to tell me all about it before you go to bed, I hope?' went on the Air Commodore anxiously. 'A lot of people at home are waiting to hear the story.'

'I'll see how I feel when I've had my bath,' answered Biggles noncommittally as the party filed into the boat.

Except for the inevitable official inquiry that was the end of what Biggles afterwards called 'their second case.' With their Norwegian allies they returned home on the *Vega*, an easy restful trip that occupied the best part of a month. Long before the carrier reached home waters Biggles had rendered a full report, with the result that much to his displeasure the newspapers had got hold of the story, and with no war news to occupy their columns had put it on the front page. The names of the officers concerned, however, were at Biggles' request, omitted.

'We've had all we want of von Schonbeck and his gang,' he told

Air Commodore Raymond, the first morning they reported for duty at their Scotland Yard office. 'As far as we're concerned it's all washed up. Think of something new.'

'I might even be able to do that,' answered the Air Commodore slyly.

'But not today, I hope?' put in Biggles coldly.

'All right – we'll leave it until tomorrow.' The Air Commodore went out, laughing.

BIGGLES BREAKS
THE SILENCE

CHAPTER I

Biggles Has Visitors

'As a job, ours is about the dullest ever. What's the use of having Air Police if there are no air crooks?' Air Constable 'Ginger' Hebblethwaite, of the Air Section, Criminal Investigation Department, New Scotland Yard, considered with moody impatience two of his colleagues, who were regarding him with sympathetic toleration from the depths of the armchairs in which they had slumped. One was Algy Lacey, and the other Lord Bertie Lissie, who for the purpose of his present duties had dropped his title.

Bertie polished his monocle with a screw of paper torn from the journal he had been reading. 'Absolutely, old boy. I couldn't agree with you more,' he agreed sadly.

'In the matter of entertainment it looks as if we shall soon be reduced to feeding the pigeons in Trafalgar Square,' observed Algy, yawning.

'For a bunch of disgruntled spivs you'd be hard to beat. Some people would call you lucky, being paid for doing nothing.' The voice came from the other side of the room, where Sergeant Bigglesworth, head of the Department, was regarding the street below through the window of his London flat in Mount Street, Mayfair. 'After all,' he went on, 'there were some air crooks when we started, which is why the air section was formed.'

'I know; but our mistake was we were in too much of a hurry to liquidate them,' grumbled Ginger.

'We did what we were paid to do,' Biggles pointed out.

'We left ourselves with nothing to do.'

'What's wrong with that? Can't you rest?'

'I shall have plenty of time to rest when I am drawing the Old Age Pension,' muttered Ginger.

'At the rate your fretting yourself to death you'll be lucky to see the colour of that money,' asserted Biggles cynically. 'But just a minute. Don't get excited, but I fancy we're going to have visitors.'

'What gave you that idea?'

'I can see two people coming along the pavement.'

'What makes you think they're coming here?'

'Deduction, my dear sir, deduction. As detectives our job is to deduct.'

'Then what about deducting a pound or two from the bank and going somewhere,' suggested Ginger.

'We may have to do that presently,' replied Biggles. 'I told you I could see two men on their way here. At any rate, they're looking at the numbers of the doors, and I've seen one of them before.'

'Where?'

'I don't know. I've seen too many faces in my time to remember them all.'

'What does this chap look like?'

'Young, clean-shaven, smart, fair-haired, walks as though he had been in one of the services.'

'That description would fit just about a million fellows in London today,' observed Ginger with mild sarcasm.

Biggles ignored the remark. 'The man with him is much older. Looks like a naval type. Yes, they're at the door.'

Biggles turned away from the window smiling faintly. 'You can

now amuse yourselves trying to guess where this visit will ultimately land us,' he added. 'You'll have noticed that our callers
usually want us to go somewhere and do something.'

'The penalty of fame, old boy, the penalty of fame,' murmured
Bertie softly.

'Well, I'm game for anywhere bar the North Pole,' declared
Ginger.

'Absolutely,' asserted Bertie. 'Beastly place. Frightfully cold, and
all that. No hot water for a bath. Miles and miles of absolutely
nothing at all – so I've been told.'

There came a tap on the door, which was opened to admit the
face of Biggles' housekeeper. 'Two gentlemen to see you, sir,' she
announced.

'Thank you, Mrs Symes. Bring them in,' requested Biggles.

The visitors entered slowly, and, it seemed, a trifle nervously. The
first was the fresh-complexioned lad whom Biggles had roughly
described. The other was much older, a shortish, heavily-built man,
with a rugged, square-cut face in which was set two of the bluest
eyes Ginger had ever seen. He wore a dark blue reefer jacket with
brass buttons, and carried in his hands a faded peaked cap.

Biggles indicated convenient chairs. 'Please sit down,' he invited.
'My name is Bigglesworth. I gather you want to speak to me.'

The younger of the two answered, in a Clydeside accent. 'Yes, sir.
You remember me, sir – L.A.C. Grimes, fitter aero. I was in your
Squadron in the Western Desert. The boys used to call me Grimy.'

Biggles' eyes opened wide. 'Of course. I knew I had seen you
before, but I couldn't remember where. One meets a lot of people in
the Service.' He held out a hand. 'How's civil life treating you?'

'Oh, not bad, sir,' was the ready answer. 'I've got a little business
of my own, a bicycle shop, in Glasgow. Trouble is, I can't get the
bikes. I've brought my father along to see you. He wants – well, we

both want – a bit of advice. I couldn't think of anyone better than you to ask. Hope you don't mind, sir.'

'Not in the least,' returned Biggles quickly. 'What can I do for you?'

The ex-airman looked at his father. 'You tell him, guv'nor,' he urged.

Biggles turned to the older man. 'Been in the Navy?'

Grimes, senior, cleared his throat. 'Mercantile Marine, sir,' he answered, in the rich Glasgow accent. 'Jumbo Grimes they call me, in the ports where sailors meet.'

'Why Jumbo?' inquired Biggles curiously.

The old man looked a trifle embarrassed. 'I once had to bring an elephant home from Bombay for the London Zoo. He didn't want to come. When we were at sea he got loose and sort of stirred things up a bit. The story got out and I've been Jumbo ever since.'

Biggles nodded, smiling. 'I see. And what's the trouble now?'

The sailor looked doubtful. 'It's a long story.'

'No matter. We're in no hurry. Take your time.'

'Well, sir, it's like this,' explained the sailor. 'I reckon I know where there's a pile of money waiting to be picked up.'

Biggles nodded slowly. 'I see. So in your travels you've tumbled on a treasure trove, eh, and you'd like to get it under your hatches.'

'Aye, that's right.'

'And what am I supposed to do about it?'

The old sailor looked a little taken aback at the directness of Biggles question. 'Well – er – I thought, mebbe—'

His son helped him out. 'We thought you might give us advice. I didn't know who else to ask.'

'What you really mean is, you thought I might do something about it myself,' suggested Biggles shrewdly. 'Am I right?'

L.A.C. Grimes moistened his lips nervously. 'Yes, sir. I reckon that's about the size of it.'

'Mercantile Marine, sir. Jumbo Grimes they call me.'

'You know, I suppose, that treasure hunts usually fail.'

'Well, it would be fun anyway,' averred Grimy.

'Very expensive fun for the man who provides the transport and foots the bills,' Biggles pointed out. 'But let's forget that for a moment,' he went on, selecting a cigarette from his case and tapping it on the back of his hand. 'Where exactly is this pile of wealth?'

Grimes, senior, answered. 'It's down near the South Pole,' he said weakly.

Biggles stared. 'Holy Smoke! That sounds like a tall order. Are you sure you're not making a mistake? I mean, what lunatic would bury a pile of gold in the South Pole?'

'Well, it isn't exactly a pile of gold,' admitted the sailor, looking somewhat crestfallen.

'What is it, then?'

'It's a crown.'

'A *what*?'

'A crown. A gold crown with diamonds in it.'

Biggles frowned. 'That doesn't make sense to me,' he asserted. 'How, may I ask, did a diamond-studded crown get to the South Pole? Have you seen it?'

'No.'

'Are you sure it's there?'

'Well, I'm not sure about the diamonds, but—'

The son, apparently not at all happy about the way things were going, chipped in. 'Tell him about it, guv'nor,' he urged.

Biggles dropped into a chair. 'Go ahead, we're listening,' he said, offering his cigarette case.

'Not for me, thanks, but I'll take a draw at my pipe, if it is all the same to you,' answered the sailor. He took from his pocket an old-fashioned silver-banded pipe, and from a coil of black plug tobacco cut with a ferocious-looking jack-knife a few slices, which he thumbed well in before applying the flame produced by a massive brass petrol lighter. He then emitted a blue reek of smoke of such pungency that Ginger backed hastily, stifling a cough.

'Well, sir, this was the way of it,' began the seaman. 'I was homeward bound from Shanghai when the Japs came into the war. My ship was seized and I was sent to a prison camp for the duration. The less said about that the better. When the war was over I had to see about getting home, but there was a lot of people besides me and not enough transport, which meant a waiting list. While I was waiting my turn in Hong Kong a fellow came to see me. His name was Lavinsky – or so he said, and it may be true for all I know. His nationality was a matter of guesswork. I could tell that from the way he talked. He spoke English well enough, although he certainly wasn't British. He mentioned one day that he was an Australian, but he didn't look like one to me. He was a bit too friendly with the Japs for my liking, too, but he explained that by saying he was in business in the Far East before the war, and I suppose that could have been true. Anyhow, he had a proposition to make, and this was it. He had got a ship, which he had sold to the Chilean Government provided he could deliver it to Santiago. I believed it at the time because I had no reason not to, and it sounded reasonable enough, but in view of what happened later I reckon that was all just a pack of lies. He was no sailor himself, you understand. He was looking for someone who held a master's ticket, and was willing to pay him well for taking the ship over. He'd be coming along as a passenger, he said. Well, it sounded fair enough, and as I had nothing better to do I said I'd go and cast an eye over this craft. One look should have told me that the whole thing was fishy, for of all the antiquated tubs I've ever seen she was about the worst. Her name was the *Svelt*, a Danish schooner with Italian engines, one of which wouldn't work and the other looked as though it would drop through the bottom any minute. My first impression was to have nothing to do with her, and I would have been right; but Lavinsky told me he had a Scotch engineer, which was true enough, and he would see that everything was all right before we started. Apart from that, I thought it might be easier to get home from South America than from China.' The sailor relighted his pipe, which had gone out.

'Well, three weeks later we put to sea with as motley a crew as ever stepped on board ship – men of every race and colour, to say nothing of half-breeds. Lavinsky had certainly collected the scum of the water-fronts. Not that that worried me. I learnt my trade in the old school and I'd handled tough crews before. The only real white man apart from myself was Neil McArthur, my chief engineer, God rest him. He also was fed up with hanging about Hong Kong. Lavinsky was there, with, if you please, a couple of Jap passengers who wanted – so he said – to get to South America. I didn't know they were below until we were well out of the harbour or I'd have put them ashore. Two smug guys they were – fairly fawned on me from the start. Not that that took me in for a minute. Not likely. It wasn't long before I twigged that these two beauties were the real owners of the ship. Lavinsky was only a stooge. I couldn't pronounce their real names, so I called them Shim and Sham for short. That was as near as I could get.

'Well, for a time it was all plain sailing. We had fair weather and it looked as if everything was going to be all right after all. Then Lavinsky started to take a particular interest in the ship's position. Trouble started when we were getting pretty close to our destination. Lavinsky came to me on the bridge and told me to take up a new course south. I asked him what for. He said there'd been a change of plan and his owners wanted him to run to Graham Land. When I'd recovered from the shock, I asked him what in thunder he expected to find in Graham Land, which sticks out from the

Antarctic ice pack. He said that was a private matter, but I should know all about it in due course. I said it wasn't in the contract, but he said he would make it right with me as far as money went. I didn't like it, and I said so. I began to smell a rat and an ugly one at that. I went below and had a word with Neil – Lavinsky and the rest of the crew watching me all the time. It began to look as if me and Neil were the only people on the ship who didn't know the real object of the voyage. Well, we could see there was going to be trouble if we refused to accept orders from the owners. I was thinking about my ticket. There wasn't a man on board who could have brought the ship to port without me and Neil, and had the ship been piled up somewhere there would have been a row over the insurance which might have put me ashore for good. Well, to make a long story short, I agreed to the new orders, but I made a note in the log that I did it under protest. The result was, a fortnight later we were groping our way through the big bergs and drift ice of the Bellingshausen Sea. When the real polar ice brought us to a stop I said, well, here we are, and I hope you like the scenery. What do we do next. But I'll tell you one thing, I said; if we get caught here in this ice your ship will crack apart like a matchbox under a steam-roller, and you'll have no more chance of getting home than a fly in a treacle jar.' The sailor thumbed the bowl of his pipe vigorously.

'Well, it didn't take me long to see what the game was,' he resumed. 'Seals. I had hitched up with a gang of seal poachers. I told Lavinsky what I thought about him and his pals. We had a first-class row, but with the whole ship's company against us, what could me and Neil do about it except threaten to report them when we got home. Mebbe I wasn't wise in saying that, as I realised later. We had still got to get home. Lavinsky offered me a share of the profits if I'd keep my mouth shut, but I told him I wouldn't touch his dirty money with the end of the mainmast. Things looked ugly.

Meanwhile, the slaughter of seals went on, and this was the state of affairs when a queer thing happened, something that put a new complexion on the whole expedition. We were drifting along near the ice ready to get out the moment we looked like getting caught, when, lo and behold, what do we see but the masts of a schooner sticking up out of the ice some distance back from the open water. She was fast in the pack, no doubt of that. Lavinsky went off to find out what ship it was. Shim and Sham went with him.

'They were away about a couple of hours, and when they came back I could see that something had happened. They were as white as ghosts and had a funny sort of wild look in their eyes. I asked them what they'd found, and they said nothing but an old hulk. There was nothing worth salvaging. I, of course, asked them for the name of the ship so that I could enter it in the log. Lavinsky said he couldn't make out the name, she was so smothered up in ice and snow – which was another lie, if ever I heard one. After that he couldn't get away from the place fast enough, which suited me, though I'd have given something to know what they'd found.'

Biggles interrupted the narrative. 'I take it they brought nothing back with them?'

'Not a thing. I'm sure of that.'

'But if they'd found something worth having they would hardly be likely to leave it behind,' Biggles pointed out.

'I think that's where you're wrong,' said the sailor thoughtfully. 'Had it been some jimcrack stuff they'd have brought it along, no doubt. But this was something big, and they didn't trust me. It wouldn't do for me to know what they'd found – not on your life. Anyway, there it was. I had orders to go back to Hong Kong. I didn't argue. I'd have gone anywhere to get off that crooked ship.

'A few nights later Neil came to me in my cabin. There was a funny look on his face. He said to me: "Do you know what Lavinsky found in that wreck?" I said "No." He said, "Well, I do. They found a gold crown studded with diamonds." I said, "How do you know that?" He said, "I've been listening to them talking outside Lavinsky's cabin. They were talking Japanese, but I happen to know a bit of the lingo, and made out something about a crown of diamonds.'"

At this point Biggles again interrupted. 'But that doesn't make sense,' he protested. 'No one would take a diamond-studded crown to the Antarctic; and, anyway, if one had been lost the world would have been told about it. Was Neil quite sure about these words – crown and diamonds?'

The sailor hesitated. 'Well, not exactly. The words were stars and crown, but he reckoned that stars could only mean diamonds.'

Suddenly a strange expression came into Biggles' eyes. 'Just a minute,' he said slowly. 'Just a minute. Stars and crown, eh? That rings a bell in my memory. Never mind. Go ahead. We'll come back to this presently.'

Jumbo Grimes, the sailor of the seven seas, continued. 'As we drew nearer to our home port I could sense a nasty sort of feeling on the ship. Mebbe it was the way Lavinsky and his pals kept clear of me, or the way the crew took to muttering in little groups. I sent for Neil. "Neil, we know too much," I said. "This crew isn't going to let us ashore knowing what we know. They'll go to jail for seal-poaching and they know it as well as we do. Keep your eyes skinned for trouble. It'll come, I reckon, when we are close enough to port for these rats to handle the ship for themselves." I was right, too, dead right. The night before we were due to dock Neil rang me on the telegraph to say that he was coming on deck for a breather and to have a word. Things were looking pretty nasty, he said. He never came. A few minutes later I heard a splash. I didn't pay much attention to it then, but as time went on and Neil didn't come I had an uneasy feeling what had happened. When I went below to find Neil he wasn't there. He wasn't in his cabin, either. Then I knew they'd heaved him overboard. So that's it, I thought. No doubt I'm next on the list. Well, I said to myself, we'll see about that. I slipped into my cabin and got the gun I always carry. When I got back to the deck there they were, waiting for me. What was I to do? Well, it didn't take me long to make up my mind. I couldn't hope to fight the whole bunch and get away with it. I knew that. So I blazed a couple of shots at them and then went overboard. We weren't far from land and I'm a pretty strong swimmer. It was pitch dark, and although they put a boat down to look for me I gave them the slip. I swam to the shore. It took me some time to make my way up the coast to Hong Kong, and when I got there I found that the *Svelt* had been in and gone. Lavinsky, I learned, had been looking for me. I told what I knew to the British Agent. What did it amount to? Mighty little. Anyway, the authorities had plenty to do, clearing up after the Jap occupation, without worrying their heads about a wild yarn such as mine must have sounded.' The sailor pocketed his pipe.

'Well, sir, that's about all,' he concluded. 'I was offered a chance to get home on the next boat and I took it. I told my boy here what I have told you, and he seemed to think that if we could get out to this old hulk we might pick up – well, some valuable salvage. The question was how to get there. Grimy said you might give us your opinion. You might even know someone who would – sort of – help us.'

A ghost of a smile crossed Biggles' face. 'I see,' he said softly.

'There is one thing I am sure of,' declared the sailor. 'Lavinsky didn't bring the crown away with him.'

'I'm quite sure of that, too,' said Biggles drily.

The mariner looked puzzled. 'Why are *you* so sure of that?'

'Because,' answered Biggles slowly, 'the crown he found would be too big, much too big, for him to handle.'

CHAPTER II

A Page From The Past

Captain Grimes stared at Biggles as if he doubted his sanity. 'I don't know what you're talking about,' he stated, with some asperity. 'How could a gold crown—'

'I'm not talking about a gold crown,' interposed Biggles quickly. 'There isn't a gold crown in the Antarctic, and there never was. Your assumption that there is one, or was one, is natural enough; but it was, after all, only surmise on your part. I suspect that the crown that Lavinsky found was a wooden one.' Biggles paused to smile at the expression on the seaman's face. 'You see, skipper,' he continued, 'unless I've missed my guess, what Lavinsky blundered on was the remains of an old schooner named the *Starry Crown*.'

Captain Grimes drew a deep breath. He looked crestfallen. 'Never heard of her,' he muttered.

'Very few people have, I imagine,' returned Biggles. 'I happen to have done so because unsolved mysteries have always interested me, and I pay a press-cutting agency to keep me informed about them or any subsequent developments. The *Starry Crown* sailed the seas in another generation. If my memory isn't at fault, she disappeared from sight about seventy years ago, on a voyage from Australia to London.'

'Well, knock me down with a marlinespike,' exclaimed the old

189

man disconsolately. 'Here am I kidding myself I'm on the track of a fortune.'

Biggles smiled again at the sailor's frank expression of chagrin. 'I didn't say you weren't,' he corrected. 'In fact, you probably are.'

The sailor looked up sharply, his shrewd eyes narrowing. 'Ah! Then there is something.'

'There was, and in view of what you now tell us, I'd say there still is. When the *Starry Crown* set sail she had on board about a ton of Australian gold, although how much of it remains under her hatches is another matter. Just a moment while I turn up my scrap-book; we might as well get our facts right.' Biggles went over to his files and put on the table a bulky album, from which the edges of newspaper clippings projected at all angles. He turned the pages slowly, and then apparently found what he was looking for, for he opened the book wide and read for some minutes in silence. 'Yes,' he said at last. 'I wasn't far wrong. The *Starry Crown* was a queer business altogether. She was a schooner of fifteen hundred tons. With a ton of gold on board she disappeared on a voyage from Melbourne to London. She was reported lost with all hands, and eventually the insurance money was paid. But that wasn't the end of the story. Twenty years later a whaler named *Swordfish* spotted the *Starry Crown* stuck fast in the polar ice-pack. The *Swordfish* herself was in a bad way. She had been driven south by northerly gales and her crew was down with scurvy. In fact, there was only one survivor, the mate, a man named Last. He died in Australia some years ago. It seems that after he got home he took into his confidence a man named Manton, presumably because he was the owner of a schooner, a vessel named *Black Dog*. The upshot was, naturally enough, that Last and Manton went off in the *Black Dog* to recover the *Starry Crown*'s gold. Things went wrong, as they usually do in treasure hunting. The *Black Dog* was caught between two bergs and crushed flat. The only two men to get ashore were Last and Manton. They may have been on the ice at the time. At any rate, after the *Black Dog* had gone down they were able to walk across the ice to the *Starry Crown*. They found things just the same as when the ship had been abandoned. The gold was intact, not that it was much use to the wretched fellows, who now found themselves prisoners on the Antarctic ice with mighty little hope of ever getting away. There was still a good supply of canned stores in the hulk, and other food which had been preserved by the intense cold, so they were in no immediate danger of starvation; but winter was setting in and their chances of being picked up were nil. To pass the time they amused themselves by dividing the gold between them. After some months the solitude drove Manton out of his mind, and he tried to murder Last. There was a fight, and it ended by Last shooting Manton dead. He buried him in the ice, built a cairn of ice blocks over his grave, and topped it with a board with the dead man's name on it. This done, to save himself being driven insane by the loneliness, he repaired the one small boat that remained on the *Starry Crown*. He then built a sledge, loaded the boat with some stores, and in the spring, when the ice began to break up, dragged the whole thing to the edge of the open water. All this occupied eight months. But his luck was in, for shortly afterwards he was picked up by an American whaler named *Spray*. He told the skipper some cock-and-bull story about losing his ship and being cast away, and eventually got home. But he never fully recovered and he died shortly afterwards. Before he died, however, he told the story of his adventures to a relation, who might well have wondered how much of it was true. Later on, apparently, this man told some friends about it, and the story got out, which is how we know what I'm telling you now. Of course, how much truth there is in it we don't know. Most people would probably take Last's story with a ladleful of salt. He may have tried to cover up some unsavoury event in his career. He may have gone really mad, like Manton, and imagined things. Anyway, as far as I know, no attempt has ever been made to check up on his story, presumably because nobody thought it worth while; but now, skipper, in view of what you tell us, it begins to look as though there was something in it. If the *Starry Crown* is still there, then the gold is probably there, too.'

'Didn't Last take any of it away with him?' asked Ginger.

'Apparently not. Would you, in such circumstances, load yourself up with a lot of useless weight? The man had plenty to haul over the ice as it was. His one concern, I imagine, was to save his life, and his hopes of that must have looked pretty thin.' Biggles closed the book. 'Well, that's all – so far. I say so far, because it looks as if the final chapter has still to be told, assuming that the *Starry Crown* is still there.' He turned to Captain Grimes. 'Did you make a note of her position?'

'Of course.'

'Did you tell Lavinsky?'

'No.'

'But he could have got your own position from the log?'

'He may have done that later, but, even so, as we were drifting all the time the position he got when we were near the *Starry Crown* would only be approximate.'

'Was the ice moving? I ask that because, if it was, the *Starry Crown* would naturally move with it. I understand that in the spring enormous fields of ice on the edge of the main pack break off and shift about.'

'That's right enough,' agreed the captain. 'It's the big danger any ship has to face – getting caught between two floes. The weight would crush any ship as flat as a pancake. There's no doubt the outer ice was on the move when I was there, but such movements are naturally slow. What you've got to watch, when you're close in, is that a piece doesn't get between you and the open sea and shut you in. That's what must have happened to the *Starry Crown*. It very nearly caught me.'

Biggles lit another cigarette. 'Well, there it is,' he murmured. 'It looks as if the gold is still there – provided Lavinsky and Co. haven't slipped back and lifted it. What are you going to do about it?'

The sailor looked helpless. 'What can I do? I reckon Lavinsky will be after it all right.'

'No doubt of that. Most men are ready to take risks when the prize is gold.'

'The gold isn't his.'

'It isn't yours, if it comes to that,' Biggles pointed out. 'What puzzles me is, why didn't Lavinsky lift it when he was there?'

'There wasn't time, or mebbe they would have done,' stated the sailor. 'The ice was closing in on me and they only just got aboard in time, as it was; but, of course, they'll go back. And they won't waste any time, either, I'll bet my sea-boots.'

'And you had an idea that you might beat them to it – by flying down, eh,' murmured Biggles. 'Was that what brought you here?'

The sailor looked uncomfortable. 'You've about hit the nail on the head,' he admitted.

'But before you, or anyone, could do anything, it would be necessary to determine the ownership of the gold,' averred Biggles.

'I reckon the stuff would belong to the underwriters who insured the ship, unless they sold the salvage,' opined Captain Grimes. 'The salvage wouldn't be much at the time, as the ship was reckoned to be at the bottom of the sea.'

'Quite so. But if the owners of the salvage knew that the ship was still afloat, so to speak, with the gold on board, it would be a very different matter. Have you told anyone else about this?'

'Not a soul. After all, I didn't know about the *Starry Crown* until you just told me. All I reported was the seal poaching.'

'Then the first thing to do is to ascertain the ownership of the salvage and find out if it is for sale. If it is, you must buy it. You ought to get it for a mere song. After that all you have to do is to go down and collect the bullion.'

The sailor looked doubtful. 'I couldn't do it – not alone. I couldn't afford such a trip. Anyway, to go by ship would take too long. I should probably find that Lavinsky had been there and gone. He'll be on his way there by now.'

Biggles nodded. 'I'm afraid you're right. Lavinsky would soon be on the job.'

'He'd have to find a better ship than the *Svelt*. She was dropping to bits and the engines were about done. But there, no doubt he'd soon find another ship.'

'I'm not so sure of that,' returned Biggles. 'Ships are expensive things. I doubt if such a man would have enough money to buy one.'

'He'd soon borrow one.'

'I don't think so.'

'Why not?'

'Because when Lavinsky went looking for a ship the owner would want to know what he wanted it for. Would Lavinsky tell him? I think it's unlikely, because as soon as he mentioned treasure the owner would want a finger in the pie. Remember, on these jaunts it's the man who puts up the money who calls the tune. Lavinsky would jib at taking second place, and from what you tell me of him, he isn't the sort of man to hand over half the profits. No; if he's gone after the gold, rather than divulge what he knows to a stranger he'd use his old ship, with the same crew. At least, that's my opinion.' Biggles tossed his cigarette end into the fire. 'And that, I'm afraid, is about as far as I can go in the matter of advice.'

The seaman drew a deep breath. 'Then it looks as if that's the end of it. I couldn't do a trip like that on my own.'

'And that's why you came to see me?'

'I thought we might do a deal.'

'Such as?'

'Well, I thought if you'd fix up a trip to fly there we could go shares in what we got. That would be fair enough, wouldn't it?'

'Certainly it would, if I could do it.' Biggles shook his head. 'But I'm afraid, Mr Grimes, putting the ownership of the gold on one side, the undertaking would be too big for me, even if I could get time off from my job to do it. I couldn't afford such an expedition as would be necessary – unless, of course, I was willing to take the most outrageous chances of losing my life, which I'm not. I don't mind reasonable risks, but I draw the line at suicide on the off-chance of getting a lump of gold, which may, or may not, be there.'

'Would it be as difficult as all that?' asked the sailor, in surprise. 'I mean, I thought aeroplanes could go pretty well anywhere.'

'A lot of people think that, and up to a point they are right,' agreed Biggles. 'But there are limits. Even though you've been to the Antarctic I don't think you quite realise what sort of place it is. We're talking about the most inaccessible place on earth. To go in a well-found ship would be a hazardous operation. To go in an aeroplane not properly equipped for the job would be asking for it. At least two planes would be needed, big planes – and aeroplanes are very expensive things.'

The sailor gazed at the floor. 'It didn't strike me as being as bad as all that.'

'Mebbe not, but you had firm planks under your feet. Let me try to make things a bit clearer. My business is flying, so I have to keep up to date with what's going on. Several Governments have an eye on the South Pole, and that's nothing to wonder at. You may say, why the South Pole more than the North? The answer is, the North

Polar regions are mostly frozen seas, no use to anybody except as a meteorological station or military base. They were always easier to reach than the South Pole, which is land, a new continent, six million square miles of mighty mountain ranges without a living creature on them. The old scientists always asserted that as nearly all the known land masses are in the Northern Hemispheres, there must be a continent somewhere in the far south to balance them, otherwise the earth wouldn't rotate evenly on its axis. Well, the continent was there, although it took a bit of finding. They call it the White Continent, because it's in the grip of eternal ice and snow; but nobody knows what metals, coal and oil there may be in that ground for the first nation to tame it. Only one or two expeditions have seen it, but even they could hardly scratch the surface. The last expedition was American, and you can judge the sort of difficulties they expected by the size of the show. I won't bore you with the details, but these fellows had a rough time, although their planes were equipped with every modern appliance, regardless of cost. There were casualties, too, due to conditions outside all human knowledge or experience.'

'Such as?' asked Ginger curiously.

Biggles lit another cigarette. 'Apparently the first difficulty is to know where the water ends and the land begins. It's all a sheet of ice, and the outer edge of the ice-pack is always breaking off and floating away, so that the coastline is never the same. Consider landing. True, most of the ice is flat, but it is covered with finely-powdered snow about a foot deep. It never rains, of course, but it often snows, and when the wind blows it flings the snow about in swirling whirlpools, so that it's impossible to see the surface of the ice. It isn't only a matter of landing. If you get down you've got to get off again – some time. On fine days, apparently, you can get visibility up to a hundred and fifty miles in every direction, due to the absolute absence of humidity in the atmosphere. For the same reason the sky is purple, not blue, and although you get sub-zero temperatures the sun may burn the skin off you. If the weather clouds up, or you get a change of temperature, you get mist, and then you've had it. You get a phenomenon which the airmen of the last expedition called a white-out. You've heard of a black-out. Well, this is the same thing in reverse. Whichever way you look, up or down, it's always the same – just a white, phantom world. The light comes from every direction, so there isn't even a shadow to help you. You can fly into the ground without even seeing it. Your altimeter is useless because you don't know the altitude of the ground below you. You may be flying over a plateau ten thousand feet high without knowing it. The mere thought of flying in such conditions is enough to give one a nervous breakdown. Navigation must be a nightmare. Remember, when you're at the South Pole, whichever way you face, you're looking north. You can't travel in any direction but north. Did you realise that? And if you happen to fly across the Pole, east immediately becomes west, and west, east. Silly, isn't it? I've never been, but I've read the reports of fellows who have, and if half of what they say is true I shan't burst into tears if I never see it. The nearest we've been is Kerguelen Island, and that's still a long way north of the Pole, but what with icebergs and fog, the going there wasn't exactly a joy ride[1]. Well, I needn't say any more; I've said enough, I think, to make it clear that not even the most optimistic pilot would hardly expect to fly down to the *Starry Crown*, pick up the bullion and come home – just like that. I could get there, I've no doubt. It's the thought of getting stuck there that I don't like.'

'No, by Jove! I'm with you there, old boy,' put in Bertie, polishing his monocle.

'I see what you mean,' said Captain Grimes sadly.

---

[1] See 'Biggles' Second Case.'

'Of course, with time and unlimited money for equipment, there's no reason why the trip shouldn't be made; but you'll understand why I'm not keen to take a chance on my own account,' went on Biggles. He thought for a moment. 'There might be one way out of the difficulty,' he said pensively. 'The Government needs gold. Governments always do, but at this moment ours needs it more than ever before. If I put the thing up to them there's just a chance that they might sanction and finance an expedition, although in that case they'd want the gold, naturally. They might give us a rake-off – say, ten per cent. – for our part in the undertaking. But even that would be better than a poke in the eye with a blunt stick. All we should have to lose then would be our lives. If you're agreeable, skipper, we could try it. The Government can only say no. If that's their answer, then as far as I'm concerned I'm afraid it's the end.'

'Aye, I'm agreeable,' answered the sailor. 'Will you do that?'

'I'll see about it right away,' promised Biggles.

Captain Grimes got up. 'All right, sir, let's leave it like that.'

Biggles, too, stood up. 'Very well. Leave me your address so that I can get in touch with you. If the trip comes off I'll make arrangements for both of you to come. I should need you, captain, anyhow, to guide us to the schooner. This boy of yours could act as mechanic and radio operator.'

'Right you are, sir. That's good enough for me,' decided Captain Grimes. 'Good day, sir.'

'Goodbye for now,' answered Biggles, seeing his visitors to the door.

'If this jaunt comes off, I shall need my winter woollies, by gad,' said Bertie.

'You certainly will, by gad,' returned Biggles grimly.

CHAPTER III

Southward Bound

Fifteen days after the discussion in Biggles' London flat, a solitary, dark, airborne object moved southward above the Antarctic sea, grey, grim and forbidding in its sullen desolation. An air cadet would have recognised the aircraft for an elderly Wellington bomber, a type once the pride of the R.A.F., but now obsolete. In the cockpit sat Biggles and Ginger. Behind, in the radio compartment, sat ex-L.A.C. Grimes, now known for the purposes of the expedition as Grimy. With him was his father, Captain Grimes of the Mercantile Marine.

The fifteen days had been busy ones, for as soon as the flight had been sanctioned no time had been lost in its organisation. In fact, the trip had been launched, so Biggles asserted, much too quickly considering its hazardous nature; but this was unavoidable if the race against Lavinsky was to be won. Biggles had assumed that such a man would return to the polar sea. At any rate, he had accepted him as a factor to be reckoned with. If nothing was seen of him, so well and good. If a collision between the two parties did occur it was as well that they should be prepared. Biggles' great fear was that the man might get to the objective first. Every day's delay would increase that risk, for which reason not a minute had been wasted.

It had not taken Biggles long to decide on what he considered to be the best plan of campaign. Not that there had been much choice in the matter. The nearest British territory to the objective – the only territory, in fact, within range of any available aircraft – was the Falkland Islands, the wild, rocky, windswept, treeless group which, lying three hundred miles south-east of the Magellan Strait, formed the southernmost colony of the British Empire. This, and the fact that frozen Graham Land, the objective, a thousand miles to the south, is a Dependency of the islands, made them the most obvious jumping-off place. As the islands were British there would be no difficulty about accommodation there, and the necessary arrangements were soon made between London and Port Stanley, the capital.

It is not to be supposed that the British Government Department responsible had accepted Biggles' proposal without question. Finance, as usual, was the chief stumbling-block; and it was not until Biggles pointed out that the cost of the trip would be relatively low compared with the profits should the raid be successful, that the expedition received official sanction. There had been a further snag when Biggles had demanded ten per cent. of the value of any gold recovered, for distribution amongst those engaged in the enterprise. In this, however, Biggles had been adamant, stating that he was not prepared to risk his life, or the lives of his companions, from a mere spirit of adventure, of which he had had, and could still find, plenty, without going to the bottom of the world to look for it. In the end he had had his way, possibly because, as the authorities grudgingly admitted, he usually brought his undertakings to a successful conclusion. But a definite limit had been set to expenditure, following the usual official custom – as Biggles complained bitterly – of risking the ship for a ha'porth of tar. He had demanded two aircraft. Nothing, he stated, would induce him to even consider the trip with one. In this he also had his way, but he had to be satisfied with two obsolete Wellingtons from surplus war stores, which could, however, be modified to suit his requirements. Actually, they suited him well enough, for the machines were types of proved reliability. Reliability was the quality which interested him most, he said; reliability and range when loaded to capacity. Speed and height didn't matter.

The modifications presented no great difficulty. They consisted chiefly of extra tankage – for they would have to take all the fuel they needed with them – to give not only the necessary endurance range but a wide margin of safety. Heating equipment had to be installed. But the biggest alteration affected the landing chassis. This involved the fitting of skis over the wheels; that is to say, the fitment of skis in such a way that a few inches of tyre projected below them, in order that the machine could land on snow as well as on hard surfaces. This, he admitted, was not his own idea. The scheme had been tried and proved in practice by the last Antarctic air expedition. It was for this reason that he decided to adopt it. The machines, of course, were stripped of their armament and war gear. They would have plenty of weight to carry without these things.

The question of equipment had been fairly straightforward, for here again Biggles went to the trouble of studying the reports of previous expeditions, by sea as well as by air. It became a matter not so much of what to take, as what could be left behind, to limit the all-up weight, taking into consideration the extra fuel and oil. The planes would in any case be overloaded, as planes usually are on such occasions, but this would only affect the outward passage. Once at the objective everything could be unloaded, and if necessary left behind at the conclusion of the operation. Indeed, this would be inevitable if the gold was found, for it would have to be transported home. But, as Biggles observed, the first thing was to find the bullion. Once they had it stowed, everything else could be jettisoned for the thousand mile run back to the Falklands.

The first part of the outward trip, to the Falkland Islands, was a mere routine flight, permission of the intermediate countries having been sought, and obtained, by the Air Ministry. The two machines had flown in consort, crossed the Atlantic by the shortest route, from Dakar in West Africa to Natal in Brazil, and then followed the trunk route on down South America until it was necessary to turn east again on the final overseas leg to the Falklands. All this was a matter of simple navigation, and as the weather had been kind, no difficulties had been encountered.

At the Falklands they had received a cordial welcome from the Colonial Secretary, the British Naval Officer in charge, and the people; indeed, such hospitality were they shown that it became a problem for Biggles to convey, without divulging what they were doing, the urgency of their mission. It had been given out officially that they were on a survey flight, which up to a point was true enough; the difficulty was to reconcile this with Biggles' anxiety to be away. In the end he left the explanations to Algy and Bertie, who were now to remain behind as a reserve, and possible rescue party.

It was for this reason that Biggles had demanded two aircraft. By no means sure of what was likely to happen when they reached the objective he had jibbed at the idea of risking a landing which, should it go wrong, would leave them all marooned on the polar ice without the slightest hope of ever being picked up. The knowledge that a reserve machine was standing by to fetch them, should it be necessary, would make all the difference to their behaviour – not to say peace of mind. It was hoped that the two machines would always be in touch by radio, but should this arrangement break down it would be the task of the second machine to fly down to see what was wrong. As Biggles pointed out, if anything had gone wrong, if, for instance, the landing had been a failure, then those on the ground – or rather, on the ice – should be able to do something to prevent the second machine from making the same mistake. It should be possible for them to mark out a safe landing area, having cleared it of obstructions in the shape of projecting lumps of ice or soft snow. This was the plan. So far it had gone according to schedule. Algy and Bertie, with the reserve machine, were at Port Stanley. Biggles, Ginger, Captain Grimes and his son, after a day's rest, were heading south for the last known position of the long-lost schooner. Grimy, being a qualified radio operator, relieved Ginger of the necessity of remaining in the wireless compartment, while his father, who had seen something of the place from sea level, was to try to locate the schooner when they reached the area in which it had last been seen.

The day was fine, with visibility fairly good, but within an hour Ginger had realised the gravity of the business in which they were engaged. Already their lives were entirely dependent on the machine and its engines. Should these fail, then that would be the end, for in water of such a temperature as that below them life could not be maintained for more than a few minutes. These conditions were bound to have a psychological effect. It was not merely that they were out of sight of land that caused Ginger to regard the scene below and ahead with an unusual degree of apprehension, for that was nothing new. It was the knowledge of where they were far beyond the limits of any regular steamship route, that caused him to imagine sometimes that the engines had changed their note.

Far away to starboard he had watched the faint shadow that was the notorious Cape Horn, southern tip of the great American continent, fade away. He had looked at the chart on his knees. The very names of everything in the region were an unpleasant reminder of what they might expect to find a thousand miles farther on – Mount Misery, Desolation Island, Last Hope Bay, East and West Furies. These were the significant names bestowed by the early mariners. He wondered what names they would have found for the great southern continent, had they discovered it. But they had not. That had been left for a later generation of seamen. Even now, he pondered, the only visitor was an occasional whaler. The thought reminded him of Lavinsky. It would be odd, he thought, if they should see him. He scanned the desolate sea around but could see no sign of a ship. Ahead, all he could see was icebergs, like ghostly sentinels guarding the very end of the earth.

He looked at Biggles, but an expressionless face gave no indication of what he was thinking. Only his eyes moved from time to time, switching from the cold grey sea below to the instrument panel, and back again. Occasionally he made a note on a slip of paper. The aircraft droned on into the sullen emptiness.

Ice, big sinister bergs and smaller 'growlers,' began to pass below. From the south came more and more, and ever more in endless succession. Some were white, some green, some blue, some weirdly luminous, some smeared with black stains as if they had been torn from the soil which no man had ever seen. Some towered high, like monstrous castles; others were flat plains on which an aircraft might land, or so it seemed. One he judged to be fully twenty miles long. It was a magnificent but soul-chilling spectacle, and there began to grow on him that feeling of human futility, when confronted by nature in the raw, that he had sometimes experienced when flying over the deserts of the Middle East. Yet even now, he brooded, the worst was yet to come.

For the first time he began to understand fully the dimensions of the task they had undertaken. Biggles, with his wide experience, had always realised it, of course. He had tried to make it clear when Captain Grimes had first come to see him. It would be hard, Biggles had said, to tell where the sea ended and the land began. It now became increasingly evident that they would not be able to tell. The large flat ice-fields were getting bigger as they neared the permanent pack-ice. Pieces, apparently, were always breaking off, pushed away by the eternal pressure from behind them. Areas of open water were getting smaller, and fewer. Presently, he perceived, there would be no water, only ice. What lay under it no man could say. It was getting colder, too, even in the heated cabin. The windows were beginning to fog up. At first he thought it was fog forming outside, but when he realised what was happening he took a rag and a bottle of alcohol, brought for the purpose, and wiped the perspex to prevent the condensation from freezing to opaque ice.

At last Biggles spoke. 'We're approaching the tip of Graham Land,' he remarked. 'It doesn't look much like land, does it? But if my navigation is correct, our time in air fixes our position. Confirm that Grimy is in touch with the base. He can give Algy our position and tell him I'm now going to alter course a trifle westerly. Ask Captain Grimes to come forward. I want to speak to him.'

Ginger went aft to obey the order, and presently returned with the information that contact had been maintained. The Skipper – as Captain Grimes was usually called – came with him.

'Take a look ahead, Skipper, and see if you can recognise anything,' requested Biggles. 'I fancy I can see rising ground. It looks like ice, but it may be a range of hills, in which case the thing should be permanent and serve as a landmark.' He passed his slip of paper. 'I make that to be our position. Your position when you spotted the wreck was about a hundred miles sou'-sou'-west of us. I'm now taking a course for it. I kept a little easterly at first because the Admiralty information is that the general drift of ice is north-east. I have made an allowance, therefore, for the wreck to move in that direction. If it has moved we should meet it.'

The Skipper subjected the region ahead to a long careful scrutiny. 'Can't say I recognise anything,' he said at length. 'But there, I wouldn't expect to, because as the ice moves the scene changes.'

'Bound to,' agreed Biggles. 'What are our chances of spotting the wreck from up here, do you think?'

'Pretty poor, I should say, particularly if there has been snow since I last saw the place. The upper works of the *Starry Crown* are bound to be under snow, anyway. Looking at her from sea level we could see her side, and the masts and standing gear stood out against the sky, even though they were iced up.'

'I'll drop off a little altitude as we go along,' decided Biggles. 'I'd rather not go below five hundred feet until I have to, for fear of hitting the tip of a big berg. Icebergs have an unpleasant habit of winding themselves up in a sort of invisible haze and then they're hard to see. You keep your eyes open for anything that looks like a ship, or anything else you saw the last time you were here.'

'Aye-aye.'

Ginger said nothing. If the truth must be told he was appalled by what he saw. To try to find a speck in such a waste – for that is all the ship would amount to – seemed hopeless. He hadn't realised until now that the *Starry Crown*, like everything else, would be white. He was not easily depressed, but had Biggles at that moment decided to turn his nose northward, he, for one, would have raised no objection.

Biggles, however, did not turn back. For rather more than half an hour he held his course, throttled back to cruising speed, down what he declared must be the western side of the Graham Peninsula, which thrusts a long arm northward as if pointing to

South America. Beyond this there was no longer any open water. It had ended in a ragged line at a sheer wall of ice, which seemed to be anything from ten to a hundred feet high. Beyond this was only a white sameness, for the most part fairly level, but with occasional piled-up masses of ice, as if pressure from below had thrust it upwards. The rough waterline was the only guide, the one mark that was any use to them. Even this was not to be trusted, because the open water was strewn with floating fields of ice, large and small. But it did at least show the limit that a ship could reach. The Skipper, on the occasion of his last visit, must have passed just to the seaward of that line. At that time the hulk had been, according to his reckoning, between one and two miles inside the ice, locked fast in it.

Biggles began to circle, slowly losing height, following the line. He followed it for some distance, with floe-covered water to the north and sheer ice as far as the eye could see to the south. Nothing that remotely resembled a ship was seen. Once Ginger spotted and pointed out a number of huge, clumsy animals. The Skipper said they were Weddell seals, the only mammals that could live so far south. There were also big rookeries of penguins. A new menace appeared when the aircraft was suddenly surrounded by large, buff-coloured birds, with eagle-like beaks and black curved claws. The Skipper said they were skuas. For a minute or two there was some risk of collision; then the danger passed.

At last Biggles looked at Ginger and said: 'Well, what are we going to do?'

'Are you asking me – seriously?' enquired Ginger in surprise.

'Yes. We've seen as much as we'll see from the air, so it's no use just using up fuel. If the hulk is still in existence it must be within twenty miles of the spot we're flying over now. She might be under a fresh fall of snow, in which case it's unlikely we'll see her. Our last hope is to land and look for her from ground level, but I'm not risking anybody's life by going down without his permission. It's for the rest of you to decide. Do we go down and set up camp, or do we go home.'

Ginger hesitated. The fact was, he was not happy about either plan, but the idea of going home empty-handed was the most repugnant. He shrugged. 'I'm in favour of going down. After all, it isn't as though we weren't prepared for a landing.'

'Suits me,' said the Skipper. 'I can speak for Grimy, too.'

'All right,' agreed Biggles. 'Go and tell Grimy to make a signal to base that we're going to land. Give him our position. You know where we are.'

'Aye-aye, sir.' The sailor went aft.

Biggles glided on to the nearest flat area. As far as space was concerned there was no difficulty. The surface was the big hazard, and that could only be ascertained by landing on it.

Ginger stared down as the machine skimmed low in a trial run. The surface looked perfect – hard, and as flat as a bowling green. He could see no obstruction. There was no wind, so the question of direction did not arise.

Biggles turned the aircraft and allowed it gently to lose height. He flattened out. Ginger held his breath. Nothing happened. Then his nerves twitched as the engines roared again and the machine swung up in a climbing turn.

Biggles laughed, a short laugh without any humour in it. 'See what I mean,' he muttered. 'I thought I was on the carpet, but I must have flattened out about ten feet too high. Landing on snow is always tricky, but here, in this grey light, where there's nothing else but snow, it's definitely nasty.'

The next time, however, there was no mistake. There was a sudden vicious hiss as the skis touched. A cloud of fine, powdery

*Ginger realised that without the skis the machine
would have finished up on its nose.*

snow, sprang high into the air, smothering the windscreen and blotting out the view. By the time it had cleared, as it quickly did, the machine was dragging, rather too quickly for comfort, to a standstill. Ginger gave a heartfelt sigh of relief. He realised that without the skis the machine would have finished up on its nose.

Biggles looked at him and smiled. 'Well, here we are,' he said lightly. 'How does it feel to be on the bottom of the world?'

'Pretty chilly,' answered Ginger.

'It'll be colder still outside,' promised Biggles. 'Let's get down and see.'

CHAPTER IV

Beyond Men's Footsteps

In two hours, clad in polar kit in a temperature that registered seventeen degrees below zero, a tent had been erected and well packed around with snow. In this, almost the entire load carried by the aircraft had been snugly stowed, leaving only enough space in the middle for the erection of a folding table. Around this packing cases had been arranged to serve as seats. Sleeping bags and blankets had been left in the cabin for the time being. It would, Biggles asserted, be warmer there.

No time had been lost in the unloading operation, Biggles being anxious to lighten the machine as quickly as possible to reduce the risk of the aircraft sinking into the powdery snow which, he was relieved to find, was only a few inches deep at the point on which he had chosen to land – about two hundred yards from the nearest open water. In this matter he may have been lucky, for there were places where the snow – tiny crystals, not unlike sugar – was much deeper. For this, apparently, the wind had been responsible. Little waves, like ripple sand, showed the direction of it.

They had this advantage, as Biggles reminded the others. There was no fear of darkness overtaking them, for the sun, at that particular period of the year, did not sink below the horizon, although it got very near to it. The result was, that every day was twenty-four hours of unbroken daylight. Nevertheless, at the normal period of night, the world was bathed in an eerie glow, through which the sun appeared as a monstrous red ball balanced on the distant ice.

From the aircraft, the landward side – if such an expression can be used – presented a fantastic picture. First, there was a gentle upward slope. Beyond this, ridges of ice, swept clear of the snow by wind, appeared as pale blue or grass-green hills. Some of these had castles and villages of ice piled on them, the illusion being strengthened by warm pink lights where facets of ice reflected the sun.

When everything was ship-shape a spirit stove was lighted and a meal prepared. It started with hot canned soup and finished with strong, sweet tea, the best stuff Biggles declared – and the Skipper agreed – for keeping the cold out.

'What do you think is our best way of trying to locate the hulk?' Biggles asked the Skipper, between mouthfuls of bread and jam.

'There's only one way to go about it that I can see, and that's to take walks out and back in every direction, like the spokes of a wheel, reckoning the camp to be the hub,' answered Captain Grimes. 'It's no use looking beyond the water line, because if the hulk ever got free she'd go down like a stone. Below her Plimsoll line she must have been crushed flat by the ice. That leaves us only half a circle to cover. We might walk a mile or two out, take a turn for about half a mile, and then come home again. In that way we ought to cover all the ground in a day or two. If we don't strike her we shall have to move camp and try again. It'll be hard going, but it's the only way.'

'What do you mean by hard going?' asked Ginger. 'It doesn't look too bad.'

'Wait till you try walking on the stuff and you'll see what I mean,' answered the Skipper. 'And I'm reckoning on the weather holding.

It can change in a flash in this part of the world. The wind's only got to rise, or veer a point or two, and anything can happen. If it starts snowing—'

'Suppose we wait until it starts snowing before we talk about that,' broke in Biggles. 'No use jumping our fences until we come to them. We'll follow your advice about the walking. I can't think of anything better. You're sure this is the right place?'

'Must be, within a mile or two. It was a clear day when I took my position and there was nothing wrong with my instruments. I took care of that. I checked up three times, as I always do, so I don't see how I could go wrong. Of course, the ice may have moved, and the hulk with it. But we knew there was a risk of that before we started.'

As if to confirm this statement, from some distance away, on the seaward side, came a grinding, splintering clash, followed by a long, low growl.

'That's ice on the move now,' said Biggles. 'Sounded like two bergs bumping into each other.'

'Gives you an idea of what a hope a ship's got when she gets trapped between a couple of chunks like that,' put in the Skipper, grimly.

'Still, from our point of view the movement is very slow,' went on Biggles. 'According to the records of the scientists who have been here the big stuff only moves a matter of a few feet a day. I'm talking of the main pack, of course – the stuff we're on now. The smaller pieces that have broken off would move faster than that, no doubt, particularly with a wind behind them. If the hulk is here, or hereabouts, she couldn't have moved far since you last saw her.'

'She was fast enough in the ice then, and had been for many a year; so unless she's disintegrated she ought to be somewhere in the region now,' returned the Skipper. 'Of course,' he added, 'if her mast came down under the weight of ice, or anything like that, she'd be harder to see.'

Again from outside came the ominous growl of colliding ice.

'All right. The sooner we start looking for her, the better,' decided Biggles. 'I've seen all I want to see of the scenery, and I shouldn't sob my heart out if I never saw it again. Let's get cracking.' He got up.

'Are we all going to walk together?' asked Ginger.

Biggles considered the question. 'I don't think that's necessary,' he replied. 'I think the best plan would be for one to remain at home to act as cook, guard and signaller. We'd look silly if we came back to find that a lot of seals had knocked everything to pieces.'

'What do you mean by signaller?' asked Ginger.

'Well, there's always the risk of fog or snow,' Biggles pointed out. 'If visibility happened to drop to zero it might not be easy for those who are out to find their way back to camp. In that case a pistol shot or two might save an awkward situation. The three walkers needn't stay together. They could walk a few hundred yards apart, always in sight of each other, so that visual signals could be made if need be.'

'That's the way to do it,' assented the Skipper. 'Safety first is the motto. You can't be too careful. I've heard of sealers getting lost within half a mile of their ship and never being seen again. It happened the very last time I was here. One of the hands was a Swede – a fellow named Larsen. Good sailor he was, too. At the last minute Lavinsky sent him back to fetch a sealskin that had been dropped. I reckon he chose him because he never did like him. Larsen didn't come back, and as the ice was closing in we went without him. Those were Lavinsky's orders, and I daren't go against the owners.'

'One would have thought,' said Ginger as he got ready, 'that nothing could have been more simple than a job like this, provided the machine always behaved itself. We knew exactly where we were coming and what we were going to do; but I've got an increasing feeling in my bones that we're up against something.'

'I never in my life heard of a salvage operation that went right from start to finish,' remarked Biggles. 'Something isn't where it should be, or something comes unstuck, somewhere, somehow. Read the records and you'll see that the unexpected is always turning up to make life harder for the people doing the job. But as I said before, we'll talk about trouble when we bump into it.' Biggles looked seaward. 'All I have to add to that is, thank goodness we didn't come in a marine aircraft. I was tempted to choose a flying-boat, because, with water within range, landing would be a simple matter. When we arrived here there was enough open water in the offing for a fleet of battleships. Now look at it.'

Ginger looked, and saw that the water was almost entirely covered by small detached floes, each an island of ice. 'Had we landed out there in a flying-boat we should have been in a mess,' he observed. 'There isn't a run long enough anywhere to get a marine craft off. But, there, most of the ice seems to be floating away, so it might be all right.'

'And what would happen to a flying-boat in the meantime?' inquired Biggles cynically. 'One touch of that ice would rip her hull wide open. There's always a lot more ice under the water than there is showing. But that's enough talking. Let's go. Grimy, will you stay in camp to wash up and get supper? You'll have to melt snow for water. Skipper, will you take the first beat to the left, keeping as near to the water as is reasonably safe. If you see anything, give me a hail; I shall be next to you.'

'Aye, aye, sir.'

'Ginger, you take a half turn right,' went on Biggles. 'Don't get too wide. If you see any sign of a change in the weather give me a shout and make for home. Keep an eye on me for signals.'

'Good enough,' agreed Ginger.

'Okay, then. Let's get weaving.'

Each member of the party set off on his respective beat.

It did not take Ginger long to appreciate the truth of the Skipper's remark about the going being harder than it looked. It was much worse than he expected. He found it hard work, although this had an advantage in that it kept him warm. One thing that he was pleased to notice as he trudged on through the powdery snow: he left a trail so plain that there was no risk of losing it should he have to return by the same route.

As he tramped on, sometimes slipping on naked ice and often ploughing through snow waist deep, the incongruity of what he was doing suddenly struck him. To look for an object the size of a ship in a snow-covered wilderness, where, he thought, a toy ship would have been conspicuous, seemed absurd. There was just a chance, he was bound to admit, that the ship might be behind one of the several masses of heaped-up ice that dotted the landscape, but the possibility of that seemed so remote as to be hardly worth consideration. The result was a feeling of hopelessness, of the futility of his task – a state of mind seldom conducive to success.

Away to his left, perhaps a quarter of a mile distant, was Biggles, as plain to see as a black beetle on a white carpet. Somewhere beyond him was the Skipper, also looking for a speck on a continent. Ginger could not see him, but he could watch Biggles. At least, he could see him for some time. When, presently, he disappeared, he assumed that either he was beyond the ridge or the higher ice towards which he had been walking. When several minutes passed and he had not reappeared, Ginger stopped, wondering if he ought to do something about it, and if so, what. He did not like to leave his beat; nor did he relish the idea of giving himself a longer march than was necessary, particularly as a slight breeze had sprung up, bitterly cold, to retard his movements. Happening to glance behind him, he noticed with a tinge of uneasiness that his trail, once so conspicuous, had disappeared; and he had not to look far for the reason. The snow was moving. At least, the surface was. The top inch or two seemed to be airborne, giving the surface a rough, blurred appearance. He was not worried about it. Visibility was still excellent; it did not appear to have disimproved in the slightest degree. Cupping his hands round his mouth he sent a hail across the waste. It had a strange, muffled sound. It was then that he noticed that he could no longer see the big pile of ice towards which Biggles had been marching. This was all the more odd because he could see the place where it had been – or he thought he could. Then, for the first time, a suspicion of the truth struck him. Swinging round he looked for the sun. It was not there. The whole length of the horizon was a dull uniform grey. That told him, beyond any shadow of doubt, that something was happening, although he was by no means sure what it was. Visibility still seemed good. But was it? Had it come to this, he wondered vaguely, that he could not believe his eyes? It seemed like it. He shouted again, and listened intently for an answer. None came. Turning about, he began to retrace his steps.

He had travelled, he thought, about two miles from camp. It had taken him rather more than an hour. He knew the direction of it, but all the same he was worried that the trail had been obliterated. Happening to glance behind him he was even more worried to see that his footprints were being filled in by whirling snow crystals almost as quickly as he made them. Feeling far from happy, he increased his pace.

It was soon evident that visibility was not so good as he had supposed, but he was still astonished that he could have been deceived so easily. Within half an hour he was struggling along through a vague world in which everything – ground, air and sky – seemed to be of the same uniform whiteness. These, he thought bitterly, were the very conditions that Biggles had been at pains to describe. He derived some satisfaction from the fact that he was on the ground, not in the air. The idea of flying in such conditions appalled him. But his exertions did at least keep him warm. Several times he thought he heard gunshots in the distance, but he could not be sure. The reports, if reports they were, and not icebergs in collision, were curiously flat and muffled. That, he soliloquised, might be due to the fog. He hoped it was so, for by now he should be nearer camp than the sounds suggested.

The crash of ice not far in front of him brought him to an abrupt halt. He recognised the sound of ice floes in collision. Floating ice meant that he must be near open water. In that case, he thought swiftly, he must be near the camp – that is, if he had followed the true course home. Had he? He thought he had, but there was no means of confirming it. How could one be sure of anything in such conditions, he mused miserably. He walked on, slowly now, and soon saw that in one respect, at any rate, he had not been at fault. Before him the ice ended in a cliff some thirty feet high. Beyond it was the sea.

Stopping again he tried to reason the thing out. He now had a landmark – the open water. The camp was not far from it, but whether it lay to left or right he had no means of knowing. He shouted. He shouted again, and there was now a ring of anxiety in his voice. What really alarmed him more than anything was the absence of gunshots, for he felt certain that Grimy, perceiving what had happened, would be firing signal shots as arranged. He would hardly fail in the main reason for his being left in camp. So there Ginger stood, a prey now to gnawing indecision, knowing that if he moved, and the direction he took was the wrong one, he would only make his case worse.

In the end he made a plan. It was quite simple. He would follow the edge of the ice-cliff for a quarter of an hour by his watch. If, then, he could not locate the camp by shouting, he would retrace his steps for the same period of time, which would bring him back to the point on which he now stood. He would then do the same in the opposite direction. In this he felt fairly safe. There would be no risk of losing his way because he had the water to guide him. His mind made up, he set off.

His nerves, already at full stretch, suffered a jolt when a great grey shape appeared suddenly out of the fog, gliding with a curious swinging motion towards him. Then he recognised it for a Weddell seal. He had seen these creatures from the air without realising they were so big. The animal stopped dead when it saw what was, perhaps, the first human being it had ever seen. Ginger also stopped. Apparently the surprise was mutual. Then the animal, with a grunt, continued on its way without taking further notice of the intruder. It passed within a few yards of where Ginger stood, reached the rim of the ice, made a spectacular dive, and was seen – no more.

Ginger's adventure ended in a rather ridiculous anti-climax. The haze began to clear as quickly as it had formed. Suddenly, to his joy, he heard voices. He let out a yell. It was answered at once. He walked on towards the sound, and presently the familiar shape of the tent loomed before him. Standing in front of the entrance were the rest of the party.

'Where have you been?' inquired Biggles.

'Where have I been?' Ginger was astonished by the question. 'I've been lost,' he announced curtly.

'Lost! Where?'

'In the fog?'

'What fog?'

'Are you kidding?' demanded Ginger suspiciously.

'No'

'Didn't you see any fog?'

'There was a little thin mist but nothing to speak of,' returned Biggles. 'I lost sight of you, but I wasn't worried. I waved to the Skipper and we came home.'

'Well, where I was the fog was as thick as pea soup,' declared Ginger. 'I couldn't see a thing.'

'Curious,' replied Biggles. 'You must have struck a peculiar slant of air. I seem to remember reading something about the fog here often being patchy and quite local.'

'Patchy or not, it had me worried,' asserted Ginger, feeling somehow that he had been cheated. He looked at Grimy. 'I listened for signal shots.'

'There didn't seem any need,' answered Grimy. 'I could see the others coming so I guessed you wouldn't be far away.'

'You're quite right – I wasn't,' confirmed Ginger. 'My trouble was I didn't know it.'

'Did you see anything looking like a ship?' asked Biggles.

'Not a sign. Did you?'

Biggles shook his head. 'No, neither did the Skipper. All I saw was snow, and there was plenty of that.'

'If we ever find this ship I'll be ready to believe anything in the future,' stated Ginger.

'We'll try again tomorrow,' said Biggles. 'Come and have something to eat.'

CHAPTER V

Into the Past

For three anxious, rather boring days, the search for the castaway schooner continued along the lines planned, but without the slightest encouragement. No one said anything, but each knew what the others were thinking. Long silences made it clear that hopes were fading. Anything like enthusiasm had certainly been extinguished. Eager anticipation had become mere labour. What was to have been a treasure hunt had become a tiresome task to be performed. However, no one had as yet mentioned failure.

At intervals, two or three times a day, Biggles ran up the engines to keep them in working order. So far, the frost had not affected them. He was concerned mostly with the lubrication system, but it seemed to be all right. For the rest, the long Antarctic days continued without incident and without any appreciable change in the weather. From the direction of the open water came the growling and muttering of icebergs waging ceaseless war with each other.

For one thing the party was particularly thankful. Visibility after the first day had remained good. Not that there was much risk now of any member of the party losing his way. After Ginger's early experience Biggles had seen to that by the simple expedient of knocking some packing cases to pieces and slicing the wood into long, thin splinters. Anyone leaving camp took a bundle of these with him, sticking one into the snow at intervals on the outward journey and recovering them on the way back. By this means, not only could a man be sure of finding his way home, but in the event of accident there would be no difficulty in trailing a searcher who failed to return.

Four-fifths of the ground to be surveyed had now been covered. All these had yielded was the sight of an endless wilderness of snow, with mountains, also snow-clad, in the far distance. One segment remained. If it produced no result, Biggles had said, then the site of the camp would have to be shifted a few miles to the east, this being the direction of the general ice-drift according to scientific investigation. The whole process would then be repeated, subject to the weather remaining fair. When the machine was in the air, making the move, Algy and Bertie could be given the new position.

Everyone was disappointed by the failure, so far, of the mission, the Skipper most of all, for he insisted on shouldering responsibility. His early confidence that he could not have made a mistake when working out his ship's position, on the occasion of his previous visit, was being shaken. Biggles admitted that the present circumstances were not exactly encouraging, but asserted that they were still far from being beaten. They were all fit, not even tired. The cold, dry atmosphere was exhilarating, and it had all been very interesting, anyway. They had seen what few mortal eyes had been privileged to see, even though the landscape was nothing to rave about.

On the morning of the fourth day the final search from the existing camp began. The party consisted of the Skipper, Grimy and Ginger, it being Biggles' turn to act as camp orderly. The Skipper took the left-hand beat. Ginger was on the extreme right, which meant that he would have to march almost due west, keeping roughly parallel with the irregular ice cliff that fringed the open water.

He set off on what had become almost a routine operation. Every hundred yards or so he pulled a stick from his bundle and planted it in the snow, leaving about eighteen inches exposed. Progress, he found, was slower than it had ever been before. This was due to several causes. In the first place, he had to more or less follow the ice-and-water line. This was as irregular as the edge of an unfinished jig-saw puzzle. Naturally, this meant that he had much farther to go than if he had followed a straight course. Again, near the water, although this had not been apparent from the camp, the ice was far from flat. Either from pressure behind, or below, it had been lifted into long, frozen corrugations. In extreme cases the ridges had burst upwards in piles of ice of every shape known to geometry. This hid what lay ahead, and as more and more ice fell away behind him his view to the camp was cut off. Otherwise he would have seen it, for while the sky was grey, with a layer of high cloud, visibility on the whole was good. So with one thing and another the going was hard, and he was soon perspiring freely. But there was this about it, he thought, as he struggled on towards more broken ice: here it would be easily possible for an object even the size of a ship to remain unobserved except from close range. Against that, however, was the fact that he was much nearer to the sea than the hulk had been when it was last sighted. At that time, according to the Skipper, it had been at least a mile inshore, whereas now he was seldom more than a hundred yards from the water. Still, he did not lose sight of the possibility of some of the ice-cliff breaking away, which would have the effect of bringing the hulk nearer to the sea.

After passing across a broad field of snow he was approaching one of the big malformations of ice when, just short of it, he struck his knee against a piece that he had not noticed. This was not an uncommon occurrence, as, owing to the absence of shadows and the resulting white flatness, small objects blended easily into the background. Muttering in his annoyance he stooped to rub his knee, for he had given it a sharp blow, although the thick stockings he wore prevented an actual wound. In stooping, he noticed something which at first did no more than arouse his curiosity. He was accustomed to seeing ice of peculiar shapes, but the piece into which he had blundered was very odd indeed. First, there was a low symmetrical mound. From this, for no reason which he could discover, rose a quite definite cross. As white as the surrounding snow, in a churchyard it would have been commonplace; but here, a thousand miles from the nearest church, he could only regard it with amazement. He stopped rubbing to stare at it. A cross! A distant bell rang in his memory. Quite recently somebody, somewhere, had said something about a cross, something, he thought, in connection with what they were doing. Then he remembered. One of the men concerned with the story of the *Starry Crown* – he could not remember his name – had killed his companion, built a cairn over his body and topped the edifice with a cross. Doubtless other men had died on the ice, to be buried by their shipmates. Was this one of them, or was it the man who had died near the schooner. He would soon see.

With pulses now beating fast he took out his heavy hunting knife and opening the biggest blade struck the point into the ice. A chip flew off. He struck again and again, causing the ice, as brittle as glass, to fly in all directions. In a couple of minutes he had reached what he hoped to see, and for that matter, what he fully expected to see. Wood. The ice was not solid. It had formed a crust over a wooden object, and from its shape that object could only be a cross. He began working on the crossbar, knowing that if there was any writing it would be here. It was. In five minutes more the board was exposed sufficiently for him to read a rough inscription, incised, it seemed, with the hard point of a lead pencil. It read:

JOHN MANTON
DIED 1877
R.I.P.

'Rest in peace,' breathed Ginger. Well, Manton had certainly done that. Straightening his back Ginger wiped his forehead with the back of a hand which now trembled slightly as his imagination ran riot. Here, then, at his feet, in loneliness utter and complete, lay the body, preserved in the eternal ice, of the man who had set out to do the very thing that he himself was now doing. Manton had come for gold. He had stayed, and would stay, for ever and ever – unless the earth moved on its axis, which did not seem likely.

Ginger shivered, glancing around apprehensively. The air seemed to have turned a shade colder. Then his imagination took a more material turn. Manton, he recalled, had been killed by the man Last. That final tragedy of solitude had occurred in or near the schooner. Last would not have carried the body of his victim far. There was no need. It followed, therefore, that the schooner was near at hand – or had been. If it was near, why hadn't he seen it? He gazed around, his eyes travelling slowly over the scene of Last's ghastly ordeal. He could picture him wild-eyed and horror stricken, dragging the corpse of his one solitary companion to the very spot on which he now stood. It was easier here, than at home, to feel the full force of that terrible moment. No wonder Last had faced the open sea in a cockleshell boat rather than leave his bones beside those of the friend whose life he had taken.

Ginger's eyes moved to the tumbled mass of ice towards which he had been walking when he had struck his knee. At first, it still seemed shapeless; so much so that had he not collided with the cross he knew that he would have walked past it without a second

glance. But now, as he stared at it, with the help of a little imagination the mass began to take form. Without much effort he could
make out the rough shape of a ship's hull. With a little more effort
he could locate the superstructure. But where were the masts on
which they had reckoned to reveal the ship's position. Certainly
they were not there – at any rate, not where they should have been.
Then, staring hard, he understood. Right across the deck stretched
a line of ice so straight that it was hard to suppose that it could
have been formed without a foundation. Ginger realised that this
must be the mast; but it had fallen, and in its new position had
soon collected a coating of ice and snow. From it, projecting downwards in rigid lines, were what had once been supple ropes.

For a moment or two Ginger stood still. The knowledge that he
had found what, in his heart, he had never expected to see, set in
motion a strange feeling of unreality. His knees went curiously
weak and he found himself trembling. What was it about gold, he
wondered vaguely, that affected men in such a way? But was he
counting his triumph too soon? Was the gold still there? Should he
return at once to report his discovery to Biggles or should he first
confirm that they had not been forestalled by another treasure
seeker? If he went back to camp to report that he had found the
ship, the first thing everyone would want to know would be, was
the gold still there? The hulk, without it, was nothing. The gold was
everything. So ran his thoughts.

It did not take him long to reach a decision. He would have a look
inside the hulk, anyway, if only to confirm that it was the ship they
were looking for. It should not take long.

He had some difficulty in getting on the sloping deck – or what
had once been a deck, for now, of course, it was under a layer of ice
of unknown thickness. He slid off several times. But in stumbling
around, looking for an easier place, he came upon something that

exceeded his hopes. It was a narrow flight of steps cut in the ice, so regular that it could only have been made by human hands.

Having gained the deck he again looked about him for some way of getting inside the hulk, and he was not altogether surprised to see that from the steps he had mounted there appeared to be a track leading to a hump of ice that must have been the cover of the companionway. He was not surprised because he remembered that he was not the first visitor to the ship after it had become ice-bound. Men had lived there for months. Naturally, they would be constantly going up and down. Walking on he saw that his surmise was correct. A hole had been cut in the ice, in the manner of a cave. Looking in he saw ice-encrusted steps leading downwards, although in his amazement at the sight that met his gaze he hardly noticed them. The place was a grotto, far exceeding in sheer fantasy those commonly pictured in books of fairy tales.

His wonderment increased as he picked a cautious way down the slippery steps and presently stood inside the ship. Here the picture presented transcended all imagination. Light and ice together made play in a manner no artist could hope to portray. Everything was ice, taking the shape of the object on which it had formed. Where the light actually came from was not easy to see, but Ginger could only assume that it came from above, where the deck had been crushed and punctured by the weight of ice on it. Through the ice that covered such gaps the light filtered, and the result was an eerie luminosity. Even the very atmosphere seemed tinged with unearthly hues never seen by human eyes. The roof and walls, floodlit by beams of daylight passing through pure ice, were sheer crystal. From the ceiling hung sparkling chandeliers ablaze with prismatic jewellery. From clusters of diamonds long pendants of precious stones hung down, in one place rubies, in another emeralds, and in another sapphires. In such entrancing surroundings, for a little while Ginger could only stand and stare, unconscious of the passing of time, unconscious of everything except an increased feeling of unreality. Then, slowly, he made his way into the fairy ice palace, following a corridor that seemed to run the full length of it.

In the first room he entered another surprise awaited him. It was, apparently, the compartment that had been used as a mess room by the wretched men who had found themselves prisoners in this world of ice. Crocks and cutlery lay about as if they might have been used that very day. There was food, too, on plates and in opened tins. He picked up a biscuit on which unknown hands had placed a slice of bully beef, and smelt it. It was quite fresh and sweet. There was, after all, nothing remarkable about that, he mused. The ship was a natural refrigerator in which food would keep for ever. Corruption does not begin below freezing point.

He walked on, looking into several cabins. The doors all stood wide open. But he saw nothing of particular interest. In one lay a pile of blankets, as if thrown aside by a man who had just slept there. The end room, however, was larger than the rest. Not only were the walls jewel-encrusted but on the far side the ice, as if melted by heat, had run down to form columns, row after row of luminous pipes in the manner of a church organ. To this weird phenomenon, however, Ginger paid little attention. His eyes were focused on the middle of the room, where stood a large deal table – or rather, he stared at what was on it. It was a stack of bars, all the same shape and size. They were black. He was disappointed that they were not yellow, for then he would have known that his quest had ended.

Stepping closer to the table he reached for one of the bars to examine it; but when he went to pick it up he was amazed by its weight. In fact, he could not lift it. He could only drag it towards him. Could this be—? His heart began to thump. He reached quickly for his knife. One snick in the side of a bar told him all he needed to know. The cut metal gleamed, and the colour was yellow. He knew then that he had found the gold. He had found it! It was only self-consciousness that prevented him from shouting.

It was at this moment, while he stood gazing fascinated at the stacked bars before him, that he thought he heard a sound. It was very slight, a faint crunch, as if a piece of ice had been crushed. He paid little attention to it, however, supposing that such sounds in such a place were only to be expected. All the ice around him was constantly subject to pressure. Then an idea struck him, one that pleased him greatly. He would take a piece of the gold back with him. He couldn't carry an entire bar. That was out of the question. But gold, pure gold, he recalled, had the quality of being soft, so that he should have no difficulty in cutting off a piece with his knife. He would take it back to camp and enjoy the expressions on the faces of his friends when they realised what it was. Making a rough measurement with his knife he started sawing at the end of the bar that lay nearest, smiling to himself at the thought that few people had a chance to saw up pure gold.

The smile died suddenly as, while thus engaged, he heard another sound. This time there was nothing natural about it, and he was definitely startled. It sounded like what is usually called a chuckle – the soft sound made by a human being who is quietly amused. Ginger stopped sawing and stood tense, while cold fingers seemed to touch the back of his neck and slide down his spine. He was not superstitious, but he remembered where he was, and the horrors that had been enacted in that very room. Perhaps the very fingers that had last touched that bar of gold were now frozen in death in the ice just outside. Could it be possible that Manton's spirit, unable to rest— He looked around furtively. Nothing moved. The silence was profound.

He tried to persuade himself that the noise had been made by a cruising skua, although in his heart he knew that the noise was utterly unlike that made by any bird. Yet, he thought, the skua was an exceptional bird to live in such inhospitable surroundings. Telling himself not to be a fool he again turned to his task, but he had not even begun when he saw, or thought he saw, a shadow flit across the room – exactly where, he couldn't say, although it seemed as if something solid had passed between the light and the pipes of the ice-organ. Could it have been the shadow of a cloud, passing across the face of the sun? But there was no sun. The sky was grey. Again he experienced the feeling of an icy hand creeping down his back. He could not deceive himself. Something, somewhere, had moved. Could it have been his own shadow? It might have been. Calling himself a child for being frightened by his own shadow he tried to laugh it off, but it was a poor effort. His nerves were going to pieces, and he knew it. He would finish the job quickly, and go. That he might not be alone in the ship was still something that did not occur to him, and for this, in the circumstances, he was hardly to be blamed.

He turned back to the bar, but found it impossible to concentrate on what he was doing. His gaze seemed drawn irresistibly to the far side of the room, to the organ, where the shadow had stopped. His eyes wandered over it. They halted abruptly, and remained fixed, staring at something that stared back at him through a hole in the ice. It was an eye. He could see it distinctly; a human eye it appeared to be, for surrounding it was the small part of a dead white face. It did not move, but it glowed, as if imbued by inhuman fire.

CHAPTER VI

Ginger Runs Away

We have already said that Ginger was not superstitious. His life had lain along lines too materialistic for that. Nor was he easily frightened. He had looked Old Man Death in the face too often. But death was something he understood. What he now saw was something he did not understand, and to say merely that he was frightened would be to say nothing at all. He was, literally, paralyzed by fright. Perhaps for the first time he comprehended fully the meaning of the word fear – the fear that comes from something beyond human understanding. He was not conscious of this. If he was conscious of anything it was an overwhelming sensation of sheer horror, a nameless dread that gripped his tongue, dried his mouth to the dryness of ashes and turned his muscles to water. He could not turn his eyes away from the awful Thing, but stood rigid, as if mesmerised. The eye, unwinking, stared back.

How long he stood there, staring, with his heart beating on his eardrums, he never knew. He forgot all about the gold. It might not have existed. He forgot everything. But in human existence everything has an end, and thus with Ginger's temporary petrification. Fear was succeeded suddenly by panic, and panic has the quality of being mobile. So to Ginger returned the power of movement, and when it came it came with a rush. An inarticulate cry burst from his lips, and, turning, he fled incontinently. Out of the dreadful chamber, straight down the passage he tore in a shower of ice-gems detached by the vibration of his flying footsteps, certain that something frightful was at his heels. He took the companion steps in three jumps, skidded across the glassy deck, and in another reckless bound reached the level ice. Nor did he stop there. On he sped, to fall with a crash as he collided full tilt with Manton's ice tombstone. He had forgotten it. He did not see it. He did not stop to pick it up. He had taken a brutal fall, for the ice was hard; but he felt no pain. Gasping, he scrambled madly to his feet and raced on. At that moment he had one idea in life, one only; and that was to put as wide a distance between himself and the haunted ship as was possible in the shortest space of time.

Once clear, he risked a glance behind, but seeing nothing, some degree of sanity returned. Panting, he steadied his pace, and not until then did he become aware that it was snowing. That sobered him. Fortunately he had not gone far, and casting about, soon came upon one of his guide-sticks. That went far to restore him, for he knew that without it he would have been lost indeed. Apparently the snow had just started, and as there was no wind he could discern faintly the trail his feet had made on the outward journey. He followed it at a run. The crash and crunch of distant bergs formed a fitting accompaniment to his shattered nerves. The snow, after all, turned out to be only a shower, and slowly died away to a fairly clear but leaden calm.

When he came in sight of the camp he saw that the others were all home. All were engaged in clearing the new snow from the upper surfaces of the aircraft, a task they had almost completed. When they saw him coming they desisted and returned to the tent, there to await his arrival.

It can hardly be said that Ginger arrived back in camp. He tumbled into it, spent and shaken. Almost sobbing from reaction he

... and in another reckless bound reached the level ice.

sank down on the nearest packing case and buried an ashen face in trembling hands.

The others gathered round, looking from one to another.

Biggles was the first to speak. 'What's the matter with you,' he asked sharply.

Ginger drew a shuddering breath and looked up. 'I'm sorry – but – I can't help it,' he blurted.

'Can't help what?'

'Being like this. I'm all to pieces. I feel awful.'

'What happened?'

'I – I don't really know,' stated Ginger. 'It must seem silly to you, but nothing like this has ever happened to me before. I've seen – a ghost.'

'You've seen *what*?'

'A ghost.'

Biggles made a sign to the Skipper: 'Get me the brandy flask out of the medicine chest,' he ordered curtly. 'I don't know what's happened but he's suffering from shock – pretty severe shock, too. Grimy, get a blanket and throw it over his shoulders, then put some milk on the stove.'

The Skipper brought the flask, poured a little of the brandy into a cup and passed it to Biggles, who thrust it at Ginger. 'Drink this,' he ordered crisply.

The cup rattled against Ginger's teeth as he complied, spluttering as the potent spirit stung his throat. Without a word he handed the cup back to Biggles and wiped away the tears that the unaccustomed liquid had brought to his eyes.

'Now, what's all this about?' demanded Biggles. 'Pull yourself together.'

Ginger drew a deep breath and held out his trembling hands. 'Look at me,' he said weakly. 'I didn't get like this for nothing.'

'I can believe that,' answered Biggles. 'What caused it?'

'I don't rightly know,' admitted Ginger. 'I wasn't so bad until I saw the eye.'

Biggles frowned, looking hard at the speaker. 'Eye! What eye? Whose eye?'

'I don't know.'

Biggles caught Ginger by the shoulders and shook him. 'Snap out of it,' he ordered. 'So you saw an eye. Okay. Where was it?'

'In the ship.'

'Ship! What ship?'

'The *Starry Crown*.'

Dead silence greeted this announcement. Then Biggles went on, speaking slowly and deliberately. 'Are you telling us that you have found the *Starry Crown*?'

'Yes.'

'Where?'

Ginger pointed. 'Somewhere over there, about three miles for a guess.'

Biggles made a sign to the others to be patient. By this time he had realised that Ginger had had such a shock, real or imaginary, that comes only once in a lifetime. 'Go on,' he invited. 'Take your time. We're in no hurry. So you found the ship. What next?'

As the brandy took effect Ginger began to feel better. He became more coherent. 'First of all I found the grave,' he explained.

'Whose grave?'

'Manton's. The cross Last put up is still there. I cut away the ice and saw the name. Then I knew the ship must be somewhere near. I found it, all covered in ice. It wasn't easy to see. I went aboard to see if the gold was still there.'

'Was it?'

'Oh yes. It's there all right.'

'Did you actually touch it?'

Ginger stared. 'What do you mean – touch it?'

'I mean – you didn't dream it.'

'Dream it my foot,' cried Ginger hotly. 'I was hacking off a lump to bring home to show you.'

'Why didn't you?'

'That's what I'm trying to tell you,' protested Ginger. 'While I was sawing away I heard a movement. I didn't take much notice of it at the time. Then I heard someone chuckle – horrible.'

'And then you bolted?'

'I did not,' asserted Ginger. 'I wasn't feeling too happy, I'll admit, remembering that a dead man was lying just outside; but I went on with what I was doing. But looking up I caught sight of an eye watching me.'

'So what?'

Ginger shrugged. 'That finished me – and it would have finished anybody.' Ginger frowned at the scepticism on Biggles' face. 'Don't you believe me?'

'Well, you must admit it sounds a pretty tall story,' returned Biggles. 'But even if we take your word for it that all this really happened, what does it add up to. You heard a sound, and then you saw an eye looking at you. What's odd about that? You've seen an eye before today.'

'Not like this one,' said Ginger warmly.

'Was there only one eye?'

'I could only see one.'

'Are you trying to say you saw an eye wandering about without a face?'

'There was a little piece of face. The skin was white – a sort of dirty fish-belly white.'

Biggles lit a cigarette and flicked the match away. 'Did you by any chance have a fall and bump your head before you found the ship?'

'Are you suggesting I knocked myself silly and imagined this?' cried Ginger hotly.

'I wondered—'

'Well, you needn't,' declared Ginger vehemently.

'I found the ship, I tell you. Aladdin's cave was nothing to it. It was marvellous, all rainbows and coloured lights, jewels—'

'Now, wait a minute,' interrupted Biggles gently. 'It sounds to me as if you've got this ship all mixed up with the neon lights in Piccadilly on a fine night.'

'All right,' said Ginger wearily. 'Have it your own way. I'm telling you what I saw. I was as right as rain until that eye squinted at me.'

'Where exactly was it?'

'Behind a sort of curtain of ice at the far end of the room.'

'Didn't it move?'

'No'

'Then why get in such a sweat about it? Didn't you go up to it to make sure that it wasn't just another piece of ice with the light shining through it?'

'I certainly did not,' answered Ginger coldly. 'That was the *last* thing that occurred to me.'

'What did you do?'

'I ran – and when I say I ran I mean I didn't dawdle to examine the icicles on the way. No, sir. I was out of the ship so fast that a bullet coming behind me would have been left standing. My jump from the deck to the ice would be a world record if it could be measured. I nearly knocked myself out falling over Manton's grave. I took an awful purler, and it was only the thought of the dead man under me, and the eye behind me, that got me on my feet again. It was some time before I realised it was snowing. That should give you an idea of the state I was in. I didn't stop running all the way home. Look at me. My nerves are pulp. It takes more than imagination to do that.'

'Imagination can play queer tricks,' remarked Biggles quietly. 'The result can be the same as reality, perhaps worse; but I must admit that when you arrived here you looked more like a corpse than a live explorer.'

'You see, the trouble was, I wasn't expecting to find anyone else on the ship,' explained Ginger.

'I can believe that,' replied Biggles. 'It wouldn't be the sort of place you'd expect to find a picnic in progress. However, I'll believe in this floating eye when I see it.'

'I tell you, there's something, or somebody, in that ship,' expostulated Ginger sullenly.

'Well, it should be fairly easy to confirm that,' retorted Biggles. 'I'm not really inquisitive by nature, but I must confess that I'm all agog to have a look at this remarkable eye. Would you mind coming back and showing it to me?'

'What – me?' cried Ginger, rising in alarm. 'Go back to that ship? Not on your life – not if she was stuffed with diamonds as big as footballs. I shall see that accursed eye leering at me for the rest of my days. I won't even dare to sleep for fear it haunts my dreams.'

'Okay – okay!' said Biggles impatiently. 'Will you take us as far as the ship. If you'll show it to me I'll guarantee to gouge out this disconcerting optic.'

Ginger hesitated. 'All right. I wouldn't mind doing that – but I shall take a gun.'

'Good enough. You can take a battery of howitzers as far as I'm concerned; but somehow I don't think you'll need anything like that. I suppose you'll be able to find your way back?'

'Easily. I left my sticks in. I came home in too much of a hurry to pull them out.'

'I see,' said Biggles. 'We'll just have a cup of tea while you're catching up with yourself, then we'll go and collect the bullion.'

CHAPTER VII

The Horror in the Hulk

It was late in the evening although, of course, it was still light, when Biggles, Ginger and the Skipper set off to investigate the mystery. Grimy had been left behind as camp guard and mess orderly. As a matter of detail, Ginger, who was still not quite himself, had suggested that the trip be postponed until the following day, but Biggles was opposed to the delay, saying that he did not like the look of the weather. This was not to be disputed, for the sun, a gigantic crimson ball hanging low over the horizon, could only just be seen through a haze. The sky overhead seemed reasonably clear, but the Skipper agreed that there was a suspicion of more snow in the air. A rising temperature also threatened fog. Biggles maintained that if they did not go at once they might never go, for if the weather deteriorated it would be madness to stay on the ice at all.

If the gold was really there, then they would carry straight on, taking it out of the ship and putting it into a position from where it could easily be picked up, Biggles had said. They would then radio for Algy, and with the gold stowed in the two machines, make for home. Ginger had protested at Biggles use of the word 'if', which implied that he was still sceptical about the gold. Biggles had admitted frankly that he was. Had Ginger merely said he found the gold, he, Biggles, would have taken his word for it without question;

but if Ginger's nerves were in such a state that he imagined he had seen a ghost, which was absurd, he might also have imagined that he had seen the gold. Ginger saw that argument was useless. He saw, too, that if the eye had vanished, or if it turned out to be an illusion created by a freak of the ice, he would look a fool, and it would take him a long time to live the business down. Secretly he hoped it would still be there; but even he was beginning to wonder if he had made a mistake. The long-abandoned ship was an eerie place, and his nerves *had* been at full stretch, he reflected.

A steady tramp of just over an hour brought the party to within sight of the mass of ice which, Ginger claimed, held in its cold embrace the remains of the doomed vessel. Biggles' scepticism as he stared at it increased rather than diminished. From a distance, at any rate, it required a big effort of the imagination to discern the shape of the ship in the formless pile of blue-and-white ice. Ginger admitted this. It was likely, he said, that he would have walked past the ice without another glance, had it not been for the cross.

But when the cross was reached, lying where it had fallen, and Ginger displayed triumphantly the name of the dead mariner on the cross-bar, Biggles' expression changed. He looked at it and then gazed long and steadily at the chaos of ice. 'By thunder! I believe he's right,' he acknowledged in a curious voice.

'Well, there it is. What are you going to do about it?' inquired Ginger, trying to speak calmly.

'For a start I'm going to winkle out this eye that seems to have put the fear of the devil into you,' answered Biggles.

'Now, you listen to me,' said Ginger, with unusual earnestness. 'Be careful. There's somebody in that ship. I began to doubt it myself as we walked along, but now I'm back I'm sure of it. I can feel it in my bones.'

'Don't talk nonsense,' snapped Biggles. 'If there's an eye there's a human being, and that's something I can't believe. It doesn't make sense. And, anyhow, even if by some incredible chance there was a man in the ship, why should he stand still and squint at you? Surely he would have shouted with joy at seeing a deliverer.'

Ginger shrugged. 'All right. Have it your own way. I can't explain the thing any more than you can. But let me ask you this: Have you ever before seen me in such a mortal funk?'

'No, I can't say I have.'

'Then what caused it? It must have been *something*.'

'Yes, I suppose it must,' admitted Biggles. 'But standing here won't solve the mystery. We'll soon settle the matter.'

'Okay. Go ahead – but watch your step,' replied Ginger. 'Don't say I didn't warn you.'

Biggles smiled. 'I won't,' he promised.

The party advanced, Biggles leading, Ginger bringing up the rear. He pointed out the ice steps by which he had reached the companion-way. Biggles did not answer, but when they were all on the deck he turned. 'Stand fast,' he said, and then went on alone to the hole in the ice that gave access to the companion-steps and the lower deck. He looked inside and let out a low whistle. 'I must say it's all very pretty-pretty,' he told Ginger, in a glance over his shoulder. Turning again he shouted, 'Hi! Anyone there?'

There was no answer, but a moment later a movement farther along the deck caught Ginger's eye. Turning quickly he was just in time to see a dark object, the size of a football, where a moment before he would have sworn there had been nothing. Staring, he made it out to be a head, human, yet scarcely human. All that could be seen clearly was the middle part of the face, for above and below was a matted crop of reddish hair. Then it was gone.

Had Ginger been able to move he knew he would have run for his life; but all he could do was let out a strangled shout.

Biggles, who was just entering the companion, looked back. 'Now what is it?' he asked irritably.

Ginger gulped. 'A head,' he managed to get out. 'A head, all hair and beard.'

Biggles stared incredulously. 'Where?'

Ginger pointed.

Biggles looked. 'I can't see anything.'

'It's gone.'

Biggles looked again at Ginger. 'So now the eye has found a face to live in,' he scoffed. 'What's the matter with you? You don't usually behave like this.'

'Things like this don't usually happen,' answered Ginger weakly. 'Come on. Let's get out of this.'

'Oh, for the love of Mike pull yourself together,' requested Biggles impatiently. As he finished speaking he turned back to the companion. 'Anyone there?' he called loudly. But in spite of the question it was obvious from his manner that he did not expect an answer. Nor for the moment was there one. He took a step forward, then, suddenly, he flung himself aside with such speed that he slipped and fell. But any amusement this may have caused died at birth when the reason for the quick move revealed itself. Out through the opening flew an axe. It struck the frozen rigging with a crash and brought down a load of icicles.

By the time the noise of this had died away Biggles was on his feet, with such an expression on his face as Ginger had never before seen. No longer was he smiling.

'Now what about it?' cried Ginger, and it must be confessed that in his tone there was more than a suspicion of satisfaction at this dramatic confirmation of his allegations.

'All you could talk of was an eye,' answered Biggles frostily. 'You said nothing about axes flying about.'

'I didn't wait for the axe,' replied Ginger emphatically. 'The eye was enough for me.'

Biggles took his automatic from his pocket and once more approached the companion-way. Gone was his earlier nonchalance. He might have been approaching a lion's den. 'Come out of that,' he shouted.

The answer was a peal of demoniac laughter that made the hairs on the back of Ginger's neck prickle. It did not come so much from the hatch as from the ice under their feet.

Biggles turned to the others. 'I know it sounds crazy, but there is somebody in this hulk,' he said soberly.

'Aye! It's a spook,' asserted the Skipper lugubriously. 'Come away, mon. Ye canna argue with a spook.'

'I have yet to see a spook that could argue with a soft-nosed forty-five-calibre bullet,' answered Biggles trenchantly.

But the Skipper, all his seafaring superstitions aroused, was as pale as Ginger. His Scotch accent broadened in his agitation. 'It's the de'il himsel',' he declared. 'I dinna like it. Let's awa'.'

'Away! Not on your life,' disputed Biggles grimly. 'I'm going to get to the bottom of this.' Again he called to the unseen occupant to show himself.

From the depths came a quavering moan. 'Go away. Go away. I found the gold. It's mine – mine.'

'I've got it,' cried the Skipper hoarsely. 'It's Manton – that's who it is. His puir numbed body lies outside in the cold ice, but his spirit canna rest.'

'Then it's time it could,' growled Biggles.

'The ship's haunted I tell ye,' cried the Skipper, backing away.

'Don't talk such rubbish,' rapped out Biggles. 'There's a man in this hulk. I don't know who he is and I don't know where he came from, but he's here, and, like Manton, he's gone out of his mind –

either gold crazy or mad from loneliness. I'm going below to fetch him out.'

'He'll brain ye, mon. Drat the gold. Let's leave it?' implored the Skipper.

'I wasn't thinking so much about the gold,' answered Biggles slowly. 'I'm thinking about the man. We can't go away and leave the wretched fellow here.'

The Skipper was silent.

Said Ginger: 'It must have been *his* eye watching me.'

'No doubt of it,' replied Biggles. 'I apologise for doubting you, but you must admit that it took some believing.'

'And to think I was in the ship with – that!' Ginger shivered.

'Seems daft to get your head split open trying to save a man who doesn't want to be saved,' observed the Skipper gloomily. 'If ye go doon into yon hulk theer'll soon be two graves outside instead of one.'

Biggles nodded. 'Mebbe. It's an infernal nuisance. Who could have imagined such a situation?' He looked at Ginger: 'Remember what I told you about the unexpected always turning up on expeditions of this sort? Here you have a pretty example of it.'

'What are you going to do with this fellow if you do get him out?' inquired Ginger.

'We'll talk about that when we've got him,' returned Biggles. Turning back to the opening he called: 'For the last time, are you coming out?'

'It's my gold you're after,' came the answer, screeched in the voice of a raving lunatic. 'I know who you are,' was the final surprising statement.

'Who am I?' called Biggles.

'Manton,' was the staggering reply. 'I saw your grave outside. I've heard you creeping about.'

Understanding dawned in Biggles' eyes. 'So that's it,' he said softly. 'The wretched fellow has gone crazy imagining Manton has returned from the grave to get the gold. Well, it's no use messing about any longer. I'm going in after him.'

'You must be madder than he is,' snorted the Skipper.

'We can't leave him here,' returned Biggles briefly; and with that he disappeared down the steps.

'We can't let him go down there alone,' cried Ginger in alarm, and ran forward to follow.

But the Skipper caught his arm and held him. 'You stay where you are,' he said shortly. 'I'll go.' Without waiting for the protest which he guessed would come, he, too, dived down the stairs.

Ginger took out his pistol and stood ready to move quickly should it be necessary. He noted that Biggles' prediction about the weather had come to pass. Fine snow was falling, reducing visibility to twenty or thirty yards. But before he had time to ponder the consequences this was likely to produce there came from somewhere below a wild yell and the crash of splintering ice. A moment later, from the place where he had seen the head, leapt the wild, unkempt figure of a man who sobbed and babbled in the manner of a terrified child. Ginger caught a glimpse of a white haggard face almost surrounded by a mane of tangled reddish hair. In his arms the man clutched an object which he recognised at once. It was one of the gold bars. Ginger moved quickly, thinking that the maniac – for maniac the man obviously was – intended to attack him. But this was not so. With a screech that was scarcely human the man jumped down to the level ice, fell, picked himself up, and still clutching the ingot, still sobbing, disappeared into the blur of falling snow. Ginger, not knowing what to do, in the end did nothing.

Biggles, followed by the Skipper, came scrambling out of the companion-way. 'Where is he? Which way did he go?' asked Biggles tersely.

Ginger pointed. 'That way. He's got a bar of gold with him.'

'Poor chap,' said Biggles sympathetically. 'A precious lot of good that'll do him out there. I'm afraid it's no use trying to follow him in these conditions. He probably knows his way about, and so may make his way back presently. That's what gold does to a man.'

'Who on earth can it be?' asked Ginger wonderingly.

'I know who he is,' put in the Skipper, surprisingly.

Biggles spun round. 'You know!' he exclaimed.

'Yes. It's Larsen, the Swede I told you about, who was lost when I was down here in the *Svelt*. Wandering about, he must have tumbled on the hulk by accident and has been living in it ever since. I only got a glimpse of him just now, but I remember that red hair. I should have known the voice. He was one of the few men I could trust. Mebbe that's why Lavinsky was content to leave him behind.'

'Well, that's settled the mystery of the sinister eye, anyway,' said Biggles.

'What happened when you went below?' asked Ginger.

'Nothing much. The poor wretch was whining like a whipped dog. When he saw us coming he bolted. I went after him, but he crashed through some ice and disappeared. Apparently he knew of another way out.'

'Did you see the gold?'

'Yes. It's there – but it isn't all on the table any longer. Having seen you, Larsen must have guessed you'd come back, so he had started to hide the gold in a hole in the ice. Another half hour and he would have finished the job, in which case the metal would probably have remained in the ice for ever. We should never have found it. I should have assumed that Lavinsky had got here first and made off with the lot.'

'I'm surprised that Larsen didn't try to hide the stuff before today,' put in the Skipper.

'Why should he?' queried Biggles. 'About the last thing he'd expect was visitors. No doubt he was as surprised to see Ginger as Ginger was to see him – or rather, his eye. Had it been otherwise Ginger might have got his brains knocked out. As soon as Ginger bolted Larsen's first thought was to save his precious gold.'

The Skipper thrust his hands into his pockets. 'What are we going to do about him?'

'It's hard to know what to do, and that's a fact,' admitted Biggles. 'I don't think it's much use looking for the chap. If we go, I imagine he'll come back. If he does, the first thing he'll do will be to lug the gold out somewhere in the snow. It wouldn't be much use looking for it then. We can't let that happen. Our plan, therefore, must be to put the gold where he can't find it.'

'You mean – take it back to camp?' asked Ginger.

'Good gracious, no. That would be a tremendous task, taking far more time than we could afford.'

'But it will have to be carried to the machine sooner or later,' argued Ginger.

'Not at all. It would be a lot easier to bring the machine here.'

'True enough,' agreed Ginger. 'What about landing, though. Is there enough room?'

'I think so. I kept an eye open for possible landing areas as we walked here. It's quite flat between the hulk and the open water. What we'll do is carry the gold to a convenient place not far away, cover it with snow and then fetch the machine. If it comes to that, there's no need for everyone to walk back to camp. With Larsen on the loose, to be on the safe side someone should stay with the gold. You're looking tired, Ginger; perhaps you'll stay. The Skipper can come back with me to help clear up the camp. I don't think you've anything to fear from Larsen. If the snow continues he wouldn't be able to find you even if he tried. If it stops, he couldn't get to you without your seeing him. How does that sound?'

No one had a better plan so it was agreed.

'Are you going to start on the gold right away?' asked Ginger.

'We might as well,' answered Biggles. 'In fact, the sooner the better. The snow isn't as thick as it was. We may get a break but I'm afraid there's more snow to come. It's not so bad at the moment, at any rate.'

This was true. The snow had practically ceased, but the sky was still grey with a promise of more.

Ginger gazed across the desolate waste of the well-named White Continent. It was possible again to see a fair distance, but there was not a movement anywhere. He wondered where the unfortunate Swede had managed to hide himself, and made a remark to that effect.

'He's probably busy hiding his lump of gold,' answered Biggles. 'There's nothing we can do about him for the time being. Let's get cracking on shifting the bullion.'

This proved to be a wearisome task, even though the gold had to be carried no great distance – merely to a point about one hundred yards from the open sea where, as the surface of the ice was smooth, and the snow thin, Biggles said he could put the aircraft down without much risk of accident. The ingots were heavy, but once hoisted on a shoulder one could be carried fairly easy. Transportation proceeded, therefore, at the rate of one bar per man per journey.

'I never thought the day would come when I should get tired of carrying gold,' remarked Ginger wearily, when, with the work finished, he sank down on the stack of precious metal.

'To move a ton of anything would be just as tiresome,' Biggles pointed out, perhaps unnecessarily. 'Still, it's finished now. I'll go with the Skipper back to camp, collect anything that we're likely to need, and bring the machine along. Sure you don't mind staying, Ginger?'

'No, I'll stay.'

'I shall be back in a couple of hours at the outside,' stated Biggles. 'As soon as the machine is in the air I'll get Grimy to make a signal to Algy asking him to fly down and help carry the stuff home. We'll light a smudge fire to show him where we are. He should have no difficulty in finding us.'

'What had I better do if Larsen comes for me?' asked Ginger. 'I wouldn't like to use my gun on a lunatic.'

'A shot or two would probably scare him,' suggested Biggles. 'Personally, I don't think he'll worry you. He seemed terrified out of his wits by the mere sight of us, poor fellow. Our problem is how to get him home. However, we'll deal with that when the time comes. We'll get along now, while the weather's fair. See you presently.'

Biggles and the Skipper set off down the track the party had made on its outward journey.

Ginger watched them go. Quite content to rest for a while he arranged the gold bars in the manner of a seat and sat down to wait for the aircraft. The whimsical thought struck him that few people had been privileged to use a ton of pure gold as a seat. Actually, little of it could be seen, because the lower bars had sunk into the snow; and the thought occurred to him that if he should have to leave the spot for any reason he might have difficulty in finding it again. A short distance away stood one of the guide sticks he had used to mark his trail earlier in the day, so he fetched it, and arranged it in the heap like a miniature flag-staff. He could think of nothing else to do so he settled down, from time to time subjecting the landscape to a searching scrutiny for a possible sight of the castaway. But he saw nothing of him. The time passed slowly, and he began to understand ever more clearly why men marooned in this white world of silence soon went out of their minds. The loneliness became a tangible thing, an invisible enemy that stood ever at his elbow. The utter absence of sound weighed like lead upon his nerves.

It was with relief, therefore, that he heard in the far distance the sound of the Wellington's engines being started, for this at once seemed to put him in touch with the world of noise and bustle that he knew. Listening, he heard the drone rise to crescendo as the motors were run up. The sound died abruptly, and he could visualise Biggles sitting in the cockpit with the engines idling while he waited for the others to get aboard. Again came the vibrant roar and he imagined Biggles taking off. Good. In five minutes his vigil would end. But instead of this the note rose and fell several times in a manner which he could not understand. Then it died altogether. What had happened, he wondered. The only thing he could think of was, Biggles had for some reason taken off in the opposite direction and in so doing had run out of earshot. Presently he would hear him coming back. He waited, listening intently. The silence persisted. Not a sound of any sort reached his ears. What could have happened? At first he was merely disappointed, but as the minutes passed and still nothing happened his disappointment turned to uneasiness, and from uneasiness to apprehension.

Time passed. Still no sound came to break the frigid solitude. Over the world hung a trance-like calm, a calm that was the calmness of death. Sitting still, the intense cold began to strike at him with silent force. He looked at his watch, ticking inexorably its measurement of time. Biggles had been gone more than three hours. He knew then that he could not deceive himself any longer. Something had gone wrong. Biggles was in trouble. He stood up, staring in the direction of the camp. But he could see nothing. A few flakes of snow were now falling from a sky as grey as his mood.

CHAPTER VIII

The Unexpected Again

Ginger was right in his assumption that Biggles was in trouble; and it was trouble of a sort that Biggles thought he should have foreseen.

There had been no difficulty about the return journey to the camp. Everything was just as it had been left. Grimy sat by the fire with hot coffee waiting. Biggles and the Skipper each paused for a cup and then straight away set about the business of packing up, which consisted of no more than sorting out the most valuable equipment and sufficient food to see them over the next forty-eight hours. By that time, Biggles asserted, they should be back at the Falklands, and there was no point in loading the machine with unnecessary weight. The value of the cargo they were taking home would render negligible the cost of anything they left behind. The work, therefore, did not take long. The things required were securely stowed in the aircraft and the rest left where they were.

This done, Biggles climbed into the cockpit and ran up the engines. Satisfied and relieved to find that they were giving their revolutions he called to the others to get aboard and at once made ready to take off. The Skipper took the spare seat beside him, while Grimy went to his place at the wireless cabin with a message that

Biggles had written for transmission to Algy, asking him to come straight out to help him to carry home the 'goods.'

When all was ready Biggles went through the usual formula for taking off. Nothing happened. The machine did not move. The engines bellowed. Still the aircraft did not move. He tried again, giving the engines as much throttle as he dare risk; but the machine remained as immobile as a rock. He throttled back and considered the situation; and it did not take him long to realise that only one thing could have happened. His landing chassis had either sunk in the snow or in some way had become attached to it. He switched off.

These, of course, were the sounds that Ginger had heard when he had supposed, naturally enough, that the machine had taken off, whereas in fact it had not left the ground.

Looking rather worried Biggles climbed down, and the others followed him. They found him on his knees examining the skis. He got up when the others joined him. 'I ought to be kicked for not thinking of it,' he remarked, with bitter self-denunciation.

'What's wrong, sir?' asked Grimy.

'The machine's been standing still long enough for the skis to become frozen to the snow. It must have been that slight rise in temperature that did it. I should have foreseen the possibility.'

'Won't the engines pull her off?' enquired the Skipper.

'This is an aircraft – not a tugboat,' returned Biggles. 'If I gave her full throttle and she came unstuck suddenly you'd see the unusual picture of an aeroplane turning a somersault. This is no place for exhibitions of that sort.'

'Can anything be done about it?'

'Yes, but it's going to take time, and Ginger is going to take a dim view of it if he's left sitting out on his own. Still, he should take no harm. All we can do is cut the ice from under the skis and slide something under to prevent them from sticking again until we can get her off. Bring me the cold chisel, Grimy – the one we used for opening the packing cases.'

Grimy brought the tool.

'Now you can start knocking to pieces some cases to get some boards,' ordered Biggles. 'We'll stick them under as we go along.' Dropping on his knees he started chipping away the frozen snow. After a little while he paused to regard his work. 'We can do it,' he observed, 'but it's going to take a little while. What has happened is, the whole weight of the machine falling on the skis has pressed the snow till it's as hard as ice. At the same time they got stuck up. I seem to recall reading of a fellow who got into a similar jam. A few pieces of board would have prevented it. However, in this business there's always something new to learn.'

The work continued. The Skipper found a screwdriver and started on the second ski, while Grimy stood by and slipped boards under as the frozen snow was cleared away. The task was purely mechanical. The aircraft was in no danger. It was, as Biggles remarked, just one of those things. What caused him more anxiety than the machine was an occasional flurry of snow. It was evident that if the weather deteriorated further they were likely to be storm-bound, and Ginger might have some difficulty in getting back. His only shelter would be in the hulk, and if the Swede returned to it, as seemed likely, anything might happen. The thought spurred him to greater efforts.

As it turned out the job did not take as long as he expected, for as the work progressed the snow came away more easily. Moreover, by using a long board as a lever it became possible to prise the skis free. At any rate, by the end of an hour and a half, although the skis were not entirely clear, Biggles thought that the machine would move under the power of its engines. He climbed into the cockpit for a test, for, while it was not actually snowing, visibility was now so poor that he feared further delay might make flying impracticable. Starting the motors he eased the throttle open cautiously. For a moment the aircraft vibrated, shuddering: then a forward lurch told him what he wanted to know. The machine was clear.

'All right,' he shouted to the others. 'Get in. Bring some boards with you, Grimy. We must see this doesn't happen again.'

The undercarriage now did the work for which it had been designed. There was a certain amount of drag when the machine first moved forward, due, as Biggles expected, to ice particles still adhering to the skis; but as the aircraft gathered speed friction soon wiped them clean and the take-off became normal.

As soon as he was clear of the ice Biggles started to turn. Visibility, he discovered, was worse than it had appeared to be from ground level, and for that reason, knowing that there were no obstructions worth considering between him and his objective, he remained within sight of the 'carpet.' There was no horizon. All he could see was a small area of snow immediately below him. The position of the sun was revealed by a dull orange glow. Flying on even keel at five hundred feet he headed for the hulk, smiling faintly at the thought of what Ginger would have to say about his being left alone so long. A minute or two later, looking ahead along the ice-cliff he expected to see him; but when he failed to do so he was not particularly concerned because, as he now realised, the snow that had fallen would cover everything with a white mantle. Still, he thought it rather odd that Ginger did not stand up to give a wave. He half expected that he would have lit a fire to mark his position. However, Biggles could see the pile of ice that enclosed the hulk, so dismissing Ginger from his mind for a moment he concentrated on the anxious business of getting down. This, to his relief, he was able to accomplish without mishap. He hoped sincerely that it would be the last time he would have to do it. With the gold on board the next landing would be at the Falkland Islands.

As soon as the machine had run to a stop Grimy jumped down and thrust his boards under the skis to prevent a repetition of the trouble that had caused the delay. Biggles asked him if he had got the signal through to Algy. Grimy said that he had, but was unable to say anything more, owing to the short time at his disposal.

'You told him we'd found the wreck?' questioned Biggles.

'Yes, sir.'

'Good.' Biggles smiled. 'That should bring him along in a hurry. He ought to be here in a few hours. Meanwhile we can all have a rest while we're waiting. The trouble about all this daylight is, one tries to go on indefinitely without sleep. I only hope the weather doesn't get any worse. If it does, the other machine may have a job to find us.'

While he had been speaking Biggles had been looking around with a puzzled expression dawning on his face. 'Where the deuce is Ginger?'

Grimy looked around. The Skipper did the same. Neither answered.

A frown creased Biggles' forehead. 'I suppose we've come to the right place?'

'No mistake about that,' answered the Skipper. 'There's the hulk,' he pointed. 'We left Ginger over there.'

'That's what I thought,' said Biggles slowly. 'Well, he isn't there now. What the dickens can he have done with himself. That shower of snow was just enough to blot out the trail we made when handling the gold. Come to mention it I can't see the gold, either.'

'Could he have got cold and gone back into the hulk?' suggested the Skipper.

'He might have done, but with Larsen running wild I should say it's most unlikely,' muttered Biggles. He gazed round the landscape. 'What an extraordinary thing.'

'What beats me is why we can't see the gold,' put in Grimy.

'It would have snow on it,' reminded Biggles. 'Wherever Ginger may be, one thing is quite certain,' he went on. 'The gold will still be where we dumped it for the simple reason one man couldn't have moved it all in the time. Ginger wouldn't be likely to move it anyway, and he wouldn't allow Larsen to touch it. Still, it's very odd that we can't see it. I wonder if there's something deceptive about the visibility? It can play queer tricks in these conditions. Dash it all, the stuff *must* be here. Ginger must have dropped off to sleep and got a coating of snow over him. This is where we left him, over here.' Biggles began walking to the spot he had indicated, his pace increasing as he advanced. But still there was no sign of Ginger. Again he looked around. Then, speaking to the Skipper, he questioned: 'Are you certain this is the place?'

'Absolutely,' declared the Skipper without hesitation. 'What makes you doubt it?'

'I've got a feeling that something has changed.'

'What *could* change.'

Biggles shrugged his shoulders, unable to find a satisfactory answer to the question. In fact, the whole thing was a mystery for which he was quite unable to provide a solution. Again he stared at the frozen sterility about him, and then at the wreck, as if to convince himself that this was the place. Cupping his hands round his mouth he shouted, 'Ginger!'

There was no answer.

Biggles, looking completely nonplussed, stared at the Skipper.

'This beats anything and everything,' he muttered in a voice of bewilderment. 'This is the place where we left him – or else I'm going crazy.'

'Aye. This is the place all right,' assented the Skipper. 'We left him sitting on the stuff.'

'I know. And had he moved, or had Larsen come here, surely there would have been fresh tracks. What baffles me is there isn't a track anywhere.'

'I'd say he got browned off sitting here and went back to the ship where he could light a fire and maybe find something to eat,' opined Grimy.

Biggles shook his head. 'No. He didn't do that. You heard what he said. I'm sure nothing would have induced him to go near the hulk – at any rate, not while that madman is at large.'

The Skipper drew a deep breath. 'I give it up.'

Biggles showed signs of exasperation. 'The whole thing is absurd. He must be here. He wouldn't leave of his own accord, and ruling out Larsen, there's nobody here to make him move.' Biggles walked on a short distance towards the open water. 'He couldn't have gone that way, anyhow,' he declared.

'If he had he wouldn't have taken the gold with him,' observed the Skipper.

'That's what I mean,' returned Biggles helplessly. 'I've seen some queer things in my time but this beats them all.'

The Skipper let out a real seaman's hail.

There was no reply. The sound died away, leaving the sullen silence even more oppressive than before.

'If he was within half a mile he would have heard that,' asserted the sailor. He looked at Biggles. 'This reminds me of the Flying Dutchman,' he said nervously. 'You remember—'

Biggles broke in. 'Now don't start any more superstitious

257

nonsense,' he requested curtly. 'There's nothing supernatural about this.' He strode away to the hulk. He did not stop when he reached it but went straight on down the companion-way. In a minute or two he was back. 'He isn't there,' he announced.

'There's nowhere else to look,' said the Skipper.

'If only the sky would clear I'd take the machine up and have a look round, but it's no use doing that in this infernal murk,' said Biggles irritably. Taking out his pistol he pointed the muzzle skywards and pulled the trigger. The report seemed dull and life-less, but he listened for a reply. From far away out over the open sea came a faint report. He looked at the Skipper.

The Skipper shook his head. 'Echo,' he murmured. 'You get an echo from a big iceberg – or perhaps you could get one from that cloud just over our heads.'

Biggles looked dubious, but agreed that it was hardly likely that Ginger could have taken to the open sea, with the gold. Putting the pistol in his pocket he remarked: 'There must be an explanation of this. We've got to find it. That's all about it.'

CHAPTER IX

What Happened to Ginger

The explanation of Ginger's uncanny disappearance was really perfectly simple. It may have been its very simplicity that caused it to be overlooked.

The statement that he had been left sitting on the gold was correct. He had not moved. There was no reason for him to move. He had no desire to see the inside of the hulk again so there was really nowhere for him to go even when he had become bored with sitting on his golden throne; and as the time passed he became very bored indeed. Not only was he bored, he was worried. He had, as he thought, heard the machine take off. It had not arrived. Obviously, something had gone wrong, and he nearly worried himself sick wondering what it could have been. But there was nothing he could do about it. Walking about would not help matters, so as he had no wish to collide with the deranged Swede he remained where he was, satisfied that Larsen would not be able to get to him without showing himself. His thoughts became sombre as he perceived all too clearly what his position would be if the aircraft never came. In that event, he pondered moodily, history looked like repeating itself. He would have to shoot Larsen or have his brains knocked out by an axe in the hands of a maniac. The prospect, he decided, was grim. He looked more often at the hulk, which he could just see in the bad light. Through the gloom, the pile of ice looked unpleasantly like a monstrous crouching apparition.

His fears took a more material turn when suddenly he experienced a queer sensation that the gold on which he was sitting had moved slightly. It was only the merest tremor yet he had been conscious of it. Or he thought he had. Was his imagination playing tricks? Why should he imagine such a thing? How could the gold move, anyway? Were his nerves in such a state? He stood up to rouse himself from the lethargy into which he had fallen, and tried to shake off the mood of depression which, he thought, must have been responsible for the illusion of movement. He promptly sat down again. He had not intended to. The movement was involuntary, induced, it seemed, by giddiness. Then he thought he understood. He was ill. Something was the matter with him – probably a recurrence of malaria contracted in the tropics. The idea took firm root when, a minute later, he experienced another quite definite wave of nausea, brought on by a feeling that the ground was rocking under him. Did they have earthquakes in the South Pole he wondered vaguely? Was that the answer? It seemed not impossible. Other countries had earthquakes, why not the Poles?

Cupping his chin in his hand he gazed across the desolation at the hulk. And as he looked at it his forehead puckered in a frown. Was it more imagination, or was the ice-encased ship farther away than it had been? Perhaps visibility had disimproved. That might produce such an affect. Then he noticed something else, something that brought him to his feet in haste. Between him and the hulk had appeared a black, irregular line, a line that widened as it appeared to cut a zig-zag course across the ice. He stood on the gold for a better view, and then he understood. A portion of the main pack ice had broken away, and he was on the piece that had come adrift.

Wondering why he had not realised at once what was happening he ran towards the line of water that now separated him from the mainland. His one concern was his personal safety. By the time he had reached the water he saw to his consternation that it was already some eight or ten feet wide, which was too wide for a jump from such a slippery take off. Swiftly his eyes ran along the gap. They stopped when they came to a place where it was still only two or three feet across. He raced towards it. But the ice was moving, too, and by the time he had reached the spot the gap was again too wide. He ran on, still looking for a place where he might get across, hoping even to find a spot where the floe had not actually parted from the parent ice. There was no such place. In sheer panic now he tore along the edge of his floating island; but it was no use. Everywhere the gap was too wide, and every passing second saw it wider. Bitterly he regretted that he had not risked a jump while there was still a chance. Breathing heavily he stared at the black water, six feet below him. There could be no question of swimming. The cold would be paralyzing. In any case, it would be impossible to climb up the sheer face of ice. So there he stood, his thoughts in a turmoil, watching the gap yawn ever wider with slow, relentless force. The hulk, his only landmark, became an indistinct object in a white, shadowless world. Presently that too disappeared.

He knew there could be no other way of escape, but in sheer desperation he looked for one. All around were floes, rafts of ice like the one he was on. All appeared to be motionless, but he knew they must be moving. Some were quite close, but all were detached, so there was no point in leaving his own. In the end he had to face the fact that there was nothing he could do. Indeed, as far as he could see there was nothing anyone could do, for while the floe he was on was not small, it was not big enough for the aircraft to land on even if Biggles should discover his predicament. He had, he thought, one

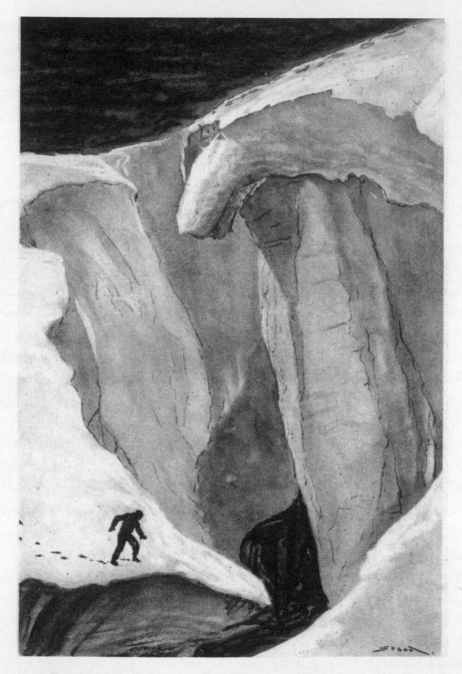

By the time he had reached the gap it was too wide.

chance, provided Biggles came quickly; for the gap between him
and the mainland told him that the floe was moving ever faster,
presumably as it felt the affect of a current. The aircraft, in view
of its long over-water journey, carried as part of its equipment a
collapsible rubber dinghy. It would take a little time to inflate and
launch, and the employment of it in the floating ice-fields would
be risky, for not only might it be crushed between two pieces of ice
but one small piece of the razor-edged stuff would certainly punc-
ture it. But before it could be used Biggles would have to find him;
and there was good reason to suppose that Biggles himself was in
serious difficulties or he would have been back long ago.

The floe was now some distance from the stable pack-ice, and he
had an idea that his drift was towards the north-east. Visualising
the map he perceived that if the floe maintained that direction it
would eventually bring up against the long, north-pointing arm
of the Graham Peninsula, the best part of a hundred miles away.
What would happen then was a matter for speculation. It would not
affect him, anyhow, because long before the ice had travelled that
distance he would have died from hunger and exposure. Should the
floe find itself in the grip of a more northerly current – as obviously
some did, for he had seen them on the way down – then the ice
would eventually melt, dropping him and the gold into the deepest
sea. The gold! He laughed bitterly. He could now understand why
Last, when he had made his desperate bid for life in a small boat,
hadn't bothered about the gold. At that moment Ginger would have
swapped all his gold bars for a dinghy, no matter how dilapidated
as long as it would float for twenty minutes.

Standing on the edge of the ice, as near as he could get to the
main pack, he watched it gradually fade into the background. He
knew it was no use shouting, for Biggles was not there to hear him.
It was ironic that the only man who might be within hail was a

raving lunatic. After a while, realising that he could do no good by standing there, he walked slowly back to the gold and sat down to think the matter over. Not that there was much to think about.

So this, he pondered miserably, was the end of their adventure – at any rate, the end of his. How many mariners, he wondered, had found themselves in the same melancholy plight, since men had begun their search for the great Southern Continent hundreds of years before his time. A good many, no doubt. And there would be more. Something of the sort had happened to Larsen. He had managed to get ashore, and a lot of good it had done him. Ginger could only hope that his fate would not be so long drawn out. A ghastly picture of himself and Larsen fighting it out in the hulk for possession of the gold, as Last and Manton had done, floated into his mind. He dismissed it with a shiver, perceiving that such thoughts were a certain way to madness.

Biggles, he feared, would never come now. Something had happened to him. He could not imagine what it was. The engines, which he had heard, seemed to be in order. Was he, too, marooned somewhere in this dismal world of everlasting ice? How he hated the stuff. All around him he could hear it growling and crunching as the floes ground into each other. Once he watched it happen, quite close to where he sat. He saw the ice splinter as the two pieces drove against each other; watched them locked in frozen embrace drift away into the murk. From an inside pocket he produced a bar of chocolate. He ate it slowly and deliberately, and was surprised to find that he could do so without emotion, although it was probably the last thing he would ever eat. He was almost glad that he had no provisions with him, for they would only prolong the inevitable end.

He did not take account of the passing of time, but it must have been about an hour later that he heard a sound that brought him to his feet with a rush. It was the drone of an aircraft. It sounded a long way off, but in his desperate case it brought a new hope, for it did at least tell him that Biggles was still alive. Listening he heard the aircraft take off, which meant that the machine was, after all, still airworthy. He could not see it, of course; it was too far off for that; but he could more or less follow its course. He judged it was on its way to the hulk. He waited for it to land, but when it did he was appalled by its distance away. It seemed impossible that he could have drifted so far in so short a time. Or was the sound deceptive, muffled, perhaps, by the low cloud? He could not even hazard a guess as to the actual distance in terms of measurement. It might be a mile, he thought; it might be two or even three. Taking out his pistol he fired a shot into the air and listened for an answering shot. None came. He knew the sound would be very faint, too faint to be heard if Biggles or the others happened to be talking, or making a noise of any sort.

He sat down again, staring in the only direction from which deliverance could come. Biggles by this time would be looking for him, wondering what had become of him. He tried shouting, but in the vastness the sound seemed a mere bleat, flat and futile. Even the skuas, with their high pitched note, could make more noise than that, he reflected bitterly. He sprang to his feet again as from the far distance came a faint pop. Could it have been a shot? Taking his pistol again he fired it in the direction from which the sound had come and then listened breathlessly for a reply. It did not come. He could have thrown his weapon into the sea from very impotence. No wonder Larsen had gone out of his mind in such a place where even a pistol seemed unable to make its usual healthy explosion.

A feeling of utter futility grew on him. It seemed to be getting colder, too, and in order to keep his circulation going he had to stamp about and buff his arms. His breath hung in the air like smoke. If only the weather would clear, he thought petulantly, as he paced up and down, stamping his feet. Even the weather was against him, although he did not lose sight of the fact that it might easily be worse. But in clear weather Biggles might still be able to see him from the shore. From the air, when Biggles took off to look for him, as he would, he would be spotted at once. Algy would soon be coming, too. There was a chance that he might see him – but not in this dismal gloom.

Time wore on. Ginger was deadly tired but he dare not rest. Apart from being buried under snow should there be another storm, or becoming frozen in his sleep, he might miss something, perhaps an attempt at rescue. All the same, with the visibility factor so low he did not think Biggles would risk flying low over the open sea for fear of colliding with one of the big bergs which, even on a clear day, were not always easy to see. To fly high would be useless.

For a long time, it seemed, Ginger paced up and down the ice, sometimes resting on the heap of gold, staring into space, striving to probe with his eyes the intangible barrier that surrounded him on all sides. And while he sat thus, brooding on the little things which make all the difference between life and death, the deceitful atmosphere played on him another trick. He saw a ship. He closed his eyes for a moment and looked again. It was still there. He could see it distinctly. A minute earlier it had not been there, he was sure of that. Now it was as large as life, as the saying goes, clear in every detail. What sort of phenomenon was this, he wondered? Could there be such a thing as a mirage in polar waters, such as he had seen in the deserts of Arabia? Or was this the beginning of madness?

For a little while yet he sat still, unable to believe his eyes – or if the truth must be told, not daring to believe them. But when he saw men moving on the deck and the throb of an engine reached his ears he knew that a miracle had happened. A ship *was* there. A real ship. Springing to his feet he let out a wild yell.

That it had been heard he knew at once from the way the men stopped what they were doing to stare at him. Their amazement, he thought, as the vessel turned slowly towards him, would be no less than his.

It may seem odd that the possible identity of the craft did not occur to him; but it must be remembered that, situated as he was, with a miserable fate confronting him, the gold and everything to do with it had for all practical purposes ceased to exist. He assumed, naturally, that the ship was one of those whalers or sealers which on rare occasions penetrated to the southern extremity of the open water in search of prey. Apart from that, his one overwhelming emotion was thankfulness that by a chance little short of miraculous he was saved. He could have shouted from sheer relief. Instead, he held himself in hand, and stood calmly awaiting deliverance.

But when his eyes wandered idly to the bows of the ship and he read the name *Svelt* his exuberance died abruptly. Even then it took him a moment or two to recall the association of the word and realise its full significance. *Svelt*. Lavinsky's ship. So that was it. Of course. What a fool he had been not to guess it at once. Not that it would have made much difference. He would still have welcomed it. He would have welcomed any craft. Anything was better than dying slowly on a floating island of ice.

Then he remembered the gold. What should he do about it? He had to think quickly because the *Svelt* was now swinging round to come alongside the ice, and a man was already standing ready to throw him a line. His brain worked swiftly. Lavinsky must not suspect the incredible truth – that the little hump of snow behind him covered the thing he had come to fetch.

Knowing something of Lavinsky's character, Ginger saw clearly that if the man realised the gold was there his respite would be short-lived. There would be no question of sharing it, or anything like that. Lavinsky would take the gold and probably knock him on the head as the easiest way of disposing of an undesirable witness.

This done he would simply turn round and sail home in triumph, while Biggles would for ever after be in ignorance of what had happened. The thing, obviously, was to say nothing. The gold would have to take its chance. It was not for him to jeopardise his life by mentioning it. Lavinsky, no doubt, would go on to the ice-pack and proceed with his search. There, sooner or later, he would run into Biggles. He, Ginger, would then tell Biggles what had happened, and leave him to deal with the newcomers. Glancing over his shoulder he saw that the gold was pretty well covered with snow. Under the pretext of stretching his legs as if to relieve stiffness he kicked a little more snow over the one or two places where it had been brushed off by his garments. One thing was quite certain, he thought whimsically. However well endowed with imagination Lavinsky might be, he would hardly expect to find the gold where it actually was – floating on the high seas on a slab of ice.

The ship felt its way alongside. A rope came swishing across the ice. Grabbing it, Ginger allowed himself to be hauled up to the deck, where he found himself facing a semi-circle of curious spectators. The men, a hard-looking lot, appeared all the tougher from the heavy garments they wore against the cold. Most wore balaclava helmets. Some were obviously Asiatics.

The first question put was the obvious one. A man in a greasy blue jacket and peaked cap stood a little in front of the others. Ginger guessed it was Lavinsky. He was not a big man. His face was pale, thin, and carried prominent cheekbones that suggested Slav ancestry. His eyes, set close together, were cold and grey, and held a calculating quality which provided a good indication of his character. He looked at Ginger as though he might have been a freak, although in the circumstances this was understandable.

'Where have you come from?' he asked in English which, while good, held a curious accent.

'From the pack-ice,' replied Ginger, noting with satisfaction that the ship was now edging away from the floe.

'What were you doing there?'

'Exploring.'

'What's the name of your ship?'

'I haven't got a ship,' answered Ginger. 'I'm a member of a British air exploration party. I was sitting near the edge of the ice, resting while the others were away, when the part I was on broke off and went adrift. By the time I'd realised it I was too far out to get back. There was nothing I could do about it. The plane was away on a flight. I heard it come back but I couldn't make the crew hear me. I'd just about given up hope when you appeared.'

'Huh! I reckon you were kinda lucky,' observed the man cynically.

Ginger agreed. But the man's next question shook him.

'I reckon,' said he, slowly, 'you're a member of the party that found the ship.'

Ginger's astonishment was genuine. 'Ship,' he echoed. 'What ship?'

'We've got radio,' was the sneering answer. 'A little while ago we picked up a message from someone saying the ship had been found.'

Then, of course, Ginger understood what had happened. Biggles had sent a signal to Algy and the *Svelt* had intercepted it. There could hardly be two exploring parties on the polar ice so Lavinsky knew who he was. In any case there seemed to be no reason why he should not stick to the truth. 'Yes,' he agreed. 'There is an old hulk fast in the ice near our camp. If you happen to land there you'd better keep clear of it though.'

The man's manner changed. 'Why?'

'Because there's a madman in it,' answered Ginger casually. 'By the way, who am I talking to?'

'My name's Lavinsky and I'm the master of this ship. What's this about a madman?'

'When we went up to have a look at the wreck, not expecting to find anybody on board, we had a shock when somebody slung an axe at us. Then he started howling. I got a glimpse of him – a biggish fellow with red hair.'

Lavinsky spun round to face his crew. 'Red hair. You heard that? I reckon we know who *he* is, boys. So that's where he went. Well, I guess we can deal with him.' Speaking again to Ginger, Lavinsky went on: 'Did you get into the ship?'

Ginger smiled ruefully. 'I was in it for about three minutes. Then I caught sight of an eye watching me through the ice so I went out again in a hurry.'

Lavinsky hesitated, and Ginger knew why. The question of paramount importance was now to come, but Lavinsky was loath to show his hand. In the end he had to – more or less.

'Was there anything – er – valuable, in this old hulk?' he enquired.

It was a tense moment. Ginger could almost feel the entire crew hanging on his answer. 'What do you mean by valuable?' he parried.

'Gold, for instance.' Lavinsky spoke as if he could not bear to wait a moment longer.

'I shouldn't think there's any gold in that ship,' answered Ginger, smiling faintly. 'I'm pretty sure there isn't,' he went on. 'If there is, as far as I'm concerned you can have it all.' In the circumstances, considering the character of his interrogator, he felt that such dissemblement was justified.

'We'll go and see,' said Lavinsky. 'You'd better get below.'

'Thanks,' acknowledged Ginger, feeling that however dangerous his position might be now, his prospects of survival were brighter than they had been half an hour earlier.

CHAPTER X

A Shock For Biggles

Meanwhile, while Ginger was having his lonely adventure on the high seas, Biggles was standing by the aircraft, completely at a loss for once to know what to do. It was another piece of ice, quite a small piece, breaking away from the main icefield, that in the end provided the solution to the mystery of Ginger's disappearance. He realised then what must have happened and he was angry with himself for not thinking of it at once. Like all problems, when the answer became available it seemed so simple.

His first inclination was to get back into the machine and make a search of the open water; and no doubt in his anxiety he would have done so, had not the Skipper pointed out two factors that counselled prudence. In the first place there was no clear indication of the size of the piece of ice that had broken away, carrying Ginger with it, for in the business of transporting the gold no one had paid much attention to the water line at that point. Had it been only a small piece, the Skipper asserted, the weight of the gold, if it happened to be on one side, might have been sufficient to overturn it. Even if the floe did not overturn, said the Skipper, it might have taken on a list at such an angle as to cause Ginger and the gold to slide off. Secondly, visibility was bad, and showed little sign of improving. With big bergs about, low flying, as would be necessary if the flight was to serve any useful purpose, would be little less of suicidal. Why not wait a little while to give visibility a chance to improve, suggested the Skipper. The clouds overhead might pass. If Ginger was in fact adrift on a piece of ice another hour would make little difference to the actual situation. A mile or two, one way or the other, could not vitally affect the issue.

This was sound reasoning and Biggles was the first to admit it. What he realised, too, even better than the Skipper, was this; once he lost sight of his position, in such a poor light it might not be easy to find again. The landing, too, would be an added risk, not to be ignored. It was not as if only his own life was at stake. There was the Skipper and Grimy to be considered. Whether he took them with him in the machine, or left them on the ice, he would be subjecting them to risks which were manifestly unfair – at any rate, unless there was absolutely no alternative. As the Skipper put it there was an alternative. He would wait a little while to see if the weather improved.

Lighting a cigarette while he thought the matter over, new difficulties presented themselves. Suppose he did find Ginger, what could he do about it? The floe would have to be a very big one for him to land on it. If he couldn't land, how was he to pick him up? If he located him, the only way of getting to him would be by means of the rubber dinghy. He then considered launching the dinghy anyway, and again it was the Skipper who pointed out the inadvisability of such a course. To paddle about haphazard amongst the ice-floes would, he alleged, be sheer madness. It would only need two small pieces of ice to close in on such a frail craft and the dinghy would be lost, and their lives with it. It would be better, he argued, to save it until they could see what they were doing.

Again Biggles was forced to agree that this argument made sense, yet it went against the grain to just stand there doing nothing.

Ginger was not Biggles' only worry. By this time Algy and Bertie would be on their way. They would expect him to be on hand, not only to reveal his position but to indicate a safe place for them to land. This in itself, in the present weather conditions, would be a serious operation. Obviously, brooded Biggles, he couldn't be in two places at once. If he went out to look for Ginger, and was still out when the reserve machine arrived, the lives of Algy and Bertie would be jeopardised. Yet by staying where he was he felt he was abandoning Ginger. However, in the end he did nothing. Leaning against the machine he smoked cigarette after cigarette to steady his nervous impatience, all the time watching the sky for the first sign of an improvement. Out on the open water ice-floes growled and splintered. Sometimes a piece of ice would drift past. He watched a floe go by.

'The experts are right,' he remarked presently. 'The general drift is a bit north of east. That means that this stuff is drifting past our old camp, and if the direction is maintained the ice may pile up against the Graham Peninsula.'

'That's about it,' confirmed the Skipper. 'If the ice drifts that way so does everything else. I've often seen bergs carrying rocks and stones which the ice must have torn from the land in shoal water. It must all end up in the same place.'

'We'll remember that when we start searching,' said Biggles. He looked up. 'Is it my fancy or is the cloud lifting a bit?'

'Aye, she's lifting,' agreed the Skipper. He glanced around. 'I can't help wondering what Larsen has done with himself. Funny where he went to.'

'He's probably watching us from a distance,' replied Biggles. 'There's nobody more cunning than a fellow out of his mind. The gold is his particular mania, of course. When he discovers that it's gone he's liable to do anything, so we'd better keep our eyes open.

I think we might have a snack and a cup of tea. By the time we've finished, if the weather continues to improve it should be good enough for a reconnaissance. Anyway, whatever it's doing I'm going to look for Ginger. We can't leave him out there. Get the kettle boiling, Grimy.'

Half an hour later the weather was no longer in doubt. It had improved considerably. The sky was clearing, due possibly to a fall in the thermometer.

'I'll tell you one thing,' observed the Skipper. 'There's going to be a cracking frost tonight.'

'It can do what it likes as long as it stays clear,' answered Biggles, who, now that he could do something, was feeling better. 'Grimy, you'll stay here and get a good smudge fire going,' he ordered, as he moved towards the aircraft. Having reached it, he paused for a last look round, for it was now possible to see for some distance. Looking out to sea, to his unbounded amazement he saw a ship creeping through the floating ice towards the main shelf. It was in a very curious voice that he said: 'Skipper, come here. Can you see what I see?'

The Skipper, who had been on the far side of the machine, joined him. 'Aye,' he said slowly. 'I can see more than you can. I know that ship. I ought to, considering the time I've put in on her bridge. It's the *Svelt*. Looks as if Lavinsky's arrived.'

'That's what I thought,' returned Biggles evenly. 'This alters things – alters them considerably.'

'What are you going to do about it?' enquired the Skipper, a hint of urgency about his tone.

'Do? Nothing.'

'They're a tough lot.'

'I've met tough people before.'

'Well, I reckon we ought to do something,' asserted the Skipper. 'If you suppose we can all settle down nice and friendly on the same piece of ice you've got another thing coming. It would be easier to settle down with a pack of wolves. Lavinsky's bad – real bad.'

'What do you suggest we do – run away?'

'Well no, not exactly.'

'I should think not,' returned Biggles frostily. 'We'll wait here and see what they have to say. They're heading this way because they must have seen the machine. They haven't done anything to us yet, so we'll give them the benefit of the doubt. If Lavinsky starts making a nuisance of himself he'll find I can be awkward, too.'

'But you can't take on that bunch,' declared the Skipper. 'If Lavinsky's got the same crew, and I reckon he has, there'll be a score of 'em.'

'Numbers aren't everything,' returned Biggles quietly. 'I've met that sort before. They're never as smart as they think they are. And anyway, Lavinsky has as much right to be here as we have, so long as he behaves himself. If we tried to stop him landing, and he made a complaint, we might find ourselves legally in the wrong. If there's going to be a rough house we'll let him start it. I'm by no means sure he will though. His only concern is the gold, so he'll probably be all right until he discovers it's gone. My main concern is Ginger. I may ask Lavinsky to turn his ship round to look for him. The *Svelt* would be a much better vehicle for the job than an aircraft.'

'I still reckon he's got a nerve, coming in here like this,' said the Skipper.

'In what way?'

'With all this loose ice about. The sea's full of it. He found a way in but that ain't to say he'll find a way out. If he happens to find himself between two big floes he's likely to finish up like the hulk behind us.'

'Men will take any risks when there's gold in the offing,' observed Biggles.

'All the same, he must be daft to take such a chance while ice is breaking off all along the shelf. I've been watching it.'

'Some people might say we're not entirely sane ourselves, bringing an aircraft to a place like this,' Biggles pointed out.

'Aye, mebbe you're right at that,' concurred the Skipper with a sigh.

The *Svelt* came on, feeling her way cautiously. That the aircraft had been seen was obvious from the way the crew had collected forward to look. Biggles returned the inspection. Indeed, he went so far as to raise a hand in greeting.

The ship came right in, for the water was deep right up to the edge of the shelf. Fenders were thrown out and the vessel edged alongside.

'That's Lavinsky, the fellow in the peaked cap,' the Skipper told Biggles quietly. 'The other two I told you about, the two I called Shim and Sham, are on each side of him. They don't say much, but they don't miss much, either. I reckon they're the partners who finance Lavinsky.'

'Lavinsky was smart enough to get the position of the hulk when you were here with him the last time,' murmured Biggles.

'He couldn't have come straight here,' argued the Skipper. 'If he had we should have passed him on the way down. I'd say he took too much westerly, and finding he was wrong, worked his way along the shelf looking for the wreck.'

Biggles did not answer. He was staring at another figure that had appeared on deck. He caught the Skipper by the arm. 'By thunder! They've got him,' he ejaculated.

'Got who?'

'Ginger. There he is, on deck. They must have picked him up. That's a load off my mind, anyway. That probably explains it.'

'Explains what?'

'Why the *Svelt* came in here. Ginger would have to tell them we were here to account for being here himself. There was no reason why he shouldn't if it comes to that. I wonder what else he told them.'

'If he's told them that we got the gold it won't be long before bullets start flying,' declared the Skipper grimly.

'He hasn't told them anything of the sort.'

'Mebbe they've got the gold. We left Ginger sitting on it.'

'That doesn't mean he was still sitting on it when they picked him up,' disputed Biggles. 'We don't know about that; but what I do know is, Lavinsky hasn't got the gold under his hatches.'

'How do you work that out?'

'Because if he had he'd have turned his ship north, not south. There would have been no need for him to hazard his ship coming here if he'd already got what he came for – unless, of course, he was decent enough to give Ginger a lift back.'

The Skipper laughed shortly. 'Ha! I can't see Lavinsky doing that.'

'Keep that muffler up over your face,' said Biggles softly. 'I don't think he's realised yet who you are.'

Further conversation of an intimate nature was prevented by the arrival on the ice of Lavinsky and his owners, Shim and Sham. Lavinsky spoke first. 'I've brought one of your boys along,' he announced.

'So I see,' replied Biggles civilly. 'Much obliged to you. I was worried about him.'

'He tells me you're down here on an exploring trip for the British Government.'

Biggles smiled faintly. 'That's right. This is a Government outfit.'

At this point, now that he was close, Lavinsky appeared to notice the Skipper for the first time. That recognition was instantaneous was obvious from the way his expression changed. So had his voice changed, when he said: 'So *you're* here.'

'Looks like it,' answered the Skipper.

Lavinsky nodded. 'Now I get it.' He hesitated as if uncertain how to proceed. Then he went on: 'Well, I reckon it's no use beating about the bush,' he said slowly. 'Where's the wreck?'

The Skipper pointed. 'She's suffered a fair bit of damage since you were here last. Her masts are down and she's well under the ice.'

Lavinsky regarded the ice that hid the actual timbers of the vessel. 'I see,' he murmured. 'Is the gold still in her?'

'No.'

Lavinsky's eyes narrowed as they rested on the Skipper. 'How do I know that?'

'Go and look for yourself.'

'Where is it?'

Biggles stepped into the conversation. 'That's just what we should like to know.'

'You mean – you haven't got it?'

'Should we be here if we had?'

'Are you kidding?' Lavinsky's eyes grew dark with suspicion.

Biggles raised a shoulder. 'There's the hulk, there's my machine. You won't find any gold in either. You have my permission to look.'

'Permission!' Lavinsky's tone hardened. 'Who do you think you are to give me permission to do anything? I do what I like.'

'I wouldn't start talking like that,' suggested Biggles quietly. 'I'd better warn you that the salvage of that ship has been acquired by the British Government. I'm here under Government orders, with Government equipment, to collect anything worth taking home. Which means, Mr Lavinsky, that before you can enter that hulk you have to ask my permission, I being the head of the salvage operation.'

Lavinsky turned an evil eye on Ginger, who had now come ashore and was standing beside Biggles. His whole attitude was one of calculating malice. 'This is a different tale from the one you told me,' he said harshly.

'Not at all,' denied Ginger. 'I answered your questions fairly. If I didn't volunteer any details it was because I saw no reason to. It wasn't my place to, anyway.'

Lavinsky considered the matter. He looked at his two companions, but their faces were expressionless and he found no inspiration there. He took a cigar from an inside pocket, put it in his mouth, lit it, and flung the match down. 'Well, what are we going to do?' he demanded viciously.

'Do about what?' asked Biggles.

'The gold? What else do you think I'm interested in?'

'If you're asking for my advice, here it is,' returned Biggles smoothly. 'As there's nothing for you to do here you'd better turn round and make for home before you get gripped in the ice and finish up like that hulk.'

'Me go home? With nothing? Not likely.'

'Please yourself. I can't stand here talking any longer. I've got things to do.'

'How about splitting the gold two ways,' suggested Lavinsky. 'I reckon you could do with some of it, and I ain't greedy.'

'At the moment there's no gold to split, even if I agreed to your proposal. Which I wouldn't, because as I have already told you, it belongs to the people for whom I happen to be working,' answered Biggles coldly.

'You say it isn't in the hulk?'

'It is not.'

'Then Larsen must have hid it somewhere. This boy of yours told me he was living in the hulk.'

'He was,' confirmed Biggles. 'I don't know where he is now. He greeted me with an axe and then bolted. He's mad, so be careful if you run into him.'

Lavinsky laughed unpleasantly. 'You needn't worry about me,' he said meaningly.

'I'm not worrying about you,' answered Biggles calmly. 'I'm just warning you, that's all. I say the man is insane, and as you know it you've no excuse for anything that may happen. To make my meaning quite clear, I'm not prepared to stand here and see murder done, if that's what's in your mind. Larsen was once a member of your crew. You abandoned him – oh yes, I heard about that – so you're responsible for what's happened to him. In those circumstances the least you can do is treat him decently and take him to a place where he can get medical attention. With a ship you are better able to do that than I am with an aircraft.'

Lavinsky drew deeply at his cigar and expelled the smoke slowly. 'I'll decide what to do with him when I've found him,' he stated. A sneer crept into his voice as he went on. 'Meanwhile, have I your permission to look through the hulk?'

'You have. That, of course, doesn't give you the right to take anything away.'

Lavinsky looked sideways at his companions and jerked his head towards the wreck. 'Come on,' he said. Followed by his companions he strode away to the hulk, went up the ice steps and disappeared down the companion-way.

Biggles watched them go. 'Things seem to be getting complicated,' he murmured. Then, turning to Ginger, he inquired: 'Well, what have you to say for yourself?'

It did not take Ginger long to narrate the unpleasant adventure that had befallen him and the remarkable manner of his escape.

'So you left the gold on the ice,' said Biggles thoughtfully, when he had finished.

'What else could I do?'

'Nothing,' admitted Biggles. 'Had you told Lavinsky that the gold was under his nose you wouldn't be here now – neither would the *Svelt*. Have you any idea of which way you were drifting when you were picked up?'

'Slightly north of east, as near as I could tell.'

'How big was the floe you were on?'

'Fairly big – say, about three acres altogether.'

'What shape was it?'

'Wide at one end and narrow at the other. Something like the shape of a pear, only the narrow end tailed off to a point.'

'Not big enough to land on?'

'No.'

'Would you know it if you saw it again?'

'I think so – provided, of course, there weren't a lot more like it. I should know for certain if I could get close because I fixed one of my sticks in the gold. I doubt if you'd see it from a distance, but it does at least mark the position of the gold on the floe. Luckily the gold was under snow; that's why Lavinsky didn't see it.'

At this juncture Lavinsky and his companions reappeared and rejoined the party standing by the aircraft. 'I reckon you're right,' conceded Lavinsky, speaking to Biggles. 'Somebody's been in since I was last there – left food and stuff lying about. The gold's gone.'

'You're telling me what I've already told you,' replied Biggles.

'Sure. But I wanted to—' Lavinsky's eyes went to the aircraft.

'You still think it might be in my machine?' suggested Biggles softly.

'It could be.'

'I told you it is not.'

'All the same, it might be.'

'If I say it isn't, it isn't,' said Biggles shortly. 'Still, you can go and look if you like. I only wish the stuff was on board because I could then turn my tail to this perishing country.'

'Yes, I suppose that's right,' said Lavinsky in a low voice, as if speaking to himself. Nevertheless, he walked over to the machine and looked in the cabin.

When he came back Biggles said: 'Well, I hope you're satisfied.'

Lavinsky did not answer. To his companions he muttered: 'Let's get aboard and talk it over.' They went back to the *Svelt*.

'We'd better talk things over, too,' suggested Biggles. 'I think the aircraft is the best place.' He led the way to the cabin.

CHAPTER XI

Move and Counter-Move

When they were all assembled in the cabin Biggles opened the debate by saying: 'Well, this is a pretty state of affairs. Queer, isn't it, how shows of this sort never seem to run smoothly. That piece of ice on which we piled the gold must have been there for years, but it had to choose today, of all days, to break off. Yesterday it wouldn't have mattered. Tomorrow it wouldn't have mattered, either. But no. It had to be today, at the very hour Ginger decided to sit on it. That's how things go. To complicate matters, Lavinsky rolls up. In a way that may have been lucky; no doubt Ginger thought so at the time, although I still think we had a good chance of finding him without any help from Lavinsky. But that's past history. The question is, what next?'

'How about looking for the gold,' suggested Ginger.

'I have every intention of looking for it,' replied Biggles. 'But how are we going to set about it without Lavinsky realising what we're doing. He's sick at losing the gold and he won't give up easily. He's boiling up for trouble even now. If it comes to war someone will get hurt, that's certain – although as long as it isn't Lavinsky he won't care. He's the type that soon gets my goat, and I'm standing for no nonsense from him. But even with Algy and Bertie here the odds would still be on his side, so if we can get the gold and clear out without a stand-up fight, so much the better. There's nothing we can do for the moment, because we've got to wait for Algy to come in. He should be here in half an hour or so. When we hear him coming we'll light a smudge fire and mark out a landing ground. As soon as he gets safely down we'll explain the position to him and then start looking for this pear-shaped floe of Ginger's. I'm afraid locating it is going to be no easy job; and even if we do locate it, to get the gold into the aircraft without Lavinsky spotting what's going on will be another pretty problem. There is this about it; we shall soon know the worst, for the simple reason we haven't enough petrol to cruise about indefinitely.'

'What do you reckon Lavinsky will do, now he's satisfied that we haven't got the gold and it isn't in the hulk?' asked Ginger.

'I wouldn't say he's satisfied,' returned Biggles. 'He must know the gold can't be far away, so as soon as he gets over the shock of finding us here he'll start looking for it, or try to work out what could have become of it. He won't leave here while there's the slightest chance of it still being in the vicinity, you can bet your boots on that. Like us, he's chewing it over from his angle. I don't think he'll guess that we've found the gold and moved it, because, on the face of it, there was no earthly reason why we should do anything of the sort. All he knows is, the gold isn't where it was when he last saw it. The stuff couldn't have moved itself so somebody must have shifted it. Only one person has been here as far as he knows, and he was here long enough to distribute the stuff all over the landscape if he felt like it – Larsen. The first thing he'll do, then, is look for the Swede. Were I in his position I should probably do the same thing, although I should ask myself why should Larsen move the gold knowing perfectly well that the chances of anyone landing here were remote.'

'Larsen's mad, and who can say what a madman will do,' murmured the Skipper.

'True enough,' agreed Biggles. 'Anyhow, the stuff has gone, and ruling out the possibility of anyone else coming here, only Larsen could have moved it. Of course, Lavinsky won't overlook the possibility of it being hidden somewhere in the hulk, so it's quite likely that he'll pull the timbers apart looking for it. There's nowhere else for him to look. It wouldn't be much use starting to search the whole landscape. I only hope it doesn't occur to him to wonder why *we* didn't pull the ship to pieces in a hunt for it, because if he starts thinking on those lines he may tumble on the truth – that we know more about the gold than we pretend. It boils down to this. I think Lavinsky will thoroughly search the ship. When that fails he'll look for Larsen, hoping that if he can find him he'll be able to tell them where the gold is hidden.'

'Larsen wouldn't tell Lavinsky anything,' put in the Skipper. 'He knows what sort of man he is. Mad though he may be, Larsen would know that once Lavinsky had his hands on the gold his life wouldn't be worth a mouldy biscuit.'

'Lavinsky will watch us,' observed Ginger.

'Of course he will,' agreed Biggles. 'And for that reason I don't feel inclined to stay where he can see everything we do. That's been in the back of my mind all the time we've been talking; and I think I've got the answer. We'll move back to our old camp. The tent is still there, and enough stores to last for some time. Lavinsky would find it more difficult to watch us. He may think we've gone. If he does, so much the better, although I don't care much what he thinks. Another point is, the old camp lies to the east, and as the ice drift is that way we shouldn't have so far to fly when looking for Ginger's floe.'

'How do you intend to get the gold from the ice to the machine even if we find it?' asked Ginger. 'That's what beats me.'

'It beats me, too,' confessed Biggles. 'Of course, a lot would depend on where we found the floe – I mean, its position in relation to the main pack. If the floe has drifted a long way out to the sea we might as well go home, because the only thing that could get to it then would be a marine craft. I doubt if we could get one here in time to save it. The floe would start melting as soon as it came in contact with warmer air and water and the gold would finish at the bottom of the sea. But let's take one thing at a time. Our first job is to locate the gold.'

'Are you going to wait here for Algy to come?' asked the Skipper.

'I don't think so,' decided Biggles. 'There's no point in it. We might as well move now. We can make a signal to him when we're in the air and tell him we're moving a mile or two eastward. We'll make a good smoke; that will show him where we are. I was only hanging about here in the hope of getting a line on what Lavinsky intends to do – not that it's really important as long as he doesn't interfere with us. The only thing about that is, we ought to know what he's doing about Larsen. The wretched fellow must be got home somehow – but we'll deal with that later on. Let's get back to the old camp; Algy must be getting close.'

'What's Lavinsky going to think when he hears us start up?' asked Ginger.

'I've told you before I don't care what he thinks,' returned Biggles. 'If he was quite certain that we hadn't found the gold no doubt he'd be glad to see us out of his way. Let's get mobile.'

The roar of motors brought Lavinsky and most of his crew to the rail of the *Svelt*, but they remained passive spectators as the aircraft swept across the snow field and into the air.

Visibility had improved somewhat, Ginger was relieved to find, but it was without success that he stared towards the north in the hope of seeing the reserve machine approaching. The old camp was at once in view, and Biggles cruised towards it while Ginger went into the

The roar of motors brought Lavinsky to the rail.

wireless compartment and sent a signal which he hoped would be picked up by Algy. This occupied only a few minutes, after which Biggles put the machine down without mishap, taxiing on and finally switching off close to the tent, which, with its contents, remained exactly as it had been left. Grimy attended to the skis while the Skipper melted snow for water to make tea. Biggles and Ginger employed themselves in marking out a landing T with old pieces of packing, and soon had a good black smoke rising from some oily rags.

The reserve machine arrived about ten minutes later. It circled once, losing height, and then came in to a smooth landing. Grimy took some more boards and slipped them under the skis. Presently Algy and Bertie climbed down and joined the party waiting for them on the ground.

'Here, I say, I hope you blighters haven't been keeping all the fun for yourselves,' greeted Bertie. 'Bit of a bind, sitting on that windy island with absolutely nothing to do.'

'We haven't had much fun so far,' Biggles told him. 'Gather round and grab a cup of tea while I give you the gen. And just remember we've got both machines here now, so if anything comes unstuck there's no one to take us off.'

'Why bring that up?' complained Bertie. 'I was trying to forget it.'

'What's that ship I noticed a mile or two along?' queried Algy.

'If you'll listen instead of asking questions I'll tell you all about it,' replied Biggles. Then, over mugs of steaming tea he narrated all that had happened since their arrival on the White Continent. 'That's how things stand at present,' he concluded. 'If anyone has a bright idea I'd be glad to hear it.'

No one answered for a little while. Then Bertie, who had been polishing his eyeglass thoughtfully, remarked: 'Deuced awkward – what?'

'I was hoping you'd appreciate that aspect,' answered Biggles, with gentle sarcasm.

'Absolutely – absolutely,' agreed Bertie. 'I'm all for getting after the jolly old gold. It's not every day a fella gets a chance to pick it up a ton at a time – no, by gad.'

'By the time you've picked up half of it you'll wish you'd never seen it,' promised Biggles. 'You two can have a rest and a cigarette while I have a look round. I'm making it a rule until we go for good that only one machine is in the air at a time, just in case of accidents, so don't go off on your own while I'm away. I'll take Ginger with me because he's the only one who has seen the particular piece of ice we're looking for.'

'Is there anything I can do?' asked the Skipper.

'Yes. You and Grimy can take turns watching the enemy camp. I don't think they'll try anything, but we should look silly if they did, and found us with no one on guard. There's a bit of a ridge a couple of hundred yards away; you can get a good view from the top of it.'

The Skipper nodded. 'Aye – aye. I know the one.'

Biggles glanced round the sky. 'The weather's still improving so let's go while the going's good.'

Within five minutes of the machine leaving the ground there occurred two events so unexpected that Ginger wondered for a moment if they could be true. Neither was really remarkable, being in the natural order of things, but they were startling in their unexpectedness. Whether or not Biggles thought they would find the gold Ginger did not know, but he himself took such a poor view of their chances that he did not even make a pretence of enthusiasm. Nor did he think seriously that the weather was improving. The temporary lifting of the cloud he took to be a mere passing phase, such as had occurred before. He was amazed therefore – not to say delighted – when, as if a curtain had been drawn aside, the cloud layer dispersed, leaving a flat mauve sky. The effect on the landscape was almost unbelievable. Visibility, from a few hundred yards, jumped to several miles. Ahead and on either side lay the deep blue water of the polar sea, dotted with a thousand glittering bergs and spreading floes. Astern stretched to the unknown hinterland of the White Continent, its southern horizon pierced by scores of mountains as yet unnamed, some rising to a tremendous height. As a spectacle, a spectacle that few men had seen, it was breathtaking.

Biggles' only remark was: 'That's better, now we can see what we're doing.'

But this was only a beginning. Happening to glance down, quite idly, a particular floe on account of its shape caught Ginger's eye, and held it. In an incredulous voice he shouted: 'There it is!'

Biggles looked at him. 'There what is?' he inquired.

'The floe we're looking for.'

Biggles astonishment was expressed in a frown. 'Are you sure?'

'Certain.'

'Where is it?'

Ginger pointed. 'That's it.'

'You're quite sure about it?'

'Well—' Ginger's eyes swept over the scores of floes visible from his altitude. 'There were, he noticed, several of similar shape, as the pieces of a jigsaw puzzle are similar, yet different. 'I'm pretty certain it's the one,' he declared. 'It's worth having a closer look at it, anyway.'

Biggles put the machine into a gentle turn, slowly losing height, while Ginger made a closer scrutiny of the floe. He could not see the stick, but that was hardly to be expected, because he realised that from his position above it, it would be foreshortened. And the ice-field was nearer to the shore than he had supposed it would be – less than a mile, he estimated. But the shape was right. Several other floes, presumably held by the same current, were close to it. Seaward, there was a wide stretch of open water. Beyond that again more floes were piling up in a wide arc; but these, he thought, were too far away to come within the same sphere of influence as the piece on which he had gone adrift.

'Take her a bit lower,' he requested. 'A side view may give me a sight of the stick. That's the only thing I can be really sure about.'

Biggles glided down towards the floe in question, lower and still lower, to flatten out eventually at about fifty feet. He then flew the whole length of the floe.

Suddenly Ginger let out a yell. 'That's it!' he shouted. 'I can see the stick. What a slice of cake.'

Biggles smiled. 'That's fine. We were about due to strike something easy for a change. Can you get an idea which way it's drifting.'

Ginger stared down for a minute or two. 'No,' he said at last. 'I don't think it's possible to tell from topsides; our own movement is too fast.'

'So I imagine,' returned Biggles. 'No matter. We'll go back. We shall be able to watch the ice from camp. We'll take a line on it from there. Keep your eyes on it or we may find ourselves watching the wrong one. I'm going in.'

I won't lose sight of it, you can bet your life on that,' asserted Ginger warmly, as Biggles turned for home. Nor did he. Even when the aircraft landed his eyes were still on what must have been the most valuable piece of ice ever to float on the surface of the sea.

'What's the matter?' asked Algy, as they jumped down. 'I thought you'd be some time.'

'So did I,' answered Biggles. 'But it happens we've found the objective – took off straight over it. As soon as the sky cleared Ginger spotted it right away. If the sun will stay put and Lavinsky keep his distance the rest should be easy.'

'What are you going to do?' asked Algy.

'For the moment, nothing – nothing, that is, except watch that lump of ice to ascertain definitely which way it's drifting. A lot will depend on that.'

'Why not launch the jolly old dinghy – if you see what I mean,' suggested Bertie.

'And do what?'

'Bring home the boodle.'

'Have a heart,' protested Biggles. 'How long do you suppose it would take us to fetch the stuff a bar at a time? The dinghy wouldn't carry more. That floe is a mile away. Of course, if the worst comes to the worst we shall have to try it, but I don't relish the job. If that floe is drifting back towards the main pack, and I have an idea it is, if we have a little patience it will come to us. That will be a lot easier than fetching it – and safer. I'm not much for putting to sea on a piece of inflated rubber at the best of times. To spring a leak in this particular ditch wouldn't be funny.'

'Too true, old boy, too true. I'm with you there, absolutely,' declared Bertie. 'I like my water warm.'

'You'd find this definitely chilly,' said Biggles grimly, as he picked up two trail sticks and arranged them in line with the floe. This done he sat behind the inner one, took a line through the other, and remained motionless for several minutes. 'It's coming in,' he announced, when at last he got up. 'I'll take another sight in a quarter of an hour. That should give us a rough idea of the rate of drift. This northerly breeze should help it. Meanwhile, we can occupy the time by having something to eat.'

CHAPTER XII

Lavinsky Shows His Hand

By the end of half an hour, which had been occupied with eating a meal more satisfying than savoury, it was evident that the floe carrying the gold was moving steadily towards the shore. The rate of drift was slow, but, Biggles thought, increasing under the influence of a rising breeze, which, fortunately, came from the right direction. The effect of this could be heard as well as seen, for there was an almost constant grinding and crunching of ice as the floes piled up together when their further progress was barred by the main ice shelf. The danger of employing the dinghy, or any craft for that matter, was now apparent.

'Lavinsky must be a fool, or else the gold has sent him stark raving mad,' asserted the Skipper once, as he watched with professional eyes the great masses of ice coming in. 'If that wind veers a point or two, and moves all that loose ice his way, he's had it, as you boys would say.'

'Well, I hope it doesn't,' said Biggles. 'Because if it does, and he loses his ship, we shall be expected to take him home.'

Biggles, too, had been watching the movement of the ice closely, and presently gave his opinion that the particular floe in which they were interested would, if its direction was maintained, come up against the ice-shelf not far from where they were waiting. There was some talk of trying to hoist a sail on the floe to hasten its progress; but the suggestion was not made seriously and was soon dismissed as impracticable. There was, therefore, nothing they could do except possess themselves in patience while they waited for the gold to come to them.

Lavinsky's movements were not ignored. Owing to the improved visibility it was now possible from the ridge near the camp to see the *Svelt*. Through binoculars it was also possible to see men moving about on the ice, some of them at a considerable distance from the ship. What they were doing, Biggles said he neither knew nor cared, as long as they kept out of the way. He supposed they were making a search either for the gold or the deranged Swede, who, Lavinsky may have thought, could tell them where it was. But when the report of a distant gunshot came through the crystal atmosphere Biggles frowned. 'What was that, I wonder,' he muttered.

'Probably shooting a seal,' answered the Skipper. 'Those fellows would kill anything for the sheer pleasure of doing it.'

'Perhaps you're right,' murmured Biggles, without conviction.

With irritating tardiness the floe crept nearer to the camp. With the aid of the glasses it was now possible to see not only Ginger's stick, but the slight hump of snow under which the gold lay hidden out of sight. Biggles sat on a packing case, smoking, until the nearest point of the ice was no more than a hundred yards distant; then he tossed the end of his cigarette aside and got up.

'We shan't be long now,' he remarked cheerfully. 'I've been thinking,' he went on. 'I'm going to load the reserve machine first. As soon as you've got a fair load aboard, Algy, you can fly it back to the Falklands. You'll be empty except for the gold so you can take most of it. I'll follow you with the remainder and bring everyone back with me. There's no need for you to hang about here waiting for us.'

'Good enough,' agreed Algy. 'I think it's a good idea.'

The floe drifted nearer, and the whole party – with the exception of Grimy who was on guard at the ridge – went to the edge of the ice-shelf to wait for it. It could now be observed that the flat piece of ice, as well as drifting shoreward was also slowly turning, so that in the end it was the narrow part of the floe that first made contact with the mainland. Actually, this did not matter. It simply meant that they would have to walk a little farther to reach the gold. But as Biggles remarked, they had no cause for complaint; they were lucky that the floe had come ashore as close to the camp as it had.

At this stage of the proceedings Grimy returned at a run from his post to report that Lavinsky and six of his men were approaching.

Biggles sighed. 'They would choose this moment to come,' he muttered. 'We'd better not let them see what we're doing. We shall probably have trouble anyway, but we'll avoid it as long as we can. Don't let them see that we've any interest in that slice of ice or we might as well tell them what's on it.'

He sat down again on his packing case and lit a cigarette.

Lavinsky and his companions topped the ridge and came straight on to the camp, the leader a little in advance of the others. His expression was hostile, and when he opened the conversation he wasted no time in preamble. 'Where's that gold?' he demanded peremptorily.

Biggles regarded the speaker dispassionately. 'What leads you to suppose that I know where it is?'

'I happen to know you know.'

Biggles' eyebrows went up. 'So what?' he inquired. 'What are you getting excited about, anyhow? The gold isn't yours.'

'It will be.'

'What you mean is, you hope it will be,' corrected Biggles. 'There's a difference,' he added.

'You said you hadn't got it,' rapped out Lavinsky.

'Perfectly true – I haven't.'

'That's a lie.'

Biggles smiled sadly. 'You're not such a smart guy after all, Lavinsky. If I'd got the gold what do you suppose I'd be doing here – sunbathing?'

Lavinsky hesitated, probably because the truth of Biggles' sarcastic observation was obvious. 'What have you done with it?' he challenged.

Biggles regarded him with a frown of disapproval. 'Who do you think you are that you can come into my camp and start slinging questions about? And what do you think I am that I should be likely to answer them? I'm trying to be patient with you, Lavinsky, but you're not making it easy. I'm the accredited agent of the British Government. Get that into your thick skull for a start. If anyone here has a right to ask questions it's me. As it happens there's no need. I know who you are and what we're doing here. I also know what happened on your last trip.'

'And I know you've got the gold,' almost spat Lavinsky.

'What makes you so sure of that?' asked Biggles curiously.

'Larsen told me. He watched you move it.'

'Ah! So you've found him?'

'Of course I found him.'

'The man's mad.'

'Not so mad that he didn't watch you find the gold and take it away.'

'He seems to have recovered somewhat since I last saw him,' murmured Biggles.

'I found a way to bring him to his senses.'

'Indeed?' Biggles' eyes narrowed. 'And just how did you achieve that?'

'Mind your own business.'

'This happens to be my business,' retorted Biggles, with iron in his voice. 'You were responsible for his condition in the first place by abandoning him here. The least you can do now is get him home, although he'd probably be safer with me. Are you going to take him or shall I?'

'Bah! There's no need to worry about him.'

'Just what do you mean by that?' asked Biggles suspiciously.

Lavinsky's lips parted as if to answer, but he checked himself. 'If you want him you can have him,' he sneered.

'Had that gunshot I heard just now anything to do with him?' inquired Biggles, in an ominously brittle voice.

'Could have been.'

'Now you mark my words, Lavinsky,' said Biggles icily. 'The man was ill. You knew it. If you've injured him I'll see you pay for it. If you've killed him, then I'll do my best to see that you hang for it. Maybe you think you can get away with murder in a place like this. Well, you can't, as you'll discover in good time. Now get out of my camp before I throw you out.'

Lavinsky's manner changed, although for what reason was not immediately apparent. 'All right, all right,' he muttered sulkily. 'That sort of talk won't get us anywhere.'

'I'll get you to the gallows if I have my way,' promised Biggles caustically.

Lavinsky's mollified tone was explained by his next suggestion. 'Look here, I'll tell you what I'll do,' said he. 'Gold's as useful to you as it is to me. You give me half of it and I'll clear out. You can have the rest. You can get a long way on half a ton of gold. That's fair enough, isn't it?'

'Your idea of fairness, Lavinsky, would make me laugh if the sight of you didn't make me feel sick,' answered Biggles contemptuously. 'I wouldn't give you one ounce even if I had it, which I haven't. Larsen was right when he saw us move it. Didn't he tell you where we put it?'

'Yes. He said you piled it up on the ice,' said Lavinsky eagerly.

'Didn't he tell you what happened to it after that?'

'No.'

'Would you like me to tell you?' Biggles seemed slightly amused.

'Sure.'

'It's still there.'

'What – where you put it?' Lavinsky's voice almost cracked with incredulity.

'Yes.'

'You mean – in the same place?'

'Well, not exactly,' answered Biggles. 'Larsen should have told you the rest of the story; but maybe he didn't know it. Anyway, as he didn't tell you, I will. And the only reason I'm telling you is to bring this futile argument to an end. I left a man on guard over the gold while I went off to fetch my machine. When I came back he wasn't there. What happened was, the particular area of ice chose that moment to break off. The man in charge didn't notice it until it was too late for him to do anything about it. He, and the gold, went adrift. You picked the man up – but not the gold. He was sitting on it. The gold is still on that same piece of ice. Now you know why I haven't got the gold and why I'm still here. Laugh that off and clear out – and stay out.'

If looks could kill Ginger would have been slain on the spot where he stood by the murderous scowl Lavinsky gave him. That he believed Biggles' story was not for a moment in doubt. It was so obviously true, not only from the way Biggles had told it but in his own experience. It explained exactly what must have been a puzzle to him all along. For a full minute he stood there staring malevolently from one to another. 'Okay,' he breathed at last. 'Okay, brother, I'll get you yet – and the gold.'

'All you have to do is find the ice floe,' said Biggles smoothly.

'I'll do that,' said Lavinsky through his teeth. 'Before I go I'll give you a tip. Keep out of my way or you'll get what Larsen got. That goes for the lot of you.'

'I'll bear it in mind,' promised Biggles.

Lavinsky turned on his heels and calling to his men strode away.

Biggles and his party watched them go, Biggles smiling faintly, the others with mixed expressions. Not until Lavinsky and his companions had topped the ridge and disappeared from sight did anyone speak. Then the Skipper said: 'Why did you tell him that?'

'To get rid of him and gain time enough for us to finish the job. What I told him was obviously the truth, and he reacted just as I thought he would. By the time he's found the floe there'll be nothing on it – I hope. Anyway, had the man stayed here arguing the thing would have ended in shooting. I could see that coming – so could he. I decided it was better this way.'

'*Phew*,' breathed Ginger. 'You were taking a chance. I nearly broke into a perspiration every time the floe bumped against the shelf. I was expecting every minute he'd see that stick. That's twice he's had the gold under his nose without knowing it. He'll go raving mad when he realises it.'

'I shouldn't break my heart over that,' asserted Biggles. 'Let's get busy. The first thing is to get organised. The Skipper, Bertie and Grimy will haul the stuff here. Algy will help me to load up. Heavy stuff like gold can't just be chucked in anyhow. It will have to be distributed. Ginger, you'll take the glasses and watch Lavinsky. Let me know at once if he moves his ship or if you see any of his men coming this way. Let's get started.'

The work began, and for nearly an hour proceeded at full speed without interruption. By the end of that time about half the gold had been moved to the aircraft. It was far from being a simple task, for a complication, a dangerous one, was caused by the constant movement of the ice floe against the solid pack. The floe did not, of course, fit flush against the main ice-shelf; it only made actual contact at one or two places, and even here the two masses sometimes swung apart leaving a gap too wide to be stepped across with safety. Again, there were times when the two masses came together with an alarming crash; on such occasions the splinters flew in all directions, at no small risk of injury to anyone who happened to be near the spot.

During this period, Ginger, who was on guard, made several reports to Biggles. First, he was able to announce that Lavinsky and his party had rejoined the ship. He next reported that the *Svelt* was on the move; it had left the pack-ice and was cruising about among the floes that littered the open water. As a matter of detail, Biggles had noticed this himself, for the ship was sometimes in view. It brought a smile to his face, for Lavinsky's purpose was fairly obvious. He was looking for the gold. After a while, however, the *Svelt* returned to its original mooring near the hulk. Ginger next reported that from time to time there was a brilliant flash of light from the crows-nest on the mainmast, although what caused this he was unable to say. Biggles, being busy, paid little attention to it at the time. He was quite content while Lavinsky kept at a distance. Ginger's final report brought an end to the operation. Lavinsky, he said, was coming back, supported by a dozen men.

'I'm afraid that means war,' remarked Biggles. He looked across the floe at the remaining gold bars which, as the top ones had been removed, were conspicuous. 'We'd better not let him see that,' he went on, pointing to the gold. 'Grimy, slip out and cover the remainder up with snow; and as you come back you might brush some snow over the track we've made.'

While this was being done the Skipper questioned the advisability of waiting for what promised to be an attack in force, supporting his argument by pointing out that as they had half the gold they had reason to be satisfied. 'We can't take on that bunch and expect to get away with it,' he concluded, not without justification.

Biggles would not hear of it. 'I'm not leaving one bar, not half a bar, for that rascal,' he asserted. 'If we lose sight of the stuff we shall never find it again. Apart from that, I'm here on official business and refuse to be intimidated by that gang of sea-crooks.' He thought for a moment. 'I think we might compromise, though,' he resumed. 'We needn't risk losing the half we've already got. Algy, you might as well take it straight away to the Falklands. I shall have to ask you to go alone because if it comes to a rough house here, and things begin to look that way, I shall need as many hands as I can muster. If Lavinsky saw he had only two or three to deal with it might encourage him to try to wipe us out.'

'As you say, chief,' agreed Algy. 'I'll unload as fast as I can, refuel, and come straight back to help you with the rest. Otherwise, with the remainder of the gold and everybody else you look like being overloaded.'

'Fair enough,' agreed Biggles.

Ginger, who had been watching the advancing men, reported that they all seemed to be carrying weapons of some sort, guns or rifles.

Biggles shrugged. 'Two can play at that game.'

'Absolutely – absolutely,' murmured Bertie. 'I've promised to join Gimlet King for a spot of deer-stalking in the Highlands when I get back so I could do with a bit of practice. Pity the blighters haven't a decent head of antlers; I'd take one home to show Gimlet the sort of beasts we shoot in the lowest of the bally lowlands – if you see what I mean.'

'Lavinsky will get his horns in the next world, no doubt,' was Algy's parting remark as he walked over to his machine. In a minute or two he took off and headed out to sea.

Shortly afterwards Lavinsky and his supporters came into sight as they topped the ridge; and from the purposeful manner of their approach it was clear that the storm was about to break. Biggles took steps to meet it by telling the others to get weapons from the arms store, but warned them to keep them out of sight. He then placed them in strategic positions. So far there was nothing in the manner of Lavinsky's advance to suggest an immediate attack, but it was fairly evident that one might develop – particularly, as Biggles told the others, if the man thought he had them at a disadvantage.

Ginger, seating himself behind a case of bully beef with a rifle across his knees, noticed that Algy, instead of carrying straight on his homeward course, had turned, and was now flying up and down as if engaged in a photographic survey of the area below him. Why he was doing this he could not imagine, and before he could arrive at a solution his attention was brought nearer to hand by Biggles calling out to Lavinsky not to come any closer. Lavinsky stopped at a distance of about ten yards with his men lined up on either side of him.

'Now what's biting you?' demanded Biggles curtly.

'You know why I've come here,' answered Lavinsky in a thin, rasping voice.

'Have you still got the gold bug in your brain?' enquired Biggles.

'Quit talking through your hat,' came back Lavinsky harshly. 'Thought you could fool me, eh. Well, think again, smart guy.

I've been watching you from the mast through my glasses,' he added, thereby explaining the flashes that Ginger had reported. Apparently they had been caused by the sun catching the lens.

'I hope you enjoyed the picture,' replied Biggles evenly.

'The metal was here all the time. I saw you loading it up,' challenged Lavinsky.

'In that case you've nothing more to worry about,' answered Biggles. 'What you saw being loaded up is now on its way home.'

'Not all of it,' answered Lavinsky. 'I'll have the rest. Are you going to hand it over?'

'I most certainly am not.'

'Then I'll—' Lavinsky glanced up as, with a roar, Algy's machine raced low over the camp. A small object hurtled down. Then the aircraft zoomed, turned, and stood out to sea.

'Ginger, pick that thing up and see what it is,' ordered Biggles.

There was silence while Ginger ran to the object and brought it back. Biggles took it. It was a small cigarette tin, the sort made to hold twenty cigarettes. He opened it and took out a slip of paper. He looked at it, smiled, rolled it into a ball and tossed the tin away. 'You were about to say something, Lavinsky, when we were interrupted,' he prompted.

'I was going to say that unless you hand over the metal I'm going to take it,' said Lavinsky viciously.

'And having got it – what then?'

Lavinsky hesitated for a moment as if he suspected that there was more behind Biggles' question than the mere words implied. 'I'll clear out and you can do what the hell you like,' he answered, his eyes on Biggles' face.

Biggles shook his head. 'You wouldn't get far, I'm afraid.'

'What do you mean by that? Do you reckon you could stop us?' Lavinsky grinned as if he found the idea amusing.

'If I didn't the ice would,' returned Biggles. 'Your ship's shut in. Between it and open water there's a half-mile-wide barrier of floes and bergs jammed together.'

Lavinsky's expression changed. 'Pah! You can't bluff me,' he answered; but there was no conviction in his voice.

Biggles raised a shoulder. 'Have it your own way.'

'How do you know?'

'You saw that message dropped a moment ago? The pilot is a friend of mine and he doesn't make mistakes. Please yourself whether you believe it or not. Personally, I couldn't care less.'

Ginger realised now the meaning of Algy's reconnaissance. The barrier could not be seen from where they were, but he had spotted it from the air and realised its significance. So did Ginger. It put a new complexion on the entire situation. If the ice barrier did in fact prove impassable it looked as if the *Svelt* would share the fate of the *Starry Crown*. In that case they would be in the curious position of having to take Lavinsky and his crew home.

Lavinsky ran his tongue over his lips. He was probably thinking on the same lines, for Biggles was obviously telling the truth.

'It's no use standing there gaping at me,' resumed Biggles. I couldn't help you to get your ship clear even if I wanted to. Instead of yammering about getting the gold out you'd better see about getting yourselves out before it's too late. You can see which way the wind's blowing. That ice must be coming in this direction.'

'It'll pack tighter, too, and get thicker as the reef shortens,' put in the Skipper. 'Once it closes in on you and nips you, you're finished.'

Lavinsky's eyes wandered to the aircraft and then came back to Biggles. It was almost possible to read his thoughts. 'If I stay you stay,' he snarled. 'I could soon shoot enough holes in that kite of yours, to keep it on the ground.'

'That would be really clever,' scoffed Biggles. 'Anyway, what do you suppose we should be doing while you were shooting?'

Lavinsky tried another tack. 'If we start shooting at each other we're all sunk,' he muttered, with a change of voice. 'There's no sense in that.'

'I was hoping that trivial point would occur to you,' returned Biggles.

'You wouldn't go off and leave me and the boys stranded here, I reckon?' There was a hint of anxiety in the question.

Biggles laughed shortly. 'Wouldn't I, by thunder! You don't know me. Why should I clutter myself up with a lot of useless scum that would be better in Davy Jones' locker? That's enough talking, Lavinsky. You're trapped. You've asked for it and you've got it. But because I've got a streak of weakness in me, if you'll obey my orders I'll give you a chance. You must have plenty of stores in your ship. Go back to it and stay there. There's a British naval sloop at the Falklands. As soon as I'm in the air I'll radio a signal and ask it to come here and take you off. Of course, I shall make a full report of what's happened here so you'd better be able to account for Larsen. That's as far as I'm prepared to go. Make up your mind what you're going to do, and make it up quickly. That's all.'

For a minute Lavinsky did not move. He glared at Biggles with hate smouldering in his eyes. Then, without another word he turned and strode away. His men followed, muttering among themselves. When he reached the ridge he stopped, and with his crew gathered round him, held what appeared to be a conference. It did not last long. Lavinsky and half a dozen men walked on towards the *Svelt*. The remainder sat down on the ridge facing the camp.

'So that's the game,' murmured Biggles.

CHAPTER XIII

Biggles Plays for Time

Biggles, sitting on a packing case, regarded the opposing force with thoughtful consideration.

'Well, old boy, what are we going to do about it – if you see what I mean?' inquired Bertie presently.

'I can see what you mean all right,' answered Biggles. 'I'm just trying to work it out.'

'What are those blighters doing, sitting on the hill?'

'Watching us.'

'But what joy will they get out of that?'

'None.'

'How long will they go on doing it?'

'As long as we don't make a move.'

'You mean, to load up the rest of the gold?'

'That's it.'

'But dash it all, we've as good as got it.'

'Yes, but not quite. Our problem is how to get the metal into the machine.'

'But is it as difficult as all that?'

'It's a lot more difficult than it looks,' asserted Biggles. 'Of course, there's a way out of the difficulty; there always is. The problem is to find it – or, shall we say, the best way. By which

I mean the safest way. Actually, there are several things we can do.'

Bertie looked disappointed. 'But look here, I don't get it. By telling that scallywag that the ice had put a cork in his bottle – if you see what I mean – I should have thought you'd have knocked his middle stump clean out of the ground.'

Biggles smiled lugubriously. 'Yes, you would think so,' answered Biggles. 'But I'm afraid he isn't the sort to accept the umpire's decision. He's got the gold fever too badly to listen to reason. He's going to get the gold, if he can, at any cost. If it would suit his book, in order to get it he'd bump us off without the slightest compunction. He's got a considerable force to back him up – and, in fact, he may have come here just now with that very object in view. But when he learned that he might have to depend on us to get him off the ice he had to think again. But that doesn't mean to say he's ready to pack up. Oh no.'

'But what can he do?' put in Ginger. 'It isn't likely that he's got an air pilot on board, so whatever happens he's bound to rely on one of us to get him home; and whoever did that would report him to the police as soon as his wheels touched the ground.'

'He isn't prepared to accept that – yet,' returned Biggles. 'I think what he's most likely to do next is confirm Algy's report that he's shut in. The fact that he's shut in now doesn't necessarily mean that he'll stay shut in. The ice may move again and give him a passage out, and he isn't likely to overlook that possibility. Even if that doesn't happen, as I see it he still has two chances of getting out. The first is to blast a gap through the ice with dynamite – I imagine he wouldn't come to this part of the world without any.'

'Quite right,' interposed the Skipper. 'We had dynamite on board when I had the ship.'

'His second resort, a more desperate one, might be to do what

Last did. Last, you remember, fixed up a small boat, loaded it with stores and dragged it across the ice to open water – or at least he said he did, and I see no reason to disbelieve it. It was possible. And if it was possible for Last to do it single-handed, Lavinsky, with several boats to choose from and twenty men to handle them, should have no great difficulty in doing it, My guess is that he's gone off to have a dekko. If he decides he can get out he'll come back here with all hands to try to wipe us out.'

'But he couldn't do that without getting some of his own men knocked out,' protested Ginger.

'Huh! That wouldn't be likely to worry him as long as he escaped himself,' replied Biggles.

'But half a minute, old boy, what's come over you?' cried Bertie. 'It isn't like you to talk as if Lavinsky and his thugs have only to come here and pop off a gun for us all to drop dead. He wouldn't get us as easy as that – no, by gad.'

'There are times, Bertie, when I think you must be sheer bone from one ear to the other,' said Biggles sadly. 'I'm not worried over-much about Lavinsky shooting at *us*, as individuals. It would be easier to hit the aircraft, and there's nothing we can do to prevent that. We can't put the machine under cover. He has only to put a few holes through the tanks and we shall be the ones to stay here, not him. He knows that, too. My talk just now to Lavinsky, about him being stuck here, was mostly bluff. Lavinsky may not have seen through it at the time, but when he's thought the matter over, he will. He just wants to confirm that he can't get out before he takes steps to make sure that we can't. Of course, if he decides he's caught in the ice, good and proper, he'll have to rely on us to get him out, whether he likes it or not.'

'Hadn't we better push off while the going's good?' suggested the Skipper tentatively.

'And leave that rascal the gold? Not on your life,' Biggles was emphatic.

'Then let's get the gold on board and take it with us,' suggested Ginger. 'I'm getting cold sitting here.'

'The moment we make a move towards that gold the fireworks will start,' answered Biggles. 'Now you all know why I'm apparently content to sit here and do nothing. Give me a minute and I may work the thing out.'

Nothing more was said. Biggles lit another cigarette. Ginger gazed moodily across the waste of snow, now pink in the glow of a westering sun. It struck him as odd that even here a mere handful of men could not exist without threats of violence. No wonder, he mused, all over the civilised world the atmosphere was brittle with fears and threats of war.

Presently he broke the silence. 'Suppose Lavinsky got away in his boats, where would he go?' he questioned. 'He's a long way from anywhere.'

The Skipper answered. 'He'd have no great difficulty in getting to South America – unless he ran into heavy seas. He's got plenty of stores. Longer trips than that have been made in open boats, many a time, and will be made again, no doubt.'

There was another silence. This time it was broken by Bertie. He stood up and buffed his arms. 'Well, what are we going to do, old boy?' he asked. 'This doing nothing is binding me rigid. It's beastly cold.'

Biggles drew a deep breath. 'Yes, I suppose we might as well do something,' he agreed. 'Let's see if we can get the gold on board. That may stir the enemy into action, anyway. I'm afraid it's going to be a longish job.'

Ginger looked at Biggles. 'You think that'll be the signal for the enemy to open fire on us.'

'I'm pretty sure of it. For what other reason would Lavinsky leave six men on the ridge? If it was just to watch us, one would have been enough.'

'If we can't get the stuff on board we could at least push off,' said Bertie cheerfully.

'You seem to be forgetting something,' remarked Biggles.

'What's that?'

'Larsen. The idea of leaving the wretched fellow here goes against the grain. But there, we'll talk about that when we've got the gold.'

'If they start shooting at us I reckon we can shoot back,' put in the Skipper grimly.

'I reckon we can,' agreed Biggles. 'Our difficulty would be to fight a gun battle and transport the gold here at the time same. We could do it, maybe, but it would be a slow business. Anyhow, let's try it and see what happens. Skipper, you're the strongest man in the party. Suppose you try fetching a bar while we keep you covered. If anything starts, drop the gold and make back for here.' He smiled faintly. 'When the enemy realises what you're doing it will be interesting to see whether they fire at you or at the aircraft. At any rate, that should tell us what Lavinsky's orders were to the men he left there.'

'Why not let me take the aircraft off the ground and cruise around while the shooting goes on?' proposed Bertie.

Biggles shook his head. 'I thought of that. We can't afford the petrol, and it would come to the same thing in the end, anyway. The machine would have to land to pick up the gold. Let's get the stuff here for a start. We needn't load it up. We could soon do that once it's here. If things get too hot, we shall have to pack up, of course. This is no place to have casualties.' Biggles reached for his binoculars and focused them on the *Svelt*. 'I wasn't far wrong,' he observed presently. 'They've lowered a lifeboat. It's on its way to the ice barrier. Okay, Skipper. Go ahead and fetch an ingot. If trouble starts, drop it and make for home.'

'Aye – aye, sir.' The Skipper set off across the ice.

That the move was noticed by the enemy was at once apparent, for they had been sitting down, and now stood up to watch. One set off at a fast pace in the direction of the *Svelt*.

'He's going to report to the boss,' conjectured Biggles.

The remaining five men, after a short discussion, disappeared from sight behind the ridge. But not for long. One by one their heads reappeared and weapons were now in evidence. A shot rang out, and a bullet flicked up some snow fairly wide of the Skipper, who, however, carried on.

'What's he doing?' muttered Biggles. 'I told him to come back if shooting started.'

'He won't come back until he's got what he went for,' asserted Grimy. 'I know my old man.'

Biggles spoke quietly. 'It's a tricky light for shooting, and shooting over snow is always deceptive; but I don't want anybody hit, so we've got to get those fellows off that ridge. The best way to do that is by enfilading them. Bertie, keep low and see if you can work your way to the end of their line. If you can do that you ought to be able to make things uncomfortable for them. Meanwhile, we'll try to make them keep their heads down from here.'

Another shot rang out from the ridge. Another feather of snow leapt up near the Skipper, who ignored it.

'Okay,' said Biggles grimly. 'If that's how they want it they can have it. Take what cover you can everybody and open fire. Don't waste ammunition. Pick your man and shoot low.'

Biggles settled himself behind the case on which he had been sitting, and taking careful aim, fired.

The man who had been his target ducked, but there was no spurt of snow to mark where the bullet had struck. 'I think I was over him,' Biggles told the others. 'Try shooting a foot below the target.' He fired again. The head at which he had aimed disappeared, but whether or not the man had been hit there was no means of knowing.

By this time Ginger and Grimy were also shooting, with the result that the heads lining the ridge no longer remained still. Only occasionally did one show, and then for not more than a second.

'I don't think they're in love with their job,' remarked Biggles. 'Hold your fire until you see something to shoot at. As long as we can make them keep their heads down the Skipper can carry on.'

Firing continued in a desultory manner.

Presently the Skipper came back, puffing, with an ingot on his shoulder.

'Nice work, Skipper,' complimented Biggles. 'Dump it near the machine – somewhere handy for the cabin door. I think we've got the situation pretty well in hand. Feel like fetching another?'

'There's nothing to it,' answered the Skipper, grinning, and set off again across the ice.

Biggles, with his rifle at the ready, watched the ridge. From time to time a head would pop up and a shot would be fired, but in such haste that the bullet usually went wide.

Presently the Skipper came back with another bar. Without waiting for an order he dropped it beside the first and set off again across the ice.

For a little while there was a certain amount of sporadic shooting. Then Bertie was heard in action at the far end of the line. There was a brisk burst of shots, then the shooting died away altogether.

'I think we've got superiority of fire, as they say in the army,' opined Biggles. 'Grimy, go and help your father. Ginger, I think you might as well go too. I'll hold the fort. If anything serious starts, drop everything and come back at the double.'

Ginger and Grimy put down their weapons and went off at a run.

Thereafter, for about an hour, there was no change in the situation. Not for a moment did Biggles take his eyes off the ridge. The stack of ingots near the aircraft grew steadily. But this satisfactory state of affairs came to an end when Ginger, on one of his homeward trips, shouted to Biggles that the enemy was receiving reinforcements. A boat was on its way across the open water.

Biggles snatched a glance. Out over the sea, beyond the floe on which the others were working, was the lifeboat. It was plain to see what was happening. Lavinsky, apparently, had made his survey of the ice reef, and having heard the shooting, instead of returning to the *Svelt* was making straight towards the floe from which the gold was being recovered, with the obvious intention of landing on it. By doing this he was saving himself a considerable amount of time. Biggles had relied on this time to finish the job he had started, but it was now evident that it would not work out that way. Another twenty minutes would see Lavinsky and his party on the floe. Not only would that put an end to any further work on it, but, what was far more serious, it would put the camp between two fires. If Lavinsky had found a way through the ice barrier, reasoned Biggles, he would first rush the remainder of the gold and then concentrate his fire on the aircraft. A target of such size could hardly be missed. Once the machine was out of action Lavinsky could pretty well finish things in his own time.

Biggles acted swiftly. To Ginger he shouted: 'How many ingots are there left?'

'About half a dozen,' was the answer.

'All right. Leave it at that,' ordered Biggles. 'Start stowing the stuff in the machine.' He gave the Skipper and his son the same order when they returned.

No shots had yet been fired from the approaching boat, possibly because the movement of it would make anything like accurate shooting impossible; but Biggles realised that as soon as the men were on firm ice the camp would quickly become untenable. At this juncture Bertie reappeared to report that what looked like the remainder of the ship's company – he had counted seven – were hurrying towards the scene with the apparent object of reinforcing those behind the ridge. These, Bertie said, he had driven to the far end of the ridge where they had found cover behind some broken ice.

Biggles counted aloud. 'Seven. There are six in the boat. That makes eighteen all told.' Turning to the Skipper who was now helping to load the gold he called: 'How many hands had you in the *Svelt*?'

'Nineteen,' was the answer.

'Did that include you and Lavinsky?'

'No.'

'Then it looks as if he's got nearly everybody here.'

The Skipper paused in his work to answer. 'He might as well have them here; there's nothing for them to do on the ship. If they've left anyone it'll be the cook. He's a Chinese, and a very old man at that – that's if he's the man who sailed under me. He's deaf, too.'

'Good,' replied Biggles. 'Buck up and get that gold stowed.'

'What are you going to do?' asked the Skipper. 'This is going to be a hot spot presently.'

'I'm going to fly down to the *Svelt*,' Biggles startled everyone by saying.

'What in blazes for?' demanded the Skipper, obviously shaken by a move so unexpected.

'The breeze is off-shore where she lies,' answered Biggles. 'I imagine Lavinsky will have made her fast with cables fore and aft.'

'That's what I should do.'

'Then if we cut her free she'll drift away from the main pack.'

The Skipper looked aghast at the idea. 'But you can't cast away a ship like that,' he cried.

'You'd be surprised at the things I can do,' replied Biggles grimly. 'Lavinsky is done if he loses his ship. When he sees she's adrift he'll have to lay off what he's doing and go back to save her.'

The Skipper grinned. 'You're right! So he will.'

'I'm playing for time,' said Biggles. 'Look lively with that gold and we'll get cracking. There's nothing like giving the enemy something he doesn't expect.'

There was a little more shooting while the rest of the gold was being stowed, but the range was long, and as far as could be seen the shots did no damage. By this time Lavinsky's boat had reached the far side of the floe, at a point about two hundred yards from the gold, and was making ready to disembark on the ice.

'Why not push off altogether?' asked Ginger. 'We've got practically all the gold.'

'I'm not thinking entirely of the gold,' returned Biggles tersely. 'Have you forgotten Larsen? He may be dead, but there's a chance that he's still alive, possibly wounded. I shouldn't sleep comfortably in my bed again if I thought we'd left him to the tender mercies of this ship-rat, Lavinsky. As I say, he may have killed him; but if he hasn't, he will. He's not likely to take home someone who could stand as a witness against him.'

With that Biggles climbed into his seat and started up. The others got aboard. Ginger, looking through a side window, remarked that the boat's crew was no longer hurrying.

'They think we're going home,' said Biggles.

'They'll move fast enough when they spot their mistake, I'll warrant.'

CHAPTER XIV

War on the Ice

Biggles took off without trouble, and after climbing to a safe height came round in a wide turn. From the air the scene below became contracted into a small area and it was possible to see every member of the enemy forces. Those in the boat had stopped what they were doing to stare upwards as the machine passed over them. Tiny spurts of smoke revealed that shots were being fired, but at such an extreme range and at such a fast-moving target, there was, Ginger thought, no cause for uneasiness.

Biggles paid no heed to those below. His big concern was to put the heavily-loaded aircraft down without damage. In the ordinary way he would not have given such a routine operation a second thought, but so much now depended on the machine remaining airworthy that what would normally be a molehill of anxiety now loomed like a mountain. Everyone realised this, and no one moved or spoke as Biggles brought the machine round in a cautious approach. However, all went well, and Ginger drew a long breath of relief as the machine skidded to a standstill about two hundred yards from the *Svelt*. Not a soul appeared on deck, nor was there any sign of life in the vicinity.

Grimy, who had brought some boards with him, jumped down and slipped them under the skis. The others were soon out, and

Biggles advanced quickly towards the ship, which, as had been anticipated, was moored fore and aft to steel pins driven into the ice. The Skipper took out his knife and moved towards the nearest rope. Biggles stopped him. 'Just a minute,' he said. 'I'm going to see if Larsen is in that ship. Lavinsky must have spoken the truth when he said he'd found him, otherwise he wouldn't have known about the gold; and I don't know where else he could be. You know your way about the ship, Skipper, so you'd better come with me. Ginger, you follow behind and guard our rear, just in case someone is hiding and tries to pull a fast one on us. Bertie, you'll stay here and keep an eye on things.'

There was still no sign of life on the ship so it did really seem as if the entire crew had gone ashore. A rope ladder hung over the side down to the firm ice. Biggles went up it quickly and stood looking about until the Skipper and Ginger had joined him.

'Anyone at home?' called Biggles sharply.

There was no answer.

Biggles walked on to the companion-way, but before going below he stopped to gaze across the water in the direction of Lavinsky's boat, which, being at the outer edge of the floe, could be seen beyond a projecting ice-cliff. Ginger looked, too, and smiled as he saw that the men who had disembarked were now back in the boat, which, judging from the flash of oars, was making back for the *Svelt* at top speed.

Biggles laughed softly. 'If we've done nothing else we've given Lavinsky a fright,' he observed. 'No doubt he thinks we're about to set fire to the ship and leave him here – and it would serve him right if we did. But let's go below. You lead the way, Skipper. You'll know where to look for Larsen if he's here.'

The Skipper now took the lead. 'Aye. I reckon I know where he'll be, if he isn't dead and under the ice,' he agreed, as they reached the foot of the steps. 'Stand fast while I go and look. There's no need for everyone to go.' He strode on and disappeared from sight.

He was away about five minutes. When he came back his face was pale with anger. 'Just as I thought,' he said in a hard voice. 'They'd put him in irons.'

'What about the key?' asked Biggles quickly.

'I've got it. I found it in Lavinsky's cabin. Let's go and get him out.'

'How does he seem?'

'Quiet as a lamb, and no wonder,' replied the Skipper grimly. 'He's been wounded, and he's half dead from loss of blood. His shirt's stiff with gore. As near as I can make out he got a bullet just under the shoulder. He's in a pretty mess, one way and another.'

Biggles drew a deep breath. 'Okay,' he said quietly. 'Let's get him up. We'll take him straight to the aircraft and fly him home. Ginger, you stay here and watch the passage in case of accidents. Lead on, Skipper.'

Ginger took out his pistol and remained where he was while the others went on. He had not long to wait. Very soon they reappeared, half carrying, half supporting a body that looked more dead than alive. Ginger did not stop to look at the unfortunate sailor closely, but taking the lead went back to the deck.

It took all hands to get the helpless Swede down to the ice, for although he was emaciated he had a big frame, and the heavy clothing he wore would alone have made a load, However, the job was done and the man carried half way to the aircraft. Then Biggles called a halt while the Skipper went back to cut the *Svelt* adrift. This did not take long, for the vessel, with an off-shore breeze on her quarter, was already straining gently at her mooring ropes. The Skipper did some quick work with his knife and the ship was free. She began at once to move slowly away from the ice.

'That should give Lavinsky something to think about,' observed Biggles with satisfaction, looking in the direction of the boat, which was now about half way to the ship.

The shore party, Ginger noticed, were also about half way, strung out like runners at the end of a long race.

'We ought to be away before they get here,' said Biggles. 'Come on, let's keep going.'

The transportation of the sick Swede to the aircraft was continued, and in a little while he was made comfortable on a bed of blankets on the floor of the cabin.

'Now let's see what we can do for him in the way of first aid, or he looks like passing out before we can get him to the Falklands,' said Biggles. 'I think we've got time.'

The medicine chest was produced, and Biggles was opening it when he paused, sniffing the air. 'Can I smell petrol?' he asked sharply, a quick frown lining his forehead.

There was a brief silence. Then Ginger answered: 'Yes, I think you can.'

'See if you can locate it,' ordered Biggles.

Ginger went off while Biggles, with the Skipper's assistance, set to work on the wounded man. The wound, it was soon discovered, had not even been bandaged.

When Ginger came back it was with the bad news that the rear main tank had been holed by a bullet, fortunately by one of small calibre. A little petrol had been lost, but not much. 'I've plugged the hole in the meantime with a piece of chewing gum,' he stated.[1]

For a moment nobody spoke. Then, without looking up from his patient, Biggles said: 'You'll have to get that hole properly plugged.'

[1] Many pilots, particularly in the early days of flying, carried chewing gum for such emergencies.

'All right, but it'll take time. I doubt if it's possible to do it before Lavinsky gets here.'

'That's awkward,' murmured Biggles. 'Still, there's nothing else for it. We shall need every drop of petrol, and I'm not starting on nearly a thousand miles of open sea with a leaky tank. Just a minute, though.' Biggles stopped work and looked up. 'It's no use staying here,' he went on. 'Once Lavinsky gets within range he'll put holes in our tanks a lot faster than we can mend them. There's only one thing we can do. As soon as Lavinsky and the shore party get close enough to be dangerous we'll fly back to the original camp and do the job there. It's a confounded nuisance, but I can't think of any other way. There is this about it, if it's any comfort to you; if we're tired of this shuttle cocking to and fro, Lavinsky's gang, who have to do it on their feet, must be even more fed up with it. Lavinsky will have to secure his ship before he can come after us again, anyway, and that will take time. We should have two or three hours clear while he's getting to her, bringing her back and making her fast, and then marching back to us – if he decides to do that. By that time his men will need a rest, too. We could pick up the remainder of the gold while we're waiting for Ginger to fix the tank.'

'There's only one thing about that,' answered Ginger slowly. 'I've just had a look at the barometer. It's falling fast. It's perishing cold, and getting colder.'

'Aye,' put in the Skipper. 'There's a change on the way. I can feel it.'

Biggles looked at Ginger. 'Make a start on that hole,' he ordered. 'Skipper, you watch the weather. Bertie, keep an eye on the enemy. I've plenty to do here.' He carried on with his first aid work. Larsen, Ginger noticed as he turned away, had lapsed into unconsciousness.

It was nearly an hour later, as Biggles was tidying up, that Bertie reported that Lavinsky had reached and boarded the *Svelt*.

The nearest members of the shore party were only about five hundred yards away. They were coming on, but very slowly, as if they were tired.

'Okay,' acknowledged Biggles. 'We'll push along. Shut the door.' He went through to the cockpit, started the engines, and having given them a minute or two to warm up, took off, heading once more for the old camp. Reaching it he made a circuit, watching the ground closely to make sure that the enemy had all gone, before landing along his original track. 'Get busy everybody,' he called, when he had switched off. 'Ginger, get that hole properly plugged. Do the job well. We can't take chances. The rest of you bring in what's left of the gold while I knock up some hot grub.' He jumped down and looked at the sky, now overcast again. His breath hung round him like bonfire smoke.

The loading of the gold was finished inside an hour, during which time the weather slowly deteriorated. But Ginger's task took longer, although Grimy went to his assistance. The trouble, as he told Biggles, was the bitter cold. It was intense. He could not work with gloves on – at least not very well – and yet it was dangerous to take them off, for the risk of frost-bite was obvious. Any metal touched seemed to burn. Bare fingers stuck to it, leaving the skin adhering after a minute or two. Ginger had to stop repeatedly to beat his hands together to keep the circulation going. Two hours later, although desperately tired, he was still at it. Biggles took him some hot coffee.

Meanwhile, the enemy had not been idle. Lavinsky had reorganised his forces for what was clearly a last desperate attempt to get the gold. The *Svelt*, now under control, had gone first to the ice shelf to pick up the men who had been left ashore. Now, under full power, it was heading for the camp, at no small risk, as the Skipper pointed out, of tearing its keel off on one of the many pieces of ice that covered the water. In this respect, however, Lavinsky's luck was in, and the *Svelt* ploughed on its way unharmed. That Lavinsky intended to launch a general attack on the aircraft from two directions became plain when, at a distance of about half a mile, he brought his ship alongside the ice and put ashore a dozen men armed with rifles. These at once fanned out in a wide semi-circle before advancing towards the camp. The *Svelt* then came on towards the far side of the floe from which the remaining ingots of gold had been removed. On this field of ice more of the ship's company were landed, and under the leadership of Lavinsky himself came on in open order towards the machine.

'This is going to be a warm spot presently,' remarked the Skipper, buffing his arms. 'As soon as they're in range the fun will start.'

At this point of the proceedings Ginger announced that his job was done. The tank was okay.

'Just in time,' returned Biggles. 'We'd better be moving.'

'Absolutely, by Jove. I was beginning to get worried,' murmured Bertie. 'Beastly cold sitting here doing nothing.'

Biggles went through to the cockpit to start up. Ginger took his place at the second pilot's seat. The port engine started, but the starboard one remained silent. Biggles tried again. Nothing happened. He glanced at Ginger. 'She's cold,' said he, and tried again. But the engine was obstinate and remained dead. 'No use,' said Biggles. He had one more try. It failed. 'How very annoying of it,' muttered Biggles. 'Get the heater.'

Ginger looked aghast. 'But while we're fiddling with that Lavinsky will arrive,' he cried.

Biggles shrugged his shoulders. 'So what? I can't get her off on one engine.'

'The temperature was twenty-eight below zero the last time I looked at the thermometer,' said Ginger morosely.

'We should have done something about it before,' stated Biggles. 'Being busy I didn't realise it was as cold as that. Still, it's no use talking about that. We've got to warm that motor before it'll start so we might as well get at it. You handle it. I'll try to keep Lavinsky at a distance.'

Ginger felt sick at heart. That they should find themselves grounded at this most critical moment was maddening, but, as Biggles had said, there was only one thing they could do about it. He climbed out of his seat and adjusted the heating apparatus which had been installed for that purpose. How long it would take to operate he did not know, but several minutes at least would be required.

A shot rang out, and, simultaneously a bullet struck the machine somewhere. Not being quite ready for it, Ginger jumped. Biggles, he thought, had not been far wrong. This was a clear indication of what they could expect.

Another shot cracked in the brittle atmosphere, but this, Ginger saw, had been fired by Biggles at the enemy advancing across the ice-floe. Shots came back, Lavinsky's men shooting as they walked. Bertie also fired, but as far as Ginger could see, without effect. This non-effective shooting, by people whom he knew to be first-class shots, was, he thought, one of the most surprising things of the expedition. He could only assume that it was due to the peculiar white light. Everything was white, the sky as well as the ground. A little breeze moaned mournfully across the frozen sterility and the penetrating cold of it brought tears to his eyes. It seemed the height of lunacy to go on fighting in such conditions, for the wind or snow – or both, as seemed likely – promised to put an end to both expeditions. Whichever side won would be lucky to get away with their lives. But apparently Lavinsky in his gold madness cared nothing for the consequences of what he was doing. More shots were exchanged. It was obvious that someone presently would be hit. Both sides could not go on missing. The range was getting shorter.

Biggles must have realised this, too, for his face was drawn with anxiety when he shouted to Ginger to start up as soon as this was possible. Ginger moved to give the recalcitrant engine another trial. But, even as he did so, a shot whistled past him to stop with that curious 'phut' which a bullet makes when it strikes flesh. Snatching a glance over his shoulder he saw Grimy sink down in the snow and then try to rise, clutching at his left arm.

'Grimy's hit,' he shouted to Biggles.

'Get him inside and do what you can for him,' answered Biggles, punctuating his words with shots. '*And get that engine going.*'

Ginger helped Grimy into the aircraft where a quick examination revealed that the wound was not serious – or at any rate it would not have been considered serious in a temperate climate. The bullet had passed through the muscle of the upper arm, lacerating it badly. Ginger clapped on a pad and bound it on with some haste, for the rattle of musketry outside made it clear that the battle was nearing its climax. Several bullets struck the machine, but as far as he could ascertain from a quick inspection, without serious damage. Perceiving that their only hope now was to get the engine started he was on his way to try it when a fresh complication arose. From overhead came the vibrant drone of a low-flying aircraft.

Ginger knew that this could only be Algy, who had now returned as he had promised. In the excitement he had forgotten all about him. It seemed highly improbable that Algy would realise what was going on below him, and Ginger's heart sank as he perceived that, far from the machine serving any useful purpose, Algy would merely land with fatal results to himself. One man more or less could make no difference to the result of the one-sided battle.

Biggles realised this, too, of course, and as Ginger jumped down he shouted to him to try to signal to Algy to keep out of it, he himself being busily engaged in trying to keep Lavinsky's men from getting any nearer. Just how Algy was to be prevented from landing Ginger did not know, for the machine was already circling preparatory to coming in. All Ginger could do was run out waving his arms wildly, but for all the effect this had he might as well have remained under cover instead of exposing himself to the enemy, some of whose shots whistled unpleasantly close.

Ginger groaned as, with no more concern than if it had been up on a test flight, the Wellington glided in to a perfect landing. And as if that were not enough, thought Ginger, with a sinking feeling in the stomach, it must finish its run right in front of those members of Lavinsky's crew who were closing in from the landward side. Instinctively Ginger yelled a warning although he knew quite well that it could not be heard. But it was all he could do, except run towards the plane firing past it with his automatic at some men who had jumped up and were making towards it. One of them fell, but the rest ran on, shouting triumphantly, as if delighted at having made such an important capture. If that was their opinion Ginger shared it, and he fully expected to see Algy shot dead the moment he showed himself. But to his stupefaction it was not Algy who sprang out, but a naval officer; and behind him, as if impelled by some hidden mechanism, came bluejackets, faster than Ginger could count. The effect was electrical. Ginger stopped, staring, making incoherent noises. Lavinsky's men stopped, too, which was no matter for wonder. They wavered in indecision, and without firing another shot retired precipitately, some throwing away their weapons. Thus might hooligans have fled on the arrival of a squad of policemen.

In a flash the whole situation was changed, and without another weapon being fired; for even Lavinsky, finding himself confronted

Bluejackets faster than Ginger could count.

by authority in a form which it is not wise to provoke, made off towards the *Svelt*, thinking perhaps that if he could get his ship clear of the ice he would be safe from pursuit – for the time being at any rate.

The bluejackets started after the attackers who had now become fugitives, but Biggles ran out and called to the officer to stop them.

'I don't think you need break your necks chasing that bunch,' Biggles told him, as he came up. 'They can't get far. They're the wrong side of the ice barrier. You can come back and pick them up later on – or you can leave them where they are as far as I'm concerned. I want to get out of this before the weather closes in on me. I don't like the look of it. I've got wounded men to get home, anyway, so the sooner we're off the better. I've got what I came for. Much obliged to you for coming to give us a hand.' Turning to Algy he concluded: 'You timed that very nicely; things were getting serious.'

'I had an idea they might be,' answered Algy. 'So did the Senior Naval Officer at Falklands Station when I told him what was afoot and who was here. Apparently he knows Lavinsky by reputation as a seal-poacher, and a bad hat altogether, so he suggested that instead of flying back empty I brought these fellows along to tidy the place up.'

The naval officer glanced round the sky. 'I think you're right about getting back,' he agreed. 'Lavinsky can't do much harm here now and we can always pick him up when it suits us. The Old Man will probably send a sloop down for him.'

'That's fine,' concurred Biggles. 'Let's divide the load and set a course for home before we all get chilblains.'

There was a general move towards the machines.

CHAPTER XV

The End of the Story

The rest of the story is soon told. The two Wellingtons returned together without incident to the Falkland Islands, where Grimy and Larsen at once received proper medical attention. Biggles straightway made a signal home through official channels reporting the success of the expedition, and this promptly brought a reply to the effect that the airmen were to make their own way home in their own time, leaving the gold to be brought back by one of H.M. ships. This decision, which relieved Biggles of any further responsibility in the matter, suited him very well. As he remarked to the others, the machines would fly better without so much dead weight, and he, at all events, had already seen enough of it. Gold, he asserted, always meant trouble. It always had, and probably always would. The thing now was to forget about it.

After a week's rest, and a top overhaul of the machines, the expedition returned home, following the route it had taken on the outward passage. Grimy, his arm in a sling, went with it, but Larsen, still being too ill to travel, was left behind.

Some time elapsed before any news came through about Lavinsky and his crew. There was, however, a good reason for this. No news was available, for following the departure of the expedition from the Antarctic came a succession of gales so severe that any attempt to reach the men would have been not only dangerous but futile. So they had remained where they were for the long polar winter. When, the following season, a Falklands Islands Dependencies sloop reached the spot only eleven men remained alive. Lavinsky was not among them, nor were his owners, Shim and Sham. The story told by the survivors was probably true in the main, although, naturally, all the blame for what had happened was piled on those who had died. The *Svelt*, it appeared, had not been able to get out, and was eventually frozen in the ice. The crew, of course, had continued to live in the ship. The result, considering the number and type of men, was inevitable. There had been quarrels, and in the end, open fighting. In one of these brawls Lavinsky had been shot by a man who had subsequently died; but who had actually killed him was never discovered.

At the trial, which came later on a charge of seal-poaching, one of the men, to save himself, had turned King's Evidence; and he stated, probably with truth, that Lavinsky's behaviour had become so brutal that a conspiracy was formed to put him off the ship, and this had resulted in shooting, in which Lavinsky and his partisans, which included the men known as Shim and Sham, had been killed. What actually happened during that dreadful period will probably never be known. Anyway, those who were brought home merely exchanged one prison for another.

In due course the gold arrived at the Bank of England, and after some delay the salvage money, as arranged, was paid to those by whose efforts the gold had been recovered. After a final dinner together the Skipper and his son returned to Glasgow, where the Skipper bought a house overlooking his home port, and Grimy acquired a motor business which is now flourishing.

The comrades, after a short leave, returned to routine duty, which, as Bertie observed, while dull, did at least permit them to have a hot bath when they felt like it.

It was some time before anything was heard of Larsen and it was feared that he must have died. Then, one day, a letter arrived from the man himself. In it he told Biggles that he had so far recovered that he was able to join a Norwegian whaler that had put in at Port Stanley. The purpose of the letter was to convey his gratitude for his salvation from a horrible fate, but in closing he mentioned a detail which, in the haste to depart from the White Continent, had been overlooked at the time. This was the bar of gold that he had seized when he had first bolted from the hulk. He said he remembered the incident quite well. He had hidden the gold under some ice. He had not mentioned the existence of it to Lavinsky so only he knew where it was. It was still there.

'And as far as I'm concerned,' remarked Biggles, as he folded the letter, 'it can stay there.'

'Absolutely, old boy, absolutely,' agreed Bertie warmly. 'I'm with you every time. There's no future in icebergs – if you see what I mean.'

'I've got a fair idea of what you mean,' admitted Biggles, smiling.

BIGGLES GETS
HIS MEN

CHAPTER I

Raymond States the Case

For some time the only sound heard in the drab headquarters of the Special Air Service, New Scotland Yard, was the sombre ticking of a white-faced clock as it numbered the seconds with dreary monotony and dropped them into the past. Sergeant Bigglesworth, one time Squadron Leader Bigglesworth, D.S.O., R.A.F., better known as 'Biggles', leaned back in a tilted chair reading the current issue of *Flight*. Air Constable 'Ginger' Hebblethwaite, hands in pockets, stared moodily across the depressing panorama of wet roofs which the window overlooked. Air Constables Algy Lacey and Bertie Lissie, in attitudes of bored indifference, idly turned the pages of the daily papers.

At length Ginger yawned audibly, and turning, remarked: 'You know, this place gets more and more like a dentist's waiting-room.'

No one answered.

Ginger tried another angle. Looking at his chief, he inquired: 'Have you no idea at all of what's in the wind?'

'None whatever,' answered Biggles, without looking up. 'But,' he added as an afterthought, 'if Air Commodore Raymond's face is anything to go by it's something unusually grim.'

'He's had something on his mind for a week,' put in Algy. 'I've met him two or three times and he couldn't even say good morning. In fact, I don't think he noticed me.'

'There have been a lot of people in and out of his office,' volunteered Bertie. 'Foreign Office messengers and official-looking blokes with their little black bags, and all that sort of thing – if you see what I mean?'

Biggles closed his magazine, tossed it on the desk and looked at his watch. 'Well, I fancy we shall soon know what it's all about,' he averred. 'My orders were to report to the conference-room at eleven o'clock. It's nearly that now.'

'What about us?' inquired Ginger.

'The Air Commodore said I'd better take you down as it would save me the trouble of telling you all about it afterwards,' replied Biggles, stubbing his cigarette in the ashtray. 'We may as well be drifting along.' He got up, and leaving the others to follow went out into the corridor.

After a walk of some distance he stopped before a door conspicuously marked Private, and knocked. A voice called, 'Come in.' Followed by the others, he obeyed.

There were five men in the long, plainly furnished room, standing together by the fireplace talking in low tones. One was Air Commodore Raymond, Assistant Commissioner of Police, and official head of the Air Section. Three were elderly men of similar type. They were unknown to Biggles, although the faces of two were vaguely familiar. The fifth man was different, being a good deal younger, and thinner, as if he had led a more active life.

'Come in, Bigglesworth,' requested the Air Commodore quietly. 'Let me introduce you. This is Lord Rutterton of the Foreign Office ... this is Mr Lucas Wetherton of the Diplomatic Service ... Colonel George Grimster, of the Canadian Army, and' – here he indicated the youngest member of the party – 'Captain Roderick Mayne.'

Turning to the first named, the Air Commodore concluded: 'This is Bigglesworth, sir, the officer I spoke to you about.'

'I've heard the name,' answered Lord Rutterton, in a deep sonorous voice that made Ginger jump. His eyes were on Biggles' face. 'Well, now that we're all here, let's get on,' he added curtly. 'We may as well sit down.'

'Will you state the case, sir?' inquired the Air Commodore, as chairs were being taken round the central table.

'No – no,' was the quick answer. 'You start, Raymond. I may have a few words to say later.'

Biggles' eyes went to the map case that occupied the entire side of one wall. He observed that the area exposed was Eastern Asia.

Lord Rutterton must have guessed what was passing in Biggles' mind, for he remarked, dryly. 'Yes, that's the part of the world with which we are concerned – very concerned. Carry on, Raymond.'

The Air Commodore cleared his throat, and looking at Biggles began in a voice pitched so low, and with such earnestness, that the gravity of the situation – whatever it might be – was at once apparent. 'Often, in asking you to undertake a mission, I have prefaced my narration by asserting that the particular case under review was of an importance that could hardly be exaggerated. All these, however, were trivial when compared with the one now before us.'

'And it's top secret,' boomed Lord Rutterton. 'You understand that?'

'Of course, sir,' answered Biggles.

'Good. Go on, Raymond,' requested the peer.

The Air Commodore continued. 'Our case, although we did not know it at the time, began in March of this year. At that date, and for some years previous to it, there had been in the service of the Government a scientist named Professor Felix Lampeter. It is unlikely that you would have heard of him because, like so many men engaged in his class of work, he detested publicity.' The Air Commodore dropped his voice a tone. 'As a matter of fact, Professor Lampeter was one of our leading experts on atomic research. He lived, very quietly, at Oxford. It was his habit after dinner to take a short walk for exercise along the river bank. On the evening of March 7th he went for his walk as usual. He did not come back. He never has come back. But we know that when he went out he had every intention of coming back because he gave instructions to his housekeeper that coffee and sandwiches were to be taken to his laboratory at eleven-thirty because he would be working late. It was only when these refreshments were taken to the laboratory that his absence was discovered. A good deal of rain had fallen and the river was high; it was a dark night, so the natural assumption, as suicide could be ruled out, was that he had fallen in the river and so met his death. There was no reason to suspect foul play. His loss was a serious blow to the department for which he was working. So much for Professor Lampeter.' The Air Commodore paused for a moment.

'Working for us in a similar capacity,' he continued, 'but specialising in remote control of rocket missiles, was a Doctor Otto Kern, an Austrian refugee who had taken out naturalisation papers and made his home in this country during the Nazi regime in Central Europe. He lived, apparently quite happily, at one of our research stations on the coast, journeying from time to time to London to make his report to the Defence Council. His only recreation was the sailing of a small boat which he kept in a cove near his home. On April 22nd he went out for a sail – to clear his brain with some fresh air, as he told his servant. He did not return. Neither he, nor his boat, has been seen since, although a few days later his cap was washed up some miles farther along the shore. Apparently he had met with a misadventure, although as he was an experienced sailor, and the sea was fairly calm at the time, it was not easy to understand how an accident could happen. Anyway, that was blow number two. Then, to cap this sequence of tragedies, in May, Squadron Leader Kerr-Watson, our supersonic aircraft designer, disappeared in somewhat similar circumstances. He was a married man who lived with his family in a small house not far from the Experimental Establishment at Farnborough. He left his home as usual after breakfast, and took, as was his habit, a short cut across the fields to the aerodrome. His wife saw him go. He was in good spirits because he had just completed an experimental job on which he had been working for months, and was confident of its success. He never arrived at the airfield. What happened to him we don't know, but whatever it was, it was something for which he was not prepared when he left his home. Naturally, in the light of this third disappearance we had to take a different view of the earlier tragedies. What was happening to these men? Could this be coincidence? It seemed unlikely. It began to look as if a sinister plot was afoot. Who were the instigators? What was their object? If it was to deprive us of our leading technical experts, why did they not murder these men and have done with it? The alternative theory, that they had in fact been abducted and were still alive, was just as alarming. You see my point? If they were dead – well, they would be prevented from doing any further work for us; but if they were still alive they might be forced to work for someone opposed to British interests. You follow?'

Biggles nodded. No one spoke.

The Air Commodore resumed. 'At this juncture we decided to warn our friends across the Atlantic in case anything of the sort should start there. It had, we discovered, already started, although there had been no suspicion of foul play. In short, we learned that

Canada had lost in curious circumstances the man responsible for the defence of its northern outposts – General John Gorton, who, incidentally, was a leading light in anti-atomic warfare. Which explains Colonel Grimster's presence here today. General Gorton went out to visit one of the northern stations. He did not arrive; he did not return, and a search has failed to find him, dead or alive.

'In view of all this you will have no difficulty in believing that the Committee of Imperial Defence became very worried. The thing had to be stopped, for if it went on it was obviously only a matter of time before we lost every good man in our service. How were we to stop it? To furnish every research worker in the country with an armed guard would be a tremendous undertaking, and hardly practicable, anyway. Moreover, it would tell those responsible for the abductions – as there was now reason to think they were – that we had realised what was going on. You must understand that no word of this has been allowed to get into the newspapers. The tragedy of the missing men has been attributed to accident. Naturally, Scotland Yard was called in. It was not easy to know what to do or where to start. The position was a delicate one. It wouldn't do to make a mistake. We dare not, without definite proof of what we suspected, impair our relations with other countries – but you will have grasped the significance of the diplomatic angle. Our first steps, therefore, were directed to find out who was behind the thing. It might have been the work of a crank, or a foreign country that was anxious to retard our atomic development. Well, this is what we did. One of our men here, a smart young sergeant of the new school named Tom Gale, was selected for an experiment. What he did was, I may say, his own idea.' The Air Commodore smiled wanly.

'In a few weeks, by what the newspapers call a build-up, we converted Gale into a top-grade atomic specialist. This was achieved by carefully prepared press and radio reports, and the like. In brief, Gale, under an assumed name, soon became known to the man in the street as our leading atomic expert. He worked at the research depot, and as far as he could he lived up to the part. Of course, he knew he was playing a dangerous game, but he was at least forewarned, which the missing men were not. He hoped, of course, that an attempt would be made to murder him, or abduct him, in which case – assuming that the attempt failed – he would be able to provide us with a clue to put us on the right track. The name Gale adopted for his plan was Vernon Victor Vale, and the reason he chose that name was on account of the simplicity of the initials. They were unusual, and they could be written quickly without appearing to be initials. They could, for instance, be a mere scrawl, such as a child might make. Should he be abducted, it would, we thought, be possible for him to leave his mark – the three Vees – *somewhere*. And in this he succeeded, or else we are in the realm of incredible coincidence.

'You must understand,' went on the Air Commodore, 'that all this happened some time ago. In fact, it is five months since Gale – or Vale, as we must now call him – disappeared.'

'So they got him?' Biggles did no more than breathe the words.

'Yes, they got him,' confirmed the Air Commodore. 'At any rate, Vale disappeared as completely, and as mysteriously, as those who had gone before him. You can imagine with what anxiety we waited for some word from him – if only the three Vees. None came. Weeks passed, and we had given up hope of hearing from him when, a fortnight ago, into the British Embassy at Nanking, in China, there walked a native in the last stages of emaciation. He made signs with his hands, and at first he was taken for a poor creature who was out of his mind. He did not speak. The reason was, he was unable to do so because his tongue had been cut out, very neatly, obviously by a skilled surgeon. Being quite illiterate, he couldn't write, either. But, as I have said, he could make signs, and these were at length interpreted to mean that he was a messenger, that his head was to be shaved, and that he was to be given a large sum of money.' The Air Commodore smiled again, bleakly.

'Well, his head was shaved, or part of it, for it was soon discovered that a small portion of it had been shaved in the not too distant past. And there, sure enough, on his scalp had been tattooed a queer-looking device, apparently with a needle and an indelible pencil. First, there was the symbol that stands for a dollar, followed by the number one thousand. This, it transpired, was the sum that had been promised to the man for his services. Below was a map as primitive as could be imagined, although in the circumstances it could hardly be anything else. Beneath this was a row of three Vees.'

'Amazing,' muttered Biggles.

The Air Commodore continued. 'Of course, our people in China knew nothing about what had been going on here, so they might well have been pardoned had they ignored a message so fantastic. Fortunately this did not happen. The man was detained. A tracing was made of the design on his scalp and sent home to see if we knew anything about it. So, unless an extraordinary coincidence has occurred, Vale has got his initials to us, as he promised. We wasted no time following up this unexpected clue, and this, briefly, is what has so far been ascertained. I will now ask Captain Mayne, our expert on internal Chinese affairs, who has spent most of his life in the Far East, to carry on with the story.'

Captain Mayne took up the narrative. His tone was clear and his manner concise. 'I saw this Chinese messenger and recognised him as an Orochon – that is, a member of a tribe that inhabits the practically unexplored territory in the region of the Manchurian and eastern Siberian frontiers. The fellow couldn't speak, but he could hear, and he made signs that he understood me when I spoke in the language used in that district. I was there myself on one occasion, and my knowledge of the country, meagre though it is, combined with the sketch map, enables me to locate the territory roughly, although not with as much detail as I would like. The key really lies in a curiously shaped lake – but I'll return to this presently. Let us deal first with the messenger, who has now gone home to his people. I tried to persuade him to act as a guide, but nothing would induce him to go anywhere near the area where apparently he had been mutilated; so as we couldn't hold him against his will we had no choice but to give him his reward and let him go. Not that he would have been of very much use, probably. Apart from not being able to speak, he was a sick man.

'You must understand that my only method of culling information from him was of the simplest possible character. I asked questions to which he could only respond by indications of yes or no, or by making signs that were not always easy to follow. As far as I can make out he was on a hunting expedition when he was seized by a party of men and taken to a district he had never seen before. There, presumably to prevent him from revealing to anyone what he had seen, should he escape, his tongue was cut out. Then, with a large number of other prisoners he was made to work like a slave, first clearing a large area of forest, and later squaring the timber, which was used for the building of huts. The place, I gather, is near the narrowest end of the lake shown on the sketch map. Actually, the whole country is strewn with lakes of all shapes and sizes, but I think I know the one. There were, according to the messenger, several white men at this place. Others came from time to time by aeroplane. Our man had no idea of what they were doing, or their nationality. Naturally, living in a barbed wire compound, where the wretched slaves died like flies, he didn't care. An interesting point is, in a perpetual hunt to get more slaves the country has been almost depopulated, survivors having fled from such a dangerous locality. The man in charge of the slaving operations is an enormous cross-eyed Mongolian who carries a whip which he uses freely on the workers. Anyone caught attempting to escape is beaten to death, yet so desperate was the plight of the slaves that several tried it, with what success is not known. Our man had an added inducement to get away. He was told by one of the white men that if he could get to a British officer in China and reveal a message tattooed on his head, he would be given a thousand dollars. That, I think, is about all.'

'What an extraordinary story,' murmured Biggles.

The Air Commodore came back into the conversation. 'Well, Bigglesworth, I think enough has been said to give you a pretty good idea of the situation,' he observed. 'Vale was abducted and taken to the remote heart of what is perhaps the most difficult country of access left in the world. We may assume that where he is, the other missing men will also be found. Vale got his message home and is now waiting for us to act. Rescue isn't going to be easy. The map, such as it is, is vague. Only by great good fortune have we a man who has actually been over the country, otherwise our task would be almost hopeless. Not only have we appalling physical obstacles to overcome, but we shall in a way be trespassers in a foreign country. If we were sure that the lake is situated in China, or Manchuria, then it wouldn't matter overmuch; but if it happens to be in eastern Siberia, which is Russian territory – well, that might be a horse of a very different colour. And it isn't as though the point could be settled with any degree of certainty, because the boundaries are still a matter of dispute – not that there are any boundary posts, or anything like that. No one can say where

Chinese, Russian, or Mongolian spheres of influence begin and end. Apart from the people we are up against, the whole country is infested by gangs of armed bandits to whom throat-cutting is the easiest and most natural way of disposing of anyone who crosses their path. But something will have to be done. First, there is the humanitarian aspect. These unfortunate men of ours will never see this country again unless we fetch them. Apart from that, we need them here. At the moment, I fear, they may be forced to work under threat of death or torture, by people who bear us nothing but ill will. At least, I can think of no other reason why these particular men should be kidnapped and taken to a place so remote that in the ordinary way they would never have been heard of again. It boils down to this. We've got to get these fellows out. What do you think of it?'

Biggles drew a deep breath. 'It sounds a pretty grim business to me,' he answered. 'What you really mean is, will I go to look for them?'

The Air Commodore nodded slowly. 'Quite right. That's it. An aircraft would cover territory in a day which overland would occupy months of time.'

Biggles shrugged. 'Obviously, someone will have to go, and I suppose we're as well equipped for the job as anyone. Of course we'll go.'

'What do you think of the situation generally, Bigglesworth?' asked Lord Rutterton, his eyes on Biggles' face. 'The first thing one wonders, naturally, is this: Are we dealing with an individual, or a hostile power?'

Biggles thought for a moment. 'I doubt if an individual would be able to provide the enormous sums of money that must have been required to abduct these men and transport them to where they are now. On the other hand, no country would assume responsibility for such a scheme. I'd say we are dealing with an individual, or a syndicate of people, financed by a power that has a particular spite against Britain. That I think is proved by the fact that all the abducted men are British. In the event of a showdown the local man on the spot would have to take the rap – not the government really responsible.'

The peer nodded. 'Quite so.'

'Still, it's the man on the spot with whom we are really concerned,' averred Biggles. He looked at Mayne. 'Do you know who normally runs this part of the world?' he inquired.

Mayne shook his head. 'No. I doubt if anyone does outside the country itself. There are local big-wigs all over China and Mongolia who want to run things their way. They may call themselves mandarins, or princes, or generals, but really they're nothing but common brigands who use the people for their own ends. Some are enormously wealthy, and are, in fact, dictators in a small way. Any of them would work in with a European nation who would dish out money and weapons, but I doubt if any one of them would on his own account think in terms of atomic bombs. No, there must be European brains behind that. It is these rascals who are giving the Chinese Government a headache. It's a vast country, and I imagine, beyond the power of any government to keep it in order. That there is some local big chief in the racket we need not doubt, because without such help Europeans of any nationality would be up against all sorts of difficulties. This slave labour, for instance. Someone must be able to speak the local language.'

'That's likely to be our difficulty,' put in Biggles. 'None of us speaks a word of Chinese, much less local dialects. If we're unable to speak to local people we shall be handicapped, if not absolutely bogged, from the start. We ought to have someone with us who can at any rate speak Chinese.'

'What about you, Mayne?' boomed Lord Rutterton. 'You've seen the country.'

'I'm willing to go, if it will help,' offered Mayne without hesitation.

'If you would it would solve a major problem,' declared Biggles. 'In this sort of enterprise one man who has been over the ground, and speaks the language, is worth more than a battalion of bayonets.'

Mayne agreed.

Lord Rutterton spoke again, looking hard at Biggles. 'I want you to understand exactly what you are taking on,' said he. 'Whatever happens the British Government must not be brought into this. If things went wrong a situation could arise that might be exceedingly embarrassing for us.'

'Such a situation would no doubt be exceedingly embarrassing for me, too, sir.' returned Biggles coldly. 'And if it comes to that, it must already be more than embarrassing for the unfortunate fellows already there.'

'Quite so – er – quite so,' agreed the peer, rather uncomfortably, glancing at the Air Commodore, who smiled faintly.

'Still, don't worry, sir. We ought to be able to stand on our own feet,' asserted Biggles. 'If we're caught – well, we shall just be a bunch of adventurers fooling about on our own account.'

'That excuse might be as good as any,' agreed Lord Rutterton. He glanced at the clock. 'Now I must be getting along. I'll leave the matter in your hands, Bigglesworth. Raymond and Mayne will give you all the help possible. Don't hesitate to spend money – should you find it necessary.'

'I won't,' promised Biggles warmly. 'I shall probably need quite a lot,' he added softly, as the conference broke up. 'One thing I shall need is a set of photographs of the missing men,' he told the

Air Commodore. 'I shall want to be able to recognise them if I see them.'

'That's easy,' promised the Air Commodore.

Biggles touched Captain Mayne on the arm. 'If you're not in a hurry I'd like you to come along to my office. There are one or two things I'd like to talk over with you.'

CHAPTER II

Distant Frontiers

'Before we start on anything in the way of organisation I thought it would be a good thing if you told us something about the country we're bound for,' explained Biggles, after the airmen were back in their own office. He offered Mayne his cigarette case. 'In fact,' he went on, 'it's no use trying to make a plan until we have at least a rough idea of the conditions we're likely to find. I've been around a bit, but what I know about this particular section of the globe you could put in your eye without noticing it. I've seen it on the map, and sometimes wondered just what was there; but that's all.'

The expert in Chinese affairs smiled. 'You're not alone in that,' he asserted, lighting his cigarette from Biggles' lighter. 'I may be the only Britisher who has ever been there. I doubt if a dozen Europeans have seen it. In fact, as far as I know, the only people who have been right across the territory were a few White Russian refugees after the Bolshevik revolution. I went ostensibly on a hunting trip, but my real purpose – as it was part of my job – was to see just what went on there, to check up on the strange rumours that occasionally trickled through to the outside world. Actually, I spent most of my time trying to get out again. Like you, I've been around a bit, and I've travelled over most of China, but this area was unlike anything I'd seen before, or have seen since. One's first impression is that it's all crazy, or else *you* are.'

'But I say, look here old man, if nobody ever goes there, how do the jolly old rumours trickle out – if you see what I mean?' inquired Bertie.

'I was referring particularly to Europeans,' explained Mayne. 'A few Orientals, mostly Chinese and Koreans, go in and out regularly, but they are only permitted to do so because they carry merchandise that the natives want – weapons and liquor, mostly – which they swap for the queer commodities the country produces. Even so, it must be a risky business, because from what I learned quite a few are murdered on the way out … not so much by the natives as by the cut-throat refugees who have found safe sanctuary there, mostly deserters from the Chinese army. One has a feeling that one is always being watched, and is never safe. There are no roads, of course, and as the country is pretty rough one is bound to follow the jungle tracks, as the local brigands know only too well. White Swan shooting, as they call it – which means the murder of returning Koreans, who wear white shirts – is the popular pastime.'

'The profits of these merchants must be pretty high or they wouldn't take such risks,' put in Algy. 'Why do they go? I mean, what are these commodities you mentioned just now?'

Mayne laughed. 'You'd never guess.'

'I wouldn't try,' returned Algy.

'There's a certain amount of gold dust, panned in the streams and gorges, but the chief items are deer antlers, ginseng, oak mushrooms, and the hearts, livers, teeth and claws of tigers.'

'Who on earth wants such things?' broke in Ginger, in an astonished voice. 'What's ginseng, anyway?'

'Ginseng is a root shaped like a human torso,' replied Mayne. 'It's thought to possess magical properties – ensures long life and immunity from disease. That may be all rot, but in China the stuff is worth its weight in gold. Deer antlers, ground up, are also medicine. The hearts and livers of tigers, dried, have the reputation of making the weak strong and the nervous brave. Tiger teeth and claws are talismans that protect the wearer from the attacks of wild beasts. Oak mushrooms – a sort of fungus that grows on old oak trees – are a delicacy in the Far East. That may sound silly to you, but some of the things people in this country waste their money on sound just as daft to a Chinaman.'

'So there are tigers there, eh?' murmured Bertie.

'Plenty. The Amur tiger is first cousin to the Bengal tiger. There are panthers, too, and bears. Their skins are another export.'

'What about the country itself?' asked Biggles. 'What does it look like?'

Mayne flicked the ash off his cigarette. 'Well, one's first impression is that nature has played a cockeyed practical joke. That is simply due to the fact that you are at the spot where the Arctic and the tropics bump into each other, so to speak ... where north meets south and east meets west. Thus, you get the *flora* and *fauna* of both; tigers, panthers, wild boars and pythons tread the same tracks as reindeer, wolves and sables. In the bird line you get most of our northern birds flying beside Chinese herons, black swans, ibis, flamingos and pelicans – pink ones, at that. In the forests, cork and palm trees rub shoulders with cedars, walnuts, wild apples and cherries, oak trees and grape vines. The whole country teems with game, large and small.'

'What about the actual terrain?' inquired Biggles. 'That's the most important thing from my angle.'

'Most of it comprises miles and miles of marsh, bog, and stagnant water, for which reason the wildfowl have to be seen to be believed. Swans and geese flight in millions, and that's no exaggeration.

From that aspect the place is a naturalist's paradise. But as for getting about – that's a different story. There are vast areas of nothing but reeds and giant bulrushes growing out of black, sticky mud. There are some mountains, too, with terrific rock gorges. There are rivers and lakes everywhere. They're full of fish. I caught a pike over six feet long which I reckon must have weighed about a hundred pounds.'

'What's the climate like, generally?' questioned Biggles.

'In summer it's blazing hot, but the winters are just as cold,' replied Mayne, 'In spring and early summer, when I was there, the country was ablaze with wild flowers, particularly lilies and peonies. I saw butterflies as big as swallows. Some of them are black. Taking it all round it's a weird, mysterious place. At night the will-o'-the-wisps hang over the marshes like lost souls. Incidentally, the fireflies are the biggest and brightest I ever saw. There is this about it; what with flesh, fish and fowl, a man with a gun need never starve. The natives produce a kind of wheat, but you have to be careful how you eat it because it makes you drunk. Apparently some sort of fungus flourishes on it which sets up fermentation and creates a strong line in alcohol.'

'What are the mosquitoes like?' asked Bertie suspiciously.

'Pretty grim,' admitted Mayne. 'Even worse is a big, red bug known locally as a *gnus*. In places they make life a misery. I came out looking as though I'd had a bad go of smallpox.'

'How long were you there?' asked Ginger.

'About six months.'

'What were the natives like – the real natives?'

'Not bad, although if what the messenger says is correct, in the area we're concerned with, most of them have cleared out on account of this slave racket. I got on well enough. That, no doubt, was partly due to the fact that I handed over to them most of the game I shot. Moreover, the fellow I had with me as a guide knew the people well, and their language, having lived amongst them for years. As a matter of detail, he was an ex-Russian political prisoner named Alexis Petroffsky who had escaped from a prison in Siberia proper. At one time he was a colonel in a crack Cossack regiment, in the Imperial Russian Army, stationed at Vladivostock – at which time he used to go into the interior on hunting trips. It was natural, therefore, that he should head for the place when he broke jail. In many ways he was an amazing fellow, and a queer piece of work to look at, having lost one side of his face in an affair with a tiger. I could never decide whether he was genuine or a superb bluffer. He told me he had spent some time in London, and he certainly speaks English well enough. I found him a grand companion. His big weakness was the bottle – but there, that pernicious brew they call vodka is the curse of the country. It's the old story of traders bringing fire-water in to barter for gold. Still, I can't complain. He got me in and out safely, although where he is now I don't know. Of course, this was some time ago, so conditions may have changed somewhat. There's a chance that I might meet some of the Orochons I got to know. They would be helpful. I could find my way, I think, to a village where I put up for a time.'

'And you learned a bit of the language?' suggested Biggles.

'If you can call it a language,' returned Mayne, smiling. 'The Orochons don't talk. They bark at each other like dogs. At least, that's what it sounds like when you first hear it.'

'Hm. All very interesting,' murmured Biggles. 'Now let's get down to brass tacks. From what you've told us it doesn't sound much of a country for flying operations.'

'I couldn't imagine anything worse,' admitted Mayne frankly.

'There's no level ground where we could land an aircraft?'

'If there is I didn't see it. What level ground there is, is either marsh or forest. What might look like a flat plain from the air would probably turn out to be reeds or bulrushes several feet high. Even the grass is waist deep. I'm not a pilot, but I'd say that a landing on any unsurveyed ground would be asking for trouble.'

'But there are, you say, plenty of lakes?'

'Lakes by the score. Practically all the lower ground that isn't marsh is under water.'

'Then it looks like being an occasion for a marine aircraft,' opined Biggles, looking at the others. 'By the way,' he went on, turning back to Mayne: 'Do any aircraft of any sort operate over this region?'

'I should think it's most unlikely,' answered Mayne thoughtfully. 'Of course I'm not including those which, according to the messenger, are being used by the slave gang. The fellow made signs with his hands which I could only take to mean aircraft. Certainly the place is far from any air route, regular or irregular. There would be no reason for one. At least, I can't imagine what sort of traffic it would take.'

'I imagine the enemy, these Europeans mentioned by the messenger, use aircraft for the same reason that we shall have to,' went on Biggles. 'On account of the time factor alone a plane must be the only reasonable form of transport. I suppose, Mayne, there are no such things as maps of this territory?'

Mayne shook his head. 'Certainly nothing likely to be of any use to us. I've never seen anything but the broad outline one finds in the average atlas. Even on these I imagine that any features marked, such as the chief mountains and rivers, are mostly guesswork. There are no towns. The village I stayed in, called Kossuri, a fair-sized place on the edge of a lake, was merely a collection of huts. The people lived by hunting, and buried their dead – if we can say buried – in trees. The body is rolled in birch bark and hoisted up out of the reach of wolves. You come across these grisly cemeteries all over the place. After the funeral everyone gets drunk on vodka. Drinking seems to be the only recreation.'

'Nice people,' murmured Biggles. 'But tell me, do you think you could find your way to this lake which is to be our final objective?'

'Yes, but I wouldn't like to promise,' returned Mayne. 'I'm assuming from its shape, and its relative position to the Ussuri Mountains, which are also marked on the messenger's map, that it is one of the lakes I passed on my journey. If I am right, I'd say it's about thirty miles long by anything from five to ten miles wide. I'm right about the area, anyhow. It was an Orochon who brought the message, and the place we're talking about is in Orochon territory.'

'You'd have no difficulty in guiding me to the general area in an aircraft?'

'That shouldn't be very difficult. If we could get anywhere near the place I'd be willing to land and make inquiries.'

'If you could find anyone to ask,' reminded Biggles. 'Don't forget what the messenger said about the people clearing out on account of the slave business.'

'There should still be a few of the tough lads hanging about, although if they saw us, there would be a risk that they might shoot first and show themselves afterwards. But that's a risk we shall have to take.'

'It looks as if there will be plenty of risks, anyway,' remarked Biggles. 'One of the biggest, from what you've told us, will be the actual landing. You see, we shouldn't be able to do much cruising about, or word of our presence, or the presence of a strange aircraft, would soon reach the enemy's ears. The only thing against an aircraft on a job like this, is, when it's in the air it's so confoundedly conspicuous. As I see it at the moment, the general idea would be to land somewhere near the objective – not *too* close – hide the plane, and using it as a base, operate on foot. Whatever happens there is bound to be some hiking at the finish.'

'I agree,' concurred Mayne. 'If you intend landing on a lake there should be no difficulty in hiding the machine in the reeds that flourish round the edge, or surround most of the islands. Nearly every lake I saw was dotted with islands. But when it comes to operating on foot we're going to be pretty conspicuous unless we do something about it. We should be recognised from a mile off as Europeans.'

Biggles shrugged. 'That can't very well be prevented.'

'I don't agree,' argued Mayne. 'Surely it would be much safer to adopt some sort of local costume – that used by the Korean merchants, for instance?'

'But the skins of these people are yellow – more or less?'

'Is there any reason why ours shouldn't be yellow?'

Biggles frowned, and thought for a moment. 'In the ordinary way I'm all against dressing up, which has always struck me as theatrical, and usually unnecessary,' he said slowly. 'But I see your point. If we made ourselves look like people who are commonly seen there we might pass without comment – certainly with less comment than if a bunch of Europeans suddenly arrived on the scene.'

'Exactly.'

'It might be worth considering. I'll think about it. Naturally, I'm willing to do anything which in your opinion would make our task easier. It would be fatal to give the enemy cause to suspect that a rescue party was on the spot. We should be hunted from the outset; the prisoners would be kept under stricter supervision, or moved to some other place, in which case our trump card, our knowledge of their position, would be lost.'

'But surely,' put in Algy, 'the very presence of an aircraft will make the enemy suspicious? You can't fly a machine across the country without it being seen or heard.'

'True enough, if the machine was cruising about obviously looking for something,' admitted Biggles. 'But there may be a way out of that difficulty. There's nothing to prevent us from painting Chinese insignia on our wings and fuselage, in which case, if we're seen it might be supposed that the aircraft is one of the Chinese Air Force that has got off its course.

'Admittedly, we could only get away with that once. If the machine hung about, and was seen too often, the enemy would soon guess that it was looking for something. It seems to me that what we really need is two machines, a big transport for getting ourselves and our equipment in and out of the country, and a small machine for reconnaissance work. I think we're bound to do a certain amount of reconnaissance in the first place, in order to locate the exact position of the enemy camp; otherwise one might wander about the country for months without finding anything. If the enemy are using aircraft then they must have a landing ground; and if there is a landing ground we ought to be able to spot it from the air straight away. We might even take a strip of photographs covering the area at the end of the lake, to examine at leisure. Having located the enemy outfit we should then work on foot. It wouldn't matter if we lost the smaller machine. We should still have the big one hidden away to get us home. After all, our job isn't to start a minor war, but to find our men and bring them back. But I think we've got enough data now to work on. The final plan will have to be carefully worked out, and that'll take a little time. I'll get cracking on it, and let you know, Mayne, when we're ready to start. Meanwhile, keep in touch. But it's past lunch-time. Let's go out and get something to eat.'

CHAPTER III

All Set

Far beyond the wild Sikhota-Alin Mountains of Manchuria, out and across the great Ussurian Plains where countless lakes interlaced by furtive streams lie hidden in a world of reeds, the day was slowly dying. To the west, the sun, its daily task complete, sank wearily into a purple horizon, followed by an immense arc of transparent colour, while far to the east, beyond a belt of purest turquoise, some shreds of clouds took fire and blazed with flames of living carmine. Below, from out of the mysterious distances, crept the sombre shades of twilight to soften the harsh outlines of the untamed land, and extinguish one by one the glowing reflected light of lakes and rivers. With the shadows came silence, a profound hush that seemed to take possession of the universe. Even the restless bulrushes, abandoned by the breezes of the day, stood erect and came to rest. The twittering of innumerable birds died away.

At one spot only was there movement, and that was near the edge of one of the larger lakes, where an islet, a mere mound of jungle held in close embrace by a belt of rushes, nestled like an uncut emerald in a tarnished silver setting. There, a figure, a human figure with an olive-yellow skin, parting the rushes to make a passage, moved slowly forward to their extremity and then stood gazing across the sullen landscape. Clad in a cotton shirt worn outside faded blue linen trousers, it was appropriate to the scene.

But a closer inspection of the little island would have revealed certain things that were by no means appropriate to such a setting. Of these, the most outstanding although not easily detected, was an aeroplane, or to be more literally correct, a float seaplane. To be specific, it was a two-seat, single-engined Birada Trainer, an American type built under licence in China, although this was not easily discernible as most of it, and all the upper surfaces, had been heavily camouflaged with bundles of reeds. Only an aerial stood clear. The undersides of the wings, could they have been examined, would have shown the twelve-pointed white star on a blue background which is the national Chinese aircraft insignia.

Near the aircraft, under a thick-leafed tree that stood on reasonably dry ground, had been pitched a tent of the familiar war-time brown and green camouflaged material. By the entrance, a second figure, clad as the first, squatted by a spirit stove on which rested a kettle just coming to the boil. It is doubtful if his best friends would have recognised Biggles, who, as the steam lifted the lid of the kettle, called softly. 'Everything quiet, Mayne?' And on receiving the answer 'Okay,' replied, 'Come and have a cup of tea.'

Captain Mayne, the pseudo-Oriental, who had been keeping watch at the water's edge, joined Biggles at the tent. 'Not a soul in sight,' he remarked. 'I don't think we could have found a better place, or a handier one.'

A month had passed since the conference at Scotland Yard, and for those taking part in 'Operation Rescue', as the enterprise had been officially designated, it had been a busy one. Briefly, the plan finally evolved by Biggles, in collaboration with Mayne, who had the advantage of knowing the ground, was this. It adhered closely to his original idea. Two aircraft had been requisitioned for

Not a soul in sight.

the task. One, the one that now stood close at hand, was a small machine which, operating from the island base, was to be used only for reconnaissance until the enemy camp had been located. The sole purpose of the other, a heavy flying boat transport, was to carry the entire party home on the conclusion of the mission. Marine types had been chosen because the nature of the terrain, as described by Mayne, obviously made the use of landplanes a hazardous business. Both types chosen were employed by the Chinese Air Force, as reorganised by the Commission of Aeronautical Affairs at the conclusion of the Japanese war. They had in fact been acquired in China. Both carried Chinese markings. The big transport, which had yet to come, was also an American type, a twin-engined 'Ranger' – a converted ocean-patrol bomber which provided ample accommodation for the purpose for which it was required.

It was not advisable, Biggles had averred, for the two machines to fly out together. One might pass where two would cause comment. Moreover, a suitable landing site had to be found, and as the smaller machine was handier for this purpose it was decided to send it out first to select and prepare the camp. Biggles was to fly it, with Captain Mayne as the obvious choice for the passenger. Somewhere reasonably near the objective the base camp would be established and the main operation conducted from it. The big machine was to allow the Birada two days' grace, sufficient time, it was thought, for the preliminary work to be completed.

Biggles, under Captain Mayne's guidance, had experienced no difficulty in finding a suitable spot, and the smaller machine was already at the chosen hiding-place. This, according to Mayne's calculations, was about thirty miles from the supposed position of the place where the abducted scientists were being held. Nearer than that Biggles dare not go. The big machine, which was to start during the hours of darkness in order to avoid being seen from the more thickly populated part of the route, was due to arrive at daybreak, flying on a compass course plotted by Biggles, who would, he promised Algy – who was to fly the transport out – be on or as near as possible to that particular line of country.

So far everything had gone according to plan. The Birada was well hidden in its nest and all preparations had been made for the reception of the transport. Camouflaged netting had been stretched from tree to tree on a small island, and on this reeds had been strewn to form a cover that should keep the aircraft safe from aerial observation. Watch had been kept, but so far there had been no indication that the arrival of the Birada had been noticed. At any rate, there had been no visitors, although in view of what the messenger had said about the country being depopulated, this was not surprising.

For the rest, Biggles, somewhat reluctantly, had accepted Mayne's advice in the matter of disguises. Being forced to operate on foot between their base and the enemy camp, in European clothes they would be conspicuous objects should they be seen, Mayne had argued. Whereas, dressed in the manner of Koreans, they would attract little, if any attention, even if their presence was reported. The country might be depopulated on account of the slave raiders, but there was always a chance that they might be seen by the raiders themselves, stated Mayne. If once the enemy got word of Europeans in the vicinity their suspicions could hardly fail to be aroused, and then anything might happen.

To the force of this argument Biggles was bound to submit, so before the start each member of the party had to have a close hair-cut, and a bath in a solution provided by Mayne, which gave the skin the required tint. Bertie had complained loudly when he discovered that the colour was in fact a stain which no amount of scrubbing would remove, but, as Mayne pointed out, what was the use of a dye which the first shower of rain would wash off? It would, he said, wear off in time, and with that consolation Bertie had to be content. It was on, anyway, said Biggles, smiling, and as no amount of protest would get it off he might as well forget about it.

Mayne had also procured the simple garments which were part of the make-up. They would, he said naïvely, get plenty of dirt on them to complete the disguise before the affair was over. The truth of this, in Biggles' case, was already in evidence, for in spite of the mosquito net, after one day and night on the island his face was so spotted with insect bites that he gave the impression of suffering from an attack of measles. The ground, too, being boggy, had resulted in a liberal distribution of mud.

Equipment, as usual, had needed careful thought and preparation. Most of it was coming out in the big machine. A boat of some sort was essential to get to and fro between the island and the mainland. A collapsible rubber dinghy had been selected for easy transport. All cooking would have to be done on a spirit stove, as smoke from an open fire would certainly attract attention if it were seen. Gunshots would have the same effect, so while every member of the party would be armed, there could be no shooting of game except in dire emergency. All the food they were likely to require had, therefore, to be brought in cans. Both aircraft were equipped with radio, although here again this was only to be used in situations that would make its use imperative – bearing in mind, Biggles pointed out, that the enemy would be similarly equipped.

Perhaps the most important pieces of equipment carried by the small machine were its cameras, for vertical and oblique photography; for in the search for the enemy camp they would enable suspicious objects to be reproduced and studied at leisure. This in turn meant developing and printing devices. That the enemy camp would be well screened against air observation was not to be doubted, averred Biggles.

The rest of the 'dunnage' comprised such articles as Biggles, in his long experience of expeditions of this sort, had found were usually worth their weight. Actually, on this occasion there was no need for them to stint themselves, as anything not required could be dumped before the homeward journey, when the big machine – it was hoped – would be heavily loaded with its extra passengers. Keeping in mind the nature of the mission, such useful tools as wire cutters, files and the like, were not overlooked.

Little had been said about the perilous nature of the undertaking, although this, perhaps, was because the dangers were obvious to everyone. In the first place, the mere act of flying over such country, with no landing, servicing or maintenance facilities, was hazardous enough. In spite of all that had been said about the country being depopulated, there was, Biggles knew, a serious risk of the machine being seen on the way out, and word of their arrival reaching the enemy, an enemy from which nothing but ruthlessness was to be expected. The only steps that could mitigate this risk had been taken by using machines which, should they be seen, would be taken for Chinese aircraft that had lost their way. The risk was greater in the case of the smaller machine, which would have to do a certain amount of flying after its arrival – how much would depend on circumstances. With luck, Biggles thought, one run over the supposed position of the objective should be enough to enable them to locate it; but this was by no means certain. When this happened, hostile eyes would certainly see the machine. That was inevitable, and he was prepared for it. They might, he thought, get away with it once – but not twice. It was possible, although he did not think it likely, that the enemy camp, on account of its sinister purpose, might be protected by anti-aircraft guns. If so, the Birada would come under fire the moment it appeared, and perhaps take punishment that would put it out of action. As an extra safety measure, therefore, the machine had been provided with parachutes for the use of its crew.

Yet this was only the beginning. Even if all went well, and the enemy camp was located, there would still be the more difficult task of getting into it, and out of it, with the men they had come to rescue. Just how this was to be achieved had not even been discussed, for to make a plan without knowing what obstacles there were to be surmounted was, as Biggles said, a waste of time. It was clear that all hands would be needed, for apart from the actual rescue party someone would have to stay in camp to mount guard, and another would be required to man the canoe between the island and the shore.

These were the known difficulties and dangers. That unknown ones would present themselves was certain. These could only be dealt with as they arose. Indeed, that very afternoon, during a casual conversation with Mayne, one had loomed up. Mayne, talking of his hunting trip, had recalled some of the native methods of killing big game. One of these was by means of pitfalls along the jungle tracks used by game; deep pits, artfully concealed, with pointed stakes in the bottom on which a trapped beast would be impaled by its weight. That such traps would be abandoned, just as they were, when the natives had left the district, was certain, and the knowledge that they were there introduced into a simple walk cause for acute anxiety.

So, as the day died, and the advance party outside their tent made a frugal meal of tea, biscuits and 'bully', Biggles had plenty to occupy his mind. His first concern was to get the big machine down safely when it arrived, for even this simple operation presented difficulties, chief of which would be to let Algy know exactly where they were. Whatever the method employed there would be a risk of the signal being seen or heard by someone outside their own party.

After a debate it had been decided to use radio for the purpose. A signal on a single sustained note, it was thought, should be enough. That the enemy, if he happened to be listening, might also pick up the note, was obvious; but even so, asserted Biggles, it ought to be possible to get the Ranger down before the enemy could bring direction-finding apparatus into action. The signal would be weak, to give an impression of distance. Anyway, a chance had to be taken by one method or another.

Little was said during the meal. Once Mayne pointed across the darkening waters of the lake to a distant shore, and remarked: 'Unless I'm off the track altogether, Kossuri, the *fang tzu* where I stayed with my Cossack hunter friend, is over there.' As an after-thought he added: 'A *fang tzu* is what in this part of the world they call a village.'

Biggles nodded, and made a slap at the back of his left hand on which several mosquitoes were also making an evening meal. 'If it's all the same to you I'm going to get into my mosquito net before these little devils eat what they left of me last night,' he said. 'We shall have to be on the move early, anyway. I want to be ready for the Ranger as soon as it gets within earshot. The weather seems to be set fair, which is a blessing.'

Mayne agreed.

'With any luck, by this time tomorrow we should know some-thing,' concluded Biggles, as he moved back into the tent.

CHAPTER IV

Danger and Disaster

Biggles was up before dawn, to discover with a shock that the land was shrouded in white, opaque mist, that reduced visibility to zero. It was chilly, too, so he lost no time in putting the kettle on for a hot drink. This done he checked the radio, and then roused Mayne, who was still asleep. Pointing through the open flap of the tent he inquired how long the fog was likely to last, assuming that during his previous visit he may have had some experience of it. 'I wasn't expecting anything like this at this time of the year,' he told Mayne bitterly. 'One thing is quite certain. No aircraft could get down in *that* – not even if the pilot was over his home airfield.'

'We're unlucky,' answered Mayne, dressing quickly. 'I've seen it happen, but not often. In fact, I used to hope it would happen because it made the wildfowl fly low, so that I could get a shot. It's caused by a slant of cold air coming in from the north.'

'I don't care what causes it, how long is it likely to last? That's all I want to know,' demanded Biggles.

'Not long. It'll disappear as the sun warms things up,' was the not very comforting answer.

'Well, until it does, the Ranger will have to sit up topsides burning petrol,' muttered Biggles. 'It should be along any minute now. Hark! What's that?'

From the distance, growing in volume every moment, came a rushing noise, as of an approaching hurricane.

'Geese,' answered Mayne. 'Geese or swans – or both.' And even as he spoke, with a tremendous clamour the birds began to pass low overhead. How many there were could not even remotely be guessed, for the swishing of countless wings lasted for several minutes.

Biggles lit a cigarette. 'Well, the Ranger has only to barge into a party like that and it'll come down all right – in pieces,' he observed gloomily.

More geese went over, the leader honking loudly. There were flights of other birds, too.

'This is something I *didn't* take into account,' remarked Biggles.

'I told you what the wildfowl population was like,' reminded Mayne.

'I know you did, but I couldn't imagine anything like this.'

'They only flight early morning and late in the evening.'

'Very obliging of them,' returned Biggles sarcastically. 'Meanwhile, it looks as if we shall have to confine our flying activities to the hours a lot of perishing birds don't want to occupy the atmosphere. An aircraft might as well fly into a brick wall as into heavyweight poultry on this scale.'

By the end of a quarter of an hour, however, the flighting had ceased, and, Biggles was relieved to note, the mist was beginning to thin. Visibility improved slowly, and they were just finishing breakfast when from the distance came the sound for which they had been waiting – the drone of aero engines. Ruling out anything in the way of coincidence it could only be the Ranger. Hurrying to the Birada's radio Biggles sent out the signal. That it had been picked up became evident when the big aircraft came nearer, although the mist was still too thick for it to be seen.

It so happened that the Ranger did not have long to wait, although to Biggles, in his anxiety – for everything depended on the machine getting down safely – it was long enough. Quite suddenly the mist began to lift, thinning as it rose. A shaft of watery sunshine struck through it; an area of pale blue sky appeared, and like magic the air was clear except for a few swiftly dispersing clouds. The drone of the engines overhead died away and the Ranger appeared like a great, grey wraith, nosing its way cautiously towards the placid surface of the lake. Biggles ran out a little way, for nowhere near the island was the water very deep, and waved a towel. Then, as the Ranger turned towards the spot he returned to the shore to await its arrival.

'Not so bad after all,' was the way he expressed his relief to Mayne as the Ranger made a good landing and surged on towards the island. He signalled it to the mooring that had been prepared for it.

Another minute and the big machine had nosed its way into its reedy anchorage. The engines died, and Algy, Ginger and Bertie, looking incongruous in their Oriental 'toggery' – as Bertie had called it – stepped ashore.

'All hands help to cover the wings with reeds,' ordered Biggles. 'I've plenty cut.'

'But here, I say old boy, what about a spot of brekker first?' protested Bertie, regarding Biggles reproachfully through his monocle. 'We started at a ghastly hour and the old tummy feels a bit emptyish – if you get what I mean?'

'You'll have all day to fill it,' answered Biggles. 'And you'd better take that window out of your face. It doesn't go with the rest of you.'

'But I shall be lost – absolutely lost – without it,' complained Bertie.

'You're more likely to be lost *with* it, if anyone sees you,' was Biggles' uncompromising reply. 'Get cracking.'

The Ranger was soon made snug, and so bestrewn with reeds that detection, except from close range, would be practically impossible.

Over breakfast Algy stated that he had nothing to report. Everything had gone off all right, although the ground mist, when it formed suddenly, had him worried for a little while. 'How are things here?' he inquired.

'Okay so far,' answered Biggles. 'We've seen nobody, and as far as we know nobody has seen us. We appear to have the place to ourselves, but to be on the safe side everyone will keep back under the trees except when handling the aircraft. Remember, in clear weather this island can be seen from anywhere along this end of the lake. Everything is dead still, so a movement of any sort would attract the attention of any odd native who happened to be on the prowl. If we're spotted, this place as a hide-out would be finished, and it would be a tricky business now, trying to move to another. How long we shall be here depends of course on how things fall out, but the sooner we get mobile the sooner we shall be away. Sharing the island with us is a real tough line in mosquitoes that should encourage everyone to put his best foot forward. You'll realise what I mean when the sun goes down. Meanwhile, we're all set to begin operations.'

'In that case let's get started,' suggested Algy. 'What's the programme? Have you worked it out yet?'

'More or less,' answered Biggles. 'Obviously, our first job is to locate the enemy camp – assuming that there is one. We can do nothing until we've confirmed it and know exactly where it is. To start blundering about on foot in this sort of country is out of the question. If it's here, or hereabouts, a single air reconnaissance should reveal it. There's no reason why that shouldn't be done today – right away, in fact. I shall do it, taking Ginger with me. The rest will stay here, get the place shipshape and watch for any movement on the mainland. You'd better know exactly what I intend to do, in case things come unstuck. The supposed position of the kidnappers' dump is about thirty miles due east from us. When I take off I shall head north, to make a wide detour before swinging round to approach the objective from behind; so, as I pass over it, I shall be already on a course for home. I shall fly straight on, having a good look, of course, while Ginger takes a strip of photos so that we can study the layout of the place in our own time. Having no map, the photos should be useful when it comes to the foot-slogging part of the operation. Having got the photos I shall wander about a bit like a lost first-soloist, so I may arrive back here from any direction.'

'And then what?' inquired Bertie.

Biggles smiled faintly. 'Having located the enemy dump, all we have to do is march to it, collect our men, return here and then fly home – but I have a feeling that it won't be quite as easy as that. We'll plan our next move when we know what we have to cope with. Of course, the objective may be well hidden, and hard to find; but we'll try the simple way first. That's enough for the moment. All right, Ginger. I'm ready when you are.'

'What happens if this trip comes unstuck?' inquired Algy. 'I mean, in case of a forced landing, or anything of that sort. What do you want me to do?'

Biggles shrugged his shoulders. 'Ginger and I ought to be able to work our way back here. I've got a pocket compass, and with a few biscuits in our pockets we should be all right for a day or two. If all goes well we should be back inside a couple of hours. If we're not, you'll know something unforeseen has happened; but don't get in a flap, and don't be in too big a hurry to do something. Give me a day or two. On no account put the big machine in the air, except to go home. Without the transport it's unlikely that any of us would ever get home. If by any chance we don't turn up you'll have to use your own initiative about what to do.'

Algy nodded. 'Good enough.'

Followed by Ginger, Biggles walked down to the edge of the lake and surveyed the shore, and the land beyond as far as it could be seen, for any sign of life. But there was none, so the Birada was cleared of its camouflage and the crew took their places.

Finding a parachute in his seat, Ginger asked: 'Do we really want these things?'

'As they're here we might as well wear them,' answered Biggles casually. 'We're not heavily loaded and they may come in useful. One never knows. By the way, don't take photos until I give the word. I want to get a good vertical strip of the far end of the long lake. You can use the oblique camera to take shots of anything that strikes you as suspicious.'

'Okay.'

The engine came to life, and in a few minutes the Birada was on its way to perform the duty for which it had been brought.

From the air, in broad daylight, Ginger watched a strange panorama unfold itself to his view, half water, half land, unmarked by a road of any sort, or, as far as he could see, a human habitation. On all sides stretched a seemingly endless succession of lakes, lakes of all shapes and sizes, many connected by rivers and brooks that meandered through vast plains of reeds. Only on the higher ground was there any actual forest, and this mostly occurred in areas seldom exceeding a few square miles. Patches of jungle on occasional knolls might have been the backs of prehistoric monsters afloat on an emerald sea, for across the plains passed wave after wave as the tall grasses and rushes bent under the pressure of a fitful breeze. There were mountains in the distance. The foothills, gashed by mysterious gorges, came down to meet the plains.

Biggles, as he had planned, first headed northward, a course which he held for some twenty minutes before swinging round to the east, and finally south, in a wide detour that would bring him over the estimated position of his objective, which, according to the rough sketch map drawn on the head of the Orochon, lay at the extremity of an arm outflung from a lake of exceptional size and peculiar shape. This lake – or so Ginger took it to be – had been in sight for some time, filling almost the whole of the eastern skyline. Indeed, it was now possible to see that this sheet of water occupied the centre of what was in fact a vast basin, perhaps a hundred miles across, hemmed in on all sides by mountains, now dwarfed by distance, but, Ginger imagined, in reality high enough to form an almost insuperable barrier to any vehicle but an aircraft.

Biggles, apparently, also assumed the lake to be the one with which they were concerned, for cruising quietly at two thousand feet he worked his way towards its western extremity where it was now possible to observe, there occurred just such a long narrow arm as was depicted on the map. Finally he turned on a new course that would take him directly over it, at the same time speaking to Ginger over the intercom. 'Use your eyes and stand by to take photos,' he said crisply. 'This is it – or should be.'

Ginger was already looking, searching the ground with trained eyes for signs of human habitation. He knew what to look for. He did not expect to see roads or conspicuous buildings; nor did he; but where people move about regularly over the same ground there come into existence tracks that are visible from the air, if not from the ground. There might be smoke from cooking fires, washed clothes left out to dry, and rubbish tips. If, as the Orochon had indicated, trees had been felled there should be some sign of that, too. He saw none of these things. All he could see was the calm surface of the lake, bounded sometimes by the eternal reeds and sometimes by wide areas of jungle.

The machine droned on, turning neither to right nor left, bringing the picture ever closer. Bending over the side of the aircraft Ginger had just convinced himself that there was nothing there, and that they had come to the wrong place when he saw a small, dark-coloured blob move swiftly from one spot to another, and then stop. It might have been a bear, or some other animal. In the ordinary way, without reason to pay particular interest, it was unlikely that he would have given the thing a second glance. As it was he watched closely, and when he saw a microscopic white spot appear against the darker background he knew that it was the face of a human being looking up at him. Then, suddenly, it was no longer there. But this only confirmed what Ginger suspected. Thus can the folly and curiosity of one man destroy the most deceptive camouflage ever designed.

'There's someone down there,' he said over the intercom.

'I saw him,' answered Biggles. 'Okay. Start taking.' Ginger applied himself to his cameras, taking photo after photo as the aircraft passed on even keel over the suspected area. Between vertical shots he took an occasional snap, with a 'pistol' camera, at several angles, covering particularly the area where he had seen the movement.

The machine droned on, and gradually the objective fell away behind.

Said Biggles: 'Did you see anything?'

'Only the one man.'

'Then you didn't notice the trench?'

'Trench? No.'

'There was a straight black line, with squared-off ends, between two patches of jungle. I took it to be a trench. I can't think what else it could be. Anyway, straight lines don't occur in nature, so there's *something* there. You should have the thing in your photos so we'll have another look at it presently. We'll get along home.'

The Birada went on. There had been no opposition, anyhow, thought Ginger, not without satisfaction. Nevertheless, he stood up to get a clear view beyond the rudder in case there was anything more to be seen. There was, but it was not on the ground, and it was on the ground, naturally, that his attention was concentrated. It may have been that a movement caught his eye. At any rate, something made him look up; and there, perhaps a mile distant, a single black spot moved against an infinity of blue. Ginger blinked and looked again, thinking it might be an eagle, or one of the larger hawks. But no. The silhouette was unmistakable. The spot was an aircraft, a monoplane, head on, well above and following them.

'Watch out, Biggles!' he warned sharply. 'There's a bandit behind us.'

'Which way is he travelling?'

'He's following us, and coming in fast.'

'Recognise the type?'

'No. It's a fighter by its cut. Painted black. Can't see any markings.'

'Okay.' Biggles' voice was quite calm.

The sinister pursuer came on, swiftly closing the gap.

'What are you going to do?' demanded Ginger, in a voice brittle with alarm. 'This chap means business.' He asked the question because the stranger was clearly a high-performance fighter, whereas their own machine, being a trainer type, carried no armament of any sort. There could, therefore, be no question of combat. Nor could the Birada hope to escape by running. Biggles had selected it for the very reason of its slow speed, robust construction and easy manoeuvrability, qualities which in view of the conditions in which it would have to operate were to be preferred to high speed and fighting performance.

Biggles' answer to Ginger's question was: 'It all depends on what he does. If he only intends to follow us we'll take him for a tour round the landscape. If he comes for us I shall have to go down. Get the cameras under your arm and be ready to jump.'

'To what?'

'Jump. We've got to save the photos. If we lose them we may never get another chance to get a fresh set. Don't bother about me. The thing is to get the cameras back to base.' Biggles' voice was now terse.

'Okay,' acknowledged Ginger in a resigned voice.

In the short time occupied by this conversation the relative positions of the two machines had altered considerably. The black fighter had increased its speed and was coming in, nose down, from the flank. Biggles, while ostensibly still on his course, was slide-slipping away from it, and clear of the lake, towards a grass-covered steppe broken by numerous groups or copses of heavy timber.

The end came suddenly, but Biggles, old at the tricks of his trade, watching the stranger in his reflector, was ready. He swerved, and only just in time, for almost simultaneously came the grunting snarl of multiple machine guns. A stream of tracer bullets, intended for the Birada, flashed behind its tail unit. Biggles continued to turn, banking steeply to pass under the attacking machine, which, in consequence, overshot, and had to make a complete turn to resume its attack.

For an instant the Birada came to even keel. At the same time Biggles' voice came over the intercom in a single staccato word, 'Jump!'

Ginger, ready, did not hesitate. With the cameras under his left arm he launched himself into space.

Ginger launched himself into space.

By the time the parachute had opened, and he was able to look around, the two machines were some distance away, the fighter turning in a tight circle to bring its guns to bear on a target, which, twisting and turning – although, as Ginger realised, under perfect control – dropped ever nearer to the ground.

He did not see the end of the affair, being too taken up with his own position which was not without its hazards. Fortunately there was little wind, but looking down to see where he was going feared that he must collide with some tall trees. In the event a puff of wind just saved him; he missed the trees by a narrow margin and made a touchdown in the long grass by which they were surrounded. He fell, but was up again in a moment, releasing himself and then swiftly piling the billowing silk into a ball for easy transport so that he could get it out of sight. With the cameras under one arm and the 'brolly' under the other, he dived into the trees. Putting his burden in a safe position he dashed out into the open to see how the one-sided combat had ended. In the last few hectic seconds of his descent he had been aware of sporadic bursts of fire, so he was not surprised when, just as he ran clear, there came the horrible, tearing, rending noise of a crashing aircraft. By the time he was quite clear of the trees there was only one machine in the air. It was the black fighter.

The matter did not end there. With a sinking feeling in his stomach Ginger watched the fighter roar down and rake its now stationary target with long bursts of fire. From the spot, into the air rolled a coiling cloud of black smoke. Only then, as if satisfied, did the fighter turn away. Either by accident or design it turned towards the place where Ginger, as if rooted to the ground by horror, was standing in full view. Perceiving his folly, having a pretty good idea of what to expect, Ginger flung himself back under the trees. Nor did he stop at the fringe, but bored his way through the undergrowth to the root of a giant oak, at the foot of which, on the far side, he flung himself flat. An instant later, through the copse came such a shattering hail of metal that he was appalled by the din it made. Branches and bark were ripped from the trees. Clods of earth sprang into the air. Hearing the fighter roar low overhead, acting under the sheer impulse of self-preservation, he reversed his position to still keep the tree between himself and the aircraft. Again came the withering blast.

Four times this happened. Ginger knew that the pilot couldn't see him, so apparently he was spraying the whole copse in the hope of killing him. Finally, either because he had used up all his ammunition, or possibly because he thought he had done enough, the fighter made off. As the noise of its engine receded, Ginger, white and shaken, picked himself up, and in a sort of frenzy raced for the spot where the Birada had crashed. There was no difficulty in finding it for it was still burning fiercely.

He was still running, dry-lipped and wild-eyed, when a voice near at hand said: 'Where do you think you're going?'

Spinning round with a gasp he saw Biggles sitting on a fallen tree, smoking a cigarette.

CHAPTER V

A Sight to Remember

'Then he didn't get you after all!' cried Ginger, almost overcome with relief.

'Doesn't look like it, does it?' returned Biggles.

'How on earth did you get away with it?'

'In the first place, probably, because the chap in the other machine hasn't had much practice.'

'You didn't jump?'

'By the time you were clear I was too low. Moreover, had I jumped he would have plastered me as I went down. As it was I preferred to remain mobile. He just couldn't hit me, that's all there was to it. Had I tried to land in the long grass I should have done a somersault, so I flattened out over it and headed for the trees. I took a gap between two of them. My wings went, of course, but they absorbed most of the shock. I've collected a bruise or two, but nothing to worry about. By the time our friend in the black kite could bring his guns to bear I was forty yards away, behind the thickest tree I could find.'

'Same here,' said Ginger, with feeling.

'Have you got the cameras safe?'

'Yes. They're in the trees, with the brolly.'

'Fine. Where did that machine come from – did you see?'

'No. I happened to look up, and there he was.'

'Well, there was no sign of an airfield yet he must have been pretty close all the time. I imagine he's got a roosting place under the trees somewhere. He's not alone there, either. It's a pity about the Birada, but it served its purpose so we can't complain.'

Ginger found a seat beside Biggles on the log, for now that reaction had set in his legs were a trifle shaky. 'It looks as if we've got a nice long walk home,' he observed. 'How far have we to go, do you think?'

'About twelve miles, as near as one can judge. Even taking it easy we ought to be home before dark.'

Ginger looked at the smoking remains of the Birada. 'What a mess,' he muttered. 'But there is this about it. We know the enemy camp is here all right, or they wouldn't have air protection.'

'Unfortunately, they also know we're here,' Biggles pointed out.

'They knew that when we flew over the place.'

'Of course,' agreed Biggles. 'They may have taken us for a lost Chinaman, but they weren't taking any chances. If that's what they thought they'll try to confirm it.'

'How?'

'Well, obviously, they won't be content to leave things as they are. Not likely. As soon as the pilot gets home – and he's probably home by now – a search party will be sent out to look at us if we're dead, or find us if we're alive. As no corpses will be available for inspection they'll know that we escaped, in which case they'll soon be after us. They won't want a Chinese pilot to go home to report that he was shot down in this area by an unknown aircraft. No fear. Someone might come out to investigate, and that's the last thing they want.'

'That being so, don't you think we ought to be moving off?' suggested Ginger.

'On the contrary, I was thinking of staying here for a bit,' returned Biggles.

Ginger stared. 'Are you kidding?' Trust Biggles, he thought, to do the unexpected.

A ghost of a smile hovered over Biggles' lips. 'No. My first inclination, like yours, was to push along right away, to get a good start. Then it struck me that this might be an admirable opportunity to have a closer look at some of the people we're up against. So far we don't even know their nationality. I decided that you should trot along home with the cameras, but on second thoughts, as the day is still young, it seems safer to keep together.'

Ginger looked doubtful. 'By staying here we're taking a chance.'

'One seldom gets anywhere without taking a chance,' argued Biggles. 'One look at these people would tell us a lot. Raymond would give his ears for that information, even if we got no more.'

'You think they'll come?'

'I'm pretty sure of it. They must be as anxious to see us as we are to see them. They should be on their way here by now. Obviously, it'll take them some time to get here, but even so, we ought to be home by nightfall.'

'Where are we going to hide?'

'What's wrong with a nice big tree? As a hiding-place a tree isn't exactly an original notion, but it's still a good one.'

'Okay,' agreed Ginger. 'Let's find a comfortable perch.'

'Plenty of time,' said Biggles. 'Let's see what's left of the machine.'

Getting up they walked along to where the Birada was just burning itself out. Nothing remained but the engine and the metal members of the airframe. Certainly there was nothing that would furnish the enemy with information.

Biggles shrugged. 'Ah well. In shows of this sort these accidents will happen,' he remarked. 'I'd like to know who made the type that shot us down.'

'Then you didn't recognise it?'

'No, and I was pretty close to it – a bit too close – once or twice. I've never seen that particular machine before, I'm certain – not that there was anything remarkable about it. The general lines were quite orthodox. There were no markings – at least, I couldn't see any.'

Turning away, they walked back to where Ginger had left the cameras and the parachute. These were retrieved, and with the burden shared, they retraced their steps to that part of the copse which held trees most suitable for their purpose. There were several from which to choose. The only essential qualification was that it should overlook the scene of the crash, for this, said Biggles, was sure to be the object of greatest interest to the search party, assuming that one came.

A tree, a massive walnut with spreading branches, was soon selected, after which all that remained to be done was find comfortable positions in it.

Ginger went up first, taking with him a long line made from the shrouds of the parachute, which, having served its purpose, was not worth the labour of carrying back to base. With the line he hauled up the cameras, and then used it to fasten them securely in a crutch. Biggles, still on the ground, cut the fabric into pieces, the purpose of which – apart from disposing of it – was to provide a softer seat than a bare branch could offer. Ginger settled himself in the junction of three branches, about thirty feet from the ground, which commanded a view, through a leafy screen, of the burnt-out machine. Biggles chose a similar position some twenty feet away from him. Each ate a biscuit. After that there was nothing to do but wait. The time, Ginger noted, was still only a little after eleven o'clock.

As the sun climbed to its zenith the air became sultry even in the shady heart of the tree. For a long time the only sounds were the twittering of birds and the drowsy hum of insects. To pass the time, Ginger, who could see the lake from his elevated position, amused himself by counting the different kinds of wading birds standing on the edge of the glassy water. Once a small brown bear caused a diversion by grubbing about under the leaves as he wandered on his way.

It was nearly two hours before anything important occurred to break the monotony of the vigil. Then to Ginger's ears came a strange chattering that puzzled him not a little. The sound came, not from the direction of the enemy camp, but the other way. However, in a few minutes the problem solved itself when into the clearing in which the wrecked machine lay stepped two figures dressed so like himself that for a moment Ginger thought that Algy and Bertie had arrived. Each carried a large, apparently heavy bag. Then the obvious truth struck him. The men were two genuine Korean traders. The chattering broke out in a fresh burst of conversation as the men caught sight of the smouldering aircraft to which, possibly, they had been attracted by the thin column of smoke that still rose into the air. Anyhow, they put down their bags and walked round the wreck talking volubly although, of course, Ginger had no idea of what the conversation was about. They seemed surprised – as well they might be – by the character of their discovery. Neither appeared to be armed – anyhow, not with firearms – and for the rest they looked harmless enough. What they were doing in the region if, as it seemed, the inhabitants had fled, he could not imagine. He concluded that either they were unaware of this or had lost their way. Finally, to his dismay, they sat down on the very log which he and Biggles had recently vacated, and like two children at a picnic proceeded to eat a meal.

It was evident that they were blissfully unaware that they were in any sort of danger.

Ginger caught Biggles' eye. Biggles made a movement with his hands as much as to say there was nothing they could do about it. Anyway, thought Ginger, since neither he nor Biggles could speak a language likely to be understood, no good purpose would be served by revealing themselves. It might make matters worse. Left alone the travellers would soon be on their way. At least, he could only hope so. What would happen if the search party arrived and found them there was a matter for speculation.

This, in fact, is what did happen, and in the event the outcome was worse, much worse, than anything he could have imagined.

Biggles was right in his prediction that a search party would be sent out to examine the crashed aircraft. Its approach was announced by a jangle and clatter of accoutrements which brought the Koreans to their feet in attitudes of alarm. They started to run, but they were too late. Round the end of the trees swept at full gallop a party of horsemen of such wild and picturesque appearance that Ginger's eyes went round with astonishment. The spectacle reminded him of a picture he had once seen in a book, of an incident in some barbaric war of olden days. There was no military order. Each rider rode his sweating beast as and how he pleased. Most of them carried rifles, although great curved swords banged against the saddle-flaps.

Only one of the men, who rode a little apart, appeared to be a European, and even he, in a tight-fitting, high-collared shirt crossed by bandoliers, and a round lambskin cap on his head, was a romantic figure. The rest were Asiatics with brownish-yellow, slab-like faces, and narrow slanting eyes. Most of them wore drooping black moustaches, some with a wisp of black hair on the chin. Ginger, searching his memory, in a vague sort of way took them to be Mongolians, or

Tartars – he wasn't sure which, if, in fact, there was any difference. As his eyes went automatically to the leader he drew in his breath sharply as he called to mind a scrap of information furnished by Mayne. According to the Orochon messenger the slave-master was a large, cross-eyed Mongolian. As there could hardly be two such men in the district, thought Ginger, this must be he. Certainly he answered to the description, and a more villainous-looking creature he had never seen. The man, who literally dwarfed his belathered mount, bristled with weapons; yet even so, in his right hand he flourished a whip with several tails, each with knots at intervals.

Watching this amazing scene a strange feeling crept over Ginger that time had somehow slipped back several centuries; that he was living in another age, the age when the hordes of Genghis Khan rode the earth on a wave of blood and horrors unspeakable. He had no idea that such people still existed.

There was, however, little time to reflect upon this aspect of the situation. The big Mongol saw the two Koreans at once, as he was bound to, and with a yell of triumph, clapping spurs already bloodstained into the flanks of his wretched horse, brandishing his whip he bore down on them. The knotted thongs curled round the legs of the nearest fugitive, who, with a scream of pain and terror, fell headlong. An instant later his companion shared a like fate. As if this were not enough the whip continued to rise and fall on the squirming Koreans who had no means of defending themselves. During this ghastly display of sheer brutality the rest of the mob dismounted, and standing in a circle roared with laughter as if the thing was a great joke. The European seemed quite disinterested. Dismounting, he walked over to the crash and proceeded to make an examination of the wreckage.

To Ginger, sitting petrified with horror in his tree, the whole thing was incredible. That any man could inflict such barbaric treatment

Brandishing his whip he bore down on them.

on his worst enemy would have been a thing to marvel at, but that he should so treat two inoffensive merchants who had done him no injury of any sort was simply beyond his understanding. Clearly, the man was not human. Ginger derived a crumb of comfort from the cold butt of his automatic, which he determined to use without the slightest compunction should he be discovered. In no circumstances would he fall into the hands of such devils alive; and the first man to die, he decided grimly, would be the monstrous Mongol. He glanced across at Biggles; but Biggles' face was expressionless and gave no indication of what he was thinking. What astonished Ginger as much as anything was that a white man, apparently a European, should make no attempt to stop this display of bestial brutality. But his examination of the aircraft concluded, the man's only interest seemed to be in the contents of a bottle which he had taken from his pocket.

The flogging only ended when the two miserable Koreans lost consciousness, or died – Ginger did not know which. The horsemen spent a little time examining the copse, drinking from black bottles which they all seemed to carry, and then remounted. The unconscious Koreans were slung like empty sacks across the backs of two spare horses with their hands and feet tied together to prevent them falling off. Their bags were then tied on with them, and the party, with the reckless abandon of a mob of madmen, rode off as it had arrived, at full gallop.

Not until the thud of hoofs and the jangle of harness had died away did Ginger move. Actually, he felt physically sick. Stretching stiff limbs he looked across at Biggles and said: 'You wanted to see the sort of men we were up against. Well, now you've seen them, and I hope you enjoyed it. I wish I hadn't seen them. That picture will haunt me for the rest of my days.' He shook his head. 'I still don't understand it.'

'At least we know what to expect if they get their hands on us,' answered Biggles quietly, as he prepared to descend. 'Mayne was certainly right when he said the country was uncivilised. No wonder the local folks have flitted. But I'll tell you this,' he went on in a hard voice. 'That big lout, who must I think be the reincarnation of Attila himself, has something coming to him. No man can behave like that and get away with it indefinitely. One day his chickens will come home to roost. I hope I shall be there to see them. Let's get out of this.'

'They didn't spend much time looking for us,' said Ginger as they climbed down.

'The same thought struck me,' replied Biggles. 'I can only think that they assume that those two unlucky Koreans were the crew of the machine. I know that doesn't sound very intelligent, but those creatures weren't normal human beings, with brains. They were beasts with the mental equipment of beasts. And after all, the pilot who saw you jump must have reported that a Korean occupied the back seat of the plane. He wasn't to know otherwise. So, in a way, the curiosity of those unfortunate travellers did us a good turn. They will, I suppose, end their days in slavery. So shall we, if we slip up. It's worth bearing in mind.'

'I'm not likely to forget it,' returned Ginger.

Biggles looked at the cameras. 'I don't think there's any need to lug all this weight back home,' he observed. 'Seems a pity to abandon them, but in an affair like this one must reckon on a certain amount of wastage.'

Ginger nodded. 'If we ran into trouble they'd only be in the way.'

'And if we should collide with the enemy he'd know just what we were doing,' went on Biggles. 'Without the Birada we couldn't use the camera again, anyway. All we need is the film packs. I'll take them out and put the cameras out of sight.' This he did, the work occupying only a few minutes. The films he put in a pocket under his shirt. 'That's all, I think,' he said, looking round.

'I hope you know the way home,' remarked Ginger.

'I've a compass, but I don't think we shall need it,' replied Biggles. 'It's no great distance to our own lake. Once we strike it, we have only to follow the edge to come within sight of the island.'

'Okay,' said Ginger. 'Let's go. We shall have to watch out we don't get bogged.'

'That's not the only thing we shall have to watch out for,' asserted Biggles. 'What frightens me a lot more than bogs are these infernal pitfalls Mayne told us about. A bog usually gives you warning, and a chance to get back. A neatly covered hole in the ground doesn't. I should hate to end up impaled on a spike like a spatchcocked snipe. I'd almost as soon walk through a mine-field. If you step on a mine you don't know anything about it. Wait a minute though, talking of mines gives me an idea. I don't see why a couple of long sticks, to prod doubtful ground in front of us, shouldn't serve as mine detectors – or rather, pit detectors.'

'I should put my feet down with a lot more confidence if I knew the ground in front of me was solid,' declared Ginger.

'Actually, I don't think there's much risk of finding any hollow spots in this particular area,' opined Biggles. 'If there were, that crew of Mongolian thugs would know about it, in which case, even if they were drunk – and I think most of them were – they wouldn't charge about at a maniac gallop. All the same, we'll play safe. Stand fast while I cut a couple of poles. It won't take a minute.'

Two bamboos about eight feet long were soon procured, and the march home began.

CHAPTER VI

Strange Encounters

In different circumstances Ginger would have enjoyed the walk, for the country, and the wild life that occupied it, was unlike anything he had seen before. The thought struck him that in the past much of the earth's surface must have been like this. At any rate, here was a place where the centuries had marked time while the rest of the world marched on. Game was everywhere. Pheasants, snipe and wildfowl rose at every step. Deer were seen frequently, and occasionally, in the trees, animals of the sable family. Once, some wild boars with much snorting rushed away from where they had been grubbing for roots of some sort. But of dangerous game none was seen.

Some miles had been covered before the first sign of human handiwork appeared, and this served as a reminder to them to be on their guard. An appalling stench assailed their nostrils. Investigating, they came upon the very thing which they had most cause to fear – a pitfall. The covering had caved in. At the bottom, in a state of decomposition, was a large bear.

'There is this about it,' remarked Biggles as they walked on, examining the ground in front of them with renewed caution, 'that trap proves that the local people have departed, otherwise the hunters who went to the trouble of digging it would have collected the poor beast that fell into it.'

By midday the air was quivering with heat, and soon afterwards a halt was made at a spring of water, where the remainder of the day's rations were eaten. Wild cherries from a nearby tree supplemented a dull meal. A short distance away a pink flamingo, as grave as a judge, watched the intruders with suspicion.

They were, Biggles estimated, getting on for ten miles on their way when the country became more park-like in character, and the ruins of primitive huts began to make their appearance. An occasional ear of wheat suggested that in the not very distant past some of the ground had been cultivated. In a glade, Ginger's pole, which he had been using automatically and rather carelessly, suddenly encountered no resistance, and he almost fell into one of the pits its purpose was to reveal. Soon afterwards Biggles discovered another, so it was evident that they were now in the region of them. The result of this was to retard progress considerably for, as Biggles pointed out, the fact that the traps had not been visited for a long time made them all the more dangerous; for over them leaves and grasses had been blown until by the eye alone it was impossible to detect them.

Rounding the end of some scrub, with their own lake now on their left hand, they came suddenly upon a deserted village of crude log huts chinked with clay. Nearly all of them were more or less in a state of dilapidation, so that disregarding a significant silence it was evident, even from a distance, that the place was abandoned. The huts were set in two rough lines some twenty yards apart, but grass and wild flowers now flourished in what might once have been called the village 'street'. Biggles and Ginger walked on slowly, for even in this wild spot there was something pathetic about the forsaken homes. It was tragic, thought Ginger moodily, that even here the ambitions of a mere handful of men could make life intolerable.

From these sombre thoughts he was jerked abruptly by Biggles' hand falling on his arm and gripping it. Looking up, startled, he saw that Biggles' eyes were on the ground, at a spot where there was a soft patch of mud. Looking at this he saw what it was that had attracted Biggles' attention. Clearly defined in the mud was the imprint of a great paw.

'Tiger,' murmured Biggles. 'He came this way not long ago. He must be just in front of us. Keep your eyes skinned.'

They walked on, looking about them, and had reached a spot about half-way through the village, when, a short distance ahead, Ginger's eyes fell on a spectacle as curious – not to say alarming – as could have been imagined. It was the tiger; but far from appearing in the furtive slinking posture in which this animal is usually depicted, it lay across the threshold of one of the huts, looking out with its head resting on its paws in the manner of a common cat. Even as Ginger watched, with his heart thumping uncomfortably, the animal moved its head slightly and he knew that it had seen them. For a minute the great striped beast regarded the two humans quizzically, its mouth half open, which gave it almost an expression of surprise. Then, rising to its feet it walked slowly towards them. There was, so far at any rate, nothing hostile about its general behaviour. Its impulse, if appearances were anything to go by, was mere curiosity. All the same, the idle curiosity of a tiger at close quarters can be disconcerting; at least, Ginger found it so, and the pistol that he took from his pocket, his only means of defence, felt utterly futile for the occasion.

'Don't move,' said Biggles softly.

Hardly had the words left his lips when, in a moment of time, the situation was transformed in a manner as dramatic as it was unexpected. The sultry silence was shattered by the report of a heavy weapon somewhere close at hand. Simultaneously, with a terrifying roar, the tiger leapt straight into the air and went over backwards. It was on its feet again in an instant, snarling horribly and biting at its side. Then, with a ferocious growling noise deep in its throat, which Ginger thought was the most frightening sound he had ever heard, it charged. The extraordinary thing was, it did not charge the two men standing in plain view. It went straight across the street towards one of the other huts, at the doorway of which now appeared the man who obviously had fired the shot, for he carried a double-barrelled rifle. The man stepped out. He would, thought Ginger, have been better advised to stay inside and shut the door.

Ginger's criticism of the man's behaviour turned to admiration when he saw with what unconcern he stood up to the charge. Quite calmly and deliberately he raised the rifle to his shoulder, and at point-blank range gave the tiger the second barrel. The bullet went home, and again the tiger was knocked over, but even though hard hit the great cat was not yet finished. Half dragging itself it still strove to reach its enemy who, without retreating a yard, dropped the now useless weapon on the grass and with a shout of defiance whipped out a dagger. How he would have fared with a weapon so inadequate was never put to the test, for at this juncture Biggles ran forward and from a distance of inches put a bullet into the tiger's ear, and so into its brain. The beast rolled over and lay still.

Ginger, who during the few seconds occupied by this crisis had remained motionless, a fascinated spectator, hurried forward to where Biggles was face to face with the most remarkable figure of a man he had ever seen. As a type he was something entirely new, something that might have appeared on the stage, or the screen, in the part of a complete vagabond. He was tall, stoutly-built, dark of complexion and full-bearded, and although he was clad only in the rags of what had once been a uniform, he bristled with vitality. Indeed, there was a poise about him, a self-confidence that amounted almost to a swagger, that would have commanded respect anywhere. How long it was since his hair and beard had made the acquaintance of a pair of scissors was a matter for surmise. Dark eyes, alert and challenging, were deeply set between high cheekbones, and although his skin was weather-tanned it carried a curious pallor. One cheek was badly scarred. A heavy, old-fashioned rifle, which he had picked up and reloaded with the slick dexterity of long practice, hung in the crook of his arm. A cartridge belt, from which the brass cases protruded, encircled his waist. He seemed not in the least perturbed by what to most people would have been a hair-raising experience.

An odd situation now developed. The man instead of looking kindly upon Biggles, who had probably saved his life, glared in frank hostility as he rapped out a remark in a language which, not surprisingly, was unknown to those to whom it was addressed.

Biggles smiled, and as it seemed in order to say something, and not knowing what else to say replied casually, in English: 'Sorry, but I don't understand.' He did not expect to be understood. Indeed, as he told Ginger afterwards, had he thought there was the slightest chance of the man being able to speak English, he would not so readily have revealed his own nationality.

But the impact of the words on the bearded stranger was almost comical. He started. He stared. He frowned. He looked Biggles up and down. Then, in a rich sonorous voice he almost shouted: 'I said what the devil do you mean by interfering with my tiger?'

If the stranger had been astonished by Biggles' choice of language, Biggles was no less amazed at this reply in the same tongue. The same with Ginger who, moreover, in the light of what had happened thought this a strange way to express gratitude for being rescued from a nasty predicament.

'I'm sorry,' said Biggles contritely. 'I thought you were in some danger of being mauled, or—'

'Danger! Pouf! Nothing of the sort, sir,' shouted the man. 'I can handle my own tigers.'

Biggles shrugged. 'Should the occasion be repeated I will bear it in mind,' he said coldly.

The man treated Biggles to a further scrutiny. 'Why do you speak English?' he demanded. 'How is this? What are you? Speak up before I shoot you.'

Perceiving that no good purpose could be served by dissembling, Biggles took the bull by the horns as the quickest way of bringing matters to a head. 'The answer to your question is this,' he said. 'We are British.'

'Hm.' The man pondered the statement, his eyes dark with suspicion. 'Then what are you doing here and why do you wear those filthy rags?' he demanded.

'That,' answered Biggles, 'is my own affair. I might ask you the same question.'

'Me?' The man struck his chest with a hand that ended in an upward flourish. 'I am a Russian, and I don't care who knows it,' said he, in a voice so loud that he obviously meant what he said for it could have been heard from one end of the village to the other. 'When I say Russian I mean a true Russian, from St Petersburg – which the rascals who now live there call Petrograd. Colonel Alexis Petroffsky, late of the Imperial Cavalry, now the Flail of God against the Bolsheviks, and the greatest killer of tigers in Eastern Asia.'

Biggles smiled at this strange boast and the way in which it was made. 'This beast nearly killed *you*,' he reminded, touching the dead tiger with his foot.

'Pah!' scoffed Petroffsky airily. 'You acted bravely, sir, I must admit, but in another instant my dagger would have been in the brute's throat, although, by the beard of St Peter, he was no ordinary beast. In his time not fewer than five hundred men, women and children has he taken to fill his stomach. Long have I stalked him, and long has he sought to add me to his collection, the only man left in Kossuri. He had the audacity to seek me here, on my own doorstep. Now he has paid for his folly. Still, he served you a good turn, for had he not appeared when he did, you would have been shot, not the tiger.'

'Shot? By whom?' asked Biggles in surprise.

'By me – who else?'

'But why shoot me?'

'Here a man shoots anyone he does not know,' declared the colonel. 'It is the only way to live in peace,' he added simply. 'But who are you, and why do you wear these preposterous garments?'

'My name and my business here are matters which at the moment I prefer not to discuss,' answered Biggles cautiously.

'Quite right,' agreed Petroffsky. 'A man should mind his own business. Pardon me for asking a question. How is London?'

'London was looking very well when I was last there,' returned Biggles. 'Do you know London?'

'Do I know London?' The colonel appeared to be almost affronted by the question. 'Why, sir,' he cried, 'in the days when men were men, and gentlemen would fight to the death for a woman's glove, London was my home. Everyone knew Petroffsky of the Russian Embassy.' He sighed. 'Ah, what days they were.'

By this time, of course, Biggles had the situation under control. So this was Alexis Petroffsky, the man who had acted as guide to Mayne on the occasion of his first visit. No wonder Mayne called him an amazing fellow. He decided to test the ground a little further before letting the Russian know that Mayne was in the country.

'You once, I think, acted as guide to a British officer named Mayne, who came here on a hunting trip?' he prompted.

Petroffsky flung out an enthusiastic arm. 'Mayne! Of course! An admirable companion, although as a hunter not up to my standard.

A trifle – shall we say – squeamish? A rascally gun-bearer insulted us. I was for putting him to death, but Mayne objected. Absurd. It is the only way to deal with such people. They're no use to anyone. Are you a hunter?'

'For what other purpose would a man come to this country?' parried Biggles.

'Why, indeed? But by the beard of St Joseph, why do you wear these disgusting clothes?'

'We thought they would attract less attention,' explained Biggles truthfully.

Petroffsky shook his head. 'It is a sad thing to see a man ashamed of his clothes. For my part, my uniform will be removed only from my dead body. Koreans are the scum of the earth. True, I allow a few to pass because they bring me cartridges and vodka, without which life would not be worth living. Two came today, so thanks be to St Thomas, I am stocked up again. Will you take a drink with me?' The colonel produced an enormous battered silver flask.

'It would be a pleasure to drink with you,' answered Biggles, 'but I think you'd better save it for yourself.'

Petroffsky frowned. 'Why?'

'Because you may get no more.'

Petroffsky's frown deepened. 'Why?'

'Two Koreans, you say, came today?'

'True.'

'And they went that way?' Biggles pointed.

'Yes.'

'A few hours ago they were set upon by a party of horsemen who beat them nearly, if not quite, to death.'

The colonel's face grew dark with anger. He cursed long and luridly. 'Why did you allow this?' he demanded at last.

'I was sitting in a tree at the time,' explained Biggles.

'Was there any reason why you couldn't get down?'

'I hadn't a rifle.'

'You had a pistol.'

'What is the use of a pistol against a score of madmen?'

'You could at least have died like a man!'

'I did not, at the moment, feel like dying,' said Biggles coldly. 'Besides,' he added, 'the purpose of my visit did not include the protection of wandering vodka pedlars.'

'But how the devil am I to get my vodka?' shouted Petroffsky.

'That, my dear sir, is your affair,' replied Biggles. 'The success or failure of your vodka supply is to me a matter of complete indifference and, may I add, if you go on bellowing like that there seems to be a good chance that we shall share the fate of your Korean liquor vendors.'

'Me? Flogged? Ha ha.' The colonel shouted with laughter. 'That's a good one. Those rascals won't come here.'

'Why not?'

'Because they're afraid of me, that's why. They know that Alexis Petroffsky fears no man. When I shoot I kill. Besides, they fear the pitfalls with which the land is beset.'

'Apparently you know these ruffians?' prompted Biggles gently, in the hope of getting more information.

'Know them? Of course I know them!' shouted Petroffsky. 'Devil's spawn, sir, that's what they are.'

'I gather you live here, in this village?'

'Certainly. Which reminds me, why do we stand here? Come and join me in some refreshment.'

The Russian strode off up the village a short distance to a house that was rather larger and in better condition than the rest.

Biggles and Ginger dropped a little behind. Said Ginger, softly: 'What an incredible fellow.'

'It's an incredible country,' answered Biggles simply.

The interior of the house, when they reached it, was also incredible – or so Ginger thought. At first glance the room into which they were invited appeared to be a museum devoted to the collection of tiger skins. Skins hung on the walls and lay strewn on the floor. Tiger skins covered the ottoman that served in lieu of chairs. In fact, tiger skins were everywhere, giving the place a musty odour. They did, at least, thought Ginger, go far to confirm the Russian's boasting of his prowess as a hunter. There were at least a dozen guns and rifles of one sort or another, mostly old patterns, standing about. Broken boxes of ammunition lay in a heap on the floor. Empty cartridge cases stood in rows on the mantelpiece.

'Be seated, gentlemen,' requested Petroffsky, producing glasses and a black bottle.

Biggles waved it aside. 'Not for me, thank you,' he said.

The Russian shrugged his shoulders. 'As you will.'

'You will not think us discourteous if we don't stay long,' remarked Biggles. 'We're still some way from camp. By the way, you'll be interested to know that your old friend Captain Mayne is with us.'

Petroffsky, who was tossing back a glass of vodka, nearly choked. 'By the beard of St Antony, that's wonderful news!' he cried. 'I must go to him as soon as I have skinned the tiger. I live to kill tigers – and Bolsheviks. There is, I think, no better occupation. The Bolsheviks threw me into prison.'

'Why?' replied Biggles.

The Russian drew himself up to his full height and laid a hand on his heart. 'Because I, Alexis Petroffsky, refused to take orders from a crew of drunken revolutionaries who climbed into the Imperial Palaces over the dead bodies of my friends. They put me in prison – me, a Cossack, a colonel of the Imperial Guard and victor of a hundred duels with sword and pistol! But they couldn't keep me there, no, by the beard of St Michael. The night I escaped I slew six of them. I killed only six because there were no more.'

Ginger listened in astonishment to this extraordinary recital. What to make of it he hardly knew. The man might be vainglorious, he thought, but there was a ring of truth in his words.

'Who are these men who flogged the Koreans?' asked Biggles, still seeking information. 'They looked like Mongolians.'

'They are,' asserted Petroffsky. 'They do the dirty work for Prince Ling Soo. Prince! Ha ha! He's nothing but a Manchurian bandit, a common soldier who deserted from the army and came here years ago. By robbery and murder he grew rich, and by employing more murderers brought the country under his control. Success has so gone to his head that he now boasts that he will conquer the whole world.'

'Is that so?' murmured Biggles slowly, for the significance of this remark was not overlooked. 'How does he intend to do that?'

Petroffsky made a disdainful gesture. 'Who cares? Yet the man is certainly getting guns from somewhere. Strange rumours have reached me from farther up the country.'

'Strange rumours have reached me, too,' said Biggles, taking a chance.

The Russian did not miss the point. 'Ha, so that's why you've come here? The British always had long ears for rumours. Well, you can rely on me for any help that I can give, for no one hates these stinking barbarians more than I do. You can see for yourself what they've done to the country?'

Biggles nodded. 'Yes, I've seen.' He got up. 'But now we must be getting along or darkness will overtake us before we reach camp, and our friends will be getting anxious.'

'Anxious? Why should they be anxious? Are you children?'

'Not exactly, but I promised to be back.'

'Then you are right to go, for a man should always keep his word,' averred Petroffsky. 'Where is your camp? I must call on you.'

Biggles hesitated. This was not because he did not trust the man. Nor did he want to offend him, particularly as he might be a useful ally. On the other hand, he was afraid the Russian might make a nuisance of himself with his noisy braggadocio. In the end he took a chance and supplied the information. 'We look forward to seeing you again,' he said. 'But you will appreciate that it would not be to our advantage to have it known that we were here?'

Petroffsky bowed. 'I understand perfectly, sir. Not a word of your presence here shall pass my lips. If there is one man in this devil's dustbin to be trusted, it is me. I, Alexis Petroffsky, am the soul of discretion. Are you sure you won't take a toothful of vodka before you go?'

'Quite sure, thanks.'

The ex-Cossack's manner became wistful. 'You will forgive me I trust for mentioning this matter so early in our acquaintance, but – er – you would not by any chance have – er – any chocolate in your pocket?'

Biggles blinked. 'Chocolate?'

'It is my one weakness,' stated Petroffsky apologetically – and not entirely truthfully. 'All my life I have adored chocolate, and here, alas, none is to be had for love or gold.'

Ginger could not repress a smile. The idea of this big bearded hermit of the wilds pining for sweets struck him as being incongruous to the point of being fantastic.

'I'm sorry I have none with me,' answered Biggles seriously, perceiving that as far as the Russian was concerned this was no laughing matter. 'But we have some in camp. You shall have some when you call.'

Petroffsky beamed. 'Now you may be certain of seeing me soon,' he declared. 'Au revoir. Remember, my rifle is at your command.'

'And my chocolate is at yours,' returned Biggles, smiling. 'Goodbye for now.'

'Adieu. Keep to the edge of the rushes and you need not fear pitfalls.'

Biggles and Ginger strode on. The rest of the march was made without incident. Just as darkness was bringing out the mosquitoes and fireflies, tired and travel-stained they reached the point of the waterside nearest to the island. A whistle brought over the canoe, and a few minutes later they were in camp, which, said Algy, had been in a fever of anxiety about them. A substantial meal had been prepared, and over it, for the best part of an hour they were kept busy recounting the details of the day's adventures.

Mayne, of course, was intrigued by the meeting with Petroffsky. 'He's a quaint piece of work,' he remarked.

'Quaint!' replied Biggles. 'He's more than that. In my opinion he's more than half-way off his rocker. I only hope he doesn't come bellowing about here.'

'He's all right when he's sober,' explained Mayne. 'It's when he gets a load of that infernal vodka inside him that he's apt to get a bit difficult. In that condition he's liable to do anything.'

'So I imagine,' answered Biggles dryly.

'But look here, old boy, what does all this amount to?' asked Bertie, when Algy had gone off to develop the photographs.

'If my arithmetic is any good it amounts to this,' responded Biggles. 'We've come to the right place. At any rate, there's something going on here. The big noise, apparently, is a Chinese bandit, but he, I'd say, is only a stooge. He may be wealthy and he may have big ambitions, but they would hardly run to the kidnapping of British scientists in England and Canada. No. There's somebody behind him, and that somebody is a European. Witness the black fighter. That machine wasn't being flown by a Mongolian tribesman. Put it like this. This fellow Ling Soo, ruler of this particular territory though he may be, is only a puppet. He's useful in that he can keep the country clear of unwanted visitors. When the white men behind him are ready they'll show him where he steps off, no doubt. I don't think Petroffsky knows this man personally. In fact, he doesn't know much about what's going on – but then, up to the present he hasn't been interested. As far as air reconnaissance is concerned the Birada is finished. That means we can do no more flying. The next move will have to be made on foot. We'll use prints of the photos in lieu of maps and do a spot of scouting. I hate walking, but there's no other way.'

'Are we all going on this beastly jaunt?' inquired Bertie.

'No. Someone will have to stay in camp to look after the place and operate the canoe. It had better be Algy, since he's O.C. transport. The rest can go – part of the way, anyhow.'

'What exactly are you going to do, if you see what I mean?' asked Bertie.

Biggles drew at his cigarette. 'If you mean have I a plan, the answer is no. All we can do is march to the place where the Birada crashed, or just beyond it, and there establish an advanced base from which we can make sorties to see anything there is to see.'

'What are you going to do about Petroffsky?' queried Mayne.

'We better ignore him for the moment,' decided Biggles. 'He shouts too much and he drinks too much. If he comes here, Algy can feed him on chocolates to keep him quiet.'

'And when do we start hiking?' Ginger wanted to know.

'We might as well start in the morning, the earlier the better. There's no point in squatting here longer than is necessary. We shall have to take some food with us. We may be away for days. I'll think about the equipment we're likely to need. That's enough for now. I'm tired, and I can't stand these mosquitoes any longer, so I'm turning in.' Biggles put his heel on the stub of his cigarette and made for the tent.

CHAPTER VII

Into the Unknown

Biggles had the expedition afoot at dawn the following morning after a night made miserable by mosquitoes which defeated all the precautions taken against them. It was really a relief for everyone to get up. Although he said nothing at the time, to Biggles these insects were more than a petty annoyance. He felt sure that they were the deadly *anopheles*, and if that were so, then it would not be long before one or the other, or even the whole party, was laid low with malaria. He had taken the precaution of bringing quinine, and his first action was to dole out a ration all round. Apart from this, the march that now lay ahead was a long one, and he was anxious to be on his way. He knew the value of an early start; that time lost in the morning can never be recovered.

The preparation of food and equipment took a little while, for it was impossible to hazard even a guess as to how long the party would be away. Even if things went well, he reckoned that it could not be less than three or four days. That he had given the matter a good deal of thought was evident from the way he mustered the articles which he thought would be needed. His own and Ginger's kit had to be carefully and securely arranged on belts to go under their shirts, for it included items not normally to be found on the person of a simple Korean hunter; such things as wire-cutters, hacksaws, files and torches, to say nothing of iron rations and automatic weapons. Wrist-watches were put out of sight. However, it was a fine morning, and by five o'clock, with long skeins of duck, geese and swans, flighting across a sky all soft pink and gold in an impressive sunrise, the party moved off. Algy transported the expedition to the mainland in the canoe, after which, as arranged, he returned to base.

'If Petroffsky turns up give him some chocolate and keep him quiet,' was Biggles' last injunction to Algy.

Algy paddled back to the island, while the rest, in single file, with Biggles leading, set off, following the trail made on the previous evening.

For the first four hours the march was maintained at a steady pace, with five-minute halts every hour for rest, and for loads to be adjusted. The only delay occurred when Biggles thought it advisable to skirt the village of Kossuri to avoid running into Petroffsky, who, with the best of intentions, might decide to accompany the party or otherwise embarrass it.

This is not to say that the march was a simple matter. Cross-country marches, even in civilised countries, seldom are, but here there were no bridges over the many streams which had to be forded sometimes waist-deep with packs held high to keep them dry. Bogs had to be crossed with care, and always there were areas of tall reeds to impede progress. On the dry ground, when it occurred, precautions had to be taken against pitfalls. Biggles employed the same method to detect them as on the previous day. One was passed, on a game trail, in which lay the mouldering remains of what had once been a man. It brought home to everyone the reality of this menace.

However, all went well, and by eleven o'clock the first objective was reached. This was the blackened area where the Birada had crashed and burnt itself out. This was approached with due care for fear of guards or scouts being placed to watch it. None was seen, although Ginger made a survey of the country around from the top of a convenient tree. After an early lunch the march was resumed, now with all the vigilance of troops moving in hostile territory. Biggles followed the trail made by the Mongolian horsemen, unmistakable in the long dry grass. Not a human being was seen, so Captain Mayne's services as an interpreter were not required, but in many ways his local knowledge was useful, and this alone was sufficient to justify his presence in the expedition. From time to time Biggles consulted the prints taken from the photographs obtained on the previous day. These, too, were a great help, for from them the nature of the country ahead could be determined with more accuracy, and with more detail than would have been possible from maps even if they had been available.

And so, without accident or a single alarm, a final halt was called on the fringe of a small forest of mixed trees, in which the dark green of walnuts was conspicuous. Here Biggles decided to establish the advanced base, for according to his calculations they were now within five miles of the enemy camp, and rather less than that from the straight trench which had been observed from the air. Nearer, he stated, it would not be safe for the entire party to go, for at any moment now they might come in contact with enemy defences, human or mechanical. In any case it would be better to have someone in reserve in case of accidents as well as a food dump on which to fall back should the need arise. So moving a little way into the trees the expedition, mud-plastered, scratched and insect bitten, sweating in the sultry heat, sat down to rest and discuss over a cup of tea the next move in the plan of campaign.

So far, averred Biggles, all had gone well, but it was only reasonable to suppose that doubts, difficulties and dangers would now crop up. First of all, he explained, he wanted a close view of the object which from the air he had taken to be a trench. He admitted that it would probably turn out to be something quite different, as he could not imagine what purpose a trench, in that particular place, could serve. It was conspicuous on the photograph, but it was still not possible to make out exactly what it was.

For rather more than an hour the party lay in the shade of the trees, resting and talking things over, by which time the sun was beginning to fall towards the west. Then Biggles got up and made ready to move on, for from here he and Ginger were to go on alone. Bertie and Mayne were to keep watch, make a bough-shelter in case the weather changed, and camouflage the position with such materials as were available.

'Any idea how long you'll be, old boy?' questioned Bertie.

'Not the foggiest,' answered Biggles. 'It all depends on what we find. We might be back in an hour or we might be a couple of days. We'll be back as soon as we can, you may be sure of that. You lie doggo. You know the rule in this sort of show. By day keep your eyes open, and at night your ears.'

'Are you hoping to bring the jolly old scientists back with you?'

'I'm afraid that's a bit too much to hope for,' replied Biggles. 'It could happen, but if we can ascertain definitely that they're here, and discover where they're housed, we shall have done enough to go on with. Come on, Ginger. We'll take it quietly. This walking makes an old man of me. My legs were made for rudder-bars, not padding the hoof like an animal.'

Leaving Bertie and Mayne in the leafy hide-out Biggles set off at a steady pace with Ginger following close behind. There was this about it, as Ginger remarked. Dirty, and mired to the eyes, they did at least look like what they were supposed to be – two miserable Koreans who had lost their way.

As far as the actual state of the ground was concerned the going was now fairly good, although there were the usual muddy streams and boggy areas to be crossed with care. Otherwise, the country ahead was slightly undulating, most of it deep in dry, rank grasses, a yard or more high, with taller bulrushes filling the lower ground, and thick jungle of palm and bamboos, sometimes overgrown with wild vines, on the drier areas. There were odd trees everywhere, and occasional small stands of timber.

From the top of each rise, approached with due care, Biggles paused to study the ground ahead before advancing. With so much cover, in the ordinary way there would have been little risk of being seen; but to Biggles' annoyance and Ginger's alarm the country was literally alive with game. Pheasants, snipe and wild-fowl rose constantly, and this, as Ginger realised, could hardly fail to attract the attention of anyone in the vicinity. There was no way of avoiding this although, as Biggles pointed out, the thing cut two ways in that no one else could move about without a similar disturbance. This, in fact, did happen on one occasion; but it turned out to be a false alarm when the disturber of the marshes was observed to be a lone red wolf, which disappeared instantly when, passing downwind, it caught the taint of human bodies. A little while later a big herd of roe deer, apparently on a migration, passed by a short distance ahead. Game tracks were everywhere, which Biggles remarked was a good thing, because it meant that the track which they themselves were making in the grass would not be noticed.

In this way a distance which Ginger reckoned to be about four miles was covered, and there was still no sign of human activity or handiwork. To all intents and purposes they had this lonely world to themselves. The terrain ahead looked much the same, except that it seemed to be getting more thickly wooded. On the right, the long arm of the lake lay like a sheet of turquoise glass, its shallow edges lined with countless birds of the wader class, feeding, squabbling, or in the case of the cranes, standing on one leg regarding the scene with expressions of utter boredom. To the left the country was mostly flat marsh and bog, although in the far distance a range of mountain peaks provided a serrated skyline.

During one of the now frequent halts Ginger remarked that if they went on any farther they would certainly not get back before nightfall. To this Biggles replied that it mattered little as a moon, nearly full, would provide as much light as they would need. He also pointed out that when it became dark any area of human habitation would almost certainly be marked by lights. Thus, darkness might serve them better than daylight, although he admitted that a light at night was a dangerous mark on which to march, since it was impossible to judge its distance, a bright light miles away having the same effect as a dim one near at hand. 'Of course,' Biggles went on, 'the enemy may have imposed a black-out, although in such a remote spot as this it would hardly seem necessary. In any case, as the war proved, a one hundred per cent black-out is almost impossible to achieve. I once carried out some tests from five thousand feet and had no difficulty in spotting a fellow lighting a cigarette a couple of miles away, if there were no other lights about. According to my reckoning,' he concluded, changing the subject, 'that trench, or whatever it is, can't be far ahead. Let's carry on.'

Grey dusk was now taking possession of the land, with seemingly endless wedges of wildfowl winging overhead to an unknown destination. Their raucous cries filled the air with clamour, and it must have been for this reason that other sounds, which otherwise must have been audible, were not noticed for some time.

Biggles and Ginger were picking their way through a thick belt of bulrushes that fringed a brook when Biggles, who was slightly in front, turned a puzzled face. 'Listen,' he ordered. 'Can you hear a queer sort of noise a little way ahead? It isn't birds – or is it?'

Ginger listened, although as a matter of fact he had already noticed the sounds to which Biggles had alluded. They were intermittent, not continuous, and when they occurred they were more like the barking of a troop of apes than the gabble made by a colony of birds. However, not having the least idea of what it could be he could only grimace and shrug his shoulders.

Biggles went on slowly for about fifty yards and then came to a dead stop, sinking lower in the rushes and at the same time making an urgent signal to Ginger to do the same. Ginger crouched, but went on slowly until he was at Biggles' side, when, peering through the screen of slender leaves, he saw the answer to not one, but two problems. First, about forty yards away in the open was what Biggles had taken to be a trench. It was not a trench, but the mistake was understandable. It was in fact the black face of what he took to be a peat hag, such as he had seen in Scotland. It formed a straight cliff some ten feet high and extended for seventy or eighty yards. On it a gang of men, some forty or fifty strong, were working – or more correctly had been working, for they were now backing away carrying their tools with them. The majority were obviously Koreans, but there were others, native types. He assumed they were Orochons, or similar local tribesmen, who had been captured and put to work. One thing was certain. This was the slave gang, for standing at intervals armed with rifles, were guards, men of the same Mongolian cast of features as those who had beaten up the two Korean merchants. They may have been the same men, for some horses were tethered close at hand. The big man in charge was certainly he who had wielded the whip on that occasion. He still carried the whip. Standing by his horse he was barking orders, as were also his assistants. The effect of this was to create a babble which at once explained the mystery of the sounds that had brought Biggles to a halt.

The slaves, apparently, had just finished their labours, although this is not to say that they were allowed to rest. Most of them were heaving on their shoulders great wickerwork baskets filled with the black bricks they had cut from what later turned out to be an outcrop of lignite.[1] Others were loading themselves up with the tools that had been used for the purpose. At the same time there was a steady movement towards a muddy path only a few yards away from where Biggles and Ginger crouched watching, and it soon became clear that this was the line on which the slaves were being mustered for their march back to wherever they were confined for the night. Filthy, in rags, emaciated, with eyes that seemed dead, they moved in silence, backs bent under their loads like weary beasts of burden – which in fact they were.

Ginger was staring with mounting indignation at this tragic spectacle when Biggles jogged his arm and whispered tersely: 'Come on, this is our chance. Remember you're dumb. Behave as the others. Watch for landmarks.' With that he stepped forward and in a moment had mingled with the nearest slaves. Ginger followed automatically, but not until, following Biggles' example, he was loading himself up with spades, did he realise fully the audacious step that Biggles had taken. For a second or two his knees went weak from shock; but the sight of Biggles moving wearily but unconcernedly with the rest, brought him to his senses, and he then played his part as well as his thumping heart would permit. Like the rest, keeping near Biggles he found a place in the line as the slave-master strode up brandishing his whip; but really his

[1] Lignite is a dark brown substance midway between peat and coal. It burns freely.

brain was still in a whirl from the suddenness of the transition. In one stride he had stepped from the peace of the quiet country into a situation so bristling with peril that he wondered if Biggles had any nerves at all. It was typical of him to make such a momentous decision on the spur of the moment. He had known many similar instances, but for sheer bare-faced, cold-blooded effrontery, mused Ginger desperately, this was hard to beat. He grasped Biggles' intention easily enough. Instead of crawling about in the marshes looking for the objective they would now march straight to it. This, at any rate, was clearly the scheme, and it was reasonably possible. What worried Ginger was, having got in, how they were to get out. He had often heard Biggles refer to the accepted military maxim of always having a line of retreat, but on this occasion he seemed to have abandoned it. They could not without taking a ghastly risk speak to each other. The wretched slaves had all been silenced by a horrible mutilation. To be caught speaking would therefore invite the same fate, if nothing worse.

By the time these sinister thoughts had flashed through Ginger's mind the ranks had been closed, and he imagined that the column was about to move off. Not so. To his unspeakable alarm a swart Mongolian came down the line obviously making a count to confirm there were no absentees. This was something which, Ginger was sure, Biggles had not taken into his reckoning; but nothing could be done about it. Apparently the guard discovered that something was wrong for he made a second check. Looking puzzled he went over and said something to the slave-master who was watching the proceedings with an expression of calculating malice. An argument of some sort ensued. There was another count. However, in the end it must have been decided that a mistake had been made when the party set out; but the taskmaster was on the right side, having two slaves too many, which was an altogether different thing from being two short. Anyhow, he allowed the matter to pass. The order to march was given and the column moved off.

The simultaneous obedience to the order revealed to Ginger a new risk. The slaves could not speak, but they could hear. They could understand orders, which he, having no knowledge of the language, could not. What would happen, he wondered with mounting apprehension, when he was given an order and failed to obey it. Perhaps it was better not to think about it.

The human crocodile wound its way across the dreary marshes, colourless in the grey twilight.

Ginger had in his time undertaken many curious and often unpleasant marches, but this, he pondered morosely, was the worst. The only sounds were the shuffling of feet and the creaking of harness as the guards rode up and down the line. The thing had all the characteristics of a nightmare, and Ginger found it hard to believe that it was really happening. He tried to pick out salient features of the landscape which might later serve as marks, but they seemed few and far between. When the end did finally come he had sunk into such a slough of despondency that he was unprepared for it. It was Biggles' arm, knocking against his own, that brought him back to earth.

They were now in a thickly wooded area, with the track keeping to forest from which the undergrowth had been cleared. Ahead and on either side lights could be seen, all downcast by overhead shades. From their steadiness, Ginger noted with surprise, it was evident that they were electric. Dimly in the shadows he could just discern several large hutments, but nothing could be seen clearly.

The march ended abruptly. The baskets of fuel were emptied on a big dump of the same material. From a nearby hut came the throb of an engine. Ginger supposed that the fuel was used to drive it. Tools were stacked under a log shelter. The slaves then passed through a gate in a closely-stranded barbed wire fence about ten feet high, into a compound from which came a stench so appalling that for a moment Ginger thought he must be sick. Outside the wire, grass still grew thickly, but inside, from constant trampling, the ground resembled a farmyard. After the prisoners had passed through, the gate was shut, sentries remaining on guard. These, it was later discovered, also patrolled the wire on the outside.

Ginger took care to keep close to Biggles, for it was evident that if they lost touch they might find it difficult to get together again. Slowly, for night had now fallen, they inspected their new quarters. There was not much to see. Near the wire on one side was a long open shed, in the manner of a field byre, and this was used evidently for the accommodation of the human animals, for most of the slaves made their way towards it. Beside it, hard against the fence so that it could be filled from the outside, was a long trough, such as is provided for pigs in a sty. Making their way towards this now appeared two Koreans, each carrying two buckets which, judging from the noise when their contents were emptied into the trough, was some sort of slop. Most of the slaves made a rush for it, pushing and fighting like so many animals in their haste to get their share, or perhaps more than their fair share. The weakest got none. Some fell, and lay on the ground making uncouth noises.

Ginger watched this dreadful spectacle with his gorge rising, yet at the same time with compassion. It is hardly necessary to say that neither he nor Biggles joined in the disgusting scramble. Presently Biggles turned and made his way through the mire to the shelter; but the smell of the place was nauseating, and he went on to the fence where he sank down to rest. Ginger dropped beside him. There was no one near, but for a little while neither spoke. The truth was, Ginger was so utterly weary that he didn't care much what happened next. Overhead the stars gleamed in a cloudless sky.

Above the coal-black wall of forest trees came the glow of the rising moon. From the swiftly emptied trough the slaves were drifting towards the shelter, so that soon the compound was deserted. Silence fell. Ginger pulled his thin shirt up above his ears. He was too tired even to think. As from a long way off he heard Biggles whisper: 'Well, we're in, anyway.' He did not answer. He could, he thought, safely leave the thinking to Biggles. He closed his eyes.

CHAPTER VIII

The Plot Unfolds

Ginger had no idea of how long he had been asleep when he was awakened by Biggles squeezing his arm; but he felt that it had not been for very long. Still, he was refreshed, and alert on the instant when he remembered where he was. All was quiet. From the shelter not far away came the uneasy noises of sleeping men.

Biggles rolled over until his lips were almost touching Ginger's ear. 'It's time we were moving,' he breathed.

'Where to?' asked Ginger, also speaking under his breath.

'I've no intention of spending the night in this filthy pen,' replied Biggles. 'We'll have a look round and see what there is to see. The camp seems to be settling down.'

'What's the time?'

'Ten o'clock.'

'How are you going to get out?'

'Cut the bottom strand of wire.'

'What about the sentry?'

'He's on the prowl, but he doesn't seem to have a regular beat. I wish he had. We'll wait for him to go past.'

'Are you coming back here?'

'Not on your life. I'm not going to spend tomorrow digging lignite.'

'Where are you going to make for when you're out?'

'Nowhere in particular. It's all the same. There's plenty of cover. The thing is to try to find out if Vale is here, and if he is, make contact with him. That's enough to go on with. We must see how he's fixed before we decide on the next move. Quiet! Here comes the sentry.'

Ginger dropped back, feigning sleep. He did not see the sentry go past but he heard him, heard his boots brushing in the grass, the sound quickly fading. He felt Biggles move and a moment later came a *snick* as his cutters bit through the wire.

Biggles pulled the strand aside and rolled under the fence. Ginger followed. Biggles replaced the wire in its original position as far as this was possible, although as a matter of detail the long grass which grew under the wire would have made the break difficult to see even in daylight. They sneaked away through the grass, making for the nearest trees. Reaching them, Biggles stood up, and the reconnaissance proceeded in more comfortable positions.

Lights were showing at many places in the trees, most of them coming from the open doors or windows of hutments, of which there appeared to be several scattered about, all inside the forest, which explained why they had not been seen from the air. It was evident that any one of these might provide accommodation for the men whom they hoped to find, but there was no indication of which it was most likely to be; so the scouting could only proceed in a haphazard manner, Biggles taking the view that sooner or later they should come to the right one.

At the door of a hut of some size, just as they were approaching it, two men appeared, and stood for a moment talking in a language which neither Biggles nor Ginger recognised. Presently they parted, one going in and the other walking away into the darkness.

Ginger found it all very confusing. There was, he felt, plenty to

Heard the sentry's boots brushing in the grass, then came a
'snick' as his cutters bit through the wire.

see, but in the darkness under the trees nothing could be made
out distinctly. One thing only became apparent. The camp was
of a considerable size and covered a large area of ground. The
huts themselves were of the temporary sort, being built of rough
timber apparently cut on the spot, and roofed with thatch or corru-
gated iron. Many of the huts showed lighted windows, in which,
occasionally, the silhouettes of the occupants were framed. More
barbed wire was encountered. Biggles, unable to find a way round
one fence, cut through it, and he and Ginger found themselves in
a veritable farmyard with horses, cows and sheep. Later, behind
more wire, they could see the shape of a large house of Oriental
design. A sentry lounged at the door. Once they had to lie flat while
a party of drunken, brawling Mongolians went past. The incident
helped to create in Ginger's mind an impression that they were
in a big military camp. For the rest, it was still all very vague.
Biggles apparently thought so too, for after a while he stopped and
remarked: 'This blundering about isn't getting us anywhere. At
this rate we shall still be here when daylight comes. We've got to
find out who occupies these huts and keep at it until we strike the
one we're looking for. Vale must be here somewhere. I'm going back
to the big house we passed just now. It must be the headquarters,
or the house of the head man. It would be something if we could
find out who he is.'

'There was a sentry,' reminded Ginger.

'I know. That's what makes me think it's a building of importance. We needn't go through the gate; we'll cut the wire and get to
the house from the far side.'

Biggles, who from the missions he had undertaken had become
something of a specialist in underground as well as overhead
warfare, led the way back to the building he had mentioned. Like
the rest, it was well hidden in the trees. From three windows on

the same side broad beams of light fell across the uncut grass beneath them. None of these windows was curtained although all were netted against the mosquitoes. One was open. Regarding this feature from fairly near at hand Ginger formed the opinion that the windows served a single room, although it would be a room of some length; and this presently turned out to be the case. From within came a faint confused murmur of voices.

What, or who, Biggles expected to see inside, Ginger did not know. He did not ask. He himself was prepared for almost anything – except, perhaps, what they did actually find. He was more concerned with the situation in which he found himself, for it is not to be supposed that moving about the camp was a simple matter. Others were abroad, too. They could not always be seen, but they could be heard. And there were the inevitable mosquitoes to make life a misery.

Biggles crept quietly forward to the dark side of the house. Here there seemed to be little risk of being seen by the sentry, who was taking his duties in a most casual manner, smoking and exchanging remarks with passers-by, and between times yawning audibly. It was obvious that he did not expect to be troubled, and consequently thought his job unnecessary.

Biggles cut the surrounding wire, went through, followed by Ginger, and then moving with extreme caution made his way to the rear of the house. There was nothing to be learned there, so keeping close to the wooden wall they went on to the side that held the lighted windows. The sills, it was discovered, were about four feet from the ground. Reaching the first Biggles sank down and remained motionless. Ginger did the same, glad of a pause, for his nerves were now at full stretch and it gave him a chance to steady them.

While he sat there an extraordinary feeling came over him that this situation had occurred before, although for a little while he could not understand why. Inside, a man was speaking, speaking with what seemed to be some asperity; and it suddenly struck him that, incredible though it seemed, he knew the voice. He knew it, but he could not place it, for somehow it did not fit into his immediate surroundings. Another reason for this, as he realised quickly, was because the speaker, who spoke in German, was interrupted frequently by a curious gibberish which he could not understand. Sometimes it actually overran what the speaker was saying. The effect was peculiar.

He felt, rather than saw, Biggles rise up slowly for a peep into the room, and even before Biggles had dropped back with a quick intake of breath he remembered the owner of that hard, crisp voice. He was Biggles' opposite number in the Nazi service during the war, now in voluntary exile – Hauptmann Erich von Stalhein, the efficient, ruthless, aristocratic German agent, with whom Biggles, by reason of the nature of the missions he undertook, had for long been in collision.

Ginger's first reaction was incredulity, complete and utter. The very idea seemed preposterous. What would the man be doing in that remote part of the globe? But very soon he perceived that, far from his presence there being remarkable, it might even have been expected. The German was now a soldier of fortune and this was just the sort of undertaking towards which, by virtue of his qualifications, he would gravitate. What of his own and Biggles' arrival on the scene? Von Stalhein, he mused, would no doubt think that remarkable, whereas in fact it was not.

In point of fact, in this respect Ginger was wrong, as he was very soon to learn. Von Stalhein had on this occasion at least foreseen a possibility which Biggles had not – the entry of a personal rival into this distant arena.

There were other people in the room, for sometimes other voices spoke; and judging from the variety of languages used they were not all of the same nationality. Ginger thought he recognised Russian, but there was another that conveyed nothing to him at all. German seemed to be the general language, and from the way sentences were echoed in a curious monotone he was soon able to grasp the situation. What was being said was being translated by interpreters for the benefit of those who did not speak that particular language. It was confusing, but he was soon able to follow the conversation because it occurred either in German or was translated into it.

Biggles drew close to Ginger, and cupping his hands round his mouth, whispered: 'Committee meeting. Von Stalhein's there, and an Oriental who I think must be Ling Soo. Ten of 'em altogether ... some Russians I think. Listen.'

At this period von Stalhein was speaking. Indeed, he seemed to be holding the floor in a voice charged with bitter denunciation. It was plain that he was angry about something. But it was the subject of his conversation that shook Ginger more than a little. 'Let me remind you,' he was saying, 'I did not solicit this work. I was invited here. You came to me to take charge of intelligence and security, of which, as apparently you knew, I am not without experience. What co-operation do I get? None. My suggestions are ignored, my orders disobeyed. Information of vital importance is deliberately withheld from me. Ach, yes, I am well aware of that. What is the use of employing a specialist if you do not put him in possession of all relevant facts? How do you expect me to perform my duties efficiently if I am not told the truth?'

There were protests at this, but von Stalhein silenced them and went on to support his allegations. 'When, at your request, I called on your agent in Europe I was assured that your organisation had the official backing of your governments. Thus, you misled me from the outset, for I know now that this is not the case. Certain members of certain governments are involved, I know, but not for the purpose you put forward. Their interests, I suspect, is entirely personal. By the control of atomic weapons they hope to intimidate – or shall we call a spade a spade and say blackmail – the rest of the world, to their financial and political advantage. That goes for you, too, of course. But do not misunderstand me. I still find the proposition attractive. I am merely endeavouring to point out that you would do better to trust me and accept my advice.'

There was another interruption, and von Stalhein went on. 'You want an example. Very well. Consider Luntz. What I suggested was an obvious precaution, yet you opposed it.'

'But you had your way,' argued a voice.

'After a struggle. And look at these drunken Mongolians. No attempt is made to control them. They are still being given unlimited vodka.'

Again a voice was raised in protest, in an unknown language. On being translated, evidently for the speaker's benefit, it came to this; that the Mongolian guards would desert in a body if their drink was cut off.

Von Stalhein went on. 'Ach, so! Very well. I warn you that if this state of affairs continues the whole thing will end in disaster. Already it may be too late to remedy the mischief already done, for that there has been a breach of security I am convinced by what happened this morning. Yet you do nothing. Lieutenant Vasilloff here reported that the men in the plane were Koreans. I don't believe it. It is assumed that they came this way by accident. I don't believe that, either. The aircraft was here for a purpose, and I know, and you should know, what that purpose was. I say it was making a reconnaissance of this area. I would even go so far as to make a guess at the name of the man who flew it.'

At this point there were several interruptions, mostly of a scornful nature; but von Stalhein went on, raising his voice, now brittle with suppressed anger.

'You say it's impossible,' he accused. 'I say nothing is impossible to well-trained agents, and, as I know to my cost, with these Britain is well supplied. She has been at the game for a long time and knows every trick. Rumour, if nothing more, of what is going on here has leaked through to the British Government, which, through its Foreign Office, has a way of solving mysteries. If, as I think, word has reached them, their first move would be to dispatch a man to investigate. I suspect that man is here, and I know the one they would send. His name is Bigglesworth. It is just the sort of work on which he has specialised. If he is not already here, he will come, and yet you are content to go on as if nothing has happened. Even now he may be in this very—'

There was a chorus of incredulous exclamations.

'Very well. You will see,' snapped von Stalhein, whose normal imperturbability was obviously being strained.

'Lieutenant Vasilloff shot down the plane and the men were brought in,' said a voice.

'The men who were brought in were not those in the plane,' declared von Stalhein. 'A dolt could see that at a glance. They were common traders. Their story rings true and the contents of their packs confirm it. They are Koreans and they speak Korean. They brought in supplies of vodka and cartridges for this mad Cossack who lives in the marshes. Had my advice been taken he would have been liquidated long ago. Any man living there would be a menace and this one talks too much. He can do no good and he may do harm. The truth is, these drunken Mongolians are afraid of him. But let that pass. The two men who were in the plane got away. They must have got away or their bodies would have been there. They must be found.'

Another voice broke in, and in it there was an element of doubt. 'This reminds me of something,' said the speaker. 'According to Ming, at the end of the day's work there were two extra men in the gang. He mentioned this to me.'

There was a brief silence. Then von Stalhein rasped: 'Why was I not told of this at once? What has been done about it?'

From excuses muttered in a surly voice it was fairly evident that nothing had been done about it.

Von Stalhein became brusque. 'This is a matter that must be settled right away,' he rapped out. 'Prince, will you please give orders for all workmen to be mustered instantly. Examine their mouths and you will find the two extra men. They will be the men who were in the aeroplane, and one of them, I would wager, will be Bigglesworth. Bring them to me. I shall know them. Let this be done at once or I will not accept responsibility for the consequences. If they are no longer in the compound the country must be scoured until they are found. Put double guards on all places that matter.'

Said another voice: 'What is all this fuss about one man, even if his name is Bigglesworth? Are we to think you are afraid of him?'

'No,' answered von Stalhein slowly. 'I am not afraid, but I have a respect for his ability. He is one of those men who, while others are talking, acts, and had he not been under the protection of the devil himself he would have been dead long ago. He is as hard to catch as an old fox, and as hard to hold as an eel. If he is about I am all the more relieved to know that Luntz is where he is.'

Ginger frowned. This was the second reference to Luntz. He wondered who and where he was.

'We are wasting time,' went on von Stalhein. 'The first thing to do, Prince, is to order Ming to examine the mouths of the workmen. You should find two with tongues. It shouldn't take long. We'll wait here.'

There was a murmur of assent, and a scraping of chairs indicated a general move.

The anxiety, not to say consternation, with which Ginger had listened to von Stalhein's arguments, calls for little imagination; but before he could dwell on them Biggles had touched him on the arm and was gliding like a shadow along the wall of the house to the rear, from where he made his way to the nearest trees. Ginger, of course, went with him. They were only just in time, for without warning unsuspected lights over the front of the house were switched on, throwing the area of the door into clear relief. A group of men emerged, talking in low tones. One called loudly. The sentry answered and hurried to the door.

Ginger, from where he lay, could now see the men for the first time. Von Stalhein was there, a tall, soldierly figure, the usual cigarette in its long holder. There were two Chinese in national dress, one resplendent in the robes of a mandarin. The rest appeared to be nondescript European types in ordinary civilian clothes. The one nearest to Ginger was a thick-set, elderly man, with a broad, slab-like, impassive face. It was impossible to even make a guess at his nationality.

For a few minutes there was a good deal of activity. The big taskmaster, whose name apparently was Ming, arrived, complete with his whip and his gang, and after a short conversation with 'Prince' Ling Soo, retired, presumably to examine the slaves in the compound. Ginger broke into a cold perspiration at the narrowness of their escape, if only for the time being. That the compound might be searched at this hour of the night was something even Biggles could hardly have foreseen. Nor could he have realised what effect the appearance of a strange aircraft would have on the enemy – but then, of course, he had been unaware that von Stalhein was in the picture, a circumstance that altered the entire situation. It was he who had sounded the alarm; and having come off second best to Biggles on so many occasions he was more than a little apprehensive, whatever he might say to the contrary. On his own statements he might almost be said to have developed a Biggles complex. Yet his reasoning had been sound enough, thought Ginger. His shrewd brain had, in fact, grasped the situation with uncanny accuracy; and this, for the intruders, was likely to have serious consequences. The enemy camp was now on the alert, and this would inevitably make the work of rescue more difficult. He wondered what Biggles' reactions would be.

He was soon to know. Again Biggles touched him on the arm and withdrew farther into the trees. 'Listen,' he said. 'We've got to get cracking. This is our chance, while they're all busy in the compound. It will take them some time to get those exhausted slaves on their feet, and round them up for inspection. When the number is found to tally most of von Stalhein's associates will be satisfied, no doubt. But not von Stalhein. If he's got it into his head that we're in the country, and obviously he has, he'll pull every trick he knows to catch up with us.'

'Imagine *him* being here,' breathed Ginger.

'Yet why not?' returned Biggles. 'This is just the sort of racket you'd expect to find him in. He had a big reputation in Germany at one time, and the people who are running this show, needing such a man, would soon get in touch with him. After all, what can the wretched fellow do? He was a Nazi. If he returned to his own country he'd be tried by a denazification court and hanged, or at any rate sent to jail for life. So he's drifting about the world like a ship without a rudder. He's got to live somehow, and the fact that he's working for this bunch doesn't necessarily mean that he's in sympathy with them. Judging from what he said just now he hasn't much time for them. He certainly said a mouthful – too much, perhaps, for he must have touched some of them on the raw, and they won't forget it. I'd say that to admit that he knew what he threw at them was indiscreet – considering the type of people he's working for. To give the devil his due, he's efficient. That's his trouble. Notice the way he worked out that I was on the job. He was right on the nail. But with some people efficiency doesn't always pay. Here we have a bunch of ambitious war-mongers, and as ambition goes hand in hand with vanity, the more often von Stalhein is right, and proves his employers wrong, the more they'll resent it. Instead of supporting him they'll oppose him, and that's where they'll come unstuck. It's an old story. But this is no time for philosophy. Thanks to von Stalhein we've collected a vital piece of information, anyway, a piece that Raymond will be glad to have. Let's get weaving. We've got to locate our men tonight; we may not get another chance.'

Standing up, Biggles made a survey of what little could be seen of the enemy camp. The compound was out of sight, but sounds coming from its direction indicated that the examination of the slaves was proceeding. The group outside the door of the house went back inside, presumably to await the result.

Ginger, too, tried to probe the darkness around him. It was all very confusing. There were several huts deep in the trees, their position being revealed in many cases by lighted windows, which were only shaded from above. But there appeared to be no way of determining which particular hutment was the one they sought. It would, he thought, be safe to assume that the scientists would be housed in a building of some sort but that was all. He expressed his doubts.

Biggles agreed that it was difficult. 'We shall just have to go from one to the other till we strike the right one,' he said. 'It's pretty certain that our men will be behind barbed wire. That should be a guide. We haven't much time. We've got to be out of this before daylight.'

With this decision Ginger was in complete agreement.

CHAPTER IX

V – V – V

The search began. In the darkness, and in the absence of any knowledge of the layout of the camp, it was a tedious, nerve-racking business, for while most of the Mongol troops had been concentrated in the region of the slave-yard there was still a number drifting aimlessly, most of them the worse for drink. Fortunately they made a good deal of noise, quarrelling and singing, which announced their approach in ample time for cover to be taken. Nevertheless, there were several narrow escapes. One in particular turned Ginger's mouth dry with shock, as well as giving him a bruise on the shin. They were crossing a patch of the deep grass which occurred everywhere between the trees when he stumbled over an object which overturned with a jangle of glass. In trying to recover himself he trod on something soft and warm that lay near it. It was a nasty moment, for he knew that it could only be a human body. Spinning round prepared to fight he saw that it was one of the Mongolians, apparently asleep. It turned out that the man was in a drunken stupor, and although he stirred uneasily, muttering, he did not attempt to rise – which for him was just as well, for Biggles had whipped out his pistol, holding it by the muzzle ready to strike should the man open his mouth. The precaution was unnecessary. The Mongol slipped back into his besotted

430

slumber. Biggles replaced his weapon with a shrug of contempt. Ginger, wiping the sweat of shock from his forehead, saw that the object over which he had tripped was a case of the now familiar vodka bottles. Two lay empty beside the intoxicated body. Biggles beckoned and they went on, leaving the sleeper to his drink-sodden dreams.

For an hour or more – Ginger lost count of time – they wandered about the camp, groping their way through trees, crawling through dry grass, creeping from hut to hut without getting even so much as a clue to guide them to their objective. There were well-used paths, carefully camouflaged where they crossed open spaces. Indeed, there was a maze of them, as there is bound to be in a camp of any size; but as these were being used by men moving about – men who, moreover, often carried torches – Biggles thought it advisable to keep clear of them. Those not covered by camouflage netting were concealed from overhead observation by the upper branches of the trees through which they ran, so it was easy to see why they had escaped notice when the Birada had made its reconnaissance. It was obvious that the camp had been established in the forest for that very purpose. It was for the same reason that the black fighter had not been spotted. Biggles and Ginger, in the course of their wanderings, came upon it near the outer fringe of the trees. It was mounted on a catapult of obsolete but quite effective pattern, facing down a short clearing which ended in open ground. There was no guard. Biggles ran a professional eye over it, and hesitated as if he contemplated doing something, but presently he passed on without a word.

Soon afterwards, Ginger, who was walking with his hands held out in front of his face to protect his eyes from the ends of broken branches which could not be seen in the gloom, encountered barbed wire. How far it extended on either side he could not see, but

*The Mongolian did not attempt to rise – which for
him was just as well.*

behind it was a log hut of some length. One window, near the end, was lighted; and it may have been due to this light in his eyes that for a time he could see nothing else. Presently, by staring hard, he could just make out the shape of a much larger hut in the background, a building not less than forty yards long. Both buildings seemed to be in the same enclosure. The ground was deep in the usual dry grass. Midway between the two huts, and to one side, apparently set in the wire fence, was yet another building, but this was tiny compared with the two large ones. He thought he could just make out the shape of a man standing by it as if it might have been a sentry outside a guardroom.

A soft hiss brought Biggles, who was slightly behind, to the spot. For several seconds they stood still side by side staring at what could dimly be seen behind the wire, for only the lighted window was distinct. By sheer concentration, after a little while Ginger could just discern what seemed to be a veranda running along the length of the nearer hut. At about the middle of this from time to time a pinpoint of light glowed to a bright orange. This puzzled him, for he could not think what it could be. It was too stationary to be a firefly. Closing his eyes for a moment to rest them he looked again, and thought he could see several vague figures in a curious reclining position. Then a match flared suddenly and he understood. The point of light was the glowing end of a cigarette. Someone was there, resting and smoking. A moment later shoes scraped on a board floor. A door was opened. Light flooded out, revealing clearly everything within its radius of influence. A man moved until his silhouette stood out black against the lighted entrance. Softly through the still air came a voice. 'Good night all,' it said quietly, in English. The speaker went in, closing the door behind him. Darkness returned. But still a cigarette glowed.

Biggles' hand had closed over Ginger's arm. 'Okay,' he breathed. 'This is it.'

But Ginger was now looking at something else, something about twenty yards away along the line of the fence, a solid-looking object which he was sure had not been there a minute earlier. While he watched it, it moved, and grew more definite in outline. He recognised it for a man walking slowly towards them, apparently along the outside of the wire. In an instant he had jerked Biggles' sleeve and was crouching back into the shadows behind them. Biggles followed. Whether or not he had seen the man approaching Ginger did not know, but there was no time to utter a warning. The man loomed up, a rifle on his shoulder. He walked straight past, and presently merged into the dark background.

Biggles waited for a good two minutes. Then he breathed: 'The fence is patrolled, but I must try to contact Vale if he's here.'

How he proposed doing this Ginger did not know, for the men on the veranda were a good twenty yards away, and to call would certainly attract the attention of the sentry. True, the wire could be cut; but if the wire was closely patrolled, the severed strands would be noticed when daylight came; so if it should happen that immediate rescue was impossible they would have betrayed their presence in the camp for no purpose. In that case extra precautions against the escape of the prisoners would certainly be taken. And anyway, thought Ginger swiftly, there was no actual proof yet that the men behind the wire were those they sought. The English-speaking voice made it seem a fairly safe conclusion, but it was not absolutely definite. There might be other English-speaking people in the camp, and it was not the moment to take risks that a little patience would avoid. Thus thought Ginger as he waited to see what Biggles would do.

Biggles' method of attracting attention was simple and reasonably safe. If Vale was there, he would understand. If not, no harm would be done. In a soft whistle such as might have been made by a night bird he sent out, in Morse code, Vale's own initial call sign; the three Vees.

There was no response. The men on the veranda, who had started to talk in low tones, continued without pause, as if the signal, if it had been noticed, had conveyed nothing to them. There was just a chance, thought Ginger, with a twinge of disappointment, that Vale was not there. Or he might have been the man who had gone in. He might never have revealed his true identity to the others, or explained the significance of his initials, in which case the signal would pass without comment.

However, this was not the case. The men on the veranda were still talking, but suddenly a shadow loomed up so close to the wire that Ginger started back, thinking it was a sentry. Then, like the breath of a breeze in the trees, came the answering signal,

. . . —   . . . —   . . . —

Biggles echoed it.

A voice said softly: 'Where are you?' and all doubts were set at rest.

'Here,' answered Biggles.

The figure moved forward. 'Who are you?'

'Bigglesworth, of the Special Air Branch. Your messenger got through. The Yard sent me out to locate you and get you home.'

'Thank God for that,' came the voice fervently. 'We're having an awful time here. We couldn't have lasted much longer.'

'Then the others are with you?'

'All except General Gorton who was shot trying to escape.'

'That leaves four of you altogether?'

'No, six.'

'Six?'

'We were four, but an American was brought in about a month ago, and a Polish professor soon afterwards. But make haste. It's a minute to eleven, and at eleven sharp we're locked in for the night.'

'In this hut?'

'Yes.'

'Then answer my questions quickly,' requested Biggles. 'Do you have separate rooms?'

'No. We sleep in one long dormitory.'

'You've no means of getting out of it?'

'No. The windows are barred. Then there's this fence.'

'You've no tools?'

'No. We're searched every night at roll-call and our shoes are taken away.'

'What happens to them?'

'They're locked in a pantry at the end of the hut. The door's on the outside.'

'Who keeps the key?'

'The guard in the guardroom at the gate. It's on a bunch. They hang on a nail. The big one is the key of the gate through this fence. The next is the key of this hut. One unlocks the workshop – that's the big building behind – and the smallest is the key of the boot pantry.'

'How many guards are on duty at a time?'

'Three. They take turns patrolling the wire. There's always a surprise visit sometime during the night, when we are counted.'

'Where are you in daytime?'

'In the big workshop behind our quarters.'

At this moment a whistle was blown and a gutteral voice shouted: 'All insides!'

'That's it,' said Vale urgently. 'I must go or they'll be looking for me.'

'Okay,' said Biggles. 'I'll get in touch with you again presently. Stand by. I'll come to a window.'

Vale walked back quickly to the veranda, where there was now a general stir. Vague figures moved in the gloom. A harsh voice spoke, and seemed to be counting. This was followed by the noises of the prisoners being secured for the night. A heavy door slammed. Keys jangled. The light went out.

Biggles backed away from the wire into the trees, pulling Ginger with him. 'Well, that's something,' he said softly. 'We know where they are and how they're fixed. With the tools we've got, when the place settles down we shouldn't have much trouble getting them out. Their shoes are the big problem. It's an old dodge, that, but effective. No man accustomed to footgear can get far without any – certainly not in country like this. Which means that as well as getting the men out we've got to open this pantry where their shoes are kept.'

'Then how about making a start?' suggested Ginger. 'We'd better wait a little while to give the guards a chance to get into their routine,' advised Biggles.

Sitting at the foot of a tree they waited. The heat was still oppressive. Fireflies danced. Mosquitoes hummed. A sentry, his rifle shouldered in reverse, strolled by, following the wire. It was evident from his attitude that he was not expecting anything to happen. No doubt he had done the job many times before.

'How about giving him a crack on the dome next time he goes by?' suggested Ginger.

'It would bring one of his pals along to see what had happened to him.'

'We could dish him out with a dose of the same medicine.'

Biggles considered the suggestion but decided against it. 'If we can get in without any fuss it'll be better that way. We'll let the sentry make one more tour and then get moving. I wish I knew how often he comes round.'

It was about a quarter of an hour before the sentry reappeared, now smoking a cigarette. As soon as he had passed out of sight Biggles rose, and in a matter of seconds had cut the lower strands of the wire. Another moment and they were both inside, walking quickly towards the prisoners' sleeping quarters. Reaching the hut, keeping close against the wall Biggles went on to the nearest window, a small one with iron bars secured on the outside in a horizontal position. A quick examination revealed that the others were the same. They were at an awkward height, the sills being some four feet from the ground, which meant that the bars could only be tackled by reaching up. It was obvious, too, that at least four bars would have to be removed to make an aperture large enough for a man of average size to pass through.

'I'm afraid this is going to be a long job,' muttered Biggles. 'If the windows are made to open, the fellows inside would be able to get to the bars more easily. I want to let Vale know we're here, anyway.' Putting a hand between the bars he tapped the V-signal very quietly on the glass.

Apparently Vale had been waiting, for almost at once the window was opened and the signal came back. Vale's face appeared dimly behind the bars.

'Everything normal?' asked Biggles.

'Yes.'

'Have you told the others we're here?'

'Not yet. I thought it better to keep mum until I'd had a word with you, to find out just what you intend to do. No use getting everyone excited too soon.'

'Quite right. Where are they now?'

'Gone to bed.'

'Then you'd better wake them up and tell them.'

'I'll do that after the inspection, otherwise Grosnow may sense the excitement and smell a rat.'

'What inspection? Who's Grosnow?'

'He's one of the head men here. He's in charge of us. He does a sort of orderly officer stunt every night about this time to make sure we're still here.'

'I see. Glad you warned me. I've cut the fence. All we have to do now is move some of these bars. They're an awkward height for me outside. Could you manage it better from there if I gave you the tools?'

'I think so – but I'll wait till Grosnow has been round before I start.'

'Good enough.'

'What about our shoes?'

'We'll attend to that,' promised Biggles. 'Here, take this file. I'm afraid a hacksaw will make too much noise.'

'Filing is going to take some time.'

'Can't be helped. Do the best you can.' Biggles turned to Ginger. 'Slip along to this pantry place to see if it looks like being difficult to crack open.'

'Okay.' Ginger crept along the wall until he reached the end. A quick survey revealing no sign of danger he made an inspection of the pantry, which, he found, was merely an extension of the prisoners' quarters. To his dismay he saw that the two windows, one on each side of the door, were tiny, not more than eighteen inches square – too small, he thought, for entrance to be obtained that way. That only left the door. It was made of rough, heavy timber, and he perceived that even with tools it would be impossible to force it open without a good deal of noise.

A slight sound took him on to the end of the gable, from where he could see the guard hut. The gate of the enclosure had been opened, and three men were entering. This, he guessed, was the inspection which Vale had mentioned. He hurried back to Biggles. '*Cave,*' he whispered. 'Grosnow is coming across. Warn Vale to watch out.'

But apparently Vale had heard. Silence fell. Biggles stood close against the wall, nerves taut, listening. He heard the door of the hut open. The light was switched on. Heavy footsteps thudded slowly, a step at a time, on a board floor. For a minute not a word was spoken. Ginger could imagine the sort of inspection that was going on. Then a voice burst out, so loud that his nerves twitched. 'Attention!' it said, in a strange foreign accent. 'I warn again, if any man tries to go he will have a bullet.'

There was no answer.

Again the footsteps, now receding. The door was shut. Silence returned.

Biggles whispered: 'What about the boot pantry?'

'I don't know what we can do about it,' answered Ginger. He explained the difficulties.

'It rather looks as if we shall have to get the keys,' murmured Biggles. 'I'll think about it. Keep your eyes skinned.'

Vale reappeared at the window. 'All clear,' he said. 'I'm going to tell the others now. Then I'll make a start on the bars.'

'Good enough.'

At this moment there came a sound which turned out to be the forerunner of others which were to put a very different aspect on the entire situation, although this was not realised at the time. The sound was a gunshot, some distance away. But it was unmistakable.

'What the deuce was that, I wonder?' muttered Biggles.

The question was soon to he answered for him. Inside a minute there came another shot. But this was nothing to what came next.

A voice was raised, shouting – nay, bellowing; and at the words, and the language used, Ginger went rigid.

'Ho there!' came the voice through the still night air. 'Ho there! Mayne! Where are you Mayne?' *Bang* went the gun again.

For a moment neither Biggles nor Ginger spoke. Then Ginger said, in a queer, thin voice: 'Petroffsky!'

'Aye, and drunk by the sound of it,' replied Biggles bitterly. 'The fool,' he went on, in his anger speaking through his teeth. 'The silly, drunken imbecile. Pity that tiger didn't get him.'

'But how on earth did he get here?'

'Heavens only knows. Blundered on our trail and followed us. I suppose. Got drunk on his last consignment of vodka and decided to call on Mayne. Probably went to the island and learning Mayne wasn't there decided to go and look for him. This means we shall have to adjust our plan. Are you still there, Vale?'

'Yes.'

'All right. Go ahead, but something is happening which may upset things. We're going to find out what's going on. We'll be back. If by any chance we don't turn up in the next couple of hours start off on your own. Head for the big lake and keep along the eastern edge. There's an aircraft waiting at one of the islands. There's a pilot with it. See you later, I hope. Come on, Ginger.'

Biggles moved quickly towards the gap in the fence.

CHAPTER X

The Velvet Glove

Having left the prison hut enclosure through the gap in the wire Biggles made for the direction of Petroffsky's approach. There could be no question of intercepting him. This had already been done by men from the camp. Others were hurrying towards the spot, from where now arose a general hubbub. Above it all rose Petroffsky's bellow, as he continued to shout for Mayne. More lights were switched on, so that large areas of the camp appeared to be floodlit, making everything plain to see. What the lights revealed, was not, in the circumstances, surprising. As Biggles observed, the Russian had certainly stirred things up.

Into the camp came Petroffsky, roaring as he fought a dozen or more Mongols who were hanging on to him like a pack of dogs baiting a bull. He had already been disarmed, but he fought with flailing arms. Time and time again he flung his assailants off, shouting what sounded like curses in his native tongue. But they always came back, striving to get a grip on the whirling arms. There was reason to suppose that orders had been given that he was not to be seriously hurt, otherwise, of course, he would not have lasted for so long. Supporting this supposition was the presence of von Stalhein. He was standing only a short distance away, watching with his usual frigid calm. Close to him, in a group, were the men with whom he had recently been in conference, when the Russian had been discussed.

At last, panting and bedraggled, Petroffsky was brought to a standstill quite close to the trees in which Biggles and Ginger crouched, watching. But this is not to say that he was in the slightest degree intimidated. He confronted his persecutors defiantly, shouting in a variety of languages what he would do if he was not taken to see 'his old friend Mayne' instantly. Once he paused to take a drink from a bottle which he suddenly produced from a pocket, afterwards hurling the bottle at the head of the nearest Mongol.

Eventually von Stalhein acted. First he said something to the men near him, then went on towards Petroffsky, and silencing the babble of voices with a gesture, addressed the Russian in the language he had used when shouting for Mayne.

'Of course – of course,' said von Stalhein gently, in such a voice as he might have used to pacify a wayward child. 'Of course you shall see your old friend Mayne. Unfortunately he isn't here at the moment, but we'll soon find him. I'm sorry you've been treated so disgracefully, but my men were under orders, and I was not to know that you were coming.' Von Stalhein patted the Russian on the arm and waved away the Mongols, who looked at each other in amazement, as well they might.

'This scum attacked me,' declared Petroffsky, in a haughty voice. 'Scum, sir, that's what they are. Do you know who I am?'

'Of course,' replied von Stalhein, who apparently knew the answer to the question. 'Everyone knows Colonel Alexis Petroffsky. I regret that these fools of sentries failed to recognise an officer and a gentleman.'

Petroffsky bowed low, and nearly fell over. 'I accept your apology,' he said gravely. 'I observe, sir, that you, too, are a gentleman. Say no more. Will you take a little drink with me?'

'With pleasure,' replied von Stalhein. 'But first, since you are my guest, you must drink with me. I have some excellent vodka. But let us not drink here. Come to my quarters, where we can talk in peace.'

Petroffsky bowed again. 'Sir, I am honoured. But what of my old friend Mayne?'

'I haven't seen him lately,' parried von Stalhein. 'Is he here?'

'He came this way.'

'Are you quite sure?'

'Certainly I'm sure.'

'How do you know?'

'His friends …' Petroffsky hesitated, as if even in his befuddled state he realised that he was saying too much.

'No matter, my dear Colonel,' went on von Stalhein smoothly. 'If he is here he shall join us as soon as he can be found. Come along. Let's have a drink.' He took the Russian by the arm, and still chatting amicably walked slowly towards a small hutment that stood alone not far from the big house. The spectators began to disperse.

Biggles drew a deep breath, and when he spoke his voice had acid in it. 'The old game. First, the velvet glove. If that fails, the iron fist. But it won't fail. Von Stalhein's a past-master at it. He went straight for Petroffsky's weakness – vanity; vanity and booze. Whips wouldn't have made Petroffsky speak if he was sober and realised what he was doing, but in his drink-sodden state he'll let von Stalhein wheedle out of him everything he knows. He'll tell him that we're here dressed as Koreans. He'll tell him we've got an aircraft, where it is, and all the rest of it. In short, he's going to turn our applecart upside-down.'

'Why on earth did Algy let him come?' groaned Ginger.

'I don't suppose Algy knew anything about him coming, or he'd have stopped him. I'd say Petroffsky paid a call, and then went home and got a skinful of vodka. Under its influence he decided to find Mayne. He's an experienced hunter, and he'd have no difficulty in trailing us.'

'Why didn't Bertie stop him?'

'I imagine he blundered past Bertie and Mayne in the dark. They might have heard him, but unless he spoke they wouldn't know who it was, and they'd sit tight – quite rightly. But that doesn't matter now. Petroffsky's here, and in half an hour von Stalhein will know all he knows. Once von Stalhein is satisfied that he's sucked Petroffsky dry of information he'll waste no time getting after us. We've one chance left, and that's speed. We've got to get our men out of this camp before von Stalhein can take action.'

'We haven't a hope,' declared Ginger bitterly. 'I can't see Vale cutting through those bars inside a couple of hours.'

'I'm afraid I'm bound to agree with you,' replied Biggles slowly. 'The alternative is to hold up von Stalhein for as long as possible. We can't be in two places at once so it means that we shall have to split. I'll go after von Stalhein. The rest of the gang will leave him alone until he's finished with Petroffsky, so keeping him where he is for a bit shouldn't be too difficult. You go and get our people out. It's now or never. You should be able to manage it. Get them out and make for Bertie and Mayne. I'll try to meet you there, but don't count on it, and don't wait for me. Push on as fast as you can to the machine. You've got to get to it before von Stalhein can send his Mongols there – unless, of course, I can prevent Petroffsky from telling him where the machine is hidden. Are you sure you can find your way back, via the lignite diggings, without me?'

'I think so. I know the direction, anyway.'

'Okay, then get going. I'll hold von Stalhein as long as I can to give you as good a start as possible.'

'I'll do my best,' promised Ginger, and turning away, keeping to the trees, made for the prisoners' quarters.

Biggles watched him until he was out of sight, and then, after a quick survey of the scene of the recent fracas, now deserted, he began to make his way towards the hut into which von Stalhein and his new friend had disappeared. A light had been switched on inside. He walked straight towards it, for there was no time for a cautious approach. It would not take von Stalhein long to extract the information he needed, and if he, Biggles, arrived too late to prevent that, his effort would be wasted.

He reached the hut without meeting anyone, although people were still moving about not far away, and halted in the shadow of the wooden wall for a final reconnaissance of the vicinity. Seeing nothing to cause alarm he went on to the window. A peep revealed Petroffsky slumped in a chair talking volubly while von Stalhein, standing up, smiling, poured liquor into two glasses from a bottle. It was obvious that there was no time to lose.

The door was on the far side. Half a dozen steps took him to the end of the building. He looked round it, half afraid there might be a guard on duty. Evidently von Stalhein did not consider it necessary, for there was none. Biggles opened the door quietly and found himself in a narrow corridor. Light showed under two badly fitting doors, one near, the other at the end of the corridor. From the far one came a clatter of crocks as if a servant was washing up. He would, Biggles could only hope, stay there. He went to the nearest door, and with a hand on the knob paused to listen.

Von Stalhein was speaking, in a casual, inconsequential voice. 'So my old friend Bigglesworth is here too, with Mayne? I was half expecting him, but he may be surprised to find me here. He's a great fellow for dropping in at unlikely places. I should be delighted to meet him again. I've been looking forward for some time to another little chat.'

Biggles felt for his automatic and quietly opened the door. 'Good evening, von Stalhein,' he said politely. 'You know, I've been looking forward to the same thing. Please sit still. Carry on. Don't let me disturb the party.'

Without turning Biggles closed the door behind him, pulled out a chair and sat down.

CHAPTER XI

Ginger Goes Alone

Ginger made his way back to the prisoners' quarters in a state bordering on dismay. He had got his orders, and he had not questioned them, but to have such a responsibility thrust upon him without the slightest warning set his brain racing at such a speed that he found it difficult to bring it under sufficient control to form a clear-cut plan of action. A dozen thoughts intruded at the same time, overlapping, jostling each other and allowing none to receive the attention it demanded – the sentries ... the keys ... the windows were barred ... the prisoners had no shoes – and so on. Each presented a problem not easy to solve. He could not get Biggles out of his mind, either. How Biggles was going to delay von Stalhein long enough for the escape to be effected, was beyond him. Yet he had a suspicion that it was by such lightning decisions as this, by snatching at passing opportunities, that he so often out-manoeuvred his opponents. One thing, however, was clear. Biggles must have thought the situation to be desperate or he would not have taken such appalling risks. Success and failure now hung in the balance. One slip, however small, would be enough to turn the scales against them, when not only the scientists, but the whole expedition, would be lost.

Striking futile blows against the ever-tormenting mosquitoes he leaned for a moment against the trunk of a tree, eyes questing ceaselessly for signs of danger as he strove to recover his composure, to think clearly and decide on the best course to take. One factor, one difficulty, superseded all others. Footgear for the prisoners. To get the prisoners away without shoes on their feet would be hopeless. They would never survive the long march back to base. Their feet would be cut to ribbons by the rough ground and the harsh grasses before they had gone a mile. To get into the room where the shoes were kept without making a noise could only be accomplished by the use of the key. There could be no question of breaking open the door. Yet it seemed that the only way to get the keys was by tackling the sentries in whose custody they were – a project which, without raising a general alarm, seemed impossible. Whichever way the problem was tackled, as far as he could see the object could not be achieved without noise. He might keep the sentries quiet by threats, but only while he was with them. The moment he left them to release the prisoners they would certainly make enough noise to raise the entire camp ... unless ...

The idea that took shape in his head did not arrive as a flash of inspiration. It began as a vague hope which, as he turned it over in his mind, crystallised slowly into a definite plan needing only nerve to carry it through. Nerve and bluff. Bluff – which he had once heard Biggles describe as man's best friend in a tight corner. But to put a big bluff over needed nerve, or no nerves at all – he was not sure which.

At first he thought that considering the amount of drinking that was going on in the camp there was a chance that the sentries might be drunk. But this was no more than a hope. The thing would be a lot easier if they were drunk. If they were sober, could he by any means induce them to get drunk? With his mind running on these lines it was natural that he should recall the fellow lying in

449

the long grass, in a drunken stupor, with a case of vodka beside him, two bottles of which he had sampled to his undoing. If only the sentries could find the liquor it was a safe bet that they, too, would be unable to resist the temptation to sample it; having sampled it they would go on drinking while any remained, or until they were in the same state as the man who had fallen by the wayside. How could he bring the two things together – the vodka and the sentries? Obviously, he would have to take the liquor to the sentries, or the sentries to the liquor.

At first he recoiled from the scheme as being too fantastic for serious contemplation; but thinking it over he perceived that the risks involved would be no greater than those that would arise if he tried to get the keys by any other ruse. After all, he pondered, he looked like a Korean. The sentries would take him for one, and they would not question him because they would assume him to be minus his tongue, and consequently unable to answer. It seemed a reasonable supposition that the men, who were probably bored with their job anyway, would be more interested in the vodka than the man who carried it. It was a gamble which, if it came off, might enable him not only to get the shoes, but save a long wait while the window bars were being removed.

Ginger realised that the longer he regarded the plan the more difficult would it appear, so, slightly breathless from excitement, he made his way to the patch of grass which the Mongolian had selected for his private orgy. Obviously, the first thing was to ascertain if he was still there. He was, snoring stertorously. What was even more important, the overturned case was still there, too. A quick survey of the area within view revealed nothing to cause immediate alarm, so he hoisted the case on his shoulder, and without any attempt at concealment marched briskly towards the guardhouse.

In the execution of his plan things did not go quite as he

intended, and for a minute or two he was afraid that he had over-reached himself. The trouble began when he almost walked into a sentry – the one, apparently, whose turn it was to patrol the wire. The encounter could not be avoided. They were too close for that. As they met, the sentry said something. Ginger, of course, had no idea of what the man actually said, but he supposed it to be a challenge. In the light of what happened next it was more likely, as Ginger then realised, that the man had simply asked if the bottles in the case were full. That he did not expect an answer, at least in so many words, was made evident by the way he reached for the case to satisfy himself on the point. With scant ceremony he relieved Ginger of his load, and knocking the neck off a bottle against the cartridge chamber of his rifle with a practised hand, he took a good swig, smacked his lips and drank again.

Now this did not suit Ginger at all, for he was afraid that the man might keep the lot for his own use. It was not enough to have one sentry drunk. He wanted them all drunk, or his plan would fail. Wherefore he made noises of protest and tried to get the case back. For his pains he got his face smacked, and a stream of vituperation. This caused him to release his hold on the case, which fell to the ground with a clank of glass. This familiar sound was something the remaining sentries understood, for they must have heard it, and the argument, the guard hut being no great distance away. Anyhow, they were soon on the scene, and the result was never in doubt. They all had a swig, and one of the newcomers lost no time in knocking off another bottle. Ginger again made noises of protest, as he considered would be natural in the circumstances; but this time he got a blow that sent him staggering.

Secretly elated by his success he abandoned the case, and moaning plaintively, to the derisive jeers of the sentries he ran away – taking care to make for the direction of the guard hut. A thought that flashed through his mind was, no wonder von Stalhein had complained about the behaviour of these undisciplined ruffians. However, it suited him well enough that they saw nothing unusual in his retreat, or in the direction of it.

Reaching the guard hut door, which had been left open, he looked back along the wire and saw the sentries coming, two of them carrying the case between them. Even as he watched them they put the case down in order to pass round another bottle. This made their intention plain, and it was with no small satisfaction that Ginger foresaw that it would not be long before most of the bottles were empty. He was particularly gratified by the success, so far, of his plan, because he had followed Biggles' precept of exploiting the enemy's weakness to his disadvantage. He had, moreover, utilised materials which the enemy himself had provided.

He looked into the hut, a bare room furnished only with a rough bench and lighted by a single electric light bulb. A bunch of keys hung on a nail just inside the door. In a moment they were in his hand, although he realised that in their removal lay his greatest risk of discovery. The sentries were not drunk – yet. Should they miss the keys they might guess what had happened. At all events, they would certainly smell a rat, as the saying goes. But there was no alternative. The keys were the most vital factor in the deadly game he was playing. The sentries were obviously returning to the hut, and once they were inside it would not be possible to get near the keys until they had drunk themselves unconscious; but that would take some time, more time than he could afford to waste, bearing in mind the situation in which Biggles had placed himself. Therefore he could only pray that the interest of the Mongolians would remain concentrated on their unexpected find to the exclusion of all else.

There was this about it, he thought swiftly, as he unlocked the gate that gave access to the prison enclosure, and closed it behind him: if after a few drinks the men did miss the keys they would hesitate to start a general alarm immediately for fear of bringing the wrath of their leaders on their heads for the drunken folly of allowing the keys to be taken.

With his heart pounding and his breath coming fast from excitement, crouching low he sped across the enclosure to the nearest point of the hut. Reaching it he did not stop, but went on to the corner, from where he made a final reconnaissance of the guard-room, some twenty yards away. The sentries were just going in. They did not close the door behind them, as he hoped they would. For a few seconds he lingered, waiting for the shout that would announce the loss of the keys, for it was now that the discovery was most likely to be made. He could hear the sentries laughing and talking, hear the chink of glass as they took the bottles out of the case; but the sound he feared did not come. The tension passed and he relaxed, breathing more freely.

Well content with the way things were going he started to move towards the door of the prisoners' quarters with the intention of opening it forthwith; but half-way he changed his mind, deciding to approach it from the far end, which, being farther from the guard hut, would reduce the chances of his being seen by the sentries should they for any reason come out again. This move, moreover, would take him past the window on the bars of which Vale would still be working. He would, he thought, be able to stop him, confirm that all was well, and warn him that he was on his way to unlock the door. This, he saw, was a necessary precaution, as to suddenly walk in would be to invite being knocked on the head in the dark by the men he had come to rescue, who would naturally suppose him to be one of the sentries. He would unlock the shoe pantry, which he would also have to pass on the way, to save time later on.

Reaching this, he unlocked it, and with eyes and ears alert for danger crept on towards the window on which Vale was working – or should be working. Actually, at the moment he was not working; of that Ginger was sure, or from where he stood he would be able to hear the file biting into the iron. Was it possible, he wondered, that Vale had finished the job already? No, it was not possible, he decided. Then why had he stopped work? Had something gone wrong? Had the prisoners been moved? Or was Vale merely taking a rest from his labours? This last surmise seemed the most probable solution. Perplexed, and worried by doubts, Ginger waited for the filing to recommence.

He waited for perhaps five minutes. Not a sound came. He couldn't understand it. Surely, he thought, considering the circumstances Vale would not waste so much time unless there was a very good reason. If all was well he would go on working even though his fingers were worn to the bone.

Keeping flat against the wall he crept on until he was almost under the window, and then listened again. Not a sound came from inside. This, too, struck him as extraordinary. Surely the men, with the prospect of escape before them, would be talking, or at least whispering, among themselves? Why weren't they? Ginger's doubts turned to fears. Something had gone wrong. He was certain of it now. He became aware of danger. He did not know what it was, or where, but it was there, close to him. He was sure of it; he sensed it, although for this he could find no logical explanation. It may have been the flickering of an age-old instinct, the instinct that wild animals have retained but men have almost lost, reawakened by nerves stretched to the limit. At any rate, he was conscious of it, and indecision took him in its grip. He looked around, eyes straining to probe the darkness, but still he could hear nothing, see nothing, to account for the dew of cold sweat that had formed on his forehead.

Another silent step took him under the window, close against the wall. Still nothing happened. Slowly his right hand went up, inch by inch, groping for the bottom bar – or rather, to ascertain if it was still there, for by now Vale should have removed it. It was there. And, moreover, there was not a mark on it. Withdrawing his hand he caught his breath when he realised what this meant. Vale hadn't even *started* work. Why? There could be only one answer to that. He had been prevented. By whom? How? When? These were questions not so easily answered.

Ginger sank down, bewildered, fearful, trying to work the thing out. He felt sure that no alarm had been given, for if it had the sentries would have known about it, in which case they would hardly be behaving as they were behaving now. For the same reason he could not believe that any of the senior members of the gang had gone into the hut since the routine inspection. The keys had been where they were always kept, in the guard hut, so presumably the door of the prisoners' quarters was still locked. If an extra guard had been put inside why should the door be locked and the keys taken away? If a man had been put inside to watch the prisoners surely the light would have been left on? The place was in darkness. How could the prisoners be watched in the dark? No, decided Ginger. That was not the answer. It didn't make sense, as Biggles would say. If anything unusual was going on, if suspicions of an attempted escape had been aroused, the guards would be on the alert instead of getting drunk. He moistened his lips and struck at the mosquitoes impatiently.

One thing at least became clear to him. He would not solve the mystery by sitting where he was. Time was passing, and Biggles might be having difficulty in holding von Stalhein. He considered giving the V-signal, and did in fact purse his lips to whistle; but he abandoned the idea because it seemed pointless. If Vale was there he would be at the window, of that there was no doubt whatever – unless, of course, he was being kept away from it by force. If someone was there to keep him away, reasoned Ginger, then the V-signal would merely betray his presence and his position to that person. In the end he decided that there was only one way of finding out exactly what had happened, or what was happening, in the silent building, and that was by going in. Towards the door, therefore, he made his way, moving swiftly now that his mind was made up. Action is always a relief after inaction.

Reaching the corner of the building, from which the guard hut again came into view, he looked across at it. Conditions there, he was relieved to note, were practically the same. The only difference was, the door was now shut. He hoped it would remain so. The voices of the sentries were raised high, as if in argument, which was also to the good, for it suggested that they were still drinking. Staring at the closed door the thought occurred to him that it was in his power to keep the men inside, for a time, anyway; and even a short time, in view of what he was going to do, might be invaluable. If he could lock the door without making a noise the sentries would not know that they had been locked in until one of them tried to get out. And in view of the din which they themselves were making it seemed unlikely that they would hear the lock turn even if it did make a slight noise. It was, he thought, a chance worth taking, and he resolved to snatch it.

He looked around. Not a soul was in sight. Bending low he ran to the gate, opened it and went on to the door of the hut. Holding the keys tight to prevent them from jangling he found the right one, inserted it and turned it. The click that it made brought his heart into his mouth, as is said; but to his unspeakable relief the noise within continued without pause. He backed away for a few yards, and after closing the gate ran to the door of the prison hut.

On the threshold he paused again for a second to survey the scene, but seeing nothing to worry him, with great caution he tried the door. As he expected, it was locked. Again finding the right key he slipped it in and very slowly turned it. It moved easily, as he thought it would, the lock being in constant use. Putting the keys in his pocket he held his breath, turned the handle and opened the door an inch. He allowed the handle to return to its original position and then stood still, listening. Not a sound came from inside. He felt for his automatic, and with it in his left hand opened the door another inch. Nothing happened. The silence within was that of a sepulchre. The only sound he could hear was the pounding of his heart. Sweat, partly the result of the humid heat and partly due to the intense strain on his nerves, trickled down his nose. He drew a deep breath and again reached for the door. He pushed it. It creaked slightly as it moved. It came to rest. The profound silence remained unbroken.

CHAPTER XII

Hot Work in Cold Blood

Quite suddenly Ginger resolved that this intolerable suspense must come to an end. It was playing havoc with his nerves. Taking a firmer grip on his automatic, making no more noise than a cloud passing over the face of the moon, he stepped inside, took a swift pace to the left and crouched low, waiting for something to happen. Still not a sound broke the trance-like calm. Nothing moved, he thought, or he must have heard it. But the very absence of sound charged the air with a tense expectancy.

How to break it, for a moment or two he did not know. Then he remembered that the hut, like the rest, was fitted with electric light. He recalled, too, that an electric light switch is usually to be found just inside a door, on the side that swings open, to allow easy access to it. The idea of switching on the light horrified him, but he could think of nothing else to do. He would at least know the worst. He *had* to see. This staring into a blank wall of darkness was not to be endured any longer. His left hand went out, groping for the switch. His questing fingers found it. They closed over the button. Edging away until he was at arm's length he held his breath, depressed the switch and jumped sideways.

Almost simultaneously with the click came the flash and crash of a firearm, and a bullet smashed into the woodwork just below the switch. In a split second he had fired back at a man, an elderly man, who stood within three paces of him, a man who he realised must have been there all the time, unless he, too, had been creeping towards the switch.

Ginger, dazed by the sudden light and the roar of the explosion, was not conscious of firing, much less of taking aim. Moving under the impulse of self-preservation his automatic had seemed to jerk up and go off. Sparks leapt between him and the man. The man hardly moved. He seemed to be making a tremendous effort to raise again the revolver he was holding. It went off, to rip a long splinter out of the floor. Then he seemed to crumple at the legs. The revolver fell with a hollow thud. Coughing, the man slumped across it and lay still.

For several seconds Ginger could only stare with eyes round with horror, feeling sure that he had killed one of the men he had come to rescue. Then they went up, and he took in the scene at a glance. Only one thing interested him. In the background, paralysed it seemed by what had happened, stood a group of men – five of them, all bearded. They stared at him. He stared back.

With an effort he found his voice. 'Which of you is Vale?' he asked shakily.

One of the men stepped forward. 'I'm Vale.'

Ginger pointed at the man on the floor. 'Who's this?'

'We thought he was one of us, but he was a traitor. His name was Luntz.'

Ginger drew a deep breath. 'Thank God,' he said fervently. Then the full realisation of where he was and what he was doing swept over him. 'Come on,' he said tersely. 'No time for talking now. Those shots will set things buzzing. Round to the pantry and get into your shoes. The door's unlocked. Look lively.'

There was a swift move towards the door.

Ginger was not conscious of firing.

'What about the sentries?' asked Vale.

'They're locked in their hut,' answered Ginger, thankful now that he had taken this precaution. 'I'll take care of them if they get out. Get cracking.'

The prisoners ran out.

Ginger went out last, switching off the light and closing the door behind him. He did not trouble to lock it. That the shots had been heard by the sentries was evident, for from within their hut came a clamour. One was beating on the door with what sounded like a rifle-butt. It did no good, for the hut was built of stout timber.

Ginger, with his nerves now under control, walked on to the angle of the prison hut, from where he could still watch the guard-room and at the same time be near his men. Naturally, he was in a fever of impatience, for time now was everything. Minutes passed. The uproar inside the guardroom continued, but as no one else had appeared on the scene he began to hope that the shots, muffled as they would be by the thick wooden walls of the building, had passed unnoticed. Still, he fidgeted in his anxiety to be away. The scientists seemed to be a long time finding their shoes and getting them on, although he made allowance for the fact that there was bound to be some confusion in the darkness.

He was still waiting, keeping watch, when three men appeared running along the outside of the wire, obviously bound for the guard hut. At first he decided that they must have heard the shots, but then, remembering what von Stalhein had said about doubling all guards, he thought that these might be the new men who, hearing the noise in the hut, were coming along at a run to see what was happening. They would not be able to get in, but even so those inside would soon tell them how they were fixed, and about the shots that had been fired. The newcomers would assume that the door of the prison hut was locked, with the keys in the guardroom;

but that would not prevent them from coming in the enclosure to make sure. In any case, he dare wait no longer, so turning to where some of his men were standing, apparently ready to move off, he asked them if they were all set to travel.

Vale answered. 'We're waiting for Major Cardwell,' he reported.

'Who's he?'

'The American.'

'What's the matter – can't he find his shoes?'

'Yes, he's got them on,' replied Vale. 'He's gone over to the work-shop for something.'

'For what?' demanded Ginger angrily.

'I don't know – he didn't say.'

Ginger swallowed hard, trying to control his impatience at this delay. 'He must be crazy,' he muttered. 'He's risking the whole show. If he isn't here in ten seconds I'm going without him. A new bunch of guards has just arrived.'

He ran back to the corner and peeped round; and he was not surprised to see the three new guards running across the enclosure towards the door of the prison hut – much too close to be comfort-able. Without stopping they went inside. Again acting on the spur of the moment he dashed along, and just as the light was switched on reached the door. He caught a fleeting glimpse of the three Mongolians standing just inside regarding with flat, bovine faces, the man who had been shot. They saw him, too, but he moved first. He slammed the door, locked it, and leapt aside just as a bullet crashed through the woodwork. Flinging aside the now useless keys he tore back to the end of the hut just as Major Cardwell reappeared.

'Come on,' he snapped. 'You've kept everyone waiting.'

'Sorry, son,' replied the officer blandly.

'You will be if we're not soon out of this,' retorted Ginger grimly, and taking the lead ran for the gap in the fence which Biggles had made on the occasion of their earlier visit. He went on to the nearest trees for cover.

Now, haste to leave the camp did not mean that Ginger could leave it at any point. In order to get his bearings, in order to find the trail that led to the lignite workings, he would have to leave by the way he came in; otherwise, as he realised well enough, he would be hopelessly lost in the wilderness of marshes. The slave compound was, therefore, his first landmark. This would give him his direction, and towards it he now led the party. Knowing that guards would be on duty at the gate he kept well clear of it; but prompted by another idea, in the hope of causing as much mischief and confusion as possible, he paused long enough to cut a broad gap in the wire, which would, at least, he thought, give the wretched Koreans a chance to get clear if they were so minded. Knowing the country, they would have a fair chance of getting away. As a matter of detail, a number of them, roused possibly by the shots, were standing about. With an astonishment that can only be surmised they watched him cut the wire.

It took him some minutes to find the rough track that led to the lignite bed – or rather, to confirm that he was heading in that direction. Having satisfied himself that this was so he hurried on. In the gloom he could dimly see figures moving about, but for the most part they seemed to be as busy as he was, making for the area he had just left, attracted, no doubt, by the commotion now going on there.

Once clear of the camp he broke into a trot, a speed that he maintained for some distance; indeed, until some of his party, who could hardly be expected to be fit after what they had endured, began to straggle. He steadied the pace to a walk to allow them to catch up. It struck him as odd, that after all that had happened, he had still only caught a brief glimpse of the faces of his companions. The only one that he could recognise was Vale.

All that they needed now, he mused, as he trudged on, was to find Biggles waiting for them beside the path. Not that he seriously expected this. It would not have occurred to Biggles that he, Ginger, could have succeeded in his task in less than an hour, which was roughly the time that had elapsed since they had parted company. It was far more likely that Biggles would still be holding up von Stalhein, supposing Vale to be busy sawing through his prison bars. Ginger hated the idea of leaving Biggles in the enemy camp; but his orders were clear, so there was nothing he could do about it.

After about three miles had been covered, and he could hear no sounds of pursuit, he called a halt to give the party a breather. He himself was deadly tired. The pause would, moreover, give Biggles a chance to overtake them. His greatest fear was that Biggles, before starting for home, would reconnoitre the prison quarters to make sure that the scientists were away. Still, he reasoned, with what was going on in the camp it should not take him long to do that.

He took the opportunity of introducing himself to the rest of the party and then gave them an idea of the general situation. The news that a plane was waiting at no great distance to take them home, should, he felt, be a tonic to help them over the rest of the march. As a matter of fact, justifiably, it must be admitted, he was feeling rather pleased with himself for the way he had managed to effect the escape of the prisoners in so short a time, by employing methods which were up to Biggles' own standards.

He turned to Vale. 'By the way, who was that man I shot?' he inquired. 'I'm still not quite clear as to who he was or why he was there. I couldn't understand why you weren't working with the file.'

'His name was said to be Luntz,' answered Vale.

Luntz. Now that he was able to think the name rang a bell in Ginger's memory. Luntz was the man named by von Stalhein at the general meeting; but he could not remember in what connection.

'Luntz was a spy,' explained Vale. 'We didn't know it. He was put in with us as if he was a prisoner like the rest of us. That's what he told us. He said he was a Pole; a research chemist by profession. He had been kidnapped in Warsaw. We believed him, having no reason to doubt his story. It's an old trick, and when I realised it I could have kicked myself for not suspecting something of the sort. He was simply a stooge, to report everything we said and did. No doubt it was through him that poor Gorton was caught whilst trying to escape, and so lost his life. You need have no qualms about what you did. Given the opportunity I would have shot the skunk myself. He had to reveal himself when I told everyone that you and your friends were here to get us away. I was just about to start work on the bottom bar when, with everyone agog with excitement, Luntz calmly covered me with a revolver and took the file away from me. He then stunned everyone by declaring who he really was. Even so, he was in rather an awkward position, because to give colour to his story he had lived with us, and was locked in with us every night. He couldn't get out any more than we could, so had you not come back he would have had to wait until the morning, when the door would have been unlocked in the usual way. No one else had a weapon of any sort, so there was nothing we could do. We were searched every night. So was Luntz, but the guards, of course, were in the know, and they left him his revolver.'

'I wonder he didn't fire a shot, or kick up a row, to bring the guards in,' murmured Ginger.

'I wondered that, too, but apparently he had a better idea – or thought he had. He knew you were coming back for us, because I had said so; so what he did was drive us into a corner and then take up a position at the window to shoot you the moment you appeared. Had he kicked up a row to bring the guards along you would have heard it, too, and kept clear. But that's only surmise. As a matter of fact his plan wouldn't have succeeded because I, too, was listening; and it was my intention, as soon as I heard you coming, to shout a warning. As it happened I didn't hear a sound. Did you come to the window?'

'I did,' replied Ginger. 'But by the time I got to it I had an uncomfortable feeling that something was wrong because I couldn't hear your file going. That was why I didn't show myself. I'd already got the key of the hut so I decided to come in through the door to find out what was happening. Lucky thing I did.'

Vale resumed. 'Luntz heard the door open. So did I, if it comes to that, but of course, I had no idea who it was. It didn't occur to me that you might have got the key, so I waited for the light to come on. Luntz must have done the same. He wouldn't dare shoot until he knew who he was shooting at in case it turned out to be one of his friends making a surprise visit – as has happened on more than one occasion. Luntz was pretty quick on the trigger when you switched on, but it happened that you weren't where he expected to see you, and you got your shot in before he could shoot again. That's about all. You know the rest.'

'I see,' said Ginger thoughtfully: 'Well, I suppose we'd better keep going. I was hoping Bigglesworth would overtake us. He's still in the camp somewhere. We were cutting things a bit fine at the finish.' He turned to the American officer who had caused the delay at the crucial moment. 'By the way,' he went on, 'I'm sorry I spoke sharply to you, but what on earth induced you to waste time going to the workshop? You nearly gave me a nervous breakdown. I'd had a pretty hectic night, one way and another.'

The American smiled. 'I thought I'd leave the rats a parting gift to remember us by – to teach them to think twice in future before manhandling an American citizen.'

'Gift?' echoed Ginger. 'What sort of gift?'

'Oh, just a little squib.'

Ginger frowned. 'Squib? What are you talking about? Please speak plainly because I'm in a hurry. I'm also very tired.'

When the American answered his tone was serious. 'There was stuff in that shed that must have been stolen from United States workshops – plans and specifications of some of our latest jobs. When I saw them I decided that it was my duty to destroy them at the first opportunity, even if it meant blotting myself out at the same time. I've been working on the idea. You see, I'm a high-explosive specialist, as well as an atomic engineer – which is why they dragged me in, no doubt. Tonight was the chance I've been waiting for, so I took it.'

Ginger spoke slowly. 'Do you mean – you put a bomb – in that hut?'

'And how, sonny.'

Ginger's legs went weak, for he could imagine what sort of a bomb an atomic expert would make. 'When is this bomb due to go off?' he asked in a strained voice.

'It isn't timed. It's wired to the electric circuit. The first guy to switch on the light in that workshop will never know what happened to him. Neither will anyone else near that enclosure. Why, what's wrong? Don't you like the idea?'

Ginger bit his lip. 'I'd like it well enough, as a means of destroying the enemy's work, were it not for one thing,' he answered wearily.

'What's that?'

'My chief is still in that camp. If I know him, he's quite likely to go to the prison enclosure to make sure that we got away before he leaves the camp himself.'

There was a brief silence.

'Well now, I guess that's just too bad,' said the American.

'There's no need to guess,' muttered Ginger bitterly, sick at this new anxiety that had been thrust upon him. 'It's worse than that.'

'I wasn't to know,' said the American contritely.

'Of course you weren't,' agreed Ginger readily. 'But that doesn't help matters. No doubt you acted for the best, but you might have told me what you were going to do, instead of—'

He got no further. From the direction of the camp a weird blue flame leapt up, it seemed, to heaven itself, flooding the world with a ghastly glare that turned the faces of the escaped prisoners to chalk-white masks. As the glow faded the thunder of the explosion rolled across the sullen landscape.

'I guess that's it,' said the American quietly.

CHAPTER XIII

Biggles Plays for Time

When Biggles made his dramatic entry into von Stalhein's room there was a silence that lasted for several seconds. Von Stalhein did not move. Imperturbable, and as immaculate as if he had been in the Wilhelmstrasse, from the cane chair in which he sat, a little to one side of a writing table, he regarded Biggles through eyes that were coldly hostile and gave the lie to the sardonic smile that twisted the corners of his thin-lipped mouth. A spiral of pale blue cigarette smoke coiled towards the ceiling from the cigarette held in its usual long holder. There was no indication of shock that must have resulted from Biggles' entrance. As for Petroffsky, he merely stared owlishly as if his befuddled faculties were unable to cope with the situation.

Von Stalhein spoke first. His voice was pitched low, but it was as sour as vinegar. Said he: 'You know, Bigglesworth, you'll do this sort of thing once too often.'

Biggles nodded slightly. 'I think it's quite likely,' he agreed. 'But this, I hope, will not be the occasion.' Actually, he had nothing to say, the object of his intrusion being merely to kill time, to keep von Stalhein in his room and prevent him from questioning the Russian.

At this juncture Petroffsky apparently recognised him, for he let out a howl of greeting. 'Have a drink,' he invited thickly, reaching for the bottle that stood on the table.

'You'd be well advised to sit still and keep quiet,' Biggles told him curtly.

The Cossack, looking abashed, sank back, blinking as he strove to grasp the purport of the words. 'Wha's the matter?' he demanded. 'Thought we were all good friends together.'

'You never made a bigger mistake,' returned Biggles grimly. 'Don't talk. Put a curb on your tongue and keep it still before these people take hold of it and pull it out.'

'But me—' spluttered Petroffsky, looking outraged. 'I'm a tiger hunter—'

'I know, but tiger hunting is child's play compared with the game you're playing now. Sober up, man, and try to get this into your head. When this gentleman has finished with you what's left will be food for foxes. If you want to leave this place alive you'd better pull yourself together and get out while the going's good.' Biggles turned sharply to von Stalhein who had edged a little nearer to his desk. 'All right, that's enough of that,' he snapped.

'Your nerve isn't what it used to be,' sneered von Stalhein. 'I was merely trying to reach a cigarette from the box on my desk.'

'Go ahead,' invited Biggles.

Smiling cynically, von Stalhein took a cigarette and fitted it carefully into his holder. 'Did you want to speak to me about something?' he inquired.

'Not particularly,' Biggles told him frankly.

'In that case, as I have nothing to say to you, why not terminate an interview, which, as far as I'm concerned, is becoming tiresome.'

'I can well believe it,' replied Biggles evenly. 'I'll decide when I've had enough of your company.'

'And that's all you have to say?'

'All, except that I see you're at your old games again.'

The German blew a smoke ring. 'And so, apparently, are you.'

'It looks as if I shall have to be while people like you are on the loose,' Biggles told him. 'But let us not waste time discussing what we are doing. We both know. On this occasion I've nothing against you, personally. As far as I'm concerned you can stay here until you fall apart from malaria; or if the mosquitoes don't like the taste of you, until your precious associates decide that you've failed in your job, when, having no further use for you no doubt they'll dispose of you in their own fashion. That's your affair.'

'Purely as a matter of detail, what's yours?'

'You should know. I'm going to remove from this unhealthy dump certain people who were brought here by force.'

Von Stalhein exhaled slowly. 'You may find that difficult.'

'Most things I'm asked to do are difficult otherwise it's unlikely that I should be asked to do them,' replied Biggles coldly.

'Aren't you getting rather tired of being given the run-around by a bunch of inefficient politicians?' sneered von Stalhein.

'They're not so inefficient that they can't keep people like you on the trot.'

'Did you come here to tell me that?'

'No. I just drifted in to make sure that you don't hinder me from doing what I came here to do. To a lesser extent I aim to get this harmless hermit out of your camp with a tongue still in his mouth.'

'You won't do that by sitting here.'

'That,' said Biggles smoothly, 'remains to be seen.'

'My batman is in the kitchen.'

'I know it. Pray hard that he stays there, because if we're interrupted I may have to pull the trigger of this gun, which might easily be pointing in your direction.'

'Why don't you pull it now?' scoffed von Stalhein. 'Were I in your position I wouldn't hesitate.'

'I can believe that,' murmured Biggles. 'Maybe that's why I don't. Call it vanity if you like, but I try to be different from people like you.'

Petroffsky, who from his expression had been trying to collect his faculties, intervened. 'Gentlemen – gentlemen,' he protested. 'If this is a quarrel let it be settled in an honourable way. I will see fair play. How about a little drink?'

'Help yourself,' invited Biggles. 'It's likely to be your last. How much have you told this man?'

'Not a word,' declared Petroffsky. 'By St Mark, not a word. I came here looking for my old friend Mayne. You said he was with you.'

'He was,' answered Biggles, 'but he isn't here now.'

'What shall I do?'

'Go home and stay there.'

The Russian looked pained. 'What have I done?' he cried wonderingly.

'You've blundered into something from which you may not find it easy to get out,' Biggles told him. 'These are the men who flogged your Koreans and cut off your vodka supply. They'll be flogging you before you know where you are.'

Petroffsky's eyes opened wide. 'I fear no man!' he cried. 'I am Alexis Petroffsky, Colonel of the Imperial Guard, the greatest killer of tigers—'

'I know – I know,' broke in Biggles impatiently. 'You've told us that before. Pull yourself together and go home while you have the chance. I shan't be here much longer.'

Von Stalhein spoke again. 'Who is this man Mayne he keeps talking about?' he inquired. 'The name is new to me.'

'I didn't come here to answer questions,' replied Biggles. He smiled faintly. 'But I'll answer that one if you'll answer one for me.'

'Try it.'

'Who's the big noise behind this racket?'

'I've often wondered that myself.'

'Are you telling me you don't know?'

'I am. It's the top secret here.'

'Then what's your angle?'

'Money. Besides, it's something to do until the next war starts. That goes for both of us, I imagine?'

Biggles shook his head sadly. 'So you're still hoping to find yourself in a victory march? Forget it. You never will.'

'Why not?'

'Because people like you will always be on the losing side, and if you haven't the wit to see why, it would be useless for me to tell you.'

Von Stalhein's lips curled. 'Are you trying to reform me with this righteous philosophy?'

'It isn't philosophy, it's a matter of common sense. But let it pass. I couldn't care less,' said Biggles curtly.

Von Stalhein looked at his watch. 'How much longer do I have to endure this?'

'Until this misguided Cossack has sobered up enough to start for home.'

'I shall stay here,' declared Petroffsky, who, as is so often the case with people recovering from the effects of alcohol, was getting aggressive.

'Please yourself,' replied Biggles without emotion. 'Remember, though, this is the crowd that flogged your Korean vodka carriers. When I go they'll flog you, too. I know I've said that before, but this is the last time I shall warn you.'

'Flog me?' Petroffsky looked shocked.

'Yes, you,' answered Biggles, wondering how Ginger was getting on. For all this talk, from which he had little to gain, was merely to kill time, to give Ginger as long as possible to do his work and get clear. He had reckoned that this might take two hours, so he was prepared to remain where he was for some time yet, should nothing occur to prevent it.

Von Stalhein moved, quite casually, a little nearer to his writing table.

Biggles looked at him. 'Listen, von Stalhein,' he said quietly. 'If you're trying to get to the gun which I suspect you keep in a drawer of that table, give up. I don't want to have to shoot you, but I shan't hesitate to do so if it becomes the alternative to you shooting me.' He turned to Petroffsky. 'Are you going home or are you going to stay here? Make up your mind. You came here bawling for Mayne. He isn't here, so try looking somewhere else. Your job is killing tigers. Trundle along and bag a brace for your old friend Mayne, just to show him that you can still do it.'

'Yes!' cried the Cossack. 'Yes, by St Peter! That's right. I'm the greatest slayer of tigers—'

'Everyone knows it,' asserted Biggles. 'Go ahead and slay some more before you lose your reputation.'

The Russian rose unsteadily to his feet and reached for the vodka bottle.

'Come – come, Colonel,' murmured Biggles reproachfully. 'Surely you're not going to abuse your host's hospitality?'

Petroffsky straightened himself. 'As if I would do such a thing!' he cried haughtily. He walked stiffly to the door, turned and bowed low. 'Good night, gentlemen,' he said, and went out.

Without taking his eyes from von Stalhein Biggles lit a cigarette.

The German considered him stonily. 'I'm beginning to find your company irksome,' he complained icily.

'I can well believe it,' acknowledged Biggles calmly, 'but I'm afraid you'll have to suffer it for a little while longer. You'll appreciate that if I could choose *my* company you wouldn't be in it,' he added.

Thereafter for some minutes they sat in silence, Biggles smoking as if nothing unusual was happening, von Stalhein slightly pale from vexation, his lips pressed together in a straight line. The camp seemed to have settled down, which suited Biggles well enough. But presently came sounds which suggested that the situation in von Stalhein's room was drawing to its conclusion. First, muffled as if by distance, came two shots in quick succession followed by a third.

The muscles of von Stalhein's face relaxed in a sour smile. 'Your Russian friend didn't get far,' he conjectured.

Biggles thought there might be something in this. What he was more afraid of was that the shots had been fired on Ginger's account, for from the speed of the first two he felt sure that two weapons had been involved; and the Russian had no weapon; his rifle, which apparently he had forgotten, was leaning against the wall in the corner behind von Stalhein. At any rate, thought Biggles swiftly, Ginger would still be in the camp, for the simple reason that Vale could not yet have cut through the barred window. It looked, therefore, as if Ginger had been discovered. He could think of no other reason for the shots. However, his face remained expressionless.

But now, from some way off came a banging and bumping that puzzled him not a little. He thought he could hear shouting, too. These noises soon mounted to what sounded unpleasantly like a hue and cry, but as no amount of conjecture would be likely to reveal the cause, Biggles could only sit still and await the explanation which, he was sure, would not long be withheld.

It arrived even sooner than he expected. From outside there came a rush of footsteps, and into the room, in a whirlwind of agitation, burst a pale-faced little man of middle age, dressed in dark civilian clothes, whose nationality might have been anything although he was almost certainly a European. Ignoring Biggles he leaned towards von Stalhein, and speaking in German, rapped out: 'The prisoners have escaped! The hut is empty. Luntz is shot – dying.' Then, appearing to notice Biggles for the first time he added sharply: 'Who is this?'

Biggles was already moving. He backed to the wall near the door. His pistol covered the newcomer but his eyes flashed frequently to von Stalhein. Speaking in the same language he said, in a hard voice: 'Stand where you are and keep your hands where I can see them.'

Expressions of surprise and consternation followed each other across the face of the new man. He looked from Biggles to von Stalhein, back to Biggles and again to von Stalhein. 'What is this?' he asked wonderingly.

'I'll leave you to tell him, von Stalhein,' put in Biggles crisply, moving to the door. He had already noted that the key was on the inside. With his left hand he took it out and put it in the outside. 'Don't be in a hurry to follow me or you may meet a piece of metal coming the other way,' he warned, and with that he slipped out, closed the door and turned the key. He caught a fleeting glimpse of a white-aproned, moon-faced Mongol staring at him from the kitchen door, a tea tray held in both hands; but paying no attention to him he went out into the darkness.

He had but a vague idea of what he was going to do, being chiefly concerned until this juncture with getting clear of von Stalhein. All he knew was that the prisoners had escaped and that a man named Luntz had been shot. How Ginger had managed to get the prisoners out in so short a time – for he was quite sure that Ginger must have had a hand in it – he could not imagine. Not that it mattered how it had been done. The fact that they were away was all that concerned him now. He wondered how far they had got. Were they still somewhere in the camp?

That there had been shooting practically proved that Ginger was with them, for the scientists would not be likely to possess a weapon between them. Just when they had gone he had, of course, no means of knowing. The alarm had obviously been given. Lights were on all over the place, and in their downcast rays he could see men moving about, Mongols chiefly, most of them hurrying in the direction of the prison hut enclosure. Their big brutal leader was with them, screaming orders. He also noticed a number of Koreans running about like frightened sheep; but these for the most part were making for the outskirts of the camp. One thing with another, it was not easy to determine exactly what was happening.

What Biggles really wanted to know was whether or not Ginger was still within the precincts of the camp. Deciding that there was only one way to find out he hurried on towards the centre of the excitement, feeling that with so many Koreans running about loose no particular attention would be paid to him. In the general uproar he would, he thought, be able to retire from the scene should that course become advisable.

Nevertheless, what he was doing was attended by a certain amount of danger, for an occasional shot was now being fired by the Mongolians at the Koreans, who were now streaming away from the camp in ever-increasing numbers. It was evident that the slaves had managed somehow to get out of their compound and were making the most of the opportunity to get away.

While from one angle this was an advantage, in that it added to the general confusion, it raised this difficulty: Ginger himself was dressed as a Korean, so recognition would only be possible from close quarters. However, Biggles resolved to make a quick reconnaissance of the area round the prison hut, and if from this he could satisfy himself that the prisoners had got clean away he, too, would leave the camp.

With this object in view, keeping as far as possible in the background, he worked his way towards the prison hut. Perceiving that, as most of the Mongolians were also converging on it, it would not be prudent to approach from the front, he made his way to the wire in the rear and followed it along until he reached the gap which he himself had made. He now had the hut between him and the crowd that had assembled either in the front or inside the building – he was not sure which; so without running any great risks he dashed across to the window at which he had spoken to Vale. But before he got half-way, as the light was on inside, he saw something that amazed him – the silhouettes of the iron bars, which were obviously still intact. Stepping back a pace or two he saw that the bars of all the windows were still in place. How, then, had the prisoners got out? There could only be one answer to that. They had gone through the door. How this had been achieved he could not think – not that he wasted time trying. He glanced across at the big hut which Vale had said was the workshop. It was conveniently close so he dashed across to the back of it with the intention of making his way round the far end to the front, thinking that from there he would get a good view of the front of the prison hut, which might yield important information. Whether it did or not, he would then carry straight on and get out of the camp, having made a complete circle round the centre of it. If he saw nothing of Ginger it would be fairly safe to conclude that he had got clear.

He reached his objective without trouble, and looking round the end of the workshop saw a considerable number of people collected in the enclosure near the door of the prison hut. They were in two groups. There were Mongolians, dominated by their leader, who was apparently waiting for orders from a smaller number of Europeans who stood, apparently holding a conference, near at hand. Of Ginger or the scientists there was no sign, and as this was all Biggles wanted to know he began to back away, having no further reason to stay. Reaching the wire he paused for a moment to watch two men, two of the Europeans, who had detached themselves from the main party and were walking quickly towards the workshop. He wondered what they were going to do. As they went in through the door he turned away towards the nearest trees; but before he had taken a dozen paces the world seemed to explode around him.

For several seconds, or it may have been minutes, he was conscious of the blinding flash only. Nothing more. With the roar filling his ears like a clap of thunder he was hurled by the blast for some distance before colliding violently with the ground. And there he lay, dazed, with the breath knocked out of his body, striving to get his brain under control.

His first really conscious impression was a terrifying one. He thought he had been blinded. He could see nothing beyond a blur of intense blue that spun before his eyes. Nor, after the clatter of falling debris had died away, could he hear a sound. Over the camp – indeed, over the whole world – hung a deathly calm, as if all movement had been suspended. This reaction to the explosion, a common one, did not last long. When true consciousness slowly returned he found himself sitting up. Things around him began to take shape. His brain began to function normally and he realised that there had been a tremendous explosion; but even so, he was by no means certain of where it had occurred, or where he was. The scene had changed. When, somewhat unsteadily, he stood up, he understood why. All the electric lights had gone out, as was only to be expected; but some slight illumination came from a patch of grass that had caught fire. The workshop had disappeared entirely. The prison hut was a flattened heap of timber. The guard hut was leaning at a drunken angle. Some men were crawling out of it. Others were lying about. A few were sitting. One or two were standing, or backing away from the spot as if afraid that the explosion might be repeated.

It was now fairly evident that the explosion had occurred in the workshop, but how it had happened, or who had caused it he had, of course, no means of knowing. He could only hope that Ginger had not been inside – that he had not been responsible for it. Anyway, there seemed to be no point in remaining where he was so he started to move away with the intention of getting out of the camp while those in it were still under the spell of the disaster. Suddenly he became aware that something was missing. He had lost something; and it was several seconds before he could discover what it was. His pistol. He recalled that he had been carrying it in his hand when the explosion had occurred. It was not in his hand now, so he could only conclude that it had been wrenched out of his hand by the blast or else he had dropped it when he had fallen. He spent a minute looking for it – or rather, groping about in the grass hoping to come upon it. But in this he was unsuccessful, and being disinclined to waste any more time decided that he would have to go without it.

Unfortunately, at this juncture, a number of Mongols who had been standing at a distance began moving towards him. Naturally, he altered his direction to avoid them. But when one of them shouted he knew that he had been noticed. All he could do was walk on, pretending that he had not heard. Ming, the Mongolian leader, now appeared on the scene, and he, too, shouted. Biggles, seeing that the situation was becoming serious, started to run, thinking that if he could reach some nearby trees he would be able to slip away. In attempting to do this he collided with a tangle of barbed wire fencing that had evidently been blown out of the ground by the explosion. He tripped and fell. Before he could extricate himself rough hands were laid on him and he was hauled to his feet to a barrage of abuse. For a moment or two he was afraid that he was going to be severely manhandled, for the men were in an ugly mood; and not having a weapon of any sort there was little he could do to prevent it. But by this time the affair had attracted the attention of a small party of Europeans who had just arrived, and they came nearer as if to ascertain what was going on. Biggles recognised von Stalhein before he himself was recognised, and tried to hide his face. But he was too late.

Von Stalhein took a quick pace forward, peering. 'Ach so!' he said in a voice that revealed the extent of his satisfaction. 'This *is* a pleasure.'

'If it is,' replied Biggles evenly, 'it's all yours.'

CHAPTER XIV

Bertie Takes a Turn

Meanwhile, following the explosion, Ginger, more than a little worried, had led his tired party on to the hide-out where Bertie and Mayne were waiting. Twice during the march they had been overtaken by escaping Koreans or Orochons. They had stood aside to let them pass. Otherwise, there had been no incident of any sort.

Bertie, of course, was delighted to see the party, for he assumed, naturally, that the expedition had been entirely successful; but his expression changed when Ginger expressed his fears for Biggles' safety. Bertie had heard the explosion, and, as he said, supposed it to have been caused by Biggles who had decided to liquidate the enemy camp.

Ginger, sitting with his back to a tree while Bertie brewed tea, ran over his earlier adventures with Biggles, and narrated his own from the time they had parted company. 'If Petroffsky hasn't come this way then he must also be in the enemy camp somewhere,' he concluded. 'Of course, he may have stayed with Biggles, but I don't think that's likely. I'm pretty sure Biggles would try to get rid of him. The fellow was as drunk as an owl and would only be in the way. Biggles was pretty browned off with him when he left me.'

'If Petroffsky was tight he might have lost himself in the beastly bogs,' opined Bertie, handing out mugs of tea.

'Personally, I couldn't care less,' asserted Ginger.

'The point is, old boy, what do we do next – if you get my meaning?' inquired Bertie. 'Do we wait here, or do we toddle along, or what do we do?'

'It isn't much use wasting time here if Biggles is in a jam back in the camp,' answered Ginger. 'I think somebody ought to go and see what's happened to him. I hoped he'd overtake us; and I think he would have done had he started soon after the explosion, which must have made a mess of things and caused a general flap. If someone does go back the chances are that he'll meet Biggles, in which case so well and good. I'd go myself, but to tell the truth I'm dead on my feet. I don't think I could do it.'

'What would Biggles say about it, I wonder?' murmured Bertie.

'I can tell you that right away,' returned Ginger. 'His orders were that the party was to make straight for the aircraft.'

'Well, Mayne could take the crowd along. He knows the way,' averred Bertie. 'If you like I'll toddle back to the camp to see what's cooking there. I know the direction. I'm browned off with sitting here, having my hide perforated by mosquitoes, flies, ticks, beetles, and what have you. Let Mayne take the party to the aircraft. You curl up here and have a snooze. I'll go back. Biggles will find you if we miss each other in the dark. How does that sound to you?'

'I can't think of anything better,' agreed Ginger.

'Good enough; then let's get it organised,' said Bertie. 'Is the idea okay with you, Mayne?'

Mayne, who had been listening to the conversation, answered that it was. He could find his way back without difficulty. Moreover he could speak the local language should his party have trouble with the refugee slaves.

And so it was decided. Mayne set off with the scientists, saying that the others would find him waiting when they got back to the island.

Ginger gave Bertie directions for finding the lignite diggings, after which he should be able easily to follow the slave trail to the camp. 'Keep on the track,' he urged, as Bertie set off, 'otherwise you may miss Biggles in the dark.'

As soon as he was alone he stretched himself on the ground with a sigh of relief and settled down to wait.

Bertie trudged along quite happily towards the scene of the recent explosion. As he had remarked, after hanging about all day, a prey to the voracious insects, he was glad to have something to do. He met several Koreans, alone or in bands, but he took no notice of them. They ignored him, no doubt taking him to be one of themselves.

But when he had gone some distance he was not a little astonished to hear a man singing. The sound came from ahead. He stopped to listen, and soon observed that the singer was coming towards him. What song the man sang he did not know, for the tune had a strange haunting lilt, and the words were in a language unknown to him. But that it was no tongueless Korean was evident.

Presently the singer could be seen in the soft moonlight, and it was the fact that he swayed slightly as he walked that provided Bertie with a clue to his identity. Being concerned only with Biggles he had forgotten all about Petroffsky. Now, as the distance between them closed, the style of his dress was certain confirmation, for Biggles had described the man after their first meeting.

Bertie now made a blunder; at least, he thought so for a time. He revealed himself, thinking that the Russian might be able to tell him something about Biggles. He might even know his present whereabouts, for according to Ginger's narrative the two had recently been together.

'What-ho, old Muscovite warrior!' he hailed cheerfully.

Petroffsky's song ended abruptly. 'Who speaks?' he demanded suspiciously.

'A friend of Bigglesworth and your old pal Mayne,' replied Bertie, still walking on.

'A friend of Bigglesworth is a friend of Alex Petroffsky,' swore the Russian. 'Have you any vodka?'

'Sorry, old boozer, not a tot,' answered Bertie.

'If you were not a friend of Bigglesworth you would be no friend of mine for admitting such a thing,' declared Petroffsky. 'In this country a man who travels without vodka has forfeited his right to live.'

'Absolutely,' agreed Bertie, 'absolutely. But tell me, my merry old toper, where is Bigglesworth?'

'Would I know that?' The Russian seemed surprised.

'But look here, I say, haven't you been with him?'

'Yes. But I have been asleep since then. I was awakened by thunder.'

'You were awakened, old Cossack, by an explosion of no small dimensions,' corrected Bertie. 'Were you near it?'

'Who knows? I might have been. Who blew up what?'

'That,' answered Bertie, 'is a long story, and I've no time to tell it now. So long.'

'But wait! Where are you going?'

'To find Bigglesworth.'

'I will come with you,' declared Petroffsky.

'Don't trouble, old warbler. I can manage,' said Bertie quickly, perceiving suddenly that this encounter was likely to have embarrassing consequences.

'No – no. Back I must go,' said the Russian. 'I have just remembered, those sons of swine took my rifle, my favourite tiger slayer. I will not go without it.'

'All right,' agreed Bertie reluctantly. 'But if you come with me, you know, you'll have to cut out the crooning. Tell me, where did you last see Bigglesworth?'

'In the house of a gentleman named von Stalhein. An amiable fellow, although your friend seemed to think he was a rascal; but at least he offered me hospitality.'

'Ah! He toted the old vodka bottle, I suppose?'

'Freely.'

'Don't flatter yourself that it was out of the goodness of his heart or because he admired your noble countenance,' asserted Bertie. 'Nor was it to tickle your palate, my jolly old shikaree. It was merely to lubricate your vocal system.'

'Could a man be so base?' questioned Petroffsky, looking aghast.

'Von Stalhein's methods are so low that no one has yet got to the bottom of them – if you see what I mean?' declared Bertie cheerfully. 'But how long is it since this display of conviviality occurred?'

The Russian shrugged. 'A short time ago. Or perhaps a long time. I'm not altogether clear about it.'

'Did you leave Bigglesworth there?'

'He sent me home,' replied Petroffsky sadly. 'I remember starting, but soon after something must have happened. Perhaps I fell asleep. Who knows? But does it matter? Let us go back. You shall find the gallant Bigglesworth and I will find my rifle.'

'Good enough, old soaker,' agreed Bertie, but without enthusiasm, for he had an uneasy suspicion that his companion was more likely to be a hindrance than a helper.

This became a conviction when, as they walked along, Petroffsky kept up a running fire of talk in a voice so loud that anything like the cautious approach he had planned had to be abandoned. They met more Koreans and Orochons who, for the most part, darted into the rushes at the sight of them. Bertie observed that it looked as if all the slaves were out and running wild. Petroffsky professed complete indifference.

As they approached the precincts of the camp more signs of disorder became apparent. At one place the dry grass was on fire, and while the flames bathed the scene in a lurid light a belt of drifting smoke made it difficult to see what was going on behind it. Men were there trying to extinguish the fire. They appeared mostly to be Mongols, although there were a few Koreans with them. A dead Korean was lying in the grass. Petroffsky said he must have been shot trying to escape. He pointed to von Stalhein's house. 'My rifle is there. I shall fetch it,' he announced. 'There is also, unless it has been removed, a bottle in which I am interested,' he added softly.

'You take my tip and keep your elbow straight while we're in this joint,' Bertie told him seriously, as they strode towards the building.

The Russian walked straight in and Bertie followed. Fortunately perhaps for both of them the place had been abandoned. At all events they saw no one. Petroffsky uttered a cry of joy, and patted his rifle affectionately as he collected it from the corner in which it stood. When he turned to the table, however, the bottle was not there, for Bertie had taken the opportunity of slipping it into his pocket. The Russian sighed his disappointment. 'Who shall we put to death first?' he asked casually.

'What's the hurry?' inquired Bertie. 'Do you have to shoot somebody?'

'It would be a good thing to do,' replied Petroffsky seriously. 'To kill a few men always discourages the others. Besides, these

Bolsheviks laid hands on me – me, Alexis Petroffsky – and for that alone they deserve death.'

'Now, you listen to me, my nimble Nimrod,' said Bertie crisply. 'If you're going to start off by pooping at people you'll get us both put to death. If you're going to indulge in a beastly orgy of wholesale slaughter you push along and play by yourself. I came here to find Bigglesworth.'

'Then let us find him first,' suggested Petroffsky. 'When we have done that we might have a little sport with the rifle. How's that?'

'All right, but wait till I'm out of the way,' requested Bertie. 'I shall save my cartridges until I need them.'

'But this rogue who calls himself a prince is nothing but a common deserter,' argued Petroffsky, as they left the building. 'He should not be allowed to live.'

'All I ask, my old sabre-rattler, is that you wait till I'm out of your line of fire,' answered Bertie wearily. He walked on hoping that the Russian would now leave him; but in this he was disappointed. Petroffsky kept pace with him, telling in a loud voice a lurid story of some Chinese deserters.

From a short distance they paused to watch the Mongols who were still striving to beat out the burning grass. No one appeared to notice them, so they walked on, with Bertie beginning to wonder if he was not wasting his time. In the darkness surrounding the fire he could see nothing. He had no idea of the layout of the camp and, as he now realised, he hardly knew what he was looking for. It was unlikely that Biggles would be walking about the camp so the chances of meeting him seemed remote. Presently his companion called attention to a large building that loomed up before them, towards which they had been drawn by a lighted window.

'This is a place of importance,' declared Petroffsky. 'Let us burn it down. A good fire is what we need for accurate shooting.'

Bertie did not answer. He stared at the building, wondering if by any chance this was the prison hut to which Ginger had referred. He was not to know that the prisoners' quarters had been demolished by the explosion; so, really, it was from lack of any definite plan that he walked on for a closer view. Petroffsky remained with him.

As they drew nearer Bertie suddenly caught his companion by the arm as from the open window came the sound of voices. 'Go easy, old sharpshooter,' he ordered. 'What have we here?' Approaching warily, the first thing he saw was an oil lamp standing on a table. This illuminated a scene that brought him to an abrupt halt. A sharp intake of breath expressed his astonishment, and perhaps dismay.

There were some seven or eight men in the room, one or two sitting, but most of them standing. In either case it was clear from their attitudes that a conference of importance was in progress, although there was nothing surprising about this considering the explosion and the effect of it on the camp. But the crux of the situation, Bertie thought, was a figure that sat a little apart from the others, for on him all eyes were turned. It was Biggles. Behind him, a revolver in one hand and his whip in the other, was the gigantic Mongol slavemaster, Ming. Von Stalhein was there, in the group, as was also the man who called himself Prince Ling Soo – at least, so Bertie assumed, from his comic-opera style of Oriental dress. He was speaking fiercely, punctuating his words with the eloquent waving of a formidable dagger. Bertie, of course, did not know what the man was saying, but he had a pretty good idea. If his gestures were an indication, he was advocating the immediate dispatch of the prisoner, the man responsible for the present state of affairs. From time to time one or two of the others present seemed to make some attempt to intervene, but without much success.

How Bertie, had he been alone, would have handled this situation, will never be known. The same may be said of Biggles. Neither had an opportunity of putting into effect any plan that he may have made. Bertie, pistol in hand, was still watching Ling Soo, who was chattering like an enraged ape, when an explosion occurred so close to his head that he thought his ear drums were shattered. As a matter of detail he suffered from the effects of it for a week. Even so, he realised what had happened. Petroffsky had fired his rifle.

Ling Soo's words were cut off short and he crumpled like an empty sack. But even before his body had reached the ground a second shot caused the oil lamp to disintegrate in a shower of glass. The room was plunged into darkness, but from it came such a medley of sounds as might be expected to result from such a situation.

Bertie's first reaction was fury with the Russian for taking matters into his own hands. But the thing was done, so no good purpose could be served by arguing about it now. Ignoring Petroffsky, who was bellowing with what seemed to be singularly ill-timed glee, Bertie tried to get in through the window, only to be knocked backwards by a man who sprang out. Picking himself up, not a little shaken, he saw that it was the big Mongolian. He fired at him from a sitting position, but missed. Ming was taking deliberate aim at him when Petroffsky's rifle came down on his head with a crack that stretched him flat on the ground. By this time others were pouring through the door of the house. Petroffsky, laughing, fired at them with such abandon that Bertie turned on him furiously, for he was afraid that one of these casual shots would hit Biggles. There was obviously a good chance of it. However, at this moment Biggles jumped through the window, and his arrival saved any further argument. Bertie called to him, and would have left the crazy Russian to his own devices, for he was still keeping up a brisk fusillade on the door. Biggles shouted to him to stop it, telling him that it was time to go. Indeed, this was made the more imperative by flames leaping up inside the room, giving more light than was desirable. Moreover, several of the Mongolians who had been trying to put out the grass fire came running towards the scene, attracted by this new commotion.

Said Biggles, tersely, to Bertie: 'Come on. Let's get out of this.' He started to walk away.

Petroffsky, to Bertie's disappointment, followed them, although he sometimes stopped to fight a minor rearguard action on his own account, singing all the while in a rich baritone voice. However, presently he overtook them, and hailed Biggles joyfully. He had an idea. There was bound to be vodka in the camp. It should not take them long to find it.

Biggles told him with scant ceremony that he could stay and drink himself to death if he liked, but he personally was going home.

Bertie silenced the bitter lamentations that broke from Petroffksy's lips at this decision by telling him that he had a bottle in his pocket, which he would give him presently if he would save his ammunition and keep quiet.

Thereafter, for a time, the Russian fell silent.

Biggles took the path that led to the lignite diggings and the others followed in single file.

From the rear, a crimson glow cast its reflection on the sky. As Bertie observed, it looked as if the ambitious Prince had lost his palace as well as his life.

CHAPTER XV

The Battle of Kossuri

Biggles and his small party marched on for some distance. It was not long before the garrulous Cossack, in spite of Bertie's warning, was talking and laughing again, and made such frequent requests for the promised bottle that it was at last given to him as the only possible means of keeping him quiet – at any rate, for a time.

No sounds of pursuit came from the direction of the enemy camp, but Biggles did not attempt to deceive himself. That a punitive expedition would be sent out after them, with orders to recapture or kill them was, he thought, a certainty, for not only had the conspirators lost all their prisoners – European and Asiatic – but the camp, with all the planning, the time and money that must have gone into its establishment, had been virtually destroyed. Ling Soo, the figurehead, and Ming, the slavemaster, had been seriously injured, if not killed. There must have been other casualties, too, for it had been one of the European executives who had switched on the light in the workshop, blowing it, and himself, to pieces. From these disasters the enemy would not easily recover, averred Biggles. Nor would they be likely to forgive those responsible.

As they walked along Biggles told Bertie how he had been

captured. Bertie, in turn, narrated what he knew about the explosion and its cause – a matter in which Biggles was in complete ignorance.

From time to time furtive rustlings and sudden rushes near the track kept the travellers on the alert. It was realised that these noises were probably caused by escaping Koreans or Orochons, but even so, they represented a danger not to be ignored. The native refugees could not be blamed if, after what they had suffered, they took revenge on any Europeans who came their way. In the dark they would be unable to distinguish friend from foe. As Biggles remarked to Bertie, the whole district was now alive with escaping slaves, although what effect this would have on the situation was not clear. When daylight came Mayne and his party would be fairly safe because he could speak the language, and so explain matters to any ex-slaves whom they might encounter. Biggles, fortunately, was similarly placed, with Petroffsky.

The first sounds of pursuit did not occur for a long time, in fact, not until they were nearing the hide-out where they hoped to find Ginger waiting. But the sounds, once heard, approached swiftly. Hoofs pounded in the soft mud; harness jingled, and the travellers had only just enough time to make themselves comfortable in the long grass beside the trail when a company of Mongolian horsemen galloped past in the pale moonlight. Where they were bound for and what they hoped to achieve by moving at such a rate was not evident, but, as Biggles observed when the danger had passed, apparently they had a definite objective in view; otherwise they would hardly be travelling at such a speed.

The little party went on, Petroffsky, now happy, singing softly what he said – when Biggles asked him to desist – was an old Persian love song. Presently, when more horsemen galloped past, it was only with difficulty that he was prevented from shooting at them. Under the influence of vodka it was obviously only a short step from love to hate.

Dawn was staining the eastern sky with pink when they came to Ginger's rendezvous. He was waiting for them, refreshed by some sleep but somewhat stiff from his exertions and from the nip of the sharp morning air. He had nothing to report, except what Biggles already knew, that a number of horsemen were somewhere ahead.

Apart from the fact that enemies were in front of them, in itself a cause for anxiety, Biggles began to wonder if Petroffsky, in his state of maudlin drunkenness, had told von Stalhein more than he admitted, or more than he himself was aware, in the short time they had been alone together in the German's quarters. If he had given away the position of their island base then the speed of the horsemen would be explained, and they could look for plenty of trouble ahead. He was afraid, too, that the riders might have over-taken Mayne and his party before they could get to the island. He questioned Petroffsky on the point, but the Russian insisted that he had said nothing about it. The truth of the matter, as Biggles realised, was this: Petroffsky had no clear recollection of what he had said because at the time his brain had been on fire with the pernicious vodka.

After a short rest and a cold, uninteresting meal, Biggles decided to push on, for the morning air was dank and chilly and there was nothing to be gained by remaining under the dripping trees with their swarms of ravenous insects. Petroffsky wanted to shoot some-thing, in fur or feathers, light a fire and cook it; but Biggles would not hear of it. It was now daylight, and it was obvious to everyone – that is, everyone except Petroffsky – that the remainder of the journey would be attended by considerable danger. As Biggles remarked, it was not so much the mobile horsemen that they had to fear, as sentries who might have been posted on high ground to keep watch over the broad marshes. Such men, if in fact they had been posted – although there was no particular reason for thinking they had – would at once see any movement on the open ground; and an exchange of shots would no doubt bring others to the spot. However, short of waiting for nightfall, a precaution which appealed to nobody, nothing could be done about this. The risk would have to be taken.

So the march continued, the party of four moving in single file with Biggles leading, followed closely by Petroffsky, whose duty it was to indicate the best path and the whereabouts of pitfalls. Biggles told the Russian jokingly that if he made any more noise than was unavoidable he would shoot him without warning and throw him in the nearest bog; but there was, nevertheless, a note of firmness in the way Biggles spoke that caused Petroffsky to look hard at his face as if to determine whether this was really a joke or a serious threat. Anyhow, the words had the desired effect, and the inebriated Cossack settled down to a sullen silence.

About half the distance to the island was covered without any serious incident. Two small parties of riders were seen in the distance, too far away to cause them any concern. A few Koreans were seen, too, and occasional flights of disturbed birds showed where others were probably moving or lying in hiding. A single gunshot far behind was heard without comment. But when, soon afterwards, there was a brisk burst of firing ahead, Biggles brought the party to a halt. The firing continued, as single irregular shots, with long or short intervals. There was, too, an occasional distant shout. It was possible only to surmise what was happening, but that it was one of two things seemed fairly certain. Either the Mongolians were rounding up escaping Koreans, or they had overtaken Mayne and his party, who were defending themselves. Biggles thought the latter explanation most likely, for the runaway slaves, having no firearms, would soon have been silenced. The sounds were too near, he thought, for Algy to be involved.

He turned to Petroffsky. 'Where would you say those shots are coming from?' he inquired.

'Kossuri,' was the answer, given without hesitation.

'You mean the village where you live?'

'Where else?'

Biggles thought for a moment and looked at Ginger as more shots were fired. 'It takes two sides to make a battle,' he murmured.

'Which means that they've caught up with Mayne?'

'I'd say so, definitely, were it not for one thing,' replied Biggles, looking worried.

'What's that?'

'Mayne is the only member of his party who has a gun – that's what I can't understand. From the volume of shooting it could hardly be one man against a crowd.'

'I'll tell you what it is!' cried Petroffsky suddenly. 'I understand such things, and I know the voices of my friends. Someone is shooting with my old Schneider rifle. I'd know its deep voice in a thousand. Besides, it fires a black powder cartridge. I should know, for I loaded them myself with buckshot, for geese.' He pointed. 'Look! There is smoke – powder smoke. Someone is shooting in my house, using my cartridges, curse them. By St Mark! I'll—'

'Just a minute,' broke in Biggles. 'Mayne knows your house?'

'Who better?'

'That's all I want to know,' declared Biggles. 'Mayne and his party have been overtaken. They have found refuge in your house where they are now being attacked by Mongolians.'

'Then it is time we were there,' swore Petroffsky. 'All the vodka I have is in that house. If a bottle is broken—'

'Your old friend Mayne is there, too,' reminded Biggles.

'I have not forgotten him,' said Petroffsky loudly. 'We shall fight side by side. This is wonderful. Onward, comrades, to battle! Charge!'

'Not so fast,' requested Biggles curtly. 'If you want to charge you can charge by yourself. I like to see what I'm charging before I break into a canter. Besides, what about these pitfalls?'

The Russian stared. 'By St Peter! What a good thing you mentioned them. I'd forgotten them myself,' he confessed.

'As you know where they are, and we shall have to hurry, would you mind going ahead to keep us clear of them?' invited Biggles.

'It is my plain duty,' asserted Petroffsky. 'Besides, it is my house that is being shot at – and my vodka!'

'Lead on,' commanded Biggles.

'Forward!' cried Petroffsky, and striding on broke into a marching song.

'We can do without the music,' muttered Biggles. 'The enemy will see us soon enough.'

The Russian shrugged his broad shoulders as if to deplore this dull form of warfare, and went on. But before he had gone far he pulled up with a shout that set everyone looking wildly for the enemy. Ginger could see no one, but he saw a saddled horse nearby, grazing. Looking at Petroffsky for guidance he noticed that he was staring at something at his feet. Stepping forward he saw that the Mongolian rider had met a dreadful fate. He was at the bottom of a pitfall, impaled by stakes. How the horse had escaped was not clear. Ginger could only imagine that the horse had jibbed when it felt the ground giving under its feet, throwing its rider over its head. The man was so obviously dead that no time was wasted extracting him from what would undoubtedly become his grave.

The advance continued, and in some twenty minutes, a period of time during which the shooting persisted in a desultory manner, it became possible to see that Petroffsky's summing up of the situation had been correct. A film of smoke hung over the Russian's house. From it, and from other houses in the vicinity, shots were being fired. A Mongolian was crawling from one house to another.

Biggles surveyed the scene. 'That's it,' he said. 'Mayne and his party are in Petroffsky's house. We'll make that the objective. Spread out, everyone; keep in line and keep your heads down.'

For a matter of a hundred yards or so, which brought the party to about the same distance from the objective, all went well. There was a lull in the shooting with no sign of the attackers or the attacked. Then Ginger spotted some horses tethered in a group of trees on his right front, and that at least told him who the attackers were. A moment later confirmation came when a swart Mongolian sprinted from one house to another, behind which he took cover. His interest was entirely on the house that was being attacked and he did not see the newcomers advancing on his flank. Ginger could have shot him, but he recoiled from the idea of shooting a man in the back, so he walked on slowly, through deep grass, waiting for Biggles, by an order or a signal, to indicate the next move.

As things fell out Biggles' decision was expedited by the enemy, who at this juncture made a direct assault on Petroffsky's abode. With a wild yell some Mongolians, numbering about a dozen, leapt up from where they had been hiding and made a rush for the door, shooting as they ran. Those inside fired an answering volley and two of the attackers fell; but the rest went on, and for a moment or two looked as if they might succeed in taking the building by storm. But this misuse of his property was apparently more than Petroffsky could stand. Before Biggles could give his orders, the Russian with a bellow of rage, charged, firing into the thick of a number of Mongolians who had reached the door and were trying to break it down. Biggles, with a shout of 'Come on!' followed him, and Bertie and Ginger were not far behind.

It was a wild moment, but it ended sooner than might have been expected. The Mongolians had, of course, looked up on hearing Petroffsky's yell. Taken by surprise at this unexpected development, after a second or two of confusion they fled in disorder towards their horses.

But now a new and unsuspected factor took a hand in the proceedings. There was an outburst of shrill cries, and these came, it was quickly revealed, from a number of white-robed Koreans and half-clad Orochons who could now be seen flitting through the trees in which the horses had been tethered.

What had happened, or what was happening, was not clear – or so it seemed to Ginger. One thing that became evident very soon, however, was that the ex-slaves were taking this opportunity to pay off old scores. There was very little shooting, which puzzled Ginger not a little at the time. Discussing the matter afterwards Biggles gave it as his opinion that a number of Orochons, accompanied by some Koreans, had made their way to the village and were hiding in the outskirts when the Mongolians had appeared. Having no firearms they took refuge in the jungle, where they would, no doubt, have preferred to remain hidden. From this sanctuary they had watched the battle being fought in the village. Some of them may have been stealing towards the horses with the object of using them to travel faster, but had been caught in their project when the Mongolians had unexpectedly bolted. The fact that there was so little shooting could be accounted for in this way: the Mongolians had emptied their weapons when storming the besieged house, and when forced to retire by Biggles' party they had not stopped to reload. Thus, they had been caught at a disadvantage which it did not take the natives long to discover.

Actually, Ginger did not see much of what happened inside the grove of trees, but what he did see gave him a good idea of what was going on there. So did the screams and yells that arose. He saw one Mongolian, caught in the act of mounting his horse, which he had managed to reach, dragged off and battered to death with cudgels.

Petroffsky, of course, had rushed into the mêlée, howling like a dervish. Then Ginger saw Biggles run into Petroffsky's house, so he went on after him, and arrived just as the door was being opened. Mayne appeared on the threshold, dishevelled but smiling. Behind him, with a strange assortment of weapons in their hands, stood the scientists, against a background of tiger skins. Explanations were unnecessary, so the whole party stood ready for action while the fracas in the trees was fought to a conclusion. When, finally, the noise died away, and Ginger took a peep round the corner of the house, he saw Petroffsky walking towards them, singing. Seeing Ginger the Russian roared: 'Ho there! The rats have fled!' He came on. 'Now what about a little drink?' he suggested.

'Just a minute before you start tilting the tumbler,' said Biggles. 'What's happened outside?'

Petroffsky struck his chest. 'Happened?' he echoed. 'What only could have happened when Alexis Petroffsky entered the battle. The Mongolian scum have fled the field – those who had legs left to carry them. Those who could not run are being carved into small pieces by my Orochon allies. If you will be advised by me you won't go near them,' added Petroffsky, with unusual earnestness. 'The spectacle is not one for the eyes of a gentleman, although in my case it could not be avoided. But then, of course, having for so long lived here I am used to such things.'

'Were any Koreans hurt?' asked Biggles.

'A few have cracked heads – but what is a cracked head to

a Korean?' answered Petroffsky lightly. 'Let us celebrate our victory!'

Biggles smiled. 'Sorry, but I've no time for celebrations. We still have some way to go.'

'A pity,' said Petroffsky sadly. 'Yes, a pity. I win a battle and meet my old friend Mayne – a double occasion for rejoicing. I must speak to Mayne.'

They went inside, and while the Russian was embracing 'his old friend Mayne', somewhat to his embarrassment, Biggles had a word with Vale and the scientists. 'I'm sorry to rush you, gentlemen,' he said, 'but we're not out of the wood yet. A few more miles and we shall be comparatively safe. I shall also, I hope, be able to give you a respectable meal, which is not available here. Afterwards we shall have plenty of time for talking.'

Mayne disengaged his arm from that of the Russian. 'I'll come back one day and we'll do some more hunting together,' he promised.

'So be it,' answered Petroffsky philosophically.

Ginger could see that Biggles was really anxious to get away, realising what Petroffsky appeared to have overlooked – that more Mongolians might overtake them, in sufficient numbers to overwhelm them after all. Everyone was showing signs of fatigue, particularly the rescued men, and it was apparent that the party would not be able to travel very fast. In any case, for more reasons than one, they should be returned to civilisation as quickly as possible.

Biggles soon had everyone lined up outside the house ready for the last lap of the journey to the aircraft. Petroffsky walked with the party to the outskirts of the village, where, with tears running down his face, he wished them farewell.

'Why don't you leave this miserable place and come with us?' suggested Mayne.

The Russian shook his head. 'This is my home,' he said simply. 'Here I must stay, for I am a man without a country. One friend remains' with me though,' he went on huskily, taking a bottle from his pocket and patting it lovingly. 'I shall drink to your good fortune, and your return. Farewell.'

The last sight Ginger had of him was a lonely figure leaning on a rifle in the long grass, holding aloft a bottle in a parting toast. As he turned away a wave of sympathy surged through him for this strange, boastful but brave man, who, for reasons known only to himself, had elected to live his life in voluntary exile.

On arrival at the shore of the lake just off the island they found Algy waiting. He was not a little relieved to see them, for he had heard shooting in the distance and was afraid things had gone wrong. He transported the party, two at a time, to the island, where he had a meal ready. While this was being enjoyed by the rest he cleared the aircraft of its camouflage and made all ready to take off.

Biggles got up. 'All right, gentlemen,' he said, 'if it's all the same to you we'll push along. The sooner we are away from here the better.'

The party trooped into the big machine. Algy took off, and the lonely land of lakes and marshes dropped away astern.

Ginger, as tired as he had ever been, closed his eyes and slept, content in the knowledge that with their job well done, they were homeward bound.

BIGGLES
FOLLOWS ON

CHAPTER I

Ginger Brings News

Air Constable 'Ginger' Hebblethwaite burst into Air Police Headquarters at Scotland Yard with an urgency that suggested he had important news to impart. 'Hold on to your seats,' he said tersely. 'You're going to take a bump.'

Biggles – and Algy and Bertie, who were with him – looked up from their several tasks. 'We're all set,' announced Biggles. 'Let it go.'

'Who do you think I've just seen?' demanded Ginger, looking from one to the other.

'You're wasting time,' Biggles told him. 'This isn't a quiz contest.'

'Erich von Stalhein.'

Lines of surprise creased Biggles' forehead. 'Are you sure?'

'Certain.'

'Where did this happen?'

'Outside Victoria Station. I was coming away from Airways House and saw him turn into the Grosvenor Hotel. I went after him and was just in time to see him step into the lift. After that I couldn't follow without him seeing me – not that there would have been much point in it, anyway. He must be staying at the hotel.'

Biggles still looked dubious. 'You're positive of this?'

'Absolutely. He was complete with eyeglass and that long ciga-rette-holder he always uses.'

'What time was this?'

'About twenty minutes ago – say, just after six o'clock.'

'How was he looking? I mean, as regards appearance? Did he look prosperous or otherwise?'

'I imagine he'd have to be fairly prosperous to stay at the Grosvenor. But somehow he looked older, a bit careworn, as if he'd been under the weather.'

'He'd probably think the same of me if he saw me,' observed Biggles, reaching for a cigarette. 'I wonder what he's doing in London. Only business of some sort could have brought him. He must be pretty hard pushed for money, or he wouldn't have come to a country which we know he detests, particularly as there was always a chance of his bumping into us. He's never got over the fact that through us Germany lost the first war.'

'If he's here on business, you can bet it's something shady,' put in Algy.

'There are people who would apply that word to some of the jobs we've had to do,' reminded Biggles.

'How about spying? Wouldn't you call that shady?'

Biggles blew a smoke ring. 'If it is, our own careers wouldn't stand close investigation. I would only call the business shady when it's applied to a man working against his own country. Let's be fair about that. There was a time when a spy was regarded as something lower than a rat, even by the military brass-hats who profited by the information the spies brought in. But not now. Today, espionage is a recognised profession, and a dangerous one at that. Spies are a military necessity. Every country employs hundreds, most of them hopelessly underpaid for the risks they take and the results they achieve. Napoleon reckoned that one spy in the right place was worth twenty thousand men in the field – and he wasn't far wrong. The truth is, an effective spy is hated simply because he is feared. But why this talk of spies anyhow?'

'Association of ideas, old boy,' murmured Bertie. 'Spying and von Stalhein are one and the same thing.'

Biggles frowned. 'All right. So what? Don't forget that when I first collided with von Stalhein I was a spy in his country, although that was not from choice. I acted under orders. But I was still a spy, although I would have called myself a soldier. So was von Stalhein a soldier in the first place. Because he was efficient, he was seconded to the Wilhelmstrasse for top counter-espionage work. He suspected me from the start. Had he been given a free hand I wouldn't be here now. As I said a moment ago, what has happened to him since was largely the result of Germany losing the war. The shock of that knocked him off the rails, and he's never got on them again. He's been fighting a sort of one-man war against this country ever since.'

'For heaven's sake!' cried Algy indignantly. 'Are you making excuses for him?'

Biggles shrugged. 'Up to a point. Who can say what we would have become had we lost the war?'

'We wouldn't have done some of the things von Stalhein has done,' declared Ginger emphatically. 'He hates the sight of you, and you know it.'

'He has no reason to regard me with affection.'

'He'd bump you off tomorrow if he had the chance.' Biggles smiled faintly. 'Okay – okay! The bumping off may come yet. I'm not really making excuses for the man, but one must be fair. Von Stalhein came from an old Prussian military family. When Germany lost the war, he lost everything – home, estate, career—'

'And his self-respect,' interposed Algy.

'What was he to do? Can you see a man with his background taking a job in an office?'

'Some people have had to do that, old boy,' put in Bertie.

Biggles stubbed his cigarette. 'Have it your own way. The real tragedy for von Stalhein was, he survived the war.'

'He must have regretted a thousand times that he didn't stand you up in front of a firing-party when he had the chance,' said Ginger.

'It's time you knew that regret doesn't get you anywhere,' returned Biggles. 'Neither does this sort of argument. Let's stick to the present. Von Stalhein is in England. Knowing who and what he is, we are bound to regard him with suspicion. He ought to be watched. Strictly speaking, that isn't our affair. It's a job for the counter-espionage people at M.I.5.'

'Why not arrest him before he can get into mischief?' suggested Algy.

'On what charge?'

'He's been breaking the law for years, and we know it.'

'Yes, we know it. But how are we going to prove it? What are we going to use for evidence? In this country judges are not interested in what people think.'

There was a silence that lasted for several seconds.

'No, it isn't as simple as that,' went on Biggles. 'Von Stalhein is no fool. He's played in some queer games, with some queer people, as we know only too well; but we should have a job to pin any specific crime on him.'

'What are you going to do about him, then?' inquired Ginger. 'Hand him over to M.I.5?'

'Our proper course would be to tip them off that he's here,' answered Biggles. 'But I must confess to some curiosity about the man. For instance, I'd like to see his passport, to find out how he got into the country.' Biggles tapped another cigarette thoughtfully. 'At this juncture I feel inclined to compromise. I mean, I'll try to get a line on what he's doing before I put the matter on official record.'

'Even before you tell the Air Commodore?' queried Algy.

'Yes. Once the Air Commodore knows about this he could act only through official channels, and that would cramp our actions.'

'Why not let one of us go down and keep an eye on him?' suggested Ginger.

Biggles shook his head. 'No use. He knows us all by sight. One glimpse of us and he'd be gone. Besides, that sort of job isn't really up our street. I'll have a word with Inspector Gaskin, of C Department. He has fellows who are experts at shadowing. Being unknown to von Stalhein it wouldn't matter if he saw them.'

Biggles reached for the intercom telephone and called the department to which he had referred. Presently he was speaking to the head of it. 'Can you spare me five minutes?' he inquired. 'Thanks, Inspector.' He replaced the receiver. 'He's coming up,' he told the others.

Presently the powerfully-built detective came in. 'What's worrying you?' he asked Biggles, as he took a seat and began filling his pipe.

Biggles explained the position. He described von Stalhein and ran briefly over his record.

'What do you want me to do?' asked the inspector, thumbing the tobacco into his pipe.

'I want to find out what von Stalhein is doing in England,' answered Biggles. 'He knows us all by sight, so we daren't go near him. For a start, I'd like to know how long he's been here, and how long he intends to stay. It would also be interesting to know how he got into the country – whether he flew in or came in by surface transport. He may not be using his own name. The reception people at the hotel must have seen his passport. We might wonder how he managed to get one, and from what country. You might find out where he's spending his time, if he's alone or with friends – and all that sort of thing. In short, any information about him would be useful. I've helped you once or twice. This is where you can return the compliment.'

'Shouldn't be any difficulty about that,' stated the inspector. 'Give me twenty-four hours. That should be long enough. I'll come round about this time tomorrow and tell you what I know.'

'Thanks a lot, Inspector,' replied Biggles. 'We'll be here.'

The detective got up. 'If that's all, I'll get back. I've plenty on my plate to keep me busy. Be seeing you.' He went out.

'That's capital,' asserted Biggles. 'All we have to do is sit back and wait for tomorrow.'

The inspector was as good as his word. Shortly after six o'clock when he walked into the Air Police office, notebook in hand, everyone was waiting, curious to hear the news.

'I've had a look at your man,' announced the inspector casually, turning over some pages of his notebook and putting it on the table where he could refer to it easily. 'Did you say he's a German?'

Biggles answered: 'He was.'

'Well, he isn't now.'

'I can't say that surprises me.'

'No, but I'll bet you'll be surprised when I tell you what he is.'

'A Pole?'

'No.'

'Austrian?'

'No.'

'Russian?'

'No.'

'Give it up.'

'He's either an American citizen, born in New York, or a Czech, born in Prague.'

Biggles' eyes opened wide. 'There's a lot of difference. How did you work it out?'

'He's got two passports, so that he can be an American or a Czech, as it suits him. At the moment he's an American.'

'What name is he using?'

'Stalek, in each case. Jan Stalek. In America he would, no doubt, say he was of Dutch descent.'

'From what you tell me, I assume you've been in his room.'

'I had a look round.'

'How long has he been here?'

'Four months.'

'Four *months*!' Biggles looked amazed. 'By thunder! I wouldn't have guessed that, either. Has he been in London all the time?'

'No. He made a trip to Paris. He first came to London from New York, via Southampton. A month ago he went to Paris by boat and train. He came back the same way after three days.'

'What's he doing?'

'According to his papers he's a salesman for an American firm of general merchants.'

'If he's been here for four months he must have some money.'

'He came armed with plenty of dollars. Useful things nowadays – dollars. They'll take you almost anywhere.'

'What on earth could he have been doing for four months?'

'I can't tell you that; but I can tell you what he did yesterday.'

'Go ahead.'

'He had breakfast in his room at nine o'clock. That's usual, I understand. He has a suite, by the way, on the third floor – rooms number twenty-five to twenty-seven. He then sent for the morning papers and read until eleven o'clock. Then he went down to the station and caught a train to Caterham, where he went to a café named the "Stand Easy", and had an early lunch of bacon and eggs. My man followed him in, of course. From the easy way he spoke to the proprietor, he's been there before. He also nodded to some troops who came in, as if he knew them.'

'Troops from the Guards' Depot, I suppose?'

'Quite right. After a bit one of them went to his table and the two of them talked for about twenty minutes, Stalek buying the soldier a cup of coffee.'

'Did you find out the name of this soldier?' inquired Biggles.

'Of course. Ross. Guardsman Ian Ross. He's a London-born Scot. Age eighteen. Four months military service. Afterwards Stalek went for a walk, spoke to no one, returned to the same café for tea, chatted for a while with the proprietor, and then went back to the Grosvenor. He didn't go out again. Had his dinner in the hotel restaurant, then back to his room.' The inspector closed his note-book. 'That's the lot, so far. Do you want me to carry on?'

Biggles thought for a moment. 'Yes, if you will,' he decided. 'That needn't prevent me from making a few inquiries on my own account, now that I have something to work on.'

'Okay,' agreed the inspector, getting up. 'I'll pass on anything that comes in.'

'Thanks very much, Gaskin.'

After the detective had closed the door behind him, Biggles turned wondering eyes on the others.

'I guessed it,' said Algy in a hard voice. 'He's still playing spy.'

'He wouldn't learn much from a lad with four months service.'

'Every guardsman at the depot would hear the barrack-room gossip,' said Ginger.

'True enough,' admitted Biggles. 'This, obviously, is where we make a few inquiries about Ross.'

'How are you going to do that, old boy?' inquired Bertie.

'By going the quickest and easiest way about it,' answered Biggles.

'You mean, you'll have a word with Ross?'

'Not on your life. At least, not at this stage. He'd only have to say one word in the café about inquiries being made and von Stalhein would vanish. Erich is an old hand at the game. No. I'll go down to Caterham in the morning and have a word in confidence with the adjutant. If he turns out to be a co-operative type, I shall at least be able to get a slant on this lad Ross without alarming anybody.'

'Have you any ideas?' questioned Ginger.

'None,' answered Biggles. 'One thing that sticks out from Gaskin's report is this. Von Stalhein has some powerful friends. Presumably he's working for them. How else could he get passports from countries other than his own; and, moreover, under an assumed name?'

'They're fakes.'

'Of course they are. I mean, the people who issued those passports must have known the real identity of the man who wanted them.'

'I smell dirty work at the cross-roads,' murmured Bertie.

'Naturally, if von Stalhein is in the picture,' declared Algy cynically.

'Why not collect von Stalhein before he can do any further mischief?' recommended Ginger. 'You were talking just now about a charge. Well, you've got one – entering the country with false papers. We could soon prove *that*.'

Biggles looked pained. 'I shall never make a good security policeman of you,' he said sadly. 'In modern practice, having located your spy, you leave him alone until you have checked up on what he is doing and how he is doing it. Sooner or later, thinking he is safe, he may betray other spies, and reveal his line of communication with his headquarters. To arrest Von Stalhein now would do more harm than good, because as soon as the people for whom he is working heard about it they would put somebody else on the job; a man unknown to us. We should then be much worse off than we are now. We do at least know our man; and, that being so, it shouldn't take us long to find out to what particular work he has been assigned.'

'But would the people he is working for know that he had been arrested?' Ginger asked the question.

'Of course. The very fact that von Stalhein ceased to communicate with them would tell them that something had gone wrong.'

'Are you going to ring up the adjutant at Caterham and make an appointment?' asked Algy.

'No.'

'Why not?'

'Because the Orderly Room telephone will go through a switchboard, and where there is a switchboard the operator can hear. One word about someone coming down from Scotland Yard, and it would be all over the camp in five minutes. If that were to happen, I might as well stay at home. I'll take a chance on catching the adjutant at his desk in the morning. Let's go and get something to eat.'

CHAPTER II

Guardsman Ross

The following morning, at half-past ten, Biggles was escorted by a reluctant but efficient orderly-room sergeant into the presence of Captain Kingham, acting adjutant at the Guards' Depot.

The officer was busy at his desk. 'I understand you want to speak to me?' he said briskly. 'Please be brief. I have a lot to do this morning.'

'I wanted to speak to you – alone,' said Biggles quietly.

'You can speak freely in front of my staff.'

'I don't doubt it, but I'd rather not. What I have to say involves a question of State security,' returned Biggles evenly.

The officer looked hard at Biggles' face and hesitated. Then, turning to the N.C.O., he inclined his head towards the door. 'I hope you're not wasting my time,' he remarked curtly as the door closed behind the sergeant.

'I hope I'm not wasting my own,' replied Biggles, putting his credentials on the desk.

One glance at them and the officer's manner changed. 'Why didn't you say who you were?' he complained.

'I didn't want anyone but you to know.'

'Not even my confidential sergeant?'

Biggles smiled. 'Not even your regimental sergeant-major. If your sergeant professes curiosity about my visit you can tell him anything but the truth.'

The adjutant offered his cigarette-case. 'Sit down. What's the trouble?'

Biggles accepted a cigarette. 'You have a recruit on the station named Ross – Ian Ross.'

'Quite right. What's he been up to?'

'That's what I'm here to find out. So far, I can only tell you that he is spending a certain amount of his off time in the company of one of the most efficient foreign agents in Europe.'

The adjutant's eyes saucered. 'Good Lord!' he ejaculated.

'You were not to know that, of course.'

'I certainly didn't know it.'

'It's unlikely that Ross knows it either, so let us not jump to conclusions.'

'What's Ross doing with this fellow?'

'That's what I want to find out. Is Ross engaged on work of a secret nature?'

'No.'

'What is he doing?'

'The usual infantry routine.'

'Could he gain access to anything secret, even through another soldier on the station?'

'No. Frankly, I don't think we have anything here that any member of the public shouldn't know about.'

'You can't think of any reason at all why a top-grade spy should seek the company of a private soldier here?'

'No.'

'What sort of a recruit is Ross?'

'He promises to turn out well. His reports are good. He is keen and intelligent and will, I believe, become an efficient soldier.'

'Was he called up or did he enlist voluntarily?'

'He enlisted as soon as he was of age, and being of the necessary physical standard put his name down for the Guards.'

'What was he doing before he joined up?'

'I'd better get his papers.' The adjutant rang for the sergeant and called for the appropriate docket.

It was brought. The sergeant went out. Biggles looked through the documents. 'Nothing remotely suspicious here,' he remarked. 'Both parents British born. References from people who have known him all his life. Served an apprenticeship as a motor mechanic. His father was a Grenadier, I see. That should be good enough.' Biggles closed the docket and put it back on the desk.

'What do we do next?' asked the adjutant anxiously. 'I don't like the idea of this boy keeping the sort of company you describe. It will end in trouble for him.'

'It certainly will if the association is continued.'

'Should we warn him?'

'That would mean warning the spy, too – unless ...'

'Unless what?'

'Unless we took Ross entirely into our confidence.'

'Is there any reason why we shouldn't?'

'From my point of view it would be taking a risk. If he's innocent there's every reason why he should be warned, even though that might put him in a position of some danger. On the other hand, if he knows what he's doing, we should have shown our hand to no purpose. What I really want to know is the drift of the conversation between Ross and this enemy agent. Only one man can tell us that, and that is Ross himself. I feel inclined to take a chance. Ross can't have known this man for very long, and it takes a fair while to persuade a fellow of Ross's type to betray his country. Could we have him in?'

'It isn't quite regular.'

'There's nothing to prevent me from questioning Ross, in my official capacity, outside the barracks. It might be better for all concerned if it were done here.'

'I should have to consult the commanding officer about that,' said the adjutant dubiously.

'Do so, by all means.'

It so happened that the Colonel commanding the Depot chose that moment to walk in. He had a good look at Biggles, who was, of course, in plain clothes, and then at the officer at the desk. 'What's the trouble?' he inquired shrewdly. 'Who's been doing what?'

Biggles smoked his cigarette while the adjutant revealed his authority and explained the purpose of his visit.

The Colonel frowned. 'I wonder, could this have any connection with the trouble we've been having?' he said, at the end.

'I should hardly think so, sir,' answered the adjutant.

Neither said what the trouble was, and Biggles did not ask.

'There's only one thing to do in a case like this, and that's to have Ross on the mat and tell him we know what he's been up to,' declared the Colonel bluntly.

Biggles looked slightly alarmed. 'But that's just it, sir; we don't know what he's been up to. If you take too strong a line at this juncture, we may never know. Let's have Ross in, by all means; but it would be better, until we know more, to give him the benefit of the doubt.'

'I could confine Ross to barracks,' asserted the Colonel. 'That would put an end to the business.'

'I repeat, sir, I think it would be better if we ascertained what the business is before we talk of putting an end to it,' said Biggles blandly. 'Ross, I grant, is within your jurisdiction, but not the man outside; and it is with him that I am chiefly concerned.'

'We'll have Ross in,' decided the Colonel.

'May I suggest that, as I know the details of the case, you allow me to ask the questions – in the first instance, anyhow?'

'As you wish,' agreed the Colonel stiffly. He turned to the adjutant: 'Where is Ross now?'

'He should be on the square, sir.'

'Send for him.'

'Yes, sir.' The adjutant pressed his bell and passed the order to the sergeant.

Five minutes later the man concerned was marched in.

'You needn't wait,' the Colonel told his escort.

The young Guardsman, a tall, fair, good-looking lad, who looked even younger than his years, stood rigid. His face was slightly pale.

'Stand at ease,' rapped out the Colonel.

The soldier complied. His blue eyes stared straight ahead.

'Now, Ross, I have here an officer from Scotland Yard. He wants to ask you a few questions,' said the Colonel sternly. 'The matter is serious and you would be well advised to speak the truth and the whole truth.' He made a sign for Biggles to begin.

The soldier did not move, except to moisten his lips nervously.

Biggles' eyes were on his face. 'Would you mind looking at me while I am talking to you?' he requested.

The eyes switched. Biggles caught them with his own and held them. 'Thank you,' he said softly, and continued. 'You are in the habit of visiting a café in this town called the "Stand Easy." Is that correct?'

'Yes, sir.'

'You have met there a civilian who speaks with a slight foreign accent. He wears a monocle and smokes his cigarettes in a long holder. He stood you a cup of coffee yesterday. You know the man I mean?'

'Stand at ease,' rapped out the Colonel.

'Yes, sir.'

'Do you know anything about him?'

'Not much, sir.'

'A little?'

'Yes, sir. Only what he told me.'

'Did he tell you his nationality?'

'Yes, sir.'

'What did he say it was?'

'He told me he was a Czech, sir. Said he fought in the war.'

'He didn't tell you which side he fought on, I imagine?' said Biggles dryly.

'No, sir.'

'Yesterday was not the first time you have spoken, I fancy?'

'No, sir.'

'How many times have you spoken to him? Or put it the other way. How many times has he got into conversation with you?'

'Yesterday was the third time, sir.'

'What did you talk about?'

A pink stain crept into the soldier's cheeks. 'We talked about the army, sir.'

'I see. You talked about the army?'

'Yes, sir.'

'What had this man to say about the army?'

'He said soldiering was a fine life, sir.'

'And you agreed?'

'Yes, sir.'

'What was this man's interest in the army? Did he tell you that?'

The pulses between the soldier's ears and eyes could be seen beating. The tip of his nose was chalk white. These signs were not lost on Biggles. 'Remember what the Colonel told you at the beginning,' he said quietly. 'You would be foolish, Ross, to try to hide anything. The truth will come out, if not from you.'

'The man told me he was recruiting for another army, sir. A better one than ours, he said. The pay was twice as much as we get here, with plenty of leave, and sport, and so on. He said the regiment was a sort of International Brigade, like the French Foreign Legion.'

Biggles drew a deep breath. 'I see,' he said softly. 'Did this man happen to mention where this unit was based?'

'He said it was in Czechoslovakia, sir.'

'Did you believe this fairy tale?'

'No, sir. Well, not altogether, sir.'

'But you were interested?'

'Well, I – er—' The man faltered.

'You were interested, even knowing that this man was deliberately trying to induce you to join a foreign army, which would have meant breaking your Oath of Allegiance?'

'There was a guarantee we should never have to fight against British—'

'We? Who do you mean by we?'

'Me and the others.'

'What others?'

'Those who have already gone, sir. That was the only reason why I was interested, sir. That's God's truth, sir. You see, sir, my chum, Hugh Macdonald, he went.'

'Ah,' breathed Biggles. 'Did this man know Macdonald was a friend of yours?'

'Yes, sir. He used to see us together in the "Stand Easy." It was because Macdonald went, I think, that he picked on me. He said he had a message for me from Macdonald to say he was having the time of his life, and if I had any sense I'd go over right away. I told him I didn't believe it. Then he said he would tell Hugh to write to me. He must have done that because, soon afterwards, I had a letter from Hugh.'

Biggles looked surprised. 'You had a letter from him?'

'Yes, sir.'

'Where is it?'

'I've got it here, sir.' The soldier took out his wallet and selected a letter from several. He passed it to Biggles.

Biggles examined the stamp and the postmark before taking out the contents. He glanced at the letter, replaced it in the envelope, and handed it back to the Guardsman. 'If ever I saw a piece of forgery, that's it,' he said. He went on. 'Did you seriously consider joining Macdonald?'

'No, sir. If my father heard I'd been posted as a deserter he'd kill me stone dead.'

'Then why did you continue to associate with a man whom you knew to be an enemy of your country?'

The soldier was now perspiring, and it was clear that he was on the point of breaking down. 'Take your time,' Biggles told him.

'I was hoping to find out where Macdonald had gone, to persuade him to come home.'

Biggles sat back. 'You knew Macdonald pretty well? Why did he decide to accept this man's invitation?'

'Well, sir, he was a bit fed up. He'd got an idea in his head that the sergeant-major had got it in for him, and he was afraid he'd never make a good soldier.'

'Did you know that Macdonald had actually decided to go?'

'No, but I was afraid of it, sir. He went sort of quiet. I told him not to be a fool.'

'He didn't by any chance tell you, before he left, how he was going to get out of the country – or where he was going?

'No, sir. He went on week-end leave. When he didn't come back I guessed he'd gone. Afterwards the man at the café told me so. He offered me twenty pounds to go, too, but I didn't take it. He said it was just pocket-money, and there was plenty more where that came from.'

'What else did he tell you?'

'He said he would make all arrangements. There wouldn't be any difficulty. I'd be hundreds of miles away before I was missed.'

'What did you say to that?'

'I said I'd think it over, sir.' The soldier added, hastily: 'But that was only to keep in touch with the man so I could find out about Macdonald.'

'Didn't it occur to you that your proper course would be to report a matter as serious as this to your Commanding Officer?'

'Yes, sir.'

'Why didn't you?'

'I didn't want to make it too black for Macdonald. I know his parents. They'd never get over it. I was frightened about the whole thing, and that's a fact, sir. I couldn't sleep at nights for worrying about it.'

'You seem to think a lot of your friend Macdonald?'

'We played at soldiers when we were kids together, sir. I did my level best to persuade him not to go; but he said he'd joined up to fight, not be ticked off all the time by a sergeant-major, who was always on to him about something or other.'

'Have any other men been caught in this trap?' asked Biggles.

'I can answer that,' broke in the Colonel, speaking through his teeth. 'In the last three months we've had to post seven men absent without leave.'

Biggles looked startled. There was an uncomfortable silence. The Colonel glared at the Guardsman. The soldier stared at the wall with glassy eyes. The adjutant made meaningless marks on his blotting-pad. Biggles considered them all in turn. When he spoke it was to the Colonel. 'Well, sir, at least a mystery has been solved for you. I'd like to speak to you alone, if I may, before you take action on the situation. I suggest that Ross waits outside. We may need him again.'

'Very well.'

Biggles spoke again to the soldier. 'Not a word of this to a soul. If you speak, I won't be responsible for your life. You're in deeper water than you know.'

'I understand, sir.'

The soldier was marched out.

As soon as the officers were alone Biggles drew a long breath. 'This is worse than I feared,' he told the Colonel, who seemed to be in some danger of having a fit.

'I'll have this infernal Czech arrested forthwith!' grated the Colonel.

'He isn't a Czech. He's a German, although the last time I heard of him he was hiding behind the Iron Curtain,' said Biggles quietly.

'I don't care who the devil he is,' raged the Colonel.

'By arresting him you will defeat your object – that is, if you have any hope of getting your men back? By this time, no doubt, they are bitterly regretting their folly. The picture is now pretty clear. A foreign power, we can guess which one, is apparently forming a unit composed of troops of other nationalities. That isn't a new idea. Hitler did it. Such men would be useful in many ways in the event of hostilities. A force of that sort could instruct others in the drill, tactics and equipment, of every other country in Western Europe. They would also be helpful as interpreters, and so on. We've got to get these men back, if only to save them from the consequences of their folly.'

'How can you get them back? Czechoslovakia is a big place.'

'These men aren't necessarily in Czechoslovakia, although I admit the evidence points that way. This agent has a Czech passport, and the letter Ross received came from Prague, although no address was given.'

'Then how the deuce can you hope to find these fellows?'

'I can think of only one way,' answered Biggles gravely. 'Ross will have to help us.'

'Ross?' The Colonel stared. 'He doesn't know where they are.'

'He will, if he accepts the proposition that has been put up to him.'

The Colonel blinked. 'Great heavens, man! Are you suggesting that Ross goes off like the others?'

'It may come to that if all else fails.'

'It would be sending the man to certain death!'

'Possibly. But what is one life against seven – that we know of? There may be other poor fools there, from other units. Naturally, before Ross takes another step he would have to be warned of his danger. In any case the decision would rest with him. I think he'd do anything to save his chum, Macdonald, although I imagine the official view will not concern itself with individuals, who are deserters, anyway. Military Intelligence will be more anxious to know for what purpose these fellows are being used.'

'You think Ross might write and tell us where they all are, when he joins them?'

Biggles shook his head. 'I hardly think he'd be allowed to do that, sir. The letter that Macdonald was alleged to have written was either a forgery or else it was produced under pressure. If Ross went I should follow him. But it hasn't come to that yet.'

'Sounds devilish dangerous to me.'

'"Danger" is a word I didn't expect to hear used here.' The Colonel flushed.

'Let's take our fences as we come to them,' suggested Biggles. 'We may get the information we want without losing sight of Ross.'

'What do you propose?'

'I suggest that we put the matter fairly to Ross, pointing out which way his duty lies – although I think he knows that already. For the moment he can go on meeting the man at the café, as if he is still unable to make up his mind. It would be something if he could learn how his comrades were got out of the country After all, it would be reasonable for him to ask questions before deciding on a step as irrevocable as desertion. If Ross fails to get any further information by these methods, we'll have to consider the next step.'

'Could we trust Ross to play the game? It's a big responsibility for a fellow of his age and experience.'

'I can see no alternative. If I'm any judge of a man, Ross is as sound as a bell. He'll do his best. After all he has a personal interest, in his friend Macdonald.'

'All right. Let's have him in and hear how he feels about it. I can put him on indefinite leave.'

'One more question,' said Biggles. 'Have the next-of-kin of these deserters been questioned, to find out if anything is known of their whereabouts?'

'We sent a military escort to the home of every man concerned, that being the most likely place to find him. In each case the escort returned saying that the man was not there, and nothing had been heard of him.'

'No letters?'

'Not a word. And that's probably true, because in some cases the mothers of these fellows were very upset.'

'Which confirms that they are not allowed to write letters, or one of them at least would have got in touch with his home.'

Ross was brought back into the room.

Biggles took up the conversation. 'Now I want you to listen to me very carefully, Ross,' he began. 'The matter we have been discussing is far more serious than you may have supposed. Because I think you can help us, and those of your comrades, who, believe me, have practically thrown their lives away, I am going to take you fully into my confidence. But before I do that I want your word that, having started, you won't go back on us.'

'I will—'

'Just a minute. What I am going to ask you to do is dangerous. One slip may cost you your life. The man you have met at the café is one of the most ruthless spies in Europe. He's a Prussian. And there are even more dangerous men behind him. They would think no more of killing you, if they thought you were working for me, than they would of swotting a fly. Now, what do you say? Are you prepared to work under my instructions? There's no compulsion about it. You are within your rights to say no, if you'd rather keep out.'

'I'll do anything you say, sir.'

'Even though the business may cost you your life before we are through with it?'

'If I'd been afraid of dying I wouldn't have joined the army.'

'That's the way to talk. Now we've got that clear, I'll go on. What we've got to do is this. We've got to find out where this fancy regiment is stationed, and bring our fellows back. They'll be glad enough to come, I'll warrant. For the moment, we'll learn all we can, here. I want you to go on seeing this man, behaving as though you can't make up your mind. In his attempts to win you over he may let one or two things drop. It would be natural for you to want to know just where you are going, and how you're going to get there. Pretend to be nervous about travelling abroad, to find out if you would go alone or with an escort. See what I mean?'

'Yes, sir.'

'Just go on talking – and listening. That's all I can tell you. You'll have to use your intelligence. I'll give you one tip. Don't on any account allow yourself to be persuaded to take strong drink. Alcohol loosens a man's tongue faster than anything – and you might say too much. Understand?'

'Yes, sir.'

'I shall be about. Tell the adjutant when you have anything to report, and he'll send for me. That's enough for now. It may be only a beginning. Eventually you may have to accept this man's offer, in order to reach Macdonald. If so, I shan't be far away from you. But we'll talk about that when the time comes. Meanwhile, this spy must suspect nothing. Let's leave it like that.' Biggles turned to the Colonel. 'That's all, sir.'

When the soldier had been dismissed Biggles stood up. 'There's nothing more we can do for the moment,' he said. 'The next move will depend on what Ross has to report. I shall be at Scotland Yard. Give me a ring and I'll come straight down.'

'You know, I can't help feeling that this matter is so serious that it ought to be reported to the Higher Authority,' said thc Colonel.

'It's because it's so serious that I've refrained from doing that myself,' returned Biggles. 'You don't need me to tell you that if one person outside this room learns what is going on, a hundred people will know, and the next thing the story will be in the newspapers. That would relieve me of a lot of trouble because the matter would then pass out of my hands. It would also save the enemy all the trouble I am going to cause him if I can handle the thing my way. Report the business to the War Office if you feel you must, sir, but, with all respect, I submit that if you do you can say goodbye to any chance of getting these spies buttoned up, or of bringing home the fools who thought they were going to a military paradise, but have found themselves in the other place. All I ask is, if you decide to report the matter officially, tip me off in time to do the same.'

'If things go wrong I shall get a rap.'

'So will Ross – on the head. And so, probably, will I.'

The Colonel hesitated. 'I'll do nothing for the moment,' he decided. 'We'll give things a day or two to see how they go.'

'Very well, sir. A final piece of advice. Keep away from the "Stand Easy." I say that because you may be tempted to have a look at this man who has reduced your ranks. If he sees you staring at him, he'll guess why. He was trained in the right school, and he's been at this game all his life. Good day, gentlemen. I'm sorry to give you all this trouble. The only consolation I can offer is, had I not stepped in it might have got worse.'

Biggles went out, got into his car, put on a pair of dark glasses and pulled the rim of his hat well down. He wasn't taking any chances of being seen in Caterham by Erich von Stalhein.

CHAPTER III

Biggles Makes His Plans

As he drove back to the Yard, Biggles decided that he had every reason to be satisfied with his visit to Caterham. To have discovered so quickly, and with so little trouble, what von Stalhein was doing in the country exceeded his most optimistic hopes. But, as he perceived, by solving this problem he had set himself some even more difficult ones. Not only difficult ones, but dangerous ones. He was more than a little perturbed by the gravity of what he had learned, and while he felt disinclined to carry the responsibility of dealing with the matter within his own department, he was equally reluctant, for security reasons, to report officially what he knew. Apart from the risk of careless talk, spies, he was well aware, were everywhere, even in the most surprising places. Von Stalhein would need only one whiff of suspicion that his activities were under surveillance, and the difficulties and dangers would be increased tenfold. Quite apart from that, with the world political situation already strained, the mishandling of the affair might do immense mischief.

Biggles wondered how many men had already been recruited from the Western Powers; for it seemed safe to suppose that if British troops were being taken, there would be others. The title International Brigade suggested troops of several countries. Again, was von Stalhein working alone in Britain, or were other agents at work at other military depots? As for the men who had been crazy enough to go, it was easy to imagine the conditions in which they now found themselves. That they would repent their action was certain. But what could they do about it? Even if a means of escape presented itself, they would hardly dare to take it, knowing that they would be arrested for desertion as soon as they landed in Britain. Once the enemy had them in his power he could force them to do anything. They would go from bad to worse until they were so hopelessly compromised that they would have to stay abroad for the rest of their lives, whether they liked it or not.

Biggles remembered that there had been more than one case of men of the Occupation Forces in Germany – British, American and French – being seized and carried by force behind the Iron Curtain. Apparently this method of getting recruits was not successful; hence the new trick. Still pondering these matters, Biggles walked into the office to find the others waiting, and looking at him expectantly.

'What's the news?' asked Ginger.

'Grim,' answered Biggles, and, sitting down at his desk, narrated the result of his inquiries. Not until he had finished did anyone speak.

'Sounds as if von Stalhein has turned Communist,' remarked Algy.

'When he worked for Hitler in the war he was a Nazi,' reminded Ginger.

'I think he would make no bones about being anything that suited him,' said Biggles. 'Primarily he was a soldier, and few soldiers have much time for politics. Von Stalhein is really concerned only with two things – himself and Germany. He is interested to some extent in money, of course, because he has to have money to live in the style to which he has always been accustomed. He has reached the stage when he isn't particular how he gets it.'

'Are you going to tell the Chief about this?' asked Ginger.

'I shall have to,' replied Biggles. 'If things went wrong I should have no valid excuse for keeping the information to myself. I'm still turning the question over in my mind. I may wait to see what tomorrow brings forth.'

'Are you seriously thinking of letting Ross accept von Stalhein's offer?' Algy asked.

'If all else fails, yes. We can't let the thing go on.'

'If you ever lose sight of Ross he'll have had it,' averred Algy. 'If the men who have already gone haven't been able to get in touch with home, he won't be able to. Once he is given a civilian hat, and a ticket to leave the country, von Stalhein won't take his eyes off him until he's on his way. What I mean is, he wouldn't be able to take any escape equipment with him. He wouldn't have an earthly chance of getting in touch with you, or anyone else. Von Stalhein would see to that.'

'We'll deal with such problems when they arise,' answered Biggles. 'We haven't come to them yet.'

The question was still being discussed at six o'clock when Inspector Gaskin came in.

'Any more news?' asked Biggles quickly.

'Nothing to speak of,' replied the detective, knocking out his pipe and putting it in his pocket. 'I went to the Grosvenor today while our friend was out and had a look over his suite. He went to Caterham again. I had a man trailing him.'

'Did you find anything?'

'Just a couple of things that puzzled me. Here's one of them.' The inspector opened his notebook and took out a loose page. 'There was a slip of paper in a drawer. It had some letters on it; looks like some sort of code. I made a copy. Take a look. Do these letters mean anything to you?'

A curious expression came over Biggles' face as he looked at the slip. 'They certainly do mean something to me,' he said in a hard voice. 'In fact, they mean quite a lot. These are the registration letters of all our aircraft.'

The Inspector whistled softly. 'Does that mean he knows you're on the job?'

'I don't think so,' answered Biggles slowly. 'I don't see how he could know. But he knows where my machines are kept. There's no secret about that. I should say he's made a note of our registration marks either for his own information, or to pass on to his friends in Europe, in case any of our machines were seen. He's very thorough, is von Stalhein.'

'The only other thing that seemed a bit odd was a box of ties — neckties,' went on the Inspector.

'What's queer about that? Most men wear a tie.'

'True. But most men buy one tie at a time, and unless it's a club or regimental tie, it's usually a different design from those they already have. I found a box with eleven ties in it. They were brand new, and all alike.'

Ginger interposed. 'Did these ties happen to be black with red spots?'

The Inspector looked surprised 'They did.'

Biggles cocked an eye at Ginger. 'How did you know?'

'Because when I saw him, von Stalhein was wearing one — possibly the one that would make up a dozen in the box. I noticed it particularly because I've never seen von Stalhein wear anything but a plain black tie.'

'We shall have to think about that,' said Biggles. 'Tell me, Inspector; what did our friend do at Caterham?'

'Same as before. He spoke to some soldiers and had a long talk with Ross.'

'Ah!'

'His movements were the same as the last time we watched him.' The detective got up. 'That's the lot. I've still got a man on the job. I'll let you know any developments.' He went out.

Biggles sat staring at the others. 'Ginger, you might take a walk round the West End shops in the morning and see if you can find any black ties with red spots. If you do, buy one or two.'

Ginger's eyebrows went up. 'What for?'

'Just an idea,' murmured Biggles.

'I've got an idea, too,' put in Algy. 'Before a man can get out of this country and into another he needs a passport. All these recruits of von Stalhein must have had one. Ross would need one if he went. How does von Stalhein get British passports?'

'There wouldn't be much difficulty about that,' returned Biggles, 'These fellows could all travel on the same passport, if it comes to that. When it had served its purpose it could be sent back and used again. The photograph and the entries could be erased and fresh ones substituted. There are plenty of spare British passports in Eastern Europe, anyway. In the Spanish Civil War, all the British contingent of the International Brigade had their passports taken from them. They didn't get them back. We know where they went.'

The telephone rang. Biggles picked up the receiver. 'Good. I'll be with you in half an hour,' he said, and hung up. 'That was the adjutant at Caterham,' he told the others. 'He's got Ross with him. Stick around till I get back.'

He was away for the best part of two hours.

'Now what?' inquired Ginger when he returned.

'We've made a little progress – not much,' answered Biggles, dropping into his chair. 'Ross had a long talk with von Stalhein today – we already knew that. I've just had a word with Ross. Under the pretence of being inclined to accept the offer, he's picked up a detail or two. When he is ready to go he is given a suit of civilian clothes, money, passport and an air ticket from London to a European airport. There he will be met by a man who will tell him what to do next. Saturday was suggested as the best time to go, because on that day Ross can get a week-end pass. That gives him plenty of time to get clear. Ross says he tried hard to get more information, but there was nothing doing. Which means that we shan't get any further along that particular line of inquiry.'

'Did you fix up with Ross to accept?' asked Algy.

'Not yet. He said he was willing to go. I told him to do nothing more until he hears from me again.'

'What's the next move?'

'I've decided to tell Raymond about it. This thing is too big for us to carry on our own hook. The Air Commodore will probably have gone home, in which case I'll go to his house. There's no need for you to stay. I shall probably be late. You needn't wait up for me unless you want to. I'll get along.'

The Air Commodore was not in his office. Biggles went to his home, and caught him just as he was leaving for the club, where he usually dined. Aware that Biggles would not trouble him at such a late hour unless he had urgent news to impart, he asked him to join him. Biggles accepted, and over the meal, in a quiet corner of the dining-room, revealed the plot he had uncovered.

The Air Commodore's expression hardened as he listened to the story, but he said nothing until Biggles had finished. Even then it was a little while before he spoke. 'This is a pretty state of affairs,' he said bitterly. 'There was a time when our enemies were content to steal our secrets. Now they entice away our troops. What do you suggest doing about it?'

'I feel inclined to let Ross go, and follow him,' said Biggles. 'I can't see any other course. For their sakes, as well as our own, we can't just abandon these fellows who have already taken the bait. Anyhow, we must find out where they are.'

'If Ross goes, he'll take his life in his hands.'

'So shall we all. Ross knows the danger.'

'Don't, for goodness sake, do anything to start a war.'

Biggles frowned. 'Surely that's what the other side is doing now? They can't expect us to sit back and do nothing about it. I doubt if any country implicated would kick up a fuss if we were caught in their territory, because if the thing became public it would mean exposing their own hand as well as ours.'

'How can you follow Ross without being seen yourself? Von Stalhein will not lose sight of him, you may be sure, until he's actually on his way.'

'That will have to be arranged. I think it could be managed.'

'You mean, as he will go by air, you'd follow in one of your machines?'

'Yes.'

'What if it comes to night flying? You'd lose your man in the dark. Or, for that matter, suppose Ross, when he's abroad, is switched suddenly to surface travel – a private car, for instance?'

'That'll be my worry,' said Biggles shortly. 'I can think of a score of unpleasant possibilities; but, as I said just now, what's the alternative?'

'We could pick up von Stalhein and so put an end to the business.'

'You might pick up von Stalhein, but how could you be sure that would end the business? The chances are that he would simply be replaced by someone else. It's better to deal with a devil we know than one we don't know. Besides, to grab von Stalhein would tell the enemy we know what's going on. That would definitely mean saying goodbye to these silly fools who have already been hooked.'

Still the Air Commodore hesitated. He looked worried. 'I don't like it, Bigglesworth. It sounds too much like attempting the impossible. You might get behind the Iron Curtain by dropping in from an aircraft; but I can't see you getting out again. Without knowing the country you couldn't arrange for a machine to pick you up. You couldn't even get a message home to say where you were. Once in, you would probably disappear as completely as a stone dropped in the middle of the Atlantic. Every hand would be against you. Think of the language difficulties. You wouldn't be able to move about, get food—'

'Just a minute, sir,' broke in Biggles. 'I've taken all these things into account. I won't deny it's risky; but someone has to take risks. The biggest difficulty of all will be keeping Ross in sight. If I lose him, he's had it. He'd never get out on his own – unless I could get in touch with him again.'

'How could you do that? Wander about Europe in the hope of meeting him?' The Air Commodore was frankly sarcastic.

'No. There's only one way. We should have to decide on a rendezvous before the start. If I lost him, I should go there and wait. On the other hand, he could make for the same meeting place.'

'What meeting place?'

'That's where you'll have to help us.'

'What do you mean?'

'I imagine we have our own agents behind the Curtain. I also imagine that they have means of getting in touch with home, or they would serve no useful purpose.'

'And I also imagine that the Intelligence Service will think twice before they give us such an address,' said the Air Commodore grimly.

'It's asking a lot, I know. But I think the occasion warrants it. If they refuse – well, we shall have to manage on our own. But such an address would make all the difference to our chances.'

The Air Commodore rolled breadcrumbs into little balls. 'Another trouble is, there is so much territory behind the Iron Curtain. This International Unit might be anywhere between Poland and Bulgaria.'

'True enough. But I have a feeling that we shall find it in Czechoslovakia.'

'Why there?'

'All the evidence we have points to it. Ross had a letter from Prague – I saw the postmark. Von Stalhein has a Czech passport, which presumably he uses. When I go I shall, with your assistance, carry a Czech passport for the same reason. We have people who could provide that I suppose?'

The Air Commodore gave ground reluctantly. 'Even if you found these fellows, how could you get them out of the country?' he argued.

'We should have to fly them out. There could be no other way.'

'That would be a nice job to undertake.'

'We've tackled worse.'

The Air Commodore drew a deep breath. 'All right,' he said wearily. 'Have it your own way. Even if you don't bring these men back, it will be something if you can find out what they're doing. Tell me exactly what you think you'll require and I'll do my best to procure it.'

The discussion was continued until the small hours. When Biggles finally reached home he found the others still up, waiting for him.

'Well, what's the verdict?' asked Algy.

Biggles sank into a chair and reached for a cigarette. 'I'm going to ask Ross to go.'

'The Chief has agreed to that?'

'Yes. He wasn't happy about it. Neither am I, for that matter. He could see the difficulties of trying to keep Ross in sight.'

'So can I,' murmured Ginger.

'If we can get a line on the general direction, or on the country to which von Stalhein's recruits are being sent, it will be something to go on with,' asserted Biggles. 'Anyway, in the morning I shall tell Ross to accept. From what has been said, he will probably start his journey on Saturday afternoon.'

'But how can you possibly keep an eye on him, old boy, without being spotted by that wily old fox, von Stalhein?' inquired Bertie, rubbing his eyeglass.

'I've been turning that over in my mind all day,' Biggles told him. 'Gaskin will have to help us for the first part of the business. I shall ask him to shadow von Stalhein from the time Ross says he's willing to go. The first thing von Stalhein will have to do is to book a passage. If he is watched, we should learn the time and place of Ross's departure. It seems certain he will go by air. I shall arrange for Ginger to be inside the machine, possibly in the radio cabin, until it is airborne. I'm assuming that von Stalhein won't travel with Ross. I shall be sitting on the tarmac in the Proctor when Ross's machine takes off. I shall follow it – or, rather, head for the same destination. You, Algy and Bertie, will stand by for radio signals from me, ready to act as I direct. That's only a rough outline of the general idea. We'll work out the details tomorrow. We mustn't forget to change our registration letters. Now let's see about getting some sleep.'

CHAPTER IV

By Air – to Where?

At a quarter to three on the following Saturday afternoon Biggles sat in the cockpit of a police Proctor aircraft that had been put in a place convenient for the observation of passengers who had booked for the three o'clock British European Airways service to Paris. The big machine was already drawn up to receive its freight, human and otherwise. Inside, by arrangement with the Traffic Manager, was Ginger, in a position from which he could not be seen from outside.

These arrangements were not guesswork. They were based on definite information, the result of a good deal of trouble on the part of more than one department at Scotland Yard.

So far, everything had gone smoothly. Indeed, as far as Biggles knew, they had gone without a hitch, and he was actually in possession of more information than he expected to get. This was brought about largely by the close and efficient co-operation of Inspector Gaskin and his highly-trained staff.

Guardsman Ross, who had thrown himself wholeheartedly into the undertaking regardless of its perilous nature, had told von Stalhein that he had decided to accept his invitation to join the International Corps; whereupon von Stalhein, watched by Gaskin's men, had lost no time in making the necessary arrangements.

These need not be dwelt upon in detail, but they exposed two more members of the spy organisation, one a photographer and the other a small printer, in the East End of London. They were left alone for the time being. What was of greater importance to Biggles was the booking by von Stalhein of a single passage to Paris, by British European Airways, on the three o'clock Saturday plane. The seat had been taken in the name of Ross. From the fact that von Stalhein had not troubled to change the name of his recruit, Biggles could only suppose that he felt he was on safe ground.

Nothing of importance had transpired at the final interview between Ross and the German. Ross told his adjutant, who passed the information on to Biggles, that they were to meet at the 'Stand Easy' café at a quarter-past one; and in due course this appointment was kept. From that moment Ross and von Stalhein were under surveillance.

They had gone together to von Stalhein's suite at the Grosvenor Hotel. When they emerged, and went into the dining-room for a meal, Ross was apparently ready for the journey, for he was now dressed in a dark suit and soft hat, and carried a suitcase. An interesting detail was, he wore a red-spotted black tie. Biggles, who was waiting at the airport with Ginger, had received this information direct from Inspector Gaskin.

'What do you make of this spotted tie business?' Ginger had asked Biggles.

'I can only think that it's for purposes of identification,' replied Biggles. 'We'll put ours on. They can do us no harm even if they do no good.'

Ginger, following Biggles' instructions to procure the ties, had found them in a shop in Piccadilly. This was only one of several minor preparations that had been put in hand as soon as it had been decided that Ross should accept von Stalhein's invitation.

Documents, which included passports, were prepared. Sums of money, in several foreign currencies, were procured. Into the linings of jackets had been inserted 'escape' equipment designed to aid prisoners of war – tiny steel files, miniature compasses, and maps which, folded, were no larger than a postage stamp. In providing these Biggles was thinking not so much of himself as of Ross, and the men he hoped to release. As he remarked with a smile: 'It's often little things like this that count.'

At the last minute he had rung up Marcel Brissac, his opposite number of the International Police Commission in Paris, and asked him to meet him off the plane at Le Bourget, the Paris airport which it seemed was to be the first stop. He had no particular reason for doing this. It struck him that it might be useful to have official assistance at the airport should there be trouble of any sort. 'There's a chance that there may be a man waiting for the London plane who wears a black tie with red spots,' he told Marcel. 'If so, check up on him and see if he books a passage for anywhere.' Marcel agreed to do this.

For luggage, Biggles and Ginger each carried only a small handbag containing nothing more questionable than small-kit—toilet things, pyjamas, and a spare shirt and socks.

Air Commodore Raymond had done all that Biggles had required of him. This was not much, but it was of paramount importance. He had obtained a name and address in Prague, which those engaged in the case, including Ross, could use as a hide-out, and from where, in dire emergency, a message could be got home. This address had of course been committed to memory.

So the stage was set for what Biggles knew was likely to prove one of the most hazardous operations he had ever undertaken.

The motor-coach bringing the passengers from London now arrived, and very soon the travellers were making their way towards the aircraft. Biggles saw von Stalhein talking earnestly to Ross, presumably giving him final instructions. For a moment a smile softened Biggles' expression as he saw Inspector Gaskin in the background, also watching.

Ross took his place in the machine. Von Stalhein retired.

Biggles waited for no more, for there was no likelihood of any change of plan on either side. He asked Control for permission to take off, and having received it, he taxied out. In a minute or two he was in the air, heading for Paris. By arriving first he would be able to watch the passenger plane come in, and have time to look over the people waiting for it. With von Stalhein out of the way there would be no danger in this. He hoped also to have a chat with Marcel.

He found Marcel waiting, and having put the Proctor out of the way he lost no time in coming to the point. 'Any clients wearing spotted ties?' he asked, as they shook hands.

Marcel grinned. 'But of course, *mon ami*. We wouldn't disappoint you. He is here.'

'Where?'

'In the booking hall. Come over and I will show him to you. I think he expects a friend on the London plane, for he has in his pocket two tickets for Prague.'

'Good work, Marcel,' acknowledged Biggles. 'At what time does the Prague machine leave?'

'At four-forty-five. *Voilà*! There it stands, ready.'

'Go and get me two tickets, if it isn't booked to capacity. I'm going on that plane, too.'

Marcel looked pained. 'Not even one night in Paris?'

'I haven't time. This is serious, and urgent.'

Marcel's expressive eyes asked a question. 'What happens?'

'Have you had any men deserting from your army lately?'

Marcel shrugged. 'How would I know?'

'Find out – but not now. I'll tell you all about it when I come back from Prague. Get me the tickets.'

'You want two tickets?'

'Yes. Ginger will go with me.'

As they walked into the main hall Marcel nudged Biggles. 'There is your man,' he said.

Following the direction indicated Biggles saw a nondescript individual with dark, restless eyes, a sallow complexion and a rather nervous manner. He was reading, or pretending to read, a newspaper; but his eyes, Biggles noted, did not linger on the printed page.

Marcel went off to get the tickets, leaving Biggles watching the man with the spotted tie.

Presently a curious thing happened; at least, it puzzled Biggles for a minute. The man he was watching looked directly at him, almost as if he had become aware that he was being scrutinised. Biggles saw him start slightly, before turning away, nearly dropping his paper in doing so. But again his eyes came back to Biggles. For a moment he fidgeted, obviously ill at ease. Then he appeared to reach a decision. After a glance to left and right he came near to where Biggles was standing, and said, in a low voice, speaking in German: 'All is well, I hope?'

Biggles was somewhat taken aback; but even as he automatically answered '*Ja*,' he realised what had happened. The man had noticed his spotted tie and had taken him for a member of the organisation for which he himself was working. This, up to a point, was the very purpose for which Biggles had adopted the tie; but he was hardly prepared for it to operate so soon, and so effectively. Too effectively, in fact; for it seemed to him at that moment that it was likely to be embarrassing. For this reason he would have avoided further conversation had it been possible, but as it was not he resolved to take advantage of the incident if this could be done without arousing the man's suspicions. It should not be difficult, he thought, for the fellow did not strike him as being a particularly bright type. Thinking quickly, he decided that to end the conversation too abruptly might set the fellow wondering, and in the end do more harm than good.

Said the man: 'We travel together perhaps?'

'Perhaps,' answered Biggles. Outwardly his manner was casual; inwardly he had qualms, for he was afraid that remarks by the man might be passwords, to which he would be expected to return the correct answers.

However, the man went on. 'Are you under orders, or are you only returning home?'

'Orders,' replied Biggles. 'I go to Prague.' He felt safe in saying this, knowing that the man had tickets for that city. His presence in the same aircraft would now appear natural.

'So. I also go to Prague,' admitted the man.

'Like me, you are here to meet the London plane?' prompted Biggles.

'*Ja.*'

'I have a fellow traveller on board.'

'And me.'

'One of the regulars, I suppose?'

'*Ja.*'

'I'm no longer doing that work,' said Biggles casually. 'I have a more important man to meet. In Prague we shall meet at the usual hotel, no doubt?'

'I go to the Hotel Schweiz, in the Moldaustrasse.'

'That's right,' agreed Biggles. 'I may see you there.'

'You were lucky to get promotion,' said the man in a surly voice.

'I have been nothing but a *Laufbursche* (errand boy) for years. I was told there was money in the business, but what I get is hardly enough to live on.' The man spoke bitterly.

'Don't worry,' Biggles told him consolingly. 'Your turn will come. Take my advice and be more careful what you say. If I reported what you said it would mean trouble for you.'

Fear leapt into the man's eyes. 'Yes, I shouldn't have said it. I try hard at my work, but sometimes I feel it is not noticed.'

'I'll put in a word for you,' promised Biggles.

'*Danke schon.*'

'Do you go with your man to the end of his journey?' inquired Biggles.

'No. Only to Prague.'

'These men must wonder where they are going.'

The man smiled unpleasantly. 'Those do, certainly, who are given fur coats.'

'That's what I think,' returned Biggles, his face expressionless.

The appearance of the London plane put an end to the conversation. The man walked nearer to the barrier while Biggles remained where he was until Marcel returned with the tickets. He took them from him. 'Don't wait,' he said quietly. 'We may be watched, and you may be recognised. I will get in touch with you later. *Au revoir.*'

'*Au revoir, mon ami.*' Marcel turned away.

Biggles walked forward, and seeing Ginger, joined him. He moved quickly, for he realised that the German to whom he had been speaking, seeing two passengers wearing spotted ties, Ginger and Ross, might be puzzled. When Biggles greeted Ginger the man went over to Ross, who was looking about him, and any doubts about identification were settled.

'Any news?' Biggles asked Ginger, as soon as landing formalities had been complied with.

'Nothing,' answered Ginger quietly. 'I had a word with Ross coming over. He still doesn't know where he's going. All he knew was, a man wearing a spotted tie would meet him here. That's the fellow he's talking to now I suppose.'

'Quite right. It was rather funny. We were both waiting here and the fellow noticed my tie. He spoke to me, but I didn't learn much.'

'Did you find out where he's taking Ross?'

'I already knew that. Marcel was here. He told me the fellow had two tickets for Prague. But that's only the next hop. Apparently Ross goes on from there with someone else.'

'Do we travel with them?'

'Of course. I have two tickets for Prague in my pocket. Marcel got them for me. I told the chap that I, too, was expecting a friend on the London plane, and was then going on to Prague. He won't be surprised, therefore, to see us on board. That's the machine over there – the Douglas with the Czech Airline markings.'

'You'll leave the Proctor here, then?'

'Can't do anything else. I shouldn't get far if I landed it at Prague. The police would be on me like a ton of bricks.'

'You decided to take me with you?'

'Yes. This is where our troubles may begin. I may need help.'

'It'll be dark when we get there.'

'So much the better.'

'Where are we going to stay when we get there?'

'I shall try to get in at the Hotel Schweiz.'

'Why there?'

'Because that's where our friend over the way is taking Ross.'

Ginger whistled softly. 'Good work. We shall still be able to keep an eye on him.'

'That's what I'm hoping. The big problem will be how to follow

Ross when he's moved on again. I imagine he won't be long in Prague. But we can only deal with that when the time comes. Let's go over to the machine. Here's your ticket. It'll be all right for us to sit together, but there can be no more talking to Ross.'

They moved on towards the aircraft bearing the O K registration letters of Czechoslovakia.

CHAPTER V

Behind the Curtain

It was dusk when the Douglas glided over the boundary lights of Ruzyn Airfield, the civil airport of the ancient Bohemian city of Prague.

There had been no developments on the journey. Indeed, Biggles and Ginger, who sat together, hardly spoke. The same might be said of Ross and his escort, who also sat together, although in that case conversation may have been handicapped by language difficulties. The remaining seats were occupied by ordinary-looking people, mostly men; but with so much political intrigue going on in Europe Biggles did not lose sight of the possibility that some of these were not so inoffensive as they appeared to be.

After landing, the usual formalities were observed. As far as Biggles was able to see there was nothing abnormal about this procedure; but knowing something of totalitarian methods he felt sure that hidden eyes were scrutinising the passengers closely. Approaching the Customs barrier he deliberately allowed Ross and his escort to go first, in order to keep his eyes on them; and in doing this he observed the first sign of under-cover behaviour. It was not conspicuous. Indeed, had he not been watching closely it would have passed unnoticed. Standing behind the uniformed

Customs official was a dour-looking civilian. As Ross put his bag on the counter, his companion's hand went to his tie, as if to straighten it. It appeared to be a careless movement: but it brought response. The civilian took a pace forward and touched the uniformed man on the arm. Forthwith the official, without even a question, put his chalk mark on the bags carried by Ross and his escort, who then simply walked on through the barrier.

Biggles, followed by Ginger, was next in the queue. They put their luggage on the counter. Biggles' hand went to his tie. For a split second his eyes met the hard gaze of the civilian watcher. Again the Customs man was touched on the arm. On the two pieces of luggage went the chalk mark. Biggles picked up his bag and walked on. Ginger did the same. Not a word was spoken.

Not until they were walking through the reception hall did Biggles speak. Then all he said was: 'Easy, wasn't it?'

Ginger, who apparently had not noticed this piece of by-play, answered: 'I don't get it.'

'Tell you later,' murmured Biggles.

Ross and his escort were now getting into a taxi. Biggles hurried after them. 'As we are going to the same hotel, do you mind if we share your cab?' he asked.

'Get in,' replied the German, in a flat voice that suggested disinterest.

Biggles and Ginger got in. What Ross was thinking of all this Ginger could not imagine. The soldier's face was like a mask.

The cab rattled along over a greasy road between misty lights, for a slight drizzle of rain was beginning to fall.

All Ginger could think was, this is going too well; much too well. It can't last.

However, nothing happened. As usual, when strangers travel together, no one spoke. The atmosphere created was stiff, and

Again the Customs man was touched on the arm.

Ginger was relieved when the taxi at last pulled into the kerb outside a hotel that was clearly of the second, or even the third, class.

Biggles said he would pay the taxi, which he did, and the time occupied by this allowed the others to enter the hotel just in front of him. The door opened into the usual small, gloomy vestibule, with a reception desk on one side, and, at the far end, a flight of stairs leading to the upper rooms. Old travel posters and notices covered most of the wall space. A table littered with papers and magazines occupied the middle of the floor. A dusty aspidistra wilted in an ornamental stand in a corner.

A heavily-built, untidy-looking man, sat in shirt-sleeves at the reception desk. He looked up as the visitors entered and pushed forward the customary forms. Biggles heard him say to the man in front of him, speaking in German, 'Good evening, Herr Stresser. The same as before? So. Number twenty-one.' As he spoke he unhooked a key and passed it over.

'*Danke*,' acknowledged Ross's escort, and thus Biggles learned his name.

Stresser filled in two registration forms with a facility born of experience while Biggles stood at his elbow awaiting his turn. The formality complete, Stresser and Ross picked up their bags and went on up the stairs. Biggles and Ginger then filled in their forms and showed their false passports.

'A double room or two singles?' inquired the proprietor.

'Double,' answered Biggles.

The man's eyes went to Biggles' tie, and then moved up to his face. 'Want to be on the same floor as Stresser?' he asked, evidently supposing them to be engaged on the same business – which in a way they were.

'Yes.'

The man unhooked another key. 'Twenty-two. First floor. Turn right at the top of the stairs.'

'Thanks.'

Biggles, followed by Ginger, went on as directed. Biggles stopped outside number twenty-two, unlocked it and went in. He switched on the light and closed the door behind him. He laid a finger on his lips warningly. 'Careful,' he breathed. 'There may be dictaphones.' Then he smiled. 'We're doing very nicely, aren't we?' he said softly.

'It's too easy,' replied Ginger suspiciously. 'All traps are easy to get into. It's the getting out that's the job.'

'I'm not thinking of getting out,' returned Biggles, taking his small-kit from his bag and putting it on the dressing-table.

'Ross and this bloke Stresser are in the next room,' said Ginger doubtfully. 'Isn't that a bit too close to be comfortable?'

'On the contrary, I think it's all to the good,' said Biggles, examining the walls. 'I want to talk some more to Stresser. I have an idea he might let something drop. At all events he seems to have a grievance against his employers. Such men are usually ready to blab to anyone who will listen to their troubles. I wouldn't trust him a yard.'

'What about something to eat?' suggested Ginger.

'Yes, we shall have to have a bite,' admitted Biggles. 'There doesn't appear to be a dining-room in this shabby joint, so presently I'll ask Stresser if he knows of a place where we can get a meal at a reasonable price. No doubt he does. I'm hoping he'll tell us where he eats himself. We could join him there. After a little food and a drink he may thaw out a bit. It should make Ross feel more comfortable, too, if he sees us around.'

In the event, this little plan did not mature; for when, after a wash, Biggles went to the next room, a tap on the door produced no response. From the proprietor he learned that Stresser and his companion had gone out. He did not say where they had gone. He may not have known. But he named a small restaurant not far away where a reasonable meal could be obtained. Biggles went to the place hoping to find Stresser there, but in this he was disappointed. He and Ginger had a mediocre meal. They lingered over their coffee, but Stresser did not put in an appearance.

In fact, to Biggles' chagrin, they did not see either Stresser or Ross again that night. They heard them come home, but it was after midnight, and Biggles could not think of a reasonable excuse for starting a conversation at such a late hour.

The night passed without incident.

The following morning Biggles was on the move early, for he had no intention of letting his man slip through his fingers if it could be prevented.

'What are you going to do?' asked Ginger, as they dressed.

'What we do will depend entirely on what Stresser does with Ross,' returned Biggles. 'For the moment I am concerned only with keeping them in sight. It's no use thinking beyond that.'

'If we go on following Ross, Stresser, unless he is a nitwit, will get suspicious.'

'I'm afraid you're right. But we daren't lose sight of him.'

'Suppose they go to Russia?'

'That's something I'd rather not think about. But, whatever happens, we can't abandon Ross.'

'Of course not.'

'Then stop worrying. The luck has been good so far. It may go on. Always ride your luck while it lasts. The time to fret is when it goes against you. There's a chance that Ross may have learned something. If he has, he'll find a way to pass the gen on to us. For the moment we'll pack our kit, pay the bill, and then stick around to see what happens, ready to move fast if necessary.'

They went down to find the front door open. The proprietor, half dressed, was sweeping the floor. When Biggles asked for his bill he showed no emotion. This matter settled, Biggles explained that he was expecting a caller, so he would, if there was no objection, leave the bags in the vestibule until such time as he and his friend were ready to leave. To this arrangement the proprietor agreed, and then went on with his work. After a while a woman called him, whereupon he stood his broom against the wall and disappeared through a door into the back premises, leaving Biggles and Ginger alone. As an excuse for being there they sat on a shabby sofa and made a pretence of reading papers taken from the table.

Soon afterwards a car pulled up outside. Glancing over the top of his paper, Ginger saw a man come in – another client, presumably, from the confident way he strode to the stairs and went up. He wore a heavy overcoat with a fur collar, and carried fur gloves, which struck Ginger as odd, for while it was not exactly hot the weather could not be called cold. It did not occur to him that the man might have any connection with his own business.

'I'd say they have some queer customers here,' he murmured to Biggles.

Biggles' eyes were still on the stairs. They switched to Ginger. 'Yes,' he said slowly.

Ginger sensed something. 'What's on your mind?'

'That fellow's fur coat and gloves.'

'What about them?'

'In Paris Stresser said something to me about a fur coat. I wonder?'

What Biggles wondered was not revealed, for at that moment the sound of voices approaching the top of the stairs caused him to break off short. Three men appeared. They were Stresser, Ross and the man with the fur collar. But it was to Ross that Ginger's eyes were drawn. He, too, now wore a heavy overcoat. It had not been buttoned, so that, swinging open, it showed that he no longer wore his dark suit. He appeared to be wearing a drab grey uniform, in the manner of a battledress. On his head he wore a round fur cap, with earflaps tied on top. Stresser wore neither hat nor coat. The implication was plain. He was not going out. The others were.

What followed occupied only a minute of time. As the three of them moved towards the door, only one showed that he was aware of Biggles and Ginger sitting there. Ross. As his eyes passed over them they seemed to flicker, as if he were trying to convey a signal. At the same time a tiny white object dropped from his fingers to the floor. There was no time for more. Ross shook the hand that Stresser held out to him and then he and his new escort were outside. The car door slammed. The engine started. Then, to Ginger's utter dismay, Stresser turned to Biggles, making it impossible for either of them to follow a natural impulse – which was to rush out and seek a means of following the car – without making it obvious that they were shadowing Ross. Nor was it possible, without the action being observed, to pick up the object which Ross had dropped.

'That's another one gone,' said Stresser, his lips parting in a twisted smile to expose decayed teeth.

'Where does he go from here?' asked Biggles, with a nonchalance he did not feel.

'The usual place.'

'Not a nice day for flying,' ventured Biggles, firing a shot in the dark.

Stresser shrugged. 'The weather is better along the route, they say.'

Ginger could have struck the man for his non-committal replies. Apparently he was not such a fool as he looked. At any rate, he was giving nothing away.

'And now, I suppose, you are free to go home?' suggested Biggles, looking at Stresser.

'Yes. I now go back to Berlin for further orders.' Stresser started to walk on, but a thought seemed to strike him. 'Which way are you going?' he asked.

'We are to wait here for the time being.'

'So. Ah, well. I may see you on the Berlin plane.'

'We'll look out for you if we go that way,' promised Biggles.

Stresser walked on. But he was not out of sight when the proprietor came back and, picking up his broom, continued his task of sweeping the floor.

Biggles moved towards the object Ross had dropped. But he was just too late to retrieve it. It had fallen on that part of the floor which had already been swept, but the hotel keeper spotted it, and with a deft flip of his broom it was in a dustpan.

Ginger, whose nerves were on edge, could have cried out.

'Hark!' exclaimed Biggles, raising a warning finger.

The proprietor stopped what he was doing to look at him. 'What is it?'

'I thought I heard someone call out in the kitchen.'

The proprietor put his dustpan on the reception desk, rested the broom against it, and then turned towards the rear of the building. The instant he was out of sight, Biggles' fingers were in the dustpan, turning over the dirt, match sticks and cigarette ends it contained. An exclamation of satisfaction told Ginger that he had found what he was looking for. Without looking at it, Biggles put it in his pocket.

'What is it?' asked Ginger.

'No time to look now,' snapped Biggles. 'Jump to it. We've got to get back to the airport. Our only hope is to find Ross there. Every second counts.' So saying he slammed on his hat, snatched up his bag, and, striding through the open door to the pavement, looked up and down for a taxi. None was in sight.

'Are you sure Ross is flying?' queried Ginger.

'No, I'm not sure,' replied Biggles crisply, 'but Stresser's remark about the weather suggested that he was. Come on.'

Together they hastened down the street towards a broad thoroughfare that crossed it at the end. Here there was a good deal of traffic, and after a brief delay they were able to pick up a cab. Biggles ordered the driver to take them to the airport.

'What's the drill when we get there?' inquired Ginger in a low voice.

'If we can't get on the same plane as Ross we might still be in time to see which way he goes,' replied Biggles.

'What was the thing he dropped?'

'A scrap of paper rolled into a ball.' Biggles took the object from his pocket, unrolled it, and smoothed it on his knee.

Ginger saw that only one word had been written. The word was 'Kratsen.' His eyes went to Biggles' face. 'Does that mean anything to you?' he asked.

'Not a thing.'

'Looks as if it might be the name of a place.'

'If it is, I haven't the remotest idea where it is on the map. It could be the name of anything, or a person. One thing is certain. Whatever the word stands for it must have meant something vital to Ross. He must have been pushed for time when he wrote it, or he would have said more. He had time for just one word, and that's it. Pity we couldn't have spoken to him; but it's no use thinking about that now. We can't expect the luck all our own way. We'll deal with the mystery later. Here we are.'

The car was now pulling up at the airport, outside the main entrance. Biggles jumped out, paid the fare, and walked on into the big booking-hall, looking around anxiously. It was, it seemed, the busy hour, and there were a lot of people about, both coming and going. From the concrete apron beyond came the clatter of aero motors. A big Berlin transport was discharging its passengers. Biggles paid no attention to them, his efforts being concentrated on finding Ross and his new escort.

It was Ginger who at last spotted them. 'There they go,' he said shortly, inclining his head towards a barrier through which the men they sought were at that moment passing. Biggles strode to the gate, but not having a ticket was not allowed to go through; so all he and Ginger could do was stare at the retreating figures as they walked towards a twin-engined passenger plane that was clearly on the point of taking off.

'Call him!' urged Ginger desperately.

'Daren't risk it,' muttered Biggles. 'If we call attention to ourselves here, we've had it. The place will be stiff with snoopers.'

'What machine is that they're making for?'

'An L I-2. Russian job. Crib of the Douglas.'

'Find out where it's bound for.'

Biggles turned to the man in charge of the barrier and put the question. But at that moment the man slammed the gate, drowning his words, and walked out on to the concrete. The engines of the aircraft roared.

Biggles stared at the machine as it began to move. There was nothing he could do. 'We've lost him,' he muttered bitterly. Ginger had never seen his face so grim.

Helpless, they watched the machine take off. Then Biggles said: 'Let's go to the inquiry office and see what we can learn there.' He turned away abruptly, and in doing so collided with one of the several passengers of the Berlin plane who were now leaving the Customs office.

'Sorry,' apologised Biggles. The word seemed to die on his lips as he found himself looking into the eyes of the last man he expected to see there. It was Erich von Stalhein.

For an instant, the expression on the German's face made it clear that his astonishment was as great as Biggles. But he had for long been trained in the hard school of experience, and he recovered his equanimity quickly. 'Good morning, Bigglesworth,' he said suavely. 'I hardly expected to see *you* here.'

Biggles smiled faintly. 'I certainly didn't expect to see you, either,' he admitted.

'I'm quite sure you didn't,' returned von Stalhein, with a sort of grim humour. His eyes were now looking past Biggles' shoulder.

Biggles knew why. 'If you're expecting friends, we won't detain you.'

'As a matter of fact, I am rather busy,' said von Stalhein. 'We shall meet again, no doubt.'

'I have quite a lot to do myself,' murmured Biggles.

'So I imagine,' came back von Stalhein dryly. And with that he walked on briskly.

Biggles made for the exit. 'Pity about that,' was all he said to Ginger.

Ginger was watching von Stalhein over his shoulder. 'He's gone to the Police Bureau.'

'Of course. We've got about fifteen seconds to get out of this.'

Outside the building Biggles looked up and down. Not a taxi was in sight, but a number of private cars were parked on the opposite side of the road, which, at this point, being a terminus, widened to a broad area. Without speaking he walked over to them. The doors of the first one were locked. The same with the second. It was a case of third time lucky. The door of the next car, a big saloon, swung open. 'In you get,' he told Ginger crisply.

Ginger, his eyes on the exit of the building opposite, scrambled in.

As Biggles dropped into his seat and slammed the door, von Stalhein, with three police officers, appeared in attitudes of urgency. They looked up and down. By the time they had turned their attention to the cars Biggles had his engine running. This, inevitably, called attention to it. The police started forward, but the car was now moving. 'Hold your hat,' warned Biggles, and the car shot forward.

Ginger saw a policeman dash back into the hall. He passed the information.

'Gone to the phone,' guessed Biggles. 'I'm afraid we've started something.'

'We shan't get far in a stolen car,' declared Ginger.

'We shouldn't have got anywhere had we waited for a taxi,' Biggles told him. As the car raced on he continued whimsically: 'There's one comforting thought when one is engaged on a job of this sort. One can do anything without making matters worse. From the moment we got the wrong side of the Iron Curtain we were booked for a high jump if we were caught. So the worst that can happen to us now is no worse than it was an hour ago.'

'An hour ago we had a chance of getting home,' reminded Ginger cuttingly, as Biggles swerved to avoid a careless cyclist.

'We've still got a chance.'

'I wouldn't call it a bright one.'

'Maybe we can do something to brighten it,' said Biggles lightly. 'Think how dull life would be if everything was always bright.'

'What foul luck we had to bump into von Stalhein.'

'Just one of those things, laddie. You can't expect jam on your bread all the time.'

On the outskirts of the city a policeman appeared in the middle of the road, arm raised. He realised just in time that this will not stop a car if the driver does nothing about it. Wisely, he gave it right of way. A bullet from his pistol *whanged* against some metal part of the vehicle.

After that Biggles went only a short distance. 'I think that's far enough,' he observed, and running the car against the kerb in a busy street, got out. 'Cars wear number plates,' he remarked. 'Fortunately, pedestrians don't have to, so we shall be safer on our feet.'

Ginger, too, got out. 'Where are you going to make for?' he asked, as they turned their backs on the car.

'I was just wondering the same thing,' replied Biggles. 'I think for a start we'll go back to the hotel.'

Ginger pulled up dead. 'Are you out of your mind?' he cried.

'Probably,' answered Biggles sadly.

CHAPTER VI

Money Talks

For a little while they walked on, threading their way along the busy pavements. At last Ginger's patience broke down.

'What's the idea of going back to the hotel?' he demanded. 'Inside an hour the police will have contacted every hotel in the city to find out where we stayed last night.'

'That's how I reckoned it,' agreed Biggles. 'It gives us an hour to do what I have in mind.'

'And what's that?'

'Have a chat with Stresser – if he's still there.'

'Stresser! Why not give ourselves up at the police station and have done with it?'

'We may arrive there eventually.'

'But Stresser! That's asking for it.'

'Possibly, but not necessarily. The point is, Stresser is the only man we know who may know where Ross has gone. If we lose touch with Stresser we've lost the trail. In a word, he is now a vital connecting link – the only one we have, in fact.'

Ginger became mildly sarcastic. 'What makes you think he'll tell you what he knows?'

Biggles smiled. 'A feeling in my bones. I have in my pocket an argument which seldom fails with his type.'

'A gun?'

'Nothing so crude. Something much more genteel and effective.'

'What, then?'

'Money. If, as they say, money talks, a big wad can fairly scream.'

'But the man's a Communist!'

'So what? I have yet to meet a Communist who wasn't interested in money. It's not having any that makes him a Communist. He wants some, and the only way he can think of to get it is, as he hopes, by getting his hands into the pockets of those who have.'

'Communists hate capitalists.'

'Of course. But they'd all be capitalists if they knew how. I know one. Apart from being a bit cracked, he's not a bad sort. How does he spend his time? I'll tell you. Filling in football coupons. For fun? Not on your life. He's hoping to get a lot of money quickly without working for it. The day he wins a big prize, if he ever does, he'll stop being a Communist. He'll be all against the Reds for fear they take his money off him. I'll wager Stresser became a Communist because he thought there was easy money in it. Now he finds there isn't. He as good as told me that he's fed up with the game because he isn't paid enough. That means he'll switch to anyone who offers him more. You watch it. Anyhow, it's worth a chance.'

'It's taking a pretty big chance.'

'If you don't take chances, you don't take anything.' Biggles raised a finger to a cruising taxi and named the hotel as his destination.

'What comes after the hotel?' inquired Ginger, as the taxi threaded its way through the traffic.

'We'll lie low while we think things over. A little foresight has provided us with a hide-out for use in just such a situation as this.'

A couple of minutes later the cab dropped them at the hotel. The proprietor was still tidying the vestibule. Biggles asked him if Herr Stresser had left. The man said no. He thought he was still in his room. Biggles went on up the stairs. A tap on the door of number twenty-one caused it to be opened by the man they were looking for. 'Oh, it's you,' he said, rather uncomfortably.

'Were you expecting someone else?' asked Biggles.

'You never know who's going to call on you in this business,' grumbled the man.

'How right you are,' murmured Biggles. 'May we come in?'

'What do you want?'

'Before I answer that question we'd better have the door shut,' said Biggles quietly. Followed by Ginger, he went in and closed the door behind them. 'Now,' he went on, facing Stresser, who was by this time looking somewhat alarmed, 'could you use some money?'

Stresser stared. 'M-money?' he stammered. 'How much money?'

'Say, a thousand West Marks.'

The German's jaw fell. 'What for?' he blurted. Then suspicion leapt into his eyes. 'Who are you?' he asked nervously, flicking his tongue over his lips. He dropped into a chair.

'We're British Intelligence agents,' Biggles told him bluntly. 'All right – sit still. We're not going to hurt you. You complained to me that you weren't paid enough for what you were doing. I can put that right.' Biggles showed his wad.

Expressions of fear, doubt and avarice, chased each other across the German's face. At the finish fear dominated the rest, and Ginger knew why. Stresser was afraid that the offer was a trap set by his own employers.

'Well, what about it?' asked Biggles impatiently. 'I've no time to waste.' He toyed with the roll of notes suggestively.

Stresser's eyes glistened. The notes seemed to fascinate him. 'How do I know you're what you say you are?'

'You'll have to take that on trust,' Biggles told him. 'You wouldn't expect me, being what I am, to walk about this city with proofs of identity in my pocket?'

'No,' conceded Stresser.

'Then make up your mind. If you feel inclined to talk you can pull out, with the money in your pocket, and be in Western Germany in an hour or two. You'd be safe there.'

Stresser drew a deep breath. 'What do you want to know?'

'Where have they taken your new recruit, Ross?'

'So you were following us?'

'Of course. But you're wasting time. Where is Ross?'

Stresser cleared his throat. 'He's on his way to Korea.'

It was Biggles' turn to stare. Suspicion clouded his eyes.

'Korea? What are you trying to give me?'

'Well, not exactly Korea. Actually, its Manchuria. But it's to do with the Korean war.'

'What's the name of the place?'

'Kratsen.'

'Did you tell Ross he was going to Kratsen?'

'Yes.'

'Why?'

'He kept asking where he was going, so I told him to keep him quiet. It was too late for him to back out, so it didn't matter.'

'Did you tell him where Kratsen was?'

'I told him it was in Poland.'

'Why lie about it?'

Stresser shrugged. 'One has to lie in this dirty game – you know that.'

'Is Ross on his way to Kratsen now?'

'Well, not exactly.'

'What do you mean by that? Don't talk in riddles.'

'Well, he should have gone direct to Kratsen, but he was a bit difficult, so he's been allowed to make a call first.'

'What was he difficult about?'

'He wanted to see a friend of his.'

'What was his name?'

'Macdonald. I brought him out some time ago.'

'I gather he isn't at Kratsen?'

'Not yet.'

'Where is he?'

'In the Soviet Zone of Berlin.'

'Doing what?'

'Broadcasting.'

'Propaganda?'

'Of course.'

Biggles' face remained expressionless. 'So at this moment Ross is on his way to Berlin to see Macdonald?'

'Yes.'

'How long will he stay there?'

'I don't know. One day perhaps. Perhaps a week. It depends. But afterwards he'll go on to Kratsen. I expect Macdonald will go with him. He must be about finished in Berlin.'

'What's going on at Kratsen?'

'Broadcasting. There's a new radio station there. Men are made to broadcast to the United Nations Forces in Korea, saying what a good time they're having.'

Ginger could now see daylight. He felt sure that Stresser was telling the truth. He had heard of such broadcasts.

Biggles' eyes were still on Stresser. 'Suppose Ross refuses to broadcast?'

Stresser shrugged.

'One last question,' said Biggles curtly. 'Where will Ross stay in Berlin? It will be in the Soviet Zone, of course?'

'Yes. The Hotel Prinz Karl, in the Zindenplatzer. I've stayed there myself sometimes. It's one of the regular places, like this.'

Ginger was looking at Biggles. His face, now set in hard lines, seemed to have aged suddenly. That the information Stresser had given him had shocked him severely was plain.

'Did you tell Ross what was in store for him?' Biggles asked Stresser.

'No. I thought it might depress him.'

'That was considerate of you,' sneered Biggles. He tossed the roll of notes on the table. 'All right, that's all,' he said. 'My advice to you is get out of this country, and keep out. Try to double-cross me and I'll remember it if we ever meet again.' With that he turned on his heel and left the room.

Outside, in the corridor, he turned for a moment to face Ginger. 'Manchuria, of all places,' he breathed. 'I wasn't thinking of anything outside Europe. Poor Ross. He'll think we've forsaken him.'

'But we haven't,' protested Ginger.

'Not on your life,' grated Biggles.

'Stresser was telling the truth?'

'I'm pretty sure of it, otherwise he needn't have mentioned Macdonald. But come on, let's get out of this place for a start.'

They went on down the stairs and into the street. The proprietor did not speak to them, and they did not speak to him. But five minutes later, from the end of the road, when Ginger looked back, he saw a car pull up outside the hotel. Some policemen alighted busily and went in. 'We cut it fine. I've an idea Stresser has left it a bit late,' he told Biggles. 'If the police find that money on him, he's had it.'

'I shan't lose any sleep on that account,' rejoined Biggles caustically, and strode on.

'You know where you're going, I hope?' queried Ginger.

'I made a point of studying a map of the city before we left home,' answered Biggles. 'You'd better not walk with me. The police will be looking for two men. Drop behind a bit.' He walked on, keeping to the main streets, where traffic, both vehicular and pedestrian, was most congested.

Twenty minutes later, after crossing a bridge over what Ginger took to be the River Moldau, they were in what was clearly the old quarter of the city. A fine drizzle of rain was now falling again. It did nothing to brighten the aspect of rows of houses that were obviously of great age. There were some small shops. Some of the goods offered in them looked as ancient as the houses. Ginger had no idea of where they were, but Biggles seemed to know, although more than once he looked up at street names on corner houses. There was very little traffic now, and what few people were about hurried along under dripping umbrellas.

At last Biggles waited for Ginger to join him. 'This is the street,' he said and, going on a short distance, turned into a drab little shop which carried over the door a board with the name Johann Smasrik, in faded paint. The establishment appeared, from the things in the dingy window, to be something between a jobbing tailor's and a second-hand clothes store. A bell clanged as he opened the door, to be greeted by the warm, sickly smell of ironing.

Ginger closed the door behind them and turned to find that they were being regarded by a mild-looking little man of late middle age, who peered at them over an old pair of steel-rimmed glasses balanced on the end of his nose. There seemed to be something wrong with his figure, and as he put down the hot iron with which he had been working, and turned towards them, it could be seen

A bell clanged.

that he was deformed, one shoulder being higher than the other. Everything about him, his threadbare clothes and his surroundings, spoke of extreme poverty and a dreary existence. Wherefore Ginger's first emotion was one of pity.

The man was still looking at his visitors questioningly. 'Do you speak German?' asked Biggles in that language, his left hand holding his lapel.

'*Ja, mein Herr.*'

Biggles went on. 'The weather is very unsettled.'

The man agreed. 'It is always raining.' He sighed.

'I have lost a button from my coat,' said Biggles.

'I wondered if you could match it for me?'

The little shopkeeper's manner seemed to change. 'English?' he asked softly.

'Yes.'

'Trouble?'

'Yes.'

'Were you followed?'

'No.'

'Come inside while I make sure.' The man spoke English in a cultured voice without a trace of accent. He opened a door at the back of the shop.

Biggles and Ginger went through and found themselves in a little living-room that was in keeping with the shop.

'Wait,' said their host, and returned to the shop.

He was back in two or three minutes. 'I think it's all right,' he said in a soft voice that in some curious way conveyed confidence. Then he smiled. 'Of course, one can never be sure. Tell me quickly, what has happened?'

Biggles answered. 'A special mission brought us to Prague. We did our work, but at the airport we were recognised by an enemy agent whom we thought was in London. He fetched the police. Not seeing a taxi, we took a car from the parking-place, abandoned it in the city, and then made our way here.'

'Which means that you are on the run with the security police looking for you?'

'Exactly.'

'What can I do for you?'

'We're looking for somewhere to lie low until we can make arrangements to get out of the country. Can you fix us up?'

'Who gave you this address?'

'Number seven.'

'I see. Then you'd better stay here,' said the man thoughtfully. 'Naturally, I don't like people using this house, but in this case I see no alternative. The address would only have been given to you in a matter of the gravest importance.'

Biggles looked at the man curiously. 'You speak English very well.'

'Naturally, since I am British,' was the reply. 'My name is easily remembered. It is Smith – yes, even when I am in England. Come this way. I cannot leave the shop for very long in case a customer comes in, but we will talk later.'

The agent led them up three flights of rickety wooden stairs to an attic which was nearly full of lumber – useless stuff most of it appeared to be. There was an old table, some broken chairs, with numerous cases and boxes half-buried under old clothes, curtains, pieces of carpet, and the like. The only light filtered through a grimy skylight in the sloping roof.

'Now listen carefully,' said Smith. 'You will stay in this room and not leave it on any account without my permission. Make yourselves as comfortable as the place permits, but disturb nothing; and leave nothing about, not a crumb, or a speck of cigarette ash, or anything that might suggest that the room has been occupied. You will realise that an establishment of this sort is subject at any moment, day or night, to a police raid, and a thorough search. One thing, however small; not in keeping with the rest, could produce unfortunate consequences.'

Biggles nodded. 'I understand. Have you any reason to suppose that you are suspect?'

'No. But it is unlikely that I would know if I was. One never knows in our business. But I shall know now, definitely, within a few hours.'

'What do you mean by that?'

'I mean this. If the secret police had any reason to suspect this house they would not show their hand at once. The only bird they would catch, perhaps, would be me. They would wait for such a moment as this. When, in an hour or two, you are not found, it will be known that you have gone into hiding. Then the police will strike at every establishment to which the slightest suspicion is attached. Such raids usually occur after dark, when a cordon can be drawn round the suspected house without alarming the occupants. In daylight such an operation could hardly be carried out unobserved.' Smith smiled. 'So you should be safe for an hour or two, anyway.'

'I follow,' murmured Biggles.

'But if there should be a raid you still have one way of escape,' continued Smith. 'All the clutter you see here appears to have been thrown in haphazard. At least, that was the intention. But far from that being the case it has been carefully arranged to provide me with an emergency exit. In the event of trouble, I want you to use this way out, because were you found here it would be the end of me as well as you.' Smith pointed to the skylight. 'That is the way you could go. Downstairs, under my counter, there is a button on the floor. When I press my foot on it, it operates a buzzer concealed in one of these boxes. Should you hear the buzzer, therefore, you will know that the security police are below. That will be your signal for a swift, but silent, departure. The table, as you see, is under the skylight. By putting this box on it the skylight can be reached. Having gone through – closing the skylight behind you of course – you will find yourself on a sloping roof. Turn to the right. It is ten yards to the end of the gable. There you will find a chimney stack. Hidden in the nearest chimney-pot there is a rope. This will enable you to descend the twenty feet to a flat roof below. Take the rope with you, for you will need it again. Apart from that, it would not do to leave it hanging there, as it might be seen from the street. Carry on along the flat roof to the end of the block. Below, there is the yard of a scrap metal merchant. A door in the wooden fence on your right opens into the street. After that you would have to take your luck.'

'And what would you be doing all this time?' inquired Biggles.

Smith shrugged his hunched shoulder. 'I should stay behind and bluff the thing out. That would give you time to get away. But don't worry about me. That's as much as I have time to say now. I shan't operate the alarm signal unless things look serious. If it should happen, what are you going to do with those?' He pointed to the two handbags. 'Should you have to leave by the roof you would find them in the way; yet should the place be searched it wouldn't do for them to be found here.'

Biggles agreed. 'What do you suggest we do with them?'

'I think you had better let me have them until the danger period is over,' said Smith. 'I have a place, where I keep some of my own things, where they would be safe. You can have them any time you want them.' He picked up the bags. 'I'll bring you some food in the lunch hour. We'll talk again then.'

'Thank you,' acknowledged Biggles.

Smith smiled again. 'No need to thank me. I'm here to do a job and I try to make the best of it. See you later.' He went out.

'Stout fellow, that,' said Biggles, finding a seat on a box.

CHAPTER VII

Over the Roof

'It's going to be a bit of a bind, sitting here twiddling our thumbs while wretched Ross is flown to the far side of the world,' remarked Ginger presently.

'We should have found it more of a bind had it not been for our friend Smith,' returned Biggles, lighting a cigarette and putting the dead match in his pocket. 'A queer type,' he went on. 'I've met several of them. But then, no normal fellow would take on such a job, spending his life in a hostile country, never knowing when an axe is going to drop on his neck. Beheading, by the way, is a common method of liquidating spies in this part of the world.'

'Why did you have to remind me of that?' complained Ginger.

Biggles smiled.

After a little while Smith returned with a basket of cold food. 'This is the best I can do,' he said as he set the basket on the box.

'Are you short of money?' inquired Biggles.

'Of course not. But if I started buying more than I could eat myself people might wonder who it was for. And here, when people wonder, they talk. They talk out of fear, hoping that by getting someone else into trouble they will avoid it themselves. You have no idea of the sort of life one lives here. The place is rotten with government snoopers and spies. No man dare trust another.'

'What on earth made you choose such a miserable job?' asked Ginger curiously.

Smith shrugged his crooked shoulder. 'With me it isn't so much a job as an occupation,' he explained. 'After all, how could I serve the country? Look at me. As a lad I was crazy to join the army, but a fall in the hunting-field buckled my spine and that was that. My people put me in the hands of a Czech specialist who thought he could cure me. That's how I came to be here in the first place. The cure didn't work, but I got to know the country, the people and the language, so I stayed on. Of course, it was all very different here then. When the war came along the Intelligence people at home were glad to have someone with my qualifications. That's all. I've been here ever since.'

'Do you never go home?' asked Ginger.

'I was just going home when Russia grabbed the country. I was asked to stay and here I am. It isn't as dull as you may suppose. A lot of quite remarkable people pass through my hands, and from them I gather interesting news.'

'But surely you are in touch with home?' prompted Biggles.

'Of course, otherwise what use would I be? I have radio. But not here. It would be dangerous to use it regularly, but it is available should an emergency arise. Why did you ask the question? Have you a message to transmit?'

'It's a matter of getting home,' answered Biggles. 'In view of what has happened it would be futile to try to get out of the country by any form of public transport. If I could make contact with home I could arrange for an aircraft to come out and pick me up. That's all laid on.'

'Are you ready to return home?'

'Yes. There's nothing more we can do here. Fresh plans will have to be made.'

'I gather you haven't actually got an appointment with an aircraft?'

'No. It wasn't practicable to make one, because when we started we had no idea of where we should end up. Aside from that, we had no knowledge of suitable landing-grounds behind the Iron Curtain.'

'I may be able to help you there.'

Biggles looked interested. 'You mean, you know of such a place?'

'Yes. It is one I have used before. You are not the first people for whom I have had to arrange transport home. By air is the best way, and the quickest.'

'Where is this place, this landing-ground?'

'It's a field, on a farm, about twelve miles from here.'

'Would you send a message home for us, giving the pinpoint of the field, a date and a time? Given that information, my own fellows could come out and pick us up.'

'Of course I'll send the message. Let me have it and I'll send it through tonight. There's no need for me to give the location of the field. My contact in London knows it. Just tell me the date and the time.' Smith got up from the box on which he had been seated. 'I must go back to the shop now.'

'What time would you send the message?' asked Biggles.

'About six. The air is stiff with radio at that hour, so my signal – which will be in code, of course – may pass unnoticed by enemy listeners.'

'Six! That means we could get a machine out tonight!'

'Certainly, if there's no hold-up at the other end. Give me your code cipher and the signal will be delivered to your chief immediately it is received. See you later.' Smith went back downstairs.

Biggles turned to Ginger. 'The sooner our people know what's happened, the better.'

'How about Ross? He'll be feeling pretty sick by this time.'

'I haven't forgotten him. Obviously, we shall have to get him out, but it may take a little longer than we expected. I don't see how we can get to him, though, direct from here.'

'I imagine you'll ask Algy and Bertie to fetch us out?'

'Of course. They're standing by. If Smith sends the message at six they should have it by seven. An hour should be long enough for them to get weaving. Another four hours brings us to midnight. Allow a margin of an hour and the machine should be able to get here by one in the morning. The only thing that might upset the schedule is the weather, but there's nothing we can do about that. We'll fix things with Smith next time he comes up.'

They did not see their host until a little after five, when he reappeared with tea and cakes. Biggles had his signal written out ready. Smith looked at it, and said he would see about getting it put into code forthwith.

'The thing that worries me most is the weather,' Biggles told him. 'It was pretty putrid this morning. What's it like now? My pilot must have reasonable visibility for a job of this sort.'

'It's still raining a little, but the clouds are breaking, and the immediate forecast is fair generally.'

'Good,' said Biggles, pouring out a cup of tea.

'I'll leave you now, to get things fixed up,' said Smith. 'The plan, as I shall try to organise it, will be this. First, I'll get the signal off. When receipt is acknowledged from the other end I'll see about the rest, which really means no more than getting you to the landing ground. I can't go with you myself for several reasons, and obviously it wouldn't be wise for you, not knowing the country, to try to find the field yourselves in the dark. At eight-forty-five you will stand by, ready to move off. At nine, a farm cart that has taken vegetables to the central market will pull up outside the scrap-metal yard which I have already mentioned. It's at the corner, about fifty yards from my door. I'd rather the cart didn't stop outside the house. If you hear the driver speak to his horse you will know that no one is in sight. Get into the cart. Cover yourselves with the old sacks which you will find in it. There's no need for you to say anything to the driver. He will indicate when you have arrived at the objective. The journey will take a good three hours. Once you have seen the field the rest will be up to you. I'm sorry if I appear to have made the thing sound melodramatic, but in my experience it doesn't do to leave anything to chance. Success in this sort of operation is more often than not determined by careful planning before the start.'

'How right you are,' agreed Biggles.

'Is there anything you can think of that you might require?'

'We're pretty well equipped, but I'd like a powerful torch, to bring the machine down.'

'I'll get you one.'

'One other thing. What happens if, for any reason, the plane doesn't turn up? Weather conditions or engine trouble might upset the timetable.'

'Yes, that's a point,' conceded Smith. 'I'll make arrangements for the same cart to come back, at dawn, with a load of vegetables. Don't try to get here on it. Just show yourselves to the driver. He'll let me know you're still in the country and I'll try to arrange something. On no account try to get back here by yourselves.'

'Fair enough,' agreed Biggles.

Smith departed.

'I don't know what the country would do without people like that,' murmured Ginger. 'Smith must have nerves of steel to stand the strain of this sort of existence. We take chances, I know, but we keep on the move and have time to get our breath between shows. He's stuck here, without friends, day in and day out.'

'And the people at home take it all for granted – except those in the know,' answered Biggles moodily. 'All the same, I wouldn't say he's entirely without friends. There must be a lot of people in Czechoslovakia who are browned off with being pushed around by the Russians.'

'You know,' went on Ginger, 'I can't help thinking what a stinking bit of bad luck it was, running into von Stalhein as we did. I bet he's fairly set things buzzing.'

'As long as he doesn't come buzzing at Smith's front door, I don't mind,' averred Biggles. 'Smith must know that every time he takes in people like us, he's taking his life in his hands. But, there, he must be well able to take care of himself or he wouldn't have lasted as long as he has.' He looked at his watch. 'The tiresome part of this sort of scheme is the waiting, with nothing to do,' he muttered.

At about seven o'clock, with the daylight fading, Smith came back with some sandwiches. 'Better have a last snack before you go,' he said cheerfully. 'We're all set. Everything is arranged. My contact in London has acknowledged my signal. Your message has been passed on to your department, with implicit instructions for finding the field. The plane should touch down at one in the morning. Come down just before nine. I'll be in the shop, keeping an eye on things. Don't leave anything about, not even a crumb.'

'What's the weather like?' queried Biggles.

'Pretty miserable, but it's improving. The sky should be clear by zero hour.'

'Thank goodness for that.'

'See you presently,' said Smith, and went out.

Ginger watched him go, not knowing that he would not see him again.

The next hour and a half passed slowly, as is always the case when important events are impending. The grey light that filtered through the skylight became weaker, and finally died. The dim twilight in the attic gave way to darkness. Not even a cigarette glowed, for Biggles had refrained from smoking for some time, rather than leave any ash about. Only his wrist watch, at which he looked with increasing frequency, glowed like a luminous eye.

At last he got up. 'Okay,' he said. 'It's a quarter to nine. Let's go down.'

So saying he walked over to the door and opened it. Simultaneously there came a peremptory knocking on what sounded like the door of the shop. Confirmation of this impression came a few seconds later when the bell jangled, announcing that the door had been opened.

Biggles did not move. Ginger, too, stood still with his heart in his mouth, as the saying is.

Up the narrow stairs came the murmur of voices, muffled by distance. Then came the sound for which Ginger was by this time prepared, although he still hoped that his fears were groundless. Somewhere in the room behind them a buzzer buzzed urgently. It was a simple sound, but in the circumstances there was something so sinister about it that Ginger experienced a feeling of chill down his spine.

Biggles closed the door carefully, quietly. 'Apparently we don't leave by the front door, after all,' he said calmly. 'The skylight it is. Up you go.'

'What about Smith?' protested Ginger.

'What about him?'

'We can't just bolt and leave him.'

'Use your head,' said Biggles curtly. 'If we're found on his premises he won't have an earthly. With us out of the way he'll hold his own. He must have made provision for this sort of situation. You're wasting time. Get cracking.'

Ginger delayed no longer. In the light of the torch provided by Smith, held by Biggles; he climbed on to the table, and then on the box that stood on it. This enabled him to reach the single large pane of glass above his head. He pushed it up, and allowed it to fall back gently on its hinges. A pull and he was through, lying flat, groping desperately for a hold on the sloping roof, aghast at what he saw. A few feet below him the roof ended in a black void. From other, similar holes of darkness rose the misshapen gables of ancient roofs, with here and there a gaunt chimney pointing like a black finger at the murky sky. What struck him at once was, Smith must have arranged his escape route in dry weather.

He could have had no idea of what the old tiles would be like after rain. The roof might have been smeared with grease.

'Move along,' said a voice at his elbow, and, twisting his face round, he saw Biggles beside him, replacing the skylight.

'Move along,' muttered Biggles again. 'What are you waiting for?'

Ginger gasped. 'This is frightful,' he managed to get out. 'If I move, I shall slide off.'

'You can't spend the rest of your life where you are,' said Biggles tersely. 'Get weaving. If the police look through the skylight they'll see us.'

The next five minutes were to Ginger something in the nature of a nightmare. Spread-eagled flat on the roof he inched his way along, fingers pressing against the tiles for any slight projection which might help him. Once a piece of moss came away in his hand and he thought he was gone; and he did in fact slide a little way before a protruding nail gave him respite. His eyes never left the chimney stack which was his objective. He thought he would never reach it. When he did, he clawed at it as a drowning man might clutch at a lifebelt; and there he clung, panting, striving to steady

Groping desperately for a hold on the sloping roof.

a racing heart, watching the black shape that he knew was Biggles making the dreadful passage. At the last moment, Biggles, too, started to slide; but with one arm round the chimney stack Ginger was able to give him a hand. For a nerve-shattering moment Ginger feared that the whole stack would come crashing down under their combined weight as Biggles drew himself up. But then the immediate danger was past, and they both paused to recover from the shock of the ordeal.

'By thunder! That wasn't funny,' remarked Biggles, breathing heavily.

'Are you telling me?' panted Ginger.

'Let's get on or we shall miss the cart,' urged Biggles.

Ginger, it may be admitted, in the anxiety of the moment, had forgotten all about the cart.

Slowly and with infinite care Biggles pulled himself erect and put a hand in the chimney-pot. It came out holding the rope which, yard by yard, was withdrawn. Ginger guided the loose end over the edge of the gable, from which the chimney was an extension. What lay below he could not see, but according to Smith there was a flat roof. He stared down, but the starlight was dim with mist, or cloud, and he could see nothing distinctly.

Biggles made a running knot round the chimney. 'Down you go,' he ordered.

The rest was simple. Ginger went hand over hand down the rope and soon found himself on a flat surface. The relief, after the strain, was almost overwhelming. 'Biggles appeared beside him, and brought the rope down with a thud. They coiled it, picked it up, and advanced cautiously until another pool of gloom appeared. Still nothing could be seen distinctly, but below them was obviously the yard of the scrap-metal merchant.

There was a little delay while a projection to which the rope could be fastened was found. Then Ginger went down, to stumble with a clatter on a heap of junk.

'Do you have to make so much noise?' muttered Biggles shortly, as he joined him.

'Sorry, but I can't see in the dark,' answered Ginger coldly, wiping filthy hands on his jacket.

Biggles buried the rope under a heap of rubbish. Then he looked at his watch. 'Five minutes to go,' he whispered. 'This way.'

They could see the street now – or, rather, the position of it – by the glow of lamps. Getting to it without making a noise was another matter, for the place was strewn with old metal objects of every description, from tin cans, bedsteads and fireplaces to the bodies of ancient vehicles. However, the short journey to a low wooden fence that ran between the yard and the street was made without disturbance, and there a halt was called while Biggles, looking over the fence, made a quick reconnaissance.

'No sign of the cart,' he reported presently. 'The corner is just along to the left. There are two cars outside the shop, which means that either the place is being searched or Smith is being questioned. There are one or two people moving about, two of them standing by one of the cars, but they are too far away for me to make out who or what they are. Police, probably. There's nothing more we can do except sit tight and wait for the cart.'

They squatted, Ginger praying fervently that the cart would be on time, and hoping every moment to hear the clatter of hooves. Instead, the sound that came to his ears was of slow foot-steps approaching. That at least two persons were responsible was revealed presently by the murmur of voices. The footsteps approached at the dead-slow pace of men who were waiting for something.

Biggles touched Ginger on the arm and got into the back seat of an old wheelless car, the door of which gaped open. Ginger joined him. The footsteps came nearer. Two voices were talking in German. Ginger's nerves twitched as he recognised one of them. It belonged to von Stalhein. He was saying to his companion: 'But you don't know this man Bigglesworth. I do. I've been trying to pin him down for years, but he's as slippery as an eel.'

'We should have found him by now,' answered the other. 'We've covered all the likely places.'

'Exactly,' replied von Stalhein, sarcasm creeping into his voice. 'All the likely places. You will never find this man by looking in likely places. He has a curious knack of appearing where one would least expect him. If you are sure that he must still be in Prague, the chances are that he is miles away.'

'All roads, airports, and even known landing grounds, are being watched.'

'If you ask my opinion, I'd say he's already on his way to Berlin.'

'Impossible!'

'I've stopped using that word where Bigglesworth is concerned.'

'But how could he know of our arrangements?'

'He could have got the information from Stresser.'

'Stresser swears he knows nothing of the man.'

'Then where did he get all that money?'

'His story is that he got it through a black market deal in Paris. It's possible. We know he was once mixed up with a gang that specialised in that sort of thing.'

'All right. Have it your own way,' said von Stalhein. The footsteps stopped. Then he went on: 'What is this place here?'

'It looks like a refuse dump.'

'Was it covered?'

'No. At least, not as far as I know.'

'Why not?'

'How could they get here without being seen? Don't worry. If Bigglesworth was in that house he is still in it, for the simple reason that I've got all exits, back and front, covered. Don't try to make me believe that this superman can fly like a bird.'

'It wouldn't surprise me to see him do just that,' answered von Stalhein in a hard, bitter voice. His companion laughed.

But it was not this that made Ginger stiffen suddenly. From somewhere not far away came the sound of iron-shod hooves on a hard road.

'What's this coming?' asked von Stalhein.

'A farm cart, by the look of it,' was the reply. Cynical humour crept into the voice. 'Are you expecting to find Bigglesworth inside it?'

'I've known more unlikely things than that,' rejoined von Stalhein grimly. 'I wouldn't let any vehicle leave this street without being searched.'

'Well, that is easily arranged,' said the other. 'We'll do it if it will steady your nerves.'

'I'd have this yard searched, too, in case he managed to slip out,' said von Stalhein.

The cart, moving at walking pace, drew nearer.

CHAPTER VIII

A Ride in the Country

Two pairs of footsteps now receded a little way, as if the men were going to meet the cart, which was coming up the street past the shop. A crisp order cut into the night air. The cart stopped.

What was said to the driver, or what the driver told the police, Ginger never knew; for at this juncture Biggles touched him on the arm and whispered: 'Let's get out of here. Now's the time, while attention is on the cart.'

There was no trouble in getting to the fence. Biggles followed this along to get as far away as possible from the shop, and then, climbing it, lay flat, close against it, until Ginger joined him. From there they wormed their way along to the corner. To Ginger it was the worst moment of all, for there was nothing between them and their enemies, and he expected every instant to hear the alarm given. The murk, which had made things so difficult on the roof, may have saved them from observation. Not until they were round the corner did he breathe freely. Looking about him he saw that they were in a narrow street running at right-angles to the one they had just left. They were, in fact, at a four crossways. Not a soul was in sight, although from somewhere farther up the street came the sound of music and singing – emanating from a café, he supposed.

Biggles crossed the street and stood in a doorway. 'We'll wait here for the cart,' he decided. 'Not knowing which way the driver will turn, we daren't go any farther.'

So they waited. They heard brisk footsteps on the pavement, followed by a good deal of noise in the scrap heap, which told them that von Stalhein's advice about making a search was being followed. Then came the clip-clop of hooves, and the crunch of wheels announced that the cart had resumed its journey.

It did not stop at the corner. It went straight on. Perhaps the driver had been unnerved by what had happened. If so, he could hardly be blamed. He may have had the wit to realise that if he stopped again the police would overtake him to ascertain why.

Realising that the cart was not going to stop, Biggles started off along the pavement, keeping more or less level with it, and as far as possible in the shadows. A short distance ahead a street lamp threw a pale radiance across both pavement and road. Ginger eyed it with misgivings, for, being still within view of the shop, although some distance from it, it obviously represented a zone of danger. But Biggles, it seemed, had no intention of crossing it. In an area darker than the rest, caused by some high buildings, he suddenly said, 'Come on,' and, darting to the rear of the cart, vaulted into it. Ginger did the same. Once more, lying on a pile of empty sacks, he waited for the signal that would announce their discovery; but when it did not come he relaxed with a sigh of relief.

The cart trundled on. If the driver had seen their furtive arrival he gave no sign of it. Ginger could see only a vague silhouette perched high in front of him. As a matter of detail, that was all he ever did see of their unknown ally. The cart went on at a speed that never varied. Clip-clop ... clip-clop went the hooves on the hard road. Occasionally the driver made an uncouth noise, presumably to encourage his horse.

The drizzle had now stopped altogether, and large, starry patches of sky showed that the clouds were dispersing. Still, the night air was chilly, and Ginger was glad to wrap himself in the sacks that still smelt strongly of onions and turnips. Not that he cared about that. His only emotion was one of relief at being out of an unpleasantly tight corner.

Clip-clop … clip-clop …

One hour, or it may have been two, passed, and still the hooves beat their monotonous rhythm on the macadam. To Ginger the sound had become part of his existence.

Eventually he must have dozed, and it may have been the cessation of the sound that aroused him. At all events, he was suddenly aware that the cart had stopped. He started up, looking at Biggles. Biggles was looking at the driver. The driver said not a word, but pointed with his whip to the right-hand side of the road. Biggles dismounted. Ginger followed. The driver clicked his tongue. The harness strained. The wheels crunched. Clip-clop … clip-clop, went the hooves.

Ginger stood with Biggles on the grass verge while the sound faded slowly into the darkness.

'Twenty past midnight,' said Biggles, his voice sounding strange after the long silence. 'We've forty minutes to spare. It may not be too long. Let's get our bearings. The driver pointed this way. Thank goodness the weather's still improving.'

They walked along a low hedge until they came to a gate. This they climbed, to find themselves in a flat field of stubble of unknown extent, for the boundaries were lost in the gloom of distance. At one point a single yellow light showed the position of a cottage, or farm. How far it was away could not be ascertained – not that it mattered.

Biggles walked a little way out into the field and tested the surface with the heel of his shoe. 'Nice and hard,' he remarked. 'I was afraid the rain might have made it soft.'

'Where are we going to wait?' asked Ginger.

'It doesn't really matter,' answered Biggles. 'We should hear the machine long before it gets here. That's the direction it should come from – unless it has run into trouble on the way.' He pointed to the west. 'There's nothing much we can do until it comes, so we might as well take a stroll round the hedge.'

They walked for some way, but, seeing nothing of interest, decided to sit down to wait.

'There is this about it; everything is nice and quiet,' observed Ginger. 'I was a bit worried when I heard that bloke tell von Stalhein that he was having all possible landing-grounds watched. I was afraid they might have included this one.'

'I didn't overlook that,' returned Biggles. 'The same conditions apply as to Smith's shop. There's no telling how much Intelligence people do know, until a situation like this arises to force them to show their hand. They don't seem to have got this place on their list, anyway.'

Hardly had the words left his lips when a motor vehicle of some sort could be heard coming down the road at high speed. Presently its headlights made the trees that occurred at intervals along the hedge stand out like pieces of stage scenery. There was of course no reason to suppose that the car was in any way concerned with them. Indeed, it did not occur to Ginger that this might be the case until it stopped at the gate by which they themselves had entered the field. There was then a good deal of noise, talking, and doors slamming, as if several men were involved. Lights appeared, and against them vague shadows.

Ginger glanced at Biggles in dismay.

'I spoke too soon,' said Biggles lugubriously. 'Smith told us that he has used this field before. Somehow the police must have got wind of it. That's what usually happens, sooner or later.'

'What are we going to do about it?' demanded Ginger.

'If Algy comes, and we signal to him to keep clear, the light will be seen and we shall almost certainly be caught,' answered Biggles. 'Let's wait to see what goes on before we get into a flap.'

'I can see four men,' said Ginger.

'One will have stayed with the car, no doubt. Call it five.'

'What are they doing?'

Two men had remained near the gate. A brittle sound, as of wood striking wood, came through the night air. The other two men began walking across the stubble, slowly, appearing to carry something between them.

'They are trapping the field,' observed Biggles.

'You mean, they're running a wire across it?'

'Yes, about a couple of feet from the ground. The trick is as old as war flying. Any machine trying to land in such a trap is bound to trip up and somersault.'

'Then that settles it,' said Ginger emphatically. 'We can't let Algy land.'

'Don't be in a hurry.' Biggles looked at his watch. 'We've still a quarter of an hour to go. I have a file up my sleeve, don't forget. It was intended for iron bars, so it should have no difficulty in cutting through soft wire.'

'If we try walking across the field we shall be spotted instantly.'

'Certainly we would, if we walked out from here. We'll work from the other side. But before we move we'll wait and see how these smart-alicks finally dispose themselves.'

The operation of trapping a landing-ground, which consists merely of stretching a taut wire across it, does not take long; and presently, after driving in a stake somewhere out of sight, the two men who had gone out into the field were observed returning. The lights of the car were dowsed.

'They're all going to wait together by the gate,' said Biggles. 'That's what I thought they'd do. They suppose they will see everything from there. Come on.' He got up and began walking briskly along the hedge away from the gate. Against the dark background there was no risk of being seen.

At a distance of perhaps a hundred yards the hedge ran into another, running at right-angles to it. Biggles turned to the left and continued on until the original hedge – the one which held the gate opening into the road – merged into the gloom. Then he struck off across the field.

'If we can find the wire and cut it I shall bring Algy down,' he told Ginger in a whisper. 'If we fail we shall have to send the danger signal. If he does come down things are likely to be a bit brisk until we get on board. The blokes at the gate won't move at once. They'll wait for the crash. When there's no crash they'll come out to see why.'

'They'll see your torch signalling to Algy.'

'Of course they will. That can't be avoided. It will probably make them smile, knowing that the field has been wired. Watch out, we're likely to walk into it at any moment now.'

A minute later Ginger felt the wire against his legs. 'Here it is,' he whispered. At the same moment, from somewhere afar off, came the drone of an aero engine.

'Help me to hold this wire steady,' ordered Biggles.

Ginger gripped the wire with both hands near the point at which Biggles' file was already biting into the metal. Two sounds only could be heard. One was the rasp of the file; the other was the murmur of a gliding aircraft.

'This is where we have to burn our boats,' decided Biggles. 'Flash the call sign.' He handed Ginger the torch and went on with his work.

The torch, upturned, cut a series of dots and dashes in the night.

'Nearly through,' muttered Biggles. 'Keep flashing till you get an answer.'

Rasp-rasp-rasp, grated the file.

'Okay. They've seen us,' informed Ginger.

Biggles raised a leg, put his foot on the wire, and jumped. The wire parted with a musical *twang*. At once Biggles snatched up the loose end and began running with it, to get as much of it as possible out of the way.

Ginger's eyes were on the gate – or the position where he knew it to be. There was no sound or sign of movement. Raising the torch again, he flashed it to show their position to the pilot, now circling overhead.

Biggles came back. 'That's all we can do,' he said. 'Watch the gate and tell me if you see 'em coming.' He took the torch and held it low to form a narrow flare path.

For the next sixty seconds, time, to Ginger, seemed to stand still. As Biggles had said, there was nothing more they could do. So there they stood, nerves tense, eyes staring into the dark vault overhead.

'He's a long time, what's he doing?' muttered Ginger impatiently.

'He's trying to avoid collision with something solid,' answered Biggles. 'Quite right. This isn't the moment to make a boob. Here he comes. Watch out he doesn't knock you down!'

The black silhouette of the aircraft suddenly appeared, hardening as it drew nearer. The wheels bumped, bumped again, and the machine ran to a stand-still. Ginger recognised the Proctor. It had overshot them a little way, but they ran on after it, and reached it just as the door was opened.

Bertie stepped out. 'What cheer, chaps!' he greeted. 'Where's this bally Iron Curtain I've heard so much about?'

'It's right here,' Biggles told him curtly. 'Get back in and cut the funny stuff. I'm in no mood for it. In you go, Ginger.'

Bertie returned to his seat. Ginger scrambled in behind him. Biggles followed and slammed the door. 'Peel off, Algy,' he snapped. 'There's no future in staying here.'

As he finished speaking several things happened at once. The engine roared. The Proctor began to move. A searchlight cut a blaze of white light across the stubble. A machine-gun started its vicious rattle, the bullets flicking dirt and scraps of straw into the air.

For a few seconds Algy held the machine low, for speed, banking with one wing-tip nearly touching the ground. Then the Proctor zoomed like a rocket, and the field, with its dangers, faded astern.

'Which way do you want to go?' called Algy.

'Grab some altitude while I think about it,' replied Biggles.

The Proctor continued to climb steeply.

After a minute Biggles went on. 'Make for the nearest German frontier. A course slightly south of east should take us to the American Zone. That'll suit me – for a start, anyway. The thing is to get outside the Curtain.'

'I'll do my best,' promised Algy.

'Do you expect any difficulty?'

'We were challenged on the way out.'

'By what?'

'Flak, when I refused to go down. Radar must have picked us up as we crossed the frontier. I saw a Russian Yak, but I dropped into a cloud and lost it.'

'Did you come across the Russian Zone?'

'Naturally, I came the shortest way.'

'That explains why they were trapping the known landing-grounds on your line of flight. No matter. Carry on. You've less than a hundred miles to go.'

Bertie chipped in. 'By the way, where's our soldier chappie, Ross?'

'On his way to China, via Berlin. They're using these fellows in the Korean war.'

'Here, I say! That's a bit tough!' muttered Bertie. 'Looks as if he's had it. How far is China from here? Never was any bally good at geography, and all that sort of thing.'

'For a rough guess,' answered Biggles grimly, 'China is about five thousand miles farther east than we could get in this kite, even with full tanks. That's why I'm going the other way.'

'But, look here, old boy, you're not going to leave Ross there, are you?'

'I am not,' Biggles told him shortly. 'But I'm not such a fool as to try to fly right across Russia. We'll get something bigger than this and tackle the job from the back door of Asia. But it may not come to that. At the moment Ross is in the Soviet Zone of Berlin.'

'Are you thinking of trying to collect him there?' asked Algy.

'It'd save us a much longer journey if we could. It would also save a lot of time. I wouldn't like Ross to think we'd let him down. Get across the frontier, and we'll talk about it.'

The Proctor droned on.

Algy's fears of interception did not materialise, due perhaps to a new front of cloud that was coming up from the west, in which he took cover. Signals ordering the machine down were received on the radio, but these were of course ignored. There was a flurry of flak as the aircraft approached the frontier, but it never threatened serious danger.

An hour later the Proctor landed, and, after explanations, parked for the night at Frankfurt, in the American Zone of Occupied Germany.

Much later in the day, just as the twilight was becoming dim, it touched its wheels on the great international airport at Berlin.

CHAPTER IX

Biggles Takes a Chance

The weather seemed determined to remain unsettled, and it was raining quietly but steadily when Biggles stepped out of a taxi in a certain street in the British Zone of Berlin. After paying his driver, he crossed the shining pavement and entered an open door over which hung a limp Union Jack.

A sergeant in British battle-dress intercepted him. 'Yes, sir?' he challenged.

'I want to speak to Major Boyd,' Biggles told him.

'Got an appointment, sir?'

'No, but if you take in my name I think he'll see me. Just say it's Inspector Bigglesworth.'

'Very good, sir. Please wait. here.' The N.C.O. strode down a corridor and knocked on a door at the far end. He went in, but reappeared at once with a finger raised. 'This way, sir.'

Biggles walked forward and entered the room. The N.C.O. retired and closed the door behind him.

An elderly man in civilian clothes, who had been seated at a desk, rose to meet Biggles. 'Come in,' he invited. 'Take a seat. What can I do for you?'

'You were expecting me, I think?'

'Yes. I had a signal from London.'

'That would be the result of a phone call I put through to my chief this afternoon. He told me to come to you.'

'What's the trouble?'

'It isn't exactly trouble. One of our operatives is a prisoner in the Soviet Zone. I'm anxious to get him out, or at any rate make contact with him.'

'Can't he get out on his own?'

'He may not try. He's an amateur, a volunteer, in a rather curious business. He doesn't know it, but as far as I'm concerned his work is finished. Through him I've got the information I wanted, so he might as well come home. It's unlikely that he could get out even if he tried. Not knowing what I know, it's more likely that he won't try. Unless I can get hold of him quickly, I may lose sight of him for good.'

'I see. How can I help you?'

'I don't know my way about. That is, I'm not familiar with the Zonal boundaries. I want you to lend me a guide who does. There are reasons why I'd rather not risk being questioned at any of the control points – our own, or Russian.'

'Where exactly do you want to go?'

'I've reason to think that my man is in the Hotel Prinz Karl, in the Zindenplatzer.'

'It shouldn't be very difficult to get you there. When do you want to go?'

'Now, if it's all the same to you?'

'It's all the same to me. D'you want the guide to wait for you and bring you out?'

Biggles hesitated. 'That's a bit difficult. I've no idea how long I shall be. How long could the guide wait?'

'As long as you like, within reason.'

'Suppose he waits for an hour? That should be long enough. If

I'm not ready to leave by then I may be over the other side indefinitely.'

The officer pushed a bell. 'Suppose you get into trouble? Do you want me to do anything about it?'

'No, thanks. It's unlikely that you would be able to do anything, short of starting a full-scale diplomatic row. If our friends over the way get their hands on me, knowing who I am, they'll keep me there.'

'Watch how you go.'

'I'll do that.'

A man came in, a youngish man in a well-worn suit. There were no introductions, but a glance told Biggles that he was a German. This was confirmed when Major Boyd spoke to him in that language, explaining what was required of him. The guide simply said, '*Jawohl*,' and went out, to return a minute later wearing a hat and raincoat. 'I am ready,' he announced, looking at Biggles.

'Thanks, Boyd, much obliged,' said Biggles, and got up.

'No trouble at all. Good luck.'

'Do you want to see me when I come back?'

'Not necessarily. I shall probably have left the office by then. The guide will come back here.'

'Fair enough. Goodbye.' Biggles followed the German into the street.

The man set off at a brisk pace. Not a word was spoken in the long walk that followed. At first the way lay through busy thoroughfares, but presently these gave way to quiet streets in what was obviously a residential quarter. In one of these the guide turned abruptly into a private house, one of a long row built in the same pattern. Three steps led from the pavement to the door. This the guide unlocked with a key which he took from his pocket. They entered. The door was closed. All was in darkness, but the guide switched on a torch, to reveal a long hall. To the far end of this he walked. Another door was opened, and another hall traversed. Yet another door gave access to a street much like the one they had just left. But there was a difference. The soldiers now encountered wore Russian uniforms, not British. The guide walked on, in an atmosphere that had suddenly become sinister. There was no need for him to tell Biggles that they were in the Russian Zone.

Ten minutes brought them to an important street of shops and bright lights. There was a fair amount of traffic. The guide stopped at a corner and spoke for the first time. 'The hotel is about a hundred paces along, on the right. It is the only one, so you cannot make a mistake. A few doors along from here there is a *bierhaus*. I will wait for you there.'

'If I'm not back in an hour, you'd better go home,' said Biggles.

'As you wish.'

Biggles went on alone and had no difficulty in finding the hotel. It was larger, and of much higher class than had been the one in Prague. The clientele was altogether different and, Biggles noticed, included a fair sprinkling of Russian officers. Several cars stood outside. There was also a patrol vehicle of the jeep type, with two soldiers standing by it.

Just how he was going to locate Ross, Biggles did not know. Apart from the name of the hotel he had no information on which to work. He had a vague hope that he might see him, or his escort, passing through the vestibule or in one of the public rooms. If these failed, he decided, he would try his luck with the reception clerk, trusting to his spotted tie to produce answers to his questions. There was, of course, no certainty that it would; but it had worked in Paris and in Prague, so it might work in Berlin.

He had no other plan, for which reason he had told the guide not to wait more than an hour. He himself was prepared to stay there all night, and all the next day, if necessary.

It was obviously not much use standing outside, so he went in through big revolving doors to find himself in a reception hall of some size, furnished with the customary appointments. The office, with its counter and rack of keys, was at the far end near the foot of a broad flight of stairs. Near it was a cloakroom. On either side were doors, one leading into a lounge and the other to the dining-room. Near the door of the lounge, a lift was operated by a uniformed attendant. The usual chairs and settees, with occasional tables near them, were arranged round the walls to leave an open space in the centre. Sitting about were, perhaps, a dozen men, alone or in pairs, some talking, others reading newspapers. So much Biggles took in at a glance.

He walked over to a settee near the lift, intending to sit and watch it for a while. It was occupied by one man, who sat at one end half hidden by a newspaper in which he appeared to be engrossed. Tobacco smoke spiralled up from behind the printed pages. Paying no attention to him, Biggles sat down in a position from which he could keep an eye on the stairs, the lift, the lounge and the dining-room.

He was feeling for his cigarette case when his companion on the settee lowered his newspaper. His attention being elsewhere, he did not notice this until a voice spoke. He paused imperceptibly in the act of taking a cigarette from his case. Then he turned his head, to meet the sardonic eyes of Erich von Stalhein.

'Good evening, Bigglesworth. I was hoping you'd look in.'

Biggles finished lighting his cigarette before he answered. He needed a moment to recover. 'It was nice of you to come along,' he replied. 'Dear me! How you do get about.'

'You're quite a traveller yourself, you know,' came back von Stalhein suavely. 'On this occasion, however, I fear you have given yourself a fruitless journey. You were, I presume, looking for a young man named Ross?'

'What gave you that idea?' questioned Biggles.

'Call it instinct,' answered von Stalhein, smiling. 'It pains me to disappoint you, but I'm afraid you won't find Ross here.'

'No?'

'No. He left here about an hour ago. By now he should be many miles from Berlin.'

Biggles' eyes searched the face of his old enemy, and he decided that he was telling the truth, for the simple reason that there was no need for him to lie. Had Ross still been in the hotel von Stalhein could have said so without risk of losing him.

'I'm sorry about that,' said Biggles evenly. 'Still, it was worth coming here if only to have a word with you. We so seldom have time to compare notes.'

'Surely that's your fault,' protested von Stalhein. 'I wonder you don't exhaust yourself rushing about the world as you do.'

'I like rushing about,' asserted Biggles, who was thinking fast. 'It keeps me alive.'

'One day it will defeat that object,' said von Stalhein gravely. 'Indeed, it may have already done so. By the way, Bigglesworth, you have disappointed me.'

'I'm sorry about that. In what way?'

'I always understood that in your country it is considered bad form to wear a club or regimental tie to which one is not entitled.'

Biggles fingered his tie, laughing softly. 'Yours looked so attractive that I succumbed to temptation. I knew, I must admit, that it was rather – er – exclusive.' He became serious. 'Tell me, why did you decide to join a club, an organisation, which at one time I am sure you would have regarded with abhorrence?'

Von Stalhein sighed. 'We are not always masters of our destiny.'

'That's where you're wrong,' argued Biggles. 'You could be yourself if you could get that grievance bug out of your brain. Do you think you are helping Germany by what you are doing?'

Von Stalhein stiffened. 'That's my business.'

'It seems a pity,' murmured Biggles. 'One day we must go into it, and I guarantee to convince you that tea tastes better on my side of the fence. I can't stop now. Don't forget I have to find Ross.'

'You will have to go a long, long way.'

'That will be nothing new to me,' averred Biggles. Actually, he hardly knew what he was saying, for his brain was occupied with something very different. He had been playing for time, and so, for some reason not apparent, had von Stalhein.

Biggles had been watching the movements of the lift attendant who, from time to time, when his services were not required, did odd jobs, such as folding newspapers thrown down carelessly. He now began to empty the ashtrays on nearby tables into a bowl which he kept handy for the purpose. Biggles had not failed to notice, too, that von Stalhein's eyes went constantly to the main entrance, as if he was expecting someone. When, through the revolving doors, marched a Russian patrol, he understood.

'Well, think over what I've said,' murmured Biggles, reaching casually for the newspaper that lay between them. 'I shall have to be going. Here's your paper.' He flicked the journal into von Stalhein's face and in the same movement vaulted over the back of the settee. Two steps took him to the lift. He slammed the gate and pressed the first button that his finger found. Von Stalhein had moved almost as quickly, but he was a fraction of a second too late. The lift shot upwards.

Biggles counted the floors as they flashed past. The lift stopped at the third. He stepped out. A long, carpeted corridor ran to left and right. To the right, a man in a dressing-gown, towels over his arm, was crossing the passage, apparently going to a bathroom. Biggles walked along, his eyes on the door of the vacated room. It stood ajar. Just inside was a hat and coat stand. Several garments hung on it. They included a Russian officer's cap and greatcoat. He lifted them off and strode on to the end of the corridor. Another passage ran at right-angles. Half-way down it a red light glowed. Putting on the cap and coat as he walked he went on to it and found, as he expected, a door under the red light marked 'Fire Exit.' Opening the door he saw a narrow stone stairway spiralling downwards. He went down. The stairway, he knew, was bound to end at the ground floor. It did, in a stone passage with doors on either side, from behind which came the rattle of crockery. A man, white clad, wearing a chef's tall hat, came out of one of the doors, singing to himself. He looked at Biggles curiously, but said nothing.

'I've lost my way,' said Biggles apologetically. 'Where is the nearest exit?'

The man pointed. 'It is the staff entrance,' he explained.

'*Danke,*' thanked Biggles, and strolled on to the door.

It opened into a dingy little side street. As he stepped out he heard whistles blowing and orders being shouted. Two soldiers came running round the corner. Biggles, already walking towards them, continued to do so, not daring to turn. The men steadied their pace as they passed him, saluting. Biggles returned their salute and went on without a backward glance.

Presently, to his chagrin, he found himself in the Zindenplatzer, with the main hotel entrance twenty yards to his right. Von Stalhein was standing on the steps, gesticulating as he spoke to several uniformed men. Biggles turned the other way. He would have done so in any case, as it was the direction of the corner where he had left his guide. He found the entrance to the *bierhaus* and, turning in, saw his man sitting alone at a small table with a glass

'I shall have to be going. Here's your paper.'

of beer in front of him. There were several other men there, mostly soldiers, but their attention was on a girl at the end of the room, singing at a piano.

Biggles touched his guide on the arm. At first he was not recognised, and the man started guiltily. But when recognition came the man moved in such haste that he nearly knocked his beer over.

'Let's get along,' said Biggles quietly. 'I'm afraid I've started something at the hotel.'

The man needed no persuasion. It was clear that he did not want to be involved. Without a word he went out into the street and hurried along, with Biggles beside him, until they came to a less frequented street, into which they turned. Several cars, travelling at high speed, overtook them, but none stopped. Once they met a police patrol on foot. The leader saluted. Biggles acknowledged.

More narrow streets and the guide turned into an iron gate Biggles recognised it as the one by which they had entered the Soviet Zone. There were, he suspected, from the length of the halls, two houses, built back-to-back. Through them they reached the British Zone.

'Take off those clothes,' said the guide in an agitated voice. 'We may meet a British patrol. Without giving you a chance to prove who you are they may hurry you back into the Soviet Zone. Russians may be watching, too. We are still too close to be safe.'

Biggles lost no time in divesting himself of his borrowed uniform. Presently he threw the cap and coat over the parapet of a bridge into a river. 'They should start a pretty little mystery when they're found,' he remarked.

'Forget everything that has happened,' advised the guide as he went on.

'That won't be easy, but I'll try,' agreed Biggles. 'I had an awkward five minutes. An old friend was waiting for me in the hotel. I had to leave somewhat hurriedly.'

'It often happens that way,' said the guide simply.

A cruising taxi came along. Biggles stopped it. Five minutes later he dropped his companion at the house where he had picked him up. He did not go in.

'Give my compliments to Major Boyd and tell him everything went off all right,' requested Biggles. 'Goodnight, and many thanks.'

Under his direction the taxi then went on to the Airport Hotel where he, and the others, had found accommodation.

'Well, how did you get on?' greeted Algy, when he walked in. 'You didn't get Ross?'

Biggles dropped wearily into a chair. 'No. Von Stalhein was there, waiting. Shook me, I don't mind telling you. My own fault. I should have reckoned on the possibility. He knows I'm after Ross. Naturally, he made things a bit difficult – or would have done, given the chance. Either his plans went wrong or else I arrived a bit too soon for him. Push the bell. I could do with a drink.'

'What about Ross?'

'He's gone.'

'He wasn't in Berlin very long.'

'No, and I can guess why. Once von Stalhein realised I was after him he'd get him out of reach – as he thinks – as quickly as possible.'

'And now what?'

'It looks as if we shall have to go East, after all. We took a chance on coming here. It didn't work, that's all. Oh, well! I'm tired. Walking never did agree with me.'

'When are we pulling out of here?'

'Right away, before von Stalhein can organise any unpleasantness. You can fly me home. I'll snatch some sleep on the way. Don't forget we've got to cross the Russian Zone to get out. Maybe I'm getting nervous, but it would be like von Stalhein to put some Yaks in the air with orders to find a Proctor. Get the machine laid on, one of you, and we'll go home.'

CHAPTER X

The Air Commodore
is Worried

The following afternoon found Biggles in Air Commodore Raymond's office, standing in front of the huge wall map of the world, narrating the events of the previous forty-eight hours, the strain of which was beginning to show on his face. He was, in fact, tired, and as a result of this his manner was inclined to be brusque. Present also at the conference was Major Charles, of the Intelligence Service, and a senior official of the Foreign Office. Their attendance had been requested by the Air Commodore, who thought they ought to hear what Biggles had to say.

'It all boils down to this,' stated Biggles, who had run over the main features of the affair. 'Our operation, from the military or political aspect, was successful in that we have good reason to think we know why these wretched soldiers were induced to desert. The scheme is not confined to Britain. I spoke to Marcel Brissac on the way home, and he has ascertained that there have been a series of desertions from the French Army, too. No doubt a check-up would reveal that the same thing has been going on in all the military forces of all the United Nations. It is a dirty business, but there it is. After all, if top scientists and government officials can

612

be persuaded to turn traitor, there is nothing surprising in the fact that soldiers, mostly men of lower education, have been induced to do the same thing.'

'These propaganda broadcasts may sound silly to people of intelligence, but they are a menace,' declared Major Charles. 'We knew the general direction from which these Far Eastern broadcasts were coming, but we haven't been able to locate the actual site of the station. It is, presumably, a new one. The general trend of the broadcasts is an appeal to the United Nations Forces to stop fighting – to refrain from killing innocent people, as they so nicely put it. We shall have to try to put an end to it.'

'Aside from the broad official aspect of the thing I have a personal interest in the matter,' resumed Biggles. 'Indeed, I should say a moral obligation. For the original deserters I have very little sympathy; no doubt they are feeling pretty sick with themselves; but I was instrumental in getting Guardsman Ross into the miserable position in which he now finds himself. I told him that, whatever happened, I'd get him out. The fact that he did a good job, all that was asked of him, makes it all the more imperative that we should not let him down. That the trail leads to the far side of the world, instead of being confined to Europe as was supposed, makes no difference. Had it been humanly possible I would have gone straight on after him; but it would have been worse than futile to try to cross the U.S.S.R. and China with such equipment as I had available. That's why I came home. What I want now is authority to make my own plans to collect Ross and bring him back here.'

There was silence for a moment. The Air Commodore looked doubtful. 'Such an operation would be in the nature of a forlorn hope.'

'You can call it what you like,' returned Biggles. 'The fact remains.'

'Just a minute,' put in Major Charles. 'Let us get the thing in perspective. It seems to me that we have here two objectives. One is the silencing of this radio station. The other is the rescue of an operative who has become involved. From the national angle the first is by far the most important.'

'From my angle, the second is the vital one,' said Biggles shortly.

'The first question to be decided,' went on Major Charles imperturbably, 'is whether to treat each operation separately, or combine them and deal with them as one?'

The representative of the Foreign Office joined in the argument, addressing himself to Major Charles. 'When you talk about silencing this station, what exactly have you in mind? You will not, I hope, overlook the fact that we are not at war with Manchuria?'

'I trust you're not going to quibble about that?' interposed Biggles trenchantly. 'Any place that is used as a base by the enemies of this country is at war with us as far as I'm concerned. If Manchuria set up a bleat, you could ask them what they're doing with our men.'

The Air Commodore forced a tolerant smile. 'All right. Let us stick to the point. We are agreed that we have two objectives before us. The question is: are they to be tackled together or separately?'

'That's not for me to answer,' said Biggles. 'My main concern is Ross.'

'What about the other fellows in the camp, if they should want to come home?' queried Major Charles. 'Are you going to bring Ross home alone, or will you give them all a chance to get out?'

'That will depend on how many there are of them,' contended Biggles. 'There would be a limit to what I could take. I certainly wouldn't try to persuade these men to come, if they don't want to. If they like Communism, they can have it – until the time comes when they wish they'd never heard of it.'

The Air Commodore resumed. 'Very well, Bigglesworth. Let us take your angle first. You want to fetch Ross home?'

'Yes.'

'How would you go about it, bearing in mind that we know nothing about this place Kratsen?'

'I should start by finding out something about it, by air photography, if nothing else. In broad terms, as Kratsen is practically on the coast according to the map, I should take out a marine aircraft, basing it in Japanese or South Korean waters. The business of making contact with Ross would depend on how much I could learn about the place. I might put someone in to get the layout of the camp.'

'Only a Chinese could do that.'

'I realise it. I have one in mind.'

The Air Commodore's eyebrows went up. 'You know a Chinese who would do that?'

'I think so. You will remember Doctor Wung Ling? I flew him out to China not so long ago to salvage his father's treasure chest.[1] When we parted he assured me that if at any time I needed his help he was at my service. That wasn't idle talk, either.'

'Go on.'

'That's all. Having got the necessary gen on the set-up, I should choose my time to go ashore and collect Ross.'

'You make it sound all very simple.'

'There's no sense in stock-piling difficulties before they arise. If I did that I'd never do anything. The longer you look at a mountain the bigger it looks.'

[1] See, The Case of the Mandarin's Treasure Chest, in Biggles – *Air Detective*.

'Very well. Let's say you find Ross. What about the other fellows?'

'I've said that would depend on the number. If there were a lot I couldn't cram them into an aircraft. There are Commandos in Korea. They've made several raids. That means they have landing craft. They might co-operate by standing by to pick up extras.'

'That means bringing the army into it,' protested the Foreign Office man. 'If there was fighting there would be casualties. Our troops would be recognised. What excuse would we have for landing on neutral territory?'

'Excuse!' breathed Biggles. 'Stiffen the crows! Has it come to this, that we have to have an excuse for getting a British soldier out of a foreign jail? This talk of excuses binds me rigid. All right. Have it your own way. We'll be civilians. If I decide I need more men I know one who'll come with me. He's an old hand at the game. Believe you me, by the time he's finished with it there won't be much left of this lying propaganda dump.'

The Air Commodore's eyes went to Biggles' face. 'Who are you thinking of?'

'Gimlet King.'

'I thought so.'

'He'll knock off hunting foxes for a while when I tell him what's cooking. He and that crazy gang of his should be useful. They're all civilians now.'

'It isn't quite regular,' objected the Foreign Office man anxiously.

'Regular! Suffering Icarus! What has regularity got to do with it? The trouble with us is, we're a thundering sight too regular. All we get for that is a kick in the pants. Don't talk to me about regulations!'

'We don't want to start a war with China.'

'Listen,' said Biggles, speaking distinctly. 'When I was a kid I hated war. And I haven't changed. But how have I spent most of my life? In wars, big and small. Why? I'll tell you. Because, instead of settling down to a quiet life as I intended I've been pitchforked into wars started by other people who have never been in a battle in their lives. I'm not starting anything. The other side has already done that. No doubt there are people who would like the police to pack up for fear of starting a war with the crooks, spivs and chisellers, who thrive like a lot of maggots on decent folk.'

'Steady. Take it easy, Bigglesworth,' adjured the Air Commodore. 'There's no need to get worked up about it.'

'Sorry, chief, but this sort of argument makes me tired,' muttered Biggles. 'Two nights ago I was sliding down a greasy roof in Prague. Last night I was dodging about in the Soviet Sector of Berlin. D'you suppose I do this sort of thing for fun? When I scrape home by the skin of my shins, what do I hear but talk of excuses and regulations? Now let's get down to brass tacks. Do I go and fetch Ross or do I not? Say "No" to that and my resignation will be on your desk in five minutes. Then I'll buy an aircraft and do the job on my own account. Afterwards I'll settle down to grow mushrooms, or tomatoes or something.'

'I don't see why you shouldn't go to fetch Ross,' said the Air Commodore awkwardly. 'But you must realise that what we are proposing is a very serious business.'

'Are you telling me? I'm the one it will be serious for if things go wrong. You gentlemen may lose your jobs. I shall lose everything from my neck up. I'm going to fetch Ross. I told him I would and no one is going to stop me. If the government wants the lid putting over the big mouth of the propaganda works at Kratsen I'll do it at the same time, if it's possible.'

The Air Commodore looked round. 'I'll take responsibility for my Department,' he said quietly. 'What about you? You need know nothing about it if you feel that it may involve you in trouble.'

Major Charles nodded. 'I have an interest in the affair,' said he. 'Go ahead.'

The Foreign Office official shrugged. 'I can't sanction the raid, of course; but I can shut my eyes.'

The Air Commodore turned back to Biggles. 'There's your answer,' he said. 'Make your own arrangements. I'll do my best to get you anything you think you're likely to want.'

'You've no objection to me bringing in Gimlet King?'

'None at all. You'd better keep quiet about that, though. Let me know when you're ready to move off.'

'I'll do that,' promised Biggles, and left the room.

He walked back to his office where the others were awaiting the result of the conference. 'Okay,' he said. 'We're going to fetch Ross. Ginger, get Gimlet King on the phone for me. If he isn't at home, you'll probably find him at the Ritz.'

Algy's eyes opened wide. 'Is he coming with us?'

'I hope so.'

Bertie whistled. 'My word! This is going to be a jolly little frolic,' he murmured.

CHAPTER XI

Wung Ling Reconnoitres

Ginger lay flat on his stomach and stared into a tenuous mist that was beginning to rise from the salt-marsh that spread away in front of him for as far as his probing eyes could reach. A crescent moon hung low in the heavens, turning the mist into a semi-transparent film that made it impossible to judge distances. Nothing was distinct. All that could really be seen clearly was the tops of coarse grasses that made a fringe at right-angles to his body. To left and right the scene was much the same, except in a few places where the dunes that lined the Manchurian foreshore of the Yellow Sea broke into gentle undulations. From behind came the gentle lapping of tiny waves expiring on a broad, sandy beach, that swung round on either hand in a vast curve that ultimately lost itself in the gloom of distances unknown.

Beside him, in a similar position, lay a figure of about his own build, chin on hand, also gazing fixedly into the same vague landscape. This was 'Cub' Peters, ex-commando, and junior member of the famous war-time troop known as King's Kittens.

For a long while neither had spoken. Apart from the fretting of the sea upon the beach the only sound that broke the eerie silence was the occasional melancholy call of a sea-fowl.

Ginger looked at his watch. 'He should be here by now,' he whispered.

'I hope he hasn't lost his direction in this confounded fog,' answered Cub. 'It's easily done.'

'He's got a compass.'

'Then he should be all right.'

Ginger moved his position slightly to relieve limbs that were becoming cramped on ground which, being damp, struck chill. Then, without relaxing his vigilance, he allowed his mind to wander back over the events of the past month.

The first week of it had been spent in making preparations for a mission which, on account of its probable long duration, required extra careful planning. In this period Biggles had made contact with Captain 'Gimlet' King, war-time specialist in delicate operations in enemy territory. The Manchurian proposition had been put to him and he had accepted it with alacrity. He, in turn, had got in touch with 'Copper' Colson, 'Trapper' Troublay, and 'Cub' Peters, of his old troop, who had welcomed the invitation that promised more adventure than was available in civil life.

Biggles had been right in his estimation of Wung Ling. The young Chinese doctor, when the scheme was explained to him, had at once dropped what he was doing in order to take advantage of an opportunity of striking back at a regime that had destroyed not only his own ancestral home, but the ancient culture of his native land.

The aircraft chosen for the enterprise was a Scorpion flying-boat, originally a military development of the Sunderland, designed for long-distance work, but later modified for civil transportation. It had not gone into production, but the prototype had for some years been on the establishment of a Royal Air Force Communication Squadron. In fact, it still was; but it happened to be one of the aircraft that had been made available under a reciprocal arrangement between the Air Ministry and the Air Police. Powered with four Bristol 'Hercules' engines, it had accommodation for sixteen passengers.

A fortnight had been spent on the journey to the Far East, for, as Biggles pointed out, there was no particular hurry. He did not know how long it would take Ross to get to his ultimate station at Kratsen and he did not want to arrive too soon. It had been decided to use South Korea as a base, this being nearer than Japan to the objective, and a mooring had been arranged at the international marine aircraft establishment of Kungching, where servicing facilities were available. There was also an R.A.F. maintenance unit, under the command of a Group Captain, who acted as Liaison Officer with the American Forces of the United Nations. So far the operation had been merely a matter of routine.

On arrival, Biggles' first step had been to present himself, and a letter of introduction that he carried, to the R.A.F. officer in charge. Asked if there was anything he needed, he said all that he required for the moment, apart from fuel, was a set of air photographs of the Kratsen area. Such photographs, he explained, were essential for the job on which he was engaged, but he was reluctant to show the big flying-boat over the objective. Apart from the obvious risk of having it shot down or damaged by enemy fighters, he was anxious to avoid doing anything that might give the broadcasting station reason to suppose that it was under observation.

It turned out that no photographs of that particular area were available. However, the Group Captain said he would see what he could do about it. That he wasted no time was evident when, twenty-four hours later, he presented Biggles with a beautiful set of pictures, both vertical and oblique, that had been taken at his request by an American photographic reconnaissance unit.

With these on the table in the cabin of the Scorpion the next phase had been planned. The photographs showed that wealth of detail for which modern photography is remarkable, but the most vital factors still remained an unknown quantity. The pylons, three of them, were plain to see from the shadows they cast; but among the several buildings which the pictures revealed, it was not possible to determine which one held the prisoners. For that the deserting soldiers would be treated as prisoners Biggles did not doubt. More information on this aspect was required before a raid could be made with any sort of confidence. This difficulty had been foreseen, and accounted for the presence of Wung Ling in the party.

He was now called upon to assume the role for which, by reason of his nationality, he was ideally adapted. Ginger had rather wondered how the Chinaman would feel when confronted by the cold, hard facts of reality; but he need not have worried. Wung Ling, like most of his countrymen, was not demonstrative, but it was clear that he was deriving no small satisfaction from this opportunity of hitting back at the people who had robbed him of all he possessed.

There were, Biggles explained, two ways of 'putting him in.' He could either be landed on the coast, a matter of some four miles from the actual objective, under cover of darkness, or he could be parachuted in. Wung Ling elected to use the parachute method, explaining, naïvely, that he had always wanted to experience the sensation of a parachute jump.

This suited Biggles, as the drop could be made from a small machine, which again would save the flying-boat a journey into dangerous waters. One trip it would have to make before the final raid, and that would be to pick up Wung (as they now called him) at the end of his reconnaissance. There could be no question, Biggles declared, of putting down a land machine, in the dark, on ground which, from the photographs, appeared to be mostly bog or paddy-fields – either of which would probably throw the machine on its nose.

It was decided that Wung should have three days in which to gather the information required. That is to say, the flying-boat would stand by, at a spot on the coast to be selected from the photographs, at midnight, on the third night after he had parachuted in. This, it was thought, would give him ample time to get the particulars that were wanted.

There was practically no limit to these, stated Biggles. Every scrap of information that could be gathered would be useful. Most important of all was the location and construction of the prisoners' sleeping quarters; the number of men occupying them; their routine, and the position, number and nationality, of sentries guarding them. Also, the number of troops at the station.

Wung said gravely that he would find out about these things, and it was arranged that he should be put in that night, as the weather was favourable and nothing was to be gained by waiting. He went ashore with Biggles to acquire a suitable outfit from the Korean refugees, whose crowded camps could be seen outside the town. Biggles, on his part, went to the R.A.F. Liaison Officer to arrange for the loan of a small aircraft suitable for the sortie. He had brought a parachute with him.

The flight was made as scheduled. Biggles flew the machine, and gliding at a great height unloaded his passenger between the coast-line, plainly seen in the moonlight, and the cluster of lights that marked the position of the radio station. The last he saw of Wung was a fast-diminishing black dot below him. He continued his glide until he was far out to sea before opening up and returned to base without incident.

The three days had now expired, and the next step in the

programme, the operation of picking up Wung, was now in progress. Five members only of the party were briefed for it, as no more were required. Biggles, with Algy as reserve pilot, flew the Scorpion. From it a rubber dinghy was launched, putting ashore Bertie, whose duty it was to stand by it, and Ginger, who with Cub for company, had advanced to the top of the dunes in order to keep watch for Wung, in case he should fail to strike the exact spot where the dinghy was waiting. They would also be in a position to help him should he arrive hard pressed, which was unlikely, but possible.

Ginger and Cub waited, watching, straining their eyes to pick out tangible objects in the miasma.

The hour appointed for the rendezvous had passed by fifteen minutes, and Ginger was just becoming alarmed, when a single, ghost-like figure loomed up with startling suddenness in the mist, proving how deceptive it was. Making no sound, he watched it advance slowly towards the beach until recognition became possible. A low signal whistle, prearranged, brought an answer, and Wung made his way wearily to him.

'Excuse me, please, for being late,' apologised Wung. 'It was the mud. I could not walk as quickly as I expected, and with the mist it was not easy to keep a straight line.'

'Otherwise you're all right?' prompted Ginger.

'Perfectly well.'

'No trouble?'

'None at all.'

'Great work,' congratulated Ginger. 'Come on, let's get home. No doubt you could do with a square meal.'

'What I need more than anything is hot water to remove this disgusting mud,' said Wung.

They made their way across the beach to where Bertie was sitting, hunched up, by the dinghy.

'Come on, you blokes, it's getting chilly,' he complained. 'How's the boy Wung?'

'Very dirty,' replied the Chinaman.

'That's what comes of getting mixed up with a bunch of scally-wags,' said Bertie cheerfully. 'Get aboard. Any more for the jolly old Skylark?'

They took their places and, with paddles busy, soon picked up the aircraft where she rode at anchor on a gentle swell. The dinghy was deflated and hauled aboard. The engines growled, and the big machine taxied out towards the open sea. Not until the long low coastline had disappeared from sight did Biggles open up. Then the Scorpion tilted its nose towards the starry sky and swung round on a south-westerly course for its base.

CHAPTER XII

Wung Reports

Six hours later, with the machine snug at her mooring, everyone foregathered in the cabin to hear what Wung had to say. Bathed, rested and breakfasted, he was back in his own clothes, and had obviously suffered no ill effects from his exploit.

'Now, tell us all about it,' invited Biggles, arranging the photographs on the table so that they could be used to demonstrate the report.

'First of all,' began Wung, 'I can tell you that Ross is there.'

'How do you know that?' asked Biggles sharply.

'I've spoken to him.'

'You've *spoken* to him?'

'Yes.'

'How did you recognise him?'

'I was working in the compound when I heard a man call another by the name Ross. I worked my way over to him and, without looking, told him to be ready because friends were near. You should have seen his face!' Wung smiled at the recollection. 'He could not think it was me, a dirty Chinese labourer, speaking in English, and he stared about him as if the voice had come from the air. He needed a tonic, poor fellow, for he looked so lonely and depressed.'

'He didn't speak to you?'

*'He could not think it was me, a dirty Chinese labourer,
speaking in English.'*

'No. I walked on.'

'What do you mean by the compound?'

'Within the barbed wire fence that surrounds the prisoners' quarters.'

'How did you come to be there?'

'I was working – emptying the garbage cans, and that sort of thing. I have been working all the time. I can't say that I liked it, but it served my purpose well.'

'How did this come about?'

'I made my way to the camp shortly after daylight. Without any attempt at concealment, I approached with confidence, knowing that no one would suspect me of being anything but what I appeared to be. There were many others exactly like me moving about, miserable, poverty-stricken inhabitants of the village – one can hardly call the collection of hovels a town. The wretched people were being mustered into gangs for labour. There must have been nearly two hundred of them. A nasty-looking man, a North Korean I think, told me to get in my place, so I joined the nearest gang. No one took the slightest notice of me. We were given a miserable ration of rice to keep us alive and then we went to work.'

'What sort of work are all these people doing?'

'They're doing many things. It is quite certain that the place is being enlarged, although for what purpose I could not find out. For one thing, a single track railway is being built. It is almost complete. From the direction it takes I would think it joins the main Trans-Siberian line farther north. An airfield is also under construction. There is already a landing-field of sorts. It is being improved. All transport comes by air, as one would expect, for there is no road worthy of the name. There is a temporary shelter for an aeroplane. An aeroplane is in it now, but I could not say what sort. There is also a petrol store. The first train, which came in while

I was there, brought in a load of petrol, also some fuel oil for the engine that makes the electricity. There is also some ammunition, which is stored in the open under tarpaulins.'

'Did you learn what this was for?'

'No. Every gang worked under a foreman, and I joined a different gang each day in order to cover as much ground as possible. That is how I got into the compound. One of the duties was scrubbing the huts and taking away the rubbish. I am not quite certain how many men live in the compound because they come and go all the time. At present there are not more than twelve. I could judge their nationality by the language they spoke. I made out five British, four Americans, two Frenchmen and one other. At one time there were more than this, but some have moved on. I will tell you where, and why, presently. First I must deal with the compound as it is of most importance to you.' Wung pulled a photograph towards him and put a finger on the spot.

'This is it,' he continued. 'First of all, you must understand, there is a barbed wire fence round the whole camp. It is of five strands and does not offer a serious obstacle. It is simply to keep the natives from wandering into the place, I imagine. Within this outer fence there is another, smaller one, also of barbed wire. It is higher and has eight strands. Inside are the prisoners' quarters consisting of three wooden buildings, two large and one small. One is a dining and recreation room; another is the sleeping accommodation; the third one is a wash-house. They are all built of wooden planks.'

'Tell us about the sleeping quarters,' requested Biggles. 'We shall make our raid at night, of course, so that is where we shall find the prisoners.'

'It is one large room with trestle beds round the wall,' explained Wung. 'The end is partitioned off to make a small cubicle for the man in charge. At present this is occupied by an extremely unpleasant fellow who, I am sorry to say, is an Englishman. At least, he speaks English. The prisoners call him sergeant. He is a bad man, ugly of face and ugly of temper. It seemed to me that he took delight in making the lives of the prisoners unbearable, shouting at them with much beastly language. This man, by the way, keeps the key of the hut, although the door is seldom locked. It hangs on a nail in his room. Work stops at sundown, when the prisoners, after a meal, retire to the sleeping hut. There is only one way in and out of the compound. It is a gate, with a sentry box. A Chinese soldier is always on duty there. He is changed every four hours.'

'Did you get the actual times?' asked Biggles.

'Yes. A new guard comes on at midnight. The next one comes at four a.m. There are about fifty Chinese soldiers altogether. There is a Russian officer, but what he does I do not know.'

'From what you tell me, the place doesn't seem very well guarded,' observed Biggles.

'Nor is it. I got the impression, from the casual way things are done, that the last thing the people in the camp expect is trouble. It would be a fairly easy matter for the prisoners to get out of their compound. They would merely need a tool to cut the wire. But even if they did this they would not get far. Where could they go? The land around is absolutely flat, and is either boggy or paddy fields. These stretch for miles, and are more efficacious than iron bars. From the camp one can see for miles. If a man tried to run away in daylight he would certainly be seen from the camp. If he tried to travel in the dark he would flounder about in the bogs and perhaps lose his life in one of them. He might also wander about in circles, for there is usually a mist at night. And as I have said, at the finish, where would he go?'

'What do the soldiers do?' asked Biggles.

'They kick a football about, mostly. They take turns at guard duty, but it is all very haphazard. Apart from the people I have mentioned there is a fairly large population of men whom I took to be mechanics and engineers in charge of the wireless rooms and the power station. They live by themselves.' Wung referred again to the photograph. 'This is the power station, here. Among other things it provides the camp with electric light. I need say nothing about the village of Kratsen. As you can see, it is some little way away from the camp. Presently I will mark on this photograph the purpose of every building shown on it, so that it can be studied by everyone at leisure. After three days in the place I could find my way about even on a dark night.'

'What is this building over here, standing by itself?' inquired Biggles, pointing.

'That is the bungalow of the overall commander of the station. I saw him only once, at a distance. I believe he is a Russian. At any rate, he is known as Commandant Kubenoff. It is said that he is usually the worse for drink.'

'I suppose the camp is on the telephone?'

'Yes.'

'You were going to say something about the prisoners who have been to the camp but are no longer there?' prompted Biggles.

'Oh yes. The talk is, these are the men who are trusted by the Communists. They are taken to Korea where, in captured uniforms of the United Nations, they are infiltrated through the lines to act as spies and saboteurs. A North Korean boasted to me of this. The headquarters of these renegades happens to be in his own village, a place on the coast called Fashtun, near the Russian frontier.'

'We'll bear that name in mind,' said Biggles grimly. 'Anything else, Wung?'

'That is all I can think of for the moment. No doubt other minor points will occur to me from time to time. I can tell you the names of most of the men in the camp should you require them. I often heard them being called. Every little while one is taken to the broadcasting room, where, I understand, he is made to read from a paper. There is much secret grumbling about this; but to refuse means death.'

'Was one of the names that you heard Macdonald?' asked Biggles.

Wung thought for a moment. 'No. I don't remember hearing that name.'

'Never mind,' said Biggles. 'You've done a great show, Wung. With the information you have provided, the job of cleaning up the place shouldn't be difficult. Personally, I see no reason why we shouldn't get on with it right away. The governing factor is the weather. At the moment it's fair. Should it change, we might have to hang about for weeks, and in that time alterations in the camp might throw our plan out of gear. I propose, therefore, that we should crack in tonight, and get the business over. Has anyone an objection?'

Only Wung answered. 'I think you're right,' he said. 'I have no definite information, but when I left there was an atmosphere of expectation about the place, as if some change was contemplated.'

'Very well,' resumed Biggles. 'Let's get the thing into line. We have two tasks. The first, is the rescue of Ross, and any other British or foreign troops who have had enough of Communism. If they all decide to come we may find ourselves overloaded – but we'll deal with that if and when it arises. The second part of the operation is the silencing of the propaganda factory. By dividing our force into two parts I see no reason why both jobs shouldn't be worked together. One part can work the rescue, and the other, the demolitions. As we have brought all the equipment likely to be required, and plenty of hands, that resolves itself into a matter of timing. I will lead the rescue party. Captain King will be in charge of the demolition squad. Has anybody anything to say about that?'

'It seems the obvious way to go about it,' observed Gimlet.

'Then we'll work out a time-table on those lines,' asserted Biggles. 'There is one other point that had better be settled here and now. The total force available will comprise eight bodies,[1] but not all of them will be able to go to the objective. One of my party will have to stay with the aircraft. Someone else will have to stand by the dinghy to deal with possible interference. That means that six men will be available for the actual raid.'

'But am I not allowed to come?' put in Wung, in a disappointed voice.

'You've already done your part,' Biggles told him. 'Do you want to come?'

'Of course.'

'Fair enough,' agreed Biggles. 'That suits me. Knowing the ground so well you'll be useful as a guide. Algy, as second-in-command, I shall have to ask you to remain in charge of the machine.'

'This being second-in-command does me out of all the fun that's going,' protested Algy.

'I'm aware of it,' admitted Biggles. 'But in a military operation either the first or second in command should remain in reserve in case things come unstuck. Ross is a personal affair of mine so I intend to go to him. That means you'll be in charge during my absence.'

'Okay,' agreed Algy.

'A member of the demolition party will have to remain with the dinghy or I may find myself short-handed,' went on Biggles. 'That

[1] Bodies. R.A.F. slang. A general term covering all ranks.

means that seven will go forward. That won't be too many, either, because there will be a fair amount of stuff to carry. Wung, knowing his way about, will act as liaison between both parties. I shall try to time our arrival on the coast for midnight. Allowing an hour and a half for the march we ought to be at the objective by one-thirty. An hour should be enough for the job. That means we ought to be back at the aircraft by four. But I'll work out the time-table with Gimlet. He knows how long it will take him to fix his fireworks. Now let's have something to eat. After that we'll see about getting ready.'

CHAPTER XIII

The Raid

It was shortly after midnight, in the soft moonlight, when the Scorpion, after a long glide, brushed its keel gently on the sullen waters of the Yellow Sea within a short distance of the flat Manchurian coast. The anchor found bottom at six fathoms, and the aircraft swung gently to a flowing tide. Not a light showed anywhere, near or far, on land or sea.

Without fuss or bustle the dinghy was launched, and Gimlet's party, with its rather heavy equipment, moved off. In twenty minutes the squat little craft was back to take the remainder of the force ashore. Algy remained in the cockpit with a Thermos flask of tea for company.

All was quiet on the beach. A quick reconnaissance was made from the top of the dunes, but nothing was seen, so loads were distributed, and with Wung leading, a prismatic compass in his hand, the party went forward in single file. It was Cub who, to his disappointment, had been allotted the task of mounting guard over the dinghy, for the reason that his older comrades were better able to carry the batteries, coils of wire, explosive charges, and other equipment. He remained at his post, a rifle across his knees.

The march that followed was a matter of wearisome necessity. It was heavy going all the way, as from Wung's experience they all knew it would be. The ground was sheer marsh. There was no actual standing water, but the earth was soft and treacherous under a blanket of spongy sphagnum moss. The only things to thrive in it were a coarse grass, which grew in awkward tussocks, and short rushes, apparently some sort of iris from the flowers it bore. The air was dank and chill. What it would be like when the icy hand of winter settled on it Ginger could only imagine. The prisoners, he pondered as they trudged on, would need their fur caps and heavy coats. They would also regret their folly when they found that this insalubrious area of the earth's surface was to be their home.

Over the vast plain hung a mist of varying intensity. For the most part visibility was limited to about a hundred yards. Beyond that everything was dim and vague. If it made the going uncomfortable, as it did, it made amends by screening their approach. At intervals long skeins of migrating geese could be heard passing overhead.

Two rests were taken before Wung announced that the immediate objective was not far ahead. This was the ruins of a peasant's hovel, built of turves, now crumbling. It stood about a hundred yards from the outer wire. Wung had come upon it, and used it, on his first sortie. He had drawn attention to it on one of the photographs as a useful place to make a dump from which to operate. The suggestion had been accepted.

The dilapidated dwelling loomed up, a mere blob rising a few feet above the level ground in a featureless landscape. Some way beyond it two lights grew slowly in the mist. One of them, Wung stated, came from the commandant's bungalow; the other from the radio station, which operated day and night. There was no sign of movement anywhere so loads were dropped while a general survey was made, Wung indicating the positions of the most important buildings. In the direction of the little township that gave the place its name all was dark and silent. It might not have been there for all that could be seen of it.

After a short rest Gimlet said he would be moving on. In working out the details of the scheme it had been decided that, as he had the most work to do, he should have twenty minutes clear start. Both parties were to rally on the ruined hovel in the event of trouble, or, if all went well, on the completion of their respective tasks. The explosive charges would then be fired, to be followed at once by the retreat to the coast.

Copper and Trapper were already on their knees arranging the batteries. This done, they moved off with their leader under Wung's guidance, uncoiling wire from a drum as they went. In a few minutes they had disappeared in the darkness.

Biggles, Bertie and Ginger squatted on mud bricks that had fallen from the walls until the twenty minutes grace had expired. Then Biggles rose to his feet. 'Time's up,' he said softly, and walked on towards the outer fence of the camp. It could not yet be seen, but its position was known.

There had been some discussion before the start as to how to make the best of Wung's local knowledge. At the end it had been decided that he should go with Gimlet, who had several objectives beside the radio station and its pylons. It was intended, if possible, to deal also with the power house and the petrol and ammunition dumps. Trapper, too, was to cut the telephone wires. Thus it was hoped that by destroying all communications nothing would be known of the raid, outside the station, for some time – long enough, at all events, for the Scorpion to reach its base without fear of interception by enemy aircraft.

Biggles had only one objective, which was to reach the prisoners' sleeping quarters, and this, compared with what Gimlet had to do, appeared to be a fairly simple matter. There was only one snag.

There was no cover of any sort. On the other hand, with one man only on duty at the gate – and he, in all probability, not very vigilant – there was reason to hope that the objective might be gained without a sound being made.

It was agreed that the sentry would have to be put out of action, for even one man in the rear, armed with a rifle, might do a lot of mischief. Copper, the big Cockney ex-policeman, had offered to attend to this matter.

Biggles' party made contact with the fence some distance from the sentry box that marked the position of the gate. They all stared at it. There was no sign of the sentry, so it could be presumed that Copper had done his work. However, to be on the safe side, Biggles decided to confirm this. He sent Ginger along.

Gun in hand, Ginger made a cautious approach, advancing on the sentry box from the rear. The man was there, unconscious, trussed up in a heap on the floor. Ginger returned to the others and reported this, whereupon Biggles, with powerful cutters brought for the purpose, in a couple of minutes had made a broad gap through the wire. The purpose of this, instead of using the gate, was to provide them with their own line of retreat in case of emergency.

With eyes and ears alert the party moved forward quietly to the inner fence – the wire that surrounded the prisoners' quarters. It was reached in a silence that was profound. Again came the crisp snick as Biggles' cutters bit through the wire. The loose ends were dragged aside and the way lay open to the final objective. The two big huts were already in plain view, silhouetted against the sky. The nearer, thanks to Wung, was known to be the sleeping quarters. To the door, which was at the end, Biggles now made his way.

It is not to be supposed that the apparent ease of these operations bereft them of any atmosphere of excitement. Far from it. Darkness is always a threat; and the very silence hung over the place like a menace. The knowledge that at any moment a shout or a shot might shatter it imposed a degree of suspense that kept all nerves at full stretch. Hearts and pulses, however, toughened by experience, increase their *tempo* at such times.

Ginger's eyes, striving to probe the surrounding gloom, were never still. They became fixed on a movement. '*Psst!*' he warned.

In a moment they were all flat on the ground, worming round the nearest corner of the hut.

'What is it?' breathed Biggles.

'Someone coming.'

They lay motionless, waiting, listening, as approaching footsteps swished through the rank grass.

Ginger allowed his breath to escape in a sigh of relief. 'It's Wung,' he announced. 'Something must have gone wrong.'

They all stood up and Wung joined the party.

'What's the matter?' asked Biggles in a terse undertone.

'There seems to be a conference going on at the Commandant's house,' reported Wung in a low voice. 'Captain King asked me to look in when we were passing, Some men are talking about you. I heard your name mentioned. Captain King could not wait as he has much to do, but he thought you should know in case some sort of trap has been set.'

'You actually looked in the room?'

'Yes, through the window.'

'Who is there?'

'The Commandant. With him is a Chinese general whom they call Kwang-Sen. I have not seen him before, but he seems to be senior to the Commandant. There is also another Russian officer, who is, I think, an aeroplane pilot. He wears wings on his uniform. There is also a German. I think he does not speak much Russian or Chinese, because there is an interpreter.'

'Did you see this German when you were here before?'

'No.'

'What sort of man is he?'

'Tall, clean shaven, well dressed. He stands and speaks like a soldier. He wears an eyeglass, and smokes all the time a cigarette in a long holder.'

'Sounds as if von Stalhein has got here,' remarked Biggles dryly, looking at the others. 'I can't say that I'm altogether surprised. After all, this is his affair as much as ours.' He turned back to Wung. 'Did you get any idea of what these men were talking about, apart from mentioning my name?'

'From what I could make out the German was trying to convince General Kwang-Sen that you would come here, so there should be more soldiers. He seems to know that you have left London, and that British Intelligence now knows about the broadcasting station.'

'What did the General say to that?'

'He seemed disinclined to do anything. I have the impression that he was drinking with Commandant Kubenoff when the others arrived.'

'Nothing else?'

'No. I did not stay long because Captain King was waiting for me.'

'All right. You'd better get back to him. Tell him to lose no time because von Stalhein is here, and if he has his way things are likely to happen.'

Wung went off and soon merged into the gloom.

Biggles faced the others. 'I'd better have a look at this in case it is decided to post extra guards right away. That might put Gimlet in a jam. Stand fast till I come back. If a flap should start, try to grab Ross and make for the ruined hut. I'll join you there.' So saying, he walked quickly in the direction of the bungalow, the position of which was clear from the light that streamed from one of its windows.

A glance showed him that his surmise had been correct. Von Stalhein, as coldly austere and as immaculate as ever in spite of his long journey, was expostulating with a heavily-built Chinaman who, in a uniform decorated with medals, sprawled in an armchair with a glass in his hand. A man in Russian uniform – Kubenoff, Biggles presumed – was sitting opposite. Standing nearby was a man who, from his actions and the way he spoke, was evidently the interpreter. Von Stalhein spoke in German.

'The matter is of importance to me, if not to you, General,' he was saying. 'Why do you think I have come all this way? For my own good, I admit, but for yours also. This man Ross is a spy, put in by the British secret agent, Bigglesworth. If it is learned in Moscow that a stool-pigeon has been introduced into the organisation it will be bad for me, and for you, too, if you do nothing about it. Stresser, one of my men in Europe, has made a complete confession. He was suspected, and has been made to talk. He now admits that in Prague he sold to Bigglesworth information about the destination of Ross, who was followed out from England.'

'We will have this man Ross before us in the morning,' said the General thickly. 'He shall tell us all he knows.'

'Why not now?' argued von Stalhein.

'Because I am tired. Nothing is likely to happen between now and daylight.'

Biggles, with his eyes on von Stalhein's face, could almost sympathise with him. It seemed to be the fate of the German that his own efficiency should be offset by the laxity of the people under whom he served.

Another man stepped into the conversation. 'It would be better to wait for a little while,' he said. 'Ross is to broadcast presently. It is important and will be relayed to all stations. He does not know this, of course. He has been told that it is only a rehearsal to test his voice, otherwise he would refuse. He is difficult. It would be better not to upset him just before the broadcast.'

'I agree,' said the General, reaching for a bottle that stood on a nearby table.

'But, at least, it would be no trouble to put on extra guards,' protested von Stalhein.

Kwang-Sen yawned. 'Very well, if it will satisfy you.'

'Why not let me have a word with Ross?' suggested von Stalhein. 'He knows me. I would tell him that his being sent here was all a mistake and that I have come to take him back to Europe. That would put him in good heart. I would learn the truth from him. Afterwards, you can do what you like with him.'

'That might be a good thing,' conceded Kwang-Sen. 'But don't worry me again tonight. I'm tired and I'm going to bed. Have a drink?'

Biggles waited for no more. He hastened back to the others. 'We were just in time,' he informed them grimly. 'We'd better get mobile. Von Stalhein is here. Stresser has spilt the whole can of beans, so von Stalhein has a pretty good idea of what's likely to happen. He insists on the guards being doubled. The General is soaked with liquor, and can't be bothered, but he has more or less agreed. What is worse, von Stalhein is trying to get to Ross. I left them all talking. But, whatever the others do, von Stalhein won't go to bed. We don't want him barging into the picture before we are finished, so we'd better get Ross and pull out right away.'

'What's the drill?' asked Ginger.

'I shall have to switch on the light in the hut,' answered

Biggles. 'We must see what we're doing. When I do, you, Bertie, will slip along to the far end and deal with this sergeant fellow if he tries to make trouble, as no doubt he will. But no shooting unless the position becomes desperate. Okay. Let's go.'

Automatic in one hand, Biggles advanced to the door. At the same moment it was opened from the inside and a man in pyjamas stepped out. Half-asleep, it seemed, he had taken two paces towards the wash-house before he noticed that he was not alone. The shock brought him to life.

'What's the idea? Who are you?' he demanded, in English, with an American accent.

Biggles showed his gun. 'Are you an American?'

'Sure I'm an American.'

'Do you like it here or would you rather go home?'

The man stared. 'Would I rather go home?' he echoed incredulously. 'That's somewhere I didn't reckon to see again. Serve me right for being a sucker. Who are you?'

'British agents. We've come to fetch one of our fellows home. The name's Ross.'

'That's right. The guy's inside.'

'Are you coming with us?'

'Am I coming? Brother, wait till I get my clothes on!'

'Stand fast for a minute.'

Biggles went to the door. Inside all was in darkness. From it came the heavy breathing of sleeping men. A few seconds sufficed to find the electric light switch. It clicked, and the scene inside the hut was revealed.

It was as Wung had described. Low trestle beds, about twelve on each side, were arranged round the walls. Not all were occupied. From those that were, men, awakened by the light, raised themselves on an elbow to ascertain the reason.

Bertie walked quickly down the centre gangway to a door at the far end and took up a position beside it.

From behind it a harsh voice shouted: 'Put that light out!'

'Put it out yourself,' invited Bertie smoothly.

A stream of threats well mixed with curses was the reply. An instant later the door was flung open and a man with tousled hair, and pyjamas awry, appeared, eyes glowering belligerently.

'That'll do nicely,' said Bertie. 'Don't move.'

The man spun round and blinked at the muzzle of Bertie's gun.

By this time the occupied beds were astir. Some of the men sat up. Others flung off their blankets and sprang to their feet.

'Take it easy, everybody,' ordered Biggles. 'Ross!'

'Sir?'

'Get your clothes on and make it snappy. We've come for you.' Biggles went on: 'Listen, everybody. Anyone who wants to go home will stand up. Those who want to stay, lie down – and stay down. No tricks. This gun's loaded.'

The sergeant in charge found his voice. He took a pace forward, but, seeing Bertie's gun move, stopped abruptly. 'What is this?' he demanded.

'Just a hold-up – just a hold-up,' murmured Bertie. 'Nothing to get excited about. Stand still unless you want to go bye-byes for a long time.'

The man stood still, staring. There was in fact little else he could do in a situation that he could hardly have imagined.

Biggles' voice rose again above the babble of conversation that had broken out. 'Not so much noise,' he snapped. 'One word of warning. Those who come with me will face a court-martial when they get home. Please yourselves. I don't care whether you come or stay.'

Practically all the men who were scrambling into their clothes continued to do so. Only two got back into their beds, and later on Biggles was to learn why. They, and the sergeant in charge, were wanted in their own countries for crimes more serious than desertion. The sergeant had, in fact, murdered a girl in Berlin while serving with the Forces of Occupation.

The first man to be ready was, from his accent, an American. His bed was at the far end of the room. Still buttoning his tunic, he advanced purposefully towards Bertie. 'Thanks for calling, pal,' he said in a curious voice. 'I was afraid I was in this dump for keeps. Show us your gun.'

Smiling, Bertie half withdrew; but with a lightning movement the man snatched the gun from his hand and jumped back.

'Nice work,' said the sergeant, and started to move; but he stopped dead as the muzzle of the weapon jerked round to cover him. 'What – what's the idea?' he faltered.

The American's eyes had taken on a queer glitter. His lips were parted and drawn back against his teeth. 'You know the idea, Sarge,' he grated. 'Remember me? Clutson's the name – Joe Clutson, from Arizona. You prodded me into this frame-up, didn't you, me and my buddy, Johnny Briggs? You remember Johnny? You croaked him, didn't you? Bashed him on the head with a hammer because he told you what you are – a dirty, lying, sneaking rat. I've prayed every night for this chance. Now I know that prayers are answered.'

'Stop that!' shouted Biggles from the far end of the room.

'Now, wait a minute, Joe,' quavered the sergeant, raising his hand.

'Wait nothing,' snarled Clutson. 'Now it's my turn, even if I fry for it. Hold this, you swine, for Johnny. You—'

The rest was lost in the crash of the weapon as it spat a stream of sparks that ended at the sergeant's chest.

The sergeant, a look of horror and amazement frozen on his face, staggered back against the wall. His body sagged and he slumped slowly to the floor.

In the shocked silence that followed Clutson handed the weapon back to Bertie. 'Thanks, pal,' he said simply.

CHAPTER XIV

Von Stalhein is Annoyed

The silence was next broken by Biggles from the far end of the room. 'You fool!' he rasped, clipping his words in his anger. 'You crazy fool! You've probably sunk us all.'

'I've sunk the rat who killed my buddy, and that's all I care,' answered Clutson, speaking carelessly, like a man who is content and has no regrets. He lit a cigarette.

In a way, Ginger could sympathise with him; but he was aghast at the price everyone was likely to pay for his revenge.

'Get the key of the hut, Bertie,' ordered Biggles. 'According to Wung it hangs in the cubicle. Tell me when you've got it.'

Bertie darted in. 'Okay!' he called.

Biggles switched off the light, in the hope, presumably of delaying the inevitable investigation. The report must have been heard all over the camp, but that did not necessarily mean that it would be traced to the compound immediately. If the light was on, however, it would speak as plainly as words – certainly to the keen-witted von Stalhein.

'Outside, everybody,' ordered Biggles. 'Come on, Ross. Any others who want to come will have to finish dressing on the way. This will be a hot spot inside five minutes. Give me the key, Bertie. Thanks. Now get these fellows through the wire and along to the hut. Ginger, you can go with them and take care of Ross if there's trouble.'

'What about you?'

'I shall try to cause a diversion. With everyone on the move, Gimlet is liable to be cut off.'

Bertie mustered his flock. 'This way, chaps,' he ordered. 'No more talking.' He set off at the double, followed by a crocodile of men hugging various garments and other possessions.

Biggles watched them out of sight and then, turning his attention to the camp, saw that the shot had done what he feared. The place was astir. Lights sprang up in several places and hurrying figures could be seen against them. Very soon three of these stood out clearly as they ran towards the compound. One of them, he saw without surprise, was von Stalhein.

Still holding his gun, Biggles took a pace round the corner and, pressing his body against the woodwork, stood still. He could no longer see the figures, but he could hear them coming. They ran up, panting, and, as he was sure they would, went straight into the hut. The light clicked on. For a moment all was quiet as the men took in the scene. Then the prone figure of the sergeant must have been noticed, for the footsteps hurried on to the far end. The next move, Biggles knew, would be a general alarm.

He walked round to the door and looked in. He saw what he expected to see. The three men were staring down at the prostrate sergeant, while the two prisoners who had stayed behind were telling them, incoherently, what had happened.

Biggles reached out to close the door and lock it, intending to depart then without revealing himself; but the movement must have caught von Stalhein's eye, for he looked round sharply and, of course, saw who was at the door. Biggles finished what he was doing, and hearing swift footsteps within, and guessing what they portended, stepped aside smartly as soon as the door was locked.

'Bigglesworth!' came von Stalhein's voice.

'Good morning to you,' answered Biggles.

A heavy revolver crashed, and splinters of wood flew from the door in line with where von Stalhein must have supposed Biggles to be standing.

'Naughty!' chided Biggles.

'I'll remember this,' promised von Stalhein, an edge on his voice.

'If your boss tries to give you a black, tell him it was his own fault for putting the camp in charge of a drunk,' said Biggles. 'I'll confirm it. You know my address? You'll find a souvenir on the door.'

He took off the spotted tie he was still wearing, hung it over the door handle, and walked away in the direction of the gap in the wire.

By the time he had reached it von Stalhein and his companions must have discovered that they were locked in, for there was a good deal of banging on the door. There was also some shouting, This was followed by several revolver shots, as someone, Biggles thought, tried to shoot the lock out of the door. He walked on. That the shots in the hut had been heard was soon apparent from the way more figures began to converge on it. He paid little attention to them, and went on to the hovel without meeting anyone. Bertie and his party were there, a huddled, silent group; but Gimlet had not yet arrived.

Biggles waited, staring in the direction from which they should come.

Wung, alone, was the first to arrive. He reported that the others were on their way. There had been some delay, he explained, because so many people were now moving about.

'Good enough,' acknowledged Biggles, 'As you know the way you can start off and get this gang to the coast. Bertie and Ginger will wait here with me in case Gimlet runs into trouble and needs help.'

Telling the men to follow him Wung set off across the marsh.

A few minutes later Gimlet and his two assistants arrived.

'Everything all right?' asked Biggles.

'Yes,' answered Gimlet. 'I was afraid at one time we might have to cut the programme short, but we managed to complete it. Did you get your man?'

'He's on his way to the boat, with some others.'

'What was the shooting about? That sort of started things.'

'Couldn't help it. A crazy prisoner shot the sergeant. Said he had bumped off his pal, or something.'

'Fool thing to do.'

'People do fool things when they lose their heads.'

'Shan't keep you a minute,' said Gimlet, and turned to watch critically while Copper and Trapper, with the aid of a small, shielded torch, made the connections to their batteries.

Bertie spoke. 'By the way, Gimlet old boy, I've been meaning to ask you for some time, have you still got that flea-bitten old grey mare you called Seagull?'

'Of course I've got her.'

'She could jump like a cat, that mare.'

'She still can.'

'Want to sell her?'

'Not likely. I'm hoping to win next year's Grand National with her.'

'Riding her yourself?'

'Of course.'

'She might do it. She's got brains, that old lady. I remember, out huntin', how she watched for the rabbit holes.'

'Here they go,' came Copper's voice from the ground. 'What did I tell yer, Trapper old chum? Didn't I tell yer we should be fox huntin' ternight if these two got tergether?'

Trapper clicked his tongue. 'You said it.'

'Not so much talking, you two,' requested Gimlet. 'Watch what you're doing.'

'We're all set, sir,' informed Copper, straightening his back.

'Good. All right. You can pull the plug.'

Copper took the sparking plunger in both hands and thrust it home.

Ginger was prepared for a certain amount of noise, but not for what actually happened. He nearly went over backwards as the earth erupted in a dozen places at once. Spears of flame leapt skyward, taking with them objects that could not be identified. Into the reverberations of the explosions came the crash of falling pylons, which gave a wonderful display of blue sparks as the electrical connections snapped and shorted. Small arms ammunition continued to crackle in spasmodic bursts from the direction of the ammunition dump. Black smoke began to roll up above a lurid glow.

'Jolly good show, old boy,' murmured Bertie.

'Looks as if we got the fuel tanks after all,' observed Gimlet thoughtfully. He turned to Biggles. 'I wasn't quite sure about them because, having got your message, I had to finish in a bit of a hurry.'

'If I'm any judge of this sort of thing you've made a pretty job of it,' complimented Biggles.

'Bent the old microphone somewhat, I'll bet,' said Bertie cheerfully.

'Yes. I don't think there will be any Music While You Work from this station for a day or two,' agreed Gimlet.

'In that case we might as well be getting back,' suggested Biggles. 'I don't think we've much to worry about. Everyone seems to be busy trying to put the fires out. From what I can see from here the place is in too much of a flap for anyone to organise anything.'

'Poor old Erich,' said Bertie sadly. 'He'll get a kick in the pants from the boys who thought out this jolly little scheme. Serves him right. Yes, by Jove! absolutely.'

'It's his own fault,' asserted Biggles. 'He will play with the wrong sort of people. Still, I hope nothing serious happens to him. We should miss him. He keeps us on our toes. But let's get mobile.'

They set off, and making good time, overtook Wung and his party just before they reached the coast. There was no pursuit; or if there was, no sign of it was seen. Which was just as well, because the dinghy had to make several trips between the shore and the aircraft to get everyone aboard. However, it was only a matter of time. When the last journey had been completed the dinghy was deflated, and abandoned to save weight, and the Scorpion, loaded to capacity, with Algy at the stick, took off and set a course for its base.

Biggles found Ross and congratulated him on his splendid work. 'By the way,' he went on, looking round. 'Which of these lads is your friend, Macdonald?'

'He isn't here, sir,' answered Ross.

Biggles looked disappointed. 'Why not?'

'He was shot some days ago, trying to escape,' said Ross, in a tremulous voice. 'He blamed himself for getting me into the business.'

'I'm sorry,' consoled Biggles quietly. 'I'm afraid that's the sort of thing that happens only too often when fellows decide to take the bit in their teeth.'

Bertie was sitting next to Gimlet. 'You were telling me about old Seagull?' he prompted.

Copper breathed heavily and nudged Trapper in the ribs. "Ere they go agin,' he said plaintively. 'This is where I snatch a spot of shut-eye. Strewth! Could I do with a nice plate o' fish and chips? My oath I could. This stayin' up all night always did make me peckish.'

Ginger looked at Cub and smiled. 'That's not a bad idea,' he whispered. 'I'm a bit weary myself.'

The engines droned on under stars that were beginning to pale with the approach of another day.

That really is the end of the story as far as it concerned Biggles and his comrades. The Scorpion reached its base without trouble of any sort, and after a day's rest Biggles took off on the return flight home. He took Ross with him. The other repentant deserters were left behind, having been handed over to the proper military authority for disciplinary action.

Guardsman Ross, it may be said here, was subsequently awarded the Distinguished Conduct Medal for the part he had played, much to the astonishment of his comrades in barracks who had supposed him to be absent without leave.

It turned out that Ross knew the names of some of the renegades who had volunteered to act as spies behind the lines in Korea. Army Intelligence Officers, with this information, soon picked them up. Their fate remained a matter for conjecture. Nothing more was heard of them.

The raid on the village of Fashtun, their headquarters, was made by a force of Marine Commandos with satisfactory results. Biggles knew no more about that than was published in the newspapers, except, of course, he knew why the raid was made. As he said to the others, when they returned to normal duties after a few days break, he had no further interest in Korea.

But he had an interest in a letter that arrived some time later. A slow smile spread over his face as he read it. 'You won't guess who this is from so I'll tell you,' he said. 'Smith, our friend in Prague. He's home, and wants us to have a meal with him.'

'Well, blow me down!' cried Bertie. 'How did he manage it?'

'He doesn't say,' answered Biggles. 'But it should be quite a story.'

And it was. But this is not the place to tell it.